THE COMPANY OF VENGEFUL CROWS

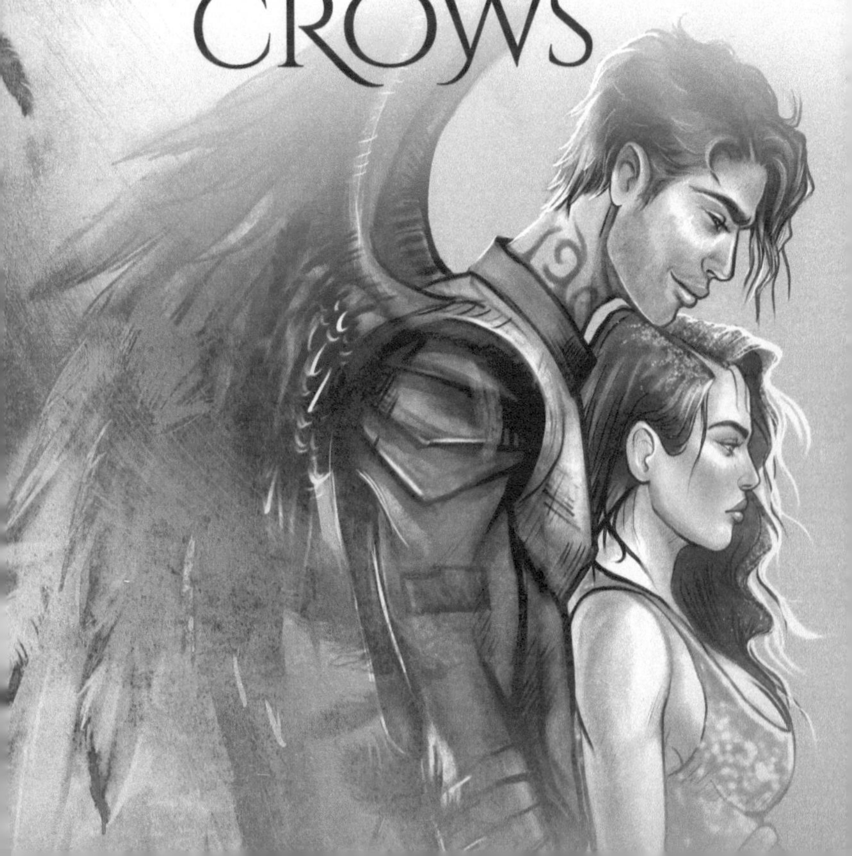

THE COMPANY OF VENGEFUL CROWS

LANA PECHERCZYK

CONTENT WARNING
A NOTE FROM THE AUTHOR

Although this is the tenth book in a series, and you may already be familiar with many of the subjects I write about and those I don't, I believe there are a few scenes in this book that may cause distress to some readers.

To avoid spoilers for those who don't wish to know, please turn the last page to find details of these scenes. If you're a no-trigger person, continue reading.

El
WINTER COU
ACONITE CIT
ACONITE SEA
ICE WITCH
THE ICE FOREST
HUMAN TERRITORY
UNSEELIE KINGDOM
SEELIE KINGDOM
CRYSTAL CITY
RUSH'S CABIN
MEANDE WOO
WHISPERING WOODS
CRESCENT HOLLOW

NE
OBSIDIAN MINE
SCENDIA
CLAW BASIN
AUTUMN COURT
RUBRUM CITY
CORNUCOPIA
TRADE CITY
FENRYSFIELD
THE CEREMONIAL LAKE
THE ORDER OF THE WELL
DELPHINIUM CITY
SPRING COURT
HELIANTHUS CITY
SUMMER COURT

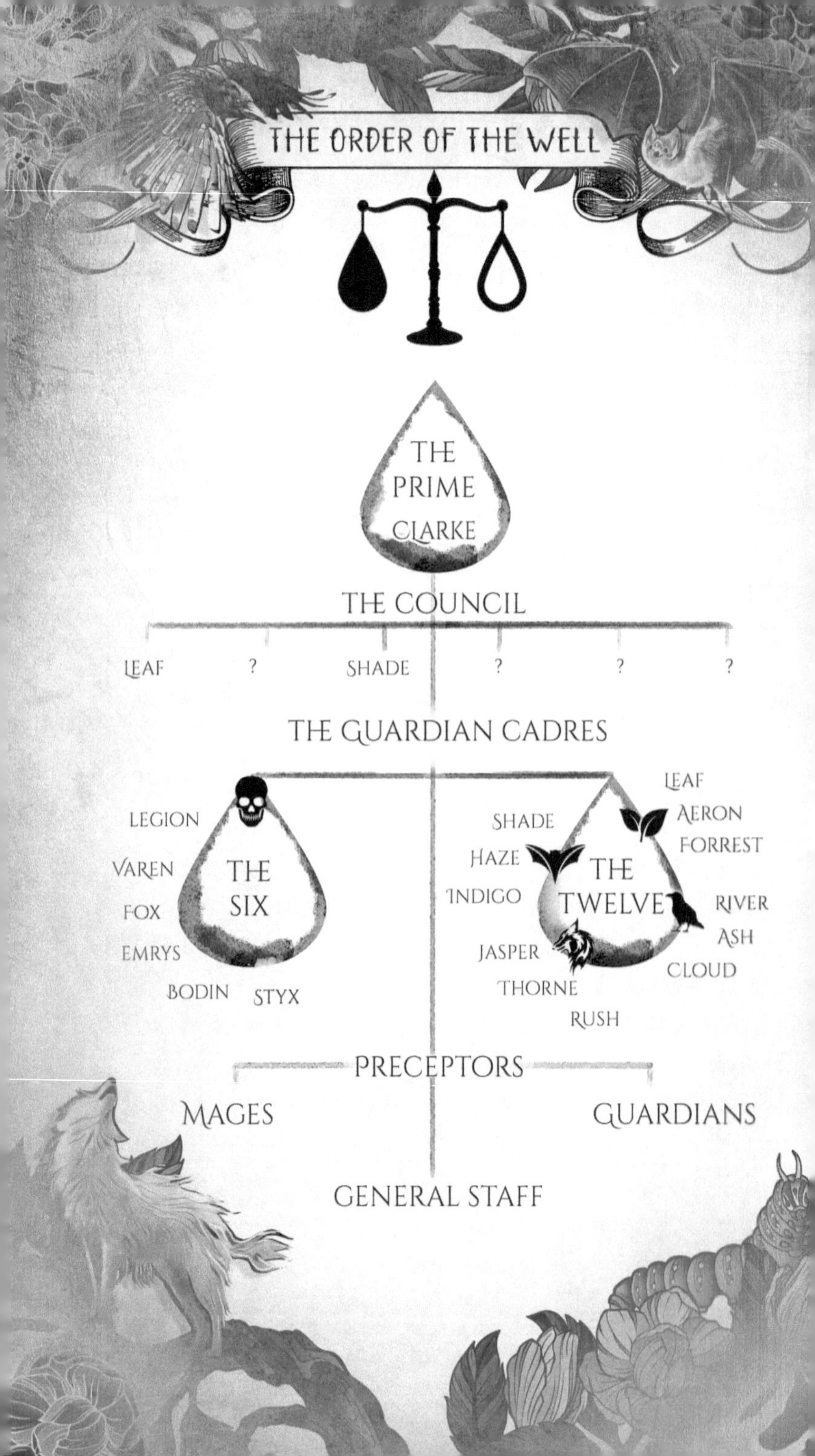

THE ORDER OF THE WELL

THE
PRIME
CLARKE

THE COUNCIL

LEAF   ?   SHADE   ?   ?   ?

THE GUARDIAN CADRES

THE SIX
LEGION
VAREN
FOX
EMRYS
BODIN   STYX

THE TWELVE
SHADE
HAZE
INDIGO
JASPER
THORNE
RUSH
LEAF
AERON
FORREST
RIVER
ASH
CLOUD

PRECEPTORS

MAGES   GUARDIANS

GENERAL STAFF

PREVIOUSLY ON FAE GUARDIANS

A RECAP OF WHAT HAPPENED IN BOOK 9.

Previously, on *Fae Guardians*, in *A War of Ruin and Reckoning*, the magical world of Elphyne was fractured, ravaged by an unstable magic source known as the Taint, and locked in a brutal war between the Seelie and Unseelie fae.

Amidst this chaos, Leaf, an elf Guardian and team leader of the Cadre of Twelve, found himself caught between his relentless quest for answers about the pioneer of their magic system, Jackson Crimson, and the Prime's insistence that he fulfill a prophecy by finding his fated human mate. Despite his deep loyalty to the Well, Leaf adamantly believed romantic entanglements were a distraction from his duty to cleanse the Taint.

Nova Morales, an environmental activist from the "old world," woke up thousands of years after a nuclear fallout to a brutal reality. Surrounded by magic, monsters, and war, everything and everyone she knew was dead. She became an unwilling prize in an Unseelie mate hunt and was forced to cook for a vile captain and his soldiers in a desperate camp.

Nova yearned for escape and answers, but her only family connection, her childhood friend Jace, was lost to her.

Their paths collided when Leaf, following a cryptic lead from the psychic Clarke, stumbled upon Nova's camp. Despite Nova's pleas and the immediate sense of recognition (she believed him to be her lost love, Jace), Leaf maintained a cold, professional distance, initially intending only to extract her as contraband due to her gold earrings. He entered the mate hunt, not out of desire, but to protect her under the guise of enforcing Well laws.

What followed was a brutal, adrenaline-fueled showdown. Leaf, despite being disarmed of his magic-cutting sword *Reckoning* and forced to fight with only a flimsy bone knife, brutally dominated the mate hunt. He decimated his competition, including the monstrous Captain Grung, with raw, untamed power. Nova witnessed his morally gray ferocity firsthand, simultaneously horrified and strangely aroused by his single-minded intensity.

Back in the mate hunt's victor's tent, Nova faced a grim choice: submit to a fake mating with Leaf to satisfy the Unseelie soldiers, or risk being returned to her vile captors. Nova chose to put her trust in Leaf, who unleashed an invisible wave of raw mana, obliterating the entire Unseelie army camp in a horrifying display of power that left nothing but bloody innards and bone.

On their journey to the Order, Nova made a shocking confession: Nero, the tyrannical human leader of Crystal City and chief antagonist of Elphyne, was her twin brother, Niles Morales. She revealed his psychopathic tendencies, his manipulations of their family, and her terrifying suspicion that he was responsible for the nuclear fallout that destroyed their world.

As they traveled, Leaf renewed his proposition for a fake mating ruse to gain an audience with the elusive Prime Aleksandra, hoping to uncover the full prophecy that would cleanse the Taint. Nova, still reeling from the devastating truth about her brother, reluctantly agreed, using cutting wit and a feigned casualness to push Leaf's buttons, subtly testing the boundaries of their forced proximity. Leaf found himself unexpectedly drawn to Nova, her vibrant spirit igniting a flicker of unfamiliar longing within him.

Arriving at the owl shifter territory, Nova succumbed to an old-world illness, a fever that left her delirious. Leaf, despite his standoffish nature, became her devoted caretaker, reading from Jackson Crimson's ancient journals at her bedside. In her delirium, Nova called him "Jace." This, combined with the entries in Crimson's journals, led Leaf to the staggering secret realization that he was, in fact, Jackson Crimson himself, or a reincarnation of him, his memories suppressed by the Well. The pieces clicked: Crimson's lost love, Estrella, was Nova.

Recovering from her illness, Nova again tested the waters of their fake relationship, suggesting they were free to "scratch their itches" with other people privately. Leaf, consumed by a burgeoning possessiveness, reacted with cold fury, reinforcing their public facade while his internal turmoil raged. This tension boiled over at a ceremonial wake, where Nova, feeling abandoned by Leaf, danced with the handsome owl shifter, Storm. Leaf, witnessing this flirtation, erupted in a jealous rage, brutally assaulting Storm and publicly claiming Nova as his "mate," a direct contradiction to his earlier vehement denials to the Prime.

Nova, enraged and confused by his erratic behavior and public declaration after he'd just disavowed her, lashed out.

She demanded he leave her alone. Leaf, his world unraveling, confessed his lost memories and his inexplicable attraction to her. He then shared his stunning realization: he *was* Jackson Crimson, a reincarnation who sacrificed his memories to continue his search for her. This profound revelation, coupled with the raw, undeniable connection between them, triggered a Well-blessing, solidifying their fated bond with glowing blue freckles appearing on Nova's skin. The emotionally charged push-pull dynamic shattered into a powerful, fated union.

Their burgeoning love was immediately tested when Maebh's demogorgon abducted the Prime Aleksandra, snatching her in plain sight during the wake's final performance. This forced Leaf and Nova back to the Order, where Nova revealed her unique gift: she was a mana amplifier, able to filter the Taint and magnify pure magic. This made her an invaluable asset, but also a dangerous target. The Council debated her involvement in the looming battle, with Leaf fiercely protective and refusing to put her in harm's way.

Amidst the rising political tensions, Leaf finally read Aleksandra's sealed letter, confirming his identity as Jackson Crimson. The letter revealed Aleksandra's profound sacrifice and her regret for not fighting for those she loved, mirroring Leaf's own journey of self-discovery and love for Nova.

The final battle descended upon the Order, heralded by a monstrous wyrm summoned by Maebh. Leaf and Nova confronted Maebh, and Nova, using her newfound gift, shared a memory of Aleksandra and Maebh's daughter, Aurora (whom they called Rory), with the Unseelie Queen, revealing that Nero had lied about their child's death and was siphoning her as a mana source. This revelation rocked Maebh to her core, breaking through her madness and obsession with revenge.

However, the battlefield erupted with Willow's terrifying power: necromancy. She raised an army of undead, mindless corpses that attacked indiscriminately, even turning on Maebh. The Six Sluagh Guardians, desperate to be free of subjugation, revealed their ultimate betrayal: they had orchestrated the entire conflict, including the Taint, to ensure Willow would rise as their new queen.

In a heart-wrenching twist, Aleksandra sacrificed herself to Legion to save Maebh, believing their unmaking was the only way to atone for their sins and give Rory a future. To clean the taint on the Well, Maebh and Aleksandra willingly chose to shed their fae forms, becoming mortal humans once more. Nova and Leaf, witnessing their profound peace, let them go, choosing compassion over justice.

The battle concluded with the defeat of the undead, but at a devastating cost: Rory sacrificed herself to save Willow from Cloud's vengeful Vendetta. River, arriving too late, was nearly killed by Cloud's unleashed fury in the aftermath.

Despite the chaos, the Well was cleansed, and the Order began to rebuild. Clarke was chosen as the new Prime, ready to lead with newfound courage and honesty. Nova revealed Nero's final weapon: she believes the location of a hidden nuclear warhead is secured within a "cryptex" puzzle, which River volunteered to retrieve. Leaf and Nova, now fully bonded and deeply in love, embraced their shared purpose and their unbreakable connection.

But as the dust settled, Nero, fresh from observing the battlefield from his airship, returned to Crystal City and discovered the empty cryopods that once held his most valuable assets. His rage, uncontained, signaled that the war was far from over, and his twisted games were only just beginning…

To all my Patreon Angels,

Your support gives me wings.
Your joy for this world refills my inner well.
Your friendship is my glitter glue.

This book is here because of you.

PROLOGUE

Blake Hartley hurried along the wharf in jewel-encrusted heels, careful not to slip.

A frigid wind cut through her short, sequined dress, but she had no time to worry about the alarming drop in temperature. She was late. Her husband, Jeff, said the yacht he'd hired was "just a stone's throw from Coco's."

But when she'd turned up, it hadn't been there.

Fortunately, her *Hidden Gems* followers went into crisis mode to figure out where Jeff had gone wrong. The yacht was moored on the *north* side of the river, near the Lucky Shag, not the *south* side. She wasn't sure how he'd mixed up something so obvious.

"G'day, hidden gems!" Her teeth chattered as she live streamed. "If there's one thing I've learned in me momentous effort to get here today, it's that nothin's gonna bring me down. Not even the end of the world!" A flurry of chimes sounded as positive and negative comments filtered through, including one from Dirk, a long-time follower but perennially sad-sack.

"Now, now," she said, "we'll have none of that today, mate. What do I always say when things get tough? We still have two feet and—?" *Ping. Ping. Ping.* She grinned as their responses finished her mantra. "That's right. As long as we have two feet and a heartbeat, she'll be right."

There wasn't much Blake remembered about her mother except for that saying, pancakes for Sunday lunch, sparkling makeup, and a whooping, opera singer's laugh. Her mother couldn't sing to save her life, but knowing that didn't stop her from trying. Somehow, those off-key attempts always ended in a laugh, which sounded more operatic than the tune.

A stab of emotion threatened Blake, and she quickly panned her phone's camera to showcase Perth's Elizabeth Quay harbor. The last thing her followers needed was to see her blubber over her long-dead mother. Especially not when she was trying to stay positive about being here instead of at home with her dad.

The usually bustling wharf was eerily quiet. Restaurants were closed. The Swan River stretched out before her, mirroring the ominous, stormy sky. In the distance, down the end of the wharf, she zoomed in on a gleaming yacht.

"Talk about razzle-dazzle," Blake gushed. "Look at that baby shine. And ... look at all those people. Wait. I had no idea it was a party." Her initial excitement waned. She shook off her doubt and forced happiness into her voice. "Jeff must have something special planned. I reckon he's gonna renew our vows. How romantic is that?"

A rush of pings stoked the fire of her expectations. Maybe she was wrong to worry about the address thing. Jeff would have a good reason. He always did.

"We made it, cunts!" she squealed, swinging her phone back to her face. "We fucking made it!"

She answered a few comments, making sure to use their names in her replies. Her followers loved her down-to-earth way of speaking despite her girly love of fashion and sparkling things. Growing up with three brothers and a widowed father, swearing had become as natural as breathing. She was the epitome of a tomboy until her sixteenth birthday, when she braved her mother's old beauty queen supplies. Her family told her to throw it all away. After sitting stagnant for ten years, the makeup was rotten. The wooden brushes had flaked.

But Blake had refused to throw away something that brought her mother such joy. She'd replaced the makeup, sanded and washed the brushes, then learned to pretty herself up and proved them wrong. After that, her brothers' friends, including Jeff, began to notice her.

A light flashed on her phone, and her heart raced. "Oh no! The battery's about to cark it. I'd better hurry up and get on board."

She tucked the bedazzled phone into her cleavage, wincing as the gems scratched her skin. Each stone was plucked from discarded treasures at a thrift shop. Most people didn't know she'd had them appraised—a few actual diamonds were hidden amongst the kitsch. It was perfectly her: a bit mismatched, a lot sparkly, but with a hidden value that most people overlooked.

With the camera facing outward and one hand cupping her jiggling tits, she focused on trotting toward the yacht—toward her husband of fifteen years, her warmth and safety in this crumbling world ... even though she was still pissed at him for forgetting her recent birthday, even though his apology effort was a hasty picnic in the backyard, even though he'd spent the evening on the phone. She wouldn't dwell on it. Not now. Not when the world was ending.

Instead, she focused on the bright boat, on the words "Boss Man" painted on the hull. Something niggled at her memory. Jeff had used that term multiple times recently on a phone call, at her birthday picnic. When she'd queried it, he'd fobbed it off as work that couldn't wait.

Shaking off her unease, she quickened her pace, heart pounding against her iPhone as she pinned it in place. The boat looked ready to leave. What if Jeff was too busy talking to those other people that he didn't see her coming? What if he left her behind?

"Oi!" she shouted, waving her hand. "Hun, I made it!"

The ex Aussie Rules football star caught sight of her and said something to one of the others on the yacht. Oddly, she didn't recognize his usual crowd. None of the boys from the club were there. No other WAGs. That seed of doubt she'd denied earlier took root, its tendrils reaching around her throat.

What was with the beige suit he wore? It looked expensive. His sandy hair was always clean-cut, but now he looked … posh. Ew, gross.

Blake stopped at the boat, panting slightly, hands still supporting her breasts as Jeff strode down the gangplank to meet her. His brow furrowed in that familiar disapproving way when he realized she wasn't wearing a push-up bra … or that she was filming.

He put his hands on his hips and stared at her. And stared.

"Hun." Her voice was tight, hesitant. "It's colder than a witch's tit out here. Shouldn't we go inside?"

"Fuck's sake." His handsome face twisted into an awkward grimace. "Babe, I really hoped to avoid this situation. Which is why I gave you the wrong address in the first place."

Ringing in her ears blended with a cascade of pings on the phone, each vibrating through her breastbone.

She shook her head. "Sorry, I think I hallucinated there for a minute. I thought you said you gave me the wrong address on purpose."

He gripped her shoulders, dipped to look at her tits—the camera lens—and then returned his gaze to her face.

"When it's the end of the world," he said, grandstanding with his voice, "your whole life flashes before your eyes. Your priorities become crystal clear. Suddenly, you know exactly how you want to spend your last hours and who you want to spend them with. Babe, that's not you." He paused, his pitying gaze taking in Blake's outfit, leaving a trail of shame in its wake. "Or your loser gaggle of fake friends."

She gasped and covered the phone's ears with her hands, but it was useless. Her followers would have heard the insult.

"Take that back, Jeffrey Donovitch," she whispered harshly.

"No, Blake *Hartley*."

He'd always been sore about her not taking his surname when they'd married. But she'd wanted her own identity outside of his famous footballer name. It was hard enough to prove herself as an influencer without his celebrity. In hindsight, maybe she should have taken his name. Maybe he'd never have become this … different person.

"I don't know what's got into you," she said.

"For the first time in years, I'm acting like myself. We're done, babe. Go home and be safe while you still can."

"You're yanking me chain, right?" A nervous laugh escaped her lips. "Come on, Jeff, we don't have time for this. A storm is coming."

"The sad fact is," he continued, slowly walking backward, "I want to spend my last moments with people who have a little more … substance."

"Substance?" The word caught in her throat.

"Oh my god, babe. You're so clueless." He stopped. Shook his head. Then, he ran a hand through his perfect hair. "You're wearing rainbow sequins and heels on the jetty while the world's fucking ending."

Blake instinctively traced the pattern on her dress. Each sequin had been hand-stitched over tiny tears in the fabric. She'd spent hours restoring it, breathing new life into something someone else had tossed away. Just like she'd spent years trying to restore the light in Jeff's eyes when he looked at her.

"This isn't about the dress," she whispered. "You've been pulling away for months."

He continued as if he hadn't heard her. "For crying out loud, even yesterday you were still gluing glitter on some kind of stupid Easter egg—"

"It's a *Fabergé* egg."

"Who gives a shit what it's called! I fucking hate glitter! It gets everywhere." He tilted his face to the cloudy sky and groaned, "Oh my god, it feels so good to finally say that aloud."

"Seriously?"

"It's not just the glitter, babe. Look at yourself." He gestured at her phone. "Live-streaming the end of the world like it's another junking haul. Do you really think anyone cares about your 'hidden gems' when a nuclear winter is coming?"

"Me followers—"

"Are a bunch of lonely blokes having a wank to your tits bouncing while you play with trash. That's not a real connection, Blake. It's not a real anything."

The word "real" hit her like a slap. She thought of her mother's dressing table, of the stars in her eyes as she watched the ex beauty queen put on makeup. She thought of the years afterward when her father could only talk to Blake when she showed interest in one of his home projects. Paul Hartley was never one for words at the best of times, and after his wife died, he'd retreated to his workshop for the solace and simplicity of carpentry. Conversations with him had always remained focused on the project, but a hidden subtext was there if Blake approached him with a problem.

The workshop was a sacred place. A place where the world's problems either melted away or righted themselves after the project was done. So what if a few undesirables watched her? So many more found solace in her work.

Those memories were real.

Jeff wasn't done shooting daggers into her heart.

"I should have seen the warning signs," he said with a scoff. "You spent your life trying to make cheap things look expensive and ordinary look special. I dunno, maybe that's why you married me—thought you could polish yourself up enough to belong in my world. But you can't upcycle your-self, babe. You still sound like an outback trucker, you still wear too much bling, and you still look like a whore with that shade of lipstick."

Blake's hand flew to cover her mouth. Her mother had loved this shade. Called it her "lucky red."

"Face it, babe. You never held down a job. You leeched off me for years while you fed your fucking razzle dazzle bullshit to other losers like you. Maybe if your dad had the guts to tell you that your mum wasn't really a beauty queen, you'd have accepted reality years ago." He gave her a pitying look. "Some things are just … common."

"You're being a dickhead, Jeff," she shot back, tears leaking from her eyes.

"Gawd, you're crying again." He gestured at her face. "See, this used to work. You cry and get your way, and then I'm miserable all over again. But that doesn't work on me anymore, Blake. I honestly don't care. You can no longer make me miserable."

Make him miserable?

Oh, hell no.

"What the actual fuck?" She gasped. "I'm crying because I have feelings. How dare you make that out to be a bad thing!" She hastily wiped her nose. "And me voice has *always* sounded like this! You expect me to change me tone just to make you feel better? Is that what's really going on here? You hate feelings because they don't make you Boss Man material?" She pointed at the boat and shook her head. " It's obviously yours. There's no use denying it."

"Who said I'm denying it?" Jeff sneered.

"B-but…" She floundered and reached for proof. "I asked you once, and you said the new company hired it."

"You think you're so smart because of your photographic memory? You just sound like an uneducated parrot."

"Nothing I just said has to do with me photographic

memory." After all these years, he still didn't understand how that worked?

"It's *my* memory," he corrected. "Not *me* memory."

A burst of laughter drifted from the yacht. A woman, also in a beige suit, whispered behind her hand to another well-dressed man. Blake recognized her as Jeff's new producer, who always called Blake "sweetie" with a condescending smile. He'd taken the sports reporting job after an injury forced him into early retirement.

The realization hit like a punch to the gut. Jeff had traded up—in his eyes, at least. With good looks, an average career, and a great body, he'd always been a superstar. After his retirement, all those little quirks of his she used to find adorable grew sharper and a little cruel. She always suspected he was jealous of her growing social media influence while his celebrity faded.

Now she knew.

"Blake." His voice softened slightly, the gentleness more painful than his earlier harshness. It said maybe he really did care for her. Once. "I want to spend my last moments alive with people who matter. People with depth. That's not you, babe. It never was."

Without a backward glance, her husband of fifteen years walked up the gangplank. He kicked it into the stormy river with a splash, and then directed a genuine smile at a group of veritable strangers. The yacht's engines roared to life, drowning out the sound of corks popping from champagne bottles and glass tinkling.

At least she had her followers. She tilted her phone's screen toward her face.

The battery was dead.

As the yacht sailed past, its wake lurched over the jetty

and pelted her with icy river water, leaving her gasping in shock. Laughter erupted on board, but she refused to give them the satisfaction of seeing her cry.

When the boat was out of earshot, she glanced down to assess the damage. The glittering sequins suddenly seemed garish and cheap. When she checked her shivering reflection, her carefully applied makeup now looked like a tear-stained child's attempt at adulthood.

Was Jeff right? Was this the reality check she needed too late? Had her father sheltered her? Had she idolized her mother too much? *Had Grace Hartley even been a beauty queen?*

The sun broke through the clouds and landed on the distant yacht, bathing it with the warmth she desperately wanted. But the passengers laughed, and her world sailed away. All she was left with was a circling crow cawing at her misfortune.

"Fuck that." Her breath clouded. "I'm not dead yet."

She clutched her phone to her chest and hobbled back toward her car with jerky, shivering strides. She still had time to drive to her dad's house. To get warm.

Never again would she fall for a nob jockey like Jeff. Never again would she give her heart, soul, and life to a man who couldn't appreciate the talent it took to upcycle trash into treasure. Never again would she put her dreams behind his.

"I'm coming, Dad." Her sob brought ice-cold razor blades into her lungs. "I still have"—another gasp—"two feet and a…"

Her numb hand pressed against her sternum, searching for a heartbeat.

Nothing.

A singular tear broke free and froze on her cheek.

ONE

"This is so random," Blake muttered as she staggered across sand. Heat from the glaring afternoon sun beat down on her face. Her sequined dress hung in tatters, but her bejeweled iPhone remained clutched in her hand, somewhat in one piece.

Keep walking. Keep moving.

Nausea swelled inside her, and she dropped to her knees, retching. Something black and viscous oozed from her throat, triggering another wave of heaving. What the hell had she swallowed? Where was she?

Vague images, fleeting glimpses, and feelings of swimming in an ocean trying to swallow her whole.

"Two feet and a heartbeat," she rasped, willing herself to focus. "I'm alive."

But not in Perth. Not near the Swan River. Squinting against the harsh light, she surveyed the foreign landscape. White sand stretched to meet a turquoise ocean. No yachts. No Elizabeth Quay. No familiar city skyline. Instead, the beach gave way to a rolling, grassy hill.

A seagull's cry pierced the air. Large, flat rocks baking in the sun were scattered across the shore. The sky above was impossibly blue, the air crisp and clean.

Maybe I drifted downriver somehow, she thought, grasping at logic. Wherever this was, the nuclear winter hadn't touched it.

She needed to tell her husband.

A crow cawed overhead, and the memory slammed into her. Jeff on a boat—without Blake. She glanced down at her rusty phone. Had he really sailed off into the sunset, leaving her stranded while the world was ending? Frantically, she tapped the screen, pressed buttons, and even tried speaking to it. "Oi, Siri. It's me, Blake." No answer. "Where the bloody hell are you?"

Silence.

Only her haggard, mascara-streaked reflection stared back.

Everything came crashing down. Tears stung her eyes. Emotion threatened to choke her. She swallowed hard and hit the phone with her fist. "Don't do this to me, Siri. Come on, you bugger."

A clash of voices drifted over the grassy embankment. She tilted her head, focusing on the sound. A crowd. Thank god. Someone might have a charger. Maybe Jeff made it out, too. Maybe that yacht business was all a weird dream because he would never leave her alone when the world was—

No.

The world was still here. That in itself meant something was wrong with her memory. They'd joked about an apocalypse, and the fallout was all anyone spoke about on social media. But her father always said Perth was the most isolated city on Earth. If any place survived a nuclear winter, it would be them.

The world hadn't ended. Her dad and brothers were somewhere laughing. Her husband hadn't said she lacked substance. He hadn't sailed away.

That was all a continuation of the same weird dream. It had to be.

But what if it wasn't…

"Charger," she mumbled, then coughed up more hot, thick goop. "Ew, gross."

Wiping her mouth, she staggered up the embankment. Keep walking. Keep moving. Two feet. But her heart was sluggish. Her limbs were heavy. She just wanted to go back to sleep, to take it easy on one of those warm rocks, like the mermaid farther down the beach.

Blake stopped. Blinked.

What?

She blinked again. Was that … a … "Yeah … nah."

It couldn't be a mermaid. Must have been a brain fart. Because if it were anything else, she had hit her head too hard or accidentally swallowed a gallon of salt water.

Blake slowly turned around.

There, lounging on a rock, was a beautiful woman with iridescent skin, her blue-green tail dipping lazily into the water. Long, wet, coppery hair covered her perky breasts. Her delicate eyes were closed as if daydreaming, one arm dangling over the edge, fingers twirling idly in the water.

A scene plucked from a fairytale.

"Not real," Blake mumbled.

She rubbed her eyes, breathed fresh air, and looked again. Hysterical laughter bubbled out when she saw nothing but ocean, sand, and an empty rock.

"It's just a mirage," she told herself.

A flying crow looped around, drawing her eye before disappearing over the embankment. Following the bird, Blake continued up the slope. A vast, glimmering citadel came into view as she crested the top. The ocean tunneled into estuaries through a patrolled citadel gate where soldiers in embroidered red and gold uniforms checked all who entered.

Her jaw dropped at the millions of tiny, swarming balls of light trapped inside the citadel's glass fortification wall. Outside it, unmistakable cries of hawkers came from a bustling marketplace. Colorful canopies and carts glimmered with reflected light from the trapped, buzzing orbs nearby, shielding people from the glare.

Blake squinted to focus and gasped, hope stirring in her soul.

People. Lots of them. Not just people, but livestock, fresh produce, trinkets, furniture, and homewares. It was exactly the kind of place she loved hunting in for hidden gems. Surely, someone here would have a charger she could borrow.

Stumbling closer, a cold dread crept up her spine as details sharpened in her vision. The marketplace—familiar in concept yet utterly alien in execution—seemed wrong in ways her mind struggled to compute. The trapped orbs hummed and pulsed like living things.

"This isn't Perth," she whispered, her voice cracking. "This isn't anywhere."

TWO

The late afternoon sun baked entrails into River's leathers and skin as he walked home through the Order campus. Two female mages approached on the same path. As they neared, they pinched their noses and scrunched up their faces. He resisted hugging them to smear his crusty mess over their pristine blue robes. Instead, he gave a jaunty wave, gesturing emphatically so the stink wafted.

"Monster guts smell good, don't they?"

They scurried away, and he grinned.

The taint-sprung monster he'd fought in Rubrum City left him covered with an unusually pungent type of blood and viscera that clung to his nostrils and itched his skin. The four-eyed rooster had phased into shadow, leaving only whispers of movement before it struck. Needless to say, it had been a handful to dispatch.

Guardians were under strict orders to debrief the preceptors of any new monsters immediately after returning from a mission. If he had to remain in festering clothes, then it was only fair that everyone else suffered too.

He ached. He stank. He was over it.

All he wanted was a scalding hot bath, enough liquor to drown his thoughts, and oblivion for a few blessed hours.

But when he finally reached the Cadre of Twelve's private training lawn, his steps slowed to a deliberate crawl. Clarke waited on the porch steps, her four-year-old twins clutching her hips like red-haired parasites. More troubling, an ornate pouch swung from her fingers. He searched for escape routes. None.

"River!"

Shit.

"Whatever it is," he shouted, "the answer's no."

He put his head down and charged forward.

Don't make eye contact.

"River," she pleaded, her voice softening in a way that burrowed under his skin.

As Prime of the Order of the Well, Clarke now wielded the power to shatter his plans, regardless of how he felt.

He stopped at the base of the steps with a deep sigh. "Fine. Tell Preceptor Barrow I'll *consider* changing the new monster's name from Cockadoom. Happy?"

"Um. Sure. Girls," she said to her children, "let Mommy give Uncle River the pouch."

"No!" shouted one—maybe Hazel? Or was she Holly?—while the other sucked louder on her thumb. The wet sound grated against his nerves.

"Girls," Clarke repeated. "I really need to give this to Uncle River."

He arched his brows. "So this isn't about the Cockadoom?"

"I have no idea what that is." Clarke shot him an apologetic look when her twins hindered her again. "They're too big to be carried, but they won't let go."

"Just kick them off." He sidestepped, but the non-thumb-sucker—definitely Hazel—blew a raspberry. He barked a laugh and nearly returned the gesture before she scrambled back up to hip level.

"These arrived today for you and Ash." Clarke finally extracted two glass coins from the pouch.

Twinkling reflections caught his gaze, sparking a war between dopamine and fury. The coins were Murder's Call, invitations to the Great Murder, a bi-annual crow-shifter gathering where scores were settled, alliances forged, and secrets traded like currency, where his inability to fly would be impossible to hide. Where they might find the Collector and trade for the cryptex.

But where Cloud might be.

Why was Clarke delivering the coins?

He left them hanging in her hands.

"Interesting timing," he said carefully, studying her pale, freckled face for hints she knew more about his true agenda. Her psychic visions had an inconvenient habit of stripping everyone's secrets bare. Guardians didn't share feelings. Feelings got them killed.

The only person River had told the truth about who'd fried him to a crisp after the battle five years ago was Ash. And even that was a mistake.

"There's something else going on," Ash had mused darkly. *"We owe it to Cloud to find out."*

"You owe it to him," River had countered. *"I owe him nothing but pain."*

Agonizing, nerve-frying pain.

Nothing could stand between River and his vengeance.

Before Clarke could answer, her gaze turned distant. "Oh no. I'm about to have a fancy. Watch the girls?"

"Absolutely not—*shit*."

White mist swallowed the blue in Clarke's eyes. Her grip slackened, and the coins slipped from her fingers, tinkling down the steps. River lunged as she swayed. He caught her shoulders, steadying her trance-locked body while the twins slid down their mother's legs, landing on the wooden porch with a thud.

Once sure Clarke wouldn't topple, River scooped up the fallen coins. Holly's thumb popped from her mouth, and her eyes brimmed with tears as he tried to step past.

"Tell us a story, Uncle Wivva!" Her sticky hand grabbed his leg, leaving a wet smear on his monster-gut-covered leather.

"That's disgusting." He scrunched his nose.

"Please?" Hazel begged.

Her voice wobbled, triggering protective instincts he'd rather deny. His gaze drifted to Cloud's empty bedroom window upstairs. A longing for simpler times weighed heavily on his chest.

"Fine." He crouched to their level. "Here's a story. Once upon a time, there was a little goblin girl who couldn't stop sucking her thumb. When her dad told her to stop, she told him to flock off and then shook her butt in his face like this."

He demonstrated with exaggerated movements, sending them into fits of giggles.

"Dad wouldn't like that," Holly said.

"He'll growl at us." Hazel nodded.

"You could always stab him," River shrugged, and feinted a dagger strike.

Their jaws dropped. For a heart-stopping moment, he thought they believed him, and they'd actually go and stab their father. He was about to remind them that the story was about goblins, clearly not them, but then Holly asked, "Can we look at your shinies again?"

Just like that, they moved on.

If only life were so easy.

"Maybe." He flipped the coins across his knuckles, their wonder fueling his grin. "These have secret messages for crows only."

He vanished the coins, then produced them from behind their ears.

Their squeals softened when he tilted the glass to catch the UV light and offered one to each of them. "I'll give you three seconds to look. See if you can decode the secret."

Clarke gasped, the vision releasing its hold.

"Oops. Too late." He snatched the coins back. "Your mother's back."

Their complaints disappeared under Clarke's strained words. "River, listen. Ash needs to be there, too. It's important. Something about a trade … the Collector…"

His jaw clenched. She'd seen the legitimate reason for him going to the Great Murder, not the vengeance burning through his veins. He wasn't sure if that was a good or a bad thing.

"It all starts and ends with you, doesn't it?" he muttered.

"Don't know what you're talking about." She gathered the twins. "Come on, girls, home before your dad."

"Wait—" The question died on his tongue. *Will I ever fly again?*

Clarke paused. "Yes?"

Say it. Ask her about your wings.

"Any word from Willow?" he asked. She'd been missing for a few weeks, but her parents weren't too worried. Their daughter had soul-searching to do, or some shit, and had left on her own volition.

"Not yet," Clarke replied. "But I have a good feeling we'll talk to her soon."

Air shimmered around the twins, and they morphed into white, rusty-patched wolf cubs. River barely dodged as they streaked down the porch and across the training lawn toward their father.

Rush's dirty Guardian uniform betrayed a recent mission. His yellow eyes narrowed at River's proximity to his mate.

"Oh, for Christ's sake," Clarke muttered, taking a giant step away.

Rush instantly relaxed and nodded at River respectfully, signaling he wouldn't attack. As if he could take a crow. River scoffed and flipped up his middle finger. The silver-haired Guardian smirked, then crouched to welcome the furry torpedoes with open arms.

"Don't mind him," Clarke drawled. "I can't even blame his possessiveness on Willow leaving on her adventure. He's always been like that."

"Mates." River rolled his eyes. "Can't live with them."

Clarke stared at him.

"What?" he said.

"Is there a second part of that saying?"

"Nope."

"River." Her pitying tone triggered every flight instinct in his body. "You know how much Rush and I appreciate that you comforted Willow after Rory died. Right?"

Appreciate. Not thank. Not enough to trigger a Well-enforced debt. Bitter anger swelled, choking him. If she were truly grateful, she'd thank him properly. Then he could finally extract answers to the questions haunting his nightmares, and force her to forget.

Tell me Cloud's descent into madness isn't my fault.

Tell me I didn't set it all in motion by letting him fall for the enemy.

Tell me how to find my best friend so I can murder his sorry ass.

But he said nothing. He just nodded and went inside, the coins burning a hole in his pocket against his thigh.

"I NEED YOUR HELP, PRINCELING," RIVER SAID AS HE BARGED unannounced into Ash's room.

The crow-shifter lounged in a battered chair by the closed window, reading in the dappled sunlight. Phantom wind whispered secrets in his ears, lifting long wisps of dark hair around his bronze face.

Without looking up, he licked his finger and turned a page. "Whose body are we burying?"

"No one died."

Cloud's bloody V-stained face flashed in River's mind, along with a stab of guilt and the urge to confess everything. But he resisted and shoved Ash's boots from the coffee table to make room. When he sat, his leather creaked. Cockadoom stink wafted.

He tossed an engraved glass coin.

Ash plucked it from the air and tilted it toward the window, catching and dispersing UV light in a way only crows understood. His pupils dilated as he took in the glittering reflections.

"Hand delivered by the Prime," River explained. "One for you and one for me."

The rainbow sparkling over their faces exposed a secret map. Every adult crow had a similar map camouflaged within their visible tattoos. It led to their trove, their life savings tucked away in a safe place.

Well, almost every crow. Cloud's lightning had melted half of River's maps, and Ash refused to end up like his hoarding mother, so he denied building a trove. The piles of his teetering belongings revealed how well that plan was going.

Ash's fist quickly swallowed the coin, the rainbow disappeared, and he glared outside.

"Why are you showing me this?" he ground out.

"Why do you think?"

"I told you, I'm not going back."

"I know." River pried open Ash's fist and reclaimed the coin. "But this isn't going back. This is meeting her on an even playing field."

"Her" meaning Ash's mother—the notorious Collector, more crow than human. The queen of hoarding had amassed treasures over millennia, guarding them with lethal claws and whatever means necessary, including chaining her son to keep watch while she hibernated. She still expected her son's return, despite it being around two centuries since they'd liberated him.

"I'm not afraid of her," Ash stated.

"Never said you were." River pocketed the coin. "You're an adopted Umbria. Ergo, I'm honor-bound to present you with Murder's Call."

"So?"

"So fuck you too."

"You're being obtuse."

"You're obtuse with your fancy book words." River snatched the volume. "What are you reading?"

"None of your business." Ash punched River in the groin.

Pain exploded. White spots danced across his vision as Ash calmly reclaimed his book.

"Cheap shot," River croaked, clutching himself. "Since when are you so sensitive? You know not to mess with the baby makers."

"You deserved it. Besides, you don't even want fledglings."

"Ew."

"Go alone." Ash found his page again.

River stared until a muscle in Ash's jaw ticked.

"Look, bro," he said finally. "We head to the Great Murder and trade with your ma for the cryptex, or we pull the Order card and go full-scale Guardian and raid her lair."

Not that they thought the cryptex was there. When Ash had lived there, he couldn't recall any treasures containing forbidden substances being stored there. They'd searched for a second trove but had come up short.

"What aren't you telling me?" Ash's voice deepened. "You've never needed me to hold your hand at these gatherings. Why now?"

"Forget it." River turned to leave.

Ash blocked the exit with his legs. "Has Clarke had a vision about me being there?"

The wind teasing Ash's hair stilled. He already knew something.

"With you there," River said carefully, "we stand a better chance of bartering for the cryptex. You don't have to speak to her. I'll do all the work, but it's this or the raid. We're running out of time to find it before Nero does."

Everything River said was the truth. Just not all of it. He needed Ash there because if Cloud turned up before they bartered for the cryptex, then someone needed to carry on with the mission. He could be dead. Or arrested. Even if Cloud was a wanted fae, he wasn't considered a traitor to the Order until he faced a democratic trial. But a Guardian murdering another Guardian in cold blood was a definite death sentence.

Not if River could get away with it.

Ash's unblinking stare promised suffering, but he stood and unfurled lustrous wings, scattering black feathers.

"Fine." He grabbed a leather satchel. "I'll meet you at the Summer Palace. They have something the Collector will want, but I'll need to convince Jasper to relinquish it. Give me a day."

"Princeling." River waited for Ash to look his way, then touched his fingers to his mouth in the fae gratitude sign. "I know this won't be easy."

Ash scowled, grabbed his supplies, and stalked out. Two minutes later, a flurry of shadows signaled his takeoff outside, wings beating into blurs before fading in the blue sky. Envy clawed at River's gut. It had been too long since he'd flown—so long that he feared it would never happen again.

Shoulders slumped, he dragged his feet down the hall to his room. When he passed Cloud's room, the door was ajar. He entered cautiously.

A shaft of light streamed through a gap between boards

covering the window. Unlike other Guardian quarters, Cloud's room held only a single mattress pushed against the wall, far from the window. One pillow. One sheet. No furniture. No trinkets. No weapons.

Nothing except the mural River had painted when they'd been promoted to the Cadre of Twelve. A sun in a cloudless sky. A river winding through a ravine. The cliff where they'd jumped together as teens—where the end of their innocence began.

Rhythmic thumping against the joining wall ruined River's moment. He tried to block it out, to admire his handiwork, but then a woman's pleasure-filled moan joined the thuds. He stomped out of Cloud's room and pounded on the neighboring door.

"Shut up!" he shouted. "Have some respect for the only Guardian actually doing his job!"

The noise stopped. The door opened to reveal a sweaty blond elf wrapping a sheet around his waist, spectacularly failing to hide his tented erection. Leaf arched his brow.

"Be careful, D'arn," he warned. "You'll sing a different tune when you find your mate."

"Not happening."

"The Well wants what it wants." Leaf gave a cocky smirk and then slammed his door.

River stalked to his room—neighboring their team leader's alternate side—and slammed his door in retaliation. Hard enough to tremble the walls. Two seconds later, the wall-banging resumed.

The Well wants what it wants?

If that were true, then he, Ash, and Cloud had devoted most of their lives to protecting something that wanted to see them suffer.

THREE

S and and grass gave way to crushed limestone that bit into Blake's feet as she stumbled toward the citadel. People here were odd. Their fashion here jarred her senses. All wore loose and light garments that seemed to be constructed with a practical purpose rather than for show. No spandex or Lycra, no denim or shiny faux leather, no stilettos or Gucci suits. Not even a hint of sequins.

Were they all farmers?

And what was with that glass wall filled with glowing, swarming lights?

Had she washed up on some remote island civilization? Crashed onto some sort of movie set? But then, wouldn't the sky still bear traces of soot? And she hadn't even been on the boat when—

"Must be dead," she mumbled.

Shocked faces turned her way as she pushed deeper into the market's core, teeth chattering and hair still dripping down her spine. Then something touched her on the shoulder. It fluttered against her skin, and she recoiled at the sensation, stumbling back into another body. More fluttering.

"Watch it," the man behind her grunted and half-walked, half-flew beyond her reach. She gaped after him, dumbfounded, as he vanished into the throng.

Cosplay wings don't flutter. Do they?

Dread coiled in her gut as she pivoted in a slow circle, registering details that shouldn't exist. Some people had pointed ears. Others sported horns spiraling from their skulls. Wings varied beyond feathers, some shimmering like prismatic dragonfly wings.

Just like the mermaid, these people had leaped straight from the pages of a fairytale. Forget Perth. This wasn't Australia or even planet Earth.

The smell was too vivid to be imagined. The pungent musk of livestock, cloying floral perfumes, briny fish, and overripe fruit saturated the air.

God, she was confused.

And thirsty.

Dizzy.

Faint.

I must be sick. Must have hit me head.

She approached the nearest person: a woman with kind eyes and twitching, fur-tipped, pointed ears.

"Excuse me," Blake croaked, waggling her dead phone. "Do you have an iPhone charger? Or maybe you've seen a tall ex-football player? I seem to have lost—"

The woman clutched her cane basket to her chest and scurried away.

"—me husband."

So much for friendly locals.

Blake scanned the nearby stalls and carts. Dirty limestone

surrendered to cobblestone. Her gaze caught on a tall, slender man with a scarf wound around his head and ears. He stroked his beard to a point as his gaze locked with hers.

Knick-knacks sprawled across the table before him, wooden furniture stacked behind. Her pulse quickened at the familiar sight. Half her life had been spent haunting antique furniture stores, workshops, and thrift shops. Finally, here was something that made sense.

Two crows swooped down to perch on his canopy, their unblinking eyes studying her approaching figure.

"Excuse me, mate," she wheezed as black spots danced in her vision. "You don't have an iPhone charger, do you? I just need to…"

Her words dried up. Her balance wavered. Why did she even need a charger? Who would she call? Her husband? The one who dumped her? Her dad and brothers couldn't operate their own phones without a crisis.

"Lady," the man said, his tone dropping to a warning bass. "I'd hide all that contraband if I were you."

She blinked. "Contraband?"

A harsh caw split the air, followed by the flutter of wings. The two birds descended, landing beside her, invading her personal space. She clutched her bejeweled brick tighter and eyed them warily.

The vendor scowled and slashed his hand through the air. "Begone, scavengers!"

More caws echoed from above as two more crows arrived, their movements as shifty as the first pair.

The bearded man jabbed a finger at Blake. "Now look at what you've done."

He tried to shoo her off, too, but the little black birds hopped to block her path.

"Bah!" he grumbled. "I don't want trouble today."

"What did I do?" Blake squeaked.

He gestured irritably at her dress. "Find something else to wear before they peck it from your body, or worse, a Guardian forcibly removes it."

"I have no idea what's happening," she cried. "And I have no other clothes."

"Find some."

"But I have no money. It's all in me phone, and no one seems to have a bloody charger!"

"Not my problem, lady." He skirted his table and physically shoved her away. "Go."

"I will. But for the record, you're a bit rude, mate."

With nowhere else to turn, she continued stumbling through the market. The four crows had now multiplied to six and stalked her like a menacing motorcycle gang on clawed feet.

"Pssst."

Blake halted and swiveled her head. Hot, prickly waves of nausea crashed over her. She put her cool palm on her forehead. God, she felt awful.

"Over here."

She dragged her exhausted gaze around until she spotted a woman leaning against a wooden pole that propped up an orange canopy. Behind her was a stall made from rope tied between canvas-covered crates of bleating livestock. The woman herself wore grime like a second skin, her long hair hanging in matted clumps. Floppy deer-like ears twitched atop her head. Several teeth were missing from her smile. She looked far too young to be in such a state of disrepair.

"Are you talking to me?" Blake pointed at herself, shuffling closer.

The woman's gaze dropped to the sequinned dress, then flicked to the still stalking crows who cawed warnings at anyone venturing too close.

"You a Rosebud Courtesan?" she asked.

"I don't know what that is."

"Then why are you dressed for attention?"

Rude.

"This is all I have." Blake threw up her hands, exasperated. "I must have fallen into the river, and it's a miracle I survived. I'm just looking for a charger for me phone." *It's my, not me*—Jeff's mocking taunt hit her along with a fresh wave of self-loathing. "A charger for *my* phone," she corrected. "Please tell me you have one."

Logic screamed for her to abandon this crusade, but surrender might crack her sanity. Clinging to common sense was all she had left.

"Are you—" The woman's voice dropped to a conspiratorial whisper. "—human?"

"Of course I am."

"Ahh." The grimy vendor beckoned Blake closer to a rickety table she stood near, then shouted something unintelligible toward the back of her stall. Someone lurked behind those crates. She popped a long stick of something hay-like into her mouth and chewed. The piece bobbed as she scrutinized Blake with shrewd eyes. Finally, she asked, "Are you one of those old-worlders?"

Old worlder.

Old.

Worlder.

The words reverberated in Blake's mind. Some kind of primal self-preservation instinct made her shake her head.

"You're not?" The woman's gaze narrowed. "You sure seem like one with all that contraband."

"I mean, I *am* human. I just … the other man had mentioned contraband, too. Do you mean this?" Blake extended her phone with trembling fingers.

"And the rest of it." She gestured at Blake's clothes. "Even the old-worlder queen follows the rules of the Well now. The Seelie High King is a Guardian … you don't know what a Guardian is, do you?"

Blake shook her head so violently that the dizziness surged. Nausea threatened to spew black goop from her lips. Her hands shot out, grasping the table edge. Her phone clattered against wood.

"Huh." The woman's skeptical gaze darted from Blake to the bejeweled phone, then widened at the engagement and wedding ring glinting on Blake's finger. "A Guardian's job is to uphold the integrity of the Well."

"Okay. You mentioned that before. What's the Well?"

Breathe. Just breathe slowly, and the dizziness will pass.

"You really don't know, do you?" She spat out the hay, plucked a sequin from Blake's dress, bit it, and then inhaled its scent. "Yep. This is plastic, alright. You're in big trouble, lady."

"Plastic is outlawed?" What kind of twisted hell dimension had she stumbled into? "But what about Spanx?"

"Huh?"

"Or acrylic nails. Me sunnies. Or—" She gaped. "Or me personal joy sparker?"

The woman held a monocle to her eye and inspected the iPhone, her floppy ears twitching. "Are these diamonds?"

"They're against the law, too?"

"Tell you what," the woman said, setting the phone

down. "You seem like a lovely lass, so I'll find you something appropriate to wear. You give me all your bits, and I'll dispose of them before a Guardian catches wind."

"What happens if they do?"

The woman sliced her thumb across her throat. "Considering our king is one, you definitely don't want to delay. Ain't that right, Shanks?"

A hidden male grumbled behind the stacked crates.

"Shanks says he saw a Guardian only two streets away at dawn, taxing the merchants. Said he'd just slain a taint-sprung monster, and we owe him. Fucking floaters. Believe me, you want to stay away from them. Not only do the Guardians hold more mana than sense, but they can crush your throat without breaking a sweat. Ain't that right, Shanks?"

Another inaudible, gravelly reply. The woman erupted into laughter, jerked her thumb toward the crates, and said to Blake, "He knows because a Guardian's hand wrapped around his throat. All the big vampire bastard did was sneeze, and he accidentally broke Shank's larynx. It didn't heal right."

Blood drained from Blake's face, leaving her lightheaded. She stared at her dead phone on the table. If plastic and metal were outlawed here, finding a charger wasn't just unlikely—it was impossible. *Old world. Old world.* Why did that phrase keep haunting her?

Blake shook her head, trying to dislodge the nonsensical words.

Maybe she should press on. If this woman recognized her as human, others like her might exist, ones more inclined to help.

The cawing intensified, growing sharper, more insistent.

She refused to turn and count how many crows had gathered, but the sound suggested a mob. The last thing she needed was to have her eyes pecked out like she was in a Hitchcock movie.

"You'd better hurry, lady." The floppy-eared vendor raised her brows. "Any minute now, a Guardian could come strolling down that street. Best be agreeing to my terms, or you'll be sorry."

Or you'll be sorry?

Blake's eyes narrowed. Years of wheeling and dealing for hidden gems in markets and antique stores had honed her bullshit radar and haggling instincts. This vendor had practically salivated over the diamonds.

Bleating from the back of the stall preceded a flash of light as if someone had parted the canvas wall. How many people lurked back there?

Warning bells clanged in her mind. This had all the hallmarks of a scam. A con. Slowly, she retrieved her phone and clutched it against her chest.

"I might just take a moment to think about it." She forced a shaky smile and turned to leave, but collided face-first with a wall of muscle.

"Well, well, well." A deep male voice rumbled above her. Meaty fingers pinched sequins on her hip. "What have we got here?"

"Oh, you've done it now," the vendor crowed. "I warned you, didn't I? Told you they were everywhere."

Heart hammering against her ribs, Blake lifted her gaze to the face of a Guardian.

FOUR

River stepped through a portal into the designated area outside the glass gates of Helianthus City. Once through, he tossed his spent mana stone. It clattered among the others littering the ground, all sacrifices to the city's hungry maw.

Briny, warm air filled his lungs as he surveyed the bustling, colorful markets. The Summer Palace loomed in the distance, calling to him like a beacon. Ada waited there —a powerful healer from the old world, now Jasper's mate, the ex-Guardian turned Summer Court King. Ada held the promise of updates on River's feather regeneration.

Beyond that, the final pilgrimage to his murder's roosting ground awaited. The sooner he dispensed with these formalities, the sooner he could begin hunting Cloud.

His stomach twisted at the thought of arriving without functional wings. River's Guardian status saved his family from being completely shunned for their "weak, lovey-dovey ways." If his weakness was exposed, he could no longer protect them. They'd likely be ostracized.

The familiar sound of cawing pierced the din of the market. Trading, no doubt. Every crow vied for the glory of bringing the rarest treasure to the Great Murder.

Travelers bottlenecked at the citadel gates, papers scrutinized by dead-eyed guards. Usually, he'd soar right over, protocol be damned. But with portal stones keyed to open outside for safety, he found himself relegated to walking in like a commoner.

He despised lines. Loathed waiting.

A gift for his sisters and mother first—that's what he needed. Showing up empty-handed after all this time would cost him more than a few feathers.

He strode into the crowded cobblestone laneway, a giant among the fae. His leather armor marked him apart. *Peacemaker*, his shiny steel chakram, hung at his hips and reflected the sunlight with his prowling gait. The blue, luminescent teardrop beneath his left eye elicited gasps. Whispers raced ahead: "Kingfisher in flight."

River scoffed at the warning. The old Guardian uniform had kingfisher blue piping on the trim. Although the leather was now black, the association clung like a stubborn shadow, as if Guardians were oblivious to the coded warning for fae to hide their contraband. The fools had no idea what was in their best interest.

It was stupid to get worked up over it now. Despite having a Guardian as their king, opinions forged over centuries wouldn't change overnight. Elphyne remained in chaos. The taint's decade-long havoc lingered in every crumbling wall and fearful glance. The vacant Unseelie winter throne and its unclaimed Well tithe left a power vacuum in the north. Mana-warped and taint-sprung monsters multiplied like vermin.

And Nero had been silent. Regrouping, no doubt. Quiet, but not forgotten.

A butterfly carved from rose quartz caught River's eye, its UV color variations shifting with each angle. As he approached the stall, he was met with a blend of fear and disgust from other shoppers.

"Fuck you, too," he muttered, blowing a mocking kiss at a couple scurrying away.

He reached for the carved figurine when the merchant spat on the ground near River's feet and said, "Your taxed coin ain't worth shit here."

River's fingers tightened. His arm trembled with the effort not to hurl the quartz at the man's skull. He'd put down three new unclassified monsters this week alone. Maybe he should have left his stained uniform on to remind them of the danger lurking beyond their walls. The public should be showering Guardians with gratitude, not spitting at them.

Without raising his head, he locked eyes with the bearded wyrm-turd. The merchant stumbled back, nearly toppling a stack of crates.

River weighed his options for delivering a lesson on respect: the *Peacemaker* method, the pointy dagger method, or the table-flipping method?

A burst of cawing yanked his attention down the market.

Few outsiders were aware of the intricacies of crow communication. Over five hundred distinct calls existed, each a coded message embedded in their DNA. River cocked his head, intently listening.

The second round sent prickles racing down his spine. It was a call to arms, specifically a hunt that rallied every cousin within earshot to join in the recovery of a rare treasure. While not always blood-related, crows formed tight-knit groups. Each murder consisted of multiple family settlements called kettles. Some murders, like the one in the Southeast where River came from, housed a population of hundreds.

"You're so generous to refuse Guardian coin," River said to the merchant, pocketing three pretty carvings without paying. "I must remember to recommend your stall to the rest of the Twelve."

"No, no, no." The merchant frantically shook his head and hands. "Take them. It's fine. Go. No recommending."

"Floater," River grumbled as he left. If Cloud were here, he'd—

His fists clenched. He took a steadying breath, forcing the thought away. It had been five years, yet he still slipped into old habits. When would it end?

By the time he reached the gathering crows, his mood had curdled beyond salvaging. Even a healthy brawl was unappealing. Considering his dick hadn't stirred since realizing he couldn't fly, a fuck to release his tension was out of the question.

He longed for simpler days, ignoring responsibilities, diving off cliffs into roaring rivers, pilfering from unsuspecting merchants, bedding their daughters until dawn, then drowning in ale with his two favorite crows until walking became an adventure.

The crowd parted, and a rainbow shard assaulted River's vision. His breath hitched from the surge of dopamine flooding his system, filling him with a mix of pleasure and visceral yearning. He blinked rapidly as flecks of prismatic light danced across his face.

Every fae was unique, from their biology to their

elemental affinity and capacity for holding mana, to their fingerprints, if any. Crow shifters had the added benefit of individual and unique reactions to external stimuli, including UV responses, courtesy of their avian side. What appeared dull and gray to one crow exploded as a riot of glittering color to another.

When the moving crowd swallowed the sparkling rainbow, it felt as if the world had stopped turning. Emptiness. Darkness where there had been light. An aching, black hole spread in his soul. Instinct propelled him forward. He weaved through the throng, chasing, hunting, needing, wanting, heart hammering for more until—

There.

He gasped. Stumbled. Stared and felt his heart ache. She was so beautiful that only a rainbow dared clothe her. Sparkling fabric hugged her curves like a second skin from shoulders to hips to…

"Fuck me," he breathed, stifling a groan as his gaze slowly dragged down, down, her smooth, toned legs.

But it wasn't just her body that stirred something awake within him. Her long, dark hair was a maelstrom of ever-shifting hues where the sunlight caressed it. Each sparkle peppered light into that dark, empty expanse trapped inside his ribcage. The colors faded as she lingered in the shade of the canopy, and all he wanted to do was drag her back into the open.

Caw caw.

His gaze snapped up to the crows lining the canopies across the way. Each locked their razor-sharp focus on the jewels adorning the pretty female's body. Deep in conversation with a vendor, she remained oblivious to their predatory interest.

She was the rare treasure a small crow army had gathered to steal.

A stirring within him gave birth to a dark, territorial urge. He flicked *Peacemaker* on his belt, launching an armada of light shards at the crows, warning them of his presence.

A clatter of cawing, scrambling, and feathers fluttering answered his warning. Some surrendered their hunt, while others merely hopped to new positions, waiting for an opportunity. A change of heart.

It wouldn't happen.

Wait.

What the fuck was he doing? He shouldn't be here stalking treasure, no matter how viscerally he'd reacted to it. He had the customary gifts for his family. He should visit the palace to check his wings so he and Ash could join the pilgrimage to the Great Murder.

Colorful dots of light swam over his face, moving as she moved.

Fuck it.

A short delay wouldn't hurt.

He only needed to wait for the sun's warmth to fade for the appeal to wear off. He casually leaned against a nearby stall, folded his arms, and returned his curious gaze to her hair. Her damp, tangled hair.

Unusual.

She was barefoot, too.

The dress sparkled, yes, but it hung in tatters. Goosebumps pebbled her olive skin as she swayed slightly. But what was that dress made of? Not glass or gems, surely. Or metal, either. They'd be too heavy to cling to her curves like that, which left ... plastic.

Air whooshed from River's lungs.

Was she an old-worlder?

The Well wants what it wants.

His eye twitched. Panic flared beneath his skin.

Run.

Fly.

His traitorous feet refused to budge. His broken wings wouldn't carry him far. And something in her body language sent alarm skating down his spine.

River glanced between the grimy vendor and the woman as she collected her bejeweled brick, clutching it as if it were her last possession. She turned to leave and slammed into a stocky satyr blocking her exit, his shoulders broad from years of hauling crates.

The remaining crows cawed angrily, warning the new horned threat away from their prize. Every instinct screamed for River to walk away. Let this local murder claim her. She was surely an old-worlder whose heart would inevitably drag him into suffering.

Yet somehow, he inched closer.

"I warned you, didn't I?" The vendor sneered at the human. "Told you they're everywhere."

The sparkling woman turned, and a riot of rainbow starlight exploded across River's face. He shielded his eyes, momentarily blinded and stunned by the surge of euphoria it wrought.

"You're a Guardian?" Her voice quivered.

River froze. Had she noticed him? But as he lowered his hand, he realized she addressed the stocky satyr.

"Give me your contraband, lady," the impostor growled, gesturing at her jeweled brick. At rings on her finger. "Or you're dead."

River's jaw slackened. This dick-monkey was impersonating a Guardian—the audacity.

And the vendor was complicit, right under his nose.

Had the whispered warnings of his arrival not reached them? Were they owl-brained?

As shock ebbed, River recognized the gift before him. A little fun was exactly what he needed to snap the sense back into him.

The dirty-faced vendor spotted him first. Her doe eyes widened to rival the moon. But the satyr remained oblivious as River stopped behind him. Good. All the more fun to peck out his eyes.

"How do I know he's a Guardian?" the human asked the vendor. "I want to see credentials."

The husky, defiant note in her voice urged him to lean over the satyr's shoulder and wink as he said, "She has a point, you know."

Wink? What the fuck was that?

"See? He agrees." The shiny human gestured at River without really looking, then did a double-take that stroked every male instinct in his body.

Her plump lips parted. Rainbow-lashed eyes widened with hot, feminine appreciation. The kind so raw and sudden, it was painted on every inch of her Well-damned, beautiful face.

Shit.

He wasn't prepared for this. He'd not expected anyone to ever look at him like that again. But the stirring her light had given him was nothing compared to the reaction inside him now. Seismic. Cataclysmic. He felt it down to the tingling tip of his cock. The bastard finally woke up from its half-a-decade hiatus, as eager to get close to this woman as the awaiting thieves and crows.

All this happened in the span of a wingbeat.

The satyr, still ignorant of a true Guardian behind him, let alone one of the Twelve, snarled, "My fist is the only credential you need."

Death possessed River's body. One moment, he was debating his dick's divine resurrection. The next, he was yanking a horn and slamming his prey to the ground. Within seconds, his knee pinned the impostor's neck. Black claws distended from his fingertips and pressed into chubby cheeks still wobbling from the impact with the ground.

How *dare* he threaten her?

Violence roared through River's veins, warping his vision. One twitch, and he'd shred the satyr's face. He'd claw into his mouth and rip out that tongue. Only the human's sharp intake of breath stayed his hand.

The last remaining crows squawked and fled. Bystanders scattered, seeking safety at distant stalls or escaping to the next market aisle, far from where one of the Twelve prepared to dispense justice.

Justice?

For what, a stranger's threat to a woman he'd never met?

No.

Justice was serving Cloud a cold dish called revenge. Not this.

The Well wants what it wants.

River's panic resurged. This human was *not* his mate. No fucking way was he doing this for her. It was a knee-jerk reaction. Some kind of rainbow drug. His parched dick was a divining rod, and she was water. That was all. The notion doused his senses, and he retracted his claws.

He straightened, glowering down at the satyr. "Give me

one good reason why I shouldn't hack your balls off for impersonating a Guardian."

"She's covered in contraband."

"And you took it upon yourself to—hey, where are you going?"

The human was already five steps away, melting into the market throng. *Well-dammit.* She moved as quietly as a mouse. But with the crowd dispersed and her prismatic dress gleaming like a beacon now that she'd hit the sun, she couldn't hide for long.

River jabbed a finger at the satyr, intending to lecture, and came up short. Only one thought occupied his mind: chase the little rainbow mouse.

FIVE

Growing up surrounded by brothers, Blake was no stranger to violence.

Once, her brother Mick tormented their other brother John for twenty minutes by flicking rubber bands at his face. John endured it silently until he exploded, breaking Mick's ribs with a single, calculated jab. The ensuing brawl left its mark on family history. Multiple Hartleys required stitches, and several pieces of furniture needed repair.

But when the Guardian brutally subdued the horned man, Blake realized that what she had mistaken for violence was merely a love tap in comparison. More terrifying was her immediate, visceral attraction to the newcomer, an instinctive lowering of her guard. He'd winked at her, and her stomach fluttered into her throat. None of this was normal, least of all the black claws sprouting from the Guardian's fingertips.

Definitely not normal.

Alarm blared, and she bolted, her bare feet slapping against sun-warmed cobblestones. A quick glance over her shoulder sent her pulse racing. His quarrel forgotten, the leather-clad, tattooed Guardian stalked a few meters behind. She locked eyes with his intense, ocean-blue gaze, startled, then whipped her gaze forward and picked up her pace. Dots swam in her vision.

Oh god. Oh god. What the hell was happening? Was he really going to kill her because of her sequined dress?

The crowd pressed in. Bodies jostled her, elbows and shoulders colliding. Voices layered over each other—hawkers shouting prices, customers bartering in clipped tones, and the occasional child's screech slicing through the din. A goat bleated nearby, and Blake flinched, nearly stepping into something sticky pooled between cobblestones.

Heat crawled up her back as she dodged a wicker basket. He remained behind her. She didn't need to look; his presence loomed like a firestorm, impossible to ignore. Her heart slammed against her ribs as she forced her aching legs onward. *Blend in. Just blend in.*

A table stacked with vibrant cushions, decor, and folded, jewel-encrusted scarves caught her eye. A scarf could hide her identity. She darted toward it, weaving through merchants and customers. Once at the homewares stall, she slowed and tried to appear like a regular shopper, but trembled as she reached for a cushion.

The woman behind the table barely glanced her way, preoccupied with rearranging products before unpacking a box farther down. Blake's attention snagged on a cracked vase catching the light. Her fingers hesitated before closing around it. The texture felt rough beneath a layer of grime, but the delicate fracture lines instantly told a story she recognized.

"She's got the razzle underneath all this muck," she murmured, rubbing her thumb over its surface.

She'd been obsessed with Kintsugi during her early days of upcycling. The Japanese pottery art captivated her with how the gold seams turned broken pieces into something beautiful. She rotated the vase, tracing fractures with her fingertips: no gold veins yet, but potential for a striking pattern.

Another shopper bumped into her from behind, nearly dislodging the vase from her grip. Her fingers clenched reflexively as she glanced back. A streak of leather and shadow moved at the edge of her vision. Her stomach knotted.

"Just focus," she told herself. "Maybe he didn't see you."

As she faced the front, a shadow fell across the vase and remained. Her breath caught as the vendor's eyes widened at something behind Blake.

Slowly, she turned, and, yep, there he stood. Cracks and wear patterns in his leather suggested years of reaching for the same weapons.

The Guardian casually rested his hand on the table beside her, so close she felt his body heat through her skin. She stared at that hand, caught by the breadth of its span. Artistic tattoos laced in intricate patterns over his skin, art broken and sliced by a network of fissures—scar tissue so fine it was almost indistinguishable.

"Interesting choice." His voice, deep and velvety, brushed against her ear. "Why that vase?"

He plucked it from her hands and edged closer, hotter, filling her vision with leather and daggers as he leaned his hip against the table, broad chest virtually in her face.

"I ... just thought it was pretty."

"This cracked thing?" He tilted the vase, inspecting it with the same precision she'd used moments before. Startlingly blue eyes flicked to her. "Funny. I thought you'd be more interested in shinier things."

The words hit like a challenge. "What's that supposed to mean?"

"Just an observation, little rainbow mouse."

"Rainbow mouse?" The absurdity of the nickname sent heat flashing to her cheeks. "Is that supposed to be clever?"

"Clever? No. Accurate? Absolutely." He leaned in, smirking. "All sparkly and scurrying about. It fits."

"I am *not* scurrying."

"No?" His head tilted, his gaze heavy as it traveled over her. "Could've fooled me with your little dance earlier."

Her hands curled into fists, nails biting into her palms.

"I liked the vase because of the flaws," she announced. "They're what makes it sparkle." Realizing she had raised her voice, she took it from him and inspected it again, hoping the familiar rush of a new project would anchor her spiraling emotions. And it did. Without fail, every time she set her mind to bringing the razzle out, she went all giddy. Her finger traced a splintered fissure. "It's in the cracks," she whispered, "where beauty hides."

"I don't see it."

"Look—" She rubbed the flaw with her thumb. "With a little polish and buff, something sparkly reinforcing the break, she's not just beautiful. She's stronger than ever before."

"So ... you *do* like shiny things." He smiled—a lazy, smug gesture—and it was worse than his smirk. It made every cell in her body clamor, begging her to inch closer.

"You missed the point."

"Which is?"

"You wouldn't get it."

His big fingers wrapped around the vase and tugged, but this time, she refused to let go. The action yanked her closer and fired a challenge in his eyes. He kept pulling. If she didn't let go, she'd fall against him.

The vendor busied herself at the far end, stacking cushions that needed no rearranging. Blake swallowed hard, released the vase, and tried to focus on anything but the Guardian. Yet her gaze drifted back, unbidden, to him, examining the vase like it held answers to questions he'd never asked. Maybe he actually wanted to know.

The strangest part was that despite the violence she'd witnessed earlier, she didn't feel like her life was threatened now. She was alive. Two feet and a heartbeat. That counted for something, right?

Forcing an exhale, her breath tickled her cleavage, reminding her of what she'd tucked there. She glanced down. Then up. He still studied the vase. Down again. Her phone had slipped deeper. Another move, another jiggle, and it would fall down her stomach to the ground. Actually, that could work. If she let it fall, and the Guardian arrested her, or whatever they did, maybe she could return later and find it. Giving it up felt like surrendering a piece of her soul.

"What you got there, Sparkles?"

She slapped her hands over her breasts. "Nothing."

The Guardian's laugh was rich and deep. His shoulders shook with mirth, his posture loose, his head tossed back. Maybe those vendors had it all wrong. He wasn't dangerous. His laugh wouldn't seem so genuine and carefree if he were … would it?

Her eyes lowered over his body, over the muscular torso hidden behind the uniform, and caught on the daggers. Lots of them were strapped to a belt beside an even scarier weapon—a sharp, curved blade resembling a frisbee.

Danger.

Also, metal. The contradiction was another in the unending line of confusion.

"Listen, mate," she said, forcing confidence into her voice. "Be straight with me. Am I under arrest?"

"Mate?" Dark eyebrows shot up. "Getting ahead of yourself there, aren't you, Sparkles? We only just met."

"It's a figure of speech. And stop calling me sparkles. Or mouse. I have a name."

"Oh? Care to share it?" His grin was infuriating.

"I don't think I will. Am I being arrested or what?"

"Or what. I'm River." He stared. Waited. "You know, like the best body of water the Well has ever blessed this world with?" He stared some more. "This is where you tell me your name. It's polite."

She rolled her eyes and tried to step away.

His hand shot out, grasping her wrist. "Not so fast. We still need to discuss your ... attire."

"My *attire* is none of your business."

"Yes, it is."

"I don't understand. You said you're not arresting me."

"I said, 'or what?'" His gaze flicked over her body, sending an involuntary shiver down her spine. One look from him and her hormones betrayed her. She hadn't felt this intensely drawn to someone since ... well, not even Jeff had made her squirm with a heated look.

"That dress has to go," River announced.

Wait. What?

"Listen here," she growled, surprising herself with the venom in her tone. "Hell will freeze over before I take me clothes off for you or anyone else."

Something flashed in his eyes—surprise, maybe even respect. But it quickly surrendered to that infuriating smirk. "I never told you to take your clothes off for me."

"Yes, you did."

"No, I said it had to go."

"Same thing."

"Your enthusiasm is cute, mouse, but let's take this slow, yeah?" He scanned the marketplace behind her and landed on a curtained area behind the vendor's wares. "You can remove the contraband behind a screen or something."

"Mate—"

"If you keep throwing that word around, I might get the wrong idea."

"Back. The. Fuck. Off."

Leather creaked as he folded his arms. A single, perfect dark brow raised. "You're the one leaning into me."

She became acutely aware of their proximity. Of her racing pulse. Of how he was right. She leaned toward him, not away. What was wrong with her?

Slamming her brows down, she stepped back and held up the back of her left hand. "Get the hint."

River's gaze snapped to her wedding band and engagement ring. She could have sworn his pupils dilated with desire. Jeff had prioritized appearances, buying the biggest diamond he could afford. It was impossible to miss. She waggled the sparkly thing and added, "I'm married."

"Married," he repeated, slowly as if tasting the word. His gaze darkened, and his voice dropped an octave. "Do I look like someone who lets anything get in the way of taking what I want?"

Oh boy. Why did his answer make her stomach flip? That reaction alone proved this must be a dream. This tatted bad-boy type wasn't for her. She preferred clean-cut, sporty men. Not the jaw-cut-from-steel-and-hair-so-black-it-looked-blue type.

Blake laughed hysterically in his face. "People don't change their type overnight!" A wave of dizziness swept inside her head as she nodded to herself and mumbled, "I'm in a dream."

He gave her a dubious look. "Okay."

"You're not real!" She jabbed him in the chest—in the hard, leather-covered, and warm chest.

"Fairly certain I am."

"Nope." She squeezed her eyes shut and tapped the phone trapped in her cleavage. "There's no place like Oz. There's no place like Oz."

"Where's Oz?"

"Australia."

"But—"

"Shh." She tapped a third time. "There's no place like Oz."

She held her breath and wished with all her might that she would wake up in bed.

"One. Two—" A goat bleated.

River's chuckle oscillated between deep and boyishly amused. Annoyed, she peeled open one eye, then the other, and found him staring at her with a smile tugging at his lips.

"Please don't stop," he said. "You're most entertaining."

"Fuck you."

"Since you asked nicely." He glanced around contemplatively. "I guess the cushions could work." He plucked a tasseled orange one and hugged it to his lap. "What were you trying to do, anyway?"

"Go home," she replied in a duh tone, waving her ring finger. "To me husband!"

The Guardian's eyes flashed with something—anger? Disappointment? Before she could decipher it, she bolted.

Didn't get far.

"For *Crimson's* sake, stop," he growled, catching her not even two feet away. "I'm not going to hurt you. You're just too easy to play with."

Her pathetic struggle had no effect against his strength. Her brain sloshed as he spun her to face him. The world tilted on its axis. Sequins snagged on his weapons, ripping and popping off, falling to the cobblestones.

"Let's try this again," he said. "You need to come with me. I promise I'll be gentle … mostly."

"No thank—"

"Tut-tut." His calloused palm smothered her lips. "That's a no-no word here in Elphyne."

Elphyne? She'd never heard of the place.

With her air supply restricted, her vision transformed from white dots to colors swimming through a white haze. Her legs buckled.

The scent of leather and something wild—pine forests and open skies—enveloped her moments before River's arm snaked around her waist. He pulled her flush against his body.

"Whoa there, little rainbow mouse," he murmured. "I've got you."

"Stop calling me that." Blake's head swam. "Not a mouse."

"No, you most definitely are not," he answered. "Sparkles fits you better."

"How about fucking cunt," she slurred.

"Only if you beg."

"I meant … you are … not … me…"

"Sure you did—wait. This isn't an escape ploy. You're really not feeling well, are you?" Concern replaced his amusement as her stomach rolled, and she heaved. "Please don't puke on me."

Somehow, she managed to avoid his leather and lurched to the side. More black gunk spewed from her mouth and splashed on the porous stone. Deft fingers gathered her lengthy hair, pulling it back. The action both anchored her and allowed cooling air in. With one arm banded around her shoulders and the other hand in her hair, the Guardian stopped her from plunging face-first into her vomit.

"I've got you," he soothed. "Let it all out."

Trying to stem the deluge proved impossible, but he stayed. He held her steady when she wanted to drift away with the shifting tides inside her head.

She vaguely registered his growled warning for someone to look the other way, or he'd curse their eyes out, but then he returned to offering soothing words and rubbing her back. This moment of compassion from a stranger surpassed anything her husband had ever shown her.

When she finished retching, he didn't flee or demand she clean up her mess. He didn't reprimand her for stinking out the house or bathroom. He tilted her face toward his and wiped tears from her eyes with his thumbs.

Caught in the snare of his ocean blues, she found herself sinking. The distant sensation of her rings sliding off her finger should have alarmed her, but as unconsciousness closed in, she only had the bizarre notion that water wasn't trying to drown her this time. It wrapped her in a calming blanket and kept her afloat.

The last thing Blake registered was the rumble of his deep voice. "Don't worry, Sparkles, I'll keep your shinies safe."

SIX

Blake opened her eyes to a strange room. Not a beach this time, but a bed in a small, curtained cubicle. It smelled like lemon and something heady. Every surface was bathed in a calm, pastel blue.

At the foot of her bed, a tattooed Guardian slouched in a chair with his head back, jaw slack, one arm dangling, and the other on his lap. His long leather-clad legs were sprawled with that instinctive dominance that men seemed born knowing how to claim. Asleep.

A bouquet of lavender sat in a vase on the side table. The same cracked vase from the markets. The same Guardian.

"Bloody hell," she croaked out. "This is real."

She pressed the heels of her palms into her eye sockets, but the memory of those affronted ocean blues drifted unbidden into her mind. He'd told her to take off her dress. Frowning, she lifted the sheet and discovered a soft gown had replaced it. *Motherfucker.*

A quick mental assessment revealed she felt physically better, not worse—no signs of pain or injury.

Pulse quickening, she scanned the small cubicle for a weapon. Nothing but the vase. Not even the arsenal he'd carried on his belt earlier. The Guardian's jacket hung carelessly open, revealing a glimpse of soft white cotton clinging to his muscular torso. A flash of a taut abdomen. His closed fist rested on his lap, clutching something tightly.

River's sculpted power made her all too aware that she'd become a faded echo of her former self. Without her concealer, contouring, and the calculated lighting that made her videos sparkle, she was just … ordinary.

Face it, Blake … some things are just common.

She turned away, adjusting her borrowed clothes to hide her stomach. That's when she noticed her ring finger was bare. And her phone was nowhere in sight.

Don't worry, Sparkles, I'll keep your shinies safe.

She glared at River's clenched fist on his lap. He'd stolen her wedding rings. That little fucker.

As quietly as possible, she slid the blanket from her body but froze when it rustled loudly. She checked on the sleeping Guardian. His brows twitched together, and he made short, hitched sounds as though he was having a nightmare.

Still asleep. Good.

She swung her bare legs over the bedside. The pale blue gown rode up to her thighs. Huh. Interesting. Her legs and feet were clean. Had he bathed her? The thought left an uncomfortable yet not entirely unwelcome feeling circling her chest.

Blake tiptoed toward him, holding her breath. Before losing her nerve, she lowered to her knees and inspected his fist more closely. He was definitely clutching something, more tightly now, but it couldn't be her phone. Strangely, she hadn't noticed the blue glittering marks on his hand before.

They swirled over his skin in a pattern that flowed and worked with his existing tattoos—tattoos she distinctly remembered.

Perhaps the market's bright light had obscured the blue marks, or maybe they were made from some kind of glow-in-the-dark ink that only showed indoors. Unable to hold the air in her lungs any longer, she exhaled … right onto River's skin.

He went utterly still. Then, a single eye popped open and focused on Blake. It closed again. He stretched his arms above his head and yawned languidly, exposing more of that obscenely toned abdomen. His foot slid out and bumped into her, knocking a squeak from her lips.

"Oh. Hello, Sparkles," he greeted, lazy heat in his amused stare. "On your knees for me already?"

Blake's cheeks blazed. "I'm just trying to get me things you stole. You know, like the wedding rings and phone."

His expression went blank. "You don't need them anymore."

She stared, wondering if he was serious. No one who flirted this much could be serious. And she wasn't in prison. So, how bad could this situation be?

"Give it back. I want to call me husband."

She wasn't sure why she kept bringing that up, but every mention of her husband made River's expression darken. Weird feelings churned in her body. She felt untethered. Irritated by her own instability.

He leaned down until his nose hovered inches from hers. "You don't need him anymore either."

"What kind of drongo thing is that to say?"

"Drongo?" He blinked.

"Just give me phone back, alright?"

"Can't." He sat back. "It's destroyed. Even if it wasn't, it's a two-thousand-year-old relic. It won't work."

Her deepening irritation brightened his entire expression. He very well might thrive on provoking people. She would have hurled something physical at him if not for those words: *two-thousand-year-old relic*. At the market, the vendor had called Blake an old worlder.

Relic. Old. Relic. Old worlder. Old. *Old*.

The ancient, cracked yet familiar vase. Her disintegrating dress. The fairytale people with animal features who dressed almost, but not quite, normal.

"What are you saying?" she asked quietly, staring at her hands. "Please just be straight with me."

Perhaps he glimpsed her emotions teetering on the edge of collapse, but he finally abandoned his games.

"What's your name?" he asked.

"Blake."

"Blake, look at me."

She didn't want to. Instinct warned her that she'd never resurface once she locked eyes with him, but she needed to know. She looked up.

"Your world is gone," he said. "It was turned into a wasteland after a nuclear winter. You're one of the lucky few humans who survived."

"Few? Like how many? A few thousand? A few—" Something in his expression strangled the words in her throat.

"I only know of nine other women from your time. Maybe ten." His eyes softened. "Everyone you know is dead."

She blinked. Stared. Then, she laughed so hard that her ribs ached. Tears blurred her vision. When she could breathe again, she wiped them away and said, "Good one, mate. For a moment there, I thought you said…" Her words withered as she caught his solemn expression. She glanced over at the cracked vase—the familiar, older, *ancient* vase.

Suddenly, her lungs refused to work.

"Where's me phone?" she gasped out, hyperventilating, eyes wide. "I need to speak to Jeff. Me husband."

"You have me."

"I don't want you!" she shouted.

His brows rose. A hardness formed in his eyes. "The feeling's mutual, Sparkles."

"I want to talk to me dad. Me brothers Mick and Johnno. Jimmy. I need to—" She lunged and palmed his chest, snarling, "Where'd you put me wedding ring? I want it back. I want—"

He seized her wrists with one big hand and held them wide so that she twisted and fell against him.

"You're not getting it back!" he shouted. "Forget about your fucking husband. He's dead!"

Tears burned her eyes. "You're an arsehole."

"So they keep telling me."

"A fucking cunt!"

"We've established that."

"I hate you."

"Mutual."

"You don't get to decide—"

"That's where you're wrong." His eyes blazed with murderous anger as he pushed her off and seized her hand, forcing it open. That's when she noticed the blue ambiance in the room wasn't natural. It emanated from glowing marks down her arm, the same as his. How had she missed that? But before she could question it, he dropped a sprinkle of tiny cold objects into her palm and said, "It's my job to decide what stays and what goes."

"Why?"

The anger drained from his voice. "Because I'm a Guardian. Metal and plastic block the flow of mana—magic. It's my job to ensure forbidden substances are destroyed so that life continues to flourish after the nuclear winter, and so your greedy human descendants don't ruin what's left of this planet." A muscle in his jaw ticked. His gaze darted down to the blue marks, then back up to her face. "Whether you like it or not, you're stuck with me. I'm your Well-blessed mate. Whoopdie-fucking-doo."

He rose, towering over her, and then strode out. The curtain swished behind him. When she glanced down at her palm, she found diamonds. Not just the ones from her engagement ring and wedding band, but every hidden gem she'd bedazzled onto her phone. He'd painstakingly plucked out each one and discarded the plastic.

Diamonds were all she had left of her world.

These little rocks held so much value back then, just as her phone had been her lifeline to people she thought were friends, family, and her entire identity.

All gone.

SEVEN

CIRCA 200 YEARS AGO, WHEN RIVER WAS KNOWN AS MANFRI, CLOUD WAS CIELO, AND ASH WAS NIKAN

Manfri ignored the wind ruffling his feathers and inched toward the cliff's edge. The river below yawned wide—at least a hundred feet down. Hit the water wrong, and the impact would crush their bodies like stone. Sounded like fun.

He looked at his best friend, Cielo Cardona, and reminded him of the deal: "We jump. No wings. First crow to wimp out and shift is a floater—and has to sneak into the Collector's trove to steal something."

"You're insane." Cielo peeled off his leather jacket.

"You're a fuck face." He grinned back.

They'd been best friends since they were fledglings, now both seventeen. Already veterans of official Gatherings, the Cardona Kettle and Umbria Kettle had grown up in the same murder and worked together. They should be tight. Cousins. Better yet, brothers.

But Cielo had been distant lately. For the past year, he'd vanished for long stretches with every turn of the moon. When the Cardonas asked about Cielo's whereabouts, Manfri covered for his friend in a wingbeat. He didn't give a flying kuturi's ass about stretching the truth. Cielo always returned with some kind of treasure to share. Crows always circled back home, no matter how far or wide they flew. And for the first time since their friendship began, Manfri noticed peace in his friend's perpetually restless eyes.

But with that contentment came softness. Cielo had stopped taking risks like he used to. Stopped spending much time with Manfri at all. It was time to remind him why crows had more fun.

Shifting his wings away, Manfri felt his inner mana supply deplete. Uh-oh. He widened his eyes at Cielo, who paused mid-unbuttoning of his leather breeches.

"What?" Cielo swiped black locks from his forehead. "Something in my hair?"

Manfri's eyes narrowed. "Since when do you care what's in your hair?"

"I don't."

"It's a female, isn't it? That's why you're always disappearing."

Cielo stripped off his breeches and strode naked to the cliff's edge.

"I was joking." Manfri gestured at the cliff. "You don't have to jump if you're out of mana."

"You're out, aren't you?"

"Maybe." He loved that word.

Wind gusted, lifting Cielo's hair as he cautiously peered over the edge, but curiosity had piqued in his blue eyes.

He slid Manfri a look. "You're empty?"

Manfri shrugged nonchalantly and finished undressing. He shivered as he joined Cielo at the edge. They stared at the cascading river, the sun beating down on their heads. The raging water sparkled like diamonds. Crimson, it was a long way down. But, fuck it. Diamonds. They were nature's apology for shit.

"What if there are actual diamonds down there?" he muttered.

"Not sure if they're worth it," Cielo returned.

"If the reward isn't worth the risk, what in the Well's name are we doing here?"

Manfri backed up from the cliff, disappointed to see the relief on his friend's face. That crow was changing too much, too fast. Soon, Cielo would be mated, knocking up some female, all nested and domesticated. They were too young for that. Hadn't partied hard enough, stolen enough, gambled enough. Fucked enough.

Hadn't lived yet.

This was another reason why having an affair with a human was bad. Just because they had short life spans didn't mean fae had to be cautious, too.

Manfri hardened his resolve and ran forward. He leaped, flipping up his middle finger at Cielo as he sailed over the cliff's edge. Airborne. Free falling, weightless, without wings to save him from a sparkling, raging river that could pulverize his insides.

Um.

This was a better idea in his head. How did he submerge correctly again? Wasn't there a way humans could safely drop to minimize impact? But what was it?

Fuck.

Gravity snatched him down. The wind stole his scream as a shadow appeared on his right. Cielo had jumped, too. Except where Manfri fell like a pinwheeling starfish, Cielo slapped his palms to his hips and squeezed his legs together, toes down like a dancer.

"Do it!" he shouted. "Feet first. Point them."

Manfri copied just before they pierced the river's surface. Water engulfed them. Down, down, slicing through the current like falling daggers. It was deep. Instead of crashing into the *riverbed, their feet gracefully touched the bottom. No diamonds beneath his toes. Just silt and smooth stones. What a shame.*

Violent bubbles overtook his vision as Cielo kicked and swam back to the surface.

Something stopped Manfri from following. It was so inviting down here. Peaceful. Quiet and comforting. No responsibility. No drama. No best friend leaving him behind for bluer skies and, no doubt, a warm pussy to sink his horny cock into.

Manfri wanted a family one day—every crow did. But not yet. Not for centuries.

Lungs burning.

Need air.

He pushed up and flailed toward the surface. He probably should have learned to swim. Oops. The current was stronger than he remembered. The flow battled his arms and legs, denying him freedom. He somehow managed to find the surface, but barely had time to gulp air when the current took him under. Oh no. He still didn't have enough mana in his reserves to shift his wings out.

If a kelpie lurked in these waters, he was in trouble. Dead.

Spluttering for air, his hand shot up to stroke. Something grasped his wrist. He glanced up, fearing the worst, but it was Cielo. Relief flooded Manfri as his friend yanked upward, pulling him out of the water so forcefully that his arm nearly dislocated.

Jet-black wings beat in a frenzy, spraying water as Cielo fought the raging current. For a long, fearful moment, Manfri feared his friend wasn't strong enough to fight this powerful force of nature.

"Just let me go," he shouted up. "Save yourself."

He would have laughed at the cutting glare Cielo sent him, but he was too busy being rescued. Cielo beat his wings harder, faster, flying them higher and higher into the sun.

"You fucking mad cunt!" he roared down, taking them up the cliff face.

They crested the top and landed in a tumbling heap beside their discarded clothes. Manfri rolled, tumbled, and saw the world spinning until they faced the blue sky. Coughing and lungs heaving, he stared up, silently thanking the Well for Cielo's stubborn loyalty. When the initial panic wore off, adrenaline still coursed through his veins, pumping life and purpose from his heart. Once he'd gathered his breath, he whooped loudly at the sun. "That was fucking awesome!"

Cielo groaned, "I think my aching wings would protest."

"Then maybe you should have flown us to the riverbank instead of up the cliff."

"Are you complaining about being rescued?"

"No."

"Well ... I didn't think of that, did I?"

Manfri sat up, grinning. Like a shaggy wolf, he shook the water from his blue-tipped black hair. His friend scowled and got to his feet, dusting his body.

"Why did you jump without mana?" Cielo grumbled.

"Humans can do it. Why can't we?"

"Because fae don't know how to do it like the humans. We're too used to relying on the Well to save our hides."

"But you knew."

Cielo went quiet.

It hurt Manfri that his friend wouldn't share his adventures. They were supposed to share everything, forever, like they used to.

He scooped up his breeches and shoved his wet, dirty legs inside, but his feet snagged. He grumbled and pushed harder. He took a moment to calm down before trying again. His shirt came next. Finally dressed, he turned to his best friend and said, "I don't understand why you can't tell me, cuz. It's not like I'll blab to anyone."

"You don't get it." Cielo sighed as he finished dressing.

"So, help me get it. Is she beautiful?"

"I can't." Cielo's wings snapped out, spraying water and sand. He tugged his split shirt over his head, accommodated his wings through the flaps, and buttoned them at the waist. "At least ... not yet."

The crafty and handsome crow was conflicted, but a layer of that peace still existed in his eyes. How could Manfri be angry if his friend was happy?

"Just tell me this: is she a diamond?"

Their gazes clashed. Cielo nodded.

Manfri kicked a pebble. "Who will do this shit with me now, then?"

"For Crimson's sake, Mannie, I'm not dead."

"But you'll leave me for a pretty pussy that probably tastes like the sweetest honey..." His words trailed off as he caught Cielo's dreamy, self-satisfied expression. "Fuck off. You've already tasted her, haven't you?"

Cielo hid his smirk by walking away.

Manfri chased after him. "Does she have a friend?"

"No."

"Crows before hoes."

"Why do you think I jumped in after you?"

"You did." He chuckled. "Fucking dumbass."

Manfri almost bumped into wings as Cielo stopped. He faced Manfri, opened his mouth, and then shut it. The emotion in his eyes was sobering. Manfri knew precisely what his friend wanted to say.

This bond they shared was more than kettle loyalty. More than the murder. It was looking into your friend's eyes and not needing to say a thing because they knew exactly what the other was thinking. It was knowing that no matter how much time passed or what mess they were in, they'd circle back home if they needed each other.

It was never being alone.

Manfri shoved Cielo's shoulder. "My feet hit the water first."

"What?"

"Bro." His tone was admonishing, but his eyes twinkled. "My feet hit the water first. Ergo, you are the loser."

Cielo looked east … to where, beyond the forest, dark canyon spires pierced the sky like jagged swords. Somewhere in that shrouded place lived the Collector—a vicious fae more crow than man. Or so they'd been told. No one had ever seen him. Only heard stories.

Ice skated down Manfri's spine.

"They say he's got claws so long," he whispered, "that they'll pierce through your heart to the other side."

"I heard he has no hands, just wings, feet, and a beak."

"I heard he's covered in feathers from head to toe."

"Cool." Cielo's brows winged up.

"Not cool. Can you imagine if your dick was feathered?"

"Good point." Cielo stared into the distance for another minute before his lips stretched into a wicked smile. "Fine. I'll steal something. Someone needs to show you how to do it properly."

Manfri crowed excitedly and clapped his friend on the back. "Then afterward, we'll celebrate in town, boast about our new fortune, and get laid!"

Well-damn, it had been a while since they'd ventured into Cornucopia and flirted with the ladies. He habitually said silly things around attractive women, such as comparing their eyes to his favorite blue crayon from childhood. What gives with that? If they rejected him or if he flirted with the wrong mated female, he felt like a complete floater, but Cielo always knew how to put the mean ones back in their place.

But the real ones that had Manfri's heart palpitating, his tongue dry, and his cock tingling like a tinger, were the females who challenged him. The ones who never backed down —from a prank, a fight, a dare, a kiss. No matter how wild Manfri became, they held their own. They pushed him toward the deep end but then jumped in first.

In truth, he wanted another best friend.

EIGHT

Three days of brooding had accomplished nothing. River circled his opponents in the Summer Palace courtyard—Aeron, Jasper, and his son Aspen—while his thoughts spiraled into darker territory.

Blake wanted nothing to do with him. Not that he gave a shit. He had places to be. Eyes to peck out. But Ash still hadn't arrived. Jasper denied knowledge of the item Ash believed worthy of trading for the cryptex. The Great Murder loomed a week away, and every day of delay carried consequences.

"You going to stand there staring, or will you toss that dagger at me?"

Jasper stood thirty feet away, sweat gleaming on his muscular chest, sword hanging heavy in his hand. Beside him, Aeron leaned on his great sword, amusement dancing in his eyes. Prince Aspen sniggered from a nearby bench beneath a rose-covered trellis.

Fuck them.

River dropped his dagger and unhooked *Peacemaker*. The

chakram was designed for versatility. Split the circular blade into a crescent in each hand for close combat, or release the full circle in a brutal, long-range attack. He'd once sliced clean through troll neck with this beauty.

His fingers hesitated when the cool metal touched his palm. Nothing felt right anymore. He returned it to his belt and muttered, "I need a drink."

Turning his back, he strode to a wooden table near the palace entrance where refreshments glistened in the afternoon light. No booze in the carafes. What kind of palace was this?

I hate you.

Blake's words sliced through his mind, sharper than any dagger. He couldn't blame her. He hated himself, too.

She had a *husband*.

He poured himself a stupid lime drink.

Of all the Well-blessed Guardians, River's mate was the only one already in a relationship. Not that he cared if her heart belonged to someone else. It should make it easier for him to walk away, to hunt down Cloud at the Great Murder. To get that thirst for vengeance out of his system and move on with his life. Or die.

She spoke weirdly.

She smelled fucking good. Like floral nectar baked in sunlight.

So good.

He glared at the clear blue sky and silently cursed the Well for his continued misfortune. What had he done to deserve this?

His triad tattoo itched, signaling an incoming message. River slammed his cup onto the table and peeled back his sleeve as Ash's scrawl appeared in his forearm flesh.

Can't do it. Go alone.

Disappointment punched River in the gut. He focused on dampening his emotions through the mate bond—something Jasper had mentioned was possible a few days ago. River immediately practiced how to build mental walls, though they crumbled whenever his focus slipped. Better than nothing.

His claw extended, pressed into his skin, ready to change Ash's mind. Nothing came out.

Aeron and Aspen continued sparring, leaving River to his thoughts. Jasper prowled in circles on the patch of lawn, his shaggy, unkempt hair flopping in his golden eyes.

"Come on, crow," he bellowed. "You wanted to train, so let's do this. I don't have all day."

River scoffed. "Yeah, you do. You're the fucking Seelie High King. You do what you want."

"I have responsibilities."

"You used to be fun."

"Fun? I'm still fun!" Jasper's tone rose defensively. "Just last week, I organized a midnight feast for my family under the stars. Aspen loved it. He couldn't stop laughing!"

"Yeah, I'll bet he did," River muttered. "A family picnic. How wild."

"Hey! I still know how to party."

"And by party, you mean host tea parties."

"It was a feast!"

"Sure. Like I said, you're no fun."

Appalled, Jasper launched into a litany of ways he was still fun, counting each on a finger. River ignored him and scratched a message to Ash on his triad tattoo: *Where are you?*

Steel clashed against mana-enforced bone, followed by a

grunt and Aspen's shout of triumph. The scent of post-magic ozone drifted on a breeze. River glanced over to see Aeron hand-sign something to the prince and bow in acknowledgment of defeat.

River checked his tattoo for a reply. Nothing. He quickly scrawled words guaranteed to grab attention: *Go and see Clarke. She has something to tell you.*

He didn't want to pull the Prime card, but screw it. If Ash skipped the Great Murder, River would get stuck with official Guardian shit, and he could kiss his revenge goodbye.

"Stop wasting time and stab my dad." The prince's voice, laced with humor, dragged River's attention to where he sat on a stone bench beside Aeron.

Since River had seen him last year, Aspen had filled out with muscle, his voice deepening. But he was still a fledgling compared to Aeron's bulk, never mind Jasper's powerful form and veins rippling beneath his skin. His son had won the sparring match purely because of his inherited, spontaneous portaling ability.

"Unless you're all talk," Aspen taunted.

The prince had a death wish. River palmed *Peacemaker's* smooth surface. A glance to the right revealed Jasper's hawk-like gaze.

Why coddle the boy? False victory would only lull him into a misplaced sense of security, leading him headfirst into danger when the real battle arrived. The last person River let win was his little sister, Lark, before she learned to fly over a century ago.

"Care to put your coin where your mouth is?" River quirked an eyebrow at the prince. "And your head?"

"No," Jasper barked.

"Why not?" River shrugged.

"Yeah, why not, Dad?" Aspen jumped up. "He can't hit me. I'm too fast."

"I said no."

Aeron hand-signed something to Jasper, who signed back. The secret exchange grated on River's nerves. He ground his teeth and focused on Aspen, who'd already paced toward the lawn.

River supposed this was as good a distraction as anything else could be. Even now, Blake's tumultuous emotions swarmed into him through their bond. Maybe he should teach her to block her emotions. Maybe they'd all be happier without feelings.

He growled.

"Name your price, crow." Aspen paced with natural-born predatory grace.

River cocked his head, contemplating. "One hundred red coin and a portal stone keyed to 'up your fucking ass' says I can slice off the tip of your pointy little fur-tipped ear from fifty paces away."

"I said no!" Jasper's voice cracked like a whip.

"Except for the portal stone, it's a deal!" Aspen grinned.

Excellent.

"River." Jasper's warning carried a hint of a plea. "Take it back."

"Maybe if you beg." River's eyes crinkled. "A king on his knees might be fun."

"Dad, it's fine." Aspen vanished, reappearing fifty paces away by the rose hedges. "It'll be the easiest coin I've ever made. I've got plenty of mana left."

"In case the 'portal stone up your ass' bit didn't give it away, son, he doesn't care about the coin."

Aspen snorted. "Dad, he's a crow. All they care about is their shinies."

River gasped. "I'm offended."

"No, you're not." Jasper's eyes beseeched him. Even Aeron's concern mounted, his hand drifting to the sword against his leg.

"Relax," River drawled, unclipping *Peacemaker* from his belt. "I'll only take the tip of his ear off. Aspen's mother is the best healer in Elphyne. Should only bleed for a little bit."

"If that weapon leaves your hand..." Fury turned Jasper's voice to gravel.

Aspen finally picked up the dangerous undercurrent. He stopped bouncing on his toes, his gaze darting between his father and Aeron as River strolled onto the lawn.

River narrowed his eyes at his opponent, then swapped *Peacemaker* for a normal dagger. Not that it mattered, but if a less lethal weapon made Jasper feel better, so be it.

"You know, princeling," River drawled, using the dagger to scrape dirt from beneath his nails, "crows never forget the faces of people who've wronged them."

"So?" Aspen swiped blond hair from his forehead, confusion evident.

"You ever wonder how it's possible?"

"Good memory?"

"I admit that helps." River flipped the dagger once, twice. "But that's not entirely the reason. I'll give you a hint. It's the same thing that helps us hunt itty bitty mice scurrying through the forest from way up high."

Or a sexy rainbow mouse through the markets.

"Good eyesight?"

"That also helps, but sadly, you're wrong again."

Aeron's palm slapped over his face in defeat.

Jasper shook his head. "Enough with the lessons, River. Fine, you win. I'm not fun. How about I get the mana weed out, and we can roll a joint just like old times? We'll forget about all this."

"Nah. I'm over that idea now. I think your son is more fun."

"What the fuck is going on?" Aspen growled. "Just throw the fucking dagger."

"Language, son," Jasper scolded.

"So uncouth for royal ilk." River twitched the dagger toward the prince but didn't release it. He studied Aspen's reaction and waited until the UV light glimmered in the air five feet to his right, just before he appeared there. River's next attempt wasn't a feint. He targeted the prince and flicked his wrist, adjusting his aim toward the shimmer mid-throw, releasing at the perfect moment.

The blade flew from his fingertips. Jasper, the son of a witch, portaled himself before his son and took the hit between his neck and shoulder.

"Party-pooper." River scowled.

The wolf king's deep rumble trembled the ground. Dismayed, Aspen jogged around to see his father as he yanked the dagger out. Blood oozed from the wound. River crouched to replay the angle of his dagger's trajectory. If it had been allowed to continue, the blade would have sliced straight across Aspen's cheekbone. So close. It might have taken off the whole ear.

"What's the matter with you?" Jasper dropped the weapon and glared at River.

"You go too easy on your kid," he countered. "It'll get him killed."

They knew exactly what River meant, which was why

neither Jasper nor Aeron lost their shit at him. Nero might have been silent, but he hadn't given up. The battle wasn't over.

Curiosity etched on the young prince's face. "How did you know exactly where to throw the blade?"

River simply shrugged. A crow never divulged his secrets.

Before Aspen could press further, his father ordered him to collect the red coin from his personal coffers. When he left, Aeron signed angrily.

Jasper watched his hands as he pressed his shirt to his wound, staunching the bleeding, and he grumbled, "I know!"

"Again, with the secret talking." River collected his dagger, hating the glimpse of blue sparkling on the back of his hand. Full of anger and exasperation, he pointed at Aeron and asked Jasper, "What is he even doing here, anyway? Don't they have midwives in the Spring Court?"

The elf king's eyes narrowed as he read River's lips, then he collected his shirt and stormed inside.

"Mating has weakened you all."

"You're out of line," Jasper returned. "Aeron is here because he hopes Ada can heal his hearing before his newborn cries for the first time."

Great.

Now River felt like shit. Fledglings were sacred and precious in crow communities, valued above all treasure. If it were him in that situation, he'd tear apart the world for a solution.

He wiped his dagger across his thigh, cleaning the blood, then sheathed it at his hip. Still unwilling to admit his mistake, he said quietly, "It's not going to work. She can't heal what's not there. I would know."

"Yet you still visit my mate for regular checkups." Jasper sat back, glaring at River. "It's either you have hope, or you're flashing your naked ass at her for other reasons. Which is it?"

The truth deflated River's lungs. No matter how many times he told hope to fuck off, it wouldn't leave. He poured himself another cup of stupid lime water.

"This is the last time," he admitted. "I'm a lost cause."

Jasper lifted his compress, checked his healing wound, and gave River a knowing smirk. "You're the patron saint of lost causes."

"What the fuck is a saint?"

"Old world thing. Ask your new mate."

"I'm leaving in the morning. Without her."

"Whatever you say." Jasper tossed the blood-stained cloth. "Now that you've blown off sufficient steam, I'll allow you to see Ada."

Allow?

River was about to remind Jasper that no one told crows what to do when he noticed the tension in his posture. Worry lines etched between his brows as he leaned forward and stared at his hands. His wolfish ears flattened in defeat.

An uncomfortable feeling squeezed River's chest. "Listen. About your son and ... stabbing you."

"It's fine." Jasper waved him off. "You were right."

"I was?"

"I've been taking it easy on him. It's just..."

Crap. This was about feelings. River searched for a quick exit. Flying was out of the question. Through the palace was worse.

The only fae he talked to about anything resembling feelings were those in his triad, which was recently reduced to a duo.

River didn't leave. He did something stupid instead and prompted, "It's just what?"

The king glanced sideways at him, then leaned back on the bench's backrest. "Have you heard about the bodies Cloud dumped around Crescent Hollow?"

River swallowed hard. "No."

"All human. All refugees from Crystal City under Silver's initiative."

That wasn't good. If Silver facilitated their escape, then those humans were innocent. The old Cloud would never have touched them. But the one who'd split the airship in half with his lightning, frying River while onboard … only the Well knew what that version would do.

"How do you know it's him?" he asked.

Jasper rifled around near his clothes on the ground and retrieved a long, black primary feather.

"Could belong to anyone." Except for the distinct UV patterns on the tip. The bastard had betrayed River, broken his wings. Yet somewhere beneath the fury, an unwelcome voice whispered: *Was there something you did to him first?*

"It could, but it belongs to him. You know it." Jasper stared hard as he twirled the feather. "Tell me about this vendetta bullshit. How far will it go?"

After Rory died, Cloud painted a V across his face using the blood of her enemies, signaling the beginning of his vendetta. At first, River thought Cloud's beef was relegated to Nero, Rory's father. But it seemed his rage targeted all of humanity.

If the Seelie High King asked these questions now, he

was preparing to deal with the problem. Cloud might be strong in mana capacity, being a Guardian with a body covered in his power-enhancing tattoos, but he wasn't Well-blessed. He wasn't a High King. In a battle against Jasper, Cloud would lose.

He'd lose against River now, too.

The knowledge didn't feel as satisfying as it should have.

"Vendettas are crow business," he said. Jasper opened his mouth to protest, but River cut him off. "Even if you knew, it wouldn't matter. What Cloud's doing … it's not normal."

"Do we need to be worried?"

Yeah. We need to be fucking terrified.

He checked his triad tattoo and sighed. Without Ash, then finding the cryptex was up to River. How the fuck was he the responsible one?

He scrubbed his face and replied heavily, "I don't know."

"When you do." Jasper stood. "I'll be the first person you tell."

"Maybe," River replied. He still fucking loved that word. "But I can promise you this—no more innocents will lose their lives if I can help it. I'll stop him, even if I have to kill him."

"Being a leader is hard," Jasper said, scrunching his nose. "But being a good mate, a good parent, is harder."

"Like I said, it makes you weak."

Noise by the rose hedge drew their attention. Jasper's worried expression melted away as Aspen appeared, carrying a small box of what River assumed were red coins.

"No, River." The king smiled at his son. "It makes it all worth it."

NINE

There were five stages of grief: denial, anger, bargaining, depression, and finally acceptance. Blake cycled through the whole gamut in two days. Whoever claimed that would be the end of it was a cunt. On the third day in Helianthus, she woke refreshed, thinking she'd accepted events and could move on. But clarity only meant she had emotional space to spiral once more.

Only days ago, Blake was married to Jeff, living a life she thought was perfect, despite the looming apocalypse. She believed herself surrounded by people who loved her. Now, her heart lay shattered in her chest, her mind fractured, and her arm covered with blue, glittering marks that tethered her emotions to a stranger by something called mana.

She wasn't sure what was worse—total ignorance of Jeff's contempt or experiencing River's emotions, even when he bristled at her existence. He hadn't returned since storming off, yet she sensed his nearby presence fluttering against her consciousness like a moth trapped against glass.

Sometimes the sense of him muffled, and she felt relieved. Other times, she was hit with a barrage of guilt, angst, and too many rapid-fire emotions that she couldn't pick them out.

It was horrifying, humiliating, and embarrassing to know her innermost feelings weren't private. Every time a memory of her father's practical, no-frills parenting or one of her brothers' stupid jokes surfaced, she had to physically clench her jaw to stop the sadness from leaking through the bond.

You cry and get your way, and then I'm miserable all over again.

On the evening of the third day, Blake shuffled toward the bathroom, still in her hospital gown. With every step, she replayed another fact she'd learned about this world. The healing center was nestled inside the palace and run by the Seelie High Queen Ada. She was from Blake's era and mated to King Jasper, who had once worked with River as a Guardian. He still had the same blue twinkling teardrop beneath his left eye. All twelve warriors of their cadre were fated to be mated to someone from the old world. This Well-blessed mating was rare, sacred, and revered above all else. It was also undeniable and irreversible. So when River had carried Blake in unconscious, they'd whisked her straight to this privileged place.

This all-powerful Well had deemed Blake important enough to drag her across oceans and millennia to be here. But she wasn't important. She didn't matter. Jeff was right. She was a shallow, glitter-obsessed upcycling influencer who'd probably fallen in the water when everything froze. Blake hadn't offered the world anything of worth. Her life held no meaning. There were people in her day who'd given up their lives to save those less fortunate. So why her?

There was no satisfying answer, which led to one conclusion. A cosmic clerical error had brought her here. Sooner or later, the Well would realize it had made a mistake and take her back.

Blake padded down a hallway overlooking resplendent palace gardens. Lush greenery cradled vibrant flowers with colors that didn't quite match anything she remembered from her world. The meticulous landscaping was only the beginning of the palace's opulence, yet the queen herself wore casual, modest clothes. At least they weren't beige.

The glass citadel walls glimmered with moving light that fractured into rainbows—a constant reminder that this world might be the same planet, but it wasn't the one Blake had left. Occasionally, she glimpsed the aerial dance of winged fae above the distant city, swooping and diving like falling stars.

Every time she passed this window, she plummeted right back into the first stage of grief.

Denial.

This couldn't be real. She pressed a palm to the cool glass, the surface fogging around her fingertips. A dream was the only explanation. The blue glittering marks spiraling up her arm were beautiful but impossible. So if they weren't real, then the slightly psychotic man with those ocean-deep eyes must also be fake. Only a nightmare would thrust her into some kind of forced-marriage situation with a dickhead like that.

After going to the toilet and glimpsing her reflection in the black glass vanity mirror, Blake cycled into rage. Her fingers gripped the porcelain sink until her knuckles whitened. What kind of world had worked out how to use magic for plumbing sewage but couldn't apply it to a clearer mirror? Or phones. Or the internet! What happened to her followers? Her friends? Her family? Were they all out there floating aimlessly in the ocean, waiting for their moment to wash ashore?

She silently begged this all-powerful Well to give her an answer. She bargained with it daily to reveal a sign. To take her back to Perth, to her world. Where she wasn't alone with her thoughts or with a stranger's emotions in her mind.

So maybe her marriage hadn't been perfect. But she'd have figured out a way to live on. She'd have gone to see her dad, to let him make her the one meal he knew how to cook —steak and eggs—and they'd sit down and speak two words to each other. He always overcooked the steak until it was tough as boot leather, but she never complained. Just ate every bite with a smile as he watched her from across the table, love hiding behind his gruff exterior.

Instead of accepting her help with doing the dishes, her dad would ask for a hand in the workshop. They'd work on some benign project until it was time for her to go. At the door, he would pull her into a bear hug and whisper, *"She'll be right, Bloss. Two feet and a heartbeat."*

In other words, she was still alive. Still standing. As long as she had two feet and a heartbeat, life would go on. Everything would be alright.

Finished in the bathroom, she shuffled back to the healing center's main room, the cool stone floor numbing her toes.

Sooner or later, she had to decide what to do with the rest of her life here. Picking one of the outfits Ada and Trix had brought her would be a good start.

Trix—Beatrix—was another woman from Blake's era.

And another queen married to another Guardian-turned-king. Aeron had fought in a battle against the man who'd nuked their world. It made Blake's blood simmer beneath her skin to know he was here, alive too, and trying to finish what he'd started. She'd never see her family again because of him.

His being here was proof that the Well made mistakes.

She wasn't a hero like the others. Regardless, she still needed to make a decision. Option one was to head to the Order of the Well, the home of some kind of magic police or military, as far as she gathered. It was where the Guardians were trained. Going there meant facing why she hadn't manifested a magical talent yet like the other old-worlders. She wasn't ready for that inevitable disappointment.

Option two was to tag along with River—no thanks.

Option three was to stay here at the palace, couch surf, or rather, ornately-embroidered-chaise surf. The furniture here was intriguing, to say the least. Exploring the palace for a hint of razzle-dazzle potential might be fun. Upcycling a hidden gem would certainly quiet the buzzing anxiety in her mind.

Then again, seeing something old and neglected from her time might crack her open all over.

As she neared the main room, a familiar deep voice stopped her mid-step.

"You sure she's not here?" River grumbled.

"*She* is the cat's mother," Ada returned, her sarcastic drawl evident.

"Whatever that means."

"A cat is like a fee-lion."

"Just say fee-lion then. You've been in Elphyne long

enough to use our words." A pause. "I know she's close. Where is she?"

"Hopefully, she's out exploring. A change of scenery and fresh air will help with her depression. Maybe you'd know if you'd bothered to check in on her, or through your bond."

The sound of a curtain moving on rails accompanied River's reply.

"This is nothing but a nuisance. I'm learning to block it."

"You males are all stubborn idiots."

"And?"

A huff of annoyance. "Did my darling mate teach you how to block your emotions from her?"

"Maybe."

That explained his random, muffled emotions.

"I doubt it." Another huff and rustling. "He knows better than to meddle."

"The sooner we separate our emotions, the faster we carry on with our lives."

"Oh, and I suppose you taught Blake how to block her feelings from you?"

Silence. Then: "She doesn't need to be stuck with someone like me."

"I'm sure you've asked her what she needs." More shuffling and a curtain drawing. "Alright, you know the drill."

"Strip. Shift. Sit?"

"Tonight on *Guardian's Anatomy…*"

Blake's hand cupped her mouth to hide her snort of amusement. She loved watching Grey's Anatomy. That she'd never see a series finale was a travesty.

"What?" River asked.

"God, I miss TV." Ada sighed. "And I miss people who

get the jokes. Trix was too busy being a brainiac in our time to watch Grey's."

"Um. Okay."

This sounded like a private examination. Blake should leave, but the only path back to her bay passed directly by River's bay, or it was back to the bathroom.

And she kind of wanted to talk about Grey's.

River's apprehension and something sharp and electric slammed into her without warning. If pain were an emotion, that might be it. Despite his claims about blocking, he wasn't doing a good job. Maybe he was injured.

She caught herself feeling concerned, then shook it off, fingers digging into her palm. He didn't deserve her sympathy, not after how he'd treated her.

Just go out there. He was the rude cunt, not her. Why should she rearrange her life to avoid him?

She pushed forward before she chickened out, but froze upon entering the room. Three healing bays filled the small, brightly lit space. Hers was farthest away. The middle was empty. River and Ada occupied the third directly in front of Blake. The curtain was only partly closed, perhaps because they'd assumed she was out exploring. No other patients had arrived since Blake.

Through the gap, she glimpsed a slumped muscular back. She gasped, her eyes widening at the great wings sprouting from his shoulder blades. Blue and black feathers glistened with an iridescent sheen, catching the ambient light in hypnotic patterns. Some primal part of her brain recognized their magnificence even as her rational mind struggled to process what she saw.

Wings.

No one had mentioned anything about River having wings. Come to think of it, she might have heard them call him a crow once or twice, but she thought it was just a weird insult. Ada's husband could shift into a wolf. Was River a crow shifter? Claws had sprouted from his fingertips. Her mind flashed to the crows following her at the markets, and she wondered if they shifted into a human form, too.

Her train of thought shattered when River's taut, naked buttocks flexed as he adjusted in his seat. Ada, impervious to the nudity, inspected his legs and then a patchy wing with clinical precision. Her hands hovered, but she didn't touch the majestic feathers. She asked questions about stiffness and flexibility, to which River replied with an innuendo. His tone didn't quite have the same mocking punch as usual. He almost sounded … vulnerable.

"Flex again?" Ada asked, leaning back to make room. His wing barely opened, but it wasn't because of an injury. The bay was too small. Blake bet a single wingspan would cover all three bays if the curtains were opened. Two open wings…

She supposed wings carrying a body like his would need the breadth and strength.

Ada crouched to inspect the patchy, less full wing more closely. Blake caught her flattened lips in profile when she peeled up a few short feathers.

River jerked away and snarled, "No touchy-touchy."

Ada exhaled, her shoulders dropping. "The touching part of this healing process would be over if you'd let me examine you outside, where you can stretch properly."

"Can't." That teasing drawl was back. "Everyone will see my naked ass and want a piece."

"As if you care, Mr. Streaking Through the Order Campus Every Other Night."

His baritone chuckle vibrated through the air, making Blake's stomach flutter traitorously.

"Besides," Ada continued, "you can put on your pants."

"Aww. So soon?"

"I'm done inspecting your legs."

"I'm not doing this outside, so forget it."

"Fine. But ... your stubbornness is not helping your feathers grow back." As Ada continued inspecting his wings, their conversation turned to how River wanted to borrow an item from the royal coffers for a special trade. Then he'd be out of Ada's hair regardless of whether someone called Ash decided to show his "owl-shit" face.

"He's not mentioned it, has he?" River asked.

"Who, Jasper? No."

River continued rattling on about particular items the king might have lying around because he didn't think there was anything here the Collector would want. When Ada bent to inspect a portion of his lower wing, Blake noticed great clumps of feathers missing in sections. Bare skin stretched over bones in patches, pale pink against the dark- ness of his remaining plumage. The sight triggered an instinctive need to touch, to fix, to understand what was broken.

She must have gasped again because they both glanced over.

River's scowl returned in full force, but Ada's face lit up.

"Great timing!" she exclaimed. "Blake, come here. I need help getting under there and comparing the regrowth to how it was at my last examination."

"Me?" she squeaked.

"Her?" River growled.

Ada's flat look landed on him. "Oh, come on. Don't tell me you didn't even know she was standing there."

"Told you, I'm shutting it down." His blue-marked hand swiped the air before him, dismissive.

"Doubt it. You flexed way more than usual." Before he could retort, Ada raised her voice. "River. You refuse to let me touch your wings because, apparently, only a crow's wingmate has the right. Well, now you have one. So suck it up, buttercup, and let me examine you properly, or you can deal with your molting problem yourself."

He stilled, and a ripple of tension filled the air.

Ada made a comical "oops" face at Blake, as if she'd poked the bird too much.

While River brooded at the wall, his back to them, Ada held Blake's stare and silently counted on her fingers. One. Two. Three.

River glanced over his shoulder at Blake, stormy eyes showering her with cold contemplation for a long, hard minute. Then he slid off the bed and collected his discarded leather pants, using his patchy wings to cover his nakedness. Once dressed, he repositioned himself on the bed and faced the wall again without another word, shoulders rigid with unspoken emotion.

"Okay." Ada smiled. "I suppose that's permission granted. Your help would be greatly appreciated, Blake." She poked River in the temple. "Right, McGrumpy?"

He flinched away, annoyed, but his eyes remained glued to the wall. If his turmoil of emotions weren't slipping through their bond—frustration, embarrassment, and something deeper that felt like shame—Blake might have told him to take a long walk off a short pier. But she couldn't resist the Grey's reference.

"He's definitely not a McDreamy," she offered, walking over.

Ada gasped and touched her chest. "You watched Grey's?"

A warmth spread throughout Blake's body, and her first genuine smile in days stretched her lips. "Religiously. What do you need me to do?"

TEN

"Put your hand here and here." Ada guided Blake's fingers to the soft, downy feathers in the crook of River's semi-folded wing. "Split them apart when he flexes."

"I usually save the splitting and flexing for the second date," River joked.

Blake tensed.

"Unless I've had a few quarts of moonshine," he added. "Then I'll split and flex for anyone."

"Ignore him," Ada said. "Continue dragging your fingers to lift the quills … yes, perfect. Keep doing that."

River's feathers ruffled moments before he tucked his wings with a snap.

"Maybe I should leave," Blake said.

"No. He's fine." Ada smacked River's head. He shot them a simpering glare over his shoulder, then flexed his wings outward again with deliberate slowness.

"See?" Ada motioned for Blake to continue.

Sensation thrummed into her fingers as they glided

through his feathers. The gentle disheveling released his woody, sky scent—earthy yet somehow warm and heady. Blake leaned closer, puzzled by its unexpected pull.

On her next stroke, River gave a full-body shudder. A flood of raw desire burst through his block on their bond.

Blake snatched her hand back. He'd said only his mate could touch his wings. Because it turned him on? The notion should have repulsed her. But instead, she returned and increased the pressure, lingering to savor the silky texture against her fingertips. Making him squirm felt like justice.

A pained groan escaped River's lips. "How much longer?"

"Almost done," Ada replied, her clinical tone distracted as she focused on writing down her observations. She pointed to a spot near the iridescent blue tips of one wing, where the feathers thinned. "Just here, Blake."

Smirking, Blake stroked the full length of his wing's bony arch to reach Ada's spot. River's sharp intake of breath was the only warning before feathers sped through her fingers, the friction stinging her palms. His wings vanished altogether.

Blake and Ada were left blinking at River's back.

He sat rigidly facing the wall, every muscle coiled tight. A webbing of scar-like fissures she'd not noticed before fractured his glossy oil-slick tattoos, breaking them into unrecognizable patterns.

Emotion slammed into Blake with staggering force: pain, embarrassment, bitterness, rage. The torrent pricked tears in her eyes. Breathing became a conscious effort.

Blake's vision cleared as the wave slowly ebbed—or rather, as he seemed to rein it in forcefully through sheer willpower. Ada's words filtered back into focus.

"...I don't think my original prognosis will change. I can't heal what's not there. As with Aeron's hearing, something missing must be reconstructed. No. That's not right." Ada tapped her lip, thinking. "With his eardrum, I can almost feel it on the other side of a chasm. That's what's so frustrating. I know I need a bridge, but with yours, it's as though the feather-making nodes are simply gone, as if they never existed. Or blocked from my senses."

"Blocked?"

Ada closed her notebook and gave him a rueful look. "As if they don't want to be found."

"You're suggesting I've put myself in a perpetual molt on purpose?"

"Have you?"

"What happened?" The question escaped before Blake could stop it.

River snorted. "Got my feathers ruffled by a lightning rod with daddy issues. Doesn't matter. Bet you'd look better naked than talking about my sob story."

She blinked at River's needling tone, then realized it was a deflection. "You can't fly?"

His facetiousness crumbled. He slid off the bed and yanked on his shirt with sharp, efficient movements, each button secured with military precision. He avoided looking at Blake until the last button was fastened. Then, he fixed her with a withering glare.

"Get out," he clipped.

Blake's lips parted.

"She's your mate, River," Ada pointed out dryly. "She was bound to find out at some point."

"I said, get out." His eyes flashed with barely contained fury, and he jabbed a finger toward the curtain.

Vulnerability warred with rage in his eyes. Despite his efforts to block their connection, she could still read his emotions.

What kind of world had she awakened to? His scars ran deeper than the eye could see, etched into his soul like the lightning marks on his skin.

She excused herself and padded back to her bay, the cool tiles soothing against her bare feet. On the center of her bed sat a small wooden chest, its polished surface gleaming in the diffused window light. Inside was full of red glass coins. Each had an intricately engraved wolf's head on one side and the Summer Court crest on the other. The emblem had been on the uniforms of soldiers and palace staff. This must be the local currency. But why was it here, on her bed? Had someone forgotten it, or was it meant for her?

Her gut tightened as possibilities raced through her mind. Was this her signal to get moving? Were they kicking her out and sending her on her way? Or was it from River— some kind of payment or bribe for her to keep away from him?

Alimony? Marital support, so he didn't feel so guilty leaving her behind?

She stared at the curtain separating her from the other bay, racking her brain for clues about what might have caused River's pain. Someone with daddy issues. But who? The fae were at war with Nero. The others had mentioned mana-warped monsters. And now that she thought of it, if this were the last habitable piece of land on Earth, survival itself would demand brutality. Gnawing her lip, she tried to suppress the building sense of fear and helplessness, but it swelled within her chest.

This era was far more dangerous than she wanted to admit.

The evidence was etched into River's very skin. And his feathers ... they weren't growing back. Fae healing in itself was still hard to comprehend. But from the hushed tones of their continued conversation, River's condition wasn't normal.

She'd wasted her life worrying about follower counts and social media reach, living through the lens of a camera. Now, she felt adrift without those things, not even a broken phone to check her makeup. A humorless laugh escaped as she touched her bare face. Makeup belonged in another life. None of the women here seemed to wear it at all.

"Heya, girl."

Trix's cheerful greeting pulled Blake from her spiral. The dark, curly-haired woman waddled into the bay, cradling a wicker basket. Her floral-embroidered blouse, which might have once been loose, strained over her swollen belly. The due date couldn't be far off.

"G'day, mate." Blake offered a small smile. Trix's British accent was comforting, a small reminder of home in this alien world. Not Australian, but like a distant cousin.

She seemed to feel the same way because she made Blake repeat her Aussie greeting twice before she sighed and perched on the edge of Blake's bed with a pensive look toward River's bay.

"That sounds serious," Trix murmured. "I'll wait until they finish before I approach him."

Unsure how to respond, Blake asked, "What's in the basket?"

Trix's eyes lit up with excitement. "It's River's chakram—his Guardian weapon. It looks a bit like a pizza cutter, or a frisbee, I suppose. Only sharper." She pulled the cloth covering the basket off. "The middle splits apart, and he can use two curved blades in battle. Or he can use it together like this."

Blake almost laughed. She'd expected some kind of knitted baby wear, but here was Trix, heavily pregnant and gleefully showing off a deadly weapon. If she didn't already like the woman, she certainly did now.

"That's both impressive and a little terrifying," Blake admitted, eyeing the gleaming steel.

"You think?"

"Fuck yeah." Blake nodded vehemently.

"I've been tinkering with it lately," Trix continued with unchecked enthusiasm. "I'm experimenting with modifications to disperse and distribute mana flow evenly across the surface area. Guardian mana is fascinating. I want to see if I can help River utilize it as a shield. I suspect it will work. River's quite good using air and water magic in tandem, so I've ensured the main conduit doesn't interfere with his casting, but I added tiny grooves here and here…"

Trix's eyes gleamed with the thrill of invention as she continued to detail the intricacies of her work, but Blake struggled to follow along. This world, with its magical weapons and strange technologies, still left her disoriented. She was caught between fascination and bewilderment.

"Right now," Trix continued, "the chakram directs all energy to the cutting edge, but with these modifications, the mana can flow any number of ways." Trix carefully placed her hand on Blake's and gave a reassuring squeeze. "Don't worry, I'll make sure it's safe before I return it to him."

Her voice was hopeful, filled with a desire to help and protect those she cared about. Blake found herself smiling at the woman's kindness and dedication, even as the effort to keep up left her feeling more than a little out of her depth. Was this what magic was supposed to be like? Or was Trix playing on a level no one else could touch?

"If he redirects the flow this way, it could be more like a net around the whole thing and not just channeled to the edges…"

Her voice trailed off as she noticed Blake's eyes glazing over. "I'm boring you. Long story short, the next time some bugger tries to throw lightning at him—"

She stopped abruptly and cleared her throat.

"You did all that?" Blake was impressed. "For a wanker?"

"He's not that bad." Trix laughed.

"Are we talking about the same person?"

"Trust me. River's one of the good guys." Trix's humor faded. Her gaze turned inward, and she frowned. "I probably shouldn't tell you this, but he was hurt recently by someone very close to him."

"The lightning?"

She nodded. "He's had every chance to walk away from this fight with Nero, but he's still here."

A small smile returned to her lips, and she touched the basket. Then she blurted out a story about a battle involving someone's kidnapped daughter, who inadvertently raised a zombie army, or perhaps under duress. River found the kid first and healed her. But then Nero attacked again, and someone died. There was more to her rambling zig-zag story, but she stopped after mentioning an exploding airship. "Anyway," Trix said. "I was part of the problem with Nero." Her gaze turned downcast. "I used to tinker for him. Created a few inventions I'm not proud of now that I know the truth about this world. The point is, River has saved more lives than we can count. He deserves happiness. I'm so glad he found you. Upgrading his weapon is the least I can offer in gratitude."

Blake wasn't sure what to make of Trix's confession. She knew as well as anyone that first appearances weren't always accurate. Not even the second and third, or all of them. Blake had never truly known Jeff. Or maybe she did, and it was herself she didn't know.

She turned their conversation back to the weapon. "You did that all in just a few days?"

Trix blushed. "I would have been faster if I were a Guardian. It's still a prototype. Aeron helped me, but I need River to test it."

The weapon wouldn't have looked out of place in an Avengers movie. Blake couldn't resist and reached for it.

"Don't touch the—"

Pain slammed into Blake the moment her fingers connected with steel. All feeling drained from Blake's body, leaving agony and emptiness in its wake.

"—metal," Trix finished.

Color dulled. Ada had thought Blake was depressed, but this was the true meaning of the word. She wanted to cry out but couldn't move, couldn't breathe. Paralyzed by darkness.

ELEVEN

Trix sighed and pried Blake's seized fingers from the weapon with the gentle care of someone handling a live wire. The instant Blake disconnected, sensations flooded back—color, feeling, hope, anger—life itself rushed into her emptied soul.

River burst through the curtain, alarm widening his eyes. Ada followed swiftly on his heels.

"What the fuck are you doing?" he growled at Trix, invading her space with dominating intent.

"Your mate's alright," Trix cooed, not backing down an inch. "She just experienced her first disconnection from the Well."

"Bloody hell." Blake gulped air like a drowning woman breaking the surface. "That's what happened?"

River snatched up his weapon and grumbled, "Serves you right for touching things you shouldn't."

Blake had spent her life placating men who pushed their sour moods onto her. Jeff had been sneakier about it, masking his contempt behind smiles while critiquing her body, choices, and existence. She'd brushed it off, made excuses, swallowed the hurt when he'd say things like, "You can't wear that dress with your old lady boobs."

Never again.

She launched to her feet and squared off with River.

"Listen here, mate." She jabbed a finger into his pectoral, her pitch rising with each word. "You'd better back the fuck up with that attitude. Your bad mood belongs to you and no one else."

His eyebrows shot up.

"This woman"— Blake thrust a finger toward Trix—"was doing something nice for you." She pointed at Ada. "That woman was doing something nice for you." She jabbed her chest. "This fucking woman was doing something nice for you." Her finger returned to his sternum, punctuating each word with a poke. "And all you give in return is being a dick dick dick."

"So were you!" he shot back, leaning into her space. "I helped you, and all you gave me was 'I hate you.'"

Her jaw clicked shut. Heat blazed across her cheeks, spreading down her neck. "You're right."

"I am?" The fight drained from his posture, replaced by wary confusion.

"Yes, that was rude, and I'm sor—"

Three hands lunged toward her mouth simultaneously.

Startled, Blake jerked back. "What the—?"

"No apologies," Ada warned.

"But I heard you apologize to Trix yesterday."

"Look," Ada replied, tension threading through her voice, "we old-worlders don't have the same rules, but I wouldn't put it past your fae mate to enforce a debt of gratitude."

Blake swung her gaze to River and found his face a mask of exaggerated innocence. His lips twitched, parting slightly as if to speak, but she jabbed him again. "I'm not done. The point is, I don't care if you've been hurt. We've all been hurt in one way or another. I lost me entire life. Me brothers *and* me father. I lost me—" She cleared her throat to avoid mentioning Jeff. "I lost *my* homeland. All the unique wildlife. Koalas, platypuses, emus, and magpies."

The word lodged in her throat like a stone. Each creature named was another piece of her world gone forever. Her final words emerged hollow. "It doesn't excuse being a dickhead to nice people."

Heat prickled behind her eyes. But the knot in her chest loosened. No more swallowing her feelings. No more polite silence. Sweeping her emotions under someone else's rug didn't make them go away. Pain existed for a reason. If wounds weren't acknowledged, they festered.

"You done?" River's tone was eerily calm.

She lifted her watery gaze and braced for the storm she'd witnessed before. Instead, she found amusement tinged with a hint of respect. She managed a shaky nod.

River faced the two women and brought his fist to his chest, where he rubbed it in a circular motion. He raised his brows at Blake. "That's how you apologize in Elphyne."

"It's fine," Trix waved him off, but the tension in the room eased.

Blake blinked, stunned. She'd spoken her truth, and the world hadn't crumbled around her.

River clipped the chakram to his belt with practiced efficiency, his body angling toward the exit. Ada exchanged a loaded glance with Trix before addressing him. "Actually, there's something you can do for us in return."

He paused, his eyes narrowing. "Now?"

Ada nodded. "You mentioned some kind of murder thing."

"Murder-what?" Blake sank onto the bed, suddenly aware of the thin fabric barely covering her thighs.

"Of crows," Trix explained.

"An annual crow gathering, I think," Ada added quickly before returning to River. "You mentioned a special market, unlike any other, where rare items are bartered. I've seen Ash and Aeron read mana-preserved books from our time. Will you see more books like that there?"

"Seen me reading what?" A smooth, male voice flowed into the room.

River poked his head past the curtain, his sharp blue eyes tracking the newcomer in from the direction of the entrance.

"About fucking time," he muttered.

The words were harsh, but Blake felt a wave of River's relief washing against her consciousness before he could block it.

The man who stepped into view matched him in height and build. He was clad in the same leather uniform with the telltale Guardian teardrop beneath his eye. But where River radiated edgy intensity, this man exuded patient menace.

His skin was darker than River's, and a thin leather cord circled his temples, holding back shoulder-length straight hair that moved as if he stood by an open window. Ash's gaze deliberately scanned River and lingered on the blue-marked arm without reaction until he looked at Blake.

A thousand emotions raced behind his brown eyes before settling on one: amusement.

The scrutiny sparked irritation in Blake's chest. Why did

everyone look at her that way, like she was both a punchline and a puzzle?

"Why do you want an old book, Ada?" Trix asked, kneading her swollen belly in slow circles.

"I had an idea when River told me about the Shadow Market." Ada's eyes brightened, her hands gesturing with renewed energy. "What if there's an anatomical medical textbook there? When I heal, I feel my way around the injury using mana. If there's no wound, I have nothing to heal. But maybe if I know what Aeron's eardrum is supposed to look like, I could—"

"Oh, I see," Blake interjected. "It's like when I run me fingers over cracks in old furniture. You're not just fixing, you're finding the original pattern underneath."

Ada nodded, a flash of appreciation crossing her features. "Exactly."

"You said you can't heal what's not there," River interrupted, his narrowed gaze fixed on Ash, who continued staring at Blake with a knowing glint.

His scrutiny crawled across her skin. She pulled the blanket higher, covering her braless chest, though he wasn't even looking there. His assessment felt deeper than physical, as if he could peel back layers of her soul, exposing everything she'd tried to bury.

"But maybe it is there and..." Ada snapped her fingers, looking to Blake for the right words.

"And you don't know what you're looking for until you feel it. Right?"

"Exactly!" Ada pressed on. "This is our last chance to give Aeron the gift of sound before his baby is born."

Guilt flashed across River's face. It was so brief, Blake might have missed it.

"Many books and items from the old world will be traded at the Shadow Market," he admitted. "But we won't have time to locate what you need. Securing the cryptex is the Order's priority."

Something sharp sliced through his emotional block. Worry? Fear? His gaze flicked to Blake before darting away, his shoulders rigid beneath his jacket.

"I'll go with you," Trix volunteered, hope widening her eyes. "I'll know what to look for."

"Trix," Ada warned. "You can barely walk with that belly. You're having Braxton-Hicks contractions and are due in two weeks. Anything can trigger labor. I'll go."

River scoffed. "As if either of your mates will let you leave their sight. It won't matter anyway. To crows, you're both outsiders. You won't be allowed within a mile of the gathering."

"What about me?" The words left Blake's mouth before she could stop them. But once spoken, they felt right, a step toward doing something worthwhile in this foreign world.

"No," he grunted, the reflex immediate.

"It could work," Ash mused, thumb tracing his jaw. "She's your Well-blessed mate."

"Precisely why she should remain here," River countered. "Bartering there is not like here. Get the offer wrong, and she'll be stabbed. This mission is too important for me to waste time babysitting."

The bitterness in his voice bounced off Ash without effect, only intensifying the amusement dancing in his eyes.

"What if I don't need to trade, just browse?" She elaborated when blank stares met her suggestion. "I have a photographic memory. I could look at the books and draw the diagrams later."

"You can draw?" Shock splashed across River's face. "Are you any good?"

She bit her lip, suddenly self-conscious under his intense focus. "I'm no master, but I'm okay. I suppose."

"What's a foto—" His brow puckered.

"Photographic memory?"

He nodded.

"Um." Blake frowned. How does one explain a camera and film to someone who's never seen it?

"I got this," Trix said, turning to River. "It's like an instant painting in her head. She'll remember the specific details long after most people forget."

River raked fingers through his hair, frustration evident in the rigid line of his shoulders. "You're still an outsider."

"Oh, come on, River," Ada cajoled, playfully slapping his chest. "She's your mate. If she can't get an invite, then who can?"

"Yeah," Ash chimed in, mimicking Ada's gesture with a mocking slap. "She's an honorary member of your kettle. Ergo, you're honor-bound to present her with Murder's Call."

River's glare could have melted steel. "I only have two invitational coins. One for you and one for me."

A gentle breeze lifted the hair over Ash's right ear. He cocked his head as if listening to it, and when his hair settled, he shrugged. "We don't need them. We're Guardians."

Doubt and panic warred in River's eyes. Trix launched a barrage of promises about "super-duper tip-top features" for *all* of his weapons while Ada murmured something about forgiving him for hustling her son.

"I'll take her if you won't," Ash offered, his tone casual but his eyes bright with challenge.

"Go near her, princeling, and I'll gut you." River stepped between them, still facing Blake. He fixed her with an intensity that stole her breath. Slowly and deliberately, he lifted his shirt all the way to his collarbone, revealing a landscape of hard muscle and intricate, yet broken, tattoos.

"Prove it," he demanded, voice deepening. "Pick a tat and draw it."

TWELVE

CIRCA 200 YEARS AGO

"*Shh.*" *Manfri pressed his fingers to his lips as he stalked around the base of the tallest spire in the canyon.*

Cielo frowned back at him. "What, like he can hear us from all the way up there! We can't even see past the clouds."

They glared at the ring of haze surrounding the spire's peak way up high. Nothing had changed since they'd arrived a few turns of the hourglass ago, except the sky's darkening color.

They'd devised a plan to survey the canyon for signs of the Collector. Ancient human ruins littered the area with forbidden substances, making some places inaccessible to the fae. All other spires had come up empty except this one, and they lacked the guts to fly into the misty barrier hiding the peak. It was the perfect hiding space for a paranoid crow monster protecting his treasure. It made complete, terrifying sense.

Cielo swiped his hand over gouge marks scarring the craggy spire's surface. "This looks like a sigil—a warning sign. Maybe a ward, but I don't feel mana in it. Do you?"

Manfri placed his palm on the gouges and felt only a cold, rocky surface. Natural stone, nothing more. He shook his head.

"*I guess the only thing left to do is go up.*" *Cielo's dark wings ruffled, and he shivered.*

Neither of them moved.

"*I also heard he's a cannibal,*" *Manfri whispered.*

"*Nah, surely not.*" *But Cielo's words carried no power, no conviction.*

"*We don't have to go.*" *Manfri's hand gravitated to his groin. "What if he eats the soft bits first?*"

"*Speak for yourself,*" *Cielo scoffed. "I have no soft bits.*"

"*Fine. Go then. You seem to be doing a lot of that lately.*"

"*Fine. I will.*" *Cielo's eyes flashed, and his wings spanned wide, but he hesitated and met Manfri's gaze. "You coming?*"

"*Always.*"

*W*INGBEATS THUNDERED AS THE CROW SHIFTERS CIRCLED UP THE *spire. Manfri pulled his bone dagger from his belt when they entered the misty top. Magic buzzed along their skin with the power of a storm. Mana. He tasted it on his tongue. This haze was magic, perhaps hiding something dangerous. Excitement and trepidation filled him in equal measure. Only treasure would be protected in this manner. This was surely the Collector's hideout.*

Two more wingbeats and they cleared the cold mist. Manfri squinted at the sudden light. When his eyes adjusted, he rubbed them to ensure he wasn't dreaming.

"*Look.*" *Awe coated Cielo's tone.*

The spire's peak was a mountain of treasure that spilled down various platforms onto lower levels. Holes and tunnels were laced throughout the mountainous peak. Sunset limned the entire collection with a golden light that sparkled in some places but seemed to absorb illumination in others. There was no actual gold. No metal. No forbidden substances. Just jewels and knick-knacks and baubles and trinkets. Treasure.

An ominous premonition shivered up Manfri's spine as they flew around, surveying the hoard.

"Hurry," he hissed. "Take something and then let's get out of here."

He wasn't psychic, but he had a bad feeling. This was too easy. Cielo only needed to grab one tiny thing, and then their wager was satisfied. But Cielo flew closer to the glittering pile and closer to the tunnels as though they called his name like a siren.

"What do you suppose is in there?" Cielo asked, pointing to the darkness.

"I don't care," Manfri replied. "Grab your shiny, and then let's go to town."

Cielo landed on the treasure. Trinkets and baubles rolled from the impact. The clink and clank sounded incredibly loud, so loud that if the Collector slept, he'd surely wake.

As always, Cielo walked to his own tune. He strolled around the treasure, picking up and turning bits as he inspected them. All the while, Manfri felt his balls shrink back into his body. His heart tested the limits of its cage.

Then a low, growling sound trembled the jeweled mountain, shaking its very foundation.

"Hurry," Manfri hissed. "Something's coming to eat us."

"It's not going to eat you."

They spun to face the foreign male voice, their daggers drawn and ready to stab. But it was only another male crow shifter, just like them. With bronze skin, dark shoulder-length hair, and dark eyes, he appeared too normal to be the Collector. And young. He had to be close to their age. Still not filling out his adult fae body, but close. He wore scrappy black clothes two sizes too small and a wary look that was beyond his years.

It could be a glamour designed to fool them.

A monster born of ink and horror lurched from a tunnel, baring its fangs at them. It moved on all fours and had the body of a canine. Acidic, glowing ink dripped from its eyes and sizzled on the ground. The newcomer leaped into action, stabbing the creature's eye as it passed him. It screeched and thrashed, but the crow shifter hung on. Manfri had never seen a Wellhound, only heard stories around the kettle campfires.

Cielo snapped out of his shock first. He launched at the hound, intending to strike and help the new crow shifter, but there was no need. Within moments, the hound was dead. Manabeeze popped from its corpse and drifted away. Only when the stranger slid from the furred corpse did they realize he'd held another dagger and had stabbed the beast in the heart. The acidic blood had narrowly missed his skin.

"I'm fucking speechless," Manfri mumbled. This barely grown fae had just dispatched a Wellhound without breaking a sweat.

"Who are you?" Cielo pointed his dagger.

The newcomer's gaze flicked to the weapon, unimpressed. He cocked his head and spread glossy black wings. "That's my question."

Shit shit shit. Manfri bounced on his toes. What should they do? Flight? Fly? Would this deadly stranger give chase? Gut them like he did the hound?

"I'm Cielo, and that's Manfri."

Manfri's eyes widened at his friend. Just go ahead and reveal our identities to the monster killer, why don't you? *Crows never forget those who steal from them. Cielo knows that, so what the actual fuck?*

The newcomer's dark eyes narrowed as he stepped to the side, seemingly weighing the situation. The sizzle of Wellhound acid, still burning treasure, filled the air. Cielo sheathed his dagger and motioned for Manfri to do the same. Fuck. He'd better know what he's doing.

Manfri tucked his dagger into his belt.

"What's your name?" Cielo asked, his head tilting as he studied their opponent. "You're not the Collector."

"How would you know?"

A single dark brow lifted on Cielo's forehead as he pointed to the stranger's feet. Manfri followed his gaze and gasped at the rune-strengthened manacles.

He shrank into himself but then straightened his spine and announced, "I'm the Collector's son."

"Your name?" Cielo pushed.

"Nikan."

"Are you a prisoner here, Nikan?" Manfri blurted.

Nikan seemed to consider answering, but then the rumble sounded again from inside a tunnel—more hounds?—and he said, "You should go. If she wakes, you're both dead."

She?

Manfri and Cielo shared a surprised look.

"Come with us," Cielo offered.

"There's nothing you can do for me." The manacle chinked as Nikan lifted his foot and showed his raw, chafed ankle. "This is my fault. I disobeyed her."

"Fuck that," Cielo snapped. "No one deserves to be in chains."

Again, Nikan seemed to consider answering. Manfri could see the plea for help in his dark eyes, the yearning to be free. But Nikan shook his head. He must be terrified of his mother.

What had that floater done to this crow to make him so frightened? A thousand horrible thoughts conjured in Manfri's mind. What if it was abuse? What if it was torture?

Manfri's mother always said he had a vivid imagination. She was awesome ... if a little spacey. She was all about love, happiness, and following one's instincts despite her love for his father ostracizing their kettle to the outer limits of the murder. She nurtured Manfri, never trapped him.

Nikan had no one up here. No friends. No food ... at least, none that they could see. Not like Manfri and Cielo had at home. What was a crow shifter without a kettle, a family? Without brothers?

His heart ached for Nikan, and he knew that with Cielo's growing distance, this might be the only time he had backup for his next daring proposal.

Manfri lifted his chin and said with a steady gaze, his hand on his dagger. "If you want to call a Vendetta against your mother, we will fly with you."

Nikan's brows furrowed. "A Vendetta?"

Crimson. Manfri and Cielo shared another shocked look. This was worse than Manfri had initially thought. What kind of crow shifter didn't know about a Vendetta? Cielo's eyes held the same disturbed note as Manfri's. They had to get Nikan out of here.

"A Vendetta," Cielo explained, "is when a crow vows revenge—"

"Justice," Manfri corrected.

Cielo scowled at him, but if he was going to explain it, then he should do it right.

"It is a time-honored tradition in the crow shifter community," Manfri added. "If one of our own has been hurt, they—or their family—have the right to call a Vendetta against the offending party. They paint blood in a V-shape across their face, from their eyebrows to their chin. Then they walk through the murder. Their closest friends and family must join the hunt until justice has been served." He stopped short of saying Vendettas were rarely called because crows could be tenacious, vicious, and single-minded in

their justice. It almost always ended in death for the opposing party or obsession and madness for the one who called the Vendetta. As Cielo said, it became more about revenge than justice. Sometimes it hurt more than it healed.

"I don't understand," Nikan said.

"He means we will kill your mother with you," Cielo continued. "Or die trying."

Nikan blinked. "You don't know me! Why would you do this?"

"We don't have to know you to see this is wrong." Manfri gestured at the manacles. He wanted to point out the too-small, tattered clothes hanging from Nikan's slim figure—he could use a good meal. But Manfri bit his words back.

"You could take anything you want from here," Nikan said, waving at the treasure hoard. "Take it and leave. My mother is asleep. I can't stop you from stealing, so do it. Don't risk your lives on a foolish notion."

Manfri fidgeted and avoided Cielo's gaze. He knew his proclamation had been hasty. Perhaps he should have thought about it first, but Cielo pressed on.

"We're not going without you."

"You'll die if she wakes and catches you helping me," Nikan warned. "There won't be a corner of Elphyne you can fly to where she won't find you."

He was right. If they failed, even if they escaped, the Collector would hunt them down and eat them. The Collector was probably in Vendetta mode every day.

"We do it now while she's asleep." Cielo unsheathed his dagger again, his eyes hard and ready to fight for their new friend.

"No," Nikan said, stopping them. "I don't want her to die."

"She chained you here for Well-knows how long." Manfri finally pointed at Nikan's too-small clothes. "There's a whole world down there. Food. Clothes that fit. More treasure. Fun. Females."

He waggled his brows suggestively on that last one.

Nikan's eyes flashed, and he snarled, "I know exactly what I'm missing. And I have plenty of food here." He gestured at the dead hound.

"Ew." Manfri scrunched his nose. "Won't that give you indigestion?"

Cielo asked Nikan, "You've been down to the city before?"

"Like I said, this predicament is my fault. I disobeyed my mother and left her alone. Vulnerable. Thieves attacked while she slept. She killed them, but her wounds forced her into hibernation. She bound me for my negligence."

"How long ago was that?"

Nikan's lips flattened, but he didn't answer.

"And what will she do when she knows you saved us by killing her hound?" Manfri pointed to the dead beast.

Again, Nikan refused to answer, but pain flashed in his eyes.

Cielo shook his head. "This is wrong, and you know it."

"She's my mother."

"She enslaved you. You're not her son but a thing she's collected." Cielo turned in circles, his arms wide at the mountain of treasure. "This is her life, not yours. I see the need to fly in your eyes. I saw the excitement when you fought the hound. Crows are not meant to have their wings clipped. Especially not by their mother."

Silence stretched between them.

"What makes her so terrifying?" Manfri asked softly. "What kind of monster—"

"None of your fucking business, crow!"

"Whoa." Manfri showed his palms, not wanting to push Nikan. But behind the defiance, hurt, and pain, flashes of something else appeared. Confusion. Longing. Yearning. Guilt. Manfri tried again, this time more subtly. "I'm just saying you have options."

"We'll leave." Cielo spread his wings.

Go? Manfri hesitated until Cielo glared at him, and he gave in. He spread his wings, ready to fly.

"Wait."

They faced Nikan. A cold breeze caught his long, dark hair, lifting it from his shoulders. He looked like a vengeful warrior king at that moment. Powerful and indomitable. Manfri would never forget it for as long as he lived.

Another sweeping tingle of premonition trailed down his spine, and he shivered. He looked around, thinking they were about to be set upon by something wicked, the Collector, or worse. But then he realized the electric feeling wasn't from danger ... it was from being around Nikan. It was the same sort of feeling Manfri had whenever he was with Cielo.

He knew in that moment, with absolute certainty, that they would be friends and in each other's lives for a long time. Their three paths would twine together for years.

They had to take Nikan with them. They had to.

"Tell me, Nikan," Manfri said, his eyes crinkling with mischief. "Have you ever seen the inside of a nightclub in Cornucopia where the females dance in cages and then invite you up for a little afternoon delight?"

Nikan's brows lifted, intrigued. "No."

"Crimson," Manfri rolled his eyes heavenward. "You are in for a treat. Fae of all kinds go there to hang loose and party. There's dancing, music, gambling, and elixirs of all kinds." He added the last one with another waggle of his eyebrows. Surely Nikan got his point by now. Shit, maybe he had no idea what a secret waggle meant. "Cielo and I are headed there now. Why don't you come for the night, and we'll have you back by dawn. Your mother won't even know you're gone."

"She'll know," he replied, scowling.

"And then there's the Rosebud Courtesans," Manfri continued as if he didn't hear Nikan's words. "They're trained in the art of sensual pleasures—if you know what I mean." Another, very obvious eyebrow waggle. "I've been trying to get Cielo to visit them. You know, just to test how good their training actually is, but he's being a prude." He dodged Cielo's dagger-like glare and hopped toward a gleaming ruby. "But if we have a red coin or a jewel like this, we can score the most beautiful and sought-after courtesans reserved for the High Fae royalty. I'll bet we can even procure King Mithras's personal favorite."

He held the ruby to the setting sun. The gem's fire caught him, scattering crimson light across his face.

"We don't want to scare him off." Cielo frowned at Manfri. "Maybe we should take him somewhere a little tamer to begin with."

See? Going soft.

This was exactly why Manfri told Nikan, "This pretty ruby will get us top-tier access. We can have a courtesan bathe us, feed us, and then suck our cocks. We can live like kings for a week."

Cielo had skirted his question earlier regarding whether his secret female was human. He'd soon reveal his truth if he refused a courtesan. Just thinking about it sent a surge of wickedness scouring through Manfri's blood. He gave his friend a dark, challenging look, waiting for him to protest his plan. But Cielo revealed nothing.

Nikan's eyes filled with longing. "I shouldn't."

Cielo smiled tightly. "Of course, it's up to you."

Manfri shrugged and pretended not to care. "We can leave you chained like this, no problems. Or you can come and have a night you'll never forget."

Nikan studied his manacle thoughtfully. "Maybe if I leave her a note..."

Manfri's simmering feelings for Cielo's growing distance melted. He felt foolish for even taking the conversation in that direction. This was more than having fun and forcing Cielo to reveal more secrets about his affair with a human. Nikan needed them.

"We don't have to see the courtesans." Manfri tossed the ruby back onto the treasure. "We don't have to take anything. But you should see what life is like out there, Nikan. There's a whole land full of excitement. You don't have to live like this."

Nikan's dirty feet shuffled toward where Manfri had tossed the ruby, and he picked it up. His eyes turned hard as he looked at the jewel. "I don't want to live like this anymore."

Before Nikan could change his mind, Cielo had the manacles unpicked and unlatched. He was a genius with that sort of stuff. Manfri hadn't met a lock Cielo couldn't pick. On the other hand, Manfri was better with a paintbrush. Not much use for that here, though.

The instant the manacle fell from Nikan's ankle, a loud squawk reverberated through the treasure tunnels.

"Oh no." Nikan's eyes widened to saucers. "She's awake. Fly!"

"Not without you." Cielo stood firm, his dagger pointed as he searched for the source of the squawk.

"Yeah," Manfri added, puffing out his chest and standing between Nikan and the tunnel. "Crows before hoes."

"She's a crow, too, Mannie," Cielo growled.

"Whatever. You know what I mean."

Nikan's eyes filled with emotion. "You should leave. You don't even know me."

"You saved our lives. You didn't know us either."

CHAPTER

THIRTEEN

This was fucked six ways from Sunday.

River found himself cornered, outnumbered, and forced to look like a complete floater just to keep this woman safe and a hundred miles away from the Great Murder. She had the prettiest face this side of the Well, a body that made his mouth water, and hair that shimmered with colors no human should possess. And she had no fucking clue how to survive in Elphyne. Tossing her into a nest of crows would be like dropping a juicy worm into a flock of starving fledglings. They'd tear her apart just to see what made her shine.

The worst part? His body betrayed him every time she entered a room. When he'd first sensed her hovering near Ada's examination curtain, his heart had hammered against his ribs like a caged animal desperate for escape.

Hunt. Collect. Take. Keep.

Ancient instincts clawed at his insides, demanding he claim what the Well had marked as his. He'd feigned ignorance, terrified she'd glimpse past his practiced indifference into the hunger that gnawed beneath.

And then Ada had called her over.

When Blake's fingers had grazed his wings, his cock hardened instantly, painfully, demandingly. Other lovers had touched his wings before, producing pleasant shivers, a hint of arousal. But Blake's touch? It had stopped his fucking heart. It was like flying too high, too fast, beyond the reach of the Well's connection.

Even now, his body thrummed with phantom sensations while she stared at his exposed torso. Her fascination and low-grade desire cascaded through their bond, despite his attempts to block it. But it seemed he could only stop the flow of emotions one way.

She'd seen his scars and pathetic, damaged wings. And somehow, impossibly, still looked at him without disgust. A longing he'd buried deep enough to forget stirred beneath his breastbone.

Then there was the way she'd stood up to him.

Well-dammit. His cock twitched at the memory.

If they were alone...

Fine. He admitted it. He wouldn't think twice about fucking her. He'd take her hard against every surface he could find. He'd part those soft thighs and sink in until his balls slapped against her ass. He'd bite those plush lips until they swelled. He'd do things to her that would make the most seasoned Rosebud Courtesan blush and beg for mercy.

But there'd be no falling in love.

And definitely no bringing her to the Great Murder, where a blade between the ribs was more common than a handshake.

Possessive fury flooded his veins. The thought of anyone else touching her, hurting her, made his claws itch to emerge. He'd eviscerate anyone who dared. The intensity of his reaction terrified him. When it came to protecting their treasures, crows were vicious. When it came to protecting their mates, they were fucking unhinged.

His teeth ground together as he dropped his shirt and raised a brow at Blake. "Go on, then. Draw it."

He'd given her mere seconds to memorize the tattoo Cloud's lightning had butchered. Once, it had symbolized the Umbria family kettle—his heritage, his identity, his bonds of loyalty. Now it resembled nothing but charred remains. His mother would castrate him when she discovered he'd hidden the damage. Tattoos weren't just decorations for crows; they were history, milestones, and a sense of belonging. They were the people they flew beside through life.

"Bloomin' hell, River. That wasn't long enough!" Trix whined. "Show it again."

He met her glare with his own. "A few seconds is all she'll get at the market. If she can't manage this, there's no point in her coming."

The challenge was impossible, and deliberately so. The Shadow Market tolerated no weakness.

River watched his rainbow mouse, waiting to see if she'd scurry away, frightened like at their first meeting. Or would she show him more of that unexpected steel?

"You're being dumb," Ada snapped. "Seriously. Blake, you don't have to do this."

"Game on, mole," Blake said to River, defiance sparking in her brown eyes as she extended her palm toward Ada. "Give me something to draw with."

One minute later, she hunched over the bed, charcoal flying across paper.

River's lungs seized at her almost perfect rendition of his tattoo. She'd even reconstructed missing pieces, intuitively adding lines that echoed the original pattern with eerie accuracy. Without a hint of shame, she tilted her head and asked if her guesswork was acceptable. She said it just *felt right.*

A fragile feeling cracked inside his chest. She'd seen the broken parts of him and, instead of recoiling, tried to make him whole again.

Ash leaned close to inspect her work and then flashed his abs, where a complete Umbria family crest remained intact. "She's good."

"See?" Ada gestured triumphantly. "She's quite capable of helping. It's remarkable, really. And you both need to spend time together, so this is the perfect solution."

River stared at Ada, suspicion prickling along his spine. Had Clarke put her up to this? These old-world women were dangerous when they banded together. It reminded him uncomfortably of his sisters back home. When his family met Blake, they'd circle her like a diamond.

Not that it was a bad thing. Fuck—he scrubbed his face. What was he thinking?

His gaze dropped to Trix's hand as she rubbed her swollen belly, and he remembered the naked hope in Aeron's eyes earlier. The elf king was ready to be a father. How could River deny him the chance to hear his child's first cry?

Then, there was the sharp, possessive heat that flared internally at the thought of Blake anywhere except beside River. In his bed.

Fuck.

"I'm going to regret this." He sighed and looked at the ceiling as if the Well might offer salvation. "It won't work. You know it."

"Maybe." Ada's voice softened. "But at least we can say we've tried everything before giving up. You understand that, don't you?"

His gaze dropped. "Yeah. I do."

Trix squealed, hands clapping with childish delight. For all of Ash's aloofness, River knew the crow secretly yearned for a family. After escaping captivity, he'd spent years with River's kettle, who'd adopted him and embraced him as their own. It was the happiest River had ever seen him.

He met River's eyes now, chin lifting imperceptibly. "I'll tell them you'll arrive with an outsider on horseback from Deyleese."

The town lay half a day's ride from the Southeast Murder's settlement. Going on horseback with a human would excuse him for not flying in. Ash wasn't just a friend, a brother; he was a Guardian. Precautions needed to be made to keep River's weakness a secret.

When everyone had left the healing bay except for River and Blake, he fixed his gaze on her. She might be sexy. She might be talented with a stick of charcoal. But she was also stubborn and fragile as spun glass.

"After you, Sparkles." He gestured toward the door.

"Now?"

"Unless you want a written invitation."

She glanced wildly around the tiny bay. "But I haven't packed. I have no clothes. I have no phone." Her brow furrowed. "I mean, I don't have any belongings."

"You won't need them where we're going. Crows travel light."

"I'm not going anywhere in this gown."

"What's wrong with it?" His gaze dropped to where the thin fabric strained across her ample breasts. He was sure the gown wasn't meant to fit so snugly, but he wasn't complaining. She had more than a generous handful. It was criminal, really—the things he could do to those breasts.

"I've not changed out of this gown in days." She crossed her arms, hiding those magnificent assets from view as she hunched. "I can't go looking like this. I'm a mess."

Mess?

Self-loathing bled through their bond like a fresh wound. Who the fuck was this husband of hers to leave her with such broken confidence? She could wear a sack and smell like the sewers, and still her beauty would blind River. Couldn't she see how she brightened every space simply by existing?

"Sparkles." He tucked a silken strand of hair behind her ear. "What you call a mess, I call a visual feast."

Goosebumps erupted across her skin. He longed to trace them with his tongue, to feel her shiver down to his marrow. His gaze caught on the open chest of coin on her bed, and his muscles tensed. He'd left them for her because he'd planned on leaving, planned on hunting Cloud alone. And if he found his former friend, River might not return at all. The money was an apology.

Reality crashed into him like a mountain of stone. He couldn't let this mating bond dictate his life. He'd seen what happened when Guardians lost themselves in romance— they grew weak, lost focus, or spiraled into self-destructive vendettas.

Love was a liability he couldn't afford, especially not

with someone as vulnerable and displaced as Blake. He was a Guardian. He had responsibilities. Vengeance to claim.

Blake deserved someone whole. Not damaged goods like him. Yet even as the thought formed, his heart rebelled. The idea of walking away, of never seeing her again, felt like gouging out his soul.

And that terrified him more than anything Cloud could do.

"Wear whatever you fucking want," he growled, stepping back. "Just be quick about it."

"Quick, like an hour?"

"You won't need these anymore." He sidestepped her to collect the chest. Her brow furrowed as she watched him. "And don't forget to bring your gift from the market."

"That's mine?" Shock rippled across her face as she glanced at the vase.

"You said you like to make broken things shine."

"You bought that for me?"

His gut twisted at her disbelief. Was she so unaccustomed to gifts, or did she think him incapable of thoughtfulness?

"Don't be ridiculous." He scoffed. "I didn't buy it. I stole it."

"Asshole."

He strode out, middle finger raised in a familiar gesture of defiance that now felt hollow. As he moved down the hallway, unease churned in his gut. Bringing Blake to the Great Murder was like leading a lamb to slaughter. His community could very well tear her apart just for being human. And if they discovered his crippled wings? That nest of vipers would strike without mercy.

But what choice did he have? Ash might change his mind

without warning. Reclaiming the cryptex was vital to defeating Nero. And while Ada had made no formal bargain, she'd asked in good faith for his help finding a book for Aeron.

At least one of them deserved a happy ending.

FOURTEEN

T he royal gardens shimmered in the afternoon light as Blake stood with River, Ash, and the Summer Court royals. The journey to their mountain farming village remained a mystery, with no obvious transportation.

Ada approached, fabric rustling as she extended a packed satchel. "You left these in your bay. All those clothes were for you."

"Oh." Heat crawled up Blake's neck as she accepted it, noting the thoughtfully included feminine supplies and a small vial of pink liquid inside. "I wasn't sure…"

"This works like contraception," Ada murmured, tapping the vial before frowning at the folded clothes. "I guess the style is different compared to your sequined dress. I only have basics besides royal attire—is this alright?"

"More than alright." Blake traced her finger along the satchel's edge. "You've been so kind."

The truth was, she'd agonized over her outfit choice. The tight gray riding pants and elegant blouse seemed like something important people wore. Back home, women of substance wore their accomplishments with subtle displays of wealth, not the disco-ball bling Blake was accustomed to.

She'd been too self-conscious to ask Ada for a better bra than the small cotton wrap supplied. It failed to support her cleavage, which explained why she clutched the satchel to her chest like a shield.

You can't upcycle yourself, babe.

Jeff's parting words still haunted her. The question of why she'd awoken in this time—why *her* specifically— nagged, especially given River's apparent preference for her absence.

Ada caught Blake's scowl directed at River and twisted her long blond braid. Her smile softened as she glanced toward her own mate. "Don't take anything River says too personally, but if you just can't handle him, I want you to know you're welcome here any time. I remember how it felt those first days." Stone entered her gaze. "Don't let McGrumpy push you around."

"Mate, I wasn't planning on it." Blake's grin felt genuine for the first time that day, the corners of her mouth lifting without effort.

Movement caught her eye as majestic black wings unfurled from Ash's leather-clad back, spanning wider than she'd imagined possible. The uniform must have hidden openings to accommodate the wings. No wonder Ada had been frustrated at River's examination. Wings that size needed space to be assessed correctly.

With a curt nod to his companions, Ash strode toward the gazebo and launched skyward, using the rose-covered roof as a springboard. Each powerful wingbeat sent air rippling against Blake's skin. The rhythmic *whoosh* faded as he climbed higher.

"I don't think I'll ever get used to seeing that." Trix's awe-filled voice came from behind.

"Me neither," Ada agreed, shielding her eyes against the sun as she tracked his ascent.

"Good to know it's not just me." Blake's grateful smile faltered as she noticed who accompanied Trix.

The tall, muscular elf king wore an intricately tailored coat in forest greens and browns. The royal insignia adorned his breast pocket. Silken curtains of brown hair framed his pointed ears. Everything about him radiated regality, from his ramrod posture to something in his eyes that spoke of wisdom.

Aeron's gaze met Blake's and his lips stretched into an awkward smile. His hands moved fluidly as he signed to Trix, *"Is this her?"*

At least, Blake thought that was what he said. Her ASL was a little rusty.

Trix nodded, passing her potted plant to Ada before signing back, *"Do you think this gift is stupid? I don't want to look desperate."*

"We kind of are," he signed and glanced at Trix's swollen belly.

The agonized adoration in his expression made Blake's heart splinter.

She should look away—eavesdropping was rude in any culture, especially when one party had no idea she understood their language. She'd picked up enough during countless hours watching the interpreter at Jeff's footy commentating broadcasts. Not that he'd watched her

Hidden Gems live streams often, but she'd wanted to support his post-AFL career.

The memory stabbed her. She'd traced each finger movement and memorized each hand position while Jeff droned through presentations, his voice fading to background noise. Their disparate levels of spousal support struck her now as glaringly obvious. Back then, she'd mastered the art of not noticing, of finding ways to entertain herself and still look supportive … just in case he would one day do the same in return.

Trix's hands moved gracefully, signing for her partner's benefit as she spoke. "Aeron, let me introduce Blake, River's mate."

Before he could respond, Blake put down her satchel and shaped the words: *"Nice to meet you."*

Sunlight broke across Aeron's face as he returned, *"You know how to sign?"*

"Only a little." She explained her learning process while continuing to sign, though Trix had to help translate the more complex parts of the story when Blake faltered. Relief visibly softened their postures, draining tension from their shoulders.

"Wow," Ada said. "You really do have a sharp memory."

"If only I'd used it to learn something more meaningful." Blake's joke fell flat, the self-deprecation tasting bitter on her tongue. Still, warmth bloomed in her chest at being believed capable of her mission, and having a purpose felt like solid ground beneath her feet.

"I wouldn't call learning to sign meaningless," Trix countered, eyebrows knitting together.

"Yeah." Ada shifted the potted plant to her hip. "Don't sell yourself short."

"Oh!" Trix startled, reclaiming the plant with a nervous laugh. "I almost forgot. I made this for you." She thrust it forward. "An appreciation gift."

Blake carefully accepted the sapling and immediately tensed upon recognizing the pot, or rather, the vase. It was River's stolen gift from the markets.

Trix's smile wilted at Blake's hesitation. "It's not right, is it?"

"The vase?" She'd purposefully left it behind, refusing to accept stolen goods. But now that it rested in her palms, cool and familiar, she knew she wanted to keep it.

"I meant the eucalyptus." Trix's fingers fluttered anxiously around the plant. "I only had memories and a book for reference. I hoped the Well would fill in the gaps, but the leaves look wrong. I remember it smelling different when I visited Australia."

"I don't understand. You make trees?"

"Sort of. I can grow plants." She waved her hand over the sapling, releasing that now-familiar ozone scent Blake associated with magic. Buds sprouted along the stem and unfurled into leaves before her eyes. "I made it with my gift. I thought you might be homesick. Since I can't conjure kangaroos or Vegemite, maybe the scent of home will help."

"You grew this?" Tears ambushed Blake, stinging her eyes and clogging her throat as she traced a leaf's veins with her fingertip. "The detail is incredible. You've captured everything perfectly."

She tried to hide how deeply homesickness had carved into her soul. But the dam broke. Tears spilled down her cheeks, and a choked sound escaped. Across the garden, River's head snapped toward her, his brow furrowing.

"I fucked up, didn't I?" Trix moaned. "I can take it back—"

"No!" Blake clutched the plant protectively. "I mean … it's perfect. It smells exactly like the eucalyptus tree from me old backyard." From the house she grew up in. "From *my* backyard, I mean. I just didn't expect…" She forced a watery smile and glanced between the two women, a foreign sense of connection unfurling in her chest. She'd never had girlfriends before. The other WAGs were competitive bitches, and there had been too many men in her life. "You cunts have been so good to me. I don't know what I would have done without you."

Ada's brows lowered. "Did you just call us the c-word?"

FIFTEEN

Blake's term of endearment felt like a live grenade with its pin removed.

Ada's wary expression deepened as silence stretched between them.

Cultural differences had never felt so mortifying. What was an affectionate familiarity in Perth translated to nuclear-level offense here.

"She means it in a good way," Trix rushed to explain, lips twitching with barely contained laughter.

"There's a good way?" Ada's eyebrows disappeared beneath her bangs.

"Ha ha." Heat swamped Blake's cheeks. "I guess you can say it's reserved for only the closest or the worst of friends." She paused. "You're the first lot." Another pause. "In case you—"

"Got it." Ada smirked.

"Thank fuck. I thought I'd put me foot in it again."

Trix looked hopefully at Blake. "So you like it, yeah?"

At her vehement nod, Trix's hands flew excitedly to sign for Aeron. "She likes it!"

His responding flood of sign language exceeded Blake's vocabulary, but his pride in his queen radiated in the softening around his eyes and the slight forward tilt of his body.

River's approach crunched gravel beneath his heavy boots, reminding Blake of their mission.

"I can't magically heal or grow plants," she told the girls softly, "but I promise I'll do everything possible to find the right book to help you both."

"Hate to interrupt this little knitting circle," River grumbled, gaze locked on the potted eucalyptus. "But we need to leave—What is that, and why is it in the vase I gave you?"

"Oh." Trix cast a nervous glance at him. "It was left behind, so I assumed it was trash."

"What?" River's jaw slackened as he stared at Blake. "You *left* it?"

The eucalyptus leaves rustled between them.

"You said you stole it," she countered, matching his affronted tone.

"So?"

"Theft is a crime, River." Her gaze darted to the women. "It's still a crime, right?"

Their laughter lightened the tension and also felt like a sign of solidarity. Ada's earlier promise—*you're welcome here any time*—gave her the courage to continue with River despite everything.

"Crows don't give a shit about rules," Jasper said, walking up behind Ada and settling his hands on her shoulders.

River's mockery dripped acid as he parroted the king's

words. When no one laughed, he snapped, "Let's go," and stalked away, weapons clinking with each rigid step.

After exchanging hugs and promises to return with good news, Blake joined River along with Jasper and his son.

River's eyes narrowed to slits when she approached, his gaze tracking from the plant to her face. She clutched her satchel and eucalyptus tighter, chin lifting in silent challenge.

His jaw worked before he announced, "Blake travels with Jasper."

The king's rebuke cut through the tension. "Unless you plan to divest yourself of metal, she'll have to travel with Aspen. He can't take you. He's not a Guardian."

"Then you take us both."

"We've been through this. It's safer with two."

Color mottled River's face, sending the prince into poorly suppressed laughter.

"Don't worry," Aspen managed between snickers, eyes dancing with mischief. "I'll try to keep my scent to myself."

"Like fuck you will," River shouted.

"Aspen, stop teasing him," Jasper growled.

"But—"

"One day, you'll feel the same. Ease up, son. River's the type to come back and haunt you."

Blake's confusion mounted. What had she done wrong? Aspen did look kind of sweaty. Maybe he'd been working out. Maybe that's what River meant by scent.

"I'm not worried about a little sweat," she said to Aspen. "Me husband—ahem—*my* husband was a football player. Trust me, mate. It's fine."

The following stretch of time swallowed every sound. Even the insects ceased chirping.

"What did I say?" Her gaze bounced between frozen

faces before landing on the women's winces, their expressions almost comical in synchronicity.

Jasper inhaled to speak but fell silent as River thrust his chakram against the king's chest.

"Don't say a word, wolf," River warned, voice dropping to a dangerous whisper.

Storm clouds gathered in his eyes as he stripped himself of weapons. Each dagger slapped into Jasper's increasingly full hands, the metal singing as steel met steel. All the while, River's gaze ping-ponged between Aspen and Blake with murderous intent.

"River," Jasper chided, juggling the growing arsenal, "how am I supposed to carry her when my hands are full of your weapons?"

"You're a clever doggy. You'll figure it out." River's dry grin never reached his eyes. He gripped Aspen's shoulders, fingers digging into the prince's flesh. "Let's go."

They vanished—no flash, no sound, just absence where bodies had stood.

"What the flying fuck?" Blake's shriek pierced the sudden emptiness as she jabbed a finger at the vacant space. "Did you all see that?"

"Aspen and I can portal ourselves with whatever we're touching," Jasper explained, struggling to tuck daggers into his belt, the weapons clinking against each other.

"Is it safe?" Her heart hammered against her ribs. "Of course, it's safe. You said it's safe, right?"

Near the palace, Ada cupped her mouth and shouted, "You'll be fine!"

Having secured River's arsenal, Jasper wrapped an arm around Blake's shoulders. His grip steadily tightened. "Here we go."

One moment, she stood in the Summer Palace's lush gardens. Next, her insides twisted like wrung laundry. Purple wildflowers blurred into being beneath her, and her stomach heaved. She doubled over, struggling to stay on her feet, but the pot in her hands felt like a support to lean on.

"Oh god." She gagged. "Not again."

Through the rush of blood in her ears, she heard weapons thudding against the dirt behind her. Then the jingle of glass coins rattled.

"Why are you returning it?" Aspen's wary voice drifted from somewhere to her right as she fought another wave of rising nausea. "You won the bet."

"Yes, and now I'm paying you for your portaling service." River's velvet tone sharpened to a razor's edge. "Does the kid know anything about commerce?"

"Consider yourself lucky, Aspen," Jasper replied, amused.

The two dematerialized an instant later.

A gust of wind smelling like ozone staggered Blake, sending fresh waves of nausea through what felt like displaced cells. She lost the battle with gravity, and her knees hit damp earth. Bile rose in her gullet. She set down the plant, shifted the satchel, and braced for vomitageddon.

Footsteps approached. Instead of mockery, gentle fingers swept her hair back from her face. River's fingertips were cool against her fevered skin as she puked her guts out.

"The nausea will pass soon." His voice anchored her to reality. "Let it out if you need to."

River had helped like this when they first met. How had she forgotten that kindness? In ten years of marriage, Jeff had never shown such care. When Blake was sick, he'd simply turn up the TV volume to drown out her retching.

It was infuriating that she continued to make these connections *after* Jeff had dumped her. Why hadn't she seen them sooner?

He's one of the good guys, Trix had said about River.

Blake hadn't believed it, but she'd glimpsed warmth breaking through his prickly exterior more than once. Reclaiming the coin chest hadn't been selfish after all. He'd simply returned it to the prince after a bet, one that the king considered a lucky lesson.

When her stomach finally settled and her brain stopped swimming, Blake sat back on her haunches, wiping her mouth with the back of her hand. River crouched before her, eyes filled with concern.

"You good?"

She groaned. "Two feet and a heartbeat."

"That's … a weird answer, but okay. Take a deep breath."

She obeyed, focusing on his continued soothing words.

"Inhale slowly. Then exhale. Good."

His praise washed over her, leaving her skin tingling in ways that had nothing to do with portaling sickness. She offered him a grateful smile.

His intense stare held for a heartbeat longer before he nodded and retrieved his scattered weapons. The new landscape beckoned—rolling hills dotted with wildflowers stretching toward a distant forest—but she couldn't tear her gaze from River as he twisted and cached daggers around his body with practiced efficiency.

The dynamic between them had shifted.

His usual anger had vanished, replaced by relaxed shoulders and an open expression. It was as though a door had swung wide between them, and somehow, vomiting had been the key?

Blake tucked her hair behind her ear, fingers lingering to wipe a smudge of dirt from her cheek. She straightened her blouse, which clung damply to her skin. God, she must look awful. But he was being nice.

"Before, at the palace," she ventured slowly, "you were angry at me."

He glanced up through blue-black locks, thoughts flickering behind his eyes. He shouldered his pack, uncorked a waterskin with his teeth, and offered it to her.

She stared at it, waiting for him to answer. When he didn't, she pushed to her feet and dusted her hands before accepting. She rinsed the sourness from her mouth, then drank deeply. The cool water felt heavenly against her raw throat.

"Thank you." She sighed, returning it to him. "For before as well."

"That's a no-no word, Blake," he growled. "Don't you feel that charge in the atmosphere?"

"No."

He tucked away the waterskin and captured her hands with his. "Close your eyes and open your senses."

"Open me—my senses. What does that even mean?"

"Just fucking close your eyes."

"Jeeze." Her eyelids lowered reluctantly. "No need to get your knickers in a knot."

A disgruntled huff tickled her lips. Smelled randomly like lime.

"Now, pay attention to the atmosphere around you," he said. "And your body, and the connection between. Then say it again."

"Atmosphere," she said. "Pay attention. Got it."

Doing that right now.

Except his hands were nice and warm. Strong. A little rough from work. Good.

Focus, Blake.

The air was warmer here than in Helianthus. Humid, too. It was a bit more like Broome up North than Perth in summer. Her body hummed with awareness, particularly the inadequate support beneath her blouse. She should have asked Ada for a larger wrap. The urge to cover herself was overwhelming, but River held her hands firmly, his thumbs resting against her wrists' pulse points.

"Repeat it," he said.

"Thank you?" She peeked with one eye and found him watching her with an unexpected intensity that brought heat to her cheeks.

He averted his gaze and gently squeezed her wrists. "You can't concentrate with your eyes open. Close them and say it again."

"Me eyes can concentrate great, open or closed, thank you very much."

Through her lashes, she caught his eye roll and the ghost of a smile playing at the corners of his lips. Oops. She'd repeated it without concentrating, but damn, that smile. Butterflies erupted in her belly. She squeezed her eyes shut before he noticed.

"Say it, Blake," he said, voice deepening, "and *feel* what happens in the air."

"Thank you."

This time, she felt it—a whisper of energy against her skin. The moment she acknowledged it, more rippled across her arms and face, raising fine hairs like static electricity.

"I feel it!" Her eyes flew open.

"That's the debt you owe me for your gratitude. The Well

acknowledges its existence and has given me control of the leash."

"Wait. What?" Her stomach plummeted. "Control?"

He released her hands and flashed a grin. "If I were truly angry with you, Sparkles, I'd collect them."

"Them?" Horror dawned as she mentally tallied each utterance.

"You've said the no-no word more than once."

"The first one, I admit, was my fault, but the rest were because you told me to say it."

His shoulders lifted in an elegant shrug. "Maybe I'll return one. But the rest I'm keeping."

"That math doesn't add up."

"Does if you're a crow."

"Far out," she managed, searching for her lost dignity. "Don't do me any favors."

"You saying you owe me a favor now too?"

"Are you for real?"

"No." Laughter burst from him, rich and unexpected. Addictive. He gestured toward a worn path winding into the hills. "Let's go before I change my mind."

Blake lingered, savoring the sound. Deep and genuine, his laughter rolled like distant thunder, curling warmth through her chest. The knowledge that she'd coaxed this rare moment from him, this glimpse behind his armor, filled her with a quiet pride she hadn't felt in years.

Maybe ever.

SIXTEEN

Nero's fingers tapped against his desktop—one-two-three, one-two-three—matching the rhythm of water dripping somewhere from the Sky Tower's greenhouse domed ceiling. He pulled open the third drawer, peered inside, then slammed it shut with enough force to rattle the wilting plants nearby.

He could have sworn he had put it there the night before.

A whisper touched his ear. *You never could keep track of things.*

He straightened, refusing to turn toward the voice. Through the grimy glass dome, the dead forest stretched toward the horizon. No movement outside. Just ghosts in his head.

"Nero," his queen said behind him. "If it's all the same to you, I'd like to finish the game this century."

"Game?"

"The chess game." A sigh. "Are you done searching?"

He turned and found Pandora sitting at the chess table,

studying the board. Her dark bob framed a face too perfect for this dying world.

"I misplaced something," he said.

She raised her brows and looked pointedly at his closed fist.

He opened it and found the mini screwdriver he'd been searching for. When had he picked it up?

Weak, the voice said. *You surround yourself with weakness.*

"You told me she tortured him," Pandora said, returning her gaze to the pieces on the board.

"She did." Nero cleared his throat and joined her at the table. "As did I. As did Bones. As did anyone I let into his cell."

"And yet he never gave her up." Her lips flattened as Nero moved his knight. She moved a pawn. "Stubborn. Or admirable, depending on which way you want to look at it."

"How can you be sure he's hunting the cryptex?"

Across the table, Pandora's fingers stilled on her queen. "What did you say his deal was when he gave you the fae military plans?"

Nero ground his teeth. "That Rory's death was his, and his alone."

She knocked over his bishop with her queen. "And what happened?"

"I don't appreciate your patronizing tone."

She held his stare. "What happened?"

"I didn't leave them alone."

You couldn't help yourself, could you? The voice mocked him. *Couldn't leave well enough alone.*

Pandora heard none of it; instead, she continued with her story. "Crows pass down grudges through generations of descendants. These immortal fae crows would hold them …

well, for eternity. Regardless of how the affair ended between him and your daughter, he admitted to stealing the cryptex. He has plenty of reasons to hold a grudge against you. If he's been robbed of his vengeance with your kin, who do you think he'll target next?"

"Hm." She was right, of course. Always was. That's why she was his queen on the board. His gambit.

"If he's caught wind that you're still after the puzzle box, he'll be hunting it too. You tortured him too much about it for him to think it's worthless."

"You think it's in Elphyne?"

"Without a doubt. My spies have heard tales of a particular crow known as the Collector—a beast obsessed with old-world treasures."

You're grasping at straws now, the voice taunted.

Nero jammed the screwdriver into the wooden chessboard where it remained, handle wobbling. Pandora blinked once, too slow, then locked her dark eyes on his.

"Was that necessary?" she asked.

A shadow formed by the grimy window. Short, kinky, dark hair. Copper beads catching light that didn't exist.

Again with the theatrics, Dad.

Sweat beaded on Nero's forehead. He turned back to Pandora. "Your move. Finish the game, and then you can tell me about this gathering."

"I have a plan," Pandora said.

She doesn't. Rory's whisper grew closer. *None of us ever do.*

"I do," he barked.

"What?"

"Nothing. Tell me your plan after you finish the game."

Pandora's jaw twitched. "I have a plan."

"I know. You just said that."

"I have a plan," she echoed. Her shoulder jerked. "I have a plan."

Fuck. He slumped. Not again.

"I have a—"

"Shut the fuck up!" Rage burst inside Nero, building with each repetition.

He launched from his chair, roaring his frustration. Nothing worked. Five years of work and nothing stuck. He struck Pandora across the face, snapping her head sideways. Her neck remained at an odd angle, and her shoulder still twitched.

You won't win. The whisper in his head sounded more like it came from behind him.

"Oh yes, I will."

No … you won't.

"I will!"

"She's right, you know," a voice said—clearer, present. Real.

Nero turned.

She perched on the windowsill, legs swinging like a child. Not the broken woman who'd fallen to her death, but Aurora, the girl she'd been before she became Rory. Sixteen and untouched by his experiments. Before the crow got its filthy, tainted claws on her.

Her caramel skin glowed against the dull light. Hair free of copper beads and braids, wild and full, framed her innocent face.

"I was never innocent, was I, Dad?" She cocked her head. "Not since you stole me from my mothers. Not since you asked me to spill the world's secrets."

"You're not real." He waggled his finger at her.

"Then why are you talking to me?" She hopped down

from the sill. "Your best assassin, your Reaper, your own daughter." She stopped before him, studying him with pity. "You drank me dry, didn't you?"

"I needed your mana."

For a brief, unnerving moment, her expression morphed into a scream. Pain. Anguish. Feathers were floating around her. The vision dissipated as quickly as it arrived.

"And what did you get instead?" She tapped her temple. "Memories you never wanted. Knowledge you can't access." She circled the room, her pale white dress dragging on the dirty ground. She eyed broken items with distaste, pitied the disarray. "Visitations you can't predict."

Nero forced his gaze away from the apparition. He brushed Pandora's hair from her nape and used the screwdriver to peel back the patch of silicone skin. A rivulet of blood oozed down her back, disappearing into Rory's old Reaper uniform. Her shoulder still twitched, a steady rhythm like clockwork gears skipping teeth.

Tick. Skip. Tick. Skip.

"Remember when you told me the madness would be manageable?" Rory appeared at his elbow. "'Family mana is safer,' you said. 'It won't drive you to hallucinate,' you said."

"Shut up."

She leaned closer, her breath—impossible, nonexistent breath—warm against his ear. "You were wrong."

"I didn't know," he muttered, focusing on Pandora's exposed control panel. The latticework of circuits and valves was tech from another era, repurposed and modified with the Tinker's designs. He pulled down the uniform collar and revealed a panel between her shoulder blades—a mix of living, human bone, and brass. He used his screwdriver to open it and connected the wires and tubes from the neural interface to the battery inside her ribs—a clockwork device of brass fueled by harvested Guardian mana.

"You knew." Rory ran her fingers along the edge of Pandora's exposed mechanics. "Look at that. The Tinker's work. You stole that too."

"She left it behind."

"Like I left behind the cryptex's location? In my memories? The ones you can't see or even access?"

Nero bit back a response, knowing it only fed the hallucination. The nuclear winter freeze had rusted Pandora's components far more than he'd expected. He'd gambled on her survival, and it had cost him five years, half their resources, the fragile loyalty of his starving people.

As he waited for her to refuel, he focused on the positive. Pandora had found him a lead. She could pass as human. But their Guardian mana reserves...

"Are almost gone," Rory whispered, now standing directly behind the still-twitching Pandora. She met his eyes. "Just like me."

Nero clenched his fists, forcing himself to inventory mechanical components. The neural network seemed intact. The Tinker's mana distribution node pulsed beneath her left clavicle—the same design he'd seen in those abandoned blueprints. The clockwork heart ticked steadily.

Wait.

He leaned closer, examining the heart's brass casing. A hairline crack had formed a complex pattern across its surface—the same design inlaid in the Tinker's weapons. He'd seen that pattern before when he'd examined her notes. It wasn't a flaw but a deliberate feature.

"Energy distribution," Rory said, voice fading as she circled behind him. "Protection."

"From what?" he whispered.

Pandora's eyes snapped open. Her head rotated with mechanical precision until she faced him, neck still at its unnatural angle. She reached up and caught his wrist, her grip calibrated to cause maximum discomfort without permanent damage.

Her other hand opened to reveal the glass coin—an invitation to the Great Murder.

"Your move, Nero," she said. Her eyes flickered, and for an instant, something alien lived behind them. Not his design.

He blinked, and then it was gone.

Behind Pandora, Rory smiled. Adult, and dressed as his Reaper once more. Copper beads clacked against each other as she faded into the shadows.

"Check," she whispered before vanishing completely.

CHAPTER

SEVENTEEN

River's jaw clenched with each step on the narrow path through the forest toward Deyleese. Blake's footsteps thrummed beneath his skin. Together, their boots crushed aromatic sweetgrass over pebbles, releasing bursts of scent that mingled with the perfume of moss and the earthy smell of dirt.

He pivoted, tracking her approach, and his breath caught. Her hair streamed like wings in flight, iridescent colors shimmering through strands. The sun outdid itself today, adding even more hues to the existing rainbow with each dappled ray. Perspiration gleamed on her skin. Her eyes lit with wonder at the forested slopes, and his traitorous heart skipped.

"This place is bloody beautiful," she said, cradling her plant against her chest.

You're beautiful, he thought, the truth burning behind his teeth.

The plant looked heavy. He took it from her, and she was too busy gawping at their surroundings to protest. He tried to surrender to the world through her eyes. Down the hill, farther across the valley, tropical trees pierced the clouds. Their trunks were wider than three men with arms outstretched. Kaleidoscope-winged insects darted through sunlight. Vegetation was verdant. The sky was blue. Farm animals bleated and mooed as they grazed in pastures by the village at the hill's base.

"A far cry from the world you left behind," he said.

Melancholy seeped through their bond. It tasted like ash. He'd learned she felt this particular brand of sadness whenever she thought of *him*.

River's fingers dug into the plant's pot, nails scraping the vase. Copper flooded his mouth as he bit his cheek. Another man's hands on Blake's skin—the image constricted his chest, strangled his lungs. His free hand found *Peacemaker*, thumb tracing the familiar curve of metal for comfort.

"We need to move." He shoved the words through clenched teeth. "Fewer horses available after sundown."

A stupid excuse. The village lay minutes away. The sun was still at high noon.

He quickened his pace and descended the hill.

Deyleese wasn't so idyllic up close. Weathered buildings circled a central square like wary predators surrounding prey. It was small, with perhaps only a few hundred inhabitants. But it was the last place they could find a horse before entering crow territory.

At the first outbuilding, River returned Blake's plant, his fingers brushing hers.

"Need both hands free for this," he said, casting a vigilant glance around. Curtains twitched. Villagers gave him a wide berth. No one wanted to draw the attention of a Guardian.

Danger lurked everywhere for a human, especially for *his* Well-blessed human.

Her hand sign of gratitude sent heat racing to his ears. Pride swelled in his chest, unexpected and addictive. He jerked his attention forward to the Drunken Drake, where merchants traded goods, secrets, and occasionally lives.

This time, River walked by her side so he could keep her in his sight. He didn't think other crows saw her so brilliantly as he did, but he couldn't be sure. He would ask Ash when they met again. The crows stalking her on the first day might have been attracted to her sparkling dress, but he didn't want to take the risk.

Blake halted abruptly. River sidestepped to avoid a collision and followed her transfixed gaze. At the tavern's entrance, over the doors and in the shadow beneath the porch, crystal lanterns pulsed with trapped manabeeze. Their light fractured into ribbons that moved across the worn wooden sign.

"Look how the light dances!" She jogged up the rickety steps, shifted the weight of her plant to one hip, and used her free hand to trace the air beneath a lantern where bright patterns split and reformed.

"It's just containment lighting," River explained as he joined her, but Blake leaned closer, wonder illuminating her face.

"Back home, me followers would send pictures of light phenomena from around the world. Sundogs, moon halos, golden hour..." Her voice faltered. "Jeff said they were just lonely people with nothing better to do, but I was honored they thought of *me*, someone they'd never met except for on a screen, to share wonder with. The world felt less empty, you know?"

An ache stirred in River's chest. When had he last marveled at anything simply for the joy of discovery?

"Sorry," Blake said, sensing his shift in mood. "I didn't mean to—" She straightened her shoulders. "Actually, no, I'm not sorry. Many inventions from my world are now gone. But the Well—or the fae, I guess—have created something new." She gestured to the swirling manabeeze in their crystal prisons. "They've made light dance without electricity. It's bloody marvelous."

Her wonder pierced his jaded armor. River stepped closer, tilting his head as ultraviolet messages revealed themselves between fracture lines in the door's wooden surface—secret communications invisible to human eyes.

"The glassmaker must have been avian," River heard himself admit. "He's added something to the manabeeze—"

"Manabeeze?"

"Those little balls of light." He nodded at them. "They erupt from Well-connected creatures at the time of death."

"Really?" She blinked. "Like us?"

He nodded. "They hold residual power and memories. If you're careful and respectful, then using them in lighting and other enhancements is permitted." Something about her avid attention kept him talking. "Here, they're used to enhance the ultraviolet light that reveals encoded messages on the door. Each prism tells a different story depending on how you look at it."

"What do you see?" Blake's fingers hovered near the light, then fell away. "What are the messages?"

"Business details," he replied, chuckling. He tapped a scrawled line near the doorknob. "This one is a crude offer for a good time. But I've seen far more interesting messages like trade routes, love notes, and warnings about bandits."

About Guardians.

She grinned. "So even what seems empty to some eyes holds treasure for those who know where to look. I love it."

The tavern door swung open, and two drunkards stumbled out. Rich aromas of spiced ale and roasting meat billowed out on a wave of air. River's hand moved to *Peacemaker* before he caught himself. He stepped between his mate and the drunks until they were long gone. Only then did he motion Blake inside.

Patrons nearest the door scattered as they entered, pressing themselves against the walls. News traveled quickly in villages, especially news of a Guardian and his Well-blessed mate. Some gazes landed on his neck tattoos and then quickly averted.

That's right, fuckers. One of the Twelve is here.

He scanned the dim interior for threats. A lone owl shifter nursed a tankard of ale near the empty hearth. His cloak failed to conceal the distinctive wings and weapons beneath. Their eyes locked briefly before the owl looked away, shoulders tensing.

River's lip curled at the stench—shit and rotting leaves. The ancient blood feud between their species burned in his veins, awakening predatory instincts that demanded satisfaction.

Not today, bird-brains.

He placed a palm on Blake's lower back and guided her toward the bar. Three men sitting there froze at their approach, drinks tilting, mouths agape. One wore the tattered uniform of a Summer Court soldier, with the insignia torn away. He was likely a deserter who had abandoned his post when Jasper gave the city's aid to the Order of the Well at the battle five years ago. Or maybe he was a

Mithras loyalist. That he still wore remnants of the red coat indicated his bitterness ran deep. Probably a—River searched and located black feathers jutting from his collar—yep, a crow.

Only one way to deal with stubborn crows. He strode to the bar and knocked the stein from the soldier's trembling hand. The ceramic shattered, ale splashing across worn floorboards.

"Oops. My bad." River's pitch lowered. "You should be more careful with that shaking hand. Though I suppose deserting your post can do that to a crow."

The soldier's face blanched. His companions stared into their drinks, suddenly fascinated by swirling amber liquid.

Blake's disapproval struck River through their bond like a physical blow. He caught her expression—not just disappointment but something that dangerously resembled pity. An unfamiliar hollowness replaced his satisfaction.

In Elphyne, strength prevented bloodshed more effectively than misplaced kindness. But the justifications died unspoken. Since when did anyone's opinion matter to him?

Lanternlight glinted off the polished horns sprouting from the bartender's temples. Heat shimmered around his massive form as he wiped the bar farther down, each swipe leaving wet arcs that instantly evaporated.

That heat revealed the bartender's mana capacity was larger than the average fae. But still insignificant compared to a Guardian. A dust mote compared to a Well-blessed woman.

"Nice place you've got here," River drawled, dropping onto a barstool. "Though your clientele could use some work."

"Guardian." The bartender spat the word like a curse. "What do you want?"

River tossed a red coin onto the counter. "A horse."

Blake settled onto the stool beside him, and River fought not to preen when she leaned closer. The bartender's nostrils flared as he assessed her, gaze flicking down to the blue matching marks on their hands.

"Got one left." He raised bushy brows. "But it will cost you three red coin."

River barked a laugh. "For a nag this late in the day? One."

"Two."

"One, and I won't mention the contraband spoons I spotted in your kitchen." River nodded toward the hole in the wall behind the bar, where a cook paused in his stirring of the pot on the stove.

The bartender's face darkened to burgundy. "Fine."

River grinned, but something in the fae's eyes set his instincts screaming. He glanced at the owl shifter, noting how he tracked their exchange with sudden interest.

Lucky for him, they were in a hurry. And apparently, Blake hated showy displays of power. Whatever. The trek to the murder was still a few hours away. River wanted to get there before dark. Ignoring his urge to brawl had nothing to do with not wanting to disappoint Blake.

Not at all.

Outside, a lone horse stood tethered in the dirt yard behind the tavern. Its coat held a glossy shimmer that seemed too shiny. Something about its gaze ruffled River's feathers.

Blake gushed, "She's a beauty."

He lunged forward, catching her wrist mid-reach. The

horse's nostrils flared, tracking his movement with unsettling focus, pupils contracting then widening again.

"Careful with animals in Elphyne," River warned, voice low. "Not everything is what it seems."

"You're just grumpy about whatever that was in there." But Blake withdrew her hand, arms crossing over her chest in that protective gesture he'd noticed she made whenever uncertain. One arm positioned slightly higher than the other, shoulders curving inward—a shield against the world.

River checked the horse, but despite his low-grade sense of unease, nothing seemed wrong with it. He helped Blake mount, his hands lingering longer than necessary on her waist as she adjusted her balance. After he'd given her the plant and secured her satchel, he swung up behind her. The curve of her spine immediately pressed against his chest before jolting forward.

Oops. The daggers strapped to his bandolier were in an awkward position.

"It's been a while since I traveled tandem on horseback," he muttered, and rearranged his weapons so they wouldn't cut into her.

Once ready, he slapped the reins and kicked the horse into a trot. They left the village for the neighboring forest. This path took them straight into the southeast crow territory. His nomadic race lived throughout Elphyne, but this latest settlement was particularly special to River.

It was where he'd grown up—where Cloud had too. Sometime in the past decade, the murder had circled back to its roots and resettled.

The forest engulfed them in a cathedral of living wood and foliage. Massive trunks soared skyward. Sunlight pierced through the canopy gaps, illuminating dancing motes of pollen. Humid air clung to River's skin. Beneath the vibrant perfume of moss and mulch lurked the metallic taste of old-world ruins.

"It's really here, isn't it?" Wonder filled Blake's voice. She pointed to a fallen signpost half-buried in fire lilies. Metal jutted from vibrant blooms. Letters were still visible beneath luminescent fungus: City Limits.

He should probably destroy the old sign, but he felt no disturbance in the flow of mana. Later. He urged the horse onward.

"I keep thinking I'll wake up, but…" Blake fell silent as parrots darted overhead, flashing crimson and electric blue against the canopy.

That ashy melancholy of hers seeped through their bond. River's jaw clenched against the intrusion.

"You're thinking about him." The accusation escaped before he could trap it behind his teeth.

"Jeff?"

She'd mentioned him earlier. "Ah, so he has a name."

She twisted to face him, surprise flashing across her features. "Are you reading my mind?"

"Don't need to." He tapped her forearm where blue marks softly glowed. "Every time you remember him, it feels like swallowing grave ash."

"Oh." Her shoulders stiffened as she faced forward again.

"You miss him."

The statement hung between them. Her continuing silence confirmed what drove splinters beneath his skin.

They continued for a while. The horse's hooves squelched against sodden earth, occasionally striking buried ancient bitumen with sharp clacks.

Like her previous life.

So her husband's name was Jeff.

Jeff-*ff*.

What kind of dumb name was that?

River shouldn't get annoyed at the distant third member of their unwanted, forced relationship.

At the time of their world freezing, the other Well-blessed women remained in this same location where Elphyne grew. As far as River knew, Blake was the only woman from a distant land. What had she called it? Oz?

More clip-clopping and squelching.

More silence and grave ash on his tongue.

Jeff-ff-*f*.

The Well wanted what it wanted, and by dragging Blake across thousands of miles to be here, with him, meant it needed something important from both of them … they must be perfect for each other. His body already agreed.

"Fucking Leaf," he grumbled under his breath.

"Did you say something?"

"Just swatting a leaf out of my face." He scowled at his flimsy excuse.

They continued at an unhurried pace. The murder's roost was about two turns of the hourglass away. They could have walked, he supposed. But then they wouldn't be sharing this horse. He caught himself leaning closer, inhaling the scent of her hair. Yep. Girly floral shit and sunshine. Perfect.

"Why did you return Aspen's coins?" she asked. "I'm guessing you won that bet fair and square. What was the bet, by the way?"

"He boasted he could avoid my flying dagger. I proved him wrong."

"You stabbed him?"

"His cursed father took the hit," he bit out. "Coddling the kid during a war will not protect him."

A pause. "War, huh?"

"Until Nero is dealt with, we're at war."

"Aspen's not really a kid anymore, though, is he?" she pointed out. "He's almost at his peak."

"Oh, you noticed, did you?"

"It was hard not to." A snort. "I don't know what's in your Well's drinking water, but all the men here are buff spunkrats."

What the fuck did that mean? River shifted uncomfortably. "Maybe I didn't want the coin."

"Right." Her laugh held unexpected warmth that curled around his spine. "Face it, you're not nearly as much of a bastard as you pretend to be."

If she only knew. Lightning seared across his memory— pain, burning feathers, the scent of his charred flesh. His knuckles whitened on the reins.

"I used to know some grumpy cunts," she continued, plucking a leaf from a passing tree and tucking it into her plant's soil. "Old mate who worked at the hardware store was so—"

"Stop calling other males *mate*," he growled.

"Seriously? I can't change me identity—" She let out a frustrated noise. "I mean, I can't change *my* identity overnight just because you're jealous."

"I'm not jealous." The denial rushed out too fast.

"Sure, mate." Her accent thickened deliberately. "Whatever you say, *mate*."

"You're doing it on purpose now."

"What gave it away?" She patted his thigh, and every cell in his body rejoiced. "Your Guardian powers of deduction truly amaze me."

He opened his mouth to retort when the horse halted abruptly. Water dripped from its mane, though no clouds marred the sky. Muscles bunched beneath them. Tension vibrated through its frame.

"Blake—" he started, warning too late.

The horse dissolved like morning mist. Its flesh reformed into something ancient and terrible between their thighs. Razor-sharp teeth flashed as the kelpie bucked, launching them skyward. River twisted mid-air, pulling Blake against his chest as they crashed into the underbrush. Her startled cry pierced his heart. But that wasn't the only sound freezing his blood.

The beating of mighty wings echoed above them, and the unmistakable shriek of an owl shifter brigade.

EIGHTEEN

Just when Blake started to believe this world was real, something unbelievable happened. Her mind reeled as she tumbled with River through loam and foliage. The horse had changed. Morphed. Where solid flesh had been, monstrous teeth emerged and snapped at her face.

Now they were airborne. Branches whipped her skin as they crashed through the underbrush. Her satchel sailed left. Trix's gift went right. The vase shattered against exposed roots. Blake's heart seized as River's powerful arms enveloped her. His body curled around hers as they continued to roll down the damp embankment.

A shriek pierced the canopy overhead. The horse-monster's whinny twisted into something disturbingly human. Ferns whipped her face, but River's cage of muscle and leather shielded her from the worst. Eventually, they rolled to a stop with his weight pinning her beneath him.

Another screech tore through the forest, silencing every cricket and bird.

River clamped his hands on either side of her face, drawing her wild gaze to his. Blood trickled down his temple, but where she expected panic in his eyes, she found calm. What kind of life did he live if this didn't faze him?

"You good?" His voice steadied her racing pulse.

"Two feet and a heartbeat."

He slid his hands down her body, checking for injuries with swift, efficient movements that sent lightning skipping across her skin. Or was that the bruising on her ribs?

"I'm fine," she managed, but her sharp intake of breath betrayed her. "I think."

Without asking permission, he tugged up her blouse and cursed under his breath. His warm hand splayed quickly against her ribs, and coolness washed through the ache.

"Better?" he asked.

She nodded.

"Good." He exhaled, dropping his forehead against hers. "I'm no healer, but bruises and scratches I can do."

No one had put her first like this, not since her mother. Her throat closed up.

The squelch of hooves faded.

"Is it gone?" she whispered.

He nodded, but looked around. "It prefers easier targets when there's no water to draw mana from."

"What was that thing?"

"A kelpie." River lifted his head, jaw tightening. "Curse that innkeeper for selling us a dud. I should have recognized it, but I was..." His gaze dipped to her lips. "Distracted." The calm in his expression hardened. "We're not out of danger yet."

He moved to rise. Instinct drove her to follow—not from

fear, but from a bone-deep certainty that beside him was where she belonged.

River calmly pressed her back down. "Stay."

"Fuck you, cunt, I'm coming with."

"Sparkles," he groaned out, lashes fluttering. After a beat, he returned his heated gaze to hers. "While your filthy mouth makes me hard, now's not the time to disobey."

Blake's outrage sputtered. "It makes you what?"

A flash of savage desire slipped through his block on their bond. His voice dropped to a growl. "You're going to hate me for this, but I'll make it up to you later…"

"Hate you for what?"

"Remember those debts you owe me?"

Her stomach knotted. She nodded cautiously.

"You're going to repay one by staying under these ferns until it's safe to come out."

The Well seized his words. Magic crackled through the air. Electricity danced across her skin as invisible bonds pinned her to the earth. He eased off her, passing through the fronds sheltering them, and settled into a crouch. He glanced over his shoulder.

"You fucking arsehole!" Blake thrashed against the magical restraints. "What have you done?"

River pressed a finger to his lips, wolfish focus gleaming in his eyes. "Trouble isn't over."

A rhythmic wind thundered overhead, shaking leaves from branches. Three massive forms plummeted earthward. Their impact vibrated the ground.

She watched River through a gap in the ferns as he straightened to his full height. That familiar crooked grin lifted his lips as he cracked his neck and flexed his fingers.

His shoulders settled into a fighter's stance, every line of his body radiating lethal grace.

"If it isn't the Well's garbage collector," said the largest newcomer as he approached River. Cream and brown feathers rippled on the folded wings behind him. White-tipped primaries brushed the forest floor. "Still scavenging through ruins like the carrion-eater you are?"

River still faced Blake's direction, giving her a perfect view of his cocky smirk.

"Careful there, moon-face." River rolled his shoulders. "Those are big words for someone who needs backup to feel brave."

Silence.

River laughed. "What's wrong, afraid to hunt alone without your mama's permission?"

The insult struck true. All three attackers bristled, their round faces flushing dark. But River caught none of it. He fixed his gaze on Blake, perhaps checking whether his magical bindings held. She bared her teeth at him, thinking shadows concealed her face, but his responding feral grin oozed male satisfaction.

"At least we hunt with honor," another spat, "unlike you thieves."

"Honor?" River's laugh held no warmth as he finally faced them. "Is that what you call ambushing travelers on the road? Here I thought you were compensating for your buggy eyes."

A hoot of outrage preceded the third's snarl. "Your kind has been stealing our prey for centuries!"

"*Your* prey?" River's tone dripped sweet innocence. "Oh, you mean the mice you're too slow to catch without our help flushing them out?"

Movement in the shadows triggered River to spit on the ground ahead. "Traitor."

The deserter from the tavern walked into view, his black wings confirming he was one of River's kind, yet nothing like him. Blake barely knew her mate but felt sure he'd never sell out his own kind.

"You're the one bringing an outsider into crow territory." The deserter sneered. "Some Guardian you turned out to be."

"As if you care who enters crow territory."

A pause stretched like death's breath.

One of the others muttered, "Floater."

River's posture went rigid. A hush fell over the clearing. Floater was the weirdest insult to sling.

He sighed dramatically and tilted his face to the canopy.

"Ancestors save me," he groaned, "from the stupidity of shriek owls." He shook his head and then addressed the offender directly. "You know I'm a Guardian, right?" He gestured down at his uniform, his teardrop mark. "By definition, I did *not* float and bloat in the ceremonial lake. I became this. A winner."

"Yeah, well," the owl shifter blustered. "That Guardian mark doesn't change what you are—just another crow thinking he's better than the rest of us."

"It makes me better at tearing owl wings from their sockets."

They attacked as one in a coordinated drive that spoke of years fighting together. But River didn't even bother drawing a weapon. He moved like water through their formations—each dodge precise, each strike devastating, every movement unpredictable and lethal.

Blake's breath caught as her mate deflected attacks with

almost casual boredom. This wasn't the controlled violence from their first meeting or even at the tavern. This was artistry in destruction. Every movement rippled through his muscles. He was raw power wrapped in snug leather.

He caught the first's wing and used the momentum to slam him into his companion. Bones crunched. An embarrassingly wimpy shriek pierced the air.

But then a hit landed on River, and playtime was over. His responding strike was a razor-thin slice across their skin with his claw. Blood sprayed. Artery hit with precision.

A wild feminine urge within Blake recognized a worthy protector in her mate. It was instinctive, base, and primal. It went against logic and the knowledge that he'd forced her to stay put, pissing her the hell off. The flash of hot desire was so unlike her that she wondered if it was part of the magical bond. Maybe even part of his animal side bleeding into her through the bond.

Her pondering vanished as she became lost again in River's brutal dance. Attraction and heat multiplied in her body like wildfire. When he spun and caught the third's throat with finesse, her mind transformed the scene into something shocking ... and arousing. It wasn't the owl being choked—it was her, pressed against silk sheets. That wasn't the shifter's arm bent behind his back—it was her wrists pinned above her head while River's teeth grazed her neck.

Blake wrenched her eyes away, cheeks heating with a realization.

She'd thought her libido had died long ago. It was just a fact of marriage. But all those times Jeff had dismissed her adventurous lovemaking suggestions, and even called her crude for wanting to fuck in his new office or to try out bondage. Or that one time she'd surprised him in a bedazzled negligee, and he'd balked. It hadn't been about propriety at all. It was about him. He'd wanted a trophy wife who looked demure and lay still. Someone who made him feel important. Not a trucker-mouthed, defiant woman with talents and desires that didn't fit his mold. His touches had been empty, mechanical, always about his pleasure while she dreamed of more. The missionary position and two-pump rhythm were as methodical as his morning workout routine.

She wasn't the one lacking substance. Jeff was.

The notion unlocked something inside her. Something she'd denied for a long, long time. Her gaze whipped back to the fight, to bask in River's physicality without shame. She didn't even feel scared. He seemed so in control. Hadn't once reached for a weapon and used only his hands and claws. Almost as if he knew she watched. As if this was a show for her eyes only.

What if it was? What if she didn't have to feel guilty over how her marriage ended? What if this was the start of her life, and she was free to be whoever she wanted to be? To desire whoever she wanted, any way she wanted him. What if he wanted her the same way?

What you call a mess, he'd said earlier, *I call a visual feast.*

Her physical attraction toward him surged with a visceral power that stole her breath. She bit her lip to stop herself from moaning.

River stumbled mid-strike, his head whipping her way, eyes narrowing.

The distraction cost him. Two owl shifters caught his arms while the crow drove a knee into his spine. They vanished behind a curtain of ferns, leaving Blake with only the sounds of a struggle and wet, choking noises to interpret.

"River!" she shouted, thrashing against the invisible restraints.

Squeezing the burn from her eyes, she forced herself to calm down. To ignore the sounds of violence. He was okay. He could handle himself. Right?

"Do something," she urged herself. "Why can't you do something to help?"

The other women from her time were all magic. It had been days since Blake thawed out in Elphyne. They said she was supposed to be like them—powerful. That she would develop a special gift, but all she had was this bond with River and a tiny spark of awareness when a Well-enforced debt triggered.

She reached for that spark, for any hint of magic that might help her mate. The Well hummed in every particle around her, in earth and air and scattered drops of blood, but remained frustratingly out of reach.

Her desperate gaze landed on the tips of the eucalyptus sapling and a shard of broken vase. The rest was hidden behind vegetation.

You like to make broken things shine, River had told her.

"Come on," she growled through her teeth. "I have to be worth more than this."

Nothing.

Tears pricked her eyes, but she refused to let them fall until she heard a sickening crack, followed by a gurgling sound nearby.

"No!" The scream tore from her throat as she thrashed. "River!"

Her restraints vanished between one heartbeat and the next. The sounds of battle had stopped.

You're going to repay it by staying under these ferns until it's safe to come out.

It must be safe to emerge.

Blake stumbled from the cover of her ferns on shaky legs. The metallic scent of blood mingled with ozone, making her stomach roll. Bodies lay broken across the forest floor, their cream and brown feathers stained crimson. Nature itself held its breath: no birdsong, no rustling leaves, just the soft pop of manabeeze abandoning corpses.

NINETEEN

Blake found River leaning against a massive trunk, flicking blood from his blue-tipped hair. His leather jacket bore fresh slashes, but his skin remained unmarked. Relief flooded her until she saw the battle light still blazing in his eyes.

"I had it under control," he grumbled.

"Clearly." Ash's dry response carried across the clearing.

He loomed nearby, darkness incarnate with his wings spread wide, ruffling feathers to shed spilled blood. River huffed, pushed off the trunk, and stalked around the carnage. He prodded each owl corpse with his boot, confirming death while sidestepping rogue manabeeze that darted through the air.

Neither acknowledged Blake's presence.

She'd thought River was dead. More relief, a dash of fury, and that stubborn animal attraction crashed through her like a tidal wave, leaving her skin buzzing and throat tight. Anger won. Anger was safer.

"You bloody nob jockey!" She jabbed her finger in his

direction with each syllable. "What kind of idiot pulls that shit? Binding me with magic while you get your arse handed to you by a bunch of fuckin'…" Her brain scrambled for the right insult. "Bunch of glorified pigeons!"

River gestured at Ash. "As I said to this party-pooper, I had it under control."

"Like hell you did." Her voice cracked, betraying more than she intended. "I bloody-well heard you choking. I thought you were going to—" The truth lodged in her throat. She'd felt so damn helpless, so utterly useless. No magic had answered her desperate prayers. No power had risen when she needed it most.

"Aw." River's brows lifted in the middle, lips forming an excited smile as he vaulted over a corpse to reach her. "Were you worried about me, Sparkles?"

When he stopped toe to toe with her, his sweaty male scent wrapped around her. It was hard to ignore that damn infernal grin spreading across his handsome face.

"No." The lie tasted bitter on her tongue. "Yes—dammit. Of course, I was worried. You're my only guide in this bloody place."

Smug knowing flashed in his eyes.

Heat crawled up her neck. The bond. He'd sensed her earlier, ill-timed physical attraction. Bloody perfect. Now he knew just how messed up she was inside.

River studied her flushed face until she squirmed. Then he slowly leaned forward until he was inches away and gently tapped a small gash on his pouty upper lip.

"I have a boo-boo," he murmured intimately, deeply. "Kiss it better?"

Peals of feminine laughter shattered the moment. Blake whirled toward the sound. Behind Ash stood three figures watching them. All had dark wings folded against their backs. Their skin was etched with tattoos, and their bodies bristled with weapons—more crow shifters.

The female with a long, blue-tipped braid cocked her hip and said to River, "Does that line ever work for you?"

"Works for me," answered the male.

"We'll finish this later." River winked at Blake before scowling at them. "Perfect timing, as usual, Sera. Dad. Lark."

Blake's stomach plummeted to her toes. She'd just cursed out River in front of his relatives. Great. She dragged her palm down her face and forced herself to look at them.

Sera's features could have been carved from the same blade as River's. Her braid glittered with interwoven charms that caught the light. A sword and a bow were strapped across her back. Two sashes crisscrossed her torso and housed an arsenal of smaller blades. Her billowing, pleated pantaloons swished with each movement, somehow making her look more lethal, not less.

The tall male, River's father, shared his son's chiseled features, but his smile radiated warmth rather than mischief. As ageless as all fae, he looked like he could be River's brother, not father. Beads clinked in his tied-back hair with each slight movement. A colorful, billowing shirt peeked out from beneath his chest plate.

The third female, Lark, curved where the others cut. She had softer edges but appeared no less lethal with the blades strapped to her thighs and arms. Wavy black hair escaped her messy top bun in a way that reminded Blake of a bird's nest. Her wide blue eyes—identical to River's—fixed on Blake with unconcealed curiosity as she propped a sashed hip against a tree.

Blake lifted her chin, refusing to abandon her point just

because of an audience. River still grinned incorrigibly, still didn't take her seriously. He'd trapped her with magic when running might have been her only survival option. If he insisted on being tone deaf to her feelings, perhaps she needed to speak his language to show him she was done being a doormat. Never again.

She pivoted to Ash and said, "Thanks for saving us, mate. I owe you one."

River's scarred hand snapped around Ash's throat before another sound was uttered.

"Touch what's mine, princeling, and I'll feed you your own entrails."

He'd moved so fast that Blake felt the air displacement against her skin.

Ash's answering smile held no warmth. He drove his knee into River's ribs with a crack that made Blake wince. Then it was game on. They crashed through the underbrush, all fists and fury. River's elbow connected with Ash's jaw, spraying blood in a crimson arc. Ash's responding headbutt would have shattered a normal man's skull. River just laughed through bloody teeth, wild and wicked, and lunged again.

This was unbelievable. Completely unhinged. They'd walked away from the owl-shifter battle with barely a scratch, but now they were carving each other up like it was a competitive sport.

"Enough!" River's father's voice boomed like thunder. Wings mantled open as he lunged between them, hauling the Guardians apart with surprising strength. He cuffed each upside the head, scattering leaves from their disheveled hair. "Almost three hundred years old and still brawling like juveniles."

Three *hundred*? Blake's jaw slackened.

"Some things never change." Sera snickered.

"Especially not River's possessive streak." Lark winked at Blake.

River shot the females a murderous glare as he dusted debris from his jacket.

"Blake," he ground out, "allow me to introduce my father, Talo. And my sisters. Sera's the one with the blue braid. Lark's got the goofy grin. Umbrias, Blake is my mate."

"Duh." Lark rolled her eyes, smirking.

"You forgot the Well-blessed bit," Sera added dryly.

"I'll forget you in a minute," he shot back.

"That doesn't even make sense."

"Welcome to the Umbria Kettle, love." Mischief danced in Talo's eyes, the same wild light Blake had glimpsed earlier in his son's. "You'll fit right in here. Our family embraces the unconventional. When River was young, we encouraged all forms of—"

"Shut the fuck up, Dad." River's nostrils flared.

"What? I think it's beautiful." Talo spread his hands. "You, Ash, and this spitfire outsider here—it's like poetry. A trinity of passion."

"Mmhm." Sera folded her arms and stared at Ash with disdain. "Now I see why it never worked out between us. One bird was never enough."

River and Ash shared a horrified glance, their postures going rigid simultaneously.

Blake's stomach plummeted as understanding crashed over her. Heat blazed from her neck to her hairline. "Oh no, that's not—"

"Don't be shy, human." Lark's grin turned wicked. "I once had a pixie orgy. They have multiple mates all the time." She scrunched her nose and shuddered. "But it ended when their barbed dicks became too much for one girl to handle."

"And remember my summer with the vampire trio?" Sera sighed dreamily.

"No, wait," Blake said. "Where I'm from, 'mate' just means friend. In a platonic way." Their expressions remained blank, not a flicker of comprehension. "It's a collo-quialism." Still nothing but unblinking stares. "You know," —she turned to River for support— "like how I call someone a cunt but mean it lovingly."

His lips curved. "You think of me lovingly?"

What? Her mind scrambled backward. She had called him that, right before he'd magically bound her to the forest floor and left her helpless.

"No, that time was actually an insult," she clarified. "But for Ada and Trix, it was friendly." Bloody hell. She was so shit at explaining. "Believe me, the Aussie version of mate doesn't have the same definition as the fae version of mate."

The bugger gave her nothing, just crossed his arms and radiated smug enjoyment over her floundering.

"Right." Lark winked. "That's why you were ready to tear apart the forest to save them both."

Blake groaned and wished the ground would swallow her. She only had her stubbornness to blame for this mess.

"Speaking of the forest." Talo's wings shook out with a soft whoosh, resplendent and dark against the dappled light. The sisters followed suit, their feathers rippling in unison. "We should head back to the roost before sunset."

Despite his casual stance, River's angst and shame sliced through the block on their bond. Blake's heart seized as understanding clicked. His damaged wings. His inability to fly home with his family.

"Actually," she blurted, "I get terrible airsickness. Could we maybe walk?"

"Of course!" Talo's head tilted, sharp and bird-like. "More time to discuss your progressive relationship choices. You girls hurry home and let your mother know we're coming."

"But we're not..." Blake's protest died as Sera launched skyward with a powerful thrust of wings, her laughter trailing behind her. Ash silently flipped off River and rocketed upward. Lark hesitated, clearly torn over wanting to stay for what promised to be a riveting conversation, before finally surrendering to the air with a disappointed sigh. Her coin pouch clinked as she disappeared above the canopy.

"Dad," River said. "Give us a moment to ourselves."

"Oh." Understanding filled Talo's gaze as it darted between River and Blake. "You two lovebirds need a post-battle pressure release. Got it."

"What?" Blake squeaked.

"That's good for the heart." Talo gave two thumbs up, wings flapping once, then stalled. "But shouldn't Ash be here for that?"

River groaned and palmed his face.

Talo waggled his dark brows. "You want me to fetch him?"

"No!" both Blake and River shouted.

Talo's gaze locked onto their blue mating marks. He frowned after the direction Ash left and then flattened his lips. "Why did your human call Ash her mate, then?"

"She's confused," River growled. "That's all."

"I'm not confused," she shot back, indignant. "I'm just Australian."

"Oh-*kay*." Talo gave another, contemplative, bird-like tilt of his head. "I'll leave you two to unravel that knot. But maybe take the shortcut."

"Why?" River tensed.

"We're on the outs with the Cardonas."

A flash of fury and something jagged with grief broke through River's block. "Cloud?"

"That too." Talo's gaze lifted with a sigh. "The Donna matched Lark to Tommas Cardona—"

"What?!" River barked. "When did this happen? Why didn't anyone tell me?"

"Don't take that tone with me."

River rubbed his fist over his heart. "But—"

"But as I was trying to say earlier, the match was called off. Carlotta Cardona took offense. And when one Cardona takes offense, their entire kettle takes offense. Ravi may have said something hurtful about Cloud's unsanctioned Vendetta." Talo scrubbed his hands through his hair. "Of course, insults about our roosting position volleyed back. Anyway, the point is, the Nesting Ceremony has been canceled."

The color drained from River's face. "Are you telling me that after hundreds of years of friendship and loyalty, our families are now feuding?"

Talo's pitying look made River's face pale. "Son, you've missed a lot."

"We're continuing this conversation when I return."

"Fine," Talo said, then launched upward with a powerful snap of wings, scattering leaves in his wake.

River growled beneath his breath. "Don't say another word."

"About what?" Blake threw up her hands. "I have no idea what you're talking about."

She collected her belongings with sharp, annoyed movements. River prowled through the underbrush, gathering his own things, jaw clenched against whatever secrets lay between him and his family.

When she located Trix's gift, she froze mid-reach. The ancient vase sat perfectly intact. Some dirt had spilled, but the baby eucalyptus still nestled in its pot, leaves trembling in the breeze.

But she'd seen it shatter against the exposed roots. Hadn't she?

"Blake," River called. "You coming?"

She nodded, shoving dirt back into the vase before carefully lifting it. Later. She'd figure it out later.

River's family thought she was in a threesome with their son and his friend. She had enough to worry about.

TWENTY

CIRCA 200 YEARS AGO

The Collector's hoard was a mountain of treasure piled atop a canyon spire, hidden by mist and a magic deterrent that both Cielo and Manfri had failed to heed. The cloudy abyss below the spire seemed bigger before. But it might have something to do with the almighty squawks of rage rattling the rocky foundations, spilling jewels over the edge like falling stars against the sunset.

"Fly!" Nikan bellowed, shoving his new friends away.

Cielo deftly caught his footing, but Manfri stumbled backward, tripping over something hard. His wings flared for balance but only succeeded in knocking over more treasure. Behind Nikan, the silhouette of a winged beast emerged from the tunnel.

The Collector walked through a beam of burnt sunlight, and Manfri gasped. Stuck somewhere between crow and human, her black feathered wings ended in taloned hands. Short, downy hair ruffled like a living crown. Stubby feathers sprouted from her cheekbones and grew in length down her neck and shoulders like a graceful capelet. She should have been frightening with that bird-

like face, but her silken dress, sharp features, feminine curves, and clinking adornments made her look more like a vicious queen than a monster.

This was her territory ... and they were the marauders.

Her beady eyes moved with preternatural speed to assess the situation. Her son had escaped his restraints, and two armed intruders were looting her treasure. Betrayal flashed in her eyes, and she opened a mouth full of stained teeth and let loose another caw of indignation.

"Mother..." Nikan started, holding his palms out warily. "Let me explain."

"My blood betrays me?" She advanced on her son, her jeweled talons clicking with menace.

Manfri wasn't sure how Cielo managed to function, but he stepped between Nikan and the Collector with his dagger pointed at her beady eye.

"He's half-starved and chained while his mother slept," Cielo accused. "If anyone's betrayed, it's him. You don't deserve to have a son."

Cielo spat at her feet in disgust.

"Fool," she screeched. "You are nothing but a hatchling. I will gut you and feed him your entrails."

"Mother—"

"Silence." She pointed a gem-encrusted talon at Nikan. "I will deal with your insolence next."

He was silenced but not cowed. Manfri liked that his spirit was still alive. But it infuriated him that Nikan had reached this level of neglect. Cielo was right. This creature did not deserve her son's loyalty. Nikan's appearance meant he could pass as a human if his wings were shifted away. The Collector couldn't. Maybe she was jealous of her son, and instead of nurturing him, she chained him.

It probably wasn't Cielo and Manfri's place to interfere in a family dynamic they knew little about. Crows handled discipline and managed their nests as they saw fit. But it was also a strict rule to treat each member of the kettle as equal. Everyone contributed in some way, and everyone benefited from it. Sure, societal rank varied for kettles within the larger murder, but loyalty within the immediate family unit was prioritized above all else. The Collector didn't understand this because if she did, Nikan would have been just as gloriously dressed and fed as she was.

"We're not going anywhere without you, Nikan." Manfri planted his feet and folded his arms.

It was a stupid proclamation because they stood no chance against her electrifying aura. She might look like Lesser Fae with that permanent half-crow appearance, but she sure as the Well had the mana of High Fae. The stories of her power must be true.

Just as Manfri was ready to grab Nikan by the scruff and escape, Cielo put his dagger away and calmly made a proposal. "I have something precious to trade for Nikan."

"What could a hatchling offer me that I don't already have?"

"Forbidden treasure from the human city." Cielo lifted his chin. "Something so valuable that it belonged to their leader. He will kill to get it back."

"You would trade me?" Nikan gasped.

Her eyes darted between her son and Cielo. She licked her cracked lips and said, "I will simply steal it from you."

"I'm not stupid enough to have it on me." Cielo bluffed ... Manfri hoped.

"Then I will gut you and force you to take me there."

Manfri laughed. "How can you gut us and then force—" Her lethal glare shut his lips. Welldammit. His mouth kept getting him in trouble. But it wasn't him she attacked.

She launched at Cielo, squawking and twirling, slashing her wings in a tornado of silk and talons. Cielo ducked and danced around her body, smiling smugly at her back while her wing sailed right over his head. His grin died as her other wing continued swiping, reaching behind her to plunge three talons into his shoulder.

His scream of pain was the jolt Manfri needed to act. He released a war cry, leaped, and stabbed toward her unguarded side. But she seemed to sense him coming and darted out of the way ... right into Nikan's orbit. He wrapped his manacles around his mother's throat and yanked hard enough to choke.

This is it, *Manfri thought.* We have her.

But she bucked her son from her body and watched him clash with the treasure mountain. He coughed, eyes watering, and tried to catch his breath. Stalking toward him, her upper lip curled in a snarl that sent shivers down Manfri's spine. He couldn't let Nikan go down for them. None of this would have happened if Manfri hadn't challenged Cielo in a fit of bitter jealousy.

Twirling his dagger, he steeled himself for another attack.

"Wait!" Cielo shouted, wincing as he staunched the blood flow at his shoulder with a hand. "I can get the treasure and be back before sun-up!"

The Collector paused but didn't face Cielo. She kept her gaze locked on her wild-eyed son.

"You don't want me." Nikan's lips twisted with disgust. "I see it in your eyes. I'm a burden. You said so yourself. Treasure doesn't take. It only gives. So just let me go."

"No one leaves this place, ever."

"We will take an oath of silence," Manfri promised.

"Forget it," Cielo snarled. "If she's not interested in the most forbidden treasure a fae could ever own, she's probably too weak even to hold it."

Her gaze snapped to Cielo and narrowed, but he continued

with his ruse, nonchalantly looking down his nose at the mighty creature.

"She's too old," he continued with derision. "She hibernates to heal. All we do to heal is shift."

Manfri added, "Even if she kills us, our murder will come. They'll call a Vendetta against her. Even if it takes every crow decades to fulfill, they won't stop until she's dead and buried in the ground."

She squawked and prowled toward Cielo, forgetting her son.

"I'm right," Cielo pressed, holding his ground and spreading his wings to make himself look more imposing. "Think about it. You're better off taking my trade, letting Nikan go, and accepting our oath of silence."

She gnashed her stained teeth in Cielo's face, but he stood firm.

"He's a drain on your resources," Cielo said. "Let us take that burden from you."

"If you're not back by sunrise, I will eat them," she announced.

The burning orb of the sun had sunk beneath the horizon, but enough light shone to see the worry in Cielo's eyes as he glanced Manfri's way.

"I'll be fine," Manfri said. "I'll stay with Nikan."

"If you dare think to bring back reinforcements," she snarled at Cielo. "I will sense you coming a mile away. Now that I am awake, I feel the wind move before the sky thinks to breathe. The first wingbeat other than your own will signal their doom."

Cielo nodded. "It's a bargain, then. When I bring you the forbidden treasure I stole from the human leader, you will immediately release Nikan and Manfri alive and unharmed."

"When I hold the treasure in my hands," she corrected, eyes narrowing at the attempted fae loophole.

"Yes," Cielo agreed. A magical snap reverberated as the Well bound their agreement in magic. Cielo shuffled closer to Nikan and started to undress, keeping one eye on the Collector.

"Take my clothes," he murmured. "I'll shift to heal and fly. I'll find another outfit before I return."

Once naked, the air shimmered around his form, and the young fae became a crow. With a caw of ominous warning, he flapped his wings and flew away.

TWENTY-ONE

The "shortcut" stretched into an hour-long trek through humid heat. Blake's borrowed clothes clung uncomfortably, and dirt grated against the damp fabric. Her arms ached from cradling the eucalyptus, but when River offered to hold it, she refused. The familiar scent anchored her and masked her unfortunate, sweaty situation.

They emerged from the jungle onto a ridge overlooking a vast natural amphitheater pit. Late afternoon sun slanted through towering trees, casting long shadows over moss-covered ruins. At first glance, the structures reminded her of Mayan or Aztec pyramids, but then recognition hit. These were old skyscrapers, hollowed out and fallen into a pattern, somehow working with the land instead of against it.

The murder's settlement, or roost as River called it, sprawled across fallen ruins and wound through ancient streets. It climbed toward the sky on living terraces. Caravans claimed each platform, creating a patchwork of color that would have sent her Hidden Gems followers wild.

Some vans flaunted elaborate tapestries adorned with sparkling jewels, while others incorporated cleverly upcycled ruins as windbreaks. At first, it seemed chaotic. But the closer she looked, the more she realized there was some kind of organization to it. A pattern she couldn't place.

Her fingers itched to document every transformation. It proved beauty could grow from destruction. It could shine. This was the living embodiment of what she'd preached about in her videos.

Her vision blurred as her throat tightened. "She's got the razz, alright."

"What?" River frowned at her.

"Nothing."

"It wasn't nothing."

Blake took a moment to process the enormity of her feelings, the strange rightness settling into her bones at being here—with him. River was hard to ignore. Especially when he was patient and waited for her words, which she sensed was unusual for him. Or maybe it was just this hidden, compassionate side of him that Blake was starting to see through his cracks.

"This is what I always tried to show people." She gestured at his home. "In my time, I mean. I showed them in my time." He still watched her, waiting. So she found the courage to explain. "Everything has a second life if you just look at it in the right way. I never had access to materials this gorgeous."

She braced, half wincing, and waited for a derogatory comment. Something like, "You can't upcycle the world, dumbass."

But River swept his hand over the landscape. "Well then, it's my honor to welcome you to the Elphyne Southeast

Murder. You're among the lucky few outsiders ever to see it."

Movement in the trees up high caught her attention. Guards or sentinels watched them in angel form, their wings in the shadows behind them. They perched on thick boughs with perfectly balanced feet. Some had bows and arrows, others daggers.

One by one, crow shifters started taking to the sky and flying around the murder in a formation.

"What are they doing?" she asked.

"Circling. Looking for changes, marking who's here and who's not. Remembering faces."

Her stomach clenched. "Is it okay that I'm here?"

He followed her gaze to where a group of nearby sentinels glared down at them. He flipped up both middle fingers and kissed the air in their direction.

"Don't worry about them. You're my mate," he said, as if that explained everything. Then, he grumbled out, "And apparently Ash's, too."

"Oh"—she blew a raspberry at him—"you know that's not what I meant. I was being petty because you ignored my feelings."

Genuine confusion crossed his face, and then he lifted his blue-marked hand. "It's literally impossible for me to do that with this."

"So then it's even worse that you forced me to stay put." Her heart raced at the memory. "I could have been stabbed, or dragged off, or worse."

River gripped her shoulders and dipped to look into her eyes. "I would never let any harm come to you. Ever."

"You can't control everything."

"Blake. Hear me when I say this: I will tear apart the

world to find you. I would tear apart my own flesh before I let yours come to harm. Understood?"

"Why would you say that? You don't know me." Hell, she didn't even know herself anymore.

"I don't need to."

"Maybe you should know me before you say things like that." The memory of Jeff's betrayal sliced. She swallowed hard and tried to step back, but River's grip held firm. Unless she dropped the plant, she remained trapped. "People change their minds all the time."

He frowned, fingers flexing on her shoulders as he searched for words. Finally, he asked, "Who changed their mind about you?"

She weighed her options in the silence. Tell, or don't tell? River kept his own secrets, after all. But something in his gaze tugged at that place deep inside her soul, the one she pretended didn't exist, the one she filled with shiny things and memories of off-tune opera singing and burned spaghetti. The place that hurt so much, she wanted to—

You can't upcycle yourself, babe.

"Jeff," she blurted, emotion clogging her throat. "Me husband." She blinked rapidly. "I mean, *my* husband. Ex-husband, I guess. He dumped me."

The confession shocked her, but an invisible thread between them kept pulling the words out. It wasn't magic. It wasn't forced. It was right.

Everything poured out: how Jeff had fallen out of love with her after deciding she was ordinary beneath the makeup, how he'd resented her success when his career faltered, how he'd forgotten every important milestone to her and then excused his mistakes by blaming it on his lack of a perfect memory like her. She told River about the jetty—

the wrong address, the casual cruelty, being abandoned as their world crumbled.

"The fucking cunt left me after fifteen years of marriage."

She trembled now, clutching the vase until her knuckles whitened and the tiny leaves shook. Great, heaving breaths tore from her throat like some kind of feral creature. Her rage refused to be contained. It burst free, wild and unstoppable, and God help River if he told her to calm down or stop crying. Or that her tears were making him miserable.

But he didn't.

He stared at her in bewilderment. Mouth agape. Closing. Opening again. Finally, he said, "He left … you."

She hugged the plant closer. "Yes."

"*You.*"

"Yes, me!"

"I just…" He scrubbed his hand down his face, shaking his head. "You?"

"Why is that so hard to believe?"

She squeezed her eyes shut against his disbelief. Every muscle tensed in her body, trying to swallow that familiar rage. Better to hide it again. Easier to pretend it never existed. Some things are just … common.

"Two feet and a heartbeat," she whispered to herself, squeezing the burn from her eyes.

Warm, calloused hands cupped her face. "Look at me, Blake."

She shook her head.

"Fucking open your eyes. I have something to say, and I want you to—Fuck it. Here."

His emotions slammed into her through their bond: rage, determination, and beneath it all, something wild and precious. Something uplifting and so good that it was almost too much. Gasping, she opened her eyes and fell into two deep blue pools. River surrounded her with comforting warmth. His presence flooded her body, mind, and soul.

"I'm glad he left you," he growled through gritted teeth. Her bottom lip trembled, but he snarled, "Listen to our bond, Blake. Listen to what I'm telling you. I'm glad he left you because—"

He clammed up.

"Because what?"

The sense of his emotions faded as he blocked the bond. But the fire in his demeanor remained. His hands slid down her face and traced the mating mark on her arm, leaving a tingling in their wake. Some kind of agony entered his expression.

He caught a lock of her sun-drenched hair and rubbed the strands between his forefinger and thumb, pupils dilating. "Did you know that crows see UV wavelengths?"

She shook her head.

"We see different colors," he continued, still mesmerized by her black hair, turning it in the sunlight. "Each crow picks up the UV differently. Where other races see the ordinary, we see a kaleidoscopic masterpiece. They mock us for our endless treasure hunt—for chasing a pot of nonexistent gold at the end of a rainbow." Blue eyes clashed with hers. The agony was replaced with something deeper that sent her soul soaring. "You are the furthest thing from ordinary I've ever seen. To me, your hair sparkles like a rainbow of colored diamonds."

"Is that why you call me Sparkles?"

A curve of his sexy lips was her answer, but then his amusement died, and he asked, "Do you still love him?"

"I hate him," she snarled. "I wish he were dead. Except

he's already dead, and I can't even go back and tell him I fucking hate him and I wish he were dead. I survived the end of the world, and he didn't, and I can't even feel smug about it because … because I don't know why! I should be able to feel good that I'm here and he's not."

Her fury burned so hot she thought she might be sick.

"It's because you're a good person," he said, and held out his hand. "Give me the plant."

"No." She spun away protectively.

His deep laugh warmed her insides. "Trust me."

Reluctantly, she handed it over. He placed it carefully at the base of a tree closer to the forest's edge, then unsheathed a dagger from his bandolier. The blade flashed as he flipped it, offering her the hilt. "Bottling it up isn't going to do you any favors."

"You can talk." She put her hands on her hips.

His lips flattened. "Take the dagger. It's reinforced obsidian. Not metal, so it's safe."

Her brow arched as she refused.

"You bottle," she accused.

"No, I don't."

"What do you call hiding your emotions from me unless it suits you?"

Silence stretched between them.

"Okay, fine," he admitted. "Let's both fucking do this."

He produced another dagger from behind his back with a magician's flourish. One flick of his wrist, and it materialized.

"How'd you—"

"Take it." He shoved the obsidian blade at her until her fingers closed around its hilt. "Good. Now that tree over there—see it?"

"Yeah…"

He jogged a few yards down and pointed to a spot above his head on its thick trunk. "Was he this tall?"

"Who?"

"The dickface we hate."

Her lips twitched. When River's own stretched into a slow, sly grin, a weight lifted from her shoulders.

"Lower," she said. "He wasn't as tall as you."

"Knew it." He dropped his hand an inch. "Here?"

"Lower."

Two inches. "Here?"

"Keep going." Another inch. "No—a little lower."

"Fuck me, was he a pixie?"

She chuckled. "He reached my height, barely."

"Ahh. That explains everything." He scratched a mark into the tree and began chipping away bark. "Small cock syndrome."

"You mean small man syndrome?"

"That's what I said. Probably why he looked like this."

She walked over to stand behind his shoulder. "Are you carving his face?"

"Yep." The tip of River's tongue poked out as he concentrated and chipped away at the wood.

"Don't you want to know what he looked like?"

"Nope."

Chip. Chip. Cut.

"Okay, but what's that weird mushroom shape on his head …? Oh. *Ooh.*" Laughter burst from her chest. "You're drawing a penis with eyes."

"Yep." He carved the final details, then stepped back to admire his work. "Spitting image, right?"

"Perfect." She had to admit, he'd captured the essence in record time.

River slanted her an amused look. "Now show that fucker what you really think of him."

"We probably shouldn't ruin a perfectly good tree."

"Feel free to fuck it up. It's not an Oak Man."

"What's that?"

"A man who is also an oak. Ergo, an Oak Man. They exist. But not here. Too warm. Okay, so here we go. Aim to put that pointy end into the—"

"But what if there *is* a man inside the tree?" Her jaw dropped. "And we just defaced him with a dick?"

Blake shuddered. Stranger things had happened in this place.

"There's no man inside that tree. Trust me. There's nothing else around here to stab except me." He pointed the dagger at his face. "And this masterpiece is the opposite of a dick."

"A puckered asshole?"

"What?"

"You know." She pointed at her butt. "Because it's on the opposite side to a dick."

He pouted. "You think I have an ass face?"

More laughter bubbled from her chest. "No, of course not!"

"Not sure if I believe you." He turned away, slumping his leather-clad shoulders.

"River!" She dropped the dagger and shoved him. "I'm taking the piss."

"Okay, now you're associating me with urine."

"It means I'm having a laugh. Stop it!" Her cheeks ached from grinning. "You know how attractive you are."

He faced her, eyes intimate, voice soft. "Yeah, I know. But do you know?"

"You don't believe me?" She deepened her voice, mocking his. "Listen to what I'm telling you."

"I am." He stepped close enough for his heat to envelop her. His sweaty, woodsy, and very masculine scent scattered her thoughts. "Emotions aren't as easy to read as you think," he murmured. "They can be misinterpreted."

Was that why he hid his from her? She supposed that made sense.

"Like texting," she offered.

"You're cute when you speak old world." His brow furrowed as his gaze dropped to her lips. "It's almost as hot as the filthy words. What's texting? Sounds naughty."

Heat flooded her cheeks. "It's a way of writing. Like sending a letter through a phone, maybe?"

"Mm." His gaze stayed fixed on her mouth. "Like my triad tattoo."

"What's that?"

"I think I know how you can convince me," he said, ignoring her question.

"Convince you of what?"

"That you don't think my face looks like an ass." His amusement slipped through their bond.

"Okay. I'll bite. How?"

"We'll save the biting for next time, Sparkles. For now—" He tilted his jaw and tapped his wounded upper lip. "Boo-boo won't get better without a kiss."

Her heart stuttered.

"I mean," she said, voice breathy as she inched closer, "it looks half-healed already."

"It's very sore. I promise."

They were so close now that barely a whisper separated their lips. Tension crackled between them, skipping along her skin. She'd only ever kissed one man in her life. Only touched one set of lips with hers.

River held perfectly still, patient enough that she knew if she backed away, he wouldn't press. He'd probably crack a joke to ease her discomfort.

She pressed her lips to his.

Contact.

At first, wrongness jarred through her. Just pressure against foreign flesh, like speaking a foreign language. Not the lips she knew. And it irritated her. She didn't want this feeling holding her back from starting a new life. She tentatively pushed her tongue past River's lips, into his mouth.

When their tongues touched, he made a sound—part groan, part purr, pure lust. It obliterated every wrong feeling in her body.

And then he kissed her back.

TWENTY-TWO

River kissed Blake like he fought, all instinct and feral control. His fingers circled her throat, pinning her with that same deadly grace he used in battle, and by god, it stoked her desire. His other hand tugged roughly at her waist, slamming her hips against his. She gasped, and he ate it up. One heartbeat, he savored her lips. Next, his teeth grazed and nipped her jaw. Each touch was deliberate. Each breath measured, yet wild.

There was no other way to describe the feeling except that he was all in. He took charge. He was violence wrapped in a pretty package. His desire peppered through his block, pelting her like bullets, injecting fire into her veins until she was left panting.

It felt too good, too right, and terrifying for reasons she couldn't fathom. She hated Jeff. She wasn't the guilty party. She should be all in for this, too, hunting River's lips as he did hers, devouring him like the starved woman she was. But a lifetime of dedication to one person, vows she'd taken seriously, and a belief that her ex's cold love was all she deserved were hard to forget. It made her angry. Indignant. He was here, ruining her new life as surely as if he stood beside her and whispered, *I should have seen the warning signs.*

River's lips froze on Blake's.

Oh no.

He knew she wasn't into this as much as he was. But she had been at the start. She wanted to get back into it. She couldn't. Awkward awareness roared between them louder than the rustling leaves, louder than the water cascading in the distance.

An apology hovered on the tip of her tongue, but River handled her change in mood exactly as she'd predicted. He cracked a joke.

"Question." His thumb traced her bottom lip, unapologetic appreciation written across his face. "How bad does my boo-boo need to be for that to last longer next time?"

Laughter bubbled up despite herself.

"Because," he added, eyes crinkling, "I think I've changed my mind about letting you stab me instead of dick-face. If it helps."

"Let's hope it doesn't come to that."

He collected their discarded daggers with fluid movements and slid the obsidian hilt of one back into her palm. He moved on from the awkwardness so easily. Must be something that came with the almost three-hundred-year age thing.

So weird.

Yet oddly comforting. It made her feel that, as an adult, she didn't need to have everything figured out. Like he would teach her and guide her, he would keep her safe. Something about that thought rekindled her desire for him.

She bit her lower lip, hid her smile, and focused on the cool feel of the dagger's hilt.

River positioned himself behind her, walking them backward until they stood halfway between the amphitheater's edge and the forest.

"Alright, Sparkles." His breath ghosted her ear. "Show me what you've got." His heat vanished as he stepped away, and she almost pouted. "Ten points if you hit the dick."

"Only ten?" Blake tested the dagger's weight as if she knew what she was doing.

"Plus one of your debts back."

"How can I resist that temptation?" She lined up her shot, then hesitated. The carved face seemed to mock her uncertainty. "But are you sure? I'm not used to destroying things. I fix them."

"Breaking things feels good. Stabbing even better."

She glanced over her shoulder. He stood two steps behind, arms crossed, narrowed gaze fixed on her with an intensity that made her breath catch.

"If it makes you feel any better," he said, "I'll kiss the wittle twee's boo-boo afterward. It's an excellent remedy."

His wink sparked heat in her cheeks. And between her thighs. Shit. She was definitely going to try kissing him again. Maybe sooner rather than later.

He clapped his hands, all business. "Let's go."

"Okay, but…" She shifted her weight. "I'm not feeling very ragey anymore."

The look he returned was pure male hubris. "I have that effect on people sometimes."

"Really? I thought it was the opposite." She threw the dagger, but it glanced off the tree with humiliating ineffectiveness.

"I meant females, not people," he corrected, striding over to collect her fallen weapon. Each movement held that lethal grace she'd begun associating with all Guardians. "Males tend to want to stab me. Go figure."

His words twisted something in her gut. Was that jealousy?

"Did he cheat on you?" he asked, returning the dagger. "Your ex?"

"I don't know." She avoided his gaze. "I mean, I don't think so. There might have been a woman. But in the end, I had no idea who he really was, so I can't be sure."

A woman of substance.

"Hmm." River kicked her feet into a wider stance. "So he was a veritable stranger."

"Exactly!"

He adjusted her grip on the dagger. "How did that make you feel?"

"Like I wasted me life on someone who wasn't that into me."

"And?"

"And it hurt."

"Release here when you throw." His body pressed against her spine as he demonstrated the action with his hand locked around hers. "Why?"

"Why what?"

"Why did it hurt when your ex treated you that way?"

"It's obvious, isn't it?"

"Tell me anyway."

"Because I felt used! Humiliated and confused. It doesn't make sense that he wasted half his life on me, someone he thought was ordinary. There's no other explanation except that he thought I was a joke. He played me."

"And that made you feel…"

"Annoyed. Angry!" She spun to face him, but he rotated her back toward the tree, his hands firm on her shoulders.

"Let it out," he murmured.

A rage-filled scream ripped from her throat, and she threw the dagger, just as he'd shown her. It struck the bark far below the face. But it was embedded, hilt wobbling.

"Argh!" She stomped over and yanked it free. "I can't even hit the right spot."

"So cheat. Fight dirty. Fucking stab him up close." River feigned an uppercut with his fist. "Cut him where it hurts."

Blake rounded on the tree. She stabbed bark. Once. Twice. Again. "You asshole!"

"You can do better. Tell him what you really think."

"I fucking will, you fucking cunt!" The blade struck deeper. "You thought you were the AFL's hottest player, Jeff, but you weren't!" Each blow punctuated her words. "Every time you packed on muscle, it just made you look shorter!" Stab. Stab. "Made your dick shrink!" Hack. Chop. "And when I told you that mullet looked good, I LIED!"

The blade bit into the wood again and again.

"I should have seen the warning signs." Chop. Chop. "Should have known a man who couldn't organize a root in a brothel was a loser." STAB. STAB. "Should have known you were no good the FIRST time you forgot our anniversary instead of the last." Her voice cracked. "Should have known better than to make you my whole world."

"Blake?"

Her vision blurred. "People keep leaving me."

She stabbed dick-face right in the eye, growling, "I gave all my attention to you instead of me dad. Me family." She choked on a breath. "I gave everything to the wrong person, and now I'll never see the right ones again!"

She screamed at the universe until the carved face disappeared beneath splinters and pulp. Warm hands enveloped hers, easing the dagger from her seized grip. "I think you got him good."

Her destruction came into focus.

"Oh no." Her breath hitched. "You wanted a turn, and I made a mess of it."

"That's okay." His fingers brushed her shoulder. "You're good. Right?"

Her bottom lip wobbled. She couldn't answer because she wasn't.

River's hands traveled up her arms to cradle her face. He lifted her eyes to meet his. Looking into those vibrant blues, so full of steadying compassion, so unlike her first impression of him, her throat tightened. Her mother had left. Jeff had left. Her whole world had left. If she fell for River and he...

"Blake." His thumbs swiped wetness from her cheeks. "You're not alone."

"Everything I know is gone, River."

His tiny smile wavered. "I can't begin to understand how shitty that feels, but this—" He threaded their blue-marked fingers together. "This means we're together until we die. I can no more leave you than I can my own body."

His expression darkened briefly, something sad in his eyes.

A knot formed in Blake's stomach. She'd heard promises before. *Forever* and *always* had fallen from Jeff's lips, too, right before he'd abandoned her on that jetty. Words were empty. She glanced at their intertwined hands, the matching marks glowing softly against their skin. Was this really different? Or just another trap waiting to spring?

River's jaw tightened, nostrils flared.

"Grave ash," he growled. In one fluid motion, he unhooked *Peacemaker* from his belt. The chakram gleamed in the fading light as he spun on his heel and hurled it at the mutilated tree.

The weapon sliced through bark with a high-pitched whine, its edges glowing blue. A heartbeat passed. Then the tree exploded, sending splinters and wood chips flying in all directions. Blake ducked, shielding her face. The blast wave rippled through the clearing, rustling leaves and scattering debris.

When she lowered her arms, the once proud tree was nothing but a shattered stump. *Peacemaker* hovered in mid-air, still spinning. River flung his hand out and called the weapon back. It slapped into his palm, the glow fading as his fingers closed around its edge.

He returned it to his belt, his eyes never leaving hers.

"Dickface doesn't deserve to exist in any form for how he treated you," he declared, voice deceptively calm despite the devastation he'd just unleashed.

She opened her mouth to say something, anything, but words failed her.

His familiar lopsided grin returned. "We'd better move if we want dinner."

TWENTY-THREE

Wood fragments littered the clearing. Blake traced the blue marks on her arm as she watched River retrieve his daggers from within the smoldering debris, his movements precise despite the tension in his posture.

"Guess that's one way to handle therapy." She gestured at the destruction. "Though I doubt that tree deserved complete annihilation."

His hands stilled over a half buried blade. "It stood in for someone who did."

"River." She stepped closer, close enough to see the muscle ticking in his jaw. "That wasn't just about me ex, was it?"

His eyes met hers. Something raw and unguarded flickered there before iron shutters slammed down.

"We need to move." He handed her the plant and strode ahead, voice clipped. "Rain's coming."

"There's not a cloud in the sky," she called after him.

He didn't turn back. "Then we're due."

Her throat tightened. After pouring out her heart about Jeff, after that kiss melted her bones, after witnessing him obliterate a tree in her defense, he still refused to let her past those walls. She'd spent fifteen years with a man who'd slowly drained her with his emotional distance. She couldn't do that again.

If this was to work between them, she needed more. Needed everything—every passion, every doubt, every wounded part of him.

All in, all the time, just like that kiss.

By the time she caught up, River stood at the amphitheater's edge, staring down at the structures below. His attention was fixed on a particular settlement in the shadows of the far side.

"Cardona roost," he said. "Cloud's family."

Blake's breath caught. A peace offering. Not much, but from River, giving her this name felt significant.

A winged figure moved between posts in the camp below, igniting torches that bloomed against dark caravans. She stepped closer, her arm brushing his. "Your father mentioned the Cardonas. Cloud was part of your family?"

"More than family." His jaw tightened, the words emerging reluctantly. "He's the missing member of my triad—a Guardian in the Twelve."

"The triad. You and Ash, too?"

He nodded, gaze never leaving the distant roost. "We grew up together. Fought together." His throat worked. "Cloud is … complicated."

"Complicated how?"

The moment shattered. River straightened, mask firmly back in place. "Everyone here is one big extended family. Everyone's someone's cousin or uncle or aunt."

"Blood related?"

"No." A quiet laugh escaped him. "We're just a tight knit community. Or were." Shadows played across his face. "Blood relatives form a kettle. Their nesting vans congregate within a dedicated roosting ground, which is part of the murder's greater roost." He swept his hand across the amphitheater. "That make sense?"

She nodded. "Roost is a place. Kettle is family. Murder is … bad."

His brows knitted together.

"It was a joke," she said.

"Right," he said, returning to the settlement. "If the Donna can't match a female to a male four times removed by blood from another kettle within the same murder, she finds a match in another territory."

"So not blood related. But close."

"Safety in numbers runs in our genes, but like most families, some of us get along, and some of us don't." He gestured toward a central tree house rising from the amphitheater's base. Platforms encircling the trunk were festooned with flags and lanterns. Opulently decorated caravans dotted the surrounding area. "That's where the Corvus and Corala reside. They're the Domatri Kettle. And a bunch of bigoted mouse-munchers."

"I sense history there."

"You could say that." Something hard entered his voice. "They're our leaders—well, they're the murder's leaders. I'm a Guardian. I only answer to the Order."

"But we hate the cunts, right?"

His grin of approval spread warmth in her body. "Yeah, Sparkles. We hate the cunts."

They continued along the amphitheater's ledge with

River pointing out which kettle settled in each roost. Over a hundred kettles filled the deep formation, each claiming multiple caravans and structures. He explained how the lowest central ring held the favor of the Corvus and were the privileged who sat dictating rules from their cushioned nests.

"And that eyesore straight ahead is the Umbria Kettle." He pointed to a colorful settlement on the highest shelf, barely a few hundred feet away. "My home before I became a Guardian."

Blake studied the roost, seeing not an eyesore but a sanctuary. Unlike the organized formations below, the Umbria settlement sprawled organically across its elevated position near a waterfall spilling from rocks jutting from the rainforest. Rope bridges swayed between crooked platforms built into the trees. Stained glass and wind chimes transformed what might have been chaos into art, like a living collage crafted from salvaged beauty.

Laughter drifted from a cushioned area beside a campfire overlooking the amphitheater's pit. Bodies bustled about, arranging decorations beneath lantern-strung trees.

River tensed. "Fuck me, they wouldn't dare."

"Wouldn't dare what?" Her fingers tightened around the vase. "Have a party?"

"We don't have parties. We have 'evening discussions' or 'weather observations' because too much fun leads to spontaneous elopements against arranged matings." Bitterness threaded his words. "My parents eloped for love. Since then, they've been relegated to the farthest spot from the Corvus."

"That's ridiculous."

"It doesn't seem to bother them. The non-parties keep coming … and so do the smiles." Something like pride colored his voice. "Not all murders have this fucked-up view about love matches, but my parents refuse to leave." His gaze flicked back to the Cardona roost before he steered her toward the forest's edge. "If we're careful, we can avoid attracting attention—"

"IS THAT MY PRODIGAL SON TRYING TO SNEAK INTO THE BACK ENTRANCE?" The deep, booming voice scattered birds and glowing insects from the canopy.

A figure launched from a high platform, wings snapping out before spiraling down. Talo landed barefoot, shirt billowing open to reveal taut abs. He certainly kept himself fit for a fae his age.

"Hello again." Blake waved.

"Heard some screeching." Talo glanced between them with knowing eyes. "You newly nested work out your kinks?"

"Dad—" River started, but a whirlwind of flowing robes and tinkling glass vials cut him off. A female with blue-tipped wings landed beside them. A decorative scarf was wrapped around her blue hair. A painted shimmering tattoo stretched from her bottom lip down her chin and throat, where it morphed into an ornate collar, tribal and elegant.

Blake attempted a quick comb of her knotty hair, but gave it up when she almost dropped the plant. No makeup. No glimmer. A glance down at her clothes made her feel ill. She raised the eucalyptus slightly so it hid the sweat marks beneath her braless, saggy breasts.

"Sweet Well, look at these wounds!" The newcomer grabbed River's chin, turning his face to inspect. Robes rippled. Glass beads and crystal pendulums chimed. "What kind of healer would I be if I let my son—" She stilled at the sight of Blake making her adjustments. No, at Blake's glowing arm marks. "Oh! OH! *Talo!*" She patted his chest without looking. "Call everyone for an emergency observation on Well-blessed healing techniques!"

"Already on it, my treasure! Table's almost set up." Talo winked at Blake before bellowing upward, "EVENING OBSERVATION OF HEALING METHODS! PURELY EDUCATIONAL!"

"So you must be Blake." River's mother beamed. "I'm Ravi."

"Um. G'day. I mean, hello."

"Such a strong name."

"Yeah, me parents thought I'd be another boy."

"And you're so beautiful too." She elbowed River. "Isn't she gorgeous?"

His gaze swept over Blake, lingering on her lips. "She puts the sun to shame."

She hugged the plant self-consciously.

"No time to lose, my love. Let's get you both sorted."

"Ma," River's voice lowered. "We're fine. We just need a wash and rest."

"Nonsense! And you!" Ravi spun toward Blake, her outfit tinkling. "Your aura is completely destabilized. You need food, too. Not a shred of meat on those bones." She whacked River as though it were his fault. "How do you expect her to see straight without the right nutrients?"

Two more figures dropped from above. The first landed with a dancer's grace, electric-blue-and-black braid whipping. The second touched down more enthusiastically, dark curls escaping her messy bun.

"New sister!" The curvy one with a messy bun—Lark—bounced. "Perfect timing! We need a subject for UV-light analysis!"

"UV what?"

"It's code for getting drunk," River drawled.

"And a proper wardrobe update." The sharper, blue-braided one—Sera—circled Blake. "No offense to those clothes, but they're a bit … dull."

"Filthy!" Ravi nodded, then shook her head at her son. "What have you put this poor human through?"

"Blame the kelpie," he shot back. "And the moon-faced fuckers who ambushed us."

"Oh, what's this?" Ravi touched the potted plant. "Is that…? But it couldn't be…"

"It's an Australian eucalyptus." Blake hugged it possessively. "A friend grew it for me."

"From the old world?" Lark tugged a dark ringlet loose and twirled it around her finger. "Tell us everything! Did you really have little people trapped inside boxes until they told stories? And those metal carriages that carried—"

"Later," Sera cut in. "First, we need to get Blake cleaned up and properly dressed before the—" She caught herself. "Before the educational discussion."

Blake looked to River for help, but he was busy batting away his mother's hands as she inspected another "injury in his aura."

"Just a simple gathering to share healing knowledge." Talo returned with a drink. "Nothing that would break any kettle rules, Well-forbid. Speaking of which…" His voice rose. "River, my boy, why don't you help me check the wards while your sisters handle the, ah, traditional welcome preparations?"

"But—" River fumbled as Talo pushed the drink against his chest.

"Don't worry." Talo winked at Blake. "Yours is waiting in River's old nest."

"My what?" River balked.

"Perfect!" Ravi clapped. "Girls, take your new sister. I'll be there as soon as I've dealt with River's injuries."

"What injuries?" Sera smirked. "Blake kissed his boo-boos all better."

"Actually." River's voice hardened, but he couldn't hide the blush staining his cheeks. "Blake needs rest. We're leaving for the Great Murder tomorrow."

"Exactly why we need to prepare her properly." Lark looped her arm through Blake's. "Can't have her showing up looking like a refugee from the Summer Court. You're a crow now, Blake. You should dress like one."

"The caravans are packed and ready," Sera added, eyes sharp between River and Blake. "Nothing left to do but wait for first light."

River growled, "We can't afford delays."

Ravi clicked her tongue, still fussing over him. "The departure beacon won't light until dawn. We have time."

"Time isn't the issue, Ma. We need to prepare for—"

"For what?" Talo's eyes glinted. "You hunting something specific this year, son?"

Blake caught River's shoulders bunching. He didn't elaborate.

"Just trying to avoid the Domatri's opening ceremony," River said smoothly. "You know how they drag on."

"All the more reason for an educational discussion tonight." Lark brightened. "We need to build up our tolerance for tedious gatherings."

River pointed at her. "You haven't explained this Tommas business yet."

"Oops!" Lark laughed, fluttering her wings and tugging Blake away. "No time. Talk later."

"Wait!" River shoved himself between Lark and Blake, then grabbed his mate by the shoulders and looked into her eyes. When it was clear that his family still watched, he glared at them and snapped, "Would it kill you to give us a little privacy?"

Each stepped back. Once. And continued staring.

"For Crimson's sake." River shook his head and then met Blake's eyes. "You've been through a lot. Are you sure you're okay going with them?"

"I…" Blake glanced at his family. They quickly averted their gaze, pretending they weren't watching but clearly invested in the outcome.

"Blake." River's voice dropped to an intimate rumble. "Crows can be a little … overwhelming. Just say the word, and I'll take you out of here, okay?"

The sincerity in his eyes was unmistakable.

Jeff had never put her well-being first like this, especially not when it meant standing against his family. Her attendance at his family gatherings always outnumbered her own, and he'd abandon her the instant they arrived. That River would shield her now, when he hardly knew her, when his own family pressured him from all sides…

She didn't feel so alone anymore.

"I'll be fine," she said, offering him a small smile. "They seem nice." And perhaps, she thought, they might help her understand the man beneath the armor, her mate.

With a sigh, he let go and stepped back. Lark and Sera fluttered in.

"Good luck," he groaned.

Blake's last glimpse of River was his fist circling over his heart.

TWENTY-FOUR

River's sisters half-flew, half-dragged Blake toward a twisted spiral staircase winding up the largest tree in the Umbria roost. It was all she could do to hold onto the vase.

A shadow landed silently by the campfire as they passed. Ash. Their eyes met briefly before Sera tugged Blake's attention skyward.

"Princeling—help!" River shouted from where their mother continued to fuss, but Ash merely chuckled and settled onto a cushion, black wings fanning behind him like a cloak.

"He needs some loving, doesn't he?" Sera murmured, climbing up worn wooden steps.

"Who, Ash?"

"Who else?" She glanced down at Blake's mating marks. "But you should know, a third wheel in a Well-blessed bond will only be hurtful to the one who's not blessed."

Heat flushed Blake's cheeks. "There is no party of three. I was just teasing River."

Sera's disbelieving hum rippled through the air.

They reached a high landing with a singular round room. Blake glanced down—no rails. At least two stories high. She should be afraid of falling, but oddly, wasn't.

"Let's see about making you look like a proper crow!" Lark pushed open a carved door inlaid with blue-tinted glass. "That ought to straighten out the confusion."

"Welcome to the crow's nest," Sera said, smirking as she tucked her wings and followed her sister.

Blake stepped inside and froze. "This is River's old bedroom?"

The sight stole her breath. Trinkets and knick-knacks were displayed with pride on shelves. His bed was wide, perhaps to accommodate the growing wings of a crow boy. The unmistakable musky scent of wood and sky she associated with River was everywhere, surrounding her as though he stood beside her.

Crystal feathers, carved charms, and polished river stones dangled from the ceiling, catching the golden sunset filtering through the windows. A cracked and worn porcelain stein looked well-used and treasured.

The circular chamber's inner walls bore hand-painted murals. One depicted three winged males with spectacular muscles facing down a giant black dog with glowing blue eyes. Except for the exaggerated musculature, the artistic talent was so realistic, she almost believed the figures would pop out and start flying.

"River painted these?" she asked, unable to hide her amazement.

"Every last one," Lark confirmed, diving into a cedar chest. "Said it helped him remember the important things."

Blake instinctively reached for her phone to capture everything, but her fingers passed through air. A hollow pang echoed through her chest. No phone. No followers. No way to share this discovery.

"What was that you just reached for?" Sera asked, eyes sparkling with sudden interest.

Blake sighed. "Me phone. It's a device from my world. I used it to capture images."

"Images?" Lark perked up. "Like River's paintings?"

"Sort of, except instant and perfect. No brushes needed."

The preserved room brought a sharp pang of homesickness. Her father had kept her childhood room exactly as she'd left it when she married, complete with her mother's old makeup brushes on the vanity. Unlike Jeff's sleek, cold minimalism that scrubbed away all traces of her personality from their home, her dad and brothers preserved her chaotic space like a shrine.

She'd been allowed to mess up one room in the house, and turned a spare room she'd hoped to turn into a nursery one day into a workshop studio. Frowning, she realized this was yet another obvious clue that her marriage wasn't a partnership. Each time she added another to her list, she felt her insides shrink. Why did she put up with that for so long?

"You okay?" Lark's wings folded slightly.

"Just reminds me of home. I miss my family."

"Families are everything," Sera agreed, squeezing her shoulder.

Ravi entered carrying a basin filled with sparkling water. She set it down on a bookshelf beside paintbrushes and ceramic pots of shimmering paste in vibrant colors.

"What's that?" Blake asked.

"Just a simple cleansing ritual first, my dear," Ravi said, arranging her supplies. "Then we'll decorate you properly. This room always reminds me of when River was still my little Manfri."

"Manfri?" Blake grinned. "What an adorable name."

Lark sat on the bed, her wings flaring behind her. "Tell her about the bathing, Ma."

"Don't encourage her," Sera warned.

"You mean how he preferred bathing buck-naked in the moonlight?" Ravi mixed pigments with gleeful abandon. "He'd stretch those blue-tipped wings under the full moon while eligible females secretly watched from the trees. My boy knew exactly what he was doing."

"Mother," Sera groaned.

"The females would practically fall out of the trees," Ravi continued, unperturbed. "And Manfri would just say, 'Ladies, there's a schedule. Alphabetical order, please.'"

Lark clapped her hands over her mouth, barely containing laughter. "I forgot about the alphabetical part!"

Blake noticed something fascinating as they dissolved into laughter—their wings twitched and fluttered with each emotion, creating subtle patterns between them. Sera's primaries flattened against her back when embarrassed, while Lark's wingtips curled inward like parentheses around a joke. Each movement conveyed nuance that human gestures couldn't capture.

"You can imagine how shocking it was to hear he had become a Guardian," Ravi concluded.

"Oh? Why?" Blake sat on the edge of the bed, resting the plant on her thighs. Her attention snagged on a carved frame hanging nearby that contained a preserved blue-tipped feather.

"Until you old-worlders came along," Ravi replied, "Guardians were forbidden to take mates."

"That's his first flight feather," Lark explained, noticing Blake's attention. "Every crow keeps their first shed feather after childhood flight. Most store them in their trove."

"Trove?"

"A sacred personal space," Sera elaborated, opening a second carved chest on the floor. "Every crow has one. It's a hidden cache where we keep our most precious treasures."

"Blake, is it true humans had boxes that kept food cold without ice?" Lark asked. "And others that heated food instantly?"

"Refrigerators and microwaves." Blake nodded. "You'd push a button, and food would be piping hot in seconds."

"What's the Well-blessed connection like?" Sera asked, changing subjects as she pulled brushes from a leather roll. "Is it true you can feel each other's emotions?"

"Yes." Blake poked the dirt beneath the eucalyptus. "Although he seems to be hiding his."

"Don't worry about that," Ravi said. "We'll sort out any confusion." She gestured between her daughters and Blake. "Remove her clothes."

"Remove me what?" Blake balked, hands instinctively covering her chest.

"Oh, honey, let them breathe!" Ravi waved dismissively. "Natural movement is essential for proper mana flow. Not to mention skin-to-skin contact with your wingmate. The Well designed our bodies for pleasure as much as function."

"Ma!" Sera's tone held more amusement than scandal.

"Now, let's find you something appropriate to wear!" Ravi nudged her daughters away from the chests and started sorting through the clothes inside. She bypassed practical options for increasingly revealing garments.

"You'll need proper windways," Lark declared, snatching one Ravi discarded. "Can't have you wearing those shapeless pants if River's going to court you properly at the Great Murder."

Blake nearly choked. "Court me?"

"Oh my," Ravi exclaimed, holding up what appeared to be a sheer triangle with buttons. "What about this? The clasps release with just the right amount of wing pressure."

"Ma, I'm sure Blake would prefer something practical for the journey," Sera suggested.

Ravi swatted her hand away. "Practical? At the Great Murder? With a new mate? Nonsense! Every crow in sight must be warned that these two are locked together."

"You might want these for more rigorous exercise," Lark cut in, holding up what looked like fat ribbons. "Nothing worse than a badly timed bounce during acrobatic maneuvers."

"Lark!" But Sera was grinning. "She's not wrong, though. We have different bindings and windways for different activities. Combat, dance, courtship ... the trick is quick-release knots."

"Easy access is essential for those urgent moments," Ravi nodded sagely, adjusting a framed sketch on the wall—a painting of River with his arms around Cloud and Ash, steins in their hands, puffy drunken eyes almost slits from grinning. "A perfect example is how just the other day, Talo and I—"

"*Ma!*" Both females blocked their ears.

"What?" Ravi pouted. "The itch must be scratched when it presents itself. These human habits of restriction..." She clicked her tongue. "No wonder their world had so many problems."

After years of criticism about Blake's "unladylike" behaviors, the Umbrias' frank discussion was both mortifying and refreshing.

"Speaking of energy…" Lark's eyes gleamed. "Wait until you try the courtship windways. They're designed for maximum impact with minimum hindrance."

"And believe me," Sera added, "our brother definitely knows." She pointed to a small crystal trophy. "First place in the Aerial Courtship Display when he was only seventeen. The older females were tripping over themselves."

"Pour your new sister a glass of moonshine, girls." Ravi waved at a crystal decanter filled with shimmering liquid before returning to her paints and pots with satisfaction. "Mm, yes. These patterns will glow beautifully."

"*Medicinal* moonshine," Sera corrected, catching Blake's questioning look. "Made from forest fruits that only bloom under UV light."

A knowing smile curved Ravi's lips. "Nothing like a little liquid courage before painting. Which reminds me of that summer River spent with the aerial dance troupe…"

"Mother," Sera warned, but she was already pouring drinks while Lark moved the eucalyptus to a shelf.

"I'm proud of my son's cultural education. Three months studying their most intimate traditions. The leader said she'd never seen such natural talent for their more vigorous movements."

Blake nearly choked on her first sip. The moonshine tasted sweet yet spicy with a hint of tropical fruit.

"Don't worry, dear," Ravi said. "River inherited his father's gift for physical expression." Her eyes narrowed on the air around Blake. "Your sexual aura feels very undernourished. Has he given you a proper wingmate welcome yet?"

"Pardon?"

"You know … sent you soaring through the clouds?"

"I think you're scaring her, Ma." But Sera was already giggling, her glass half empty.

"A healthy orgasm is essential for—" Ravi caught Blake's expression. "Oh, sweet ancestors, he hasn't, has he? I'll need to have a word."

"No, it's not…" Blake took another fortifying sip. "I mean, we haven't even…"

"She had a husband," Sera supplied helpfully. "A wingmate in her world."

Blake's gaze snapped to her. How did she know?

"Yes," Blake replied. "His name was Jeff. Jeffrey."

"Was he this tall?" Sera dropped her hand to hip level, exaggerating River's gesture from the forest.

Blake smiled into her cup.

"Surely this *Jiggery* person didn't fail to…" Ravi studied Blake with concerned eyes. "Please tell me you've experienced the wild, passionate, break-every-piece-of-furniture-in-the-nest kind of pleasure that's every female's right?"

The moonshine loosened Blake's tongue. "Jeff was more … efficient."

Silence. Crickets.

"Efficient?" Lark whispered, horrified as she refilled Blake's cup.

"Mate," Blake laughed, "he was a two pumps and a grunt sort of man." Her hand clapped over her mouth. "I didn't mean to say that."

"That's the moonshine talking," Lark said. "Also, that's absolutely tragic."

"No wonder your aura's so knotted." Ravi looked personally offended. "A female of your passion going undernourished … it's practically criminal. Well, my boy may be stubborn about some things, but he knows how to worship at the altar of feminine pleasure."

"Again, Ma!" Sera rolled her eyes. "We don't need details."

"What? Orgasms are nourishing. It's a medicinal fact!" Ravi tested a brush on her skin, the pattern glowing as the room darkened with twilight. "These patterns will highlight your beautiful form and guide River's attention to all the right places."

The right places? Blake blinked. "What?"

"It will help with the confusion. Do you have special human markings for mating?" Sera asked, reaching for a jar of shimmering blue powder. "Or do you just … find each other in the dark?"

Blake laughed. "Some humans get tattoos or wear perfume, but nothing like your UV patterns."

"If they can't swoop," Lark asked, "what did the males do to announce their interest in courting?"

"Some brought flowers or wrote songs," Blake said. "Jeff once scored tickets to the grand final. That was his big romantic gesture where he proposed."

The sisters exchanged puzzled glances.

"It was a footy game," she explained.

"A game with feet?" Ravi's head cocked.

"That's … it?" Sera asked, clearly unimpressed.

"Enough about that. Time for some crow education." Lark flicked out flowing silk trousers resembling a pleated skirt, cinched at the ankles with intricate embroidery along the sides.

"These"—she waggled her brows—"are your courtship windways."

"Oh, good choice." Sera hiccuped and squinted at her empty glass.

"Perfect for optimum blood flow and easy access," Ravi added.

Blake glanced at the other pairs of pleated pants. "They look the same."

"For the most part, they are," Sera said. "Unless you change one thing."

"You're supposed to wear modesty shorts with them," Lark explained, her expression serious.

All three crow shifters looked at each other, then burst out laughing, their wings rustling and disturbing hanging trinkets.

"What's so funny?" Blake took another sip of moonshine. The bitterness had gone. It was all sweet now. Yummy.

"She's an expert at forgetting her modesty shorts." Sera refilled Blake's cup. "Almost every pair of windways she owns is of the courtship variety. Show her, sis."

Lark poked out her bottom and flicked one pleated panel. Her wing snapped, gusting wind to blow the flap wide, flashing the curved naked flesh of her underbottom. "Oops." She glanced over her shoulder, covering her mouth in mock surprise. "The wind caught my ways again."

Sera waggled her finger in Blake's face. "A well-timed flash will surely wipe the confusion from your mate's eyes."

"Now," Ravi said, holding up a delicate brush, "let's clean you up and get those patterns started so you can join your Well-blessed mate."

Blake noticed Ravi put a strange emphasis on some of her words. But the moonshine made her feel a little loose. It burned away her last reservations. "Fuck it. Can't be any more awkward than Jeff's annual birthday inspection of me lady bits."

She reached for the hem of her borrowed blouse, hesitating just a heartbeat before she pulled it over her head in one fluid motion.

TWENTY-FIVE

CIRCA 200 YEARS AGO

Hours after Cielo left to find something worth trading for Nikan, Manfri was still sitting on the treasure hoard with their new friend under the watchful Collector's eye.

The moon hung high in the night sky, cold air nipped their skin, but their spirits remained oddly buoyant, considering their circumstances. Manfri liked to think he had something to do with that. His innate facetiousness tended to anger opponents yet humor allies simultaneously. It was all entertainment.

Never once did he doubt Cielo would circle back for them.

He occupied the time by telling stories about the adventures awaiting them in Cornucopia once Cielo returned, from exotic food to potent drinks, and high-stakes gambling to delicious mischief. These inevitably spiraled into tales of carousing he and Cielo had already shared.

Upon hearing his stories of debauchery, the Collector squawked bitterly, "You're an imbecile. You waste your treasure on experiences you will not recall."

"Better than to be isolated here from everyone," Manfri fired back, braver now that he knew they'd escape soon. Surely Cielo wouldn't be long.

"And this is what you want?" she asked Nikan suddenly. "Instead of being heir to my fortune?"

"I never wanted this—" Nikan gestured around them at the jewels still shimmering in the darkness. "I hate it. I hate what you've done to me. I would have murdered you in your sleep if it wasn't for some stupid sense of..." His words trailed off, lips flattening.

The Collector canted her head, studying her son as though he were a puzzle she couldn't decipher.

How could she not understand his emotions?

Bird brain, Manfri concluded. That must be it. Too many feathers upstairs.

"He returns," she announced, standing to face the direction in which Manfri could see nothing but stars and distant clouds beyond their canyon spire.

As she hopped toward the platform's edge, Manfri pressed his hidden dagger into Nikan's palm and whispered, "We can still..."

They might stand a better chance of maiming her while she was distracted by a new treasure.

But Nikan shook his head. "I just want to be done with this place."

Cielo landed with a flurry of feathers and wind-blown hair, huffing and puffing. He pulled a small metal cylinder from his jacket with a wince. Manfri stepped closer to see better in the darkness. His friend's cheeks burned bright from windburn, but his eyes appeared dull, his lips pinched with pain. While shifting helped heal a crow, it wasn't always complete—he might still be injured after what had been done to him earlier.

Metal glinted in the moonlight as Cielo tossed his prize to the Collector. His sigh of relief echoed against the hoard as the Well reconnected with him, flooding his system with life-saving energy. Mesmerized by the sparkling item coming her way, the Collector captured the forbidden item with her winged, taloned hands. Unlike Cielo, who'd trained himself to master the debilitating pain from losing magic, she cried out and seized with shock, drooling as her eyes bulged.

"Go!" Cielo roared.

All three crow shifters launched into the sky, beating their wings furiously until their limbs burned and nothing filled their ears but rushing air and pounding hearts. Even though the Well enforced their bargain, safety lasted only as long as the distance between them and the Collector continued to widen. She could be right behind them now.

Cielo surprised them again by activating a portal stone in mid-air. The three sailed right through the electric circle, only turning back upon hearing a screech of fury. Cielo quickly deactivated the portal stone. The last thing they saw was the silhouette of the crow queen standing atop her treasure hoard, hunched over her prize.

They flew through darkness, hearts hammering with fear. While Cielo refused help initially, by the time they neared Cornucopia, his wings had faltered too many times. Manfri and Nikan took hold of his arms and carried him the rest of the way.

When the city's bright manabee-powered lights appeared, Manfri couldn't hold back his thought: "I hope she fell from her spire before she recovered."

"Nah," Nikan answered under his breath, wind buffeting his long, dark hair as they descended. "She's too indestructible. She's probably already taken the treasure to her secret trove. I've seen her transport items in a bag and return empty-handed."

"What did you trade?" Manfri asked Cielo. He wouldn't put it past his crafty friend to have somehow tricked the Collector. To have tricked them all.

Cielo shrugged. "It was the item I stole from Crystal City the first time I visited a few years back."

Manfri made the hand sign for an apology. "I know it meant a lot to you."

"It's fine. I'll just have to return and steal something else."

Manfri was the only one who knew how hard Cielo had trained to claim it, only to be unable to boast to his family because it was made from forbidden metal. Someone inside Crystal City—probably that girl—had warned him not to take it. Of course, the fastest way to get Cielo to do something was to forbid him.

None of them wanted to be punished by the Guardians. Despite being raised by a violent father who demanded perfection, Cielo defied expectation and became the most daring thief Manfri had ever known. The thought of following his friend's example—of being that brave—sent equal parts admiration and envy coursing through him.

"Thank you," Nikan's sharp words pierced the air.

Manfri's wings faltered at the acknowledgment of a debt. It tipped the balance between them as they carried Cielo during their descent. Being close to public eyes, Cielo shirked out of their hold and stubbornly flew the rest of the way.

"We didn't do this because we expected a favor," Manfri said.
"I know."

They dropped onto a street in Cornucopia, stumbling in their haste. Each shifted their aching wings away and stretched. Manfri still couldn't believe they'd entered the Collector's trove, thinking her most prized possession would be a jewel or even her son, but it was something else entirely—her greed.

"You good?" Cielo asked Nikan.

"I should ask the same of you."

"I'll be fine once I get a drink."

"Maybe this will help." Manfri pulled a palm-sized, jewel-encrusted bottle from his rear pocket.

They gaped at him.

"When did you get that?" Cielo asked, swiping the bottle and uncorking it.

"While you were gone, I talked Nikan's ear off and—"

"Say no more." Cielo burst out laughing. "Manfri's artful distraction to the rescue."

They shared the stolen liquor, finding it potent enough to make the ground tilt beneath their feet instantly. But they felt good. Alive. Hungry. Ready for more adventure.

"We fucking rescued you from the Collector!" Manfri blurted, bumping shoulders with Nikan.

"Shh." Cielo put his finger to his lips, glancing around to see if anyone heard. The ramshackle street they'd landed on was nearly empty, save for a drunken elf pissing on a wall twenty yards away.

"Come on." Manfri slammed his palm against Nikan's back. They stumbled forward, laughing. Maybe a little drunk. Definitely drunk.

"What did you say this was again?" Cielo squinted like a pirate at their new friend as he held up the empty bottle.

Nikan shrugged. "Something she told me not to drink."

"You want it back?"

"I want nothing she touched," Nikan declared. "I'm done. So done."

"Good." Manfri clapped him on the back again and waggled his brows. "Let's see about getting you laid."

"Eat!" Cielo scowled at him. "We need food first."

"I've never..." Nikan blushed. He glanced down at his borrowed attire. "I don't even look..." His stomach growled. "I have no coin."

"Don't worry about that." Cielo winked and held up a palm-sized ruby that looked almost black in the moonlight.

"You sneaky little fucker." Manfri shoved him, loving this triumphant feeling. This is what he missed—the adventure, the danger, the camaraderie, the celebration.

"We were there because I lost the bet," Cielo drawled, all puffy eyed from the liquor. "I had to come away with something." He tossed the ruby to Nikan. "You said you're done, so we'd better spend it. But it's your choice. Whatever you want."

Nikan looked at Manfri. "What do you think we should do?"

"Stupid question. Let's party."

TWO ELIXIRS AND A PINT OF SOUR ORC ALE LATER, WITH BELLIES full of food, the three victorious crows stumbled down Cornucopia's main street. They'd won a velvet cloak off a posh traveler's back (which Manfri promptly lost in a canal), started a brawl with dumb owl shifters, and pilfered an empty stein as a trophy—something to remember this night. Manfri hadn't decided if it would go to his trove or if he wanted to look at it every night before going to sleep.

Since Cielo had somehow convinced Nikan to forgo the Rosebud Courtesans in favor of general mischief, and dawn approached, they should probably find their new friend somewhere to live. Manfri's backup plan was taking him home to the family roost, but doubt flickered in Nikan's eyes whenever he mentioned it.

As they passed a late-night clothing merchant, bright buzzing manabee sconces drew their attention to a faceless mannequin in a *store window that wore leather battle gear. It was too clean and pristine, but something about it had them inching closer.*

"It reminds me of a Guardian's uniform." Manfri touched the glass.

Cielo spat at their feet. "Fuckin' cunts. Taxing us coin for nothing."

They all knew the stories—Guardians were just puppets of the Prime and the highest level of party poopers known to fae. Crows hated them because they enforced the no-metal rule, and some of the greatest treasures were made of gold, silver, steel, and copper. The list went on. It didn't matter that they were cut from the Well for holding it. As Nikan said, crows found ways to carry it without being affected. But as much as they wanted to hate the Order, the leather battle gear called to them. They couldn't look away.

Guardians were free to hold any treasure they wanted, including those made of forbidden substances.

"Do you think it's for sale?" Nikan asked quietly.

Manfri glimpsed movement inside the shop. Two females—a busty blonde with rosy cheeks laughed at something a dark-haired elf said. Likely young, still getting into the kind of trouble Manfri excelled at cultivating.

A wry grin formed on his lips. "Why don't we go in and ask?"

Before Cielo could protest, he dragged Nikan inside by his sleeve. A porcelain bell dinged above them as they squeezed through the doorframe. Giggling and fire-warmed air greeted them, scented with lavender, cotton, and candle wax.

Both females looked up, conversation halting. Manfri resisted puffing his chest when their eyes widened with appreciation. His mother had always teased him and Cielo, saying they'd steal hearts with their faces but invite murder with their mischief. And now they'd added Nikan to their group, right when Manfri had been furious about Cielo moving on.

Ask the Well, and it would provide…

After introductions and flirtations that made Cielo's eyes roll and Manfri's blood heat, the shopgirls—Adeline and Selene—agreed to help outfit Nikan with proper clothing befitting a princeling. One thing led to another, and soon Manfri found himself on a chaise with Selene while Adeline took Nikan's measurements with increasingly bold hands.

Somewhere in the background, as Nikan looked his way with bewildered excitement, Manfri noticed Cielo inching toward the exit like the thief he was.

"Where the fuck are you going?" *Manfri caught him at the door.*

Cielo rounded on him. "It's late."

"Past your bedtime, hatchling?" *he teased.*

"Three's a crowd."

"I'm sure they don't mind sharing."

"I do."

"Fine. You take one of them. I'll watch." *Manfri waggled his brows.*

"That's not what I meant, and you know it."

"I won't leave Nikan alone. They'll eat him alive. Probably swipe all his new coin while he's getting his cock sucked. Besides, he deserves tonight to end like this. Didn't you see the look on his face?"

Cielo folded his arms. "So, you wanting to join in has nothing to do with it?"

Manfri's eyes crinkled. "Maybe."

Best word ever.

"Whatever. Like I said, I need to get home."

"Whatever," *Manfri snarked back, even though he knew Cielo had sacrificed a lot tonight. He was probably still sore from his wounded shoulder.* "As if this has nothing to do with your secret hoe."

"Take that back." Blue lightning flashed in Cielo's eyes.

"The part about the secret. Or the part where she's a hoe?"

"I'm going to murder you."

"No, you won't," Manfri drawled confidently.

"And why not?"

Manfri opened his mouth just as Nikan shouted for them to come back. Something about being undressed and having another drink. Crimson. Those females meant business. Manfri pointed in that direction with his thumb. "That's why—crows before hoes. I'm taking one for the team. He wants to stay. I'll stay with him."

Cielo laughed bitterly. "I'm sure you and the princeling can handle it without me. I'm out."

As he walked away, Manfri called after him, "When that human breaks your heart, you know I'll be here."

"In the shop?" Cielo pivoted and flashed a grin, walking backward before spreading his wings.

Manfri wanted to tell him to fuck off, but instead, he said, "Just promise me, whatever happens, that you'll circle back."

Something like respect flashed in Cielo's eyes. He gave a curt nod and beat his wings. Two seconds later, he was gone.

Manfri closed the shop door, making sure to lock it tight. He sighed heavily, thinking about the future fun lost to Cielo's new obsession. But then giggling females and a low-pitched male rumble drew his attention.

Things were changing. But not necessarily for the worse.

TWENTY-SIX

River slouched on a giant cushion by the campfire, brooding at the scenery below their elevated position. The dying sun touched everything in the amphitheater with a golden brush. It should be a glorious sight, but all he could think of was that vast amount of open space where he used to fly. Tonight, the sentinels in charge of circling were just dark specs. He and Cloud used to volunteer for the job, which meant they could spy on the other kettles and plan their midnight raids.

Then Ash came along and everything changed. No … it changed long before that. When Cloud's father, Salvatore, forbade him from going on an official gathering, a raid. That's when the restless spark ignited in Cloud. After that, he was always hunting.

River knocked back another sip of Talo's moonshine. It burned sweeter than usual tonight, leaving a bitter aftertaste in his mouth. He sighed as the liquid went to work, easing his tension. He slouched further, spreading his legs for comfort. He supposed that getting used to change was inevitable when fae lived for millennia.

Ash spoke with Talo—each on either side of River—making quiet bets on how long it would be before curious stragglers started flying in for the observations. Ash was clean of blood and owl brain matter, out of his Guardian uniform, and now in a fresh linen shirt and drawstring pants to suit the balmy weather. Unlike River, though, his wings spread out behind him, dark blotches against the low light.

Movement a few levels down the amphitheater at the Cardona roost drew River's gaze. He sat up, thinking maybe … but no, it was Carlotta, Cloud's mother. Tall, wavy black hair, and with a steel spine, she ruled her roost with as much love as her mate did discipline.

She once made River swear to protect her son from human harm. He wondered if she thought River had failed that promise. Rory broke his heart. Did that count?

"The Valentis will fly up first." Talo pointed at a kettle one level down, where several winged figures puttered around their caravan, preparing it for tomorrow's procession. "Nobody needs to check their wheel bearings three times in five minutes."

He waved openly when they glanced up.

"Nah." Ash jerked his chin in the opposite direction. "Reed Faelin's already working out how to make his injury look natural so he can join the 'healing observations.'"

"Isn't it educational observations?" Talo tapped his chin.

"You said both," Ash reminded him.

"What do you think, son?"

"Who gives a flying fuck?" River took another sip of moonshine. It burned less now. His mind was elsewhere, specifically on Blake. Since they'd separated, he'd felt no less than a gazillion fluctuations of her emotions through their bond. Were his sisters spilling his secrets? Was Blake spilling hers? And what in the Well's name were they dressing her in that took this long?

He shouldn't have kissed her earlier; he hadn't planned on it. But when she stood in that sunlight, her skin catching prismatic light, instinct and hunger had overwhelmed his better judgment.

Now, he floated in a mess of his own confusion. The Well had blessed and marked them as mates, but he shouldn't have kissed her. It gave her the wrong idea.

Nerve-frying pain. Agony. Fire in his blood.

Every night, that's what River saw when he closed his eyes to sleep. His best friend had looked at him like a stranger.

Cloud could go fuck himself.

The Well-blessing had to be wrong this time. Had to be. River was damaged goods, a Guardian who couldn't fly, whose wings hung in tatters. Just as he'd failed to protect Cloud, he'd inevitably fail Blake too.

"Not you, I'm guessing, son."

"Huh?" River's gaze drifted to his father's amused expression.

Ash roared with laughter, nearly toppling backward if it weren't for his wings saving him. It took River several seconds to catch up through the growing haze of moonshine in his mind. But he could see he'd walked into that trap with his "Who gives a flying fuck?" comment.

Talo launched into a detailed demonstration of his favorite exercises to "reinvigorate blood flow" to his groin to help return River a few of his fucks.

"Dad!" River growled, heat crawling up his neck.

"How long's it been, son?"

"Five years," Ash quipped, his dark eyes twinkling with mischief.

River glared at the princeling. How in the Well's name did he know about the drought? River had thought he'd been clever in hiding his problem. But there was no use wondering—Ash had a way of knowing things he shouldn't. That damned wind of his was sneaky. And now the whole kettle would know.

Great. Fucking peachy.

"Mm." Talo stroked his chin. "Five years is definitely a dry spell. Have you seen your mother about it?"

"I don't have a problem," he muttered while silently miming to Ash that he'd stab him in his sleep tonight. The gesture came out sloppier than intended. "And if I did, why in the Well's name would I tell Ma?"

"Nothing to be ashamed of," Talo continued. "Why, once your mother and I—"

"For *Crimson's* sake, Dad!" River dragged his palm down his face. "Can we change the subject? The bastard downstairs works just fine!"

"Now ... but earlier..." Ash's smirk widened.

"You call your cock the bastard?" Talo's frown deepened as he stared at River. "That's not healthy, son."

"Kill me now."

"Wait," Talo continued, "if blood flow's not your problem, then are you worried you're too rusty to handle your new wingmate's youthful appetite? Is this why she calls other males mate?" He gestured to Ash.

River didn't think he could slump lower on the cushions, but he did. He sank until the world tilted oddly. "Wake me up tomorrow."

"Again," Talo persisted, "it's nothing to worry about. Especially with what I heard earlier."

River groaned beneath his hand. "She attacked a tree! Not me."

"Not that."

"We aren't a throuple!" he shouted.

"I'm wounded," Ash drawled.

"Stop encouraging him." River pointed at his face, then swung his finger to Talo. "Finish your story."

"Oh yes. That." Talo leaned closer, lowering his voice conspiratorially. "I'm talking about what I heard when I delivered the moonshine to your old bedroom and—"

"My bedroom." River blanched. He'd forgotten about that part.

"Apparently, Blake's previous mate was a two-pump-and-dump sort of lover." He clapped River's shoulder with a wink. "You see? You have nothing to worry about. Anyone coming after that will look good."

"Your faith in me is … astounding."

"Don't worry about a thing." Talo gave Ash a conspiratorial wink. "We've got it all sorted."

River's gaze darted between them. The movement made his vision swim. "What's that supposed to mean?"

"It means," Talo said, his usual jovial tone softening, "that your mother and I won't let another chance at happiness slip through our kettle's fingers. Not after…" He glanced toward the Cardona settlement, his wings rustling with unease. "Well."

River's jaw clenched. "Lark and Tommas."

"We suspected they were meeting at Lover's Roost." Talo sighed. "Would have been a perfect match. Your sister's healing gift, his strength. But perhaps our flocks aren't as compatible as we thought."

"I can't believe the Donna changed her mind about the match." River's fingers curled into fists on his lap.

Talo's eyes sparked. "Violence begets violence, son."

"Not according to *Peacemaker*." He scoffed.

"There are better ways to seek justice."

"Like what? Turning the other cheek? Living in peace and harmony while our kettle remains at the top of the amphitheater?" River gestured at their elevated position, his arm feeling unusually like jelly. "Face it, Dad. Your 'make love, not war' philosophy hasn't worked out for us."

"Hasn't it?" Talo's gaze settled meaningfully on River's glowing marks. "The Well chose you as a Guardian. It blessed you with a mate. That's not nothing."

Talo smoothly changed the subject and launched into unsolicited tips on improving stamina beyond two pumps so that River's new mate was well looked after in the bedroom. Ash mimed explicit suggestions when Talo wasn't watching. River wanted to throttle them both, but … not really. The moonshine made it hard to get riled up, which he suspected was his father's intention.

It had been too long since River had seen Ash laugh and enjoy himself. *Crimson*, it had been too long since River had done so either. This past day with Blake, he'd laughed more than he cared to admit.

Ash suddenly cut off mid-sentence, tensing as his gaze snapped to the air above the inner amphitheater. Alert, River instinctively reached for mana, preparing for battle. The sudden movement made his stomach lurch. Had the kelpie returned?

TWENTY-SEVEN

When the Faelins crested the ledge, River almost wished it were the kelpie returning.

"Yoo-hoo, cousins!" Reed Faelin called, landing with an exaggerated limp that his wing-mate, Skye, fussed over. "I heard you're having a healing observation tonight. I wouldn't mind Ravi looking at my knee. I'm hoping to be in perfect shape for tomorrow. Hope we're not intruding."

Talo sprang to his feet, grinning. "Not at all, Faelins. Our roost is your roost. Come on in."

"We brought a gift." Skye handed over something small and sparkly, which Talo accepted graciously with a dark look sent River's way—a silent dig at the shitty "rocks" River had brought as gifts for his family.

In River's defense, he'd been a little distracted.

"Perfect timing," Talo said. "We're about to dish up a feast like no other! Ravi's got something special in store tonight. Won't you join us?"

River watched them walk toward the long table, their

figures growing hazy in the twilight. Bioluminescent mushrooms had been cultivated to grow over the tree trunks and boughs. Their light complemented the soft atmosphere that manabee lanterns provided, gently swaying from branches.

Music started somewhere—percussion on wood and the intricate plucking of a lyre's gut strings. The Faelins had brought their instruments, and Sera began to sing in her low, haunting way. Lark conversed with another couple who had recently flown in.

Wait.

If they were there, then where was Blake? Should he find her? What was the protocol?

River turned back to find Ash staring into the amphitheater's abyss, specifically toward the Cardonas.

"You think he's over there?" River asked, his tongue feeling oddly thick. He tipped his moonshine back and gulped down the last of it.

Ash shook his head but didn't elaborate.

So many thoughts warred in River's mind: righteous payback, guilt over his potential happiness, and Blake's prolonged absence. The feud. In the end, all he could muster was, "This bullshit with Cloud sucks."

"You'll see him soon enough."

"When?"

"At the Great Murder."

River checked the triad tattoo, but there was no message from Cloud. This news from Ash was either passed on from Clarke or from the wind.

"What did you hear?" he asked.

"There's a rumor he'll appear at the Tribunal to exonerate his family." Ash checked over his shoulder to see if anyone was listening nearby, but they were all busy at the table. "He doesn't want them ostracized to the top level like your family."

"How magnanimous of him," River drawled. "Wait. Exonerate them from what? His Vendetta?"

Rules had to be followed for a Vendetta to be legally binding in the community. Otherwise, any old crow could kill another and claim it righteous. Cloud refused to include his kettle, his murder, or his triad. His Vendetta wasn't even against another fae. The elders shouldn't give a shit.

Ash's sigh spoke volumes.

"You don't believe that's why he's coming," River stated, fighting to keep his thoughts clear, "which is why you changed your mind about coming to the Great Murder."

Ash's jaw clenched, but he nodded. "Cloud's up to something."

River gasped dramatically. "You mean beyond the blanket murderous rampage?"

"Yes."

"Clarke told you that?"

"No."

"Did you see her?"

"Maybe."

"You going to elaborate?"

"No."

"Well fuck you too."

Ash chuckled. He tossed a pebble across the campfire at River. It hit him on the head.

"What was that for?" River rubbed the ache.

"Just checking."

"For what?"

"If you still have your wits."

"You're the one with rocks for brains."

He wanted to find the pebble and toss it back, but his arms felt too heavy. He followed Ash's drifting gaze to the lone, ornate caravan parked beneath the twisted branches farther down the roost. The Crow's Dowry nesting caravan had likely cost his family a small fortune in coin. The gift was given to the newly mated couple to help them start a life together. Worthy trinkets and gems made it shimmer like starlight, but it now sat empty. Forgotten. Sad.

Something bitter and unexpected lodged in River's throat. He never thought he'd want that for himself—the traditional courtship, the thrill of swooping for his chosen mate, the community's and the Donna's blessing. But now that the Well threw him and Blake together without any of those moments, he couldn't help feeling like he'd been cheated out of something vital.

He snatched the moonshine decanter Talo had left and shook it. When did it get so low? He shrugged and tipped the last of it into his cup, drinking deeply to wash away the bitterness.

"At least the inside's practical," Ash noted, gesturing at the nesting van. "Private washing area, kitchen, sleeping quarters. Everything a newly mated couple needs for their bonding tasks."

"Sounds like torture." River's voice came out rougher than intended. "Locked inside until you complete arbitrary rituals with someone you barely know? Nope."

"We both know that's not what you really think."

"Maybe."

"Maybe she's the right person for you..." Ash's gaze flicked to where Talo and Ravi slow danced, wing to wing by the table. "To dance under the moonlight with."

"There is no right person for that tradition." River knocked back the rest of his moonshine.

"You're only trapped if you fight it."

"Lark and Tommas should have kept fucking in private. The Donna has it in for our kettle. Trying to seek her approval only made things worse."

There were two ways to become mated in the crow community. The first and most respected was the Donna's strategic arrangement. The second still needed to be approved by her, but petitions were allowed.

"It wasn't the Donna who caused the feud," Ash remarked.

"She still denied every petition my parents made after they eloped," River pointed out, his tongue feeling like cotton.

"Until Lark and Tommas."

"Why can't you let me wallow?" River groaned. "You're being a warada's tail."

"And you're being a cunt. What crawled up your ass and died? I thought you and Blake were getting along."

"We are." River scowled at him.

Ash glowered back.

A balmy, girly-scented wind tickled River's nose, cutting through the smoky campfire. The impact of his mate's unique smell floored him. Every cell in his drunken body awakened, vibrating with hot, male need. He hunted for a glimpse of her rainbow sparkle beneath the sparkling lanterns. Twilight was still young. Her hair should still hold a touch of UV warmth. He didn't realize he'd leaped to his feet, didn't even notice his erection, until Ash growled, "Get that thing out of my face."

River's crotch bulge hovered inches from Ash's head.

Wincing at the throbbing protest, he adjusted himself. All this from one whiff of his mate's scent in his lungs.

An image of his scarred, patchy wings attempting flight flashed through his mind, and panic choked him. For all their joking about performance anxiety, they had a point. What if his cock decided this little reawakening was temporary? What if he couldn't even make it to two pumps?

What if Blake decided that mourning her ex was easier than hating him? What if she refused to be near River again?

"I'm no good for her," he muttered, the words coming thick and slow.

"For *Crimson's* sake, stop feeling sorry for yourself."

The animosity in Ash's voice pulled claws from River's fingertips. He was ready for a fight despite his unsteady stance.

Dark, steady eyes dropped to River's hands. Ash's brow arched. "You'd rather fight me than deal with your shit?"

"So?"

Ash straightened to his full height, coming face to face with River, and said, "You think you're the only one with problems?"

"I think that moonshine is getting to your head, princeling."

"Get over yourself."

"This isn't about me."

Ash used two fingers to shove River's shoulder. "Who's it about then?"

"Duh." River flung his hand toward the Cardona Kettle, nearly losing his balance. "He's made everything about him. Since the beginning."

"Wrong." Another hard poke. "Try again."

"Don't fucking touch me." He shoved back, definitely

slurring now. "Of course, it's about him. It's always about him, and I'm sick of it."

"Wrong again." Another shove. "It's about your own shit, and you need to sort it out before you fuck everything up."

"I'm going to find that cryptex."

"I'm not talking about that."

"Cloud deserves what's coming to him."

"Not talking about that either." Ash's narrowed eyes darted to River's Well-blessed mating marks.

Blake. Her name, her scent, her taste. *Her.*

"My mate is none of your business," River growled through increasingly numb lips.

"Maybe she's not." Ash's stare was infuriatingly steady. "Or maybe you should start acting like she's yours."

"Are you threatening to steal my mate?"

"Only you would think that."

River shoved him. "Should have left you in chains."

Ash's expression went flat. Dead.

Silence.

Oops. River shouldn't have said that. Guilt hit him hard in the chest, stealing his breath. Moonshine made any deep-seated fear seem like the truth in the moment. But the truth he'd neglected to voice was that his self-destructive pattern of protection had begun. How he pushed away those who mattered before love grew too real, saying things he couldn't take back.

Love meant that inevitably, someone's heart would break. Whether ostracized by the community, like his parents, or whether fate turned love into betrayal. Into obsession. There was no perfect, happy ever after like everyone dreamed of—only pain.

And no matter what River tried, what he said or did, he ended up failing. Just like he did with Cloud on that airship, nothing he said mattered. He couldn't take the words back. Nothing would make them right.

"It's a good thing you didn't," Ash said, his voice quiet. "Otherwise, I'd never have had the chance to do this."

His fist connected with River's stomach, exploding eye-watering pain throughout his body.

"I deserved that," he choked.

"Yes, you did." Ash calmly dusted his wings and straightened his shirt. "It's because of the Umbrias, because of you and Cloud, that I learned a good life was possible. It didn't have to be about accumulated things. It could be more." He stared down at River, who was still doubled over and wheezing. "And now both of you are so caught up in what you've lost, you don't even appreciate that you had it in the first place."

"Great," he groaned. "Now I feel like a floater."

"You owe me another hit."

"What for?"

"For sticking your dick in my face. Seems to work fine to me."

At least Ash's eyes twinkled with humor instead of that dead look from earlier.

River glanced down. His cock was still hard, even through the moonshine. He grinned. "Yeah, it works fine, doesn't it?"

"One punch."

"Fine. Last one, and only because I'm two quarts sloshed to the moon. Three quarts. Maybe four." River straightened and tensed his abdomen, ready for the hit. "Otherwise, you'd be mouse meat, brother."

"Whatever you say." Ash hit River in the stomach again. Not as hard, but it still hurt on the heels of the earlier blow. Weirdly, though, River struggled to straighten this time. His head swam too much. In the end, he dropped to his knees.

"I feel a bit…" The campfire and cushions circled him.

"Don't worry." Ash's voice sounded distant. "You have nothing to worry about."

"What makesh you fink 'shat, prinsh-*sh*—" Fuck. Why couldn't he talk properly?

"You heard your father. He has it all under control."

Aw, shit.

The moonshine was spiked.

River faceplanted into a cushion.

the Newly Nested!

TWENTY-EIGHT

Blake woke to gentle rocking and birdsong. Something click-clacked nearby while something else clip-clopped outside. The rhythmic sounds nearly lulled her back to sleep as she rolled over, hugging her pillow with a lazy smile.

Clip-clop. Clip-clop.

A horse?

Sunlight sliced across her face. She opened her eyes to a curved wood-slatted ceiling, and farther beyond her bed nook was the interior of an ornately decorated caravan. Strings of beads hung across the ceiling and clacked together with each sway. The sunlight in her eyes came from a clear strip atop a stained glass window above a kitchenette on the left. It cast colorful reflections over the polished wood surfaces of a dining booth against the right wall, cupboards, a chest on the floor, and several larger doors. Hopefully, one led to a bathroom.

Bloody hell. This habit of waking up in strange places needed to stop.

Blake rifled through her foggy brain for clues to how she ended up here. Her last memory was of being in River's old room, hesitating over Ravi's clothing selections. None had seemed the sort that a woman of substance would wear. But something had changed—the moonshine, perhaps, or the catharsis of stabbing dickface Jeff's tree effigy, or Ravi, Sera, and Lark's infectious enthusiasm. Her resistance had evaporated.

"Oh my god," she mumbled. Did she flash her boobs at the new in-laws?

No time to ponder. Her bladder pulsed with urgency. She slipped from the bed and dashed over a pretty woven rug to the opposite end, where she opened the first door to reveal a tiny bathroom including a shower stall. The second door opened to a toilet.

Removing her pants proved challenging. The space was cramped, the van rocked, and layer upon folded layer of fabric had been wrapped around her like origami.

"The fuck?" She turned in the small cubicle, chasing her tail.

Another memory bubbled up.

"Lark's an expert at forgetting her modesty shorts," Sera had explained, refilling Blake's cup. *"Almost every pair of wind-ways she owns is of the courtship variety."*

Easy access. Blake found the splits and separated them, cheering at the discovery of no modesty shorts beneath. She plonked down with a groan of relief.

"Fark, that feels good," she moaned.

Christ. If she had waited any longer, she might have pissed her pants.

Looking down the length of her body, she finally took in the rest of the outfit. The fabric at her waist and ankles glittered with intricate beading. Pretty. The jewels were the sparkly sort that made her heart flutter. Silk crisscrossed over her breasts, lifting them into drool-worthy cleavage. The straps knotted behind her neck and left her midriff bare. Shimmering painted patterns emulated her Well-blessed markings on every inch of her exposed skin. Some lines became arrows pointing downward into her pants, others toward each breast.

"Oh my god," she gasped, as flashes of memory entered her mind. Hadn't Ravi said something about guiding River's attention to all the right places?

Blake lifted her gaze and caught her reflection in a black glass pane over the tiny wash basin—messy hair, no makeup, no filter—nothing to hide behind.

She washed her hands and returned to the main cabin, arms folded beneath her breasts in case the straps gave way. This second pass across the van, she noticed more curious things. Fresh food in bowls and sacks, wicker baskets on the booth's tabletop. Two steps from the bed, she froze.

River lay face down on the covers, fully clothed. His collar was crumpled at the back of his neck as if someone had grabbed him by the scruff and dumped him there. New beard growth peppered his square jaw. His blue-black hair lay disheveled, covering his eyes. The same luminous ink patterns decorated his skin.

He was dead to the world despite the caravan's jostling.

Blake quickly finger-combed her tangled hair.

Maybe they'd both drunk too much moonshine last night, except … she frowned, trying to recall seeing River out of his Guardian uniform. Surely, she'd remember that. After the way he'd kissed her, seeing what he looked like under that leather was all she'd thought about.

Nothing. Blank space where memories should be.

Something was very wrong with this situation.

They were likely on their way to the Great Murder, but she needed to know for sure. She reached for his shoulder but hesitated. He looked peaceful. Vulnerable. Kind of adorable. No darkness burned behind that wicked smile—just a beautiful man with rosy cheeks and impossibly long eyelashes that seemed to sparkle a little in the shaft of sunlight.

The last time she saw him sleep, he'd woken at the tiniest sound, but the van's rocking and light in his eyes didn't wake him. Perhaps this moonshine hangover had gifted her a rare opportunity to study her mate unguarded.

A paper-thin fractal scar spiderwebbed across his face like a drunken snowflake. Previously, she'd only noticed the thickest one near his cheekbone, almost invisible. Now she saw tiny fissures spreading to his upper lip.

Blake brushed her thumb across his skin but felt no raised flesh. Ada had healed him well. It was strange she couldn't do the same with his feathers when his hair and flesh had regrown. Perhaps wing follicles differed from hair follicles. Then again, internal scars often lingered longest.

She settled beside him and tucked a lock of hair behind his ear.

More fine scars.

Muscles rippling, River snapped awake and seized her wrists. "Moonshine!"

Blake shrieked.

"What happened?" His gaze darted around the caravan. "Why are you screaming?"

"You shouted in me face!"

"I did?"

"And you're hurting me."

Wide eyes dipped to where he gripped her wrists.

"Oh." His hold loosened, but he failed to release her. Probably because his attention had diverted to her strappy top, specifically, what it struggled to contain. Hot, male appreciation darkened his eyes and deepened his voice. "*Oh.*"

"They gave me this to wear."

"You say that like it's a bad thing," he mumbled. Then frowned. "Wait." His gaze snapped up to hers. "I feel like I'd have remembered seeing you wearing this last night because you look—" He cleared his throat. Blushed. Swallowed hard. "You look *really* good."

"That's exactly what I thought!" She looked at his open shirt, at flashes of tattoos and hardened abdominal muscles. "About you, I mean. When I saw you after I woke up. I don't remember anything after getting dressed."

"Fucking moonshine!" He slapped his palm over his face and flopped back with a groan.

For a long moment, silence reigned. Eventually, the rhythmic crunching of rocks, lazy clip-clopping, and gentle cabin rocking soothed them. River's fingers drummed against his face.

"You know what's weird?" Blake said. "I feel pretty good for someone who drank herself blind."

His fingers split to reveal one eye. "You're blind now?"

"No," she laughed out. "It's an old world saying. Maybe just Australian. It means we drank so much we blacked out."

He relaxed but pushed up on his elbows, glaring past her at the van's interior.

"We didn't drink too much," he said flatly. "We were drugged."

"Get fucked!" She shoved him in the chest. "By who?"

His lips twitched, eyes lingering on where she'd touched him. "My guess is my parents, but Ash knew. My sisters probably helped. Again … welcome to the Umbria Kettle."

Blake's stomach clenched. His family drugged her? But she thought they liked her. "Why?"

"You don't want to know." River sighed, avoiding her gaze.

"Yeah, nah." She folded her arms and raised her brows.

"Which is it, yeah or nah?"

"I'm not buying it."

"Buying what?" His black brows knitted innocently, reminding her of how he'd looked while sleeping.

"Yeah, I hear what you're saying. But nah, I'm not accepting your answer."

"Just say that, then."

"Why did they drug us, and more importantly, why the bloody hell aren't you ropeable about it?"

"Ropeable?" His gaze dipped to her mouth. "I can't understand a word you're saying today, Sparkles, but you look sexy all worked up. Keep talking."

She shoved him again, square in the chest. Big mistake. The Guardian caught her wrists and flipped their positions faster than she could blink. She ended up pinned beneath his warm, hard body with her hands trapped above her head, his amused blue eyes inches from hers.

"Naughty mate," River murmured. "Getting violent with your male."

She wriggled, trying to squirm free, but he easily adjusted his hips and legs to trap her completely. She felt like a mouse in a lion's jaws. Her ex's muscles were nothing compared to River's effortless strength. Not that Jeff had ever manhandled her like this. Not that she was complaining about River doing it.

None of this should feel right.

Yet everything did whenever he touched her. The way he looked at her, all hot and wanting, made her body ache to surrender. Being desired this intensely, becoming the object of someone's obsession after years in a cardboard relationship, made her pulse quicken. She silently begged him to manhandle her again, to move her like his plaything while having his wicked way with her.

She inhaled deeply, arching her breasts into him. His eyes dipped, and he released a strangled groan. For a moment, she thought—hoped—he'd go all feral and take her mouth like before.

Instead, he pushed off with a muttered curse, scrubbed his face, and slid from the bed.

After composing himself, he strode straight for the exit door with zero concern that they were in a moving vehicle. His fist closed around the bejeweled knob, turned, and pulled.

"River!" Blake leaped after him, stumbling on the decorative rug.

The door remained shut.

She slapped his hand away. "Are you nuts?"

"You know I am."

"I'm not kidding. You open that door and—"

"Worried I'll fall out?"

"Of course I am." Annoyed he couldn't see that, she slipped under his arm and pressed her back against the door. The protective move filled his eyes with arrogance, provoking her to blurt what was really on her mind. "One minute, you look like you want to kiss me. Next, you're attempting to leap out of a moving vehicle. I'm insulted."

She truly was. This outfit made her look good. Made her *feel* good. Better than she had in days. If he wasn't into her, then—*You can't upcycle yourself, babe.*

Blake folded her arms across her midriff, hating how that disparaging voice still lingered in the corners of her mind.

River held her gaze and slapped his palm against the door beside her head, caging her. His other hand reached around her waist to grasp the doorknob. The heat of his body scalded her front. She clutched his shirt as he jiggled the door, squeezed her eyes shut, and waited to fall. Nothing happened.

"Door's locked, Sparkles."

She opened her eyes to an annoyingly handsome face, struggling to contain laughter.

"I knew that," she said.

"Oh really?"

"Yes." She folded her arms. "And you're missing the point."

"The point is"—he lowered his lips to her ear—"that we're not going anywhere for a very … long … time."

Excitement and unease tangled through her. "What do you mean?"

"Stand back, and I'll show you."

She hesitated.

He raised a brow. "Remember my promise back in the forest?"

"Not really." She blew a lock of hair from her eyes. "Too bloody busy fearing for me life." She cleared her throat. "*My* life."

"Not that part. Afterward, when I said I'd never let you

get hurt." He harrumphed, then scowled, as if something in her words bothered him. "Stand aside, and I'll demonstrate why we can't leave."

"Fine. No need for dramatics."

River's expression went blank. A stillness came over him that triggered warning bells in her mind. Then he clenched his jaw, grunted and grabbed her shoulders. He lifted her clean off the floor as if she weighed nothing and deposited her behind him near the kitchenette. Then he patted her head and said, "Now be a good little rainbow mouse, and no more squeaking until the big bad birdy finishes his lesson, okay?"

She pouted. "Get fucked."

"Gladly." Heat flared in his eyes.

"Finish your lesson, bad bird."

"I will."

"Good."

"I'm finishing it."

"I'm waiting."

His stare intensified. His hands flexed at his sides. Tension crackled between them, hot enough to combust. Then he shook his head, cursed under his breath, and returned his attention to the door.

"As I was about to demonstrate," he ground out, "we're stuck in here."

River gave Blake a pointed look to ensure she paid attention, and then rammed his shoulder against the door. It rattled, but held firm. He checked if she still watched, then stood back and kicked it. Nothing. And it wasn't a soft kick, despite his bare feet. The entire caravan rocked when his heel struck the wood.

"Maybe it's jammed," she offered weakly.

Huffing, he joined her by the kitchenette but positioned himself between her and the door. When she tried to side-step for a better view, he reached back with a large hand and pinned her against the counter.

"Stay behind me," he ordered, suddenly all serious.

Before she could protest, his free hand swung toward the door. A thunderous gust of air exploded from his palm. It hit wood without effect and rebounded, gusting back in their faces, and up her pants and hair. Beads and decorations clattered. Objects and papers tumbled from the booth. The horse whinnied outside.

She'd glimpsed enough over his arm to see the blast had come from his hand. *Mana*. Magic. It was only the second time she'd witnessed it used. The explosion had rocked the van hard enough to tilt it and frighten the horse. *This* was the power they said she would hold?

Wait.

"Is the horse alright?" Alarm jolted through her.

"It's fine," he muttered.

"What about the driver?"

"There's no driver or rider."

"What?"

He faced her, and she nearly laughed at his windblown hair standing on end.

"There's no horse, either." He caught her looking and quickly fixed himself. "There aren't enough to pull every carriage to the Great Murder. Some vans run on mana. After we travel a certain distance, we'll portal the rest of the way. Evasion tactics."

"But I heard a whinny outside."

"A few years back, Trix and Peaches—another Well-blessed woman—discovered how to capture sounds in mana stones. What you're hearing isn't real."

"Come again?"

A boyish, cheeky lowering of his lashes. "I can make you come all night, Sparkles. Just say the word."

"How is it possible you're almost three hundred and still have a horny teenager's mind?"

River's lips quirked. "Talent."

"Naturally."

"See? You get me."

"I was being sarcastic."

"Mmhm. And I'm being facetious."

"Why?"

His humor vanished. "Because we're stuck here against our wills."

TWENTY-NINE

Blake watched River prowl through the caravan, systematically opening cupboards and rifling through their contents. His actions grew more agitated with each cabinet opened. Each held a range of supplies, from tools, food, clothes, medicines, linen, and more. It looked like they'd be well stocked for weeks.

Finally, she couldn't take it anymore. "What exactly are you looking for?"

"Yes!" Triumph lit up his face as he yanked his Guardian uniform from an open chest on the floor. He brandished his chakram before her like a prize. "Look what I found."

"Yes, very impressive. But you still haven't told me why we're locked in here."

"Because if I can get us out…" He split the chakram into two deadly crescents and flashed her a grin. "It won't matter."

He shooed her back with an impatient gesture. It might have annoyed her if he didn't look so cute, being all determined and shit.

Blake retreated to the bed nook. "Far enough for you?"

"Yep." His eyes found hers again, checking—not showing off as she'd first thought, but ensuring her safety. The realization sent warmth blooming in her chest, followed by a sharp pang of longing. She'd not felt his emotions travel through their bond for a while now. But she knew he felt hers. Why did he hide his feelings?

"Nothing to worry about," he assured her, misinterpreting her angst. "We'll be out of here in no time. Metal cuts through magic."

He spun, all grace and deadly power, and slammed his right blade into the door. The impact sounded like a thunderclap. She flinched, hands flying to cover her face.

"What the—?" River gasped.

Blake lowered her hands and found him staring at his blades, confusion in every line of his face. "Did Trix break them?"

He brought one down on the booth's bench seat, testing the sharpness. The blade sliced through leather and wood like tissue paper, sending stuffed feathers exploding outward. He winced. "Oopsy."

"Why won't it work on the door?"

"I don't know." He tested the blade's edge with his thumb. "Metal *always* cuts through magic. Always." His frown deepened. "Unless..."

"Unless what?"

"No." Disbelief colored his voice, and he started pacing. "I've never seen a spell like this. She must have used Guardian blood—*my* blood, but..." He halted, staring at the open chest. "Ah, shit. My uniform is clean."

"Planning on filling me in this century?"

"Um."

He looked lost, nervous, and unmoored in a way that sent alarm bells ringing through her head.

"River, sit down." She guided him to the dining booth. In a daze, he allowed her to push him onto the intact seat.

"Now give me those sharp thingies," she said.

"Yeah, sure," he mumbled, extending them.

The instant she touched metal, agony ripped through her. The Well's power drained like water through a sieve. Her cry of pain snapped River back to awareness.

He snatched his weapons back. "Why are you touching *Peacemaker*?"

She gripped the table, heaving in lungfuls of air until her connection to the Well was restored completely. "You said I could."

"You're right. I did." He hand-signed an apology, horror replacing the fog in his eyes. "I wasn't thinking."

"No worries. Neither was I." She eyed the chakram warily as he searched for somewhere to set it among the baskets and boxes crowding the table. "You're starting to scare me."

"You might want to sit down."

"Uhh." Her gaze fell on the mangled bench seat.

"Right." He vacated his spot, stowed his weapon back in the chest, and gestured for her to take the bench seat.

"We can both squeeze in," she offered, sliding across the leather. "It fits two. Sort of."

"You won't want to be near me after this."

"Oh my god, spit it out before the suspense gives me an aneurysm!"

He pulled a handwritten letter from one of the baskets. "Read that."

"Okay..." She unfolded the paper. "It's from your parents."

"Makes sense. They're the ones who supplied the dowry." He kept pulling items from the basket—ink bottles, wooden skewers, a leather-bound book. "Keep reading."

She scanned the first lines. "Dearest lovebirds, we're so thrilled that the Donna approved a union of our two families. The Cardonas and the Um—"

"It's not for us?" River snatched the letter, eyes brightening. "Maybe us being trapped here is a mistake." His eyes narrowed again. "But then, why can't we leave?"

She reclaimed the paper with a sharp tug. "I wasn't finished."

"Be my guest." He busied himself at the kitchenette's sink, filling a bowl with water. "This will go faster if I speak straight to the source."

Blake scanned the letter. "Okay, where was I ... ah, yes. *The Crow's Path: Four Trials of the Heart.*

"First comes sustenance, craft with care
A meal that shows your soul laid bare.
One must cook while one must wait,
As ancient customs dictate.

"Two brings broken objects whole,
Proving worth between two souls.
For in healing what's torn,
Bonds of trust are born.

"Three is a mark of feathered kin.
Family crests must be etched within the skin
With sacred ink that binds and burns,

As each other's loyalty is earned.

"Four, each shares three fantasies to explore,
One, a gift of pleasure your mate will adore.
Then let your primal instincts out to play,
With sexual chemistry now guiding your way."

Blake's eyes widened the more she read. When she reached the end and saw Ravi and Talo's special bedroom tips for Lark and Tommas, she stopped reading and refolded the letter.

"Good on 'em," she said. "It's kind of nice that you have these customs to help a new couple get to know each other, especially since most are arranged matches."

Perhaps she wouldn't have ended up in a loveless marriage if there were customs like this back in her day.

Silence.

Blake glanced over and found River drawing blood from his fingertip with the distended claw on another, letting it drip into the water bowl.

"Great," she muttered. "Now you're summoning demons. You know what? Don't even explain."

A ghost of a laugh escaped him, but his focus remained on the bowl. "Summoning my parents, more like it."

"Sure," she intoned. "Because that also makes sense."

While he conducted his spell, Blake's curiosity got the better of her, and she examined each basket's contents more closely. The wooden skewers River pulled out earlier were tattoo needles. The book contained intricate illustrations, including individual family and kettle crests of the Southeast Murder. Various food ingredients filled another wicker basket. The third, she liked. It was filled with construction tools like hammers, saws, nails, and knives. None were metal, only naturally found substances like flint, bone, and wood. Like River's obsidian blade, mana-enforced glyphs reinforced each tool's strength.

River growled at the water, looking ready to punch it before resetting his stance and drawing fresh blood.

"Nothing yet?" she asked.

He grumbled.

Blake thrummed her fingers on the table and watched him glare at the bowl for a few more minutes, but the remaining unopened basket drew her curiosity. Each of the others held items relating to the first three challenges. But when words like primal and pleasure were included in the fourth, she was dying to know what was inside its accompanying basket.

Her gaze darted to River, but his brow was tense with concentration, eyes locked on the bowl.

Should she look in the basket? Was it prying? She'd already looked at the others. Technically, she'd already pried.

Another glance to see if River noticed her. Nope. She lifted the basket lid and nearly swallowed her tongue. "Now that's … ambitious."

She dropped the lid, but images of fae sex toys were seared into her retinas. How did they make the dildo so velvety soft without using plastic? And the furry wrist cuffs, were they real fur? Then there were the glossy, round balls, pegs, straps, masks, tickle feathers, oils, and sparkling, studded things—she had no idea what they were called. She tentatively opened the lid again and stared. Blinked. And muttered, "Far out, crows are kinky."

"What?"

"Nothing." Blake dropped the lid, heat crawling up her neck.

"Sure, it is." Sarcasm dripped from River's tone, but still, he didn't break his concentration.

"What exactly are you doing?"

"Triggering a blood-communication spell with my family."

"Oh." She joined him at the bowl. "Cool. Do they appear like little people floating above the water?"

"No, little mouse." He snorted, eyes crinkling. "They do not."

"Well, I don't know. That's how Obi-Wan and Princess Leia did it."

"One of your old-world moving storytime fillems, I presume?"

"Fillems?" She giggled. "You mean films?"

"That's what I said."

"Aw." She patted his head. "You're cute when you try to speak human."

Scowling, he dodged her ruffling hand just as a blue light flashed in the bowl's water, revealing Talo's rippling face as if he looked up at them from beneath the surface.

"My son!" he boomed. "How'd you like our newly nested gifts?"

River plunged his arm into the water. And kept going. The shallow bowl somehow accommodated his entire limb.

Blake's jaw dropped. "What kind of Mary Poppins shit is this?" She opened the cupboard beneath the kitchenette. Nope, no hand dangling there. Had River reached through a portal in the water?

He snarled like an animal, face contorting with rage. His shoulder tugged as if something tried to pull him down through the bowl—or someone. Violence rippled in his posture. Blake stepped back.

"That escalated quickly," she muttered.

River pulled his father's head out, gripped by the throat, and held it above the bowl. Water cascaded from Talo's sputtering face.

"Oh. Hello, Blake." He managed a nervous laugh. "You look good."

Awkward didn't begin to cover it.

"G'day, Talo." She started to wave.

"Eyes on me, Dad," River growled.

Instead of fear, pride shone in Talo's eyes. "Just look at you, son. Strong enough to pull matter through a blood-borne water connection! Such a rare talent."

"Dad."

"Of course, my boy would develop a gift like this. Umbria flock is a sturdy stock. We are truly blessed indeed." He shouted down his body through the water. "Do you see this, my love? See our son?"

"Dad!"

"No need to shout. I'm right here."

A vein pulsed in River's forehead. "Tell me how to break the nesting spell."

"Why would you want to do that?" Genuine confusion colored Talo's voice.

"None of your fucking business." River squeezed. Blood trickled from claw marks down his father's neck.

"River." Blake touched his rigid bicep. "I don't think he meant harm."

Angry blue eyes flashed her way, peeking through mud-stained locks of hair. The bowl of water was now swamp-like. River must have seen or sensed her simmering fear, because his gaze softened. His grip loosened enough for Talo to say, "See? Nothing to worry about."

"She has no idea what you've done," River shot back.

"River Manfri Umbria, you let go of your father this instant!" Ravi's voice warbled through the water. *"Inviting that toxicity into a new nest is a bad omen, mark my words."*

"It's alright, my treasure," Talo called down. "He's just nervous because of that issue I had to—"

River's renewed grip cut him off. "This is not a fucking joke!"

"We know it's not, son." Talo wheezed, eyes darting to Blake. "But when we heard your mate's having trouble identifying your bond, we knew we had to help."

River dunked his father and then brought him back up to shout in his face, "There's nothing wrong with our bond!"

"She calls other males her mate!" Sera's underwater voice filtered through.

Uh-oh.

Now it made sense why they kept talking about fixing the confusion with her mate.

"Mm." Talo nodded sagely. "And you clearly haven't bumped tail feathers yet, or else you'd be a little less tense, hmm?"

"Tell them about the basket!" Ravi's voice filtered through. *"It's just as well that I added those extra toys on a whim last night."*

"We knew you were having trouble sealing the deal," Talo continued.

"We only just met!" River shouted at them.

"Wasn't that a week ago?"

"A few days!"

"Son." Talo dipped his chin. "You're using that tone again."

"Fuck my life." River inhaled deeply, eyes closed. When he spoke again, his voice carried a deadly calm. "If you don't break the nesting spell now, only the Well will save you from my wrath if we miss the Great Murder."

"Ah … about that." Talo winced. "We might have made a boo-boo."

River's expression blanked. "You made a what?"

"You're going to laugh. Ha ha. The spell to lock the van usually needs the blood of both newly mated—"

"You made my mate bleed?" River snarled. Murder was promised in every syllable.

"*Of course we didn't!*" Ravi shouted, annoyance clear. "*That's the problem. We used only yours, assuming we could unlock it with just one blood sample, but it doesn't work that way. This is the first time we've planned a Crow's Dowry. We might have gotten a few things wrong.*"

"What are you saying?"

"*Regardless of whether you accept our gift, the door won't unlock unless you complete the nesting rituals.*"

River opened his fist, and Talo's head splashed beneath the surface. Muddy water sprayed River's face and dripped down his front. Without a word, he emptied the bowl into the sink, cutting off his parents' warbled, enthusiastic praise and encouragement. Then he braced his hands on the counter, his back to Blake. From his locked-up muscles and the white knuckles of his grip, he was not a happy chappy.

It was hard not to take his mood personally. Did this all start because of her? Because she'd called other males mate? She'd called lots of people mate. River had warned her, been downright annoyed at her for it, and now he refused to look at her.

"What a fucking joke," she whispered, eyes burning.

River's grip tightened hard enough to creak the wooden counter.

"Why is it such a big deal?" she asked.

He slammed his palms on the counter and stalked to the end of the caravan.

"I'm taking a shower," he grumbled before yanking open the bathroom door and disappearing inside.

The sound of running water filled the silence.

Blake sniffed and wrapped her arms around her painted midriff. This was her fault, but she had no idea how to fix it. Nothing to offer. No magic yet. No way to make this right. No … substance.

THIRTY

Scalding water cascaded over River's back as he stood in the cramped shower cubicle, rinsing away the muddy remnants. But it couldn't wash away the shame, self-disgust, and general shittiness he'd felt since Cloud's lightning bolt sliced into his heart.

Ash told River to sort himself out, but whenever he felt like he could finally let go of his issues, maybe get close to Blake, something like this happened. He called himself a Guardian, a protector, but he couldn't protect shit.

Couldn't stop his friend from going mad. Couldn't keep his new mate safe.

He should have seen his family's gift coming a mile away. It was so obvious to him now … the side comments about him being unhealthy, about him being too rusty to handle Blake's appetite, about them having it all '"sorted."

Once again, he'd arrived at the conclusion too late.

This spell expected intimacy. It wanted them to share secret fantasies when Blake's heart had been broken mere days ago. He didn't care what his family considered an appropriate time for Well-blessed mates to consummate. Blake needed time to get used to being with a loser like River—a crow who couldn't fly, and until recently, couldn't even get it up.

He gently pounded his fist against the shower enclosure, watching water droplets scatter.

The whole situation made him sick. He'd never been the sort to manipulate females into his arms and never liked having to chase them, either. If they desired him, he let them come. If they weren't interested, neither was he. Simple. Done.

It was one thing to see his parents so in love that the mess didn't touch them. It was another to figure out a way *through* the mess first. This confusing feelings bullshit was why he never wanted to be mated in the first place.

He should be interrogating every member of the murder for information on Cloud's whereabouts. If that failed, he should be locating the cryptex. Being a Guardian was the only thing River knew how to do well, and even that was slipping through his fingers.

Crimson, it had been years since Cloud's betrayal, and River still wasn't over it. Why did he care so much? Why did he feel guilty, as though what happened was his fault? They were just friends, not lovers, not partners for life.

River dropped his forehead against the cool tiles, letting the caravan's rocking soothe his nerves. He couldn't believe he'd almost killed his father. He'd somehow pulled matter through the blood connection spell—something he'd never had the skill or potential for. But the moment he saw his father's dopey, grinning face beneath the water, he knew Blake's world was about to come crashing down again, and there was nothing he could do to stop it.

Too little, too late.

Always too little, too late.

What a fucking joke... He didn't blame Blake for thinking that. As far as blessings went, she got the short end of the deal.

This kind of trickery might be expected among crows, but Blake wasn't just human; she was fresh from a traumatic relationship. They'd dressed her up, painted her with newly nested UV symbols, and treated her like kin. It both angered him and made him proud.

When he woke up and realized it was her leaning over him, her expression full of compassion, her breasts abundant in that tight top, his cock had swelled with eagerness. He winced and glared at the thick, angry shaft pointing toward the door. It was doing its divining rod thing, telling him she waited on the other side.

The other Well-blessed Guardians could locate their better halves through the mating bond, but for River, it was this thing between his legs leading the way. Had been since he first laid eyes on her rainbow hair in that marketplace.

"Down, you bastard." But it never cared much for listening to his brain.

Maybe if he released tension, he could think clearly about escaping without ruining Blake's opinion. He took himself in hand and squeezed, but it didn't feel good. It felt empty. It wasn't Blake's fingers wrapped around his shaft. He sighed as the caravan jostled over a bump, and he still felt nothing.

Glass shattered in the main cabin, followed by Blake's muffled apology that stabbed him in the gut. Back to saying she's sorry again.

He turned off the faucet and wrapped a towel around his waist. Then he gathered his mud-stained clothes, took a steadying breath, and stepped out to face yet another person he was destined to disappoint.

Three steps out, he stopped short. Blake stood at the kitchenette, her shoulders slumped, halfway through preparing the nesting recipe his mother had left. Her black hair was pulled into a messy bun, revealing more UV-painted patterns on her mostly bare back. Painted arrows pointed down to her curved ass.

He inhaled deeply and exhaled to gather his focus. What had broken?

Vegetable peelings, broken eggshells, and glass shards were swept into the trash basket beside the kitchenette. Waves of Blake's melancholy traveled through their bond. *Well-damm* if that didn't make him feel worse.

She glanced over her shoulder, briefly locked red-rimmed eyes with him, and then returned to peeling a potato.

"While you were in the shower," she said, voice brittle bright, "I re-read the letter and realized why you were so angry." She cleared her throat, still not looking at him as she peeled with jerky movements. "We need to do the rituals in Lark and Tommas's place." Another clearing of the throat. "So I thought I may as well start with the meal. I hope that's okay?"

"Sure." He kept his tone neutral, afraid any hint of humor might shatter whatever fragile thing was happening here.

She sniffed, nodded, and attacked the potato with more determination than skill. The ceramic blade skittered across the vegetable's surface, removing chunks and leaving a masticated mess.

"I also thought about the other rituals," she continued, words tumbling faster as her shoulders curved inward. "The tattoo challenge looks simple enough. You have experience with that. I'm sure you can teach me. And the repair job will be the easiest. I can repair things with me eyes closed." Her tone was no longer bright. "*My* eyes closed."

He scowled. She kept doing that—correcting herself and feeling shitty. Why?

"As for the final challenge," she said. "I pulled out a few items I think I'm brave enough to try."

River's gaze drifted to the booth where she had, indeed, laid out various toys. His brain screamed for him to look away, not even to consider this an option, but something deeper than curiosity held his attention.

She hadn't chosen the tamer items—no simple blindfold or tickle feather. Instead, she decided on fur-covered cuffs, a bejeweled plug, and a sparkling string of anal beads. Blood rushed south again.

But this wasn't how he wanted to learn her secrets.

He shook his head, scrubbing his face with his palm. This was Blake trying to give him what she thought he needed. His bastard cock could shut the fuck up.

A sharp crack drew his attention to Blake's hand over the sink, yolk from an accidentally crushed egg oozing between her fingers. "Fuck you, you fucking egg," she sobbed, flicking the mess toward the trash. "Fucking cunty-cuntfaced egg."

The movement gave him a glimpse of her profile and the fresh tear tracks glistening on her cheeks.

"Hey." He tossed his clothes on the floor, moved behind her, and reached around her.

Blood.

His breath caught.

On her hands.

Mixed with the egg yolk and peelings.

She must have cut herself on the glass thing that broke while he was in the shower. He turned on the faucet and guided her fingers under running water.

"We'll figure another way out," he murmured. "It's not worth hurting yourself over."

She remained silent but leaned a fraction against his chest. Her black hair caught a stream of sunlight filtering through the window. Glittering rainbows danced across the strands. He closed his eyes and inhaled her warm scent like a balm. It wiped away the mess in his mind. Cleaned it right out.

And it wasn't just him feeling this way. He sensed her soul grow calmer. For the first time, he understood why the mess never seemed to touch his parents. It was this. She needed him, and he was here. She hurt, and he surrounded her with his arms. Just like she had cared for him when he'd sat there dumbly, staring at *Peacemaker*, not knowing what was happening.

No one else had shown him this. No one else had reacted to him like this. Needed him like this.

He shut off the faucet and wrapped her hand in a dish towel embroidered with gaudy palm trees. Once dry, he held her fingers to the light and examined her wounds. His throat tightened at the bright crimson against her olive skin. Despite his mother and sister having a healing gift, River could barely knit together a scratch. If these cuts were any deeper, he'd be helpless in here.

His heart squeezed. "Bleeding for this ritual isn't worth it."

"There's no other way out of here." She ducked her head. Hair fell from her bun, hiding her eyes. But not before he caught a fresh tear spilling down her cheek. "I need to fix this so you can return to your mission for the cryptex."

Cloud's V-painted face flashed in River's mind, and he frowned.

That was the real reason he'd been desperate to get to the Great Murder. Ash was here to provide the backup plan for the cryptex. But Blake didn't know that.

He searched for a place to set her down, but the counter was covered in the aftermath of her meal preparation. With one mighty sweep of his arm and a little mana for coralling assistance, he shoved everything into the sink. The clatter of ceramic and vegetables echoed his internal chaos.

"Not worth it, Blake." His voice came out rough with emotion. "But you are."

THIRTY-ONE

River gripped Blake's waist, so small in his scarred hands, and lifted her onto the cleared counter. The domesticity of the moment hit him like a punch to the gut.

This should have been different. He should have courted her, showered her with gifts, publicly swooped to announce his claim, danced, and made love under the moonlight.

"Let me look at this properly." He cradled her injured hand, searching for fragments that might cause infection. "Even fae get sick if they don't heal fast enough. We need to remove the shards."

"I thought fae were immortal," she said, then quickly muttered, "but I'm not fae."

"Fae aren't immortal," he replied, drawing on his mana. The familiar warmth tingled through his palms as he fed the magic into her raw flesh, so many cuts. "They just live long."

She watched him work. "Do you think that's why I haven't developed magic yet?"

"That you're not fae? No. The other Well-blessed women are human."

"Oh yeah." She sniffed. "When the kelpie attacked, I swear I saw the vase break. But when I collected it, I found it fixed again. I thought maybe I'd done it with magic, but I must have hallucinated." She glanced at the floor by the bed nook where the little plant sat, its sapling wobbling from travel.

Her disappointment was tangible in its weight.

"Something will develop." River squeezed her arm. "I sense your power, Blake. It's there. I can even siphon it off if I need to." He paused, unsure if the next part would hinder or help, but she should know. "You're probably the first to thaw after the taint almost ruined the Well. We don't know what effect that might have."

Maybe no one else would receive a specific gift like the first nine women. Perhaps they'd ruined their chances by not stopping Nero sooner. Maybe River should have done more instead of plotting to take down Cloud.

As he moved to Blake's next cut, she started babbling again. "I'm sorry I fucked up the meal. Your mother's recipe said the potatoes should be sliced like straws, but I've never peeled potatoes with a knife before. So it looks all hacked up and ugly. Never cooked much in me old life at all." Her voice cracked. "Couldn't keep up with Jeff's dietary demands. Never could prepare the chicken, add enough protein, or slice the onion thin enough. So he just took over. It was easier that way. At least it was done how he wanted."

"He never let you cook?" River's words came out sharp with disbelief.

"I'm not good at much." She wiped her eyes, shrugging.

"Except renovating things." A sniff. "Bedazzling them. Maybe. I don't know. He was probably right."

Rage bubbled beneath River's skin. Obliterating that tree had not been enough to punish Dickface for his treatment of Blake.

"I'm sorry you're stuck with me," she whispered.

"Stop fucking apologizing." His growl came out harsher than intended. "You've got nothing to be sorry about."

"I have everything to be sorry about."

"You?" The word exploded from him. "Like what?"

Could she not see how damaged he was? His wings were missing half their feathers, scarred and too useless to fly. His tattoos were broken, just like the promises he'd made to protect those he loved. And that was just on the outside.

He took in their prison—the locked door, the sex toys wobbling on the table, the ritual requirements laid out like a checklist of his inadequacies. Everything about this situation was his fault. His family's interference. His inability to protect her from this. His weakness was in wanting her despite knowing she deserved better.

"Blake…"

Her name came out like a prayer, heavy with everything he couldn't say. But like every time he tried to open up, nothing came out.

He was a coward.

The need to let it all out clawed beneath his skin. He longed for someone to share his pain with, but how could he do that to someone he cared about? How could he articulate all the feelings he avoided for good reason?

His emotions were a storm without wings to ride it.

"Can I ask you to do something?" Blake's voice was hesitant.

"Of course." He was powerless to do anything but wait for her instructions. If she wanted to stay in this van for longer, but they missed the Great Murder, he'd do it. If she asked him to get down on his knees, on broken glass, he would. But if she asked him to leave … he wasn't sure he'd be able to walk away.

As it turned out, she wanted something far less dramatic. She lifted a cut finger in front of his face. "Kiss it better?"

Laughter burst out of him, and he brought her fingertip to his lips. The strangest thing happened when he kissed it—he found his courage.

"I know you think being with me is a joke." His lips bumped over her skin. "But I'll prove I'm someone you can rely on. Someone worthy of being your mate."

Her gasp needled him.

"I don't think you're a joke," she said.

"You said so earlier. I believe your exact words were, 'What a fucking joke.' I felt your disgust, Blake. And it's okay. I get it."

"That's *not* what I meant." She shook her head, anger flashing in her eyes. "I keep saying the wrong thing. Saying mate to everyone was normal five days ago, but it's causing so much trouble now. I'm angry at me, River, not you. In case you haven't noticed—" She folded her arms, shrinking in on herself. "I'm not adjusting very well."

"Only days ago, you were married to someone else. Now you're expected to be with someone like me."

She jabbed him in the pectoral. "You're not as bad as you think."

"Yeah." His chin dipped. "I am."

She stared at him with far too much understanding, seeing parts no one else had. It scared the shit out of him. He pushed away, intending to find clean clothes, but her hand snaked out and grasped his wrist.

"I get that it's too painful for you to share your emotions with me." She tugged him back to her. "I won't push it, but I need to know. Why do you avoid being with me? I mean—" She hesitated. "Should I dress differently? Should I work on understanding why I haven't developed magic? Should I have picked something a little bit wilder?" She glanced nervously at the basket.

He gaped. "You're actually considering this?"

"I mean…" She sniffed. "Sure. If that's what you want."

"You're blushing." He brushed her colored cheek with his thumb, marveling. His gaze dipped to her lips and found them parted, panting ever so slightly, nervous or scared, or … was that her desire he detected trickling through their bond? "Tell me, Sparkles, what's making you so nervous?"

"You're *obviously* more experienced than me…"

"Why do you think that?"

"Oh, fuck off," she scoffed. "I might be younger, but I'm not dumb. You're sex on a stick. Just look at you." She swept her appreciative gaze over his body, biting her lower lip when she reached his abdomen. He bit back a groan as his damned divining cock tried to burst through the towel for her attention, but her gaze had already returned to his face. "River, I lived around blokes who played professional footy for years, but your muscles are so big and shredded that you'd wipe the field with them."

"I'm not sure that makes sense."

"Don't even get me started on your sexy scars and tattoos. My point is, you look like *that*, and you've lived for almost three hundred years. Going by what's in that kink basket and your family's *very* liberal way of life, I'm guessing crow shifters aren't afraid to explore their sexuality. Often." She took a deep breath as if steeling her resolve. "Mate, I'm fucking nervous because my experience pales in comparison. I mean, shit, you have a dildo the size of a King Brown snake in there. I've had one dick inside my vagina—*ever*—and let me tell you"—she snort-laughed—"he ain't no King Brown."

Any blood left in River's head flowed south. His brain stopped working. He couldn't understand half of what she said. He would have stopped her right there and kissed her until she whimpered, but she was on a roll.

Another self-deprecating snort slipped out of her, and she rolled her eyes. "Take yesterday, for instance. I was all hot and bothered watching you fight, wishing it was me beneath you instead of that owl shifter, fantasizing about you pinning me and half-choking me while you had your way with…" She trailed off when she finally noticed his face, the raw hunger bleeding from his every pore. "Um. How naive of me, right? Ha ha. I mean, that's the lamest fantasy, right? I mean … fuck. I keep saying, 'I mean.'"

"Blake," he growled.

"Hm?" She tucked a lock of rainbow hair behind her ear and averted her gaze.

"You had a fantasy about me?"

"Maybe." Her blush returned, and she folded her arms over her chest.

"Yesterday. *Before* we kissed."

"Maybe."

He was so fucking hard it hurt. "The only reason I'm not ripping off your clothes and worshipping your body with my tongue is because I'm…"

She leaned forward, hanging eagerly on his next words.

But nothing came out. He was too busy falling in love with her. Eventually, she said, "Because you're all nice and freshly showered, but I'm stinky and covered in food goop and blood?"

River blinked. Processed her suggestion. And snapped.

"You could be covered in shit, blood, or dripping with my cum, and still, I'd want to lick every inch of your body." His fingers speared into her hair and tightened on reflex, driven by the way her pupils expanded, by her desire bleeding into him like a mortal wound. "The only reason I'm not is because—" Again, it was on the tip of his tongue to tell her everything. Again, he choked up.

"Because?" she prompted, breathless, waiting for him to be her knight in shining armor.

Shame coated his insides. He relaxed but couldn't let go. "You said it yourself. You're not adjusting well. Once you get out of this fucked up caravan, you'll think differently about wanting to do the nesting ritual."

THIRTY-TWO

CIRCA 200 YEARS AGO

The bundle landed on the table before Manfri with a thud, followed by a worn book that Cielo slid toward Nikan.

The three of them sat there for a long moment, staring at the items. The rowdy tavern sounds grew and ebbed. A clang from the kitchen. A crackle from the fireplace. A shout from the gaming tables a few yards away.

"What's this?" Manfri touched the fabric-wrapped package.

"My latest haul from … you know where." Cielo's fingers drummed against the table. His eyes skittered toward the tavern door every third beat. "Gifts."

Nikan's expression brightened with reverence as he traced the book's binding. He hated collecting objects, treasure, or any physical thing except for books. Reading was a treasure that stayed with him long after the book had gone. It was something his mother could never take. He devoured anything he could find.

Manfri couldn't look away from the bundle before him, dread and anticipation tangling in his gut.

"What is it?" he asked again, struggling to keep his voice steady despite the ale fuzzing his edges.

"Fuck'sake, Manni." Cielo nudged it closer. "Open it."

Inside the wrapped fabric lay delicate bamboo needles, ink pots, and hollow thorns sharper than any he'd seen. Manfri's breath caught. It was a perfect replica of the Donna's tattooing instruments, without a single ounce of forbidden metal. Instructions for use were nestled inside Nikan's book.

That nagging tightness he felt every time Cielo slipped into human territory alone eased, only to be replaced by a sourness beneath his tongue. The tools gleamed in the tavern light. Beautiful. Perfect. Acquired elsewhere.

"All this time." He traced the needle's point, watching his fingertip dimple without breaking. "You weren't just treasure hunting. You were searching for another way."

"Well, can you blame me? You haven't shut up about the triad link." Cielo curved his hands around his stein. "Now we don't need the Donna. You can do it tonight. Tonight is good." His knuckles whitened. "I'm flying out again tomorrow."

"Again?"

"So you'll do it?" Cielo leaned forward.

"Sure..." Manfri would need to sober up first. But tonight ... if they completed the triad tattoo, then tonight, they would be brothers for real. He gulped back a sip of ale, thinking of the adventures the three of them would have now. His lips curved into a smile. "Tonight."

"It was her idea," Cielo blurted. "The gifts."

Silence crashed between them.

"Her?" The stein suddenly felt fragile in Manfri's grip.

"The human?" Nikan's perceptive gaze tracked between them.

Instead of his usual denial, Cielo lifted one shoulder, a half-smile playing at his lips. "She's not afraid to ask questions—like you, Mannie. She's not afraid to leap without wings."

Manfri shared a look with Nikan. This was the most Cielo had offered up about his human in months. Usually, when they queried it, they were met with the same answer. Not yet.

It seemed yet had arrived, but now Manfri wasn't sure he wanted to know more.

"What questions?" Nikan asked.

"She once asked what it feels like to fly." Cielo stared into his stein, thumb circling its rim.

"And?"

"I told her it's like freedom." Something raw edged into his voice, a crack Manfri had never heard before. "She didn't laugh. She just ... nodded. She understood even though she'll never..." His gaze remained fixed on a point beyond the tavern walls, once again traveling where the others couldn't go.

A treacherous ache bloomed in Manfri's chest. This human felt pain. This human understood Cielo. This human wasn't just one of the Untouched anymore. She'd reached places in his friend that Manfri's wings couldn't carry him.

"I'd have told her it's like being king of the sky." Manfri lifted his stein with a bitter smirk. "Free to shit on anyone below." He gulped down the ale, the burn failing to cauterize the wound opening inside him. "But risking your neck for treasure like this is stupid."

"Worth it." Cielo's eyes flashed as he gestured at his gifts.

"Is it?" Manfri's stein hit the table hard enough to slosh.

Spilled ale seeped toward Cielo's side. Their gazes locked across the table's divide.

"Diamonds always are," Cielo said.

"Not if they're cut wrong—if they make you bleed."

A shimmer of firelight caught the edge of Cielo's distending claws as they scraped against his stein.

Nikan's gaze darted between them, clearly understanding no actual diamonds lay amongst the gifts. Just when Manfri expected *the tension to snap, Cielo's expression softened. His claws retracted.*

"You fuck faces still know that I'll always circle back. Right?" His brows raised. "I'll always come home."

Home.

The word meant something different for crows than for other fae breeds. It wasn't a brick or mortar house, wasn't a place or a treasure or a feeling. Crows circled overhead nightly for a reason. They mourned their dead for a reason. They reminded themselves of where they had been, where they were going, and, most importantly, who they were with.

Home wasn't a journey but the people it was shared with.

Home was this—the three males around this scarred tavern table—the ones Manfri would always circle back for.

But it hadn't always been three. It had once been two. Before that, the kettle, the murder. One day, they'd each find a mate and a new home. Nothing was written in stone. And if Cielo's path took him places no one else could follow, then ... where did that leave the rest of them?

He lifted his gaze to his friend's. "How can you be sure she's worth the trouble?"

"Your parents think it's worth it, right?"

It, meaning obsession. The one thing. The all. The core of existence every crow yearned for.

It, meaning love.

The question hung between them like a blade. Manfri's throat tightened around a truth he rarely admitted.

"Yeah, they think it's worth it. But look where love got them. Banished. Ostracized. Treated like shit by their own kind." His claw dug into a crack in the table, deepening it. "Maybe love conquers all, but it leaves a fucking mess."

Silence stretched until it threatened to break him. Cielo stared into his stein with a long face. Nikan flicked the edge of his book, eyes distant and empty. Manfri couldn't stand knowing he'd caused either of his friends to give up the hunt for the ultimate prize. He still wanted it himself. He was only afraid. So he summoned his courage and admitted, "They still dance under the moonlight. My parents. Even with nothing, they dance like the mess can't touch them."

The admission burned his tongue, too raw, too honest. He reached for a crude joke to cover the exposure, but Nikan surprised him by murmuring, "I'd like to see that. A love like that."

The air between them thickened. Maybe Manfri hadn't ruined everything, after all.

Cielo reached for the pitcher and poured himself another drink, ale cascading too quickly, foam spilling over the rim. "Don't get too sentimental on us. You'll ruin the ale."

"Fuck your ale," Nikan returned, scowling.

"Look at us," Manfri joked, "talking feelings and shit. Better look out, or we'll start laying eggs."

Cielo raised his stein as if to toast their brotherhood. Instead, with his eyes never leaving Manfri's, he blew a raspberry and tipped it slowly, deliberately. Ale spread across the wood grain, racing toward their new gifts—two distinct rivulets splitting from a single source. Manfri snatched the bundle while Nikan dabbed at the book with his cloak.

"The fuck?" he growled.

"Bad birdy!" Manfri inspected the wet implements, which were now dripping with sticky, sour liquid. He glanced down at his breeches, at the wet spot around his crotch. "Fuck'sake. It looks like I pissed myself." He waggled his finger at Cielo. "No triad tattoo for you!"

Their laughter scattered between them like fallen feathers, and for the next few minutes, they cracked jokes and tried unsuccess-

fully to wipe away the sticky brown liquid oozing into all the cracks. Cielo bellowed for another pitcher. When it came, he poured another stein for everyone and then raised his to his lips.

"Yeah," he murmured into the cup. "You're not ready for the mess."

Manfri strained to catch the words. "What?"

But Cielo had already leaned back, lazy smile fixed, gaze distant once more.

THIRTY-THREE

When Blake was twelve, a particularly territorial magpie had claimed their front yard eucalyptus as his domain. The neighborhood kids called it "Scarface" and gave the tree a wide berth during swooping season, racing past with schoolbags held over their heads like makeshift helmets.

"Mad as a cut snake, that one," her dad had muttered one Sunday afternoon, nursing his beer as the one-eyed bird dive-bombed Mick, who dared to venture too close to the tree. "Bloody menace needs putting down."

Her brothers agreed and plotted revenge with their cricket bats. But Blake, still grieving her mum and feeling isolated, saw something different when she watched the magpie from her window.

It wasn't aggression driving those territorial swoops. The bird guarded something precious—a nest without a mother.

She'd started leaving scraps of mincemeat on the porch steps and sitting quietly nearby with her sketch pad. For weeks, the magpie watched from a distance, its head tilting suspiciously, that damaged eye assessing Blake's intentions.

One quiet afternoon, when everyone else was at Johnno's footy match, the magpie landed beside her. Up close, his scar wasn't frightening. It reminded her that he'd once fought for what mattered and lived to tell the tale. It was proof that he didn't need two feet to have a heartbeat.

"You're not scary," she'd whispered. "You've just been hurt, haven't you?"

Over that summer, Scarface became her unlikely friend. Her brothers thought she was mental. Her dad barely noticed, but Blake recognized that beneath the battle scars was something beautiful and fiercely loyal.

Now, as Blake stared into River's eyes in the caravan, processing his words, she recognized that same damaged beauty. His hands could destroy, but instead, they treated her with gentleness. Everyone else might see the scars, the broken wings, the facetious Guardian. But she saw the loyal heart beneath … even if he couldn't.

Blake had trouble breathing.

River no longer leaned into her space, but he still consumed the air around her. He still had his hand in her hair. Still looked at her like he would die if he couldn't kiss her.

"So … just to be clear," she said slowly, deliberately. "You're not avoiding being with me because you're not into this."

She gestured down her body.

His brows slammed down. "What do you think?"

"I think you're avoiding—" She gasped as his fist tightened in her hair.

He tilted her face down, forcing her to look at his

tattooed torso, abdominal muscles flexing with rapid breath, down to where the tightly wrapped towel trapped his erection against his thigh.

Her mouth dried.

"Far out," Blake murmured, eyes widening. "Yeah." She licked her lips. "I can see why you're waiting for me to adjust."

"Not funny."

"Kind of is, Mr. Brown."

A frustrated, stunted growl caught in his throat. His fingers flexed against her scalp as if he considered pushing her down further, what she kind of hoped he'd do—take charge and order her to open her mouth, to take him deep.

The thought made desire flood her system. Her clit pulsed. She grew wet. Hot. Needy. A moan slipped from her lips, and she pressed her thighs together, hoping to ease the ache.

River let go and took a giant step back, running both hands through his damp hair. Flexing biceps short-circuited her brain and spiked her pulse. Desire ran rampant in her body, tightening her nipples, her skin. Dark, blue eyes met hers.

"You think you want this, Blake, but you don't know me."

"So let's get to know each other, then. That's what these nesting challenges are for, right?"

Why did that sentence seem to frighten him more than a monster?

"Right?" she pushed.

"Yeah," he admitted, relaxing his shoulders.

"We can take it slow. Start with one challenge. See how we go." She glanced at the mess in the sink and sighed. "I'm not going to sugarcoat it. If you wanted a mate who could cook, it's not me."

"I can cook." He turned toward the ruined bench seat. "But I'm shitty at repairing furniture. More of a slice and dice sort of male."

Possibility fizzed through her. She slipped off the counter. "I'm excellent at it!"

"Oh yeah?" His small, hesitant smile filled her with warmth. "Then we've been approaching this all wrong."

"We have?"

"You repair. I'll cook."

"But your mother addressed the recipe to Lark. Doesn't that mean a woman should cook?"

"Fuck the letter. Do what you want." His brows drew together. "Wait. Unless you want to cook?"

She shrugged. "Maybe you can teach me?"

"Whatever you want."

For a long, blissful moment, they stared into each other's eyes with the same dopey, hopeful grin. Then River's eyes widened, ruining the spell.

"Ma said something I'm starting to wonder about." He rummaged around the table, found the letter, and scanned it. "Could be another thing I've been wrong about."

His self-deprecating tone didn't sit well with her. "What do you mean?"

"She said my blood was used for the spell, and that I had to complete the rituals. Not us." River folded the letter, determination settling over his features. "That means you probably don't have to do any of it."

Her disappointment clashed with his hopeful eyes.

"But Ravi also said they got it wrong," Blake mumbled,

twirling her hair. "Maybe we shouldn't risk it if you're not one hundred percent sure. Right?"

Intense blue eyes stared into her soul, to all the secret, hidden places she never dared examine before. Just when she thought he'd deny her suggestion, he flashed a heart-stopping grin and said, "Maybe."

She exhaled.

"Okay, good." She joined him at the table and picked up the bottle of ink.

The brush of his fingers on her jaw lifted her gaze to his.

"You're really okay with this, aren't you?" Wonder threaded through his voice.

"I am."

"Hungry?"

"Not for food," she teased.

He groaned and palmed his face.

"River?"

"I'm trying to be good," he mumbled through his fingers, then glared down his body, "but this fucking bastard won't shut up."

"Your penis talks to you?"

He shot her an apologetic look. "He's just angry that he waited so long."

"Five days?"

He froze, eyes wide. "Um ... so, have you had a tattoo before?"

"No."

A certain *someone* in her old life thought they looked cheap. He mistook her angst and dipped to meet her eyes. "You afraid?"

Glass bottles tinkled as the caravan went over a bump.

Blake looked around, noticing more jiggling things. They weren't traveling at breakneck speed, but still…

"It's just, these aren't the conditions I imagined getting one in."

"Mm," he agreed, scowling at their surroundings and flicking beads irritably. He picked up the letter again. "Let me go over that challenge."

"Three is a mark of feathered kin," she recited, not needing to read. "Family crests must be etched within the skin with sacred ink that binds and burns, as each other's loyalty is earned." She pointed to the book. "Do you want the page numbers your parents referred to in their notes?"

He blinked. "And I thought crows had good memories."

"Maybe I'm part magpie," she joked, snorting.

"Those docile things?"

"Docile!" she scoffed. "Mate, I don't know what you call a magpie, but in Australia, they're about as vicious and terri-torial as you can get." Remembering her old friend, she added, "To be fair, they usually have a good reason."

"Oh yeah?"

"They're protecting their nests."

"Sounds fair."

As they finished unpacking supplies, she told him the story about Scarface. When she was done, hiding the melan-choly in her soul was hard. She'd lost so much of her world in the nuclear winter.

"Human or bird," River said softly. "Magic or not, your mind is incredible."

"You say that now," she intoned. "But in a few years, when I remember details about something vital to our argu-ment from yesterday, you'll complain that you always"—she made air quotes with her fingers—"'lose by default' and will end up resenting me for it."

It's what everyone eventually did. Not just Jeff. People hated feeling inferior, and recalling more details was the quickest way to make them feel that way. Since Blake couldn't change how her brain worked, she'd grown to avoid having an opinion about much. Except for her Hidden Gems.

"Well, it's a good thing I don't win arguments with words." River waggled his dark brows.

She laughed. "And I suppose Mr. Brown wins arguments for you?"

"Such a dirty mind, Sparkles. But no. I wasn't talking about the bastard downstairs. I was talking about flashing the ones upstairs." He flexed his biceps, posing like some kind of Michelangelo statue. "Males fear them." He kissed one. "Females go nuts for them … as you demonstrated earlier."

When she had no snappy comeback, he said, "See? I win."

"You haven't seen me flash me tits yet. So … jury's out on that one."

He slapped his heart as though he'd taken an arrow. "She talks *and* fights dirty."

THIRTY-FOUR

Pain lanced through Blake's wrist with each tap of the bamboo needle. River's calloused fingers steadied her arm, his concentration absolute as he dipped the thorn tip into blue-black ink. The caravan swayed, yet his hand remained perfectly steady, tapping a rhythmic pain into her skin with practiced precision.

He'd put on pants, which was a crime in Blake's mind, but at least he'd left his shirt off. Studying his broken tattoos gave her something to focus on.

"Almost done," he murmured, adding the final touches to the feather design she'd chosen from the history book. "You shouldn't have picked your wrist for your first. Thin skin and bony parts always hurt worse."

"Worth it," Blake whispered, transfixed by the emerging pattern. Her first permanent mark in this new world—chosen, not forced upon her like the Well's blue glow.

River blew gently across her skin, clearing excess ink. His breath sent shivers racing up her arm. The tattoo shimmered in the slanted light filtering through stained glass—blue-black lines against her olive skin, feathered edges delicate.

"Looks good on you," he said, voice low. "Traditional crow pattern. Means 'protection.'"

Pride bloomed in Blake's chest. "I probably should have asked what it meant before choosing it."

His gaze flicked up to hers. "I wouldn't have let you choose something stupid."

"When did you learn to do this?" she asked, noting his hands' expert precision.

"Every crow knows basic hand-poking. Can't remember when I learned."

Blake snorted. He was too old to remember. She mumbled under her breath, "Old fart."

"What?"

"Nothing. And what about those?" She pointed to the different tattoos on his arm, the ones swirling with prismatic color.

His tone shifted, grew distant. "Guardians can use metal needles with power-enhancing ink."

"Why doesn't everyone have them? Seems like a no-brainer."

"They're not exactly what you would call safe. The process of extracting the ink includes dipping into the inky side of the Well. It's dangerous and forbidden, but Guardians get away with it." He traced a broken pattern on his biceps where lightning had disrupted the flow. "Used to have more, but Cloud…"

His voice trailed off, but Blake caught the almost imperceptible tightening of his jaw. The way his pupils contracted slightly.

"Does it still hurt?" she asked, brushing her fingers near the scarred, jagged edges of his disrupted tattoo.

River's eyes met hers—startled, wary, then guarded again. "Nothing important does."

Not wanting his attentiveness to end, she returned her focus to her wrist and asked, "Can you make the tattoo bigger?"

"Sit on this one for a while. Decide what you really want because now that you're connected to the Well, mistakes last a very long time." He cleaned her finished artwork with gentle strokes. "And so does regret."

Maybe that explained why he delayed Blake's turn to control the needle. Instead, he gave a pointed look at her massacred meal waiting on the counter.

"Come on," he said, abandoning the tattoo supplies to rescue her culinary disaster. "Help me clean this up. We'll start fresh, and I'll guide you through proper cutting techniques."

She joined him at the kitchenette, and the moment the old mess was cleared, he positioned himself behind her.

"Hold the blade like this," he demonstrated, his chest pressed against her back, hands covering hers. "Let the knife do the work. Don't force it."

Heat bloomed where their bodies connected. His voice vibrated against her spine as he answered her endless questions about mana stones powering the stove, about how fae had adapted without metal or plastic. Everything ran on mana. The plumbing. The lighting. The heating and cooling. If supplies dwindled, they'd be fucked.

After they'd eaten, River insisted on washing dishes while she tackled the bench repair challenge.

Safety first was her motto in her workshop, so she fixed

her topknot and borrowed one of River's shirts to cover her midriff. She tied the tails around her waist to prevent dangling bits from catching in imaginary power tools. She even slipped on shoes, picturing dropped hammers or errant nails.

The bench seat awaited her attention. The leather was split, and feathers spilled from its guts. The wood frame was completely cracked in half from where River had tested his blade. Blake assessed the damage, mentally cataloging each required step. Without thinking, she angled her body as if positioning for an invisible camera.

Laughter burst from her throat when she realized what she'd been doing.

River glanced over from the kitchenette. "What's so funny?"

"Almost started talking to a nonexistent audience." Heat crept up her neck. "This used to be me job."

"Talking to yourself?" He arched his brow as he placed his dish in the cupboard.

"Sort of. I was a social media influencer back home."

He frowned. "Influencing? Like a type of power?"

"Some would say." Blake smiled, remembering the rush of connecting with thousands of strangers. "I had a large following—people who valued me opinions. I called the segment Hidden Gems." At his blank expression, she added, "Like a film? A show?"

Recognition flickered in his eyes.

"I'd find old furniture," she continued, running her fingers along the bench's damaged seam. "Or I'd hunt for broken objects at markets that others overlooked."

"Like how you mentioned putting something shiny in the cracks." River set the dish towel aside.

Something fluttered in Blake's chest. "You remember that?"

"I remember everything you tell me." His gaze held hers, unwavering. "And I understood what you meant. About the cracks." He studied his palms, tracing a thin scar that bisected his right hand. "You think resilience is what makes something beautiful, that drawing attention to damage can transform it."

Tears pricked behind Blake's eyes. She turned quickly to the bench. "I'd restore them and make them stronger. I'd show me followers how to do it themselves."

"These followers," River cleared his throat. "They all just stood and watched?"

"Sort of. From their own homes, though. Remember me phone that you stole?" She shot him daggers.

He showed his palms. "Don't shoot the messenger."

"They'd watch from a screen. I guess it's like one of your Obi-Wan water spells." She tried framing an imaginary shot with her hands. "Hard to explain without a phone to demonstrate."

"So show me anyway." He leaned his hips against the counter, arms folded across his chest, biceps popping. "Pretend I'm one of your followers."

Heat crawled up her neck. "It's embarrassing."

"Come on, Sparkles." Something softened in his face … genuine curiosity. "Show me how you work your magic."

The eagerness in his expression broke through her hesitation.

"Sit there, then. Pretend to look at me through a screen." She gestured to the intact bench. "And don't laugh."

"As you wish, m'lady." He dropped onto the seat with

exaggerated attention, leaning forward with elbows on the table, chin in hand. "Talk to me like you would them."

Blake took a steadying breath, then brightened her expression as naturally as breathing. "G'day, hidden gems! Blake Hartley here with another restoration that'll blow your socks off." She mimed holding up a phone to the damaged bench. "Today, we're tackling this little beauty. She's rough as guts now, but wait till you see what she looks like when we shine her up."

"Your expertise sounds kind of hot," River purred.

"Shh! Followers don't talk back."

"What do they do?"

"They comment on posts. Like—" She grabbed the letter, flipped to a blank page, and handed him a tattoo needle with ink. "Write me a message."

"Got it." He winked as she continued outlining the fix-it project, using animated gestures to demonstrate the measurements.

"See this pattern in the wood?" She traced the grain with reverent fingers. "That's how you know she's got the razz. Underneath all this damage, she's just begging for someone to notice her potential."

The words caught in her throat, suddenly too personal.

"Wood." River nodded, scribbling something that brought a smirk to his lips.

When she hesitated, he shooed her on. "Keep going. Back to your influencing."

"Focus on the project!" Blake warned.

"Got it."

"And only appropriate comments. I blocked any rude cunts. River. Are you paying attention?"

"I *am* focused." He leaned back, eyes wide with feigned innocence. "But you keep talking about wood and cunts."

"Stop it!" But she was grinning despite herself. "As I was saying, that tells us—"

He lifted his hand like a schoolboy.

"Yes, River?"

"I have a comment."

"Oh-*kay*. Do I want to read it?"

He held up his paper with the words: *Your tits look great in my shirt.*

The words cut too close to Jeffrey's criticisms. Her smile faltered. "Me ex said that was the only reason anyone watched."

River's playfulness vanished. He stood and crossed to her in one fluid stride, lifting her chin with his fingers. "Your ex was a dickface who couldn't handle you being smarter than him." His eyes blazed with conviction as he gestured to the bench. "Keep going. Show me how to fix this thing properly. I promise I'll behave."

Taking a steadying breath, Blake squared her shoulders and faced her imaginary audience. "Now, the trick with joining these pieces is all in the angle..."

River settled back, but his demeanor changed, transformed as it had during tattooing. Concentration and genuine interest replaced the teasing. His appreciative sounds came when she demonstrated a clever joining technique or explained why certain types of woods split along predictable patterns. With each passing minute, each demonstration, Blake's voice grew stronger. For the first time since waking in this strange world, she felt anchored to who she'd been—the parts worth keeping, anyway. The parts she didn't like could stay behind.

With dickface.

The hours melted away as she lost herself in the restoration. With River holding pieces steady, she repaired the bench and reinforced its structure. After stuffing spilled feathers back inside, he traced a finger along the split leather. Blue flame sizzled from his fingertip, fusing the tear with an ornate pattern that transformed the scar into decoration.

"That's it." He sat back, admiring their work.

"You gave it the razz," she said, grinning from ear to ear as they locked eyes.

The bench wasn't perfect, but considering their limited tools, it would hold.

They finished an hour ago. Now, Blake straddled River's hips while he reclined in the bed nook. His hands braced behind his head against a pillow as he watched her tap the bamboo needle into his left pectoral. The caravan's gentle sway didn't concern him at all.

"I'm fucking this up," she muttered, dabbing away excess ink. The broken Umbria crest she tried to restore looked more like a child's drawing than the intricate pattern in the book. It had been so much easier using charcoal on paper.

"It's perfect." His gaze never left her face. "Every time I look at it, I'll remember this day."

He'd insisted on reclining while she worked. Hadn't even tried hiding the fact that he wanted her "perfect tits" in his face while she "pricked him" because it was an effective distraction technique.

Blake had to admit she felt good, too. Being trapped with him in a moving caravan was the best time of her life. She never wanted to leave. But still, she was acutely aware that he'd not yet revealed anything about himself ... including sharing his emotions. Apart from their intense sexual chemistry, the bonding was one-way.

"If I can finish your crest without looking at the book," she said, dabbing excess ink, "drawing ear anatomy from memory should be easy." She traced where lightning had erased the intricate design near his nipple. The muscle jumped beneath her touch. "You're certain about this?"

"Mmhm." River's response sounded strangled as she shifted position to get comfortable.

"You okay? Am I hurting you?" She glanced up from the tattoo, breath catching at the midnight that had devoured the blue of his eyes. No longer relaxed but smoky with desire.

"Never." His hands found her thighs and slid upward, bunching the windways. His thumbs found the splits and slipped beneath.

Bare skin. Electric contact.

Blood roared in Blake's ears as he stroked lazy circles on her flesh. "But don't let me distract you."

"We're almost done." Her voice remained steady, but the bamboo needle trembled when she aimed the next tap. "Though you're breathing too fast."

"Because you keep wiggling."

"I do not…" Her denial died as she caught herself mid-wiggle. Heat flooded her cheeks. Arousal pulsed between her thighs.

"See?" His fingers flexed, branding her skin. Voice dropping to gravel. "Driving me fucking insane."

Her pussy clenched at that growl. *Focus.* She had to focus. But his taut abdominal muscles bunched beneath her hands. His throat worked as he swallowed. His lingering gaze burned hotter than a summer sun.

"Almost done." Her whisper barely carried over her thundering heart.

"Good." His jaw tightened. "Because that's about all I can take."

She dabbed away the last traces of ink with unsteady hands. The restored crest gleamed against his skin, perfect and whole despite a few wavering lines from bumps in the road.

"What do you think?" She bit her lower lip.

A pure animal sound rumbled from the base of his throat. He caught her wrist and pressed her palm against his jackhammering heart, just left of the fresh tattoo.

"I think we've tortured ourselves enough, Sparkles."

CHAPTER
THIRTY-FIVE

River ached everywhere, and it had nothing to do with the new tattoo. His mate had been straddling him for the past turn of the hourglass, pressing soft curves against his chest. He'd lured her into that position as a distraction, claiming it accentuated her full breasts. But a darker part of him craved her closeness while she delivered pain.

The problem was her arousal grew stronger, too—in scent, in signs, in the way her body spoke to his. For his life, he couldn't understand why he'd tried playing the decent male before. With her palm pressed to his chest, her eyes filling with heat, her thighs clamping around his midsection … he saw nothing else, wanted nothing else, but her. Especially that slight gap between her two front teeth. He'd not noticed it before, but now that he had, all he could think of was how it would feel pressed against his skin.

"River," she scolded, tapping his jaw. "You should look at what you're getting stuck with."

"It's perfect."

"I messed it up." She winced, tracing her finger along the raised flesh of his newly inked chest. "You shouldn't have let me do this big one."

"Say big one again."

"Stop it."

"Never."

"Take a look. Please?"

Holding her palm captive against his skin, he glanced down. Stray ink marks were scattered across his chest. A wobbly line curved where it should have angled. That crow's beak looked more like a wolf's muzzle. But every time he would look down or catch his reflection, he'd remember how she'd looked above him now, how she smelled, how she smiled at him like she didn't see the cracks.

"Maybe someone else can fix my mistakes when we get to the Great Murder." Her sigh stirred the fine hairs on his chest.

"Don't you dare say that." His voice hardened. "It's my honor to be the canvas for your mistakes." He guided her finger to a splotchy mark. "When I see this one, I'll remember that first bump lifting your hips off mine. You made that little breathy squeak when I caught you."

He slid her finger to a wobbly line. "This wasn't even from a bump. I cracked a joke about you pricking me, and you laughed so hard you slipped."

She snorted. "Oh yeah."

He traced her finger down his abdomen to another spot, his voice deepening. "And this one, remember?"

She bit her lip, failing to hide her smile. "I dropped the needle, and it stabbed you."

"Mm." His hands slid up her thighs, fingers slipping

beneath the slits in her windways. "And you learned a valuable lesson on proper prick grip."

Her laugh was the sun breaking through storm clouds.

She knew nothing of his past. Nothing of nights spent drenched in sweat, heart hammering, memories of betrayal and violence clawing through his mind. The distant ones haunted him, but the recent ones—Cloud's lightning strike, the empty look in his former friend's eyes—carved deeper, demanded more blood.

If he were any kind of hero, he'd warn her about the darkness coiled inside him. But right now, all he could focus on was her pussy soaking through her pants to his, her softness squirming against his hard shaft, those plump lips forming words he craved to taste.

"Yeah." The word came out breathy as her palm slid across his abdomen. "I think we're done here."

"Tell me what's next, Sparkles."

He waited for her to recite the challenge details from memory, preferring to watch her lips shape words rather than read the pages himself.

She squirmed again, lower lip dragging through teeth as she tried to focus while he pulled her hips against his.

"Out loud," he rasped. "I need to hear you say it, need to know we won't cross lines you're not ready for."

"Four, each shares three fantasies to explore. One, a gift of pleasure your mate will adore." Her cheeks flushed.

"And?"

"Then let your primal instincts out to play, with sexual chemistry now guiding your way."

The truth tasted bitter, but she deserved to hear it. "There's a lot of space between those lines, Sparkles. The toys are just suggestions. Explore can mean discuss. Fantasy can mean a daydream. Just because it says sexual chemistry doesn't mean we have to—"

Her growl cut through his words, vibrating against his chest.

"Stop putting this off, or I'll think you're avoiding me again." She jabbed a finger against his sternum. "Don't think I haven't noticed how I've spilled me guts while you've barely whispered a word about your past." Her accent thickened with frustration. "You have to give me something real here too. Not something accidental. Something deliberate."

He'd hoped she hadn't noticed his evasions. "Am I in trouble now?"

"No." Her eyes flashed as she untied her hair, letting the cascade tumble around her shoulders. "Unless that's one of your fantasies? Being punished?"

"If by punish, you mean sit on my face, then yes. Fuck yes."

She finger-combed her hair and glanced over her shoulder at the booth, where the baskets remained beneath scattered books and tattoo supplies. "So we don't have to use what's in there?"

"Do whatever you want."

Her gaze snapped back to him. "I love it when you say things like that. Like you give zero fucks about what anyone thinks."

"All my fucks are yours."

"You say the most romantic things," she joked, but a gleam of satisfaction bled into him through their bond.

The caravan jolted over a particularly rough patch, throwing her forward. Her palms slapped against him to catch herself. Their faces were inches apart.

"I love it when you look at me like that." He groaned as

his hands found her plump bottom, kneading the flesh through silk. "Like … like you really want this."

"I do," she whispered.

He ground his erection against her core until her breathing quickened, until her lashes fluttered and her lips parted. How the fuck would he last more than two pumps after five years of abstinence? Panic squeezed his heart with icy fingers.

"What's wrong?" Hair cascaded over one shoulder as she looked down at him, concern creasing her brow.

He must have let his emotions slip through their bond. He'd been doing that more frequently lately.

"It's been a while," he admitted.

"A while for what?" Innocence colored her voice.

Had she not figured it out? He'd danced around the truth, hiding behind clever words. Maybe he'd been better at concealing than he thought. Fuck it. She wanted to know something real about him—here was his chance.

"I haven't had sex in five years," he confessed.

"Okay." She straightened and returned to clearing the tattoo supplies, methodically arranging them on a nearby plate.

His brow furrowed. "You're not bothered?"

A simple shrug. "Should I be?"

I'm so hard for you, I'm going to destroy you. "No."

"Okay, then." She flashed that devious grin of hers and slid off him, leaving him aching as she finished clearing the supplies.

Through the window, moonlit shadows whizzed past. The Great Murder's location drew closer with each passing minute. If they didn't complete these rituals soon, they'd miss their opportunity to find the cryptex. And Cloud.

River's breath caught as Blake lingered in a moonbeam by the table. Daylight screamed. It showed everything. Punched hard. But under the moon, she was still, a whispered secret. Beautiful in a way that hurt.

He saw no rainbows at night, only the echo of them. Black had softened to pale lilacs, ash, and pearl. Every strand of her hair was dipped in ghostlight. He blinked once, then again, but it didn't fade.

His chest and throat ached.

Because that was it. The moment. The reason his parents still danced in the moonlight, despite the mess.

This was his soul catching up with his body and whispering, *It's her.*

He schooled his expression as Blake brought over what she'd dubbed the kink basket with a bounce in her step. The jostling caravan tinkled the basket's contents like forbidden treasure. She arranged the toys in neat rows across the bed—first by size, then by how brightly each adorned jewel sparkled. She gave them all a razz rating, narrating her reasons, something to do with hidden gems.

He pushed onto his elbows and watched her, feeling that familiar vertigo of falling without wings. It was like that day in his youth when he'd jumped off a cliff with Cloud. And just like then, River had no idea how to survive the plunge without shattering.

Wanting something too much always came with a cost.

Blake would eventually discover he was a disappointment. He'd inevitably fuck up, and then she wouldn't look at him with such bright-eyed hope. When the ghostlight faded, she'd remember he was the reason things broke, not the one who fixed them.

"So I was thinking..." She tapped her chin, studying

their options. "I know we don't technically have to use these, but I reckon we may as well give some a go, right? I mean, when will we get a chance like this again?" Those bright eyes found his. "Okay, you go first. Tell me your fantasies."

His mind emptied like a bucket with the bottom kicked out. "Me first?"

She picked up a toy, testing its weight in her palm with a deliberate smack. "What about this one?"

He reluctantly dragged his gaze from her face and nearly choked. She wielded a long, curved dildo studded with diamonds down its considerable shaft.

He coughed. Thumped his chest. "No."

"No?"

"Sparkles, I might be open to a lot, but not that."

"You sure?" Evil glinted in her eyes as she stroked the toy's length. "We have oil and everything."

"Wait … are you serious? Is that your fantasy … to put that … in me?"

"What if it was?"

Blood drained from his face, pooling somewhere near his feet. "Then I guess..." He swallowed hard. "I guess we're here to get to know each other. Whatever you want."

"Oh my god, you dork." She snort-laughed and gave him big, watery eyes. Affection flooded their bond like warm honey. "I wasn't being serious."

"My ass is safe?"

"For now." She tossed the toy aside, prowled to him over the bed on hands and knees, and straddled his hips again. Her windways flared around her thighs as she leaned forward, hair falling around them like a silken curtain, her breath warm against his mouth. "I was just trying to break the ice."

He arched up, closing the gap between their lips. The contact fried his brain, but when she kissed him back, all slow, deep, and slippery tongue, her taste fried his entire body. If her eyes and emotions didn't convince him she was all in this, her kiss did. It was his new addiction.

"Fuck the basket," he growled against her mouth. "I only want this."

"But we have to share three things. It was specific." She pulled back to meet his eyes, but he wasn't looking. His attention was trapped by the way her swollen lips formed the perfect, O-shaped pout that made his cock throb.

"River?"

His head fell back against the pillow, and he glared at the slatted ceiling, mind racing, fingers flexing on her hips. The caravan rocked beneath them, its gentle sway mocking his internal chaos.

"Okay," he said. "Three things. Should be easy since you know nothing about what I like."

"Wait." Her finger pressed against his lips, silencing him. "I want three secret, *personal* things. Not normal things because I'll share something I've never told anyone else."

His brows lifted, a thrill dancing through his soul. Against her finger, he asked, "Not even dickface?"

"Especially not him."

Hot, possessive pleasure shot to his groin. "Personal things or sex things first?"

"Sex things." Her playful smile faded to something deeper, more serious. "But I want personal things later."

"Here's my first sex thing." He surged upright so fast that she tumbled backward, but he steadied her spine with his splayed hands. The movement inadvertently arched her back, pushing those full breasts like an offering through his tied shirt. Since their first meeting, he'd imagined countless ways to worship them, but one fantasy burned brightest.

"I want to fuck your tits," he growled.

"Really?" Uncertainty colored her voice. "But they're so…"

"Big, full, perfect?" His mind spiraled into delicious darkness. He dropped his face into her cleavage and spoke from there, voice muffled against warm, feminine flesh. "I want to lather them with oil, sit on you and fuck between them until I paint a messy masterpiece on your face." He pulled back, arching his brow. "That good enough for you?"

A blush bloomed across her cheeks. Her excitement surged through their bond.

Fuck, she wasn't just open to it—the idea turned her on. His demanding cock jerked, eager to make this fantasy a reality.

"Yeah," she breathed. "I mean … that's good."

"You next." He tugged his shirt off her, and then worked at the strappy knot behind her neck while kissing along her jaw. He whispered against her skin, "I love this game."

Blake's fingers tangled in his hair when his tongue traced the hollow of her throat. She rocked her hips against him, grinding along his shaft with little squeaking moans that made his heart race. Too many fucking clothes were in the way. The knot unraveled, and he pulled back to unwrap her like the gift she was. "Your turn, Blake."

She quickly cupped the falling strips, stopping them from revealing more.

"You still okay with this?" He searched her eyes for any hint of hesitation.

"I'm just having a hard time focusing."

His lips curved wickedly. "Of course you are. I'm irre-sistible."

"We have to reveal three first, then choose one to explore." Her gaze sharpened with delicious authority. "So, no more exploring until we're ready to choose, okay?"

"Fine." He lifted his palms in surrender, though his body screamed in protest.

"Good. Now, give me two more. I want to do this right."

Blake's bossiness ignited conflicting urges within him. He hated being submissive but loved it when she challenged him. How did that work? But the more he dwelt on it, the more he realized that he loved her pushing his boundaries, especially when it might end in her pleasure, when he gave her something she needed but never really had. That sparked deeper thoughts. The realization must have shown on his face.

"Okay, out with it," she demanded, retying the strips at her ribs. "Were you thinking of a fantasy?"

"I'm not sure," he admitted. "Maybe."

"What crossed your mind?" Her gaze softened with the kind of honest affection that stole his breath.

That look was everything. The kind that stopped the mess from touching you. He would die to keep that look in his life. He would kill—

"River?"

"Hm?"

"You were saying?"

"I like you bossing me around," he said slowly, testing his words against the truth in his heart. "But I don't like being dominated. I'm not sure what that means."

A shy smile curved her lips. "I like it when you take charge."

"Oh yeah? Like how?"

"Like when you just … you know … move me about however you want me." She guided his hands into her hair, her eyes never leaving his. "Like when you want me so bad that you grab me and…" Hesitation threaded through her voice. "Maybe even force me to do hot, sexy things to you?" That sass returned full force. "But only if you're communicating properly. And if I'm not in the fucking mood, then back off and let it go."

Amusement twitched his lips. That's all he showed on the outside, but inside, pure satisfaction and joy unfurled. His instinctive behavior had already set her on fire. He prompted, "And what else? You said there was something no one knew?"

"That was the thing."

"Oh." His gaze wandered to the toys spread across the bed.

She caught his look and laughed. "Oh, those? Ha ha. I have no idea what half of them do. But I guess you can mark me third fantasy down as exploring everything." Her eyes brightened with wicked inspiration. "Ooh, and maybe some spanking. Or dressing up. And I did like the idea of you tying me up. Even a bit of—" She bared her teeth and growled.

"What does that mean?"

"It means flip me over and then use me like a whore."

"Of course it means that."

The caravan lurched over a bump, sending several toys rolling toward them. One tumbled into River's leg—a bejeweled plug that made his blood simmer.

"Oh, no, wait. I think that was the specific thing." She scrambled off him and presented her round bottom, throwing a sultry look over her shoulder with another growl. "Call me a whore. He thought it was an insult, but hah! The joke's on him because I kind of like it. It makes me feel desired, especially when you use me like you'll die if you can't have me." Another excited gasp as inspiration struck. She crawled back onto his lap, straddling him like she belonged there. The strips had already loosened. "And I want you to choke me." Her fingers wrapped around her throat, making an exaggerated strangled sound. "Like that, and—"

"Whoa." He chuckled, placing aside the plug. "Slow down."

"Oh my god. That was too much." She covered her face with her hands. "I'm so embarrassed."

"Don't be."

"I don't know what happened. Everything came crashing out like a wave."

"You never had much chance to let loose, did you?"

He gently pried her hands away, and she squirmed beneath his gaze.

"No."

"But you want to."

A nod. A nervous lip bite that was fast joining his list of addictions. "I never had a partner willing to … spend more time with me in the bedroom than he had to."

Anger blazed through their bond—his, hers, he couldn't tell anymore. But it ignited a shared purpose that burned away their hesitation.

"That's about to change," he declared. "So I pick one of yours to explore now, right?"

"Uh-uh." She waggled her finger in his face. "Finish your fantasy list."

"I've told you my three."

"No, you haven't." She counted on her fingers. "Tits, bossy but not dominating—which, for the record, what does that even mean—and that's it."

"Licking my dripping cum off your body," he corrected smugly. "Three."

"No." She shook her head. "That was earlier today. Don't be a cunt. Tell me something specific for this challenge. Something deep."

"Hearing you say words like cunt and deep makes that impossible."

"Are you being deliberately difficult?"

"As in naughty?"

His eyebrows raised. She challenged him with those fierce eyes, a goddess refusing to yield … it made him so close to blowing he thought he might die.

"Punish me," he dared, reclining with his fingers laced behind his head.

"What?"

"If I've been naughty, punish me," he repeated, certainty slipping even as he pressed on. She'd started something kindling in his mind earlier, and now that he'd thought it a few times, it wanted out. Fuck it. She wanted to go deep? Here was the abyss. "Use sex as a weapon."

"Making you orgasm doesn't sound like a punishment."

"Oh, you precious thing." His heart swelled knowing he could still teach her about new dark desires in this world. He reached for her thighs. "There are thousands of ways to use sex as punishment. Make me come, don't make me come, sit on my face and suffocate me unless I make you come or until I spill all of my secrets, my … mistakes."

The last word ambushed him. Once spoken, it froze his limbs. His eyes widened.

He couldn't take it back. She might have believed it was a joke, except his reaction betrayed him. Terror paralyzed him. Was that really his fantasy, for Blake to wrench out painful memories he was too cowardly to voice? The answer thundered through his soul—yes. Just like her straddling him when she pricked him with the tattoo needle, he wanted to feel pleasure when he cut himself open and laid his heart bare.

The revelation squeezed his lungs until breathing became torture. What now? Say more? Say less? Pretend it never happened? His grip flexed on her thighs, his eyes fixed on some distant point beyond the caravan walls.

Each turn of the wheels brought them closer to the Great Murder. Closer to his past and all its jagged edges.

Blake cupped his face between her palms, her touch anchoring him to the present. She melted against him, her body fitting to his like it belonged.

"It would be my honor," she whispered, "to be the canvas for your mistakes. Tell me more."

THIRTY-SIX

Blake watched the change come over River. His face emptied the moment his confession left his lips. His muscles locked beneath her thighs, jaw clenched tight enough to crack teeth. He breathed shallowly through his nose, gaze fixed on a point beyond her shoulder.

"Tell me more," she urged, threading fingers into his hair.

Slowly, deliberately, she tightened her grip until his pupils dilated and swallowed the blue. When she crossed that edge where pleasure met pain, he gasped. Blake captured that sound with her mouth, pouring everything into the kiss. She used her whole body, whimpers, and moans to tell him what words couldn't. His hands slid up her bare back, and he kissed her harder in return, teeth clashing with urgency.

She broke away, panting. "Tell me."

"Sometimes I can't—" He bit off the words with a self-disparaging frown, but she tugged at his hair and he finished his sentence. "I can't share what's bothering me."

"So your fantasy is..."

"For you to force it out of me." He yanked down on her already loose strips, baring her breasts with a growl of triumph.

Wicked eyes met hers before he lifted her by the waist, aligning her nipple to his mouth. Hot, wet suction on the sensitive nub wrenched a moan from deep within her throat. Her clit throbbed, heavy with need.

"To be clear," she panted, fingers digging into his shoulders, "your fantasy is for me to force you to spill your secrets by using sex?"

"Yes." He came off her breast with a pop and moved to the next one, but Blake had heard enough. She covered his mouth with her hand and pushed him down against the pillow. His eyes flashed with indignation so vivid that she nearly laughed.

"River," she chided, eyes crinkling. "I think we need a safe word because I choose this fantasy of yours to explore, and I can tell you'll be a hard nut to crack."

He muttered an innuendo against her palm and retaliated by pinning her hips, thrusting up hard, grinding his erection into her pussy through their clothes until she whimpered, "You get to choose my fantasy next."

His fingers dug harder into her hips, but he didn't wrestle control. After a deep inhale, he nodded. Slowly, she removed her hand from his mouth and reared back.

Fear still lingered in his eyes, but something else glimmered—cautious hope. The moment hung suspended between them, filling with tension until his retreat appeared like a storm over the horizon.

"Oh no, you don't," she said, slapping her hand back on his mouth while the other worked at the laces on his pants. Like a woman possessed, she slid her hand beneath the loosened waistband and found his erection. Hot, hard, yet silky soft against her palm. They groaned in unison.

He grunted approval against her hand, and pride flooded her veins. This turned him on. Good. She stroked him, increasing pressure and speed until his eyes clouded with lust. He tried mumbling something against her palm.

"What's that?" She pulled her hand back.

"Use that dirty mouth on my cock, Sparkles." His voice dropped to gravel.

"Safe word first."

His eyes narrowed.

She stopped stroking, let go, and sat back with raised eyebrows. He looked more annoyed with himself than with her. She softened the blow by untying her windway's laces. Even though he could find his way through the side splits, the show was what he needed.

"Ah, fuck," he murmured, smoldering eyes dragging down from her breasts and avidly watching her progress. "You're a cheater."

Her careless chuckle made her realize something. Here with River, she felt beautiful, desired, and confident. With Jeff, she always felt a layer of anxiety, a need to cover herself after the deed was done, despite the sexy things he said in the heat of the moment.

"My pants come off next if you're a good birdy," she teased.

"You win at this game."

"Not a game." She swatted his hand away when he reached for her breast. "Tell me your word, and then we both feel good." At his hesitation, she added, "Just a word for now. No deep, dark secret mistakes spilled yet."

"Fine," he ground out. His eyes darted around the cabin before locking onto her hair. "My word is … rainbow."

"Rainbow," she echoed, testing the weight of it.

He nodded. The hunger in his gaze made her feel powerful and sexy enough to rise to her knees and untangle the folded fabric, stripping it from her legs. Looking down at him, she noticed his stillness differed from his usual control. He was so hungry for her that he could hardly breathe, hardly move. When he finally did, his fingers trembled as they traced reverently up her thighs.

But she still had to guess if his emotions matched his body language, which drove her insane.

"I want you to drop your block on our bond," she announced. "For good."

Blue eyes lifted to hers, that familiar animal lurking in their depths. No, he didn't like being bossed around. Not really. But fae couldn't lie. He'd admitted his fantasy. His reluctance had to be from fear.

"Suck my cock," he growled, "and maybe I will."

She laughed. "That's not how this works."

"It is if I say it is."

"No, it's not. And nice try." She wasn't concerned. He'd made no move to touch her despite his hands on her thighs. "And since you haven't said your safe word…" She walked her knees up his body until her naked thighs straddled his face. His heady, hitched intake of breath gave her the courage to grab his hair and hold him still as she lowered her hips. But just as he extended his tongue, eager for his first taste, she lifted out of reach.

"River. I'm the one in control. You're going to—oh, *fuck.*"

He struck like lightning, hands gripping her bottom to pin her against his mouth. He devoured her pussy with hungry sweeps of his tongue. Wet, tantalizing pleasure exploded through her core.

Blake gasped, panted, and struggled to see straight. She braced against the caravan's wall behind his head. She hadn't even finished her sentence, and now she couldn't remember what she'd been saying. Every flick and swirl of his tongue brought her closer to bliss, blurring her thoughts until she yanked his hair and scrambled back, whimpering at the loss.

Defiance flared in his eyes. He pointed to his glistening lips. "Get back here."

"No."

"You'll pay for this when it's my turn."

"I'm looking forward to it."

"You're so fucking perfect for me, Blake Hartley-Umbria." His grin was feral.

She returned his smile, loving how right this felt. A flash of his emotion cut through their bond—hot and fast and full of something that felt like—then nothing. Was he playing with her now? Pushing her resolve? She growled and trailed kisses down his stomach, over muscles that jumped beneath her touch. He lifted onto his elbows to watch but made no move to force her lower.

Hooking her fingers into his waistband, she dragged his pants halfway down his legs. His erection rested against his thigh, long and heavy, veins distended, crown dusky. She continued her kisses along the shaft, lifting her gaze to his face.

If this fantasy scared him, the reward would surely be worth it.

Her first taste of him jerked his hips forward.

"Fuck," he gasped. "Do that again."

She swirled her tongue around his tip and then pumped his shaft. She continued lavishing attention on his cock until his whole body quivered and he sucked in short, fast breaths, head thrown back, throat working.

Then she stopped.

"Keep going," he moaned.

"You know what to do." She squeezed his shaft. "Lower the block and then promise to keep it down for good."

"That's not fair." He scowled, thrusting into her hand, chasing more friction.

"Your fantasy was for me to force out what's bothering you by using sex. Am I wrong?"

A pause. "No, but—"

"So, lowering the block on your emotions is the first step. We're exploring."

"Fine. I'll lower it."

"But you have to also keep it down for good."

"Fuck."

"I'm not stupid, River. You're the one who told me there are many ways to interpret words. So I want to be clear." She paused. "It's okay if you change your mind. Say your safe word, and we forget this. No judgment. I just want to help."

A guilty look splashed over his handsome features, but no rainbow. This seemingly simple act caused him pain. The choice paralyzed him.

"I have an idea," she said. "What if I let you fuck my mouth or tits, or whatever you want, and when you come, you drop the block then. That way, you feel so good that you don't even feel the pain."

His jaw clenched. "Fine."

"But you need to vow now that you'll do it and not be

all, 'Ooh, my bad. The orgasm distracted me too much. I forgot.'"

"You're good, Sparkles." His lips curved. "Fuck, you're good."

"I know." She hovered her lips over the tip of his cock and glanced up at him. "Your oath?"

"With the Well as my witness, I vow that when I blow my load into your sweet little whore's mouth, I'll lower the block on our bond and never put it up again." His big hand landed on her head. "Now suck me so hard that I won't see straight."

Somewhere between the start and the end, River took control. It was less her and more him. Less stroking and sucking, more fucking and growling instructions on how to angle her throat, to lick a certain way, to swallow, to fondle. None of it mattered because she knew he'd keep his vow. She felt desired, aroused, and wanted so deeply that she writhed with need.

His breath hitched, his cock twitched, and when he tried to pull out, she realized her mistake. His vow only worked if he finished in her mouth.

Oh no, he didn't.

She relaxed her throat and took him deep. His body bowed over her, spilling hot jets of his salty release into her mouth. His emotions slammed into her like a tidal wave, stealing her breath.

Too many to decipher. All she could do was ride it out.

When it ebbed, she sat back and gingerly met his eyes. The blue burned bright enough to steal her soul. Everything about him was perfect, from his face to the wobbly tattoo over his heart.

"That wasn't so bad now, was it?" she asked, wiping her lips.

His response was a crushing flood of desire, need, and triumph through their bond.

"Safe word," he growled.

"Why do I need one?"

"Give it to me now or forever hold your peace because I'm about to make you come so often you'll forget your name." He crowded her space, easing her onto her back, prowling over her body. His teeth grazed her jaw. "Safe word. Now."

"Um." She hesitated. "I don't know."

His nibble on her earlobe made her shiver.

"I would say to use my name," he said, "because I want to be the only safe word you need. But we both know that won't work. You'll scream it every chance you get."

"Your mother mentioned another name. Before you became a Guardian?"

He reared back to look at her. "My birth name?"

"Yes." She smiled hesitantly. "I want you to be my only safe word too."

His hurricane of emotion slammed into her again, stealing her breath. But despite the angst she sensed, he didn't hide a single thing. He kept his promise to keep the block down.

"My name was Manfri. I hated it."

"I love it."

"Then remember it. Because I won't stop for anything else."

"Are you okay?" she whispered, touching his jaw. "With what I did?"

"I don't know yet," he admitted. "But I need you for this, Blake. I just hope you're not the one who regrets it."

"Manfri."

"Already?"

The look of honest confusion on his face, the disappointment, his messed-up hair, and pouty, full lips—it made her fall in love. "I'm just testing."

"You little—" His growl cut off. His mouth had better uses than words.

THIRTY-SEVEN

The caravan still rocked gently. Wooden joints still creaked in the midnight rhythm. Hooves still clip-clopped. Beads clacked.

Blake woke up from sleep, wrapped in River's protective arms. His fingers moved lazily, drawing gentle patterns across her shoulders in the dark. She had been dreaming of something she couldn't remember, but his musky pine scent grounded her in reality. What kept her anchored most was the rise and fall of his emotions stirring alongside her own, no longer hidden. When they flurried like scattered snow, she knew he sensed her wakefulness.

"I fell asleep," she murmured apologetically, rubbing her eyes.

"You did." His deep voice held a note of humor, though darker currents churned beneath. He tightened his embrace.

Their bond hummed with raw intensity. He'd opened himself to her completely, a choice that felt like their first real step toward forever. That notion felt good. Safe. Blissful.

Smiling, she slid her hand over his abdomen, watching her blue mating marks shimmer against his skin.

"Did you sleep?" she asked.

"I felt the spell on the door break." His jaw tightened against her temple.

"That's good, right?" Too awake now to temper her excitement, she grinned. "That's exactly what we want … right?"

His nod came slowly and unconvincingly. The shadows beneath his eyes deepened as he stared at some invisible point beyond the caravan walls.

"Then why aren't you happy?"

"It's not safe now." He pulled her closer. "Why are you so full of joy?"

She blinked. "What do you mean?"

"Even when you're asleep, your happiness vibrates into me." He brushed back an errant lock of her hair when she looked up at him, his throat working with unspoken words. "How can you possibly feel one thing that much that it remains while you're unconscious?"

She pressed her palm over his thundering heart. "Because you make me happy."

"Not that happy," he noted dryly. "You fell asleep after one orgasm."

She tried to hide her embarrassment by saying, "Sex isn't everything."

"You're breaking my heart."

"Har har," she said, lifting to kiss him. "I'm happy because you trusted me more than anyone else ever has. Coming down from that high might take a while."

At his silence, she traced her fingers around the new tattoo on his pectoral. It was already healed. Remarkable.

His emotions flickered. Though unsettled, she sensed no regret. Still, she had to ask.

"You don't regret what we did … do you?"

"No. Do you?"

"Not a chance." A slow smile spread on her lips. "Except we didn't try a single toy."

"You don't need one when you have me."

"So arrogant."

He rose, and the blanket slipped from his naked form.

"Where are you going?" she asked, pouting.

"Getting dressed."

"What time is it?"

"Around midnight." He glanced toward the thin slice of night visible through the window crack, nostrils flaring as if scenting danger beyond.

"How long until we arrive?"

He shrugged. "Maybe a few turns after dawn. Hard to say, depending on when the Corvus uses the portal stone."

"So we have hours." She reached for him, palm sliding against his warm skin. "Come back to bed. Get some rest."

"I can't."

"Because the door's unlocked?" She softened her tone. "River, what's wrong?"

He scrubbed a hand down his face, frown lines deepening around his mouth. "You won't feel like this forever, Blake."

"Why do you say that?"

His gaze locked onto hers. "I'm not someone you should feel safe with."

"Of course you are."

He grumbled something and stalked to the chest at the back of the caravan, pulling out his Guardian uniform. She crossed the creaking floor to his side in an instant, slamming down the lid.

She glared at him. "I call bullshit."

His jaw clenched. "I'm not in the mood."

"I can see that." Moonlight caught the sweat beading at his temple, the tremble in his fingers as he gripped his uniform.

He straightened to his full height, magnificent and imposing in his nudity. Shadows played across the planes of his body, deepening the broken tattoos.

"Rainbow," he said.

Blake's eyes narrowed at his sharp tone. "You can't just toss that word at me when you don't want to talk. It's specifically for use in the bedroom."

"I'll use it however the fuck I want."

"River," she said quietly, stepping closer, arms slipping around his waist. "You don't have to share everything. You don't even have to have sex with me." Her embrace tightened. "You can just sleep. Rest. Lie there awake if that's what you need. Just ... don't leave."

The silence stretched between them, broken only by rolling wheels crunching against dirt and trotting hooves. Finally, he cradled her face, his touch tender but resolute. "I told you that wouldn't happen."

"There's more than one way to create distance."

He exhaled sharply. "I don't sleep well, Blake. When I do ... I have nightmares. You might hear things, feel things you won't like."

She took his large hand and tugged him back to the bed nook.

"Okay," she said, "so tell me what to do if you're having

a nightmare. Do I wake you up, tuck you in tighter? What do I do?"

He stared at her as if she'd spoken in tongues. Confusion, disbelief, and something like wonder crossed into her through their bond. "You should be running in the opposite direction."

"Not going to happen. Tell me how to help." She pulled him down beside her, the mattress dipping beneath their combined weight.

"I don't know."

She tugged him down beside her and settled into the soft covers. "What did your other partners do?"

"I've slept beside no others," he confessed. Pain flickered across his shadowed features. "Unless I was on a mission, out in the wilderness or something. I rarely had nightmares then."

"Why do you think that was?" She nestled close.

He lay back stiffly, muscles coiled against her. "Maybe I was too exhausted from killing monsters and entitled floaters who defied the Well."

She drew the blanket higher over them and rested her head on his chest, listening to his steady heartbeat. "Or maybe it was because you were with people you trusted."

He stilled.

"You trust me, though, right?" she asked.

"Of course." No hesitation.

She traced a faint scar along his torso. "But Cloud broke your trust," she murmured. "And that piece of you … it's still missing."

He caught her hand. "If only it were that simple. I had trouble sleeping long before he attacked me."

"Then maybe there's no easy answer." She rolled on top of him. "Or maybe I should find a way to exhaust you."

Earlier, he'd made her come with his tongue. They hadn't had sex, and she desperately wanted to.

"Sparkles—" His warning was cut short when she parted her naked thighs and pressed down, letting him feel how wet she was.

"I know you don't want to talk about it," she whispered near his ear. "So don't. Just … take me instead."

"Blake…"

"Use me, River. Like you need me."

His palm flew to her sternum, pressing just enough to remind her who held control. But he didn't push her away. His gaze darkened as his thumb traced the hollow of her throat. He trembled with restrained hunger. She felt it simmering beneath his sadness, growing with each passing second.

They remained like that for a long moment, his hand on her collarbone, thumb swiping, testing. She idly traced the web of scars on his torso, feeling out the raised striations in the blue-washed shadows.

"Can I ask you something?" His voice was so quiet she almost didn't hear it.

"Of course."

"Earlier, you said my scars were sexy."

"Yes."

"Am I one of your projects?"

He contemplated her throat like a puzzle too complex to solve. Confusion, unease, and something else he tried to suppress kept surfacing, dragging him back to that sad place he slipped into. A question like this was rare from River, so she gave it the weight it deserved and thought hard. Her answer came when she remembered how they'd first met—what he'd done.

"When we first met, that fae tried to scare me with a story about ruthless, dangerous Guardians. Alarm bells went off in my head. I knew I was in trouble. I thought I was alone and that no one was coming to save me." She sniffed, thinking about her ex. "No one was ever going to come to my rescue. They never had. But then I heard your voice, taking my side." She frowned as the memory came back to her. "I was so lost and afraid, and here was this scarred, tatted, lethal, and handsome stranger standing up for me like no one ever has." She lifted his chin so he met her eyes. "You were the one the bad fae tried to warn me against, but I knew the moment I saw you that he was wrong. A man like you, a Guardian, receives scars from fighting for what he believes in, for protecting it. A man like that is good."

River's every muscle beneath her tensed. His shuddering breath warred for restraint as his fingers wrapped around her neck. "I'm not good."

"You're good for me. You're the only safe word I need, and I want to be the same for you. I want to be your whole world, River. Because it's safe, it's happy. It's knowing that no matter what, you have my back." She pressed her throat against his grip, voice dropping to a husky dare. "Let me fight for you, too."

"Careful what you wish for, Sparkles." His grip tightened. "You have no idea what you're asking."

"Then show me."

His eyes narrowed, feral and unyielding. "Your safe word?"

"Manfri."

The word barely left her lips before he moved, all that

bottled tension exploding raw and unleashed. He flipped her beneath him and pressed his weight down. He smothered her with his body. Violence thrummed in the air. She felt his strength, the hard edge of his control slipping as he stared down at her, his face a mask of unhinged beauty.

"Do you still want to know," he whispered, "what it's like to be a crow's whole world?"

Her nod snapped whatever thread he still held.

"No, you don't." He notched his cock against her slick entrance. "But you will." His gaze met hers, dark and unrelenting. "After tonight, you'll know."

THIRTY-EIGHT

River entered Blake with a single, powerful thrust that ripped a cry from somewhere deep in her lungs. He stayed inside her, cock buried, pinning her with a hand against her throat while she writhed, on fire, adjusting to the intrusion.

"There is only this," he growled. "Only me, deep inside you." Each whimper she made, every squirm he coveted. "So fucking deep you cease to exist, Blake." His mouth dipped to her throat. "I will possess you." Grazed with his teeth. "Obsess over you."

The instinct to fight him surged. She bucked, but his impossible grip held her firm. His musky scent flooded her senses until his declaration became a reality. Nothing existed but him, around her, inside her, everywhere. He consumed her world.

The more she reacted, the more he craved, and the more she was reminded of why she wanted him in the first place. This was the passion she'd missed her whole life.

"I will own you, Blake. Do you understand?"

"Yes," she moaned, hands mapping the corded strength of his back.

"No, you don't." Ragged, stilted breath against her neck. "Tell me."

He reared back, drinking in the sight of her beneath him like a prize, a treasure. At that moment, he appeared other-worldly—a tattooed god of darkness and pain, bound by nothing but his own burning need. She could only imagine how he'd look with his wings filling the cabin.

"You are all I think about." His fingers traced her throat with unexpected reverence, softening his intensity. "You and your Well-damned weird words." He pinched her peaked nipple, a quick, wicked tug that made her gasp. "Your filthy mouth." He lowered again to her neck. "And your heart."

Hot, wet, open-mouthed kisses down her throat made her shiver. He savored her now, drawing out each moan, each trembling gasp with unhurried exploration. His touches turned adoring as his hands roamed her body. Finally, when she was mindless with the need to feel him moving inside her, he did—long, measured strokes until she arched beneath him, begging for more.

"I'll worship the ground you walk on, Sparkles," he promised, devotion in his deep voice. "I'll give you anything you want. I'll give you the world."

Her heart swelled as his words filled empty spaces she didn't know existed. But his gentle reprieve waned. When his hand returned to her throat, there was no tenderness, only a fierce possessiveness, a beastly growl.

"Being my whole world means you'll never be free of me."

His gaze bore into her as they stared each other down,

lungs heaving, drawing ragged breath. Waiting for her safe word, she realized.

Not bloody likely.

"You don't scare me," Blake whispered harshly. "You're only turning me on."

She shoved two palms against his chest, rolling them so she was on top. She refitted his cock to her entrance and sank. A bone-deep, pleasure-soaked moan escaped her lips.

"Fuck, Blake," River groaned, eyes fluttering. "You feel so good."

"I want this," she said, voice husky. "Give it to me."

"If you change your mind," he gasped out, "I won't let you go."

"Good." She rolled her hips. "For the first time in my life, I feel caught. Like I belong."

A growl. A hard, punishing thrust up. Another spark of pleasure burst inside her body. She matched his rhythm, riding him with equal fervor until his hands locked around her waist, reclaiming control. And she let him. She fell against his chest and submitted to his pounding need. Knowing he would take care of her was so freeing.

"You're mine, Blake." A jagged snarl in her ear. "Even if you turn against me, even if you grow to hate me, pluck every feather from my wings, I still won't let you go." His rhythm grew desperate, almost frantic. Breathless. "I'll hunt you to the ends of the earth, and even then, if you refuse to return with me, if you forget,"—his voice cracked—"I will fucking end you."

He buried his face in her neck, cradling her head, and became completely still except for his ragged breaths.

These weren't a tyrant's words. They were a plea for help

from a wounded soul. She held him close, trembling from him being still buried inside her, still hard. "River?"

"There is no world without you, Sparkles." His arms banded tighter around her. "And I don't want to be left in darkness. I don't want to end up like him."

"Oh, honey." Her heart shattered for him. Tears stung her eyes at the agony he could no longer hide. "I'm so sorry."

"You're mine. *Mine.*" He reversed their positions again, fisted her hair, and squeezed her throat, reminding her how this all started, a challenge in his wild, desperate eyes. "This is what it means to be a crow's whole world, Blake. To be *my* whole world. If that's not what you want, then say it. Say the word."

Indignation flashed through her. She slapped his face, hard. But he was immovable as stone. He rose to his knees, leaving her achingly empty as he loomed above her, hands flexing at his sides, angry erection jutting before him.

After everything, he still couldn't see.

"I'm bloody-well yours, arsehole," she shouted in his face. "I'm not going anywhere."

"Blake—" His eyes widened, and his breath hitched with what looked like pain. For a heart-stopping moment, she thought something was wrong. But then his eyelashes fluttered, and he released a long, drawn-out groan of pleasure. White ropes of cum spurted from his cock. "Oh, fuck," he gasped. "Look what your words do to me."

Seconds ago, he was a god. Now, he was undone.

All this from her words.

From his desire for her.

His fear that he'd lose her.

Her with the outback trucker voice. *Her* with the saggy tits. *Her*, the woman without substance.

"I'm so fucking turned on right now," she growled.

Their gazes clashed.

"Say that again," he demanded.

When she did, he stroked his pulsing shaft to milk more from his release. Even as his strength wavered and his knees buckled, as he caught himself above her, his eyes remained locked with hers. Like she was the only thing grounding him.

And she felt it too—this intensity, this aching need that ran deeper than desire. Her hands slid over his sweat-slicked back.

"You're mine too," she whispered.

A tremor passed through his powerful frame, dark yet achingly vulnerable. It was all she needed from him tonight. She sighed with contentment and tried to gather him against her, but he settled back on his haunches with a baffled expression.

"You think we're done?" He dashed a lock of hair from his sweaty brow. "We're not done."

"We're not?"

"I said I want you dripping." He spread his release across her stomach, mixing it with swirls of the shimmering paint. "I'm going to mark you," he murmured, almost to himself. "I'm going to own every part of you."

"God, yes."

He flipped her onto her stomach and pressed her down with firm yet gentle hands that traced reverent patterns over her spine, her thighs. Each touch felt like worship.

Desire hummed through her veins as he slid backward, dragging her with him. Only her torso remained on the bed, legs dangling over the edge.

"Yep." He splayed his big hand across her lower back,

then gave her bottom a quick, biting smack. "This is mine too."

Blake sensed movement, heard his knees hit the floor, and then he parted her folds and claimed her pussy with his mouth. Pleasure paralyzed her. All she could do was clutch sheets and surrender as his skilled tongue brought her to a screaming climax, leaving her throat raw.

When her tremors finally subsided, and she lay boneless and panting, his touch disappeared. The creak of an opening wicker basket made her lift her head, but he pressed her face back to the sheets with a gentle command. "No peeking."

"More?" she whimpered.

"I warned you." A pause. "Unless you have something to say to me." Warm oil dripped onto her lower back, onto her bottom. His calloused hands worked it into every curve, every hollow. "A particular word?"

She shook her head, biting her thumb to hide her smile.

"You asked for it." He swatted her ass again, then took his time apologizing by kneading deep into her aching muscles until she groaned, blissed out. Just as she felt herself drift off, his touch slipped into the crack between her cheeks. Her pulse quickened as he gently massaged the rim of her tight back entrance, pausing again for a beat, waiting for her word. Did he forget *she* suggested trying the toys?

His oiled finger breached the first tight ring, and she moaned, pushing back into him for more.

Another nip on the pillow of her bottom to remind her who was in control. And then he owned every part of her, worshipped at the altar of her pleasure, painted a messy masterpiece all over her.

Hours later, after he'd cleaned them both and collapsed beside her, his heavy arms pulled her close and his legs entwined with hers. Peace settled over them like a blanket. The gentle rocking of the cabin was the perfect lullaby.

Only when his breathing evened out and his body fully relaxed did she allow her guarded emotions to surface—ones she'd held back, even as she screamed in pleasure.

He'd find a way to fly away if he knew how much she worried.

Her fingers traced the lightly haired area around his steady heartbeat. An undercurrent of his truth pulsed through their bond—a shadow lurking beneath his calm. His desperate need to possess her was armor, masking the fear behind his confession: *"I don't want to be left in darkness. I don't want to end up like him."*

THIRTY-NINE

River thrashed in the darkness, trapped in a storm of memory. Lightning crackled, but he wasn't its target this time. He stood on solid ground, watching Cloud spiral downward through rain, wings failing. River's arms remained locked at his sides despite his desperate need to reach out.

"You're never here when it matters," Cloud's voice warbled, distorted, like it came through water. "You never stay for the mess."

The scene shifted.

They sat at a tavern, Cloud's ale untouched.

"I need to tell you something about her," he whispered, eyes haunted.

River heard himself laugh, slapping his best friend's shoulder. "In a minute. The princeling's stuck at the bar with a handsy pixie."

FRANTIC CAWS JOLTED RIVER AWAKE. THE CARAVAN'S unnatural stillness registered first—no fake clip-clopping, no tinkling beads. Every nerve in his body sparked to life.

Danger.

He lunged for *Peacemaker* on the clothing chest, instincts primed for battle. No intruders burst through their door, but distant screams confirmed his fears. The threat lay elsewhere in the cavalcade.

Blake stirred beneath rumpled sheets. Messy hair framed her face, lips still swollen from his kisses, eyes blinking into awareness. Last night's sanctuary crumbled beneath the weight of reality, what he'd revealed to her, what he'd become in her arms. What she'd become to him.

He pressed his finger to his lips in warning. The languid heat in her eyes hardened into alertness. She clutched the blanket to her chest.

River yanked on his leather breeches, but they clung to his sweaty skin. His shirt followed, then his Guardian jacket. The caws intensified. Shouts and screams carried through the caravan's walls. He cocked his head, calculating distances. Voices echoed from too far ahead, never behind. They must be positioned near the train's rear.

"River?" Blake's voice quavered behind him. "What's happening?"

"I don't know yet." His fingers flew through buckles and ties. "Get dressed."

She nodded and dressed, her movements quick and efficient. She helped tighten his bandolier while he laced his boots. Working in tandem gave him a flicker of control until a bloodcurdling scream shattered the illusion.

River wrenched the door open and burst outside. Morning air slapped his face, sharp with pine and dew. His eyes adjusted to the dawn light as he scanned their misty surroundings. They'd left tropical growth behind. Towering pines now dominated the landscape. Ghostly spiderwebs glistened between branches. The path behind their caravan stretched empty.

Ahead, destruction carved a grotesque path. The nearest caravan lay split in two, belongings and blood splattered across trampled earth. Farther down the line, intact caravans stood abandoned, doors swinging in the breeze.

A harsh call pierced the sky. River's head snapped upward to track a crow sentinel perched high in the canopy, wings mantled with stress.

"What happened?" The question tore from his throat.

The sentinel plummeted. Air shimmered around its form. Halfway down, black feathers retracted into skin, wings transformed to arms, and a body elongated. Sera landed naked and trembling, her familiar face contorted in terror he'd never witnessed from her before.

"Sis?" His stomach twisted at her expression.

Fingers dug into his elbows as she stumbled into him. "It was the horse."

"The fake horse?" His pulse thundered in his ears.

"No—I mean yes." She choked on the words. "We found a kelpie wandering near the murder. It looked like a normal horse. Lark thought it would be perfect to pull the nesting caravan."

"Fa-*ark*." Blake's curse slithered from behind him. "So it *was* a real horse."

"Get back inside," he barked, spinning toward her.

The dark look she returned could have frozen fire. She'd dressed against the morning chill in boots, thick windways, and layers beneath her shawl. Rainbow hair flew like a red flag. One glance at her stubborn stance told him running wasn't in her plans.

"It's gone." Sera's voice cracked. "The kelpie broke free and—" Her hand slapped over her mouth as tears carved paths down her cheeks.

River's spine stiffened. Sera never cried. Not when she'd broken both wings at twelve. Not when she'd been passed over for sentinel duties. Not even when their grandmother died. She was the toughest female he knew, while Lark wore her heart on her sleeve. Dread clawed up his throat, threatening to suffocate him.

"Where's Lark?" he asked.

"Helping the others."

Air rushed from his lungs. She was alive for now.

Blake moved past him, wrapping her shawl around Sera's shoulders with murmured comfort.

"Which way did it go?" He forced his voice to remain steady.

Sera pointed past their caravan to the dense forest beyond, but something in her expression iced his blood. "Where's everyone else? Ma? Dad?"

Her face crumpled. "They're looking for the fledglings."

"What do you mean?"

"You know how they are—impossible to control, up at first light. A group snuck out to explore some passing ruins, and the kelpie…" She swallowed a sob. "It saw its chance."

River crouched to inspect the reins trailing in the dirt. Teeth marks shredded the leather. Not torn in panic, but intentionally chewed through.

"Did Ash travel with you?" Sometimes he bunked with Sera, and their casual intimacy was an open secret.

She swiped tears with trembling fingers. "He didn't want to stay. Flew ahead to the Great Murder from home."

"Shit." That meant Ash had already used a portal stone. There'd be no way he could return. River straightened, touching his mate's shoulder. "Stay in the van. Sera's going to shift and lead me to where the others went."

"Not bloody likely." Blake's chin jutted forward. "I'll go with you."

"But why aren't you shifting?" Fear sharpened Sera's voice as her gaze raked over him. "There's something wrong with your wings, isn't there?"

His muscles seized. It was only a matter of time before someone figured it out. River had only hoped it was after he'd destroyed Cloud.

But there was no time to think about vengeance or damaged wings, not when young lives hung in the balance. Ignoring the question, he sprinted into the forest, vaulting over splintered wood and scattered belongings. *Peacemaker* slid into his palm, and he stretched his senses outward for any sound or movement.

Blake's boots crunched behind him.

"Get back to the van!" he snarled.

"It's okay!" Her breath came in ragged puffs. "Sera gave me a knife."

What the fuck? River spun and snatched her wrist before disaster struck, before her blade found his gut. She'd been focused on her footing rather than the path ahead. A growl rumbled from his chest. "You can't be here, Blake!"

"Why not?" Her voice faltered despite her defiant stance.

He shoved her back, stomach clenching. "Why do you think? The van is safer."

"It's safer with you."

"I can't protect you and do my job at the same time!" Even now, her rainbow hair soaked up the sun's rays, brightening with each passing second. She might as well have carried a sign that said, "Here I am. Come eat me."

"I can help!"

"You can't." The words sliced between them. "You have no training, no powers. You're a liability, Blake. Go back."

"But…" Her eyes glistened. "You're my only safe word."

"And that's not healthy."

He'd tried to warn her. Obsession was the beginning of madness.

Another scream ripped through the forest, startling birds and insects. Winged figures darted between branches ahead.

He ran toward them, silently cursing when Blake's footsteps followed.

Three sentinels in angel form clustered ahead, their leather armor gleaming in the dappled light. He recognized Tommas instantly. He had the same unruly black hair as his brother, the same natural fuck-off demeanor carved into his features. But where Cloud burned cold enough to freeze blood, Tommas merely chilled. No wonder Lark had matched with him.

"Thank the Well you escaped the nesting spell." Relief saturated Tommas's voice. "We could use a Guardian."

River's jaw locked. No crow admitted to needing Order help unless disaster had reached apocalyptic proportions.

"Somebody fucking explain. Now." He jabbed at the bloody shirt clutched in another sentinel's hands. "How many dead? Any survivors? Where did they go?"

Each answer stabbed like a blade. Four adults dead. All fledglings were alive, except maybe one whose shirt they'd found. The mother's scream had been the one echoing through the trees earlier.

River pressed his palms against his eyes until stars burst behind his lids. "Timeline?"

The sentinels' gazes kept sliding past him to Blake, to her Well-blessed marks glowing faintly against her skin.

He snapped his fingers in front of Tommas's face. "I asked a question."

All three glared, but Tommas answered, eyes stark. "The kelpie, it just melted into water, then reformed. Impossible to fight." He shook his head. "We tried, but—"

"*Timeline,*" River repeated.

"Right." Tommas scrubbed his face. "I don't know how Lark spelled it to … right, timeline."

Another sentinel cut in. "Beast hit the caravan ahead of yours first. The sentinels on duty tried to stop it. For a moment, they succeeded. Kelpie only escaped five minutes ago."

"The fledglings?"

"Left about half a turn ago. Down by the riverside ruins."

"Fuck me." River's pulse hammered. A kelpie in water amplified its power tenfold. "How many?"

"Four."

"Search party?"

"Started a quarter turn back. No news yet."

Some relief loosened his shoulders. No news meant the children might still be safely hidden. "Which way?"

They pointed east. One last attempt. River grabbed Blake's arm and thrust her toward Tommas. "Keep her here."

She wrenched free, eyes blazing. "I'm coming with."

"Let her go," one sentinel barked, gesturing at Blake's

marks. "She's Well-blessed. Aren't they meant to boost your power?"

Having two High Fae royals mated to Well-blessed old-worlders meant word had spread throughout Elphyne. Blake's magical ability remained dormant, but her inner well overflowed. If things went wrong, he might need to tap that reservoir.

"I can't believe I'm agreeing to this." He shook his head. "Stay behind me, Blake. Shout if you see it, then get clear. Climb a fucking tree if you have to." To the others, he ordered, "Follow me."

River raced through the woods, mapping each sound and movement that didn't belong. The terrain wasn't unfamiliar. They'd roosted nearby in his youth, but the murder had abandoned this site after the ruins grew unstable. As he neared the churning river, more crows appeared—some shouting directions, others in bird form, cawing warnings from tree branches.

Evidence of the kelpie's rampage grew with each step. There were flooded patches where no water should exist, broken brush, and wounded crows drowning on dry land in both forms. River couldn't stop to check. This much destruction meant the kelpie had advanced beyond mere hunger to rage.

Despite what Sera thought, Lark hadn't trapped the creature. It willingly became their nesting caravan's steed, biding its time for the perfect feast. It likely remembered his and Blake's scent, wanting to finish what it started.

Blake had been right. She'd heard a real horse, and River had dismissed her warning with arrogant certainty. Too wrapped up in his head.

They broke free from the forest and raced toward a cliff's

edge. River dropped to his belly, inching forward to peer over. The kelpie lurked in the churning water two hundred feet below, horse-like snout and eyes above the surface. It dodged arrows and daggers with unnatural grace, slipping into liquid form whenever attacks drew too close.

Apart from Tommas, the other sentinels dispersed, likely to report to whoever commanded the rescue. Probably the fucking Domatri Corvus.

Winged shifters dove in military precision, their choreographed attacks useless against a creature that fed on water. It would never tire, never bleed, never yield—not unless a Guardian used metal to block its mana flow.

River's jaw clenched as he spotted why the kelpie lingered. Fledglings huddled inside an old storm drain near the cliff base, trapped between rock and predator. They must have fled the riverbank and managed a partial flight upward.

Aerial advantage offered the only viable strategy. Kelpies couldn't fly, their jaws only reaching so high. But the drain was not quite out of that dangerous range. If the cliff weren't so steep, the monster would have crawled up to feast.

"Don't just lie there," Tommas growled from behind. "Do something."

"I'm thinking."

"What's there to think about? Swoop down and—"

"He can't fly!" Blake shouted. "And it's your brother's fault, so shut the fuck up. Think of another way down."

The secret he'd hidden from the murder now lay exposed like a wound. River's vision tunneled. Blood roared in his ears. Centuries of respect, of authority—gone. The crows would never follow his lead now. A Guardian who couldn't fly. A joke.

Tommas's expression shifted from shock to pity.

"Tell the others I'll come at it from downriver," River said, but Tommas was already leaving. "Wait for my signal."

Black wings snapped out, and the sentinel launched without a backward glance.

River pivoted and jogged to find an access path down the cliff. If memory served right, there was an easier slope somewhere nearby.

"I shouldn't have said that." Regret tightened Blake's voice as she followed.

"It's fine." Cold sweat broke out on his skin, but he couldn't fault her for protecting him. "It was bound to come out sooner or later."

Farther downriver, the cliff face gentled into a sloping ravine. They found a narrow ledge and began their descent, jagged rock biting into River's palms. Blake moved with surprising confidence, her trust in him radiating through their bond, oddly settling his shame rather than amplifying it.

Halfway down, she gasped and pointed to an opening in the rock. "Another storm drain." Her finger swung further down. "And another. Do they all network to the same drain the children are in?"

"Probably."

"Why isn't anyone trying to enter through a different point?"

"Structure's unsound." Even as he spoke, sunrise crested the forest's edge, illuminating their precarious position. The way would become treacherous if they didn't reach the bank soon.

"Wait, are the tunnels drains or windows?"

"Both," he explained, scrabbling for another handhold.

"This cliff is an overgrown fallen group of buildings, much like at the amphitheater."

A rock crumbled beneath his grip. The sense of Blake through their bond flickered. She hissed in pain behind him, pulling her hand to her chest.

"What happened?" His gaze snapped to her.

"Touched metal." She nodded toward a square rail protruding from the rock face.

River cursed for missing it.

"I should have remembered," he said. "Cloud and I explored here when we were young. The ruins drew us in, but the abundance of metal made navigating dangerous." His gaze tracked the river's course. "Not far downstream is a waterfall. A big one."

Blake still cradled her hand.

"It's too dangerous for you to continue," he said.

She should be able to return the way they'd come without him. He opened his mouth to send her back when high-pitched screams and violent splashing erupted below.

The rescue had begun without him. Lark darted among the other swooping crows, her aerial skill unmistakable even at this distance. She must have volunteered to regain favor, to make up for her mistake. The Corvus must be seething. Sentinels renewed their attack on the kelpie while others lined up on the top of the cliff for a rescue formation, aiming to swoop close to the drain.

Shame deepened. It should be him down there.

A boy appeared at the tunnel opening, readying himself to jump. He looked older than the others, poking their heads out beside him. Maybe eight or nine years old. Scratched up. He was likely the bravest of the lot and was trying to lead by example. The bloody shirt might have been his. One wing hung at an odd angle.

River's throat tightened. This could go wrong in too many ways. The monster wouldn't fall for the distraction. The fledglings might mistime their jumps, miss the outstretched arms. The rescuers could clip their wings against the rock.

"No!" Blake's gasp echoed his thoughts.

The fledgling leaped too early, missing Lark's outstretched arms. He pinwheeled through empty air, broken wing useless against gravity's pull. If the kelpie didn't get him, the water would drag him under.

The water surged—no, the kelpie itself transformed, scattering sentinels like leaves. Teeth snapped toward the falling child with hungry precision. The circling crows adjusted their trajectory, murder hardening their eyes as they positioned themselves between predator and prey.

But Lark was closer.

Wings tucked tight against her body, she dove.

FORTY

Time sharpened into a single, horrifying choice for River. Save his sister or the boy?

In the end, he stood by and did nothing as Lark's leg intercepted the kelpie's snapping jaw, taking the hit while the fledgling fell into the river.

Cold sweat beaded along River's spine. His vision narrowed to pinpricks, blood roaring through his ears. Blood. Screams.

Blake's voice cut through his spiral. "Why aren't the others diving after him?"

He forced his gaze down to where the fledgling thrashed against the current, fighting to return to his family. Though he'd cleared the immediate danger zone, the river's fury claimed him inch by inch. A small hand broke the surface before disappearing again. Two crow shifters hovered anxiously overhead, attempting to snatch at the flailing limb, but it proved too slippery.

"Crows can't swim," River said through gritted teeth.

The rescue had begun without waiting for his signal.

Tommas hadn't trusted him to lead, and now everyone knew River couldn't fly.

"But you can, right?" Blake grabbed his arm. "You can swim?"

"I'm a Guardian…" What kind of Guardian couldn't soar through the skies? "And not exactly what you'd call sane."

He'd almost drowned once if not for Cloud. They'd later learned how to swim properly at the Order, but the skill remained rare among their kind.

"That's what makes you the best person for the job." Her voice held steady and sure, no hint of doubt. She grabbed his collar and jerked his attention toward her, eyes searching his. "I've seen you fight, River. You don't need wings to fly when you can jump."

We jump. No wings.

River studied her face. This human knew his greatest shame, yet looked at him with unwavering trust. No judgment. No pity. Just conviction.

"We can jump," she repeated, shaking the sense back into him.

He grinned. "Let's fucking do this."

"I'll go after the boy." She kicked off her boots. "You handle the monster."

She backed up, her muscles tense for the leap.

"Wait—" River caught her arm. "Can *you* swim?"

A cocky, sexy as fuck smirk. "Mate, I'm a sandgroper. Got me bronze medallion dodging sharks before other kids learned how to tie their bloody shoelaces."

"I don't know what that means, but unless it has to do with flying, you won't clear that cliff alone."

They looked down. The current dragged the boy closer by the second. His hovering parents were frantic, failing to pluck him from the water. Blake had about a minute's window to reach him before the waterfall's gravity pulled them faster than anyone could swim.

"I have to try," she whispered, and River fell deeper in love.

Calculations clicked into place. "You jump. I'll boost you with mana. One, two—"

Blake launched herself into the air, taking his heart with her. He thrust his hands forward, channeling mana into a powerful gust that propelled her further, compensating for her mortal strength. His breath held as she arced through the air.

She splash-landed right where he'd hoped, front and center, before the approaching boy.

Grinning like a maniac, he ran in the opposite direction and leaped into the unknown. His damaged wings shifted out with a snap. They couldn't give him true flight, but they could help him angle his entry.

Relief and anxiety knotted his stomach at the approaching scene. Lark was wedged beneath the storm drain's mouth, backed up against the cliff. Her windways were nearly ripped off. Blood ran dark ribbons through the water and down her leg.

Fierce respect cut through River as Tommas floundered toward Lark in the water. Arranged match or not, the male's determination revealed his true feelings.

Five seconds to impact.

Fuck! The monster lost interest in Lark.

Four.

It swam toward Blake and the fledgling.

Three.

River found *Peacemaker's* grip and angled into a dive.

Two.

The weapon split with familiar comfort.

One.

Impact. Twin crescent blades struck flesh—a blessing, considering the kelpie's semi-liquid state. Red bloomed through the water, mixing with bubbles as River submerged and swiped again for a follow-up.

He hit nothing but water.

Using mana to power his swim, he kept himself within reach as he hacked. But his third and fourth strikes failed. Reconnecting *Peacemaker*, he used his free hand to grip the beast's seaweed-like mane and concentrated on holding on. He sucked air into his lungs whenever they lifted above the surface. But the kelpie switched tactics. It knew he needed to breathe, so it dove.

They spun round and round, barrelling downward. Water crushed against his chest as they plunged. The surface light dimmed.

River clung to any solid flesh that formed, stubbornly refusing to let go. His mate—his world—would likely be dead if he did. Desperately grappling, holding on for dear life, their spiral destroyed calmer waters at the bottom of the river.

A sense of déjà vu hit him.

He'd first noticed these calmer waters the day he'd jumped off the cliff with Cloud. No mana left. No care for his safety. Angry because his best friend was growing up and falling in love ... leaving River behind.

Down here, none of it had mattered. There was only peace.

His lungs burned. Lashing pain erupted where the kelpie's morphing claws thrashed against his body. Panic tried to force its way in, but he leaned into the peace of this place and gripped harder. He emptied his mind, and an idea struck—Trix's upgrades. She'd warned him not to use too much mana. A power blast could extend farther than the shield parameters.

But that's what he wanted. If he angled it right, the kelpie's morphing body wouldn't be able to escape a hit.

Risky. Insane. Dangerous.

That's what makes you the best person for the job.

He gathered his bearings through the rotating chaos of bubbles and blood. With the Well-blessed bond, he could pinpoint Blake's exact direction. The others were the opposite.

He angled *Peacemaker* against the kelpie's liquid flesh and let go of everything holding him back. Mana surged through his arms into the chakram and exploded outward. The force of the blast rocketed him up, up, up into the open air. Gasping through the spray, he glimpsed a geyser of viscera and gore. Scattered, dismembered horse limbs hurtled in all directions.

With no time for a victory cry, he landed back in the water. He snapped *Peacemaker* to his belt and kicked off, following the direction of the current—and the bond— toward his mate. His leather uniform and weapons weighed him down like anchors, so he pumped more power into his strokes. It didn't matter if he emptied his inner well, not with Blake here to borrow from.

So long as she remained alive.

Closing the distance, he registered her lifting the fledgling to the safety of his hovering parents. But Blake's assistance ruined her rhythm. The moment the child was out, nature's fury dragged her along in its grip.

The father glanced worriedly at Blake's struggle, his hand briefly leaving his son. The extra weight caused an imbalance, and the mother's grip slipped. The fledgling cried out.

"I've got her—go!" he bellowed.

When his eyes met with the father, River was shocked to recognize the Corvus. A nod of respect passed before he returned to his family.

River's muscles screamed as he fought to close the gap, but sensing Blake's increasing panic drove him harder. She'd saved the boy; now it was River's turn to save her. The roar of the approaching falls drowned out the thundering of his heart.

His fingers brushed her arm, just missing as the current yanked her away. "Blake!"

"River!" She managed to face him, eyes wide. "Tunnels underwater—" Her words disappeared underwater.

He surged after her, gripped her wrist, and lifted her to the surface.

"I've got you," he said, holding her afloat.

"Tunnels," she spluttered.

"Where?"

"Every few meters." Another spluttering gasp. "More storm drains."

Of course, she'd noticed. Even drowning, his mate's mind worked faster than his.

The same ancient human engineering on the cliffs created a maze of underwater passages. These ruins had been some kind of amusement park in Blake's time. Most of the passages were death traps, but some weren't. During low tides, River and Cloud explored them in their youth, searching for treasure.

Water ricocheted off rocks, spraying their faces as the river became rapids. Debris struck their legs and ripped at their skin. Nothing was immune to the waterfall's pull.

In no future would they survive that drop, not even with working, drenched wings. Maybe if he shifted into his crow form, but that meant leaving Blake to die. Fuck no. The current brawled with him, but he'd been born for this—the Well had named him for this.

River relied on his friend to save him from drowning last time.

This time, he relied on himself. He summoned mana and formed eddies in the water, pushing them toward the ravine's jagged cliff face.

"Hold your breath," he roared as they neared the wall.

When a collision was imminent, he dragged them under. His shoulder took the hit against the rocks, saving Blake as he searched for their opening. *The drain. The drain. Where was it?* There—a dark splodge.

His broken wings snapped out, exploding into the water like parachutes and slowing their pace. He tucked one like a rudder and angled toward the drain. Blake fisted his shirt, her trust absolute despite the lack of oxygen. They'd been submerged for too long. His lungs burned. Hers would be dying.

Once inside the drain, he used mana to propel them away from the source. His wings pulled at the joints. Dim light glimmered ahead. Hope. He angled upward and pumped more mana. They broke the surface just as Blake's grip weakened, her presence fading through their bond.

His lungs heaved in damp air. Shadows. Space. Blue bioluminescent worms dotted the ceiling, but that's all he had time to glimpse. Nothing else mattered but the woman in his arms.

"Breathe, Blake. Breathe."

Her slack face failed to respond.

"Blake!"

Need to heal. Need to breathe for her. Terror filled him as he kicked toward the edge of their dark pool. This had to be an old maintenance tunnel, not a storm drain. His feet touched the ground. He held her afloat and breathed into her lungs. She convulsed and choked, spitting water from her lips. Wild eyes locked onto his as she gasped.

"You're alive," he croaked. "We're alive."

She threw her arms around him, legs too, clinging like a bear, sobbing into his neck. Cupping her head, River waded through the last distance and lifted her onto the dirt platform. Then, with her help, he hauled himself up beside her.

They collapsed side by side, facing each other. He felt so heavy. Barely had the strength to rest his hand on her shoulder, but he needed to touch her. Needed to be sure she was there.

Only then did he allow himself to close his eyes and silently thank the Well for wanting what it wanted.

FORTY-ONE

Jagged, burning throbs of pain forced River's eyes open before he was ready. He tasted copper and river silt, felt hard dirt against his cheek, and registered a steady drip of water. Each breath dragged in the scent of minerals, old paper, and something else he couldn't name—something familiar that skittered at the edges of his memory.

He inhaled, and pain stabbed him beneath the ribs. The kelpie's claws had cut deeper than he'd realized. Blood pooled beneath him, sticky and warm.

"River?"

"Still alive, Sparkles," he croaked, throat raw from swallowed river water. He forced a confident smirk onto his lips. "Wouldn't leave you alone in this shithole."

Relief softened Blake's features. She kneeled beside him, hands cupping his jaw.

"Thought I'd lost you for a minute."

"Takes more than a pissed-off water horse to kill me."

He surveyed their surroundings for the first time since awakening. They'd washed up in some kind of underground chamber, larger than any storm drain he'd ever seen. He'd thought it might be a maintenance tunnel, but now he wasn't so sure. Smooth stone walls curved overhead into a domed ceiling crawling with glowworms. "Help me stand."

Blake slid her shoulder under his arm, and together, they staggered to their feet. The world tilted. Darkness crowded River's vision. Her arm locked around his waist, steadying him with surprising strength.

The chamber stretched into shadows beyond the small pool where they'd emerged. Not just glowworms. Blue light emanated from phosphorescent fungi clinging to walls, casting shifting shadows with their movements. Stone shelves had been carved into the rock, bearing objects River couldn't immediately identify.

"What is this place?" Blake asked, voice hushed with wonder.

"Part of the farm park ruins—"

"Fun park?"

"Yeah, that." His words felt thick, copper-coated. "Storm drains are sometimes connected to maintenance tunnels. Maybe."

Blake guided him toward a flat stone surface that might have once been a bench. "Sit before you fall."

"Bossy," he grumbled, but sank gratefully. His patchy wings drooped behind him.

"Someone has to be the sensible one." She wrung water from her hair. "And considering I'm not the one needing help to stand, that's me."

"Your heroics have gone to your head."

"Maybe they have." Something fierce crossed her face, a certainty that struck him silent. "I saved that kid. Me."

Pride—vibrant and deep—surged into him. "You did."

"*Me.*"

He grinned.

"Oh no. Not again." She covered her mouth, eyes widening, and lurched toward the water's edge. She vomited water and bile into the pool they'd emerged from.

He winced, pushing himself halfway up before his body rejected the movement. "I'd help, but I can't move."

She waved him down between heaves. "I'm good."

"You puke a lot."

"Wish I could say it's new," she managed, sucking in deep breaths. "Me brothers loved finding new smells and textures to test me gag reflex." She retched again. "Always been easily triggered."

River slumped, fighting a wave of dizziness. "I think it's safe to say we won't be exiting the same way we arrived. Not for a while."

"Gross." Another deep inhale. "I think it's passed."

"Come here."

She stumbled back to him on shaky legs, dropping to her knees beside the stone bench. His fingers tangled through her wet hair, and she instantly rested her cheek against his thigh, eyes fluttering closed.

"You good?" he asked, stroking her hair.

She moaned and nodded. "Two feet and a heartbeat."

A smile tugged at his lips. "You've said that a few times."

"Dad used to say it." Her eyes opened, fixing on the ceiling. "After Mum died."

"You miss your family."

"Yeah."

"I'm sorry."

Her eyes snapped to his, widening. "You just gave me a debt. Right?"

"Maybe." His eyes crinkled at the corners.

Something shifted in her expression, shadows darkening her gaze. "You said I'm a liability."

Fuck, he was a bastard. "I'm sorry about that, too."

"You said it wasn't healthy to want to be with one person too much."

"It's not. But you're mated to a crow. We're all unhinged like that. I guess." He paused, guilt churning in his stomach. "I fucked up, Blake." He twirled a strand of her hair, hunting for the last of her rainbow before it faded beneath river silt. "I do that a lot."

"You were right," she whispered. "I am a liability."

"You just saved a child's life."

"And almost killed you in the process." She sighed, gaze drifting back to the ceiling. "But he's alive."

His vision blurred at the edges, wounds demanding attention. He needed to shift soon or risk passing out.

"When we get out of here," he mumbled, "remind me to thank Trix for that weapon upgrade."

"When we get out of here," Blake countered, "remind me to thank the Order for teaching you to swim."

"Guardian training." He snorted. Then paused. "Or possibly further back when my idiot friend and I jumped off a cliff without wings."

"Cloud?"

"Yeah."

The name hung between them, laden with unspoken history—Cloud, who'd saved River from drowning that first time. Cloud, who'd taught him to throw a dagger properly because Talo was too much of a pacifist. Cloud, who'd been there for every stupid adventure until…

Guilt twisted through River as he recalled his nightmare

this morning. Had he ever been there when Cloud needed him? Or had he turned away, too caught up in easy distractions?

"You two were super close, huh?" Blake's question pulled him back from the edge of memory.

He nodded, grateful she didn't push further.

"River, you're bleeding!" Blake pushed herself upright. She peeled back torn leather at his ribs. "A lot."

He winced. "Might have taken a few hits from the rocks."

"That's not from rocks." Her face paled. "These slashes—I can see bone."

"Oh yeah. That." He tried to smile but failed. "Kiss the boo-boo?"

"River, it looks bad."

"I'm fine."

"You're not."

"I just need to shift, that's all." He struggled upright, blinking against dizziness. "And I might need to borrow your mana if that's okay. I'm low."

She shrugged. "I can't use it anyway."

He nodded, strengthened by her easy acceptance but also concerned. "One last thing: Don't, under any circumstances, cuddle me."

"Why?"

He arched a brow. "Because I'm a big birdy now and too old for coochy-coos."

"But not boo-boo kisses?"

"Never."

Blake's chuckle finally lit up her face—exactly what he'd intended. She shuffled back, lowering to her haunches.

He hesitated. It was one thing for her to see his patchy wings, but another to witness a mangy crow missing chunks of feathers. Still, she was his mate. If not her, who could he trust with his crow form?

Inhaling deeply, he sank into the Well's embrace, letting mana pull away the parts he didn't need. Fire scorched through his veins, illuminating every wound with excruciating clarity. Blake was right—he'd been ignoring the severity of his injuries. Darkness crushed him as his body compressed and was caught within his uniform's confines.

He cawed in frustration, struggling against wet leather until he finally emerged. Freedom at last.

Two wide eyes and an excited face greeted him. Blake planted her hands on the floor and leaned forward, her dripping hair framing her face. "You're so bloody cute!"

Before he could escape, she scooped him into her arms and pressed him against her chest. He squawked and flapped, but when she scolded him for scratching her, he folded his wings and surrendered. The last thing he wanted was to cause her more pain.

"That's better." Her fingers found a spot behind his neck, scratching gently. "Such a good little birdy. Yes, you are."

He cawed in protest, dignity crumbling.

But her fingers felt too good, and when she pressed him closer to her cleavage—well, the view suddenly held compelling advantages. Warmth seeped through his feathers, and he leaned into her touch, allowing himself this guilty pleasure.

Her finger brushed a wound, and he squawked in surprise.

"Oh no, River, you're still bleeding." She placed him gently on the floor. "Do you need to shift again? I wish I could help. I'm so bloody useless."

Blake climbed to her feet, hugging herself as she turned

away. The desolation in her posture carved through his thoughts. Making her feel needed, wanted, and valuable rocketed to the top of his priorities.

He surged back into fae form, wings snapping out for balance. The shift had helped close his wounds, though the deepest gashes were at risk of rupturing. Exhaustion clawed at him, but seeing Blake's dejection hurt worse.

She wandered deeper into the chamber, trailing her fingers along the stone wall. The blue glow intensified wherever she touched, following her movements like a living thing.

"There's something weird about this light." She frowned, examining her fingertips. "It's reacting to me."

"Probably the Well-blessed mark." He dressed slowly. "Your abundance of mana likely makes them glow brighter."

"That's ... kind of amazing." Wonder filled her voice as she explored further. "And comforting. Wait, there's something on these walls farther in."

As the light brightened in her wake, River noticed markings on the stone weren't random cracks, but deliberate lines, symbols, patterns. Something cold slithered down his spine. He knew those markings.

"These aren't natural." Blake's fingers traced an intricate spiral. "Someone carved these."

His throat constricted.

"Blake." His voice emerged sharper than intended. "Come back here."

She ignored him, moving deeper into the chamber.

Shit. He quickly finished dressing, shoving on his boots but leaving his bandolier behind and his jacket open. He clipped *Peacemaker* to his hip.

"There's another tunnel ahead. I see more light." Her

voice echoed back to him. "And something else—papers? I think there are papers on the walls."

"Blake!" He surged forward, ignoring fresh pain. "Don't—"

"I'm fine." Her voice drifted from around the corner. "There's a whole other room here. It's bigger, and—"

Silence dropped like a stone.

River stumbled forward, one hand pressed against his ribs, the other trailing the wall for support. As he approached the tunnel mouth, the markings grew more elaborate, no longer simple lines but complex diagrams and formulas. Dread mounted with each step.

He found Blake standing frozen in the center of a vast, circular chamber, surrounded by thousands of glowing marks that covered every surface. Papers had been pinned to the walls in obsessive patterns, diagrams, and equations spanning centuries of work. Tables around the perimeter held artifacts and trinkets—old-world technology, Guardian weapons, and things he couldn't immediately identify.

"River," she whispered, not turning. "What is this place?"

Words and patterns marked in UV ink glowed softly, adding to the bioluminescence. The meticulous organization, the precise calculations: he'd seen it all before, in a childhood hideout they'd discovered once together.

"This isn't a maintenance tunnel," Blake continued, voice wavering. Her attention was caught by something across the chamber.

River followed her gaze to a massive diagram dominating the far wall, a detailed rendering of a woman. Red lines traced her nervous system, blue lines her veins, and green lines her lymphatic pathways. Beside it hung a gallery of sketches—the same woman in different poses, captured with obsessive precision.

Not River's style of art. Something more than skin deep.

Blake approached the central image slowly. "She's beautiful."

"She was," River agreed.

"Was?" Blake turned, confusion furrowing her brow. "You know her?"

"Her name was Aurora. Also known as Rory, Cloud's…"

He couldn't find the right word to explain her, so he didn't.

Blake faced him, her expression shifting from confusion to dawning horror as she absorbed the obsessive detail of the chamber around them, the years of collected research, the shrine-like quality of the space.

"Cloud fell in love with her, didn't he? A human?"

"He didn't just fall for her," River said, the truth settling around them like stone. "She consumed him."

They hadn't stumbled across an old maintenance tunnel. They'd fallen into Cloud's secret trove—his obsession lay bare.

FORTY-TWO

CIRCA 200 YEARS AGO

Manfri kicked aside a discarded bottle. He flinched at the clatter that struck a dozen more pieces on his bedroom floor.

Three days of hard drinking had left him numb, which was the point. No dreams meant no guilt. And if the dreams came anyway, another bottle waited.

His mother had stopped knocking, stopped asking if he'd join what they pretended wasn't a party outside—just another observation of lunar phases or some shit. From his window, he watched his family gather beneath strung lanterns in the roost's central clearing. Moonshine flowed. Laughter rose. Life continued despite the gaping absence beside him.

Two empty spaces where friends should be.

Cielo gone.

Nikan gone.

One crow missing for months in human territory, the other fed up with Manfri's descent into self-pity.

"Eat a fungus-crusted dick, Nikan," he muttered, eyeing the space on his forearm—the very place they'd sworn would keep *them connected forever with a triad tattoo. Forever blank, mocking his weakness.*

The morning after Nikan had departed for Cornucopia, Manfri woke with resolve burning through his hangover. He told himself that day would be different, that he'd travel to Crystal City, over desecrated ground where no fae belonged. If Cielo could do it, so could he.

How he'd been wrong.

At the wasteland where tainted land met the blessed, Manfri made it three steps before collapsing. Blood boiled in his veins. His lungs refused air. His wings writhed against his back, feathers trying to retreat into his flesh. He crawled back to the nearby dead forest's shelter and vomited until nothing remained.

Three heartbeats. Three fucking steps.

Cielo had been gone for weeks by then.

Manfri had stopped counting days, remembering only moments: that final argument when he refused to acknowledge the secrets in his friend's eyes. The tightness in Cielo's voice when he mentioned his human lover. How Manfri had rolled his eyes, changing subjects rather than risking the truth—that he feared being left behind.

Now, a decade later, he'd been left behind anyway. He lifted his father's moonshine to his parched lips and savored its burn, secretly hating the momentary solace it brought. The sting felt righteous, a deserved punishment for his cowardice.

The only solace that felt good was knowing Cielo must be happy with his human. Why else would he stay for so long?

Movement outside his window.

Manfri stumbled over and peered out into the first rays of dawn cracking the amphitheater's horizon. A shadow dropped from the sky and struck his nest's balcony floor with a wet, sickening thud.

A crow.

Not the glossy, healthy black bird from his murder, but a creature more bone than flesh. Raw, bleeding skin stretched over fragile wing bones. Its remaining patchy plumage hung dull and brittle, lacking the identifying iridescent shimmer all crows should possess.

He stepped outside and froze. His bottle slipped from numb fingers and shattered at his feet. Crimson puddles formed beneath the bird with each shallow breath. It shuddered, one wing twitching in weak, abortive attempts at movement.

The bird's beak parted, releasing a strangled caw that sliced through Manfri's drunken haze. He dropped to his knees, reaching with trembling hands.

Everything in him recognized what his mind refused to accept, until dawn splashed its first light across the balcony, bringing to life the unmistakable UV patterns he knew like the back of his hand. The crow lifted its head and fixed Manfri with familiar eyes.

"Cielo?" The name emerged broken, disbelieving.

The bird's head dropped and paved the way for light to reveal something clutched in its bloodied claws—a dark strand of hair with a distinctive curl. Colors shimmered across its surface like an oil slick.

Manfri knew that pattern. Had once seen Cielo rotate it beneath the sun. It must belong to her.

His stomach lurched. "You circled back."

Something flickered in the crow's eyes—recognition, pain, something more complex that Manfri couldn't decipher. The twisted remains of one foot uncurled, allowing the strand to drift into his palm.

All these years, Manfri had thought Cielo had eloped.

"She did this?" He couldn't keep the rage from his voice.

The bird's eyes fluttered closed. Its head slumped against Manfri's palm.

Carefully, he gathered the broken creature against his chest, wings falling protectively around them both as he carried his friend inside. Blood seeped into his shirt as he lay the crow on his bed, placing the precious strand of hair in a small wooden box on his nightstand.

"I'll fix this," he vowed, voice rough with emotion. "I'll make it right."

THE WEEKS BLENDED TOGETHER, MARKED ONLY BY THE PATTERN *of Manfri's failed attempts to heal his friend. He tried everything— salves stolen from his mother's supplies, ancient restoration rituals performed at dawn and dusk, begging the crow to shift back to fae form. Nothing worked.*

Cielo's wounds closed but never truly healed. He remained in crow form with raw patches forming scars that refused to sprout new feathers. The first three days, he refused food and water until Manfri resorted to mixing broth with healing herbs and feeding it drop by drop from a dropper.

"Hey fuck face, remember when we stole that ox shifter's prize mushrooms?" Manfri talked constantly, filling the silence with memories. "He chased us halfway to Cornucopia before his breeches fell down." He laughed, the sound hollow in the stillness of his room. "Or the time we convinced Nikan that moonberries would turn his skin purple, and he avoided them for a year?"

No response. Just empty, haunted eyes tracking his movements.

Manfri's kettle had noticed his absence from their gatherings, but he'd fabricated excuses. Currently, there was a note pinned to his door saying, "Advanced hangover underway, leave food outside."

Ravi left healing drafts that he promptly fed to Cielo. His sisters tried picking his locks until he threatened dismemberment. Talo stood outside his door each evening, lecturing him about venereal diseases.

On the fifth day, Manfri began to paint.

"You need something to look at besides my ugly face," he explained to the silent crow.

Midnight blue paint stained his fingers as he worked, sketching three young males—himself, Cielo, and Nikan—clustered around a Wellhound they'd hunted. Nikan had taught them all the tricks for a swift and speedy dispatch. They'd saved their murder from being overtaxed by the Order that year. His brush captured each memory with obsessive precision: the way Cielo's head tilted when proud, how Nikan checked every shadow twice, Manfri's own cocky stance and glorious blue-tipped wings.

Each brushstroke felt like atonement. Each completed scene, a prayer.

"Remember this?" he asked as beige wings emerged beneath his brush. "First time you outflew that owl patrol by diving through the waterfall." He chuckled, adding shadows to the cliffside. "You looked like a half-drowned rat, but so fucking proud of yourself."

Sometimes, when Manfri painted late into the night, he caught the crow watching with fragments of recognition flickering in its gaze. Other times, it stared at the strand of hair as though drawn to a flame both mesmerizing and deadly.

On the fifteenth day, Manfri tried one last desperate measure. He created a trail of trinkets—shiny buttons, glass coins, polished gems—leading from his nest to the waterfall pool behind his kettle's roost. It was a source of power. If ordinary water couldn't heal Cielo, perhaps the Well's direct power might.

"The source is pure, Cielo," he called, dropping shiny objects between rocks and roots at midnight. "Come and see the shinies I found for you."

He jogged back to find the crow still motionless on his doorstep, unmoved by treasures that once would have sent him diving with delight.

Not dead.

Just lost the will to live.

On the eighteenth day, the crow finally shifted.

Manfri had fallen asleep at his mural, brush slipping from limp fingers. He woke to a hoarse scream ripping through the stillness.

"It burns!"

He launched toward the sound, bare feet slipping on discarded brushes. Cielo thrashed on the floor, his emaciated human form twisted as he fought invisible attackers. His skin bore the same scars as his feathers had—pale patches where flesh had healed wrong, patterns of systematic torture.

"Cielo!" Manfri reached for his friend's shoulders, dodging flailing limbs. "You're safe. You shifted. You're safe."

Wild eyes found his, recognition dawning gradually through pain and confusion. Cielo stilled, chest heaving with shallow, panicked breaths. He clutched Manfri's arms hard enough to bruise, nails drawing blood.

He tried to speak, but his voice was shredded from disuse.

Manfri scrambled for a cup, returning to find Cielo collapsed against the wall, staring at his hands with blank incomprehension. He accepted the water with trembling fingers, drinking in desperate gulps that left him coughing.

"Slow," Manfri cautioned, steadying the cup. "You're safe here."

Cielo's gaze finally focused, taking in his surroundings—the paintings covering the walls, the scattered art supplies, the wooden box on the nightstand holding that single strand of hair.

"You came back," Manfri whispered.

Cielo's expression remained fixed, empty of everything but exhaustion. He slumped forward, and Manfri caught him, easing him toward the bed.

"Rest," he urged. "We'll talk when you're stronger."

That night, Cielo's nightmares began.

Manfri woke to screams unlike anything he'd ever heard—raw, animal sounds torn from a throat that had witnessed horrors beyond imagination. He thrashed against tangled sheets, fighting invisible restraints while howling the same word repeatedly.

"Stop, stop, stop."

Manfri ran to him, pinning his arms before he could tear his healing wounds open. "Wake up. You're dreaming."

The struggle continued until Cielo's eyes snapped open, vacant with terror. Sweat plastered his overgrown hair to his forehead, his skin burning with fever.

This pattern repeated for days. Cielo would wake, drink water, refuse food, then collapse into tortured sleep. Occasionally, he'd watch Manfri paint with hollow eyes, his silence more damning than any accusation.

In those quiet moments, Manfri's rage grew, directed not at Cielo but at himself. He should have listened. Should have followed sooner. Should have recognized the danger of a human stealing his friend's heart.

"Tell me," he finally begged during one of Cielo's more lucid moments. "Tell me who did this. We'll call every crow we know— Nikan, Carmine, and Tommas. Your father. My family. We'll call *them all and rain bloody murder from the sky. On them, on their descendants." He gripped Cielo's shoulders. "Just say the words, and we'll paint your enemy's blood on our faces."*

"No," Cielo croaked. His fingers flexed against the blanket, knuckles whitening. "Her death belongs to me."

Her. The only confirmation Manfri needed.

Manfri nodded, understanding blooming between them. He wouldn't push. Wouldn't question. His friend had claimed this vengeance, and he would honor it.

But he would help. Would strengthen Cielo for the battle to come.

"I'll make you strong again," he promised. "We'll make Aurora pay."

Something flickered in Cielo's eyes then. Before Manfri could decipher it, the moment passed, and exhaustion reclaimed his friend.

FORTY-THREE

Entering another crow's trove violated more than privacy. It peeled back layers of their soul, exposing every secret they'd collected across centuries. Treasures, memories, and dreams they dared whisper only to starlight were all gathered in one sacred space. Trespassing didn't just break some unwritten rule. It sliced open their heart and devoured it raw.

If Cloud discovered River and Blake there, lightning would be the kindest punishment he'd deliver.

They should leave.

Yet, River couldn't help thinking that they had a little time. Cloud had likely departed for the Great Murder already. He wouldn't return soon. Besides, it wasn't as though River had deliberately sought out this place. The river's fury had chosen their path, almost as if it wanted them here.

"What is this place?" Blake's words bounced off stone walls.

A single mattress with a rumpled blanket at the chamber's center was the only functional furniture.

"Cloud's trove." River kneeled and pressed the blanket to his nose. His friend's scent flooded his nostrils—ozone, rain-soaked earth, and woodsmoke.

"Over here." Blake beckoned River closer. "I think this is where it begins."

Walk away. Don't look.

He shuffled to her side. "How can you tell? It's chaos."

She gripped his arm and pointed to trinkets dangling from a taut string. "These look like a child's treasures. See the crude craftsmanship?"

River lifted a dangling stone dagger carved in the shape of a feather. Dried blood still crusted its porous edges. "A remnant from our Blooding Ceremony."

"What's that?"

"A coming-of-age ritual. Juvenile crows face a series of challenges to earn their place as adults in the murder." River pulled aside his jacket to reveal a tattooed dagger covering a pale scar. "He stabbed me here to win. Classic Cloud—always first."

"He sounds awful."

A small, bittersweet smile touched River's lips. "He's not. Just competitive. I'd have done the same. I think I even have a similar memento in my trove."

"You have a trove too?"

Heat rushed to his cheeks. "Maybe."

"Will I get to see it?"

He wanted to say no. He'd never planned on having a mate, so his trove was embarrassingly personal. And bare. He was a bit of a romantic in his youth. Looked up to his parents far too much. Painted a few embarrassing things on the walls. Couldn't decide what was worth keeping and what was worth tossing. Then, after Cloud's betrayal, River had stopped going there altogether. Stopped caring.

"Shit, you're blushing."

"It's personal, that's all."

"This place is too." She touched a trinket with a child's drawing on it. "It's nice when you think about it. Photographs just aren't the same. What I wouldn't give to revisit objects from me past—Mum's makeup brushes. Dad's hammer. I'd feel less alone."

She sniffed.

"Are you crying?" River asked.

"I'll stop." She wiped her nose.

He hooked a finger under her chin and brought her eyes to his. "Do whatever the fuck you need to do to feel better, Blake."

"Do you ever take your own advice?"

He smirked, let go, and faced the darkness. The weight of her stare remained with him a little longer before she asked, "Should we leave?"

"Probably, but … it can't be a coincidence we found this place. The Well has an interesting sense of timing, and…" He thought about all the times he had feelings and intuition that were validated. Rory, for one. He'd always known something was off with her, that she'd break Cloud's heart. And the moment he'd seen that shadowy figure flying after the retreating airship five years ago, he knew Cloud was about to break her.

"And?" Blake prompted.

"And I sometimes wonder if I've got a touch of psychic powers. My mother was almost the Donna before she eloped. I'm sure you noticed the chin markings and how she reads auras. The point is, if we're here, the Well wants us to see something."

The bioluminescence wasn't bright enough to see clearly. Cloud would have prepared another light source. He focused on his connection to the Well and sent his awareness outward. Nearby, he felt the telltale buzzing of a concentration of mana. He crossed to the shadowed wall and peeled back a tattered, dusty tapestry to reveal a lever attached to a pipe. He held his ear to it, and the buzzing amplified.

"This must be it." He pulled the lever, opening a valve, triggering a whooshing and tinkling sound through the pipe. Two seconds later, light erupted around the room as lanterns around the trove filled with escaping manabeeze.

"Whoa," Blake blurted as previously invisible UV scripts blazed across every surface. Cloud's handwriting grew more frenzied deeper in the chamber.

River's people believed that if a circling crow's shadow touched theirs while they were grounded, they were marked for an unlucky life. They never left home without shiny objects on their belts for this reason. Distracting a circling crow prevented their shadows from crossing paths.

At the ripe old age of ten, River had once spent a weekend terrorizing his murder from above, casting his shadow over the grounded just to watch them scatter like mice. His kettle's low social status had barred him from a stupid event he couldn't even remember now. But he'd retaliated by seeing how many destinies he could ruin.

Every single target shone their shiny in his face. All except one.

River had found Cloud sitting alone, nose bleeding from his father's fist—punishment for attempting to join a Gathering before he was of age.

When Cloud didn't react to their shadows crossing paths, River shifted into fae form and berated him for inviting trouble.

"What's the point?" he'd replied, sniffing through his bloody nose.

"Fuck your dad. Do what you want."

"It's not that easy."

"Everything's easy with someone to watch your back."

They'd sketched plans in the dirt, seizing control of their destinies, laughing off shadow-crossing superstition. But now, seeing the evidence of Cloud's madness in chaotic discord on the ruin's internal walls, River feared they'd been wrong.

So very wrong.

"What's this?" Blake whispered, indicating papers pinned beneath a blue feather. "Are these yours?"

"That's the stupid stick we used to plan out our first heist in the dirt on the day we first met." His fleeting smile died as his gaze landed on another item: an old, hand-drawn map. "He's the most meticulous planner. He thought of every variable before he made a move. It's why I've always trusted him, always followed him when he led us." River cleared the emotion from his voice and tapped a circled mark on the map. "Here's where he recovered during his conditioning. He knew breaching Crystal City meant enduring separation from the Well. He tested his limits by flying toward the city until the severing drove him back. He'd collapse, sleep, then start again. He was twelve. I couldn't even do it when I was an adult."

"All that pain. Just to steal something?"

"Blake," River chided. "There is no *just* when it comes to thieving. Only glory. But to be fair, I think Cloud overcame the pain because he wanted to prove his father and older brother wrong."

She snorted. "And I thought me brothers were stubborn."

Memories cluttered every surface, hanging from threads, perched on stools, pinned to walls, or scattered across the floor.

Among the artifacts, a set of bamboo needles caught his eye.

"It's his life's museum," Blake murmured, reaching for a leather-bound volume.

"In chaos."

"Not to him."

A letter fell out of the book when she opened it. River picked it up, hesitated, then unfolded it. A childish scrawl filled the page.

Crow Boy,

I put an orange lantern in my window like I promised! Did you see it? I found more crystal animals—a giraffe this time. Do you want to trade? I have so many questions about Elphyne.

From,

Your Friend in the Tower

P.S. You forgot your dagger. I named it "Sparkles" instead of Murder. Much prettier, don't you think?

"Aww." Blake tapped the letter. "She called it Sparkles. Did you know when you gave me the nickname?"

"No."

A sense of unease prompted him to fold the note. He didn't want to read anymore. He returned it to the book, taking it from Blake and closing it with a snap. Dust bloomed. When it settled, he realized it was stupid to ignore the letter. A thousand more were fixed to the wall in various shapes and forms. Some stuck to string, others folded into animals, and simply tacked on. He stalked to the next letter, shoulders rigid as he read.

Hello, Treasure Hunter,

The guards changed their patrol route, but I've mapped their new pattern. Two bells past midnight, the east wall is clear. I have something special to show you—an old book about wings. The drawings remind me of your friend's pretty blue. He might like this book.

Your Little Song Bird.

River's upper lip curled. He'd always known Cloud spoke to her about him and Ash, but seeing it in her handwriting made his skin crawl. She might have sounded sweet here, but he knew how things turned out.

Over a century had passed, but River still remembered the sickening thud of a featherless crow landing broken and twitching at his feet. His hands still felt the trembling, fragile body. His soul still cried when it replayed the moment he recognized Cloud's eyes staring back at him—the friend he'd thought eloped, the friend he'd given up on finding, the friend he should have tried harder to find.

Above them, pale threads dangled in intricate patterns.

Glowworms crawled down each strand, illuminating what initially appeared to be a child's mobile. A closer look revealed darker elements like braided bloody feathers, with black and white bound together. Under UV light, they transformed into swirls of green, pink, and purple. A mana-preserved photograph hung from one thread. He gasped when he recognized the faces of Maebh, Aleksandra, Nero, and young Aurora all posed together before an old-world vehicle.

A letter dangled beside it, handwriting catching the light:

> Dearest Cielo,
> I found a picture in my father's locked drawer. Meet me in the garden tonight. I need to see your face when I tell you everything.
> — Aurora

Star maps covered the next section of the rocky wall. Old-world constellations aligned with modern fae patterns, each compared and analyzed with Cloud's meticulous hand. A letter was nestled among them:

> My Midnight Prince,
> The thought of you fills every quiet moment. When you're gone, I trace the constellation patterns we learned together. I pretend we're still flying above the trees. Father grows more suspicious each day. But he can't cage my spirit—it soars with you,

always.

Forever, Your Star Gazer

River's chest constricted. Another note waited:

Hey, You,

Meet me at our usual spot. Father's guards change shift at midnight. They're so clueless. It's almost too easy. I've learned a new trick with mana that will make you smile.

— Love, Me.

"They wrote love letters. That's so cute." Blake touched the wall.

"Cute?" he snarled. "She manipulated him from the start."

"I don't…" Blake's voice softened. "You still haven't told me the details. Not really."

Rage roared in his ears, choking his response. He strode deeper into the trove, each discovery a fresh wound. These mementos aligned with Cloud's happiest moments, including River's first draft sketch of their triad tattoo on a tavern napkin.

The farther he went into the trove, the heavier the air became with blood, mold, urine, and decay. White, spindly shapes covered the far wall. River's lungs fought for air, but he pressed on. He had to see. If only to understand, to know the path of madness, especially if he wanted any hope of avoiding it himself. But there were too many letters, too many notes written in Cloud's handwriting on the wall. And over it all, in any free gap, more words that made no sense. Fly. Trees. Seas. Away. Please.

A flash of red caught his eye, stopping his heart.

He moved to the wall like a moth to a flame, his hand landing beside a picture frame without glass. The empty chalk outline of a shape was inside. Something cylindrical he recognized should have been there. The cryptex. He knew it with all certainty because in its place was the ruby Cloud pilfered from the Collector. River thought they'd spent that on clothes for Ash. But perhaps he'd assumed. Maybe Cloud, a master thief by that stage, had funded the new wardrobe from his own pocket.

Below the frame in UV ink: *I fucked up.*

FORTY-FOUR

Cloud's admission of guilt didn't make sense until River read another letter in Rory's handwriting.

Cielo,

These walls feel closer than ever since Father's first treatment. I ache with phantom pain. My head is filled with clouds. I fear he took something more precious than wings. But last night ... you gave me the sky, Cielo. Not just to look at, but to touch. When we soared past the city walls, past the seas, over the trees—I finally understood what freedom tastes like.

The Milky Way spread before us like a road to forever. Mars burned red with possibility. I know you blame yourself for Father's punishment. Don't. That moment we became one beneath the stars?

How they shimmered like diamonds? Worth every scar. Worth every pain.

The guards watch closer now, but I won't let them take what we shared. He doesn't know that I'm learning to be better than him. He thinks he's a step ahead. But we flew high. I saw everything differently from the sky.

Every star holds our secret. Every breeze carries my heart to you.

Yours,

Aurora

"What is that?" Awe in Blake's tone drew River's attention.

Something deeper in the trove caught the blue light. A skeletal structure, delicate and precise, dangled from the ceiling. Not bones, but preserved wood meticulously crafted to mimic the curves and joints of wings.

"That's..." He stepped closer, examining the intricate mechanism.

"Leonardo da Vinci's flying machine," Blake whispered, joining him. She ran her fingers along the framework's base. "It's a working replica, but modified. See how he's reinforced the joints with something that looks like sinew instead of canvas?" Her eyes narrowed as she leaned closer. "It's stretchy. Maybe some kind of glue or latex. Clever."

River's brow furrowed. "Who's Leonardo?"

"An old-world genius." She ducked beneath the contraption, studying its craftsmanship. "He was a human who dreamed of flying like birds. He designed this centuries before the freeze." Her voice quieted. "I wonder if it worked."

"Cloud would have tested it," River murmured, spotting detailed blueprints pinned to the wall behind the replica. Cloud's handwriting covered every inch and included calculations for weight distribution, lift patterns, and adjustments. Sketches of human figures with grafted wings filled the margins, alongside diagrams of bird anatomy. "These aren't just copies. He improved on them."

Dried herbs and powders in small ceramic vials were scattered at the base of the wall. River recognized ingredients used in healing salves, the kind his mother made.

Blake pointed at a letter under a carved wooden box filled with feathers.

My Beloved Cielo,

I found your sketches hidden beneath my pillow. The way you've mapped every feather, every hollow bone, is beautiful and heartbreaking. Your dedication to restoring what Father stole from me takes my breath away.

But my love, what's gone is gone. I'm not like you. Each attempt burns deeper than the last. I can't endure this pain, not even for flight.

Perhaps it's better if you let me go. The treatments Father gives me … they make my memories blur at the edges. Sometimes I wake not knowing my name, but I always remember yours. Always remember us beneath the stars.

When the world is safe again, then we can think about our hearts once more.

Until then, keep your wings strong for both of us. Fly higher than anyone has before.

Until our stars align again,

Your Aurora

"River, look."

He spun toward Blake and saw her gaze locked on something in the shadows, an outline of something pinned on the wall that poured icy cold dread down his spine. Before he could stop her, she moved closer.

River lunged forward, his shoulders dislodging papers from the wall in his rush to shield her, but she planted her feet.

"Tell me they're not his," she whispered.

Moonlight-pale bones branched like winter trees, black feathers clinging to their macabre architecture.

"Not the bones. The feathers are. I recognize the UV patterns."

She touched a tear-stained and crumpled letter pinned beneath the skeletal remains.

Crow Boy,

If you find this, remember: even wingless birds dream of flight.

I will always choose you.

Always.

But if I can't ... if I forget ... then let me go.

Look for me in the stars we claimed as our own.

Our lyrics fade with the sun, but the tune lives forever on.

Don't return to Crystal City. He will be waiting.

Your Songbird.

P.S. I hope your two friends like my gifts. With them, you're never alone.

A masculine scrawl beneath it: *Fuck the mess. Tomorrow, I'm bringing her home.*

Ringing started in River's ears. The cryptex. The wings. The admission of guilt.

"I know you blame yourself for Father's anger. Don't." Rory's words bounced around his head. *"…restoring what Father took…"* Faster and faster her words flew, blending with Cloud's. *"Fuck the mess. Tomorrow I'm bringing her home."* Merging with River's memories. *"Even with nothing, they dance like the mess can't touch them."* Back to Cloud's. *"No matter how far I fly tomorrow, I'll circle home. Always."* Rory: *"I hope your friends like my gifts. With them, you're never alone."*

River—*"Bad birdy! No triad tattoo for you!"*

Cloud—*"You're not ready for a mess."*

And finally, her warning: *"Don't come back. He will be waiting."*

River's fingers went numb. He rocked unsteadily on his feet. Rory had warned Cloud away. He stole Nero's secret cryptex, used it to save Ash, but she took the punishment. She suffered. For years, she suffered. Had her wings cut off, wings River never knew she had, but…

It made sense.

They always knew Rory had mana. It was how she'd lived far longer than the average human. Nero had siphoned her supply to keep himself young. Something about blood relatives made manabee consumption avoid the madness. Maebh and Aleksandra were Rory's mothers. One was the surrogate. One was the egg donor. One mutated into a vampire after the Fallout. One mutated into an owl shifter.

Rory had wings.

Wings.

River's throat clogged with emotion.

Blake crouched and dusted the cover of a nearby book. "River, this is the original *Gray's Anatomy* textbook." She read the title on another. "*Avian Surgical Anatomy and Ortho-pedic Management.*" She slammed the book closed in her excitement. Dust bloomed as she picked up another. "More anatomy books. Surely there's an inner ear diagram in one."

Pages flipped as she kept talking, but River couldn't hear. His body was shutting down from shock.

That night in the tavern, Cloud had come to them for help. He'd shared more with them than ever about Rory. And that moment, when Cloud had tipped his ale…

It was a test to see how River reacted, and he'd failed.

He screwed his eyes shut and shook his head against the knowledge. It hurt to breathe. Hurt to admit how stupid he'd been. Cloud, the one who kept his feelings to himself more than River, had been screaming for help. But River had spent that evening throwing shade on love. Telling Cloud she wasn't worth the risk. She, who'd been mutilated on their behalf.

Fuck, he was an asshole, and he didn't even realize it.

He pressed his hands into his stinging eyes and shook his

head. No, none of this mattered. It didn't matter. It didn't change what happened in the end. Rory still tortured Cloud. His obsession with her never faded. It only became toxic. His betrayal cost the lives of so many innocent people. Thousands! All to lure Nero and Rory into Elphyne, all so he could manipulate a situation where he would have his vengeance … only to lose. Only to have it slip through his fingers.

"River, look." Blake was in her own world, crawling along the ground back the way they'd come, collecting papers River had knocked off the wall. "These are regeneration experiments. Research notes." Her tone softened. "He was trying to help her regrow what her father took. Maybe your wings—"

"No," River choked out. It didn't matter.

"Yes, look. Here he wrote, 'Regeneration possible if mana flow restored. Source must be pure.'"

Her words triggered a memory for River.

"The source is pure, Cielo," he called, dropping sneaky crumbs between trinkets and making a path at midnight to the waterfall pool behind his roost.

"Come and see the shinies I found you," he sang.

"It doesn't matter," he mumbled. "Doesn't rewrite the past."

But Blake read on. "'She winced today when drinking her father's mana. Said it burns.'"

"It burns," Cielo screamed, thrashing his head. "It burns!"

"Wake up. You're dreaming." Manfri ran to his friend's bed.

He fought with tangled limbs and sweat-dampened sheets, but his friend kept screaming: "Stop, stop, stop."

"Stop, Blake," River growled, blocking his ears as if that would stop the deluge of memories. "Stop reading."

"'Father's tainted supply causing…' I can't read that bit. It's smudged. Maybe if you tell me who did this…"

"Tell me," Manfri begged. "Tell me who did this. We'll call every crow we know—Nikan, Carmine, and Tommas. Your father. My family. We'll call them all and rain bloody murder from the sky. On them and their descendants. Just say the words, and we'll paint your enemy's blood on our faces."

"No," Cielo croaked. "Her death belongs to me."

"Oh, this is so sad," Blake sighed. "It says, 'Memory loss hindering—'"

"I said it doesn't matter!" River bellowed, ripping the papers from her hands, hating how she flinched in fright. Her bottom lip wobbled, and he pointed at her face. "Don't you dare apologize. Don't you dare!"

But his mate stood. She faced him with resolution in her eyes and steel in her spine.

"Why won't you just tell me everything?" She grabbed fallen papers and shook them in his face. "Why do I have to puzzle it out?"

"Because it hurts!" he shouted. "And this shit is making it worse!"

"Show me. Help me understand."

He grabbed her hand and dragged her deeper into the trove, into the descent of Cloud's madness. The parts that were created *after* his abuse. A metal hairpin with dried blood. A torn scrap wrapped around a dagger. Crystal City soldier badges that were obviously trophies. Sheet music, handwritten on military plans—airship schematics. Two conflicting, repeated, jagged phrases clashed, growing in intensity: *"Boy, I got to get away"* and *"Don't let me go."*

Pain sliced through River's chest. Guilt. Agony. Grief.

They kept walking. He stopped abruptly before an old

sketch of a young Aurora sleeping, hair tucked around round ears, something clutched in her hand. More recently, a brown, crusted V had been painted over her face. Dried Blood. More of Cloud's manic scrawl:

She looked right through me today. Those big eyes that used to light up … nothing. Empty.

More words.

She laughed with the guards. MY laugh. The one she saved for me. She doesn't remember. She doesn't remember anything. How could she forget so quickly?

River scanned the chaotic walls for what he needed to show Blake, but all he found was more evidence of a double life. All these years, River thought Cloud was happy with him and Ash. Happy-*ish* being a Guardian. He had a purpose.

LITTLE BIRD WITH BROKEN WINGS
DOESN'T REMEMBER HOW TO SING
DADDY'S POISON IN HER VEINS
TOOK MY LOVE, LEFT ONLY PAIN.

River made it to the end of the trove, a curved wall. He flipped through useless diagrams, more schematics. "Where is it?"

"Where is what?"

"He saved all this shit, but not the truth."

"What truth?"

"*She* was his torturer." He dashed his hand at the ramblings. "I know because he told me." He pounded the wall beside the hand-carved word HATE. "He told me how she plucked his feathers. She made him beg for her to stop. He talked in his sleep. I heard his nightmares."

He pounded his fist against another spot, the carved words, *HER DEATH IS MINE.*

"This just shows … what happened after. It shows his hate. But you can't see why." He started ripping pages off the wall, looking for hidden messages behind them. "She messed with his mind. She killed so many of our kind and then laughed about it. She—"

He found a note and choked up. The ink was fresh and sharp, the words more painful than any others he'd read.

YOU DIED SAVING SOMEONE ELSE'S CHILD.
WAS I NOT WORTH SAVING?
OR DID YOU JUST FORGET?

"He wrote this after she died," River whispered. "No mention of me. No mention of what he did to me. It's almost like … he feels nothing."

"You might be right."

Something in her tone lifted his gaze. Blake pointed to a final set of posters on the wall—nuclear warhead schematics. River recognized them because Violet and Silver had briefed the Twelve on what to look for, what they needed to find before Nero did, and what they'd hoped the cryptex would lead to.

No more crazed words. No more wobbly lines.

Everything in this section was clean, premeditated. Planned. Different maps were marked with potential detonation locations. One had obsessive calculations about blast radii. A time and date. Another map circled the secret location of this year's Shadow Market. The distance between the Collector's known trove and a second location with a question mark. A circle around the words cryptex and codes.

And finally, the madness itself bled onto the paper. Cloud's recent handwriting—

THERE'S NOTHING LEFT TO HATE.
NOTHING LEFT TO LOVE.
NOTHING LEFT AT ALL.

I LET HER GO.

FORTY-FIVE

Blake stared at the writing on the wall with a dawning sense of dread. Cloud's final words, the maps, the plans. The heartache. The confusion. The guilt. The bitterness. The emptiness.

There was nothing left for him, so why not burn it all down?

She locked eyes with River, and his emotions flooded through their bond. One stood out more than the rest, the same one he couldn't shake during his sleep: fear. No, more than that—terror.

"Hun, are you okay?" she asked.

He fell to his knees and buried his face in his hands. Broken wings splayed behind him, brushing the dirt, feathers molting. Crooked jacket. Haphazard shirt. Broad shoulders hitched as he fought for control, trying to barricade the emotion, to put that block back up.

She sensed his struggle as if it were her own, but the dam had already cracked.

Here kneeled her warrior, a creature who'd lived ten lifetimes to her one. With his whip-fast banter and endless confidence, River never lacked a quip. He projected indifference, but the fresh scars mapping his skin, the wobbly tattoo she'd made on his chest, and these bottled emotions proved otherwise. The mementos he'd kept in his old bedroom. The way he held her hair back when she was sick. He cared too deeply in a world where love bowed to strategic matches and was killed by the enemy, where love became an obsession and ended in madness.

I don't want to be left in darkness. I don't want to end up like him.

Panic squeezed her heart. What should she do?

When her feelings overwhelmed her, she usually retreated to the solace of social media. Everything seemed so much safer with a screen separating her from reality.

But River was different. He'd encouraged her to release her pain, cracked jokes until she smiled, and showed her how to channel anger into strength. A joke wouldn't heal him now, and neither would stabbing practice, but maybe that wasn't the point.

She glanced around at the heartbreaking madness, an obsession born from love. Or maybe it was the other way around. Fragments of Cloud's story still puzzled her, even with the evidence surrounding them. But it was clear these three crow boys had a special bond. And it was breaking.

Blake sank to her knees and gripped his thighs. "I'm here."

He yanked her roughly onto his lap, crushing her against his chest.

Then, her blue-winged warrior buried his face in her neck and confessed everything. The agonized story rushed from him in desperate bursts. He spoke of his childhood friendship with Cloud, of the jealousy poisoning him when his best friend fell in love. Guilt saturated every word. Guilt for thinking Cloud had eloped. Guilt for abandoning the search when he never returned, for delaying the triad tattoo, for misinterpreting Cloud's cry for help about the messiness of love. Cloud had spent his life trying to prove himself to his family, especially his older brothers and father. River had been his ally, his friend, his co-conspirator. But in the end, River had become exactly the kind of selfish bastard he despised. He'd tried to dictate how Cloud should live.

His voice cracked as he described that day at the river, the day they jumped with no wings.

"I was selfish, trying to uncover his secret affair with the enemy. I orchestrated the dare, something so stupid and reckless that I assumed he would buckle and confess. But he didn't. I almost drowned, but he saved me. And instead of getting angry, he still held up his end of the dare. We rescued Ash that day, but that fucking cryptex—" He gestured at the empty space in the frame on the wall. "That never would have been lost if I had never made that dare in the first place. Rory would have kept her—" he gasped, face contorting with pain, unable to speak the words.

Blake touched his tear-stained face. "But then Ash wouldn't be here, right?"

"I still can't shake the responsibility that this is my fault. Cloud was happier than I'd ever seen him, and I couldn't celebrate that. Why couldn't I have just been happy for him? I should have supported him. Maybe if I had, he would have confided in me sooner. Maybe I could have stopped him from making the worst mistake of his life. He went alone, and even then I assumed he'd eloped." River's shoulders trembled as he recounted nursing Cloud to health after he plummeted from the sky, a broken crow. "He didn't speak for so long. Wouldn't even shift from his avian form. That's what she did to him." A sob tore from his throat. "She cracked open his heart and watched it bleed. Sure, it didn't start like that. But that's how it ended. Because of me. Nero sank his hooks into her, changed her, and she let him. She twisted everything, yet Cloud couldn't kill her in the end. His obsession, whether it was hate or love, ruined everything. Look around. This shit just proves they're two sides of the same cursed coin." He jerked back, his storm-dark eyes locking with Blake's. "I can't end up like that. I can't."

"You won't," she whispered.

"You don't understand." His voice roughened. "I tried to warn you last night. We're not like the other fae races. Crows hold onto *everything*. I'm already following in his footsteps, have been my whole life. But I can't follow him there. Not there."

"Where?" Blake struggled to understand.

He scrubbed his face, trying to wipe away tears that leaked through his defenses. "Do you know why I was so furious when I first met you? Your very existence ruins my revenge. He hurt me, so I want to hurt him back. But it's more than that now. If putting him out of his misery also saves everyone else..."

"River—"

"There is no good answer." His manic eyes darted to and fro, seeing only his thoughts. "No matter how you look at it, there is only death. We can't go back in time. Only forward. He's a dead crow flying."

She gripped his shoulders until her fingers ached. "Don't think that way."

"Promise me, if you die first, take me with you."

"River, stop it. No one is dying."

"Everyone is dying."

"I'm not dead. You're not dead."

"Crows aren't supposed to fly alone."

"I'm here."

His expression darkened with creeping anger. "You could leave me. You could change your mind, but I won't let you. I told you last night, but you didn't get it. Can't you see it around us? This is your future. There is no escape."

"We're not like them," she insisted. "We won't end up like them."

"How can you be sure? You've known me a week."

She thrust her hand between their faces, the one covered in blue glittering marks. "Did they have this?"

One heartbeat of silence. Two.

"No," he whispered.

"Well, there you go. They're not us."

"A blessing wouldn't have changed anything for him." Bitterness edged his words. "She still tortured him. Still forgot everything he was to her while his obsession grew deeper. She used his love to turn him into a monster."

He rambled, half to himself and half to her. He shook her shoulders, speared fingers through his hair, and plucked at his feathers.

It pierced her heart that she couldn't heal his wounds or bring him comfort.

He was wrong. Love wasn't madness. It was only that without trust, without communication. She knew that in the deepest parts of her soul. If only he could see that, too.

"River." She lifted his face until his red-rimmed eyes met hers. "I love you."

"What?"

"I know we haven't known each other for long, but with this"—she glanced at the mating marks—"I feel like we have."

"You can't," he blurted. "You're lying."

She pressed his hand against her heart. "I'm telling the truth."

Emotion battled on his face and through their bond. Tenderly, she brushed her thumbs over his tear-stained cheeks.

"I love you, River. I love your sense of humor. Your energy. Your face. Your body. I love Mr. King Brown downstairs. I love your spontaneity, and I love how you adapt." Her hand traced down his neck, circling over his chest. "I love how you don't give a fuck what other people think. Only me. Only your closest friends. I love how you care for me, hold my hair when I'm sick. I love how *your* hair changes color between blue and black." She threaded her fingers through his locks, watching the strands catch the manabee light. "I love how sometimes they seem to have other colors in there, like turquoise and green." A soft laugh escaped her. "Almost like they're playing with me."

Her gaze filled with wonder as it landed on the splendid wings sprouting through the leather jacket on his back. She sighed, trailing her hands down his strong neck, over his shoulders, along the smooth ridges of the top of his wings. He shuddered beneath her touch and released a sharp exhale. "And I love these." Her lips curved. "They're so beautiful. I know you don't want anyone else to see them, but I hope you'll always have them out when it's just the two of us. For me." She slid her palm over his bare, warm chest and rested it over the beating organ beneath. "But most of all, I love your heart. Maybe you made mistakes. Maybe you have regrets. But if you didn't care, you wouldn't be here on the floor, feeling like your world is crumbling. If you weren't one of the good guys, you'd have burned this place to the ground. I know you feel lost right now, but I believe you'll find a way to glue everything back together. I believe in *you*, River." She tapped his sternum. "Because of this."

His expression crumbled, eyes brimming with fresh tears.

"If you need to cry, do it," she whispered, hands sliding over his shoulders and finding the ridge of his wings. "Don't hold back."

"I don't…"

"Then what do you need?"

"I need—" He shuddered as she stroked his wings. "I need—"

"Yes?"

His breathing grew labored as he slid his hands around her waist. "I need you."

"You have me."

"No. I need you, not like before." He glanced at the trove, fear slicing through. "Not like that. I need you … not like last night."

"I understand. You need to see that it can be different between us, that we don't have to push each other to the edge of obsession. We don't need words to keep us safe. We can just love without the danger."

Relief dropped his shoulders, wings sagging, muscles unknotting beneath her palms.

"I want you to keep touching my wings." His shaky admission trembled through his body. "If that's not too disgusting."

"I told you, I love them." She started removing his jacket, but then paused. "May I?"

His throat worked, and he nodded.

She peeled off his jacket, then his shirt, careful not to rupture his newly healed and fragile wounds. Before he could change his mind, she reached around his torso and traced the ridged spine between his wings, fingers finding the downy transition where pebbled skin became feathers.

"Yes," he groaned out, trembling. "Like how you did that first time."

She worked her nails beneath the feathers, raising quills until she found warm skin. "Like this?"

He nodded, drawing her hips down until her core pressed against his erection. The contact pulled a gasp from her throat.

River kneaded her breasts over her blouse until her nipples tightened against his palms. When she arched into him, whimpering for more, he lowered his mouth and suckled the sensitive nub through the fabric. Hot bolts of heat shot directly to her womb, eliciting a moan of pleasure from deep in her throat. Their arousal built in their shared breaths, in the gentle exploration of each other's bodies.

His mouth made its way up her neck, tongue swirling against flesh until he captured her lips in a hot, slow, and deep kiss that left her dizzy and breathless.

"More," she gasped, overcome with sensation.

Pure, male satisfaction glimmered in his eyes as he parted the pleats on her windways, fingers hunting through the volumes. Every teasing swipe of his fingers against bare skin drove her mindless until he finally found the access she craved. Three fingers swiped through her center folds, finding her slick and ready.

"Fuck, Blake," he groaned into her mouth, and then pulled back again to watch her face as he plunged a single finger inside her tight pussy. "Now, you tell me what feels good."

He worked her clit with his thumb.

"All of it," she whimpered.

A breathy laugh escaped him. "Need to be more specific, Sparkles."

But she couldn't talk. His fingers were too adept, sliding through her pussy lips, stroking her inside, gliding around outside, and finding all the sensitive spots.

The musty cave air sweetened with their rising desire. She found herself rocking against him, eagerly chasing the tightening of pleasure from every angle.

"Don't stop," he growled. "My wings."

Her hands had stilled. He nipped her jaw, jolting her back to work. When her touch swept outward from his spine, along the lengths he usually kept folded close, he kissed the area he'd bitten on her jaw. Apologizing, she realized. A splash of his shame came through their bond. He felt bad for asking her to touch him this way. He shouldn't feel bad for wanting to feel loved. She found a bare patch on his wing and traced circles against the velvet-soft skin.

"Even here," she marveled, "you feel like silk."

He groaned, hips jerking upward.

"Shit," he mumbled. "Pants still on."

He quickly freed himself from his leather breeches. She rose on her knees when he fumbled again between her thighs, this time, clumsy and trembling with his own arousal. Both panting hard, both eager to feel more, she helped part the windways' pleats, exposing herself while he guided the blunt head of his cock to her slick entrance.

"Yes." She tried to sink down on it, to feel complete

again, but he grumbled and lifted her, grinning against her lips, playing with her, delaying their gratification.

"You tease," she muttered.

"Always." His brows flicked together. "But I need to see you naked first. Stay on your knees."

He ripped away her pants completely, tossing them aside. Her shirt came off next, leaving her bare. "Fuck, Sparkles. You look so good like this, spread and ready to take me."

He splayed his fingers, spreading her pussy lips while his other hand rubbed the blunt head of his cock against her slickness. He circled her clit, and had her feeling so damn aroused she couldn't see straight. Only when he had her a whimpering mess did he notch at her entrance and let her sink. Their joining transcended physical connection—she felt it in the charged air, in his quivering muscles, his shallow breaths, his fingers digging into her hips, voice rough as he said, "Ride me." More breathlessly. "I love watching your tight little pussy take me."

"But your wings."

"Forget them for now." He leaned back on his palms, eyelids heavy, staring where they joined. "Make yourself come on my cock."

This wasn't the first time he'd handed her the reins. Sex with him would never be a one-way street. Never be boring. Her palms flattened against his flexed abdomen, and she gave herself over to the feel of him inside her, stretching her, emptying her, and then filling her. She thrust and undulated, rocked and ground. She tested every movement she'd never had the opportunity to explore. And when she found the sweet spot, good god, did she ride it out. Pleasure coiled hot and tight. She whimpered and grunted in unflattering ways.

Her heavy breasts bounced and jiggled. Her thighs burned and trembled. But he lapped it up. He growled words of encouragement, commending her for looking so good while she used him.

And when she couldn't support herself any longer, he lurched forward and helped her with guiding hands on her hips and more hot words in her ear.

She felt beautiful. Desired. Accepted. Their emotions tangled until she couldn't distinguish his from hers. Want. Need. Understanding. They merged into a single truth. This. This felt like home. She cried out when her climax hit, and her hands slapped over the ridges of his wings for balance. The building pressure released in a wave of bone-tensing, nerve-searing sensation. Her grip on his wings tightened. She might have bitten him somewhere—she wasn't sure, but whatever she did triggered his release.

With a long, drawn-out groan, he held her pinned until every last drop spilled inside her. And then he held them together, basking in the moment. They were two sweaty, dirty, half-naked hot messes surrounded by a trove of tragedy.

But they noticed none of it.

Not while wrapped in each other's arms.

FORTY-SIX

River lost track of time with his mate nestled against him, tucked into his side. His wings cushioned them both from the cold, gritty floor. Sleep claimed them both, but now reality demanded attention. Or rather, demanding his. Blake, being her beautiful self, simply gave whatever he needed. Her intuition about him was keen as ever.

Her youth struck him anew. Where his edges had grown jagged, she remained resilient and optimistic, open to new experiences and ideas, and even to love in the face of her recent heartache. Truth had rung in every syllable when she'd whispered those three words. His feelings ran just as deep, just as intense. He'd never felt this way, which could only mean one thing. He loved her too.

But any time he thought he could confess his feelings, his throat closed up. He kept thinking about how they'd only known each other for days. Their love was fragile, new, and precious like Blake's eucalyptus sapling. What Cloud and

Rory had shared was an ancient oak with roots that stretched beyond comprehension. Look how that ended.

His chest tightened.

Anything was possible, including having their hearts shattered and their world destroyed. Maybe that's why he hoarded those words, clutching them like a shiny object used to ward off circling crows and bad luck.

River's gaze drifted across the ceiling. For all of Cloud's darkness, he'd surrounded himself with beauty. Glowworms dotted the rocky backdrop like a constellation of scattered stars.

Had Cloud lain here too, agonizing over what he'd lost, reliving those first precious moments of his daring relationship with the enemy? Had he wondered where it all went wrong, what he could have done differently? Had he wondered if there was a reason the Well chose him for this fate, targeting him specifically?

River, Cloud, and Ash once stargazed together. When ale or mana-weed had loosened their tongues on rare nights, they shared their hopes and dreams. Ash had slipped into their friendship as naturally as breathing. Like he'd been there from the beginning.

Crimson.

River's stomach churned. If Ash knew what trouble the cryptex had caused, he'd never forgive himself. He would have moved mountains to prevent another soul from suffering for the sake of his freedom. Rory had taken the blame for the missing cryptex. Cloud probably didn't learn about Nero's punishment until it was too late to stop.

Wings.

Rory had *wings.*

Like her two mothers, she was born in the old world.

The Well wiped the slate clean for everyone. It gave everyone an equal chance to abide by its rules. Even Nero had that same opportunity, waking in this time to find out he could hold mana. But he'd depleted it permanently through his deplorable choices, which spoke volumes about his character. If he needed to replenish from stolen mana, it meant the Well blocked him from refilling naturally.

Leaf's collection of Jackson Crimson's journals detailed a firsthand account of old-world humans mutating into fae after the Fallout. That first generation wasn't born. It was made. Whatever Rory had become might have surprised them all.

River's gaze flicked to the winged skeletal remains on the wall, and he exhaled.

Why did Cloud torture himself with thoughts of what might have been? Why hold onto this tragedy as if it were a treasure? Rory was still dead, and Cloud had still been cheated out of his vengeance. Now he sought revenge against the world—maybe even the Well.

Regardless of the conflict between them, River had to stop Cloud. Simple as that.

They had to find a way out of the trove first.

Cloud had either brought portal stones into the trove each time he visited or, with practice, shifted into crow form and flew directly after submerging. He'd always been good at that stuff. Better than River, better than anyone. Faster, stronger, could fly higher. It's what made him such a great thief. He stayed humble about it until he used it to his advantage.

Waiting for the tide to lower wouldn't help them. The lowering water levels were seasonal. They'd starve before that happened.

Blake stirred in his arms. She looked up at him and smiled, melting away all his troubles.

"Hey," she said, running her hand over his stomach. "How are you feeling?"

He suspected she wasn't asking about physical sensations but was done analyzing his head.

"Wounds are mostly healed," he replied, offering a smile.

She checked his wounds, systematically moving around his body, mothering him. It had been a long time since he'd allowed anyone to look at him like this without feeling defensive. It was nice.

"Yeah," she confirmed. "You've healed."

"I think the Well flows strongly here," he noted, "despite the metal threading through the ruins. There's something about this place. The glowworms are a good indicator."

"Maybe because it belongs to a Guardian," she suggested.

"Could be."

After long moments of silence, River asked, "Do you think someone can betray you if you betrayed them first?"

He regretted the question immediately, but couldn't take it back.

Blake gave a sleepy yawn. "I guess it depends on whether the betrayal was intentional. Maybe. I don't know. Why do you ask?"

His gaze flicked to the wall of doom. He lifted her from his side to lie over his front. "How are you feeling?"

A contented sigh answered him. She dropped her head to his chest and dangled her hand over the side of his body, skimming her fingers through his feathers.

His instinct was to tense, to shift his wings away, to hide the damaged parts. But he didn't. For some crazy reason, she loved them. He palmed her curvy buttocks instead, slightly annoyed she'd redressed before dozing. Couldn't she just walk around naked for him?

"They're so beautiful. Really," she mused, idly stroking his wings. "Not as bad as you think."

Hot pleasure zipped through his body, waking nerve endings that sleep had dulled.

"Sparkles," he warned, already breathless, his skin tightening with arousal. "Stop stroking unless you want to part those windways again and sit on my cock."

She laughed.

"I'm not joking."

"Does it really make you that horny?" she asked, still tickling his wings.

He held her waist firm and gently ground his arousal into her until she gasped.

"You have no idea." His voice roughened to gravel. "You could probably make me come just by rubbing my wings."

"Ooh, that might be fun," she breathed, sliding him mischievous eyes.

"You're so perfect for me. But we need to get out of here first, and then I'll let you do whatever you want to my wings."

"Really?"

"Whatever you want, Sparkles."

She pressed her smiling lips against his, and he was flying without wings. His lashes fluttered as he palmed her luscious buttocks, savoring the moment.

"I am kind of hungry," she confessed, head back on his chest. "How are we going to get out of here?"

"I don't know," he admitted, "but I'm thinking."

The problem was that between her and the things

written on the wall, all the blood in his body had been diverted to unhelpful parts. He wasn't doing a good job of developing a plan. No matter where he looked, sadness surrounded them.

"I know it's none of my business," she whispered, "but don't write off your friend just yet. Please."

He craned his neck to look down at her. "I have to stop him. You see the same thing I do."

"I know, but … I can't explain it. Something doesn't feel right about all this. For all we know, this is just like a diary— a place to vent. I don't think we should jump to conclusions."

"There's no jumping. The proof is on the walls."

"But you said it yourself—when it came to that battle on the airship, he couldn't go through with killing her. Would he burn the entire world just because she's not in it?"

"Yes." He threw up his hands. "We're crows. That's what we do." He gently rolled her off him and walked to where the diabolical words were written at the end of the trove. A sick feeling rolled in his gut as he re-read them. "Jasper said he killed innocent human refugees."

"Did he?"

He nodded, slumping. "There's nothing left for him."

"I mean, are you *sure* that Cloud killed the refugees?"

Irritation swam in his chest. He hadn't seen the bodies himself, so no, he wasn't sure. But Cloud—and every Guardian—had killed humans. Before the Well-blessed humans came along, they'd executed the enemy for infiltrating Elphyne. It was their job. More recently, Cloud had betrayed the fae to lure Nero into Elphyne, who, in turn, used Willow to raise an army of undead and almost destroyed them all.

Blake never saw the emptiness in Cloud's eyes when he struck down his closest friend with lightning.

"Why are you defending him?" River growled. "You don't know him."

Her flinch cut him deep. He hadn't meant to sound so cruel.

"I just think something is missing here." She joined him by the wall, hugging herself. "All these shimmering words, I think they're lyrics to a song from my time. But … some words are missing." She walked to the beginning, to where Rory's letters were more evident. Her eyes darted to and fro, rereading. "She says things in here … things that don't quite make sense but that remind me of the song, too. I don't know. It just feels like something is missing, and Cloud knew that."

River forced his blood pressure to lower, to address his mate without anger. "It doesn't matter if we stare at it all day. It won't bring her back, nor will it erase what she did to him, what Nero did to her. Cloud will still feel like there's nothing left worth saving."

His voice cracked on the last word, and he closed his eyes.

Blake wrapped her arms around him and pressed her forehead against the spiny ridge between his wings.

"Sometimes things break," she murmured, "so they can be put back together stronger than before. But first, you need to acknowledge the break. You can't fix it if you can't see exactly where it happened and why."

"We know why. Wait—" His throat tightened as her words settled. "You said I wasn't one of your projects."

"You're not!"

"Blake…"

"I just think you shouldn't give up on him yet."

"Like I gave up on him before?" he clipped.

"I'm sorry. I overstepped."

An incredulous laugh burst out of him.

"Oh shit, sorry." She covered her mouth. "This is so annoying."

"It's fine." He kissed the top of her head. A laugh was exactly what he'd needed to snap him out of his mood. "I stopped collecting your debts a while ago. And I think the Well has too."

"Hm. Yes, I felt no zip of recognition. What does that mean?"

"You and I don't need debts paid between us because we're in this together. All in."

His gaze flicked to the wall, to his future. Maybe Blake was right. Maybe acknowledging the break was the only way they could repair this. But maybe she wasn't. Either way, he shouldn't have taken out his mood on her. Squeezing her tighter, he murmured against her head, "I shouldn't have snapped. I laughed because I keep fucking up, yet you're the one who apologizes."

She rubbed his back. "You're upset."

"But not at you."

"I know." Blake lowered to a crouch by the stack of anatomy books. "I want to take the textbook with me when we leave."

"Far as I know," he said, glad for the change of subject, "there's only one way out of here: through water."

"Oh, bugger." She paused. "The paper will get soaked. I'd better study the right page. And I puked in there. Have you thought of a way out?"

"Not really. The water seems clean now. If we swim out,

maybe we can avoid the waterfall if I use *Peacemaker* and claw my way up the ravine with you hanging on my back."

"Or!" she countered, eyes wide with an idea. "Maybe you could do one of those communication spells and contact your parents?"

"I didn't think of that," he admitted. He showed her his triad tattoo. "I could even use this to contact Ash and ask for his help to lift you from the river. How did I not think of that? It's so obvious."

He definitely wasn't the forger of new paths like his namesake.

"Get fucked." She shoved him playfully. "You're perfect. But also, have you wondered if you can travel through the water the same way you pulled your dad out of the bowl?"

He stared at her. Stunned. More than stunned.

And then his cock got hard again. This woman, this *perfect* woman, was his. And for some Well-damned reason, she loved *him*.

He cupped her face and gave her a slow, deep kiss that left her breathless, and him wondering if it was too late to change his mind about leaving so soon.

"Your mind is so fucking sexy," he said. "I don't know how I'd do this without you."

"Imagine what I could do with me own magic." Blake's lips trembled when she smiled.

"Don't worry about that," he promised. "The first thing we'll do at the Great Murder is visit the Donna for a reading. We'll figure out what's happening with your mana."

She pulled at a pleat on her windways, avoiding his gaze. "It might not work."

"Until we get your elemental affinities tested at the Order, it's our best option."

Feathers rustled softly as he shifted his wings away. He considered finding a portal stone at the Great Murder and returning to the Order with this new information about Cloud, but Clarke needed the cryptex. He had to trust her reasons for sending both him and Ash after it.

He scrawled a greeting to Ash on the triad tattoo:

PRINCELING

As the welt sank into his skin and disappeared, another message written in Ash's familiar masculine scrawl appeared.

Kelpie didn't eat you then.

River's lips stretched, and he replied,

I'M NOT THAT EASY TO GET RID OF.

Blake?

It warmed River's heart that Ash was already inquiring about Blake's health.

SHE'S GOOD. YOU AT THE GREAT MURDER YET?

A few minutes later, Ash's handwriting appeared.

Yes. As is the cavalcade. The Corvus didn't want to risk ground travel and portaled them immediately.

Even better. Time to get out of this place.

TELL SERA TO WAIT FOR ME NEAR A PRIVATE BODY OF WATER. WE'RE COMING THROUGH.

Not your messenger bird.

River's smile faded when he scratched in the next bit.

AFTER THAT, MEET US AT THE DONNA'S. WE NEED TO TALK.

HALF A TURN LATER, RIVER AND BLAKE STOOD IN A FOREST clearing with water dripping from their clothes. The pond they'd emerged from was filled with tadpoles and mosquitoes, but otherwise, they remained incident free.

River's parents, Talo and Ravi, waited with pinched, worried faces. Sera had sent them instead, probably hoping they'd reconcile, but he wasn't ready to forgive them for the nesting caravan incident. Even if everything turned out fine, forcing Blake into a situation like that without her consent was unforgivable.

He quickly dried Blake with his mana, drawing every ounce of water from her clothes and hair before he dried himself.

Wings overhead cast fleeting shadows on the ground. Beyond the shelter of their trees, hundreds of crow shifters in various forms swooped through a valley between evergreen mountains. The ruins of an ancient dam loomed in the near distance, its abandoned concrete forms defined against the blue sky. Water trickled from the top of the dam's wall and gathered in sporadic pools on moss-covered ledges, raining down streams that caught the sunlight and sparkled like diamonds.

Hundreds of caravans were camped in the valley in murder districts, and within them, kettle congregations. Some had flown up to the concrete and grass ledges, camping with colorful tents. Winged fae were in the process of festooning the dam and trees with bright banners and intricate decorations that fluttered and twinkled in the breeze, transforming the eyesore into something alive and beautiful.

Finally, they'd arrived at the Great Murder.

FORTY-SEVEN

"Invitations." The sentinel's wings mantled wide, blocking Blake's path.

River angled protectively toward Blake. He pulled coins from his pocket and flipped them over his tattooed knuckles. She didn't need the bond to sense his irritation. It seethed from his every pore. Eventually, he tossed the coins with deliberate force.

The sentinel caught them and then held them to the light until prisms sparkled and dispersed shards of rainbows. Her gaze lingered on River's weapons, particularly *Peacemaker* at his hip.

Blake's pulse hammered as she watched them, half expecting battle to erupt.

"And the outsider?"

Attention shifted to Blake, who clutched the anatomy book against her chest.

"Obviously, she's my Well-blessed mate." River's voice dropped dangerously low. He flicked his blue-marked wrist dismissively. "Or are you blind as well as stupid?"

Blake lifted her chin, allowing her marks to catch the sunlight. The sentinel's eyes widened and instantly narrowed to slits.

"Proceed, Guardian." She stepped aside with apparent reluctance.

With a grumbled insult tossed her way, River placed his hand on Blake's back and guided her forward.

"What was that about?"

"Just reminding her who's boss." He stopped and slid his hand along Blake's jaw until his fingers curled around her nape. "You okay?"

"I'm fine. Why?"

His gaze flicked to where his parents hovered nearby, worry tightening their faces. Blake hadn't missed the uncomfortable silence when they'd emerged from the pond. River's greeting had been arctic.

"As long as they don't drug us again, I'll be fine."

"They're in an early grave if they do." His gaze never wavered from hers, deadly serious.

Blake released a tentative laugh. "I'm joking, River."

"I'm not."

She patted his hand. "Seriously, I'm fine."

It seemed like he wanted to say more, but he inhaled deeply and nodded on the exhale. "Ash is meeting us at the Donna's."

She shifted her anatomy book to one hand and offered him the other, half expecting him to scoff about being too old for such gestures. But he laced his fingers through hers with a grateful smile.

"Will you join us for the evening feast?" Ravi asked him as they passed.

"Maybe."

"The Corvus has called a general meeting afterward." Talo's words fell carefully. "We'll save you seats."

River acknowledged this with a distracted nod, already guiding Blake forward. "Let's reach the Donna's before the lines grow long."

Blake tried to give them a friendly wave, but River dragged her forward with urgency. It didn't take long for her to get distracted. Magic saturated the atmosphere, prickling her skin.

Too many wonders competed for her attention. Afternoon sun glimmered through shifting leaves. Black-winged silhouettes flew against the sun's golden glare, their caws carrying messages across the gathering. Feathers floated downward and swirled with impossible colors. Families moved about, setting up temporary homes as they chattered, laughed, and argued with passion.

The energy was infectious. Blake's cheeks hurt from grinning. This was crow territory in its purest form—the Great Murder—and she, a human, was *here*.

A nearby marketplace grew by the minute. New stalls, canopies, carts, wagons, and more arguments over which murder had certain territorial rights. Vendors hawked treasures gathered or stolen from every corner of Elphyne. A brawl nearly broke out when one crow accused another of stealing a jeweled shoe. Blake even recognized some objects from her era, preserved in glass casings and marked as antiques. Her fingers twitched to investigate.

Before conscious thought stopped her, she pulled away from River and stepped toward a stall displaying crystalline figurines. The vendor looked up with a bright smile until her gaze landed on Blake's Well-blessed markings. She turned away, suddenly rearranging pieces.

"Blake." River's hand found her elbow. "Later."

They continued past more stalls. Another fae caught sight of her mating mark and quickly placed his antique compass beneath the counter. Conversations fell to whispers. A mother pulled her child closer, wings spreading protectively. Two young crow shifters went silent, gazes tracking Blake's movement before spotting River and averting their attention.

The book's spine dug into her ribs as she hugged it tighter.

"They're staring."

"You want me to stab them?" River asked, completely serious.

A part of her preened at the protective, earnest gesture. But she didn't want another owl-shifter brigade situation. And stabbing was wrong. That too.

"No."

"You sure? I think one of them looks like dickface."

She laughed and shook her head.

"Alright then." His fingers brushed her lower back. "Let's keep walking."

Beyond the market, nestled between towering pines carved with watchful crow totems, were caravans arranged in a perfect circle. Macabre curtains made from bones, beads, and silken feather strands linked each caravan, hiding the space beyond. A crow hidden in the branches announced their approach with three sharp caws.

Fae lined up at each van's steps. Wary gazes slid toward them, some fixating on River in his Guardian uniform, his metal weapons, but most still wary of Blake. It seemed the Well-blessed marks gave her humanity away more than anything else.

River took Blake's hand and gently nudged her forward. "Almost there."

"She's in one of these vans?"

"Yep. Each belongs to the Donna from a different murder. Ours is the eldest." His voice dropped. "And the creepiest."

Creepy was an understatement. The caravan he led her to was bathed in darkness, black paint and decor oozing from every surface. The faces carved into obsidian wood tracked their approach, eyes following with unnatural awareness. The entire structure pulsed with power and dread.

But there was no line at the door. No one stood a foot within the allotted space.

"Maybe we should leave." Blake spun around. "I don't belong—"

She collided with leather-clad muscle, narrowly missing a sheathed dagger's hilt. Black feathered wings rustled as Ash steadied her shoulders, his touch impersonal but firm.

"There's no point," he said, releasing her and dismissing his wings in a shimmer of darkness. "She'll be expecting us."

"Us?" River's brows raised. "I thought you and I could talk while Blake has her reading."

Bones dangling over the caravan's closed door swayed, clicking ominously. Dark strands of hair floated around Ash's face long after the wind had settled. His narrow gaze shifted to River, and he repeated, "Us."

Neither Guardian seemed thrilled with the prospect of seeing the Donna. And if they weren't, then what the fuck was Blake doing here?

"Ugh, fine," River groaned, and then led the way up creaking steps.

He didn't knock, just swept aside the dangling charms

and pushed the door open. Smoke curled from within, thick with clove and something older.

He hesitated before entering and looked at Blake. "Don't lie to her. And whatever you do, don't touch the birds."

"What birds?"

Despite every instinct in her body urging her to run, she had no choice. Ash was behind her, his big frame leaving her nowhere to go but inside. Once in, he closed the door.

It took a moment for Blake's vision to adjust to the low light. No windows. Illumination came solely from jars of pulsing manabeeze suspended from hooks.

The layout differed from the nesting caravan. To the left of the door was a sitting area with scattered cushions. Very casual and inviting. But to the right, a kitchenette covered in carved-up game and chewed pulp glimmered beneath a ceiling hung with drying herbs and more lanterns.

A woman with her back turned to them was grinding something in a mortar and pestle, humming softly to herself. Bones, feathers, and curling fragments of ancient American dollar bills adorned every inch of her shoulderless black dress. Three elongated feathers served as hairpins, their quills disappearing into a severe topknot of black hair. No wings, just knobby shoulders crawling with tattooed crows.

Blake's mouth fell open when one blinked at her.

Not tattoos. But living birds, each somehow trapped beneath skin. The one perched on the Donna's left shoulder lifted its head. Another cawed softly from the woman's nape.

"Come in." The Donna's voice rasped like sandpaper. "Sit, child of the old world."

Blake hesitated, then shuffled to the van's comforting end and settled onto a cushion with the anatomy book in her lap.

The Guardians remained by the door. River folded his arms and glared. His family held a deep grudge against this woman for ostracizing the Umbrias because Talo and Ravi had eloped.

The Donna clicked her tongue and faced them.

She was a striking woman. Her ageless face was truly beautiful, complemented by her all-white eyes and black-painted lips. A shiny black streak of ink traced her skin from her lips to her throat and then branched across her collarbones.

When she'd turned, the tattooed birds flew beneath her skin and settled on the branches. Every inked crow mimicked her as she narrowed her eyes at River.

"Boy, you always were a stubborn crow." She gestured to the cushions. "I won't peck. Sit."

River's fear flashed through their mating bond—sharp and unexpected. Ash looked equally uneasy but elbowed him in the ribs.

"There's a spot here." Blake patted the cushion beside her.

His stubbled jaw clenched, but he walked over. Leather creaked as his large frame filled the small space, his thigh pressing against hers. Ash stayed by the door with a relaxed stance, watching Donna's every move.

Her smile revealed too many teeth. "The prodigal son returns. With a mate, no less."

"Well-*blessed* mate."

"So protective of your little bird, aren't you?"

"She's human."

"Is she now?" The Donna's tone sounded like Jeff's fake producer, all condescending superiority.

Blake's fingers tightened on the book's spine until her

knuckles blanched. The Donna's unnerving, milky eyes dropped to the movement. "And what have you brought me, child?"

"It's for Aeron," she blurted. "I'm studying it to help Ada heal his hearing."

"Ah. So not a gift for me." The reproachful look she gave River could have stripped meat from bones. Before he could respond, she inhaled deeply, nostrils flaring. "And your Summer Queen thinks to heal what is not there, hm? With old-world medicine, hm?" She laughed at River's tensing fists. "Interesting."

"Not with medicine." Defensive heat climbed Blake's neck. "With knowledge."

"Hm." The Donna's gaze traveled over Blake's face, lingered on her mating mark glinting at her throat. "You're not supposed to be here."

"Wh-what?"

"You're not what they think you are."

The words drove air from Blake's lungs. "What do you mean? What am I?"

"You're impatient for your feather tracing, yes?" The Donna scooped paste from her mortar and reached for Blake with startling speed.

River's hand shot out, fingers encircling the offending wrist. "Touch her, and I'll end you."

"Protective, indeed." The crows inked into the Donna's skin flapped their wings and cawed in agitation, but he wouldn't let go. Ash tensed. Violence crackled in the air.

"The ritual requires marking," the Donna calmly explained to River. "Or does the Guardian no longer respect his ancestors' ways?"

"Not without her consent."

"I give my permission," Blake babbled, eager to defuse the hostility. "We can't do the feather casting without it, right?"

River's expression darkened, but he nodded and released his grip and eased back. His hand found Blake's and squeezed once, letting her know he remained coiled to strike.

"A feather tracing reading reveals what is already known but unseen." The Donna dipped her fingers into thick, black paste.

Cold fingertips touched the top of Blake's lips and painted downward over her chin. The substance tasted bitter and earthy, like ashes and cloves with an undertone she couldn't name. It numbed her skin instantly. Warmth coursed through her veins.

"Your ancestors speak through your feathers." The Donna reached for a small pouch hanging from her neck. "The past whispers to the present." She untied the pouch and poured iridescent black feathers onto her palm. "Since you have no feathers, the magpie collects what others discard."

"Pull out those which call to you." She offered Blake the feathers. "Then scatter them on the stone."

This must be like a tarot reading, Blake thought. The association calmed her nerves. She hovered her hand over the feathers, but nothing called to her. Trying not to feel disappointed, she randomly selected a few and scattered them onto a flat circular stone between them.

A gust of wind hit Blake's face as if the feathers had displaced a boulder's worth of air.

"What do you see, child of the old world?" The Donna's raspy voice sounded distant, as if speaking from across a void.

Blake's vision blurred at the edges, the caravan's interior stretching and contracting. The familiar scent of eucalyptus oil drifted across her senses. It reminded her of her dad's workshop back in Perth, her childhood home.

The scent intensified as the caravan melted around her and morphed into the workshop's wood-paneled room. Her dad's hammer was pressed against her palm, worn smooth from years of use. Broken furniture waited to be restored on the cluttered workbench. The radio played golden oldies in the corner, and her father hummed off-key from somewhere. A warbling, musical sound drew her attention to the window. Outside, Scarface, her old magpie friend, hopped about on the grass, hunting for worms.

She remembered this day. She'd been thirteen, taking the hammer to wood too recklessly, splintering a join, ruining the plank.

"She'll be right, Bloss." Her father's voice whispered from her memories. She felt his large, callused hand on her shoulder, smelled eucalyptus, sweat, and cedar shavings. *"The break will make it stronger, you'll see."*

"Dad?" She reached into empty air.

"The feathers." The Donna's voice cut through the vision. "Tell me what you see."

"Dad, it's me." Blake blinked hard, trying to focus, desperate to hold onto her father's presence.

"The feathers, girl. Look at the feathers."

Blake wrenched her gaze downward. Scattered feathers swirled like a kaleidoscope.

"Colors," she said. "Light. Patterns that move."

"Good. What else?"

Blake leaned closer, drawn by something beyond rational

explanation. The feathers distinguished themselves, moved, and rearranged.

"The feathers form a spiral. Three parts connecting."

"And what else?"

"A wing." Blake traced the air above one formation. "But broken. Stars, trees, and a song—also broken. But there—" Her finger drifted to another cluster. "A shadow. Something dark is moving between the feathers and stealing them." Rising terror built, racing her heart. "It's not part of them, but hunting them."

"Hm," the Donna mused. "Something with borrowed feet and no heartbeat."

"This is supposed to be about Blake's mana." River's hand found hers again and squeezed hard.

"The enemy stands among friends." The Donna gestured to two bloody feathers joining to form a V, splitting apart the three. "What blinds the Guardian is not darkness, but his own wings."

River's breath hitched, his face draining of color. "That's enough."

The feathers shifted again, and for an instant, in the glossy surface, Blake saw her father's weathered hands holding the broken wooden plank. The workshop dissolved around him, replaced by vast open skies. Her father stood beneath their eucalyptus tree, watching her with eyes full of pride and sorrow. He looked down at his hands. The hammer was gone, replaced by Scarface—motionless, lifeless.

"You can't fix stupid." His voice resonated through her mind as the dead bird fell from his fingers.

Blake screamed, but no sound came out. Moments before Scarface hit the ground, his wings snapped open. What had been a free fall became a swoop. Black and white feathers fluttered, and the bird plucked out the morning worm wriggling from the grass and flew into the sun. Blake's father bellowed with laughter.

The sun's glare grew so bright it swallowed them whole.

"Dad!" she shouted, tears spilling down her cheeks. "Don't go!"

But the vision faded, leaving nothing but a deep ache between Blake's ribs and dead, oily feathers on flat stone. Her sob caught in her throat.

"You're upsetting her." River's accusation carried a lethal edge. "We didn't bring a gift, and now you're fucking with us, just like you always do."

"Always?"

"You punished my parents for eloping. You approve of Lark and Tommas's match, but then take it back. You haven't even officially approved mine. We came for answers about Blake's gift, not more of your petty fuckery."

"Sorry and thanks go to waste." The Donna tapped a curved fingernail against her temple. "The magpie knows. She sees the patterns."

Ash shifted uncomfortably by the door. "Maybe we should—"

"The crow speaks of approval when he already knows what I see." The Donna pointed a long, bony finger at the empty space between River and Blake. "The bond exists, whether I approve or not. Umbria and Cardona flocks entwine as always, existing to balance that which flows, grows, and binds. Look inside your kettle for what broke the match because it wasn't me. But what you seek"—her gaze shifted to Blake—"is not what you think."

The paste on Blake's chin tingled and burned. The caravan's interior shifted and swayed. Manabeeze pulsed in jars faster and brighter. Like the sun in the vision, threatening to swallow her whole.

"I'm taking you out of here." River lifted Blake to her feet and pulled her toward the exit. Ash moved quickly to avoid a collision.

The Donna's birds took flight, peeling from tattooed skin and materializing into three-dimensional forms. Their wings beat furiously as they circled the caravan. Feathers molted everywhere. Blake gasped and ducked as one swooped near her head, catching her hair. River pulled her against his chest and shielded her with his body.

"The crow flies blind when the Guardian refuses to see the truth!" The Donna cackled over the cacophony of caws and beating wings. "The magpie collects treasures she doesn't understand. The vulture looks for death in the stars above instead of those below."

Ash yanked the door open. River thrust Blake outside. She glanced back to see a crow land on Ash's shoulder and hunt through his hair with its ebony beak. Feathers continued to shed from its body until nothing remained but bones, but Ash dared not remove it.

The Donna clasped his wrist, her silver eyes widening. "When the dead crow takes flight, the owl sees through the darkest night."

The skeletal crow on Ash's shoulder flew onto its mistress as she shoved him outside.

"What did it see?" he demanded, voice raw as he stumbled back.

The Donna tilted her head. "It saw grief. Yours. So now it lives with me."

She slammed the door shut.

All three of them stood frozen. Stunned.

"What the fuck was that?" Blake muttered.

The world tilted sharply. Every reflection, every trinket, every glass surface flared with painful brightness. She staggered and clutched River's arm.

"Blake?" He steadied her, but his voice sounded distant through the blood rushing in her ears.

"I'm fine." She straightened, fought the sensation. Then she remembered. "The book!"

It wasn't in her hands. Not in River's or Ash's.

River's gaze darted between her and the Donna's caravan. "I'll get it."

The ground shifted as he jogged back up the porch steps and pounded on the door. Ash joined him, but no answer came. People stared. Judged.

You're not supposed to be here.

Blake had one job: to protect the book. She hadn't even studied the pages.

You can't fix stupid.

Panic squeezed her throat.

"I need air," she said, then spun on her heels and ran.

FORTY-EIGHT

Blake's heartbeat thundered in her ears as she ran. Bodies materialized in her path, solid obstacles she couldn't process fast enough. Her shoulder connected with a female carrying glass trinkets, then a faceless male whose wings she clipped. Angry cries pursued her retreat.

"Watch yourself!"

"Outsider!"

Direction meant nothing. Only distance. She pushed deeper into the thickening crowd, drawn to the clamor of commerce. When the Great Murder's marketplace engulfed her, she expected peace. Instead, the paste burned her chin. Each heartbeat pushed the substance deeper into her bloodstream. Colors intensified. Blues became electric, reds throbbed with impossible depth. The scent of feathers, smoke, and thousands of bodies pressed against her nostrils until she could taste them.

Her steps faltered. The world tilted.

"The book," she whispered, fingers clutching empty air where the anatomy text should have been. Or her phone?

No substance.

One purpose. One task. She'd abandoned it in that nightmare caravan. Her one chance to do something meaningful in this world—gone. Because she'd been too worried about why she had no magic like the other women from her time.

Shallow.

The familiar vice of failure tightened around her chest. She pressed her palms against her temples, trying to recall the diagrams of inner ears and cranial structures, but the images dissolved into ribbons of light. The burning sensation spread from her chin to her throat. Her bones itched beneath her flesh.

Singing pierced the market's din. She stumbled toward the sound, following it past stalls of shimmering fabrics and weapons forged from strange substances. The music emanated from a small, shadowy tent where two fledgling crow shifters sat cross-legged on woven mats. Not singing. Laughter. They threw carved bones into a circle of salt and laughed as the shiny river stones inside skittered after them through some kind of magic. Their mother stood nearby, showing beaded fabrics to a potential buyer.

Blake stepped closer, drawn by their joy. The blue glow from her mating marks spilled across the children's upturned faces, illuminating their features.

Their laughter died.

"Mama!" The smaller one recoiled, wings erupting from his back in a flurry of glossy feathers. "It's a human!"

The mother dropped her merchandise. Fabric panels billowed to the ground as she lunged between Blake and her children, wings spreading to their full terrifying width.

"Get away from them!" she snarled.

Blake raised her hands. "I didn't mean—"

The mother's caw pierced the air. Her warning rippled through the marketplace, triggering a chain reaction. Heads snapped toward them. Wings unfurled. Daggers brandished. Conversations halted mid-syllable.

"Human!" someone shouted. "In the nursery quarter!"

"What?" Blake gaped. "I didn't know—"

But now she saw more young crawling about, playing beneath tables, hiding behind legs. More wings snapped open. Bodies and feathers closed ranks. The space around Blake expanded as the crow shifters backed away, their defensive postures creating a widening circle with her at its center.

Blake backed away, staggering as the world tilted beneath her feet. The market's colors blurred and separated, fracturing her vision into prisms. The crowd's angry murmurs transformed into a single deafening roar.

She needed to find River. She needed to breathe. She needed—

Her hand closed around something cold and smooth, a discarded glass coin that winked at her from beneath a merchant's table. She couldn't remember reaching for it, but its weight in her palm centered her, anchored her against the dizzying rush of sensation.

The mother's eyes tracked the movement, narrowing with dangerous understanding.

"Thief," she hissed, pointing at Blake's closed fist. "She steals from us!"

"Blake!"

A figure blocked her path, curvy with a black topknot, leaning on a cane.

"Lark." Relief momentarily cleared the fog in Blake's mind. "Thank god."

"Why do these people think you stole something?" Lark's gaze dropped to the glass coin clutched in Blake's fist. Her brows arched.

"I didn't realize I took it." Blake opened her palm, revealing the shimmering disc. The ground pitched and rolled. "I just … I don't feel so good."

"Oh dear. You've been to see her." Lark squinted, zeroing in on Blake's mouth. "That shit needs to come off your skin. Now."

Lark jabbed her cane toward the crow mother. "Get some water. Hurry."

The crowd's hostility receded like an outgoing tide. Something clicked in their recognition. The intensity in their eyes diminished, wings folding against backs as one of their own defended the outsider. The mother still ushered her children deeper into the tent, maintaining eye contact with Blake as she disappeared through the back flap. Seconds later, she emerged clutching a wooden bowl filled with water.

"Don't you know who this is?" Lark's voice carried as she grabbed a cloth from her windways pocket and dipped it in the bowl. "This is the Well-blessed human who saved the fledgling from drowning. She's Umbria Flock."

Irritation tightened Lark's features as she scrubbed at Blake's mouth and chin. "This shit is toxic," she muttered between swipes. "I can't believe River let you walk around with it on."

With each stroke of the cloth, clarity returned to Blake's senses. Colors stabilized. Sounds split into distinct notes rather than overwhelming discord. The burning sensation retreated from her skin, replaced by blessed coolness.

"Bloody hell." Blake pressed her palm against her forehead, still feeling a touch feverish. "What's in that paste?"

"You don't want to know."

"That look on your face makes me *need* to know."

Lark tossed the blackened cloth into the bowl and then hand signed her gratitude to the still-wary but now curious mother.

"It was guano," she said to Blake.

"Guano?"

"Otherwise known as vampire bat shit. Plus a few mana-cultivated herbs and spices."

Blake's hand flew to her mouth, gagging. "She put *bat poop* on me face?"

"You must have ingested some." Lark's lips twitched. "The hallucinogenic properties are quite potent. Explains why you're collecting shiny things." She nodded toward the coin still clutched in Blake's other hand. "Makes you go a bit bird-brained."

"I wasn't—" Blake stopped. Had she been gathering things? She couldn't remember. She forced her fingers to release the coin, watching it drop to the dirt with unexpected regret.

"Don't worry, I'll pay for it. I owe you anyway for saving my life." Lark dug into her pocket and tossed a few coins to the vendor.

"I didn't save your life."

"You mated my pain-in-the-tailfeather brother. That means he's now pestering you, not me. So you see? You saved my life." She returned the stolen coin to Blake's pocket with a pat and raised her voice loud enough to carry. "You saved many lives this morning when you jumped into the river. Not only did you draw the kelpie away from the fledglings, but you saved the Corvus's boy from drowning."

Gasps and sounds of awe rippled over the crowd. Murmurs and whispers morphed from hostile insults to praise. The mother picked up her fabrics from the ground and straightened her stall. She whispered something to her children, who stared at Blake with their little jaws dropping. She grabbed a bolt of pretty beaded silk and knelt before Blake, offering it with a bowed head. Her two children mimicked their mother, but each held a glimmering river stone from their game in their chubby little hands.

"Um." Blake's eyes widened.

She glanced at Lark, who gave no help, only grinned with pride.

Then the weirdest thing happened. More parents joined the first. A father with a small child on his shoulders kneeled with a jewel-adorned ink bottle in his outstretched hand. Then came another female, with a jar of something pearlescent. One by one, parents from around the nursery quarter arrived with an offering. Their children started creeping closer, touching Blake's hair and giggling over her blue, glowing marks. One even licked her arm until her mother swatted her away.

A nervous laugh slipped out of Blake. "What's happening?"

"They're showing their gratitude," she replied. "Fledglings are sacred in our community. Fae don't conceive as often as humans. Protecting their innocence is one of our most honored values." She collected the bolt of fabric and dropped it into Blake's arms. "Of course," she added wryly, "after their Blooding Ceremony, they're on their own."

After the parents retreated to their stalls, a few fledglings remained poking feathers and trinkets into Blake's hair before Lark shooed them away. Hushed mutters of bravery and blessings occasionally carried on the wind as word traveled.

"Where's River?" Lark asked, scanning the marketplace. "He shouldn't have left you alone after a reading."

"The book." Reality crashed back. "I accidentally left Aeron's anatomy book with the Donna. River went back for it."

"Then we should go find him." Lark looped her arm through Blake's. "The Donna's readings leave impressions. What did you see?"

Blake's throat tightened. The vivid image of her father standing beneath the eucalyptus tree returned full force.

"I saw me dad," she whispered. "He said … I just miss him."

Lark's expression softened with understanding. "Come on. Let's get you back to my idiot brother before he tears apart the Donna's caravan."

They retraced Blake's steps through the marketplace, the crowd parting before Lark's authoritative limping stride and cane. Blake's head cleared with each step, but her shoulder blades cramped—a persistent, shifting weight that refused to settle. The sooner she could put down the load of gifts, the better.

They didn't need to search far. River charged through the crowd, parting bodies with his glare alone. Ash followed in his wake, no book in sight.

River's eyes locked on Blake, his relief flooding their bond. He was with her in two quick strides, shouldering his sister aside, cupping Blake's face.

"Where have you been?"

Lark's cane cracked against his shoulder. "You left her with that toxic shit on her lips! What were you thinking?"

River ducked another swing. When Lark attempted a third strike, his patience snapped. He thrust his palm toward his sister, and a gust of air knocked her backward.

He returned to Blake, gathering her against his chest, squashing the armload of gifts.

"You scared me," he murmured into her hair. Fear pulsed raw and unfiltered through their connection. The intensity reminded her of his reaction in Cloud's trove, that edge of madness when he spoke of losing her.

Lark dusted her windways, scowling. "You're lucky I found her. Another minute and they'd have fed her to the fledglings."

River eased back, gaze dropping to her armload as if seeing it for the first time. "What's this?"

"Um." She bit her lower lip. "They kinda…"

"Thanked her," Lark finished. "You know, for saving the Corvus's son's life."

"Anyone would have done it," Blake muttered.

"No, they wouldn't," Ash countered matter-of-factly.

River relieved Blake of the heaviest items, a warm smile stretching his lips when he looked at her. "Crows don't swim, remember?"

"Yeah, but you killed the kelpie."

"I'm a Guardian." He said it like it meant nothing, and plucked a decorative feather from her hair. "What's all this?"

"The little ones couldn't stop touching me."

River stepped back for a better vantage. His eyes moved over her with reverence. "They *let* their fledglings touch you."

"Trust me, sis." Lark touched Blake's shoulder. "What you did went above and beyond the call of duty. The Well might have blessed your union with this mouse-brain, but what you did made you one of us."

River waved a young shifter over, paid him some coin, and instructed him to take Blake's armload of gifts to the Umbria roost. Once he was gone, he slung his arm around Blake's shoulders and asked Lark, "Why aren't you at the roost, anyway?"

"Oh, you know." Her gaze drifted toward a distant row of caravans. "Things aren't exactly peaceful there. The Cardonas settled nearby, and…"

"I thought with everything that happened—" River's words died as Lark laughed.

She flipped open her windways, revealing what remained of her leg after the kelpie attack. "Turns out a wing-mate with a leg like this isn't exactly appealing."

Rage slammed through their mating bond. River's fingers dug into Blake's shoulder. "You're telling me those fuckers are using this as an excuse to call off your mating? We just came from the Donna. She said the match was still on."

Lark blinked. "Still on?"

"It was never broken in the first place," Ash explained.

"Which means," River said, urging them eastward, "someone else is blocking your match. I can think of only one family in our murder with a centuries-old grudge against us. Considering I killed the damned monster, and strangers are thanking my mate for saving their son, I think it's fair to say they owe us."

A war cry shattered the marketplace's steady murmur. Blake's head snapped up as a massive shadow eclipsed the sun. A black-winged male plummeted from above, talons extended, trajectory aimed directly at the crowd. Her muscles tensed, ready to duck and take cover, but no one else reacted. Not a wing flared. Not a face showed alarm.

The predator swooped and snatched a woman examining decorative sundials at a nearby table. She shrieked, her wings erupting from her back, snapping so violently that molting feathers exploded in a cloud. The pair spiraled upward in a tangle of limbs and beating wings.

"Shouldn't we—" Blake clutched River's arm. "Shouldn't we help her?"

Lark's laughter melded with an unexpected sound— Ash's deep chuckle. Even his typically stoic face softened with a rare smirk.

"What?" Blake asked, heat climbing her neck. "What am I missing?"

River's hand settled at her waist, his lips lowering to her ear. "That, my treasure, was a courtship swoop."

"Ooh. But … she's fighting him." Blake watched the woman twist against her captor's grip.

"Because that's how their suitability is measured." River's breath was warm against her skin. "If she succeeds in breaking free, they're not a good match."

"Doesn't the Donna decide that?"

"Even with her approval, they must still prove to the community they're suited."

The pair descended behind a row of caravans, the woman's protests fading into the distance. Blake's eyes widened. "But the males are stronger—"

"Believe me," Lark drawled. "We crows know how to fight off unwanted advances. Right River?"

"I don't know what you mean."

Lark shared a humorous look with Ash.

"I'm serious," River replied. "The ladies love me."

Something hot and possessive boiled in Blake's blood. She didn't like this talk about previous partners. And he said love. Present tense.

"The book?" she snapped.

Guilt splashed over River's face as he circled his fist over his heart. "The Donna claimed it. We couldn't get into the caravan."

"Shit." Blake tugged her hair. "It's fine. I'll just … draw what I remember." She stepped forward, but the ground tilted beneath her feet, and she stumbled.

"First," Lark interrupted, pulling Blake from River's grasp. "You both look filthy and exhausted."

"And hungry," Blake admitted, her stomach twisting.

Her mate's face paled. "I should have thought of that. I brought you straight here from—"

"How about I take her back?" Lark suggested, gaze darting between the two Guardians. "You clearly need to be somewhere. Meet us at the roost."

Blake noticed Ash waiting with unease etched into his features. Perhaps his mother had arrived. Or Cloud. Or maybe River hadn't finished telling him what they'd found in the trove. Maybe he did.

"I won't leave you alone," River told Blake.

"I'll be fine." The truth was, she still needed some space after the reading. Nothing felt right. "I might even take a nap."

He nodded, the wildness in his eyes receding. Then he took her chin and lowered his lips to hers, pouring every-thing unsaid into his kiss: love, need, and relief. But the instant his tongue delved into her mouth, she pulled back with a scowl.

"Ew! Did you forget what she put on me?"

"Vampire shit."

"Don't you mean vampire *bat* shit?"

"Is that what she told you?" Amusement crinkled the edges of River's eyes. His sister's face was suspiciously blank.

"What's the difference?" Blake asked.

"When you meet a vampire, you'll see."

"I'm going to be sick."

"Trust me." He gathered her into his arms, eyes softening. "It's all gone." His smile dropped. "But Blake, remember what I said in the nesting caravan?"

Her thoughts scattered beneath that intense, heat-filled gaze. When she shook her head, he lowered his lips to her ear, his voice deepening to a rumble. "You could be covered in shit, blood, or dripping with my cum, and still, I'd want to lick every inch of your body."

FORTY-NINE

Pandora moved between the market stalls and tents, adjusting her stride to match the peculiar gait of the Tainted Ones. The stolen plumage adorning her shoulders rustled with each step, marking her as one of them. The stench of carrion was hard to swallow, but it did the job well enough. Beneath her skin, something stirred. A rhythm she had learned to ignore.

Tick-tick-tick.

The Great Murder heaved with life. Worthless trinkets were exchanged as if they were prized possessions. Sour liquors were sipped from crystal goblets. Laughter carried on the night breeze. Conversations faded in and out as she passed—talk of territory disputes, matings, and precious stones.

"Quite the collection you have there." A female with purple-tipped braids materialized at Pandora's elbow, gesturing toward her feather ornaments. "Northern murder pattern, but your scent…"

Pandora's fingers twitched. "My travels have taken me far."

The female's eyes narrowed. "Strange. Most crows circle back home before attending the Great Murder."

Tick-tick-tick.

"Some nests aren't worth returning to." Pandora pressed her fingertips against her sternum, steadying the sensation within.

She moved on quickly, palming the steel dagger concealed in her sleeve. The blade had already dispatched countless tainted enemies.

Three stalls ahead, a commotion rippled through the crowd. Carrion parted, opening a path to a striking pair—a dark-haired woman and a Guardian. The blue marks spiraling up their forearms glowed, even under the sunlight. A shorter female stood to the side, arguing with the Guardian.

Pandora selected a weathered tome from a nearby merchant's table, angling her body to watch the pair while feigning interest in the merchandise.

"Rare copy," the merchant chirped, edging closer. "It was engineered before the Freeze. Protected by a preservation spell. Worth every…"

His words faded as Pandora focused on the other conversation. The human stood close to the Guardian. Her shoulders tensed whenever fae drifted too near. Clearly, she was not entirely comfortable in her skin.

Another Guardian materialized from between two tents. This one was bronze-skinned with wind-swept hair. Something about him seemed familiar…

The book crumbled in Pandora's hands. The preservation

spell failed, and time eroded the paper, causing it to disintegrate.

The merchant cried out, distraught. "What have you done?"

Tick-tick-tick-tick.

"Looks like your spell ain't worth the feathers on your wings," Pandora muttered, dusting her hands. Her hidden metallic finishings must have disrupted the magic.

When she glanced back at the group, the Guardians were all that remained. They walked away, almost out of sight. Pandora abandoned the merchant's whining mid-sentence and stalked them. She circled the market until she found a narrow gap between structures and pressed against the rough wood, melting into the shadows. Deep voices carried through the late afternoon air.

"—confirmed sightings," the second Guardian said. "Three more disappearances near the western perimeter."

"Cloud?" The first's voice hardened.

"Or something else."

"Nero knows we're here."

"Maybe."

"That's my line."

A short laugh held no warmth.

"The Collector is here," the second Guardian continued. "She'll be at the Shadow Market tonight. Midnight. I doubt she'll have the cryptex—"

"But we can talk to her," the other finished. "Did you bring that thing you wanted to trade?"

An extended pause. "Yeah."

"Where?"

"Up your ass."

"Fuck you."

The duo moved away, their voices diminishing. Pandora remained frozen, processing this revelation. The Collector—the very target Nero had dispatched her to find. The Guardians had done her work for her. Tonight at the Shadow Market. Perfect.

Tick. Tick.

Pandora slipped deeper into the shadows, calculating. The cryptex remained her objective, but this unexpected development altered her approach. It would be better for her to observe this Collector first to understand what would make a valuable trade.

"Find the cryptex," she whispered. "Deliver it to Nero."

And then what?

"I knew you weren't one of us."

The purple-braided female blocked Pandora's path, her eyes narrowing. "Your feathers. They're not yours."

Tick-tick-tick-tick.

"I have claws, just like the rest of you." Pandora's voice remained flat.

"Prove it." The jeweled crow's hand drifted toward her hip, where a dagger hilt waited to be claimed.

Pandora struck. One hand clamped over the crow's mouth while the other clamped around her throat, driving her backward behind a stack of wooden crates. The female kicked, scratched, and drew a wound across Pandora's cheek, but no blood came out.

Her eyes widened with terror, but she made no sound. Pandora still covered her mouth.

Electricity flared in the atmosphere, skipping and crackling. Wings started to manifest. Shadows and shimmering light formed shapes behind the female.

But Pandora was faster. Warmth flooded her joints. Her

fingertips tingled, then split open, and five metal claws ripped through the female's throat. Blood welled around polished metal. The Tainted One's wings disappeared, her access to the Well cut off. Her struggles weakened, then eventually ceased.

"See?" Pandora whispered as the body slumped. "I told you I had claws."

FIFTY

Blake hunched over the table in the nesting caravan, her fingers tight around a quill as she drew another diagram of the inner ear's anatomy. Her hand trembled. Wavy lines replaced the precision she needed. Fucked up again. *Gah.* She crumpled the paper and tossed it onto the growing pile of failures.

"Bloody hell." She massaged her throbbing temples.

The Donna's paste had washed off, but the aftereffects lingered. Nausea churned her stomach. Feverish flushes made her sweat. Colors brightened until they seared her retinas. The marketplace gifts sat in neat piles around the caravan, mocking today's failures with yesterday's accomplishments.

She dipped the quill in a crystal inkwell, a gift from one of the grateful parents, and pulled out a clean piece of paper. She stalled. "How am I supposed to help Ada if I can't even draw a bloody ear canal right?"

Saving that fledgling from drowning had been easy in comparison. Every child in Perth learned to swim during their school years. Drawing medical diagrams from memory while battling bat shit toxins? Not so easy.

Beside her on the table, Trix's eucalyptus sapling still thrived in River's vase. She ran her finger along the cracks in the ceramic, willing her magic to activate. A strange tremor ran up her arm through the Well-blessed marks, but then dissipated.

You're not meant to be here.

The feather casting gave Blake no solace, only an ill feeling that something wasn't right. Her dad, the warped memories, the strange signs and symbols. It seemed more like a nightmare than a vision.

She shoved the papers away and pressed her forehead against the cool wooden table. What good was her photographic memory if she hadn't given herself enough time to study the diagrams?

The caravan door swung open.

River?

Her hope faded when Lark limped inside.

"Still nothing?" she asked.

Blake slid blank papers over the map she'd been recreating from Cloud's trove. When she couldn't recall the anatomy diagrams, she'd found herself reproducing other things. Words. Lyrics. Maps. Things she couldn't get out of her mind.

"It's shit," she replied. "Everything keeps blurring together."

"Aftereffects of the Donna's paste." Lark offered a steaming cup. "This helps."

Blake accepted the drink with a hand sign of gratitude. She smelled the bitter liquid and grimaced. "It's not spiked, is it?"

"Just a herbal relaxant."

"What I wouldn't give for a hot choccie with marsh-mallows."

Lark slid onto the mended bench seat opposite. "How are you feeling?"

"I should be asking you that." Blake gave a pointed look at the injured woman's leg. "You were so brave. I can't believe you leaped between the kid and a monster."

"You're the one who almost drowned."

"Not really. I know how to swim."

"Don't sell yourself short. I know how to fly, but that doesn't make what I did any less brave. Does it?"

The last words sounded hesitant. Blake lifted her gaze from the mug and met those unsteady eyes.

"Look at us," she blurted. Scoffed. "Two badass cunts doubting ourselves." She glanced outside the window and caught a glimpse of Talo arguing at the boundary between the roosts. "I didn't see any of them jumping between a kelpie and a child."

"Not even Tommas." Lark snorted. Her humor faded. "He's not a fighter like his brothers. But that's why I love him." She sighed. "Dad's accusing him of *letting* me get hurt."

"I thought I saw Tommas swimming to you."

"He did. But if it weren't for River and you, he'd have been eaten. Me too." Her eyes watered, and she cleared her throat. "Anyway, these gifts are beautiful. I think you actually have a few valuable items here."

Blake glanced at her marketplace treasures. The beaded silk caught the afternoon light, scattering tiny rainbows across her failed drawings. "At least we did something right yesterday."

"*You* did."

"What does that mean?"

"The Corvus will offer you a debt for saving his son's life."

"But not you?" Outrage flamed Blake's cheeks.

Lark held up her palm. "Before you lecture me about the unfairness, let me tell you something else about crow economics. There is only one winner. River might be brave, but that's expected from Guardians. You're the one who will receive the glory." Her hand dropped to the silk scarf, and she stroked it. "But I'm not angry. It's well deserved. A win for you is still a win for the kettle."

Shouting erupted outside, voices crescendoing with volleyed insults.

"For *Crimson's* sake," Lark groaned, reaching for her walking stick. "The Cardonas have pitched their camp right beside ours."

"That's not normal?"

"Usually we're relegated to the end of our murder's territory, but this year the Cardonas have been ordered to camp here too. I think Cloud's unsanctioned Vendetta is affecting their social standing." She paused near the door, shoulders tensing before she met Blake's eyes. "Sera and Ma are also arguing with Carlotta. I've never seen them all filled with so much … hatred."

Pain bled from those dark eyes. Blake would be the worst person in the world if she ignored it, even feeling as shitty as she did. "You want me to come with?"

Hope filled Lark's round eyes. "If you're not too busy."

"Babe, you saved me bacon at the market today. Of course I'll come."

Lark's tentative smile felt like the beginning of something

Blake was too afraid to name, but desperately wanted. Needed. She followed her new sister outside, blinking against the slanting afternoon sun spearing light through the trees. The Umbria roost buzzed with activity. Distant cousins erected colorful awnings farther down. Winged children darted between supply stacks. Sentinels perched in nearby trees, watching their territory while in crow form.

But the most beautiful sight was the dam in the distance, caught between two mountains. Water trickled down the ancient wall and uneven ledges, glittering like falling stars into random pools before spilling over. Fae splashed about playing or sat dangling their legs. Blake imagined family reunions, tales of adventure being passed on, and boasts around their latest scores. It looked far more inviting than the disturbance shaping up here.

As Lark mentioned, the Cardona kettle had begun establishing their camp next door in rigid, precise rows at the boundary line. Their black caravans created a stark, military presence against the Umbrias' bohemian sprawl.

At the contested line, Talo faced off against Carlotta's wingmate, Salvatore. The two couldn't look more different. Talo wore his usual colorful garb, while his opponent sported a leather vest with bone studs. Salvatore had dark, slicked-back hair that emphasized his sharp, ageless features and thick beard. He seemed like the kind of man Blake avoided at the local pub in Perth, the kind with an unlawful firearm tucked into his Harley's saddlebag.

"Your central post stands six inches over the boundary," he growled and thrust a measuring cord against the dirt beside the stake. "Move it back."

"Ah, but what's six inches between old friends?" Talo hammered the stake in deeper.

"That's what he tells all the ladies," Ravi joked, emerging from Blake's neighboring caravan with a tray of filled crystal goblets.

"We've used this exact configuration for centuries," Carlotta said, walking up to stand behind her wingmate. Somehow she made a simple black pair of windways and wrap top look stunning.

Tommas sat above the Cardonas on a branch, legs dangling, wings drooping, gazing longingly at Lark.

Talo's smile tightened. "You Cardonas might be new to this ... distance from the Corvus, but the boundary markers remain precisely where my grandfather established them."

"Precisely?" Salvatore snorted, his massive knuckles whitening around the cord. "Precisely a fucking joke."

"Yes, I'm sure that's why your roost resembles a military encampment designed by a drunken pixie with a ruler fetish."

"At least we maintain order," Salvatore grumbled. "Not like this..." He gestured at the Umbria encampment. "Rainbow vomit."

Something pinged near Ravi. She ducked as a pebble ricocheted off the caravan roof, feathers puffing. Scanning the opposing roost, she located the culprit and pointed. "Your son is throwing rocks at our caravan!"

Another Cardona—same dark unruly hair, handsome features, and menacing eyes as the rest of them—launched another pebble from his perch on a black caravan's roof. Sera arrived with a tray of moonshine, saw the projectile, and swatted it away with a deft flick of her wing. Her grimace transformed into smug satisfaction when the stone ricocheted into a Cardona hanging lamp.

"Rocco's just testing structural integrity." Salvatore

folded his arms. "If your caravan can't withstand a few pebbles, perhaps it's not up to code."

"Code?" Talo laughed. "There is no code at the Great Murder."

"There should be, starting with minimum distances between kindling and sleeping quarters. Your piles are a fire hazard."

"That's rich," Sera shot back, "coming from a male who almost burned down his nest after a three-day bender."

"That was over a century ago!" Salvatore's cheeks darkened. "Your memory stretches inconveniently long when it serves you."

"And yours is conveniently short," Ravi countered, defending her daughter. "Especially about who taught your sons to fly when you were too busy with gambling debts."

Lark groaned and blocked her ears. The argument intensified. Farther down the boundary line, two crow shifters engaged in a tug-of-war with some kind of sash or curtain, while younger cousins on either side hurled increasingly creative insults ... and pebbles as per Rocco's instructions.

"Your kettle's aura is black as ink," Ravi hissed at Carlotta. "No wonder one of your sons rots in a dungeon and the other—"

"How dare you!" The Cardona matriarch surged forward, wings snapping open, only to pause when River and Ash emerged from between two Umbria caravans.

The Guardians stopped short.

River's fingers twitched toward *Peacemaker* as he scanned the gathering. When he saw Blake, relief washed through their bond. He crossed to her in four long strides, anyone in his way scattering. Ash prowled behind him, glaring at anyone and everyone, the wind stirring fallen leaves in his wake.

"You good?" River's fingers brushed Blake's cheek.

She nodded, warmth spreading in her chest. "Thank god you're here. I feel like things are escalating."

His gaze flicked to where the Cardonas still tried to measure the distance between roosts. Talo discarded his mallet and tied a stone onto the stake he'd installed.

"What is he doing?" Blake asked.

"Proximity stones. He's setting up an alarm in case anyone tries to cross into the Umbria roost."

Lark's face paled. She limped closer. "Do they think Tommas's family will steal from us?"

"Who the fuck knows?" He shook his head and motioned Ash in closer. When he arrived, River pitched his voice low. "We had a word with the Corvus. About Lark and Tommas's match."

"You did?" Lark whispered.

"It wasn't the Corvus *or* the Donna who blocked the match," Ash announced.

Loudly.

Silence crashed over the gathering. Even the feuding cousins farther down froze mid-tug.

"What do you mean?" Tommas launched from his perch, wings snapping open to ease into his landing.

"Who did it then?" Lark clutched Tommas's arm. "Who hates us that much?"

"No one hates you, love," Ravi said. "Sometimes a match isn't meant to be."

Blake's mate's fury and outrage roiled through their bond. She never expected him to turn to his mother and say, "Tell them."

Color drained from her face. "This isn't the time."

His voice dropped to that dangerous purr. "Is there a right time to tell your daughter you interfered with her love match?"

Ravi fretted with a vial on her sash. "I was protecting our family."

"Protecting me?" Lark stepped toward her mother. "From what?"

"From them!" Ravi's wings snapped open as she gestured toward the Cardonas. "From their toxic influence. From their cursed bloodline."

"Cursed?" Carlotta hissed. "It wasn't my son who urged others to abandon their kettle and walk into the ceremonial lake!"

"No, it was your son who abandoned the Order of the Well to go on a murder spree!" Ravi shot back. "After he broke my boy's wings!"

The words echoed. A lone crow cawed in the distance. The wind rustled leaves. Blake sensed her mate's horror dawning, despite his expression being blank.

"You knew." His voice emerged barely audible.

His mother's silence condemned her more than any confession.

"You *knew* what Cloud did to me." River's hands curled into fists. "All this time."

Talo stepped forward. "Son—"

River raised his hand and looked at his family's faces, noticing his father's guilty grimace, his sister's shock, and Ash's eyes avoided him.

"You told them." He glared daggers at his adopted brother.

"To be fair, you never said not to."

"River, please." Ravi reached for her son, but he flinched away.

"How. Long."

She darted a nervous look at Ash. "He came to us the night you were injured."

River's wide eyes found Blake's, latching on like a drowning man spotting shore. Without a word, she took his hand and tugged him away from the gathering, behind the nearest caravan.

"They knew," he rasped, bracing one hand against the wooden panel. "All of them. I stayed away for five years. Thought I was keeping some big secret, but they fucking knew." A bitter laugh escaped him. "All this time, I was acting like a good little Guardian so they wouldn't catch on when I finally got my chance for revenge. What a waste of time. I could have been hunting him down, could have ended this sooner."

"Ended what?" Blake snapped. "His life? Yours? Only one of you is coming out of that battle alive." Her throat constricted. "And if you did hunt him down, then I might never have met you. I can't lose you."

"He deserves to pay for what he did to me. For his betrayal. For making a mess of everything! And now…" He held up his blue-marked hand. "Now there's no doubt who'll win."

"Maybe." Fury and fear clashed in her veins, causing her to tremble. "But if you think the mess is bad now? Imagine what it would look like if you actually went through with it. If you murdered your best friend."

He turned his back on her and paced the length of the caravan, boots crunching on dirt and twigs, fingers spearing through his hair, weapons clanking. His emotions were so knotted up that she couldn't identify them. When he turned back with an agonized look, her heart melted.

"I know you're hurting," she whispered. "But Lark is out there right now, learning that her parents betrayed her. *Your* parents. The couple who everyone believes value love above all else. Lark's happiness was sacrificed because of secrets and shame, and all this … all this *bullshit* bickering has nothing to do with their love."

River's gaze fixed on Blake.

"You're right." He nodded. "Fuck this fucking shit. Not on my watch."

But he remained rooted, eyes stark with that same vulnerability she'd glimpsed in Cloud's trove.

"River?"

His chest heaved. "I can't do this. They won't listen to me. I'm half a fucking—"

She smacked his chest. Hard.

"Ow." He pouted, rubbing his chest.

"Oh, stop it. As if that hurt. And stop feeling sorry for yourself. You killed the kelpie when it seemed invincible. You're here, trying to save the world! You're a fucking machine." She lowered her voice in case anyone was eavesdropping. "Both in and out of the sack."

That caught his attention. His lips twitched, blue eyes crinkling. "Keep talking."

Blake rolled her eyes. "One stroke of your ego and look at you."

"Stroke me more, Sparkles." He gathered her into his arms, eyes alight with affection.

She laughed despite herself. "River, you're me mate. The bravest, funniest, sexiest damn—"

His lips crashed down on hers, tongue driving in. The

sudden, hot male taste short-circuited her brain. River gripped her face and deepened the kiss. When he finally relaxed and pulled away, she was left dazed and speechless.

"After I sort this out," he murmured, idly toying with her hair and holding it to the sun, "remind me about the surprise I have for you."

"A surprise?"

He nodded, grinning in that disarming way of his. "Been working on it all afternoon. Consider yourself booked until midnight."

"Midnight?"

"When I have to work. Shadow Market." Mood broken, he scowled at the sky. "Ash's psycho ma is here."

"Well, that's good, right?" she said. "He'll need you with him."

River nodded, took her hand, and pulled her after him as he strode back into the fray.

When they arrived, the crowd had grown. Neighboring families gathered to watch the drama unfold. Lark stood rigid between them, tears brimming in her eyes. Tommas held his father back from pressing a dagger to Talo's throat. Rocco goaded Salvatore on. Ash sat on a chair outside the nesting caravan, expression blank until he caught sight of his adopted brother. Something like approval flickered across his features.

River gave him a curt nod, then barged toward the warring families. He flicked *Peacemaker* at his hip, the shiny reflections drawing every eye.

"*Enough!*" His bellow shook leaves from nearby trees. Crows took flight. Once he held everyone's attention, he continued. "The match between Lark and Tommas will proceed. As a Guardian of the Twelve, I invoke the right of making up the fucking rules myself. These two love each other. The Donna approves of their match. So I repeat, it *will* proceed." He looked at Lark. "Congratulations, sis." Glared at Tommas. "You break her heart, and I'll rip yours from your ass. Got it?"

Tommas nodded slowly. No one spoke. No one else moved until Carlotta folded her arms. Her wingmate shrugged his son off. Talo pulled Ravi under his wing. Lark and Tommas gravitated toward each other, hesitant, but with barely contained excitement in their expressions.

River watched, hand on *Peacemaker*, daring anyone to challenge him—especially his mother—until the couple reunited. Then he waited a full minute after Tommas grinned and yanked Lark to his side.

Blake was about to breathe a sigh of relief when Salvatore pointed at the boundary line and barked, "He's still six inches over."

Arguments erupted anew, each side squawking as though nothing had happened.

The shouts compounded in Blake's ears, ringing and blaring. The sun's glare brightened through swaying leaves. Her skin felt too hot. Her clothes clung. Everything annoying bubbled up inside her until it exploded from her mouth.

"Shut the fuck up!" she screamed, pulling at her hair. "All of you cunts, just shut *up!*"

Mouths opened and closed.

"Look at yourselves," she said. "Fighting over posts and bloody boundary lines while your children suffer. You *have* them. You're all *alive*. Don't lose sight of what matters here."

River tugged her close. Ash unfolded from his seat and strolled to their side. "She's right. Listen to her."

Salvatore grumbled, "I think we'll let the tribunal sort this out."

"No," Blake said. "Find another way. This isn't about the boundary line. It's about all the grievances you two kettles leave unsaid. Find a way to settle this amongst yourselves, or it will never end."

The words hung in the air like smoke.

Her stomach dropped as the silence stretched. Every face turned toward her—not just the feuding families, but the gathering crowd of neighbors who'd come to watch the drama. Ancient eyes. Powerful wings. Centuries of crow politics and blood feuds.

And she'd just told them all what to do.

FIFTY-ONE

"Alright." Salvatore sneered at Blake. "You seem to know everything. What's your grand idea?"

River took a step forward. "Watch your tone with my mate."

The last thing they needed was more discourse.

"An idea," Blake muttered, mind racing. "Of course, I have one."

River lowered his head to her level. "You don't have to do anything they tell you to."

"It's fine. I have an idea."

"You do?"

"Yeah. Sure." She faked a smile, but she started this. She should finish it.

Idea. Idea.

A way to settle their dispute. She tapped her thigh, thinking.

Idea. Idea.

The memory hit her. Christmas Day. Her brothers, three sheets to the wind, challenged the Johnsons next door to a game of street footy. They used wheelie bins for goal posts. The winning team claimed cul-de-sac parking rights for a year.

Perfect. Sort of.

She pointed at her mate. "Don't let anyone move. I'll be right back."

Peacemaker appeared in River's hand. His feral grin promised consequences to anyone who disobeyed. His instant support left a warm, gooey feeling in her heart as she jogged back to the nesting caravan and headed inside.

The gratitude trinkets were so beautiful that she almost hesitated, wanting them for herself. She snatched the beaded silk first, then a crystal figurine, and anything that looked valuable until her arms were loaded.

When she returned outside, a storm had rolled in from beyond the dam wall. She dumped her treasures onto the ground between the two roosts. Before she could explain, the first fat raindrop splashed her forehead. Another followed, landing on her cheek.

The feuding families began retreating toward their caravans.

"Fuck'sake," she bemoaned, looking up as the sky opened. "Just me luck."

"Wait." River's command froze everyone in place. He assessed the rain with narrowed eyes, then shrugged. "A little water won't hurt us. It's not like we have to swim in it. We settle this now."

Blake stared at him, surprised by his willingness. And his bossiness. To be honest, it was getting kind of hot. Already soaked, his leather uniform must be uncomfortable and heavy. But he looked at her with unwavering patience and trust.

"Explain the game, Sparkles."

Summoning her courage, she faced the crow shifters and shouted over the steady downpour, "Where I come from, we settled disputes with a game."

Eyes lit up. Several males shuffled forward, especially Salvatore and Talo, who eyed each other warily.

"What kind of game?" Rocco asked, flicking dripping hair from his eyes.

"Football." When no signs of recognition answered her, she added, "Think of it as a battle for territory."

Someone scoffed. "Who uses their feet in a game?"

"Or a ball," another said. Paused. "What even is a ball?"

Blake resisted slapping her palm over her face. Did these fae not play sport? Had that been lost over time? She tried to size up an imaginary ball between her hands and explained. "A ball is like a stretchy, air-filled sack that you bounce around and throw and kick."

"You throw around trapped air?" a Faelin asked.

"With your feet?" another cousin gasped. "Not wings?"

"Forget the ball and feet part," she amended and pointed at her sodden treasure pile. She'd been explaining this all wrong. "I've changed the rules anyway. Think of this game as a heist." That earned her more *oohs* and *aahs*. "You steal a shiny from the middle, get it to your team's goal—I mean trove—on the other side without being tackled or having your shiny stolen."

"Tackling, you say?" Talo narrowed his eyes at Salvatore.

"Can I use daggers?" a young Cardona cousin called.

"No."

"Claws?"

"No."

"Wing attacks from above?" another asked. The number

of players had grown exponentially in the past few minutes, each lured by the potential of treasure. And violence.

"No wings," Blake insisted. "And no mana allowed. Just regular physical strength and skill on the ground."

"Yes!" Rocco blurted, swinging his finger between the two Guardians. "You two are just normal mouse-munchers without your fancy metal and inflated mana shit."

Ash stared at him through rain-slicked hair, tattooed arms folded, his bulging biceps doing the talking.

"Great!" Blake clapped her wet hands, grinning at River. "You captain one team. Ash can captain the other. Each side will have a trove."

River started to protest that Ash belonged to the Umbria kettle, not the Cardona's, but then he caught her intention. The game would remain fair and controlled with a Guardian on each side. She hoped. Maybe if they mixed up the families on different teams, they'd forget about the feud altogether.

"We'll crush them," Sera whispered to Talo, stripping off her weapon's sash to reveal a skimpy wrap top, earning her an appreciative whistle from somewhere in the back.

Sera responded by flicking out her claws and giving a toothy grin that showed her relation to River.

"No claws," Blake reminded.

"Kill 'em, sis!" Lark shouted from the sidelines beneath a waterproof canopy Ravi and Carlotta were setting up. "Get Tommas in the nuts for me!"

"What?" His eyes widened.

"Love you!" Lark kissed the air in his direction.

"First, we need to clear a field." Blake pointed to a muddy area between the edge of the forest and the roosts.

The transformation was immediate. Feuding families

dissolved into strategizing teams. Insults morphed into competitive boasts. A makeshift field materialized with startling speed. And then, the glorious shedding began.

Sodden leather jackets hit the dirt. Tunics followed. Wings shifted away for safety. Males stripped down to leather breeches or linen pants, revealing landscapes of sculpted muscle glistening from the rain. Sera, the only female brave enough to join the game, sliced off her windways at the thighs and strutted about, bending over strategically to clear random pebbles from the field. More than one male on the opposing team stopped to stare.

With the rules laid out, Blake left the game in the hands of the two Guardians and retreated to a hastily erected canopy stretching between each roost. It had the best vantage point and welcomed spectators from both families. Lark and Ravi already poured out the moonshine to anyone who joined.

"I have to say, sis," Lark said, patting a cushion beside her. "This is a spectacular idea."

Blake grinned into her cup. "Let's just hope it works."

"Who cares if it works?" Ravi purred. "Look at my Talo, still in peak physical shape."

"Gross, Ma." Lark scrunched up her nose.

"I simply meant it's the perfect time for a little anatomy observation."

"Of course." Blake nodded solemnly. "That's exactly what this is for."

Talo argued tactics with a Faelin. Ash, whose warrior's body rippled with power, discussed war with the Cardonas. Salvatore's raw strength was undeniable, even at rest. Tommas moved with an earnest intensity that made Lark squirm beside Blake.

And River. God, River. Her mate. His perfectly proportioned body. His languid stretches. The rolls of his shoulders as he sized up his opponents. Every line of him was honed and perfect. He moved with some kind of raw, animal grace that made Blake's mouth go dry, and her insides flutter. This was better than watching him fight the owl brigade. This time, he was shirtless.

All hers.

She fanned her face. The rain did nothing to cool her down.

"They're just showing off now." Humor laced Lark's voice. "Like juveniles with their first flight feathers."

Since Sera was participating, a cushion remained free beside Ravi. Lark pointed it out to her new mother-in-law, who stood alone beneath her nearby caravan's awnings. Carlotta hesitated, but settled awkwardly, her black wings folded tightly against her back. She remained stiff and formal until Ravi handed her a glass of moonshine. Carlotta accepted with a cautious smile.

"How are you holding up?" Ravi's gaze flicked toward the Cardona roost. "With the tribunal hearing approaching for … well. You know."

Blake's shoulders went rigid. But Carlotta's shoulders sagged almost imperceptibly.

"Every day I wonder," she whispered, twirling her glass, "if this unsanctioned Vendetta will end in exile for us, or him." Her breath hitched. "*If* he turns up."

"He'll turn up," Ravi said, briefly touching Carlotta's hand. "And when he does, we'll figure it out. Together."

A pause. A held breath. Then, Carlotta whispered, "I've missed our evening observations."

"Me too."

A whistle blew. The game exploded into chaotic action. It started less football, more full-contact and high-speed larceny. Tackles landed with bone-jarring force. Dodges defied gravity. After a few rounds of Blake barking rule amendments, they settled into an organized rhythm.

Two imposing figures approached the canopy during a natural lull between rounds, drawing curious glances from the muddy players. Decked out in bejeweled robes with feathered shawls, the Domatri Corvus and Corala stepped directly beside Blake. He looked down his long nose, but his eyes flickered with recognition and something close to respect.

"Blake Umbria," he stated simply, a little awkwardly. "Our son lives because of you. The Domatri Kettle *thanks* you."

A buzz zipped over Blake's skin as the Well acknowledged a debt. Blake's jaw dropped. Her gaze darted to Lark and Ravi, to Carlotta, and then to the field where every single player tried not to stare—including River. *Debt. He owes me a debt.* Heart hammering, Blake seized the moment.

"There is something," she said quickly, before she lost her courage. "That I would like to claim."

"Now?" the Corvus raised a brow. "You do not wish to think it over?"

"River's kettle shouldn't be ostracized for following their hearts." She glanced at Ravi. "For eloping against the Donna's wishes."

The Corvus and Corala exchanged a meaningful look. After a pause, he inclined his head. "Agreed. They shall be restored to their proper place within the murder."

Another zip of magic buzzed over Blake's skin as the Well acknowledged his promise. Looks of shock bounced around. Someone cleared their throat on the field. Rain pitter pattered on the canopy.

After a few more awkward moments of silence, Blake asked, "Would you like to join in?"

Imperious brows raised. The Corvus glanced at the mud-streaked players. Just when she started to wonder if maybe games were illegal here too, the tall leader shrugged out of his ornate ceremonial cloak.

"It has been decades since I participated in something so frivolous." His eyes gleamed with unexpected mischief as he shifted away his wings. "Perhaps I can take a break from responsibility."

With a parting kiss on his mate's head, he jogged onto the field. The teams reshuffled and pulled another player from the crowd to remain even. The Corala settled gracefully onto a hastily vacated cushion, her gaze lingering on the moonshine with slight disapproval. Before she voiced a reprimand about this being a party, Ravi quickly interjected, "Anatomy observations. Purely educational."

Carlotta nodded solemnly in agreement. "Essential for understanding physical conditioning."

The Corala's expression softened with understanding.

"I prefer to observe," she said, voice like smooth honey, accepting the offered glass. "But I will judge which team demonstrates superior technique."

The Corvus proved surprisingly agile for one accustomed to leadership over combat. He dodged between players cunningly, stealing a trinket from beneath Talo's nose and sprinting with unexpected speed toward his chosen trove. River intercepted a jeweled comb that Tommas was sprinting with. The two collided in a tangle of limbs, sending them rolling through the mud. Nearby, Ash executed a move so fast that Blake barely tracked it. He left Sera blinking dazedly in mud, minus her polished river stone.

"You're slowing down, princeling," River taunted as he sprinted past, snatching the stone from Ash's grip.

"Just giving you a fighting chance, *old mate*," he called back, lips curving in a rare smile.

Blake gasped and pointed. "He learned that word from me!"

Instead of getting possessive and aggressive, River's laughter erupted, raw and genuine. The humor was infectious. Jokes and insults mingled with grunts and curses. The rain had lessened to a gentle mist, but mud now spattered every participant, creating tribal-like patterns across bare torsos and arms.

The next round, River snagged the beaded silk—the one the first mother had offered Blake. He tucked it under his arm, proclaiming loudly that he'd win it back for her, and broke free from a pile-up to sprint for the Umbria trove. He was magnificent. Muddy, sweaty, dark hair plastered to his temples, eyes blazing with competitive fire as he checked to see if she watched him.

He was so magnificent, in fact, that Blake wasn't the only one who noticed. A cluster of females had gathered at the field's edge. Their feathers fluffed as they chattered behind their hands, pointing and aiming sultry eyes at him.

River ran directly toward them and executed a completely unnecessary but undeniably hot mud-spraying slide past their feet as he evaded capture from the opponent. The females shrieked and giggled, wings flaring in delight. He flashed them a devastating wink, then veered toward the Umbria trove.

"What the actual fuck?" Blake sat up straight, eyes narrowing to slits.

Was that flirting? Did River *wink* at them? Like how he'd winked at her on the first day they met?

Mine.

Possessiveness burned through her veins before she could stifle it. Her fingers curled tightly around her still-full glass. She wanted to hurl herself onto that field and tackle those preening bitches.

She'd never been enough for Jeff. Not pretty enough. Not sophisticated enough. Now that she knew how he'd truly felt about her, she wondered how many of those football groupies were 'just annoying fans' as he'd claimed. How many had he actually fucked behind the locker rooms while Blake waited in the dedicated area for WAGs?

"I'm going to fucking pluck out their eyes," she snarled.

"Whoa there, sister-matriarch." Lark's voice carried rich amusement as she leaned closer. "Deep breaths. Ruffle your feathers later. Let him see you watching."

Lark subtly adjusted her position, angling toward Tommas, who was on his way to do the same thing. "Remember when I laughed at how you thought a courtship swoop was unfair on the female?"

"Yeah." Blake forced her fists to unclench and took a shaky sip of moonshine. The burning beneath her skin intensified, spreading across her back like wildfire.

Lark casually waved at Tommas, black claws extended from her fingertips. His face paled, and he quickly changed trajectory, heading to the opposite side of the field. "That's because their hands are busy grabbing us during the swoop. But ours aren't. Their balls are free game."

Except that Blake didn't have claws.

As River triumphantly slammed another prize onto the Umbria trove pile, the air changed. Electrified. A visceral wrongness scraped across Blake's nerves.

Her mate felt it too. He froze mid-celebration, arm still raised in triumph. His attention darted to somewhere beside the canopy she sat beneath and widened.

His silent scream of danger pierced her through their bond.

She followed his gaze to a lone figure. Tall. Clad in tattered Guardian leathers. Black, wavy hair stuck to a handsome face. Who else could it be but Cloud? Two bloody stripes slashed from each brow to join at a stubbled chin. Somehow, it remained intact despite the rain.

"Oh shit," Lark muttered.

Blake thought the Corvus had presence, but this guy—this menacing, tattooed and leather-wrapped dark angel—was a force unto himself. He was the axis on which this world turned. He pulled gravity with his gaze as it swept the field.

Slowly, deliberately, he unbuckled his weapon belt. Daggers thudded softly onto the damp earth. Knuckle dusters. A sword. More knives. More sharp things. He peeled off his jacket and then his undershirt. Almost every inch of revealed skin was riddled with ink—the oil slick, power-enhancing kind.

At River's glare, a small, almost imperceptible smile touched Cloud's lips. It held no warmth, only a chilling vacancy. His voice was quiet, but somehow still carried across the sudden, absolute silence.

"Room for one more player?"

FIFTY-TWO

How quickly things changed.

One moment, River was floating, drunk on physical exertion, mud slicking his skin, basking in the territorial heat in his mate's eyes as she tracked his every move. More than his mate, she was part of the murder. A crow. And he was already planning how this new possessiveness of hers would add to the surprise he'd planned later.

Then his intuition spiked, and everything felt cold.

Like an apparition from his nightmares, Cloud appeared at the edge of the makeshift field, stripping off weapons from his dirty Guardian uniform as if he belonged. As if nothing was wrong. Daggers thudded. Jacket and shirt went next. Power-enhancing tattoos pulsed over pale skin. Dark curls, longer now, clung to his damp face. And the V—those fucking strips of preserved human blood mocked the rain. Mocked time itself.

River's gaze snapped to Blake beneath the canopy. She sat frozen, hand half-raised as if to warn him. Or to call him close. Unease scampered through their bond like a skittish mouse. Fear trickled down his spine. Had Cloud noticed her? Had he noticed the blue glow of their mating marks?

The blue-eyed, rogue Guardian ignored the collective gasp. Down to his low-slung leather pants and boots, he moved onto the field with unnerving calm. He walked straight past River and stopped beside Ash.

On the other side.

Talo sputtered, "Uneven numbers! Someone needs to switch!"

The Corvus spat at Cloud's feet and crossed sides. He pointed at some poor, nameless Umbria cousin and waited until the player scurried off the field.

Not that Cloud noticed. He stared vacantly, head tilted toward Ash, already listening to the rules with detached interest.

The Umbria team shuffled nervously, pretending nothing had changed.

This *wasn't* normal.

Fuck it. No more waiting.

River stalked into the no-man's land between the teams.

"That's it?" he shouted across the misty night. "You stroll back after five years of *nothing*?" He jabbed a finger at his triad tattoo. "No answer. Not a peep. Now you crash the party, invite yourself to the game, and for what?" He gestured at the dwindling pile of treasures, gifts his mate earned by saving a child's life. "To show off what a big, bad fucking bird you are now?"

Who had Cloud saved?

No one.

In fact, *negative* people.

As if he heard River's thoughts, Cloud's eyes narrowed and zeroed in on Blake.

River's fists clenched at his side. He took a threatening step forward. If that bastard looked at her for one more second, took one step in her direction, he was dead. But the crow-shifter dug into his rear pocket and pulled something out, concealed in his fist. He held River's gaze and strode toward the treasure pot three feet away.

"This should cover the buy-in." His fist opened. A heavy object dropped onto the mud. *Squelch.*

They were barely a wingspan apart, close enough to feel the tension crackling between them. Or maybe that was just Cloud's powerful aura, the same power that had once summoned lightning and seared River's flesh.

"Fuck me, is that real?" Rocco blurted.

River refused to break eye contact, but when he sensed his mate's shock, his gaze drifted downward.

A single, enormous ruby sat innocuously in the muddy grass.

The same one they'd stolen from the Collector's hoard centuries ago. The same one River had assumed they'd used as payment for Ash to start his new life. The same one that had been in Cloud's trove when they'd left.

He knows.

He knows we were there. He knows I saw everything.

Ash's eyes narrowed, darting between his fellow Guardians.

Excited whispers about the ruby's value spread among the players and beyond the field, all unaware of the real challenge unfolding. Smug satisfaction shone in Cloud's eyes, cold and sharp as he stared at River.

He wants a fight. He came back to finish what the lightning started.

Worse, he wanted to do it with Blake watching.

"We playing," Cloud said, tone hardening, "or we gonna keep eye-fucking each other from across the field?"

Snickers erupted from the Cardona team.

The Corvus stepped forward, regal despite the mud clinging to his skin. "D'arn Cloud Cielo Cardona." Each official name fell like a hammer blow. "Evading the tribunal … showing up like this…" He waved dismissively at the bloody V. "You have much to answer for."

"I'm here, aren't I?" The casual insolence was pure Cloud. "Hearing's still a few turns away. These could be my last moments of freedom. You're wasting them."

"Let's play!" Rocco yelled, bouncing impatiently. "I'm starving. Let's get this fuck-off fest over with."

The sun had fully set. Torches blazed across the Great Murder. Around the field, growing crowds brought jars of manabeeze for light. Crow shifters settled in the trees, watching from the boughs with dangling legs swinging through darkness. Someone took bets nearby. Typical. These crows would gamble on a fight between two raindrops.

River knew Cloud had a hidden agenda, some secret knife waiting to twist. He wouldn't let the violation of his sanctuary slide. But Blake's power hummed beneath River's skin now, and he'd be damned if he bowed to a madman's manipulations.

Fuck it.

"Game on!" he shouted.

The two teams huddled. He stood slightly apart, feigning attention. Every sense remained locked on the other side, where the remaining members of his triad stood shoulder to shoulder, whispering strategy.

"...double back while Rocco..." Talo's voice faded to background noise.

The Corvus jabbed River's ribs. "You listening, Umbria?"

He nodded curtly, watching Cloud sketch the play in mud with a stick—old habits.

"Two options," Talo declared. "Hard and fast through the center, maximum violence—"

"Violent," Sera grinned. "I like violent."

The Corvus bumped fists with her.

"—*or* flank wide with a timed strike," Talo finished.

"Why play if you're not playing to win?" River clipped. "We hit hard. We hit fast. We break them."

Murmurs rippled through their huddle, but his decision hardened into consensus. Talo shot his son an odd look, but the Corvus clasped River's shoulder, sealing the strategy with a silent nod.

They broke formation. Mud squished beneath their feet. River crouched, muscles tensed as his team took their positions, ready to defend his drive. Cloud mirrored him across the imaginary line, face a stoic mask as he smoothly took over as the lead hunter. Ash and the others lined up beside him. Ready.

Every reflective surface in the treasure pot caught the manabee lantern and torchlight. Glistening sparkles shimmered and shone between the two teams. The first item lifted would be the only one in play until it landed in a trove.

A whistle pierced the air.

Go.

Chaos erupted. Bodies slammed together. Mud flew in sheets. River moved instinctively, ducking under Tommas's clumsy grab, weaving through the fray. His target: the sapphire pendant, winking like a fallen star. It had a cord, making it easier to grab.

He lunged, momentum propelling him forward. His fingers closed around the cold, faceted stone just as another hand grabbed him, tattooed knuckles cracking against his, fingers curling around the cord.

Cloud. Face inches away. Dirt, blood, and that familiar smoky ozone scent. Time fractured. Five years ago. Order of the Well. Back to back they stood, surrounded by Nero's undead and Maebh's army.

"Left!" Cloud's dagger whizzed past River's ear.

"Mine!" Peacemaker severed bone.

Ash thundered past, blade high — "Done."

A knee drove into River's gut. Air exploded from his lungs, but his grip on the sapphire held. Neither would yield.

"Let go," Cloud snarled.

"Fuck yourself raw." River twisted.

They rolled, a tangled mess of limbs and hatred in the mud.

"Where'd he go?" River turned, spinning on his heels.

Ash pointed. "There."

A single speck chasing fading airships. The world tilted.

"He left us?" Disbelief colder than the grave.

River wrenched the pendant. The cord snapped. Leather burned against his palm, but the sapphire remained his. They tumbled apart, gasping for breath.

He had it.

He fucking had it.

The crowd's roar was a distant, meaningless sound beneath Blake's possessive pride pulsing through their bond.

He surged upward. Three strides. Two. He dove toward the middle of two flags representing his trove. He slid through the mud as Ash lunged from the side, fingers snatching empty air where River's ankle had been.

Thump.

He slammed the pendant onto his team's treasure pile. Victory.

Across the trampled battlefield, Cloud remained kneeling where they'd fallen. He didn't move. Just watched River through the cheering chaos, torchlight, and dark drizzle. His eyes weren't angry. Not hateful.

Just … empty. Hollowed out.

Lost.

FIFTY-THREE

CIRCA 200 YEARS AGO

"Hold still." Manfri dipped the bamboo needle into black ink. "This will sting."

Nikan returned three days ago after receiving a message through Sera, who had been partying with him in Cornucopia. Now the three males sat on Manfri's balcony beneath a waning moon, finishing what they started years earlier.

"If this works," he explained as he wiped the ink and blood from Nikan's forearm. The design was now complete. He glanced at Cielo. "We'll never be alone again."

Months had passed since Cielo's first words. His strength had returned gradually. He was still a shadow of his former self, but his wounds had closed, he'd gained weight, and he could walk the length of Manfri's room without faltering.

Nikan nodded, studying Cielo with careful eyes. "Are you certain? Once done, it can't be undone."

Cielo simply extended his arm.

Manfri went to work, replicating the same design. The tattoo took shape beneath his skilled hands. It was an intricate pattern of spirals, feathers, and sharp angles forming a stylized triad symbol.

Every tap drove the sacred, mana-infused ink deeper, binding them together with magic older than their traditions.

Long minutes passed in silence as Manfri worked.

"The Untouched want to kill us," he eventually muttered. "They fear what's different. But we can become what they fear most." He blotted excess ink from Cielo's skin. "Guardians."

Nikan's sharp inhale cut through the night. "You mean join the Order of the Well?"

"I've been thinking." He sat back, examining his work. "We need more power. The three of us should enter the ceremonial lake."

"Not sure that's a good thing," Cielo muttered.

"Eight out of ten float and bloat in those waters," Nikan added.

"Not us," Manfri said. "This link will convince the worms we're a single entity. One trial, not three individual judgments. They'll have to choose all of us or none."

"And if they choose none?" Nikan pressed.

"Then we float together." Manfri's eyes found theirs.

A spark ignited behind the emptiness of Cielo's eyes. His fingers traced the pattern, smearing fresh ink.

"When?" His voice remained rough, but determination replaced resignation.

"As soon as you're strong enough." Manfri began cleaning his tools. "The Order is calling for tributes at the next full moon. If we succeed, we gain access to metal weapons without pain. To plastic. To places where the Well doesn't reach." His gaze locked with Cielo's. "To human cities."

"No," Cielo said, staring at his fingers. "A Guardian can still be cut from the Well. Desecrated land is still desecrated."

"Then we'll be waiting for them," Manfri declared. "As Guardians, we'll be powerful enough to take down any human coming into Elphyne."

Cielo nodded once, decisively.

Manfri resumed his work, carefully finishing the final lines of the tattoo. His mind churned with possibilities and plans. With this link, with the Well's blessing as Guardians, they'd be invincible. No one would hurt any of them again. Even the Donna and the Corvus bowed to the Order of the Well.

As he connected the last mirrored stroke between their matching marks, energy flowed between them. Their separate inner wells briefly linked into a shared ocean of power before fading away. They were connected, but still separate. Not exactly what he'd envisioned when they came across the ancient, dark spell, but the sense of change had begun.

"Who's going to test it?" Nikan whispered, already looking at Manfri. Cielo did the same.

"For Crimson's sake," he muttered. "You fuck faces can't do anything without me, can you?"

He distended a claw and scratched a message onto the designated space of his forearm tattoo. Two words appeared on the other's arms.

Never alone.

FIFTY-FOUR

Two treasures remained. The ruby and a jar of trapped colorful beads, crystal shards, and manabeeze. Fractured rainbows. It sparkled, just like Blake.

River glanced over his shoulder and locked eyes with his mate. Concern and encouragement surged through their bond, warming his chest. Her hands fretted with her windways, eyes wide and watching. She had no idea how much her steady presence anchored him, how her confidence settled his raging thoughts. A tentative smile lifted one corner of his mouth, and he waved. When she returned the gesture, his lips stretched into a full-blown grin.

He turned back to the sparkling jar. *Mine.*

At some point, the rain completely stopped, but the field was still filled with slippery hazards. No problem. He would just have to run faster, dig his boots in, and use his claws for grip. His team huddled closer, shoulders bumping, breath fogging in the cool night.

"The glittery one," he rasped. "Easier to target."

Sera's grin bared teeth. "I'll run interference on—"

"No." River cut her off, his tone like ice. The thought of anyone else touching Cloud, even Sera, felt wrong. "I'll handle him."

Talo's gaze weighed heavily. "Son, vengeance makes a poor strategist."

River ignored his father and focused on the jar until the whistle shrieked. He lunged forward through sucking mud, ignoring the ache in his ribs and the burns in his muscles. The glittering prize pulsed like a beacon. A shadow leaped. He ducked, evading a second blow while someone on his team intercepted a third. Bodies clashed around him. Sacrifices were made. Rainbow glitter jar in sight. He reached—

A shoulder connected like a battering ram. Tommas. Not Cloud. River jerked to the side, hit the ground, breath knocked out, stars dancing behind his eyes. He twisted, grabbing Tommas's ankle and yanking hard.

"Traitor," River hissed. "I just saved your relationship!"

His new brother-in-law laughed. "Maybe I'm just bait."

What?

Heart hammering, River surged upward, climbing over Tommas to get to the prize. His fingertips grazed glass, but a boot stomped down, pinning his forearm in cold mud.

River glanced up.

"Pathetic," Cloud muttered, then scooped up the prize and launched it downfield to Ash. Five years melted away in that single, coordinated movement. Ash caught it, pivoted, and tossed it onto their trove's pile.

Cheers erupted.

River pushed himself up, spitting mud. He turned, looking around. Cloud hadn't joined the celebration.

Instead, he was already at his team's starting point, watching River and waiting.

Only one treasure left.

The ruby.

It sat accusing in the mud at centerfield, gleaming like fresh blood under torchlight. More spectators from around the Great Murder had formed a wider circle, sensing the game had become more dangerous. And they were right.

When the final round began, the other team moved with vicious intent. An elbow caught River under the chin, snapping his head back. A knee drove into his kidney as he stumbled. He saw Talo go down face-first after a brutal, deliberate trip. No whistle. No foul. Blake's human rules had abandoned the field.

"They're playing dirty," Sera panted, hauling River upright after another bone-jarring tackle.

"Just playing by crow rules now," he replied, copper tang of blood coating his tongue. "Watch for sharps. Sneaky claws. Hidden weapons. I don't want anyone losing an eye, got it?"

Five years earlier, he would have known exactly what strategy Cloud implemented. They'd fought back-to-back against Nero's undead army, their movements synchronized like wings sharing the same air current. He still remembered the taste of death, the burn of depleted mana in his tainted inner well, the way Cloud had pressed a dagger into River's palm without looking, knowing exactly what he needed.

"Umbria, focus!" The Corvus's roar cut through his thoughts as Cloud launched toward the ruby, a streak of lethal darkness across the field.

River pumped effort into his legs and raced to intercept. They collided in the airspace over the treasure, the impact sending shockwaves through his aching body. Mud and wet grass splattered his face, cold and slick. Limbs flew, fists jabbed. Cloud's forehead snapped forward and connected with River's nose. Pain exploded. His head jerked back, spraying blood. Through blurry vision, a figure approached, taking out River's backup. One by one, the Umbrias fell to the Cardonas.

Blake's terror spiked through their bond, distracting him from Cloud's second attack. A palm heel to the solar plexus, knocking the wind from his paralyzed lungs. His swinging fist went wide. He slumped sideways, wheezing and collapsing.

Through the haze, he saw Cloud pluck the ruby from the mud, stroll calmly downfield uncontested to his team's trove, and place it down. Finality.

Game over.

Point made.

Cloud had always been better at this—harder, more stubborn, more vicious. More willing to hurt in order to understand weakness, to sacrifice everything for the prize, more willing to stab his friend in the guts. He was the son of a bitch who'd told suffering to fuck off long enough for him to infiltrate Crystal City. River was weak, preferring to stay cozy and safe, wrapped in ignorance.

River struggled to his knees. The world swam. Mud became his second skin. Players limped off the field, nursing wounds. Ash assessed injuries, ever the pragmatist. And the crow of the hour stood apart, untouched by the fray he'd orchestrated.

Watching.

Waiting.

Fury ignited River's blood as his vision tunneled to that

fucking, perfectly preserved bloody V. Suddenly, all he could see was lightning arcing down from the sky. All he could smell was burning feathers. Scorching flesh. The heartbeat when he realized his best friend had meant to kill him.

"We're not friends," River choked out, swaying slightly. "We're not family." He stalked forward, crossing the invisible line. "We never were."

Before thought, before reason, before Blake's terrified face flashed in his mind, he lunged. His fist connected with Cloud's jaw. A solid, satisfying crack. Savage relief. Finally.

But Cloud barely stumbled. He spat blood onto the field near River's feet, where it mingled with rain-slick earth in a dark pool. Thunder rumbled overhead, matching the tension coiling between them. It felt like the airship all over again.

"You haven't changed." Cloud's lips curled into something too cruel to be a smile. "Still thinking you're defending everyone when really"—he gestured at the crowd, the splintering teams, Blake watching from beneath the canopy—"you're just making a bigger mess."

"Fuck. You."

"That all you got?" Cloud circled, beckoning with his tattooed fingers, but River refused to take the bait. "You sure get quiet when the truth bites back."

"What's that supposed to mean?"

Cloud's gaze dipped to River's chest. "Who's your new tattooist? A two-year-old?"

Rage.

Flames on the sides of his face.

He flicked his hands out, claws distending from his fingertips. "Leave my mate out of this."

"Crows before hoes, huh, River? Funny how your rules

change depending on who's spreading their legs for you in my trove."

"Don't. Fucking. Look. At. Her." Each word ripped from a dark place in River's soul.

"Why not?" A step closer, voice a venomous whisper. "Afraid she'll see her future? Afraid she'll turn on you, too?"

Something inside River snapped. The carefully constructed dam holding back years of grief, rage, confusion, and gut-wrenching guilt shattered. He roared and charged. His fist connected. Bone grated against bone. Pain shot up his arm, and he ignored it. All he cared about was turning that smirking, smug face into a pulp.

Cloud met him blow for blow. No finesse. Just raw, ugly violence. Knee to his ribs, elbow to the temple. Stars exploded behind his eyes, but he didn't go down. He gouged Cloud's thigh, shredding leather.

"Stop!" Talo bellowed, trying to intervene.

"No." Ash blocked him, arm extended. "Let them."

Sort out your shit.

River wanted to laugh. This wasn't them sorting out feelings. This was hate. This was vengeance. He rolled, pinning Cloud, and rained blows down on that impassive, emotionless face.

"You're fucking insane," he shouted, spittle flying. "I saw inside your head! Your sick fucking shrine! My mother was right—you Cardonas are cursed! Black fucking rot inside!"

A fist to his ear. "Yet you're the one who got off on it."

"Like you get off on misery? You think I don't know your plan?" River grappled him, legs and arms locked tight. "Think I didn't see the maps?" He put Cloud in a chokehold, growled in his ear, "You want to burn it all down."

Cloud smacked his head back, butting River's nose,

threw him off, and gained the upper hand in a scramble of mud and limbs. They were like fledglings grappling, all heart and no skill. But it didn't stop them from trying to decimate each other, from finding a weak spot to exploit.

"You know shit," Cloud snarled, kicking toward River's dodging face. The boot glanced off his jaw. "Too busy licking your wounds to hear anything but your own fucking whining!"

"I know you're here for the cryptex," he countered. "Think we're stupid?"

"*Know* you're stupid." Tattooed knuckles split against River's cheekbone. He rolled back. More blows, targeted, vicious. Kidneys. Throat. Temple. Places that wouldn't heal fast. Places known to hurt.

"Stop this madness!" Talo's command was again ignored.

River surged, tackling Cloud low, driving him back. They crashed through boundary flags, then through a forgotten supply table. When had they left the field? Wood and pottery flew. Screams erupted from bystanders. The torch-light dimmed as they tumbled farther from the gathering's center.

He dug his claws into Cloud's forearms and swung him against a wall. Not a wall, the nesting caravan. Wood cracked. Beads inside clacked against stained glass. Some-thing green inside flashed against the window, warping colors—Blake's special plant.

It survived so much already. If River broke it now…

Reality came crashing down.

Suddenly, they weren't opponents in a game. They weren't even enemies. They were two losers covered in mud, bloody and bruised and fucking miserable enough to violate a precious gift.

The fight expelled from River's lungs. His fists dropped to his sides.

"I would have followed you anywhere," he choked out.

When Cloud merely stared, fists up, River gripped his shoulders and shook him, trying to make him see sense. He forced his friend to his knees, pinned him there, and shouted down, "We're *triad!* More than fucking brothers. Why?"

Cloud gripped River's wrists, claws piercing skin, oozing blood, and snarled, "You said it first. We're not family."

Lightning split the sky, momentarily illuminating Cloud's face. River saw it then, the same face looking up at him on the day they'd met—stark eyes filled with hopelessness, bloody nose dripping.

"What's the point?"

"Fuck your dad. Do what you want."

"It's not that easy."

"Everything's easy with someone to watch your back."

River sheathed his claws, fell to his knees, and slumped his shoulders. Breathing heavily, they stared each other down, just inches apart between two caravans in the darkness. Distant voices traveled on a breeze, concerned, wary. Ash must still be holding them back.

"Just tell me why?" River whispered, shaking his head as he looked down at the fine scars on his torso. "Why?"

"Because you weren't fucking listening!" A roar. A bellow of anguish that shook the earth. "You didn't get it!"

That flicker of emotion in Cloud's eyes fled. He rose to his feet, a dark stain against the stormy night sky, until lightning flashed again. This time, it began inside his eyes, turning the blue white. Electricity skipped across his skin, zipping through oil-slick tracks on his body, lifting each strand of black, wavy hair.

Stand.

Get up and face him head-on.

But River couldn't get up. Maybe he deserved this.

"I was begging for you to tell me!" Air heaved into his lungs. "I just wanted to help."

"Help?" Cloud's laugh was cruel. "You wouldn't know the meaning of the word."

"I was there for you when you were broken. I nursed you back to health." River gaped. "And do you know what? You never even thanked me. Not once." The buried and festered words exploded out. "Months I spent, pulling you back from the edge. Watching you scream in your sleep. Cleaning your *actual* shit because you couldn't fucking move. Not. Once." His eyes stung, his throat clogged, but what was the point in pretending he didn't feel this way? "Maybe I don't fucking know all the answers, but I just wanted to help."

Cloud exhaled.

His head dropped.

The raw fury binding them together seemed to lessen, replaced by exhaustion.

"It was an accident," he whispered.

FIFTY-FIVE

An accident.

Cloud's confession echoed in River's head. He stilled, letting it soak in. Letting himself understand. Forgiveness, a fragile, impossible thing, hovered.

Then exploded.

"A fucking *accident*?" His fist struck out, rising with an uppercut, connecting squarely with Cloud's dipped jaw. He never saw it coming. Bone crunched. Head snapped back. Staggered. Body slumped against the side, against the caravan's cracked panel. But River wasn't done. "Five years! Five fucking years of silence, and that's your excuse?" Another hit. "An 'oopsy'?" Fingers around his tattooed throat, pinning him against the caravan's wall. Rage, clean and absolute, surged back. "An accident wouldn't have kept you away for so long. An accident wouldn't have made you ignore me! Ignore us!"

Cloud's brief submission evaporated. He snarled in River's face, pushing against the stranglehold. "Grow some wings and get over it."

"I can't! You *ruined* my wings, fuck face." Unhinged rage magnified in River's veins, trembling his grip, pushing his thumbs deeper into soft flesh. One twist. Snap. Silence the ghosts. End the pain. His muscles screamed, tensed for the final act—

"Manfri!"

Blake's voice. Sharp. Terrified. His name. His *birth* name, not the Guardian's.

I want you to be my only safe word, too.

River froze, his grip slackening. His head whipped toward the sound. She stood ten feet away, horror etched on her face. Wind whipping her hair, slashing streaks against her tear-stained face.

"You said it," he muttered, surprised.

"I shouted 'River' first, but you weren't listening!"

Not listening.

Not...

River's eyes clashed with Cloud's.

Because you weren't fucking listening! You didn't get it!

The trove. All the secrets kept. A sickening lurch of self-loathing hit River as his fingers slackened around Cloud's throat. But the bastard, he held River's hands there. He forced the chokehold, eyes flashing with silent, bitter challenge.

Do it, his eyes seemed to say. *Put me out of my misery. I'm alone.*

River tensed. Steeled himself. Maybe this was a kindness. Maybe this was River listening now.

Blake's disappointment sliced through their bond like a physical blow. He glanced back at her in time to see her pushing through the gathering onlookers, melting into the darkness beyond the torchlit caravans. Gone.

She thinks I chose this. Chose vengeance.

All that kindness and understanding she'd given him, given his family, when her own world had been ripped to shreds…

"Don't come crying to me," Cloud spat, "when she breaks your heart, *Manfri*."

His words should ignite fury in River. Even guilt. But all he could think of was all of the mementos Cloud had saved in his trove—experiences with this kettle, with his triad, but a ton more of Rory.

And River … he'd not listened. He'd…

You have to acknowledge the break first. You can't fix it if you can't see exactly where it happened and why.

Cloud still held River's wrists, pushing his hands against his throat. A one-handed chokehold. Willow told her parents this was how he'd gripped Rory, dangling over the airship. He had her by the throat and Willow by the arm. He'd tried to save them both, but had to make a choice—save an innocent, or the enemy.

Be a savior or a villain.

And he couldn't. He'd roared in Rory's face, bellowed his rage, refusing to sacrifice her.

So Rory chose for him.

She became the villain so he didn't have to.

"I know why," River whispered, the realization hitting him, "why you didn't let me help you. Why you shut me out."

Cloud shoved River away, eyes narrowed. "Because you're a predictable, self-serving cunt?"

River laughed, wet and ragged. "Yeah."

"What?"

"I promised you'd never be alone." The truth hurt. "But

when you were drowning in it, drowning in her … I fucking panicked." The confession tore through him. "Long before they locked you up in Crystal City, before we were a triad, I was jealous. Afraid of losing you, losing us. So I pushed you away first. Like a fucking coward."

Uncertainty flickered in Cloud's stunned eyes.

"I saw the signs," River pushed on, the truth pouring out. "Knew something had happened between you and Rory. You tried to tell me about something special, but couldn't. And then you were spiraling. And I…" His voice cracked. "I knew deep inside, but still I let you fall alone."

Cloud's jaw worked. "Save your pity."

"Not pity." River leaned closer. "You needed me. Trusted *me*." He pounded his fist against his chest. "The one who always ran his mouth about love being the only treasure worth a damn." Vulnerability flashed across Cloud's face, but River plowed on. "I convinced you—jump with no wings. The mess can't touch you. Do what you fucking want. Join the Order. Triad tattoo will keep us safe. *Never alone*." He shook his head, guilt a physical weight as he realized he had it all wrong. "I would have followed you anywhere," he repeated, the words tasting like dirt. "But you were already following me." Pain lanced through him. "And when you needed me most … needed someone to understand that love was worth the risk … I failed you." He sagged. "I made it worse."

Cloud snapped. He lunged, tackling River hard. His fists pounded down, clumsy and full of desperate, raw anguish. For a moment, River took it. He basked in the corporal punishment. It was what he deserved. Too little, too late, his realization had come.

But this wasn't the way to fix a break. And he wanted it fixed. He wanted his triad whole again.

With a final surge of strength, he flipped their positions, pinning Cloud beneath him. Mana, unwanted but surging, flooded his veins, amplified by his mate's latent power.

Wings exploded from his back, unfurled, stretched wide, tips scraping the caravan walls on either side of them.

"This," he roared, "this is what happens when we don't fucking trust each other! When we don't communicate. This is *my* fault! You might be too proud to acknowledge a debt, but I'm not. I pushed you into love, pushed you high, then watched you fall and blamed you for the landing." He heaved in an agonized breath. "I'm sorry! Fuck, Cloud, I'm so sorry I wasn't there! I'll never fly again, but that's okay. I forgive you for ruining my wings."

Cloud's gaze drifted over River's shoulders. "Yeah. They look ruined, alright."

Slowly, fearfully, he twisted to see.

Wings. His wings. Impossibly whole. Glossy, perfect feathers, blue-black catching the softer UV moonlight, stretching from shoulder to tip, vibrant, quivering, and alive. Not a single inch of bare, pebbled skin remained visible.

"Blake," he muttered, gaze lifting to the stained glass window, to the eucalyptus plant squashed against the pane. She swore that the vase had cracked. Perhaps she was right after all. "She fixed me."

They're so beautiful, she'd said in the trove, idly running her fingers through the soft down. *Not as bad as you think.*

Her touch had felt so good, so right. Healing.

Beneath him, Cloud stilled. His gaze tracked the impossible span of River's wings, expression utterly unreadable. "What do you mean she *fixed* you?"

Joy, fierce and overwhelming, surged. River shouldn't feel it, not now, not here. Shouldn't rub Cloud's face in this miracle. But fuck it. He looked down at his oldest friend, brother, and tormentor, and had to share the joy. "This must be her gift."

"Healing?"

"Restoring! She made something from nothing. The Donna said something about her bringing back what was lost." River grinned so hard it hurt. "Her gift manifested after all. And it's … it's going to be life changing."

He had to tell her. Had to—River froze, realizing what this meant.

"I can fly," he breathed, dazed. "Holy fucking Well, I can do something I never thought I'd be able to do." He babbled. "Never even wanted to do it before. But now … I really wanna do that thing."

He pinned Cloud's jaw between his hands and smacked a kiss square on his lips. Hard. Fast. Loud.

Cloud's eyes widened with comical shock.

"What the fuck?" He shoved River back. "*That's* why you were jealous?"

Laughter, raw and real and deep, banished five years of shadows from River's heart.

"Not that, fuck face." The words tumbled out, shaky but true. "I love you, bro. Hope you can use the apology. Said it too fucking late."

"You're the insane one," Cloud grumbled, dusting his shoulders.

River flashed him a grin. "You love it."

"Fuck off."

"Exactly." River waggled his brows and only stopped

when Cloud turned to hide his smirk. That old glimpse of brotherhood was enough. A small truce. A minor repair.

River stepped back, testing his wings, stretching them gloriously and wide behind him. He pointed at Cloud's still stunned face. "I know I said I'd never leave you alone, but I gotta go. When I get back, you're talking."

"Maybe."

"You're talking because I'm listening."

Cloud averted his gaze, staring into the darkness. When he realized River still stared at him, he sighed and said, "Fine. I'll be here."

Heart hammering, River searched the darkness in the direction Blake had vanished, sensing the pulse of her bond through their connection like a UV trail glittering on the ground. Feral, predatory instinct flared his new feathers to their fullest—time to swoop the little rainbow mouse.

FIFTY-SIX

Blake stormed away from the sickening fight, down a dark path on the outskirts of the settlement, away from River and the newly arrived … *him*—the one who shattered everything. The game, the fragile truce she'd brokered between the warring families, the tentative steps towards peace. It was all ground to dust the second Cloud had appeared.

Just like that.

Gone.

She dashed annoying strands of hair from her hot face. Maybe River had been right. The guy was toxic. A menace to society. But an ache deep in her chest had wanted things to be different. She'd wanted this world to be better because if it was, then losing everything she knew wasn't so bad. Like, maybe, just maybe, there was a point to this world. Like maybe, there were things on that trove wall more important than a nuclear blast radius, things that could save them all from a cycle of self-annihilation. Things Blake wanted to be a part of.

Things that gave her life meaning.

The low-grade fever still hummed beneath her skin, an insistent, maddening itch. She felt … unhinged. Ready to detonate. Like her body wasn't entirely her own anymore.

Like *she* was the blast radius.

Mud sucked at her boots, and each step sank deeper with a fury that felt foreign and terrifyingly potent. Her hands clenched and unclenched. *Useless.* Everything she did was bloody useless. She'd tried to fix things, tried to bring the razz, tried to make them see sense, and what happened? Males reverted to peacocks showing off for bimbos who batted their eyelashes.

Mine.

Blake bared her teeth at the empty night air. Her reaction to watching River preen near those females hadn't lessened. It warped with a possessive, selfish urge to distract him from the bitter feud with Cloud.

Mine. Mine, mine, fucking mine!

Where did this come from? This need. This obsession. It was never there with her ex. Jeff had only ever cultivated a dull ache of insecurity. But this was fierce. Territorial. An urge to bite, to mark, to claim. And since she knew she'd lose to Cloud, all her anger filtered toward the flirting females.

A burst of laughter. A woman in a cream suit whispering behind her hand.

"I'm going to tear those bitches limb from limb," she announced to no one. "Fucking slags. Dirty moles."

A shriek of bottled emotion tore from her lungs and scared crows from nearby trees. Some cawed angrily. Others just melted away into the darkness, heading toward caravans filled with nosy busybodies looking at her through their windows.

"You hear that, cunts?" she shouted. "I'm coming for you."

Blake doubled down on her stalk. Glared back. Maybe even flipped two middle fingers their way.

Somewhere, deep in the corner of her mind, she knew something was wrong. This feverish madness wasn't her.

It hurt. It scraped her heart raw. It grew claws.

A low rumble vibrated through the soles of her boots, stopping her in her tracks. Thunder.

"Great," she mumbled. "Just bloody perfect."

Fat drops of rain began to splatter against the pine needles in the forest to her left, releasing the sharp, clean scent of wet earth and resin. She hadn't brought an umbrella, not that they existed in this magic-addled version of her world.

Blake looked around and had no idea where she was, somewhere on a trodden path circling the Great Murder settlement. Forest on one side. Caravans on the other. Feminine laughter drew her attention to a nearby roost, and that urge to gouge out eyeballs resurged. The laughter came from a family enjoying a meal together beneath a tasseled canopy, their happy faces warmed by glowing manabee lanterns.

The ache in her chest faded.

A flutter of small wings caught her peripheral vision. Since she'd stopped, three fledglings had crept closer, sneaking up behind her. They couldn't be older than six or seven. How long had they been trailing her?

When they realized they'd been found out, their little dark eyes widened with the kind of reverence usually reserved for mythical beings. But they didn't run. Didn't fly away with their tiny, downy wings. They whispered among themselves in hushed, excited tones about "the human who swims" and "the blessed one who saves drowning birds."

Blake's jaw clenched. Even the children treated her like some fucking saint when all she'd done was jump in water. The weight of their innocent expectation pressed against her already fraying nerves. She didn't want to be anyone's hero right now. She wanted to rage, to claim, to tear something apart with her bare hands.

"Go away," she grumbled, shooing them. They scattered in a fit of giggles.

"They didn't mean to offend you," a woman shouted from the nearby table. "They're just curious."

"It's not them," she said. "I'm just… I should go."

In her haste to escape, she almost stepped on the little crushed flower left behind by one of the children. Giggles beneath the nearby table drew her attention. Wide, curious eyes watched Blake, waiting to see what she would do.

Was it … an offering?

Great. Now she felt bad.

She inserted the floppy stem into her wet hair and then sighed. The woman who had shooed the fledglings looked at Blake's blue, Well-blessed marks. Like falling dominoes, the rest of her companions stopped their conversation and stared.

"Would you like to join our storytelling?" she asked Blake. "We'd love to hear about how you rescued the Domatri boy."

It was hard to stay furious when they waited with such honest eagerness. Blake had always loved a good yarn. Jeff had been right about one thing: forging quick and fast connections through the safety of her phone had not built lasting connections. Not the way she'd approached it. But this was real life.

She smiled through the rain. "Sure."

Two steps toward the table, Blake realized the thunder was getting worse. Rumbling grew louder, vibrations closer, impossibly rhythmic. The crow family searched the night sky. When one of them pointed, Blake realized it wasn't thunder but *wings*.

Whoosh.

A startled scream ripped from Blake's throat as strong hands hooked beneath her armpits, lifting her. Her stomach bottomed out. The world dropped away. The fledglings chased after her, proclaiming that they'd protect her, until a stern voice called them back.

Just as Blake was about to release a second scream for help, River's upside-down face appeared above her—incorrigible grin, utterly feral, eyes alive. Rain plastered strands of his hair to his temples. Exhilaration pulsed off him, lashing through their connection, jarring against her inner turmoil.

He lowered his lips to her ear. "Trying to run, Sparkles?"

Her lips parted. Closed.

"Didn't I make it clear?" His chest vibrated with possessive satisfaction, infuriatingly charming. "There's nowhere you can go that I won't find you. You're *mine*."

Something inside Blake snapped. Hard.

"Put me the *fuck* down, River Umbria!" Her hysterical shriek sounded foreign, even to herself. She slashed blindly at his face, kicking and bucking. "I want off."

Her nails scraped stubble. He laughed and tightened his iron grip.

"You think this is a joke?" Globs of rain splattered her face, mingling with tears of sheer rage. "I was making friends! I was … gah! You parade around like some prize cock, try to rip your best mate's throat out. Oh my god, is he dead? And now … now this! You can't just snatch me from the sky like some kind of—"

"Rainbow mouse?"

"—shiny trinket you found!" She flailed at him. "I am *not* your fucking property!"

She thrashed and kicked, throwing them off balance.

"Shit." He banked and then corrected his flight path. "Easy there, Sparkles." A flash of fear through their bond. "I haven't flown in years." Then quieter. "Might need to get used—"

He repositioned her, scooping her beneath the knees and lower back. Self-preservation tossed her hands around his neck, gripping hard. Great, feathered wings beat steadily behind him, blocking out the moonlit storm clouds.

She stilled.

Wings.

River had wings.

Manabee lanterns, torches, and campfires twinkled below like stars. Caravans soared past. Faces looked up. Some pointed. A man bellowed something about being insane to fly in a storm like this.

"Oh my god, we're flying," she blurted, sputtering. "River. Your feathers are back."

"Yeah, they are." Deep and soft. Joy pumped from his heart to hers. His lips fluttered against her ear, making her shiver. "As soon as I knew, the first thing I thought of was finding you."

"What about—"

He cleared his throat. "I apologized to him."

"You what?"

"You were right." He shrugged. "I needed to acknowledge the break before it could mend, and I … I broke it first."

Blake blinked rapidly, fighting the prick of tears. River had made the first step toward reconciliation. He'd listened to her.

And now he had wings. They filled the dark sky around them. Magnificent, black feathers tipped with shimmering blue flapped above him, shedding raindrops like diamonds. She instinctively moved her fingers from his neck to brush the lush ridge beating slowly, then gasped at the contrasting sensations—soft yet hard, downy feathers mixed with strong muscles, tendons flexing.

A whimper caught in River's throat. He nuzzled into her neck, hiding his vulnerability, but she felt his need and desire as if they were her own. With his head lowered, his wings became her whole world.

"They're perfect. How?"

"You fixed me." He pulled her tighter against his chest. Inhaled against her skin. Released a husky growl. "Must have been all that"—his voice deepened—"hands on therapy in the trove."

"I didn't do anything!" This wasn't her magic. She knew it deep in her soul. "That wasn't…"

"Doesn't matter how. Point is, I swooped you." He growled against her skin, "Crow tradition, Sparkles. I just claimed you in front of the whole damn Great Murder." He nipped her jaw, making her gasp. "You're supposed to be fighting me now. Trying to escape." Another low, male rumbling sound. "Show everyone your strength like you did before." He pulled back, eyes glittering with challenge and arousal. "So I can overpower you and claim you good and proper."

Hot, liquid need pooled between her thighs. It scorched through her blood, tearing up her veins, shooting fire into her already feverish body. But it also reminded her of why she'd been angry in the first place. He'd had the nerve to preen in front of other females, then he'd ignored Blake's safe word, and now he was making her walking away about him.

"No!" she shouted.

He merely looked enamored. She exploded again—a shriek, a scream, a chaotic mix of rage and a foolish lust so insanely feral and furious that she felt inhuman. How could she want him and not want him? Her nails carved welts into the back of his neck, but the pain only intensified the sense of his arousal through their bond.

"Fuck yes, Blake." He tightened his grip. "Give it to me."

"Don't you fuck yes Blake me!"

"That's the whole poi—"

She slapped him across the face. Hard. His hold on her slipped, but she wasn't afraid. Falling didn't even enter her mind. This was about *her*. About her need to be heard, her need to be his one, to come first. Maybe it was irrational, maybe it was validated, maybe it didn't matter.

"Put me. The fuck. Down!"

His flight path shifted abruptly. He banked hard and dove, startling a squeak from her lips as she latched onto his neck again. Wind whipped her face. Rain pelted like bullets. She had no choice but to shelter her face against the solid expanse of his bare chest.

God, he smelled divine.

No, he doesn't.

Another change in momentum lifted her gaze. Coming in fast was the ancient dam wall, a space between two long, jutting concrete platforms. Water spilled from the top slab like a shimmering curtain, collecting in a reservoir formed by the upheaval of invasive roots. Bioluminescent plants and moss deep in the alcove's wall backlit two figures nestled in the pool, lost in their own world.

River didn't hesitate. He descended fast, bursting through the waterfall, landing with a jarring thud on the concrete a few feet away from them.

"Out!" he bellowed, wings snapping wide with a loud crack, displacing rain. "This perch is taken."

Blake barely registered warm air, surprised faces, and bodies scrambling away. She was too busy doing the same thing. She wriggled out of River's arms and fell onto the platform. The impact knocked her teeth, but her fury overshadowed the pain.

The trespassing bathers burst through the curtain of water and leaped off the ledge, shifting into crows. They squawked irritably, but otherwise disappeared into the stormy night.

Heart pounding, Blake followed them through the waterfall, but skidded to a halt. Lightning cracked in the sky beyond, briefly illuminating the vast campsite fifty feet below.

Spinning, she ran toward the ancient dam wall and slapped her palms on the surface. Rain continued to pour, soaking her. Water streamed down the wall as she searched for a way to climb, but it was all slippery. Her touch activated a glowing response, leaving a trail of blue, green, and purple in the bioluminescent moss. It gave her enough light to see that the wall was enormous and impossibly high. She couldn't see the top. The ledge above theirs, where the water spilled from, only covered half of their platform. It was too high to reach.

River emerged from the curtain of falling water. Sparkling rivulets trickled down his warrior's body, caressing every curve of tattooed skin. Dark eyes met hers with knowing.

Trapped.

FIFTY-SEVEN

Rain beat down on the settlement below. Blake tried to focus on it, tried to slow her breathing, but River was everywhere —inside her mind, in the air, and inside her aching and fevered body. His torrent of emotion flooded their bond. His need, affection, and desire infected her.

This was what she'd prayed for. This was the kind of love she wanted, something so visceral that it would rip her apart.

But if it was love, then why hadn't he said it? Why had he flirted with those other females? He'd promised her obsession, possession. She wanted to be consumed. She wanted to feel safe. Kept. She didn't want to feel left behind.

Fae couldn't lie.

So why hadn't he said those three little words back to her?

River watched her through strands of dripping blue-black hair. His wingspan opened against the backdrop of falling water and bioluminescent moss. His fingers flexed at his sides, pumping his muscles into hard relief, stomach so fucking defined it begged to be licked.

Blood from his recent fight had washed away. Most wounds had closed, but a few angry welts remained like the claw gouges on his forearms. Made by another. Made by someone Blake couldn't even remember right now because she was blind with territorial need. Blind with rage because the wounds had ripped through the blue Well-blessed mating marks. *Her* marks.

That's what hurt the most—that everyone else had a piece of him, too.

This was just like Jeff all over again. She'd tried to fill the gap of his attention with her followers, but it was never the same. She wasn't enough. Rather than admitting how inadequate she felt, she stalked toward him and shoved him hard. Eyes burning. Throat tight.

"You can't just—you stupid—gah!" She pounded her fists against him and screamed.

"Not sure what's happening here..." River captured her wrists, effortlessly stopping her assault. "...but I like it."

His gaze raked over her, heating with every increment of her soaked body.

"Not sure what's happening?" Her jaw dropped. She wrenched out of his grip and walked forward, forcing them through the curtain and into the alcove with the steaming pool. "You *like* me feeling like this?"

It glowed in here, too. Stifling. Hot. Her vision blurred. Warped.

"Blake." His brows drew together. "Why do your emotions feel so..."

"So real? Like this isn't part of your swooping ritual?"

"Well, I figured..." His feathers ruffled, throwing off rain.

"You figured those bloody wings would fix everything? I ripped me heart open for you, and you gave me nothing!" He tried to answer, but she wouldn't let him, just continued advancing on him because she couldn't do anything else. "I helped diffuse an ugly family feud down there, and what did you do?" She prodded his pectoral. "You flashed your buff body for the first bit of tail looking your way!"

She planted her palms against his chest and shoved hard. He stumbled backward, wings flaring for balance, surprise flashing across his face as his foot caught on an exposed root. He fell backward with a magnificent splash into the pool.

Water and steam displaced over the edges, briefly dampening the bioluminescent moss. Light dimmed and then flared. River's wings spread wide as he tried to balance his footing in the water, but the waterlogged feathers dragged him down. He floundered, splashed, searching for footing or something to grasp around the edges. But as she'd learned, the moss-covered rocks were slippery. It was almost comical if she wasn't so annoyed.

When he finally managed to sit still, back against the ancient wall, the shallow water came up to his waist. Blake hopped into the pool and waded toward him, feet slipping, half falling. She made it to him and somehow managed to climb onto his lap and lean close enough to feel his breath against her face.

"*Mine*," she growled. "You're mine, River Umbria. Not those sluts perving on you, not—"

"Whoa, whoa." He cupped her face, eyes widening, darting over her face. "What sluts?"

"The ones you flirted with during the game!"

"That I purposefully splashed mud on—"

"Yes! Those—wait. What?"

"—to make them unappealing to anyone with eyes."

Why was he smiling?

"You winked at them," she accused.

"At *you*," he corrected. "To show you I knew you were watching. That I felt your emotions through our bond."

"You did?"

"Oh, Blake. You sweet, darling human." His hands slid from her face to her shoulders and held her back so he could stare into her eyes with amused affection. "Why do you think crows like violent displays for claiming their wingmates?"

"Because you're all bird brains?"

"It's a warning. Both to the males who think a weak female is free game, and to the females who think the same of the male." His approval washed through their bond, darkly satisfied. "You did good warning off rivals, Sparkles."

The praise shouldn't have affected her, but it did. A flush of warmth spread through her chest, annoying the hell out of her.

"That's not why I fought you!" She huffed. Swiped wet hair from her eyes. "When you swooped me, I mean. And…" Her body felt too hot, skin too tight, as if something wanted to burst free. "And I'm still angry at you because I used the safe word and you ignored me."

Worst excuse. She blinked, shaking her head.

"No." His jaw tightened. "I did listen to you. I stopped short of killing Cloud."

"But—"

"I still let you walk away," he finished, understanding dawning in his eyes. "And when he provoked me again, you thought I'd chosen vengeance over you."

The truth of it cracked something open inside her chest. "You *let* me walk away."

"I did." He scrubbed a hand down his face. "You're right, I did. How can I make it up to you?"

Say the words.

Say you love me.

You'll keep me.

Nothing.

She threaded her fingers into his wet hair and yanked his head back until his throat was exposed. Vulnerable.

"You promised me obsession." She tightened her grip, watching his pupils dilate with each painful tug. "You don't get to pick and choose when or how that applies. If I'm yours, then you're mine. We're all in or we aren't."

Her heart couldn't take anything less.

River's hands found her hips beneath the water, his grip gentle but firm. "I won't let you walk away again."

"Show me you mean it," she challenged, wading off his lap and finding her footing.

With deliberate, provocative intent, River stretched his arms wide along the pool's edge, sliding his hands through glowing moss beneath his splayed wings.

"How?" he asked.

The sight of him—proud, powerful, and offering himself sent a fresh wave of need beneath her skin. Her windways suddenly felt heavy, the fabric a cinderblock pulling her down. Her blouse was an irritant, suffocating her.

She planted a foot on his chest, forcing him back against the wall.

"Take it off," she ordered, glancing at her boot dripping colorful mud on his stomach.

His gaze dropped, then lifted to meet hers. "This is my punishment?"

"Shut up." She applied more pressure with her boot. "You don't get to talk right now. Do as I say."

Never had she seen laces undone so quickly. He tossed her boots beyond the waterfall, likely over the ledge entirely. Then he sat back, arms resuming their sprawled position, eyes gleaming with an intensity that both challenged and worshipped her.

How could he look at her with such devotion, flood her with it through their bond, and not say it? Canting her head, she studied him. He mentioned punishment.

Sometimes I can't share what's bothering me.

Was this another one of those moments?

She peeled the soaked silk top from her skin, every nerve ending hypersensitive as fabric dragged across her hardened nipples. River's sharp intake of breath sent a spike of satisfaction through her core.

His hungry gaze tracked her movement as she worked the knots of her windways. Undone, the volumes slid down her legs to float in the pool. His arms twitched as if the effort to remain still was too much. Yet still he waited for instructions. For permission.

"Blake—"

"I said no talking."

His jaw clicked shut.

"And no touching with your hands."

His lips curved wickedly. She waded closer until she stood between his spread thighs. Holding her balance on his head, she lifted her foot and slid it onto the mossy edge beside his waist, exposing herself directly at his eye level.

River's eyes turned molten as she parted her pussy lips.

"Show me how sorry you are." Her command came out breathless. "Use that clever mouth and make me forget that you let me walk away. Make me forget the things you're not saying. Earn it."

Blue eyes flashed, dark, defiant, aroused, reverent. River leaned forward, slowly closing the gap. Just as his breath ghosted her sensitive flesh, he stuck out his pink tongue and stopped. He lifted his gaze to hers—checking to see if she watched—and then licked a slow, deliberate path through her center without breaking eye contact.

Sweet. Fucking. Christ.

Hot pleasure exploded from his touch. She bit back a moan, hips instinctively rocking forward. Another teasing lap, mapping her shape, learning her taste. He licked again, slower, deliberate, pressure firmer, making little sounds of satisfaction, savoring her like a delicacy.

"More," she gasped, fingers tightening in his hair.

He obeyed and closed his mouth over her clit. He suckled her sensitive bud, fluttering it, teeth grazing with a maddening tease.

"Faster," she groaned. "Harder."

She felt him grin against her flesh before he leisurely pushed his tongue deep inside, mimicking the slow thrust of a cock. He gave her just enough friction for a maddening electric pleasure that went nowhere.

"River—please," she sobbed, sanity fraying.

"Please, *what*, Sparkles?" His deep voice vibrated, dark with satisfaction. "Beg properly. Tell me what my good little rainbow mouse needs."

"Fuck you," she managed, the words dissolving into a gasp as his tongue found that exquisite spot again.

"Not yet." His smirk pressed against her flesh as he

renewed his assault, tongue circling, flicking, building her higher. "Haven't made me earn it yet."

Fury pierced through her haze of pleasure.

He was a manipulative, alpha, psycho bastard. Controlling, selfish sonovabitch who loved playing games. Bloody hell, it was *hot*.

"You think," she panted, wrestling her control back, "that this makes up for letting me walk away? For not saying it back?"

His tongue stilled. He looked up, eyes narrowing dangerously.

"Saying what, Blake?" he asked softly.

She wouldn't give him the satisfaction, wouldn't give him the answer. Not yet. Instead, she shoved him away hard, snapping his head back, breaking contact. The abrupt absence of his touch made her body scream in protest, but her pride demanded it.

"Don't pretend you don't know the answer." Her words were shaky but resolute.

River allowed the distance. He leaned back against the pool wall, arms still wide, feathers partly floating on the water's surface, partly over the glowing, mossy ledge.

He stared at her through entitled eyes. Waiting.

And it wasn't enough.

What was wrong with her?

She'd never felt this territorial, this possessive, this *angry* with her ex. But with River, every emotion was magnified to extremes she couldn't control.

"Tell me," she demanded. "Tell me why you can't say it."

CHAPTER

FIFTY-EIGHT

Blake's question hung suspended in the humid night air, echoing in their private alcove along with the churning waterfall, the distant growl of thunder.

River avoided meeting her eyes. His emotions were a mix of pain, guilt, and a love so deep it made her throat clog with emotion.

Tell me I belong here.

Tell me you'll fight for me.

Tell me you'll never let me go.

He finally looked up. Agony and desperation warred in his eyes. His throat worked. But the words remained prisoners behind his teeth.

Blake waded back to him, disturbing the water into luminous eddies. Beneath the water surface, his erection strained against his leather breeches. The tip breached the water's surface, a pearl of precum catching the uncanny glow. A wicked thought tugged at her lips.

He shifted uncomfortably, trying to hide the evidence. Too late.

"Blake…" he warned.

"Yes, wing-*mate*?"

"What's that look in your eyes for?"

Her smile stretched into a feral grin as she reached for his right wing. Damp feathers yielded beneath her fingers. She sank her fingers into the delicate underside of the trailing edge, stroking slowly, teasing the sensitive quills.

River's reaction was visceral. His pupils blew wide, the tendons in his neck grew taut, and he dropped his head against the wall. His cock jerked violently, the exposed tip darkening to a dusky purple against his abdomen. "Blake … fuck … don't you dare…"

"Don't?" She pressed closer, lips brushing his ear. "Just say 'rainbow' and I'll stop."

"You're so perfect for me," he mumbled, breathing turned ragged, chest heaving. Sweat beaded across his brow.

"Not the words I'm looking for." She added the other wing to her attentions.

She found the sensitive junction where they connected to his back, massaging the hidden hollow there. Muscles spasmed beneath her touch. His skin flushed crimson from chest to throat, the broken tattoos darkening as blood rushed to the surface. The tented leather of his breeches strained impossibly tighter.

Crows respected shows of power, of dominance. So it's time River learned a lesson. Blake might be female, but she was not submissive.

"You like me on top," she observed, voice dropping to that husky note she'd discovered drove him wild. "Look at you—Guardian of the Well, mighty warrior, reduced to a trembling mess by a human's touch."

A broken sound escaped him, part growl, part whimper.

"Beg me," she whispered, trailing both hands from his wings down his tense shoulders.

Muscles leapt and quivered as she explored his slick chest, traced the intricate wobbly tattoo she'd inked, and followed the arrow of dark hair to his defined abdomen. She stopped just above where his cock breached the water, its tip taunting her, waiting to be licked.

"Beg me to stop," she said. "Or beg me to suck you off."

When he gave no reply, she returned to his wings. She climbed onto his lap, the position bringing her breasts level with his face. She pressed against his chest and slid her hands beneath his arms to fondle his primaries. His hips bucked violently. The hard ridge of his cock ground against her thigh, the wet leather rough against her bare skin. Still, his hands remained gripping the ledge, knuckles blanched with restraint.

"Please…" The plea broke from him, high-pitched and desperate. "For *Crimson's* sake, Blake … please…"

Something in his tone made her stop. She eased back slightly and glanced down. An inch of shaft had worked itself free from the leather confines. A vein pulsed visibly along the underside, throbbing in time with his racing heart. His chest heaved with each ragged breath, nostrils flaring as he fought for control.

"Say it," she whispered. Hoped.

"I'm yours, Blake," he whimpered, squeezing his eyes closed.

He'd not said his safe word, but was there any point in continuing? With final, almost cruel deliberation, she stroked the hypersensitive leading edge of his wing, dragging her nails firmly along the bone.

He threw his head back and slammed his hips forward,

abdomen muscles seizing. His face contorted in agonized pleasure. Cum spurted from the tip of his cock, pulsing against his tattooed stomach, into the churning pool. The water clouded briefly with pale tendrils before dissolving into the current.

Outside their haven, rain continued its steady percussion. Blake watched River recover, face tilted to the rough ceiling, broad chest heaving. She'd pushed him beyond control. She'd made him surrender his body. And still, the words she desperately needed to hear remained locked away.

Words had power in this world. True words, spoken aloud. Words that created debts and sealed bonds. Words that made magic.

"I guess you won that round," she mumbled, unable to hide her self-doubt.

River's eyes opened, his pupils contracting as they focused on her face. He took in her nakedness, her defiant posture, the disappointment etched into her soul.

A low growl started deep in his chest and vibrated through the air between them. "You think I'm done?"

Before she could respond, he exploded from the water, hands clamping around her hips, as he lifted her with him. His wings flared wide for balance, spraying droplets like diamonds. Her legs instinctively wrapped around his waist, ankles crossing at the small of his back, hands around his neck.

He slammed her spine against the frost-cold wall, making her gasp.

He snarled, face inches from hers, breath searing her lips. "You think that was me groveling?"

His mouth crashed down on hers, tongue driving inside. He kissed her with brutal demand, stealing her breath. Only when she gasped for air, tapped his arms, did he move his lips to her jaw, her neck, his teeth nipping the tender skin.

"River!"

"No talking." He nipped her collarbone. "My turn now."

His mouth enclosed her left nipple, suction so intense it shot lightning south, pulsing her clit. She bucked and cried out. He suckled until pleasure blurred with pain, until her thighs trembled, until her slick arousal coated his stomach.

Her next protest came out as a moan. She threaded her fingers into his hair, trying to pull him away, but only succeeded because he dropped to his knees in the water, slung her legs over his shoulders and wings. He fit his face between her thighs, mouth over her pussy. The move was savage—no finesse.

Then his tongue invaded, filling her up, one thrust, two. He sucked hard until she screamed and thrashed against his hold. Her nails scrabbled uselessly on slick stone, dislodging fragments of phosphorescent growth that tumbled into the churning water below.

Somehow, she ended up positioned half on the ledge, half against the wall, one leg dangling in the pool and the other stretched toward the concrete slab ceiling. River's eyes stayed locked on hers the entire time, challenging, claiming, owning. He forced her to witness her undoing beneath his tongue's relentless assault. The hunger in his gaze held an edge of desperation, as if he believed this—this *physical* connection—could bridge what unsaid words could not.

It only proved he knew exactly why she was upset.

It only hurt more.

One hand slid from her hip to dip between her folds alongside his tongue. She gasped at the stretch, moaned as he pushed another finger inside. The sensation was exquisite, bringing a fresh flood of arousal.

"Don't you dare stop," she rasped.

His response was to curl his fingers inside her, finding that spot that made her vision fragment. His tongue flattened against her clit, giving her the perfect pressure until her body seized. Her orgasm tore through her body, from her lungs, a scream that reverberated through their private space and beyond.

She ground against his face, riding out her pleasure. But when the world finally solidified around her, she shoved weakly against his shoulders, chest heaving. "Get. Off."

He released her instantly, pulling back into the waist-deep water. His chest expanded with each harsh breath, wings held rigid for balance. He wiped his glistening mouth with the back of his hand, belligerent eyes still locked on her.

They stared at each other. Hating each other because they were too broken to be mended. Still wanting each other, even if pieces of their hearts were missing.

Simultaneously, they surged forward, meeting in the middle. Their mouths clashed—desperate, bruising, animal. Their tongues tangled in a frantic battle, a kiss of iron and salt and the savage truth of their obsessive connection.

River fumbled with his wet breeches. Blake helped him, shoving down leather to free the full length of his shaft, hard again. Already. This time, he didn't leave her bare skin exposed to the wall. His wings curled around her, shielding her from the icy surface. He notched his cock at her entrance and thrust in. Deep. She cried out at the sudden breach, and he swallowed her sound. He kissed and fucked her with intense, irrefutable drives against his wings, against the wall. His scent, his warmth, his heart pounding against hers.

"Only this," he snarled hotly against her mouth. Thrust. "Only me." *Thrust.* "You." Each drive pushed her higher, took him deeper. "I'm yours, Blake." His voice broke on her name as he buried himself to the hilt and held, trembling against her. "What else could this mean?"

In that fractured moment, his walls crumbled. Her body answered what her heart understood. She locked her ankles at the small of his back, pulling him impossibly deeper.

She wanted to hate him for his silence, for not saying the words, but she needed him too much. Maybe this was River giving the only way he knew how.

Who was she to ask for more?

CHAPTER

FIFTY-NINE

A quarter turn after midnight, River soared toward the Shadow Market, savoring the bite of cold air against his newly feathered wings. Each powerful beat sent ripples of contentment down his spine—a sensation he'd nearly forgotten.

A path between towering conifers appeared below, worn smooth by countless footsteps and wagon wheels. He descended, tucking his wings an instant before his boots hit the ground.

"You're late." Ash emerged from the shadows, wings ruffling as he tugged his high collar.

"No need to get your windways in a twist." River's eyes crinkled. "What the fuck are you wearing? I said dress inconspicuously, not in a conspicuous dress."

Since Guardian leather would scream their presence at a black market peddling forbidden wares, they had to disguise themselves. River wore dark woolen trousers, an embroidered tunic, and a hooded coat concealing the *Peacemaker* on his belt.

Ash, however, wore ceremonial pleated windways cut for male crows attending their mating ceremony. The hem flared wide enough to mimic a female's skirt. A black band cinched around his flat stomach. Glossy crow feathers adorned the shoulders of his cropped, patterned jacket. At least the fluffy nonsense hid his power-enhancing neck tattoos, considering his hair had been swept back into a knotted bun.

"You better have daggers hidden in those pleats."

"Don't worry about me." Ash's jaw tightened.

"I do." River paused. "Seriously."

"You said to look like the opposite of me."

"So you raided the Donna's ancestral closet?"

"I'll raid your face in a minute."

"Moody much?"

"It's Tommas's," Ash grunted, took a breath, then brushed the feathers at his shoulders. "A family heirloom or something."

"I'm suddenly very grateful the Well-blessed bond means I don't need a mating ceremony."

Ash shouldered past him. "Don't ask me to source my own disguise next time."

"Wait." River scooped up a finger of mud and jogged after him. He smeared the mud over Ash's Guardian mark, concealing its blue glow, and then gave him a patronizing pat. "There."

"Great." Ash jerked back. "Now I look like I've got shit on my face."

"Glamour doesn't work on Well-blessed marks."

"Whatever. Let's go."

"What's eating you?" River blocked his path, arms folded. "It's me who should be pissed after what you did."

Ash's eyebrow arched. "After what *I* did?"

"You know." River gestured toward their roost. "Picked sides."

"Still sore that you lost?"

"Two of the triad against one. Definitely not fair." River scanned the surrounding trees and shadows. "Where is he?"

"Probably at the tribunal."

River's fingers worried at the laces of his tunic. "Is he … okay?"

He'd rushed off after promising Cloud he wouldn't be alone. He'd abandoned Ash too. Left him to clean up the mess.

How could River protect both his mate and his triad? He had no idea how to manage this.

What blinds the Guardian is not darkness, but his own feathers.

The Donna probably meant River needed to stop second-guessing himself. Following his instincts was how he forged a path ahead of the others. If his instincts weren't talking, then jumping with no wings also did the job.

"Come on," he said, circling behind Ash. "The sooner we find your psycho ma, the sooner we help Cloud sort out his shit, and the sooner I get back to my mate."

They walked in silence, boots crunching over dirt and twigs, wings rustling in the tight space. The crowded branches overhead provided excellent cover for aerial discovery of illicit acts but made flying awkward.

River's gaze slid sideways to inspect the ridiculous outfit. Where he expected to find Ash tugging at his collar, the princeling held his chin high, shoulders relaxed. He looked more at home in mating garb than Guardian leathers.

Interesting.

He tried to recall what the Donna had said to Ash. If she'd been right about River, perhaps there was more to her ramblings.

The wind—or the Well itself—whispered to Ash. By that logic, this "accidentally embarrassing" outfit might not be a mistake at all. He opened his mouth to question it when Ash asked, "How's Blake?"

A spike of possessive jealousy gripped River's throat. His eyes narrowed on the ceremonial mating outfit. "What's that supposed to mean?"

"Did you—"

"Fuck her senseless?" River's lips curved. "Of course I did."

"I was going to say, did you give her your gift?"

River grabbed himself crudely through his pants. "Sure did."

"Stop fucking around."

Of course Ash wouldn't make a move on Blake. That was ridiculous. River circled his fist over his heart. "I'm edgy."

"Why, she didn't like your gift?"

"I didn't give it to her. Didn't feel right. She was…"

His stomach knotted at the memory of how he'd left Blake stretched across their bed—sweat-dampened hair in wild tangles, lips swollen from his kisses and cock. After returning from the springs, they'd fucked again. On the bed. Against the table. On the Well-damned floor. Her need for him raged until he mentioned leaving. Then her gaze kind of … emptied. She tracked his every movement as he dressed, never wavering even as she'd padded to the table and reached for her sketching tools.

He told her to stay in bed and rest, but she scoffed, inked nib already scratching across parchment.

"I need to finish these drawings before I forget. And I want to write down everything she said."

"Who?"

"The Donna."

The fact that Blake had sat nude at the table hadn't seemed to register in her mind. After placing a plate of cheese and bread beside her, he'd tucked her tangled hair behind her ear. Her skin burned against his fingertips. When he'd questioned if she felt ill, she'd simply asked him to prop the door open for cooler air.

Regardless, he attempted to heal her, but sensed no illness. If the Donna's bat-shit paste still affected her, wouldn't he have detected a toxin? When she finally met his gaze, he searched her eyes and asked what was wrong.

Tell me I'm your whole world. Tell me I belong here.

Her unspoken plea had echoed through their bond. That grimy sense of grave ash he once associated with her ex slithered into him through their connection. Because of him.

I love you, he'd wanted to say. But saying the words aloud would paint a target on her back. Saying them meant promises he wasn't sure he could keep. Not until he dealt with Cloud. Not until he secured their future.

He'd kissed her instead—a simple, lingering press of lips. He fussed over her comfort, cleaned up debris from his fight with Cloud, righted the toppled eucalyptus, and reshaped the dented wall.

Actions, not words. But her eyes begged for both.

The weight of her need still pressed against his chest.

He'd tell her when the moment was right, when he'd secured the cryptex, helped Cloud overcome his grief, and they understood what was happening to Blake's body. He owed her the perfect moment, and he wanted to do it right.

"And?" Ash prompted.

"Something's off with her body," he admitted. "I think she's unwell."

"As in … a mortal affliction?"

"You don't think that's what the Donna—"

"Fuck off." Ash froze mid-step, eyes boring into River's. "What?"

"Nothing out of the Donna's twisted mouth is straight-forward. I just meant a human illness."

A crow's harsh warning call pierced the night, silencing them. The path ahead appeared to end abruptly. Each Guardian snapped out their wings, sure to display the glossy feathers.

The crow cawed once. An acknowledgment—entrance accepted.

River tugged his hood lower, concealing his face. He glanced at Ash and mumbled, "You brought the item to trade, right?"

"I brought something."

SIXTY

River and Ash passed the crow sentinel, and the forest became unnaturally quiet. They'd entered the warded area that blocked sound, even the rustling wind. Another few steps and sound returned. Ordinary underbrush and trees transformed into the Shadow Market. Glamours fell away to expose crude wooden structures festooned with hanging wares. Patrons moved with furtive purpose, wings bound tightly to avoid recognition, or shifted away altogether.

UV markings glowed along the tent flaps, indicating which forbidden goods waited inside. Cages containing contraband hung from branches—metal trinkets, old-world technology, and preserved specimens pulsing with mana.

The sense of forbidden grated against River's nerves. It went against everything they stood for as Guardians, but the land was still rich in mana. The objects were simply transient passengers. If they remained long enough in one spot, the Well would withdraw mana. The land would become desecrated. Crows loved finding workarounds, which was why the Shadow Market was open for one night only.

River recognized faces from his murder's lowest roosts bartering alongside those relegated to the amphitheater's highest tiers. Each came prepared with insulated bags to carry their Well-cutting treasure safely home. Status meant nothing here, only what treasures you brought to trade. Unless, of course, you were a Guardian.

Wrongness continued to pulse through River, making his gut squirm. But destroying this time-honored crow tradition felt like a betrayal. Besides, not all wares here were made of metal or plastic. Some were forbidden for entirely different reasons.

They moved through the crowd, pretending to study trinkets while keeping each other in their peripheral vision. A master thief's tent caught River's eye. Polished lockpicks were arranged like surgical tools beside wingtip silencers. A sign proclaimed dark journals bound in leather held family weaknesses inside. River stopped, fingers hovering over a book with the Winter Court crest visible beneath layers of dust and dirt.

"Could be useful on a mission," he murmured, glancing back.

Ash's jaw flexed, shoulders rigid, gaze fixed ahead. "Maybe."

River abandoned the journals. "Can you sense her?"

Ash nodded curtly toward the far end of the market, where a tall female crowned with feathers and glittering beads squawked at a trader's stall. Even from this distance, her energy distorted the air, creating ripples that patrons avoided. The trader cowered before her, wings tucked tight against his spine as they bartered.

"Fuck me," River whispered. "She hasn't changed a bit."

The Collector's birdlike face was still as oddly beautiful and terrifying at once. Even the way her wings and arms were the same didn't seem so odd. Ash ground his teeth so hard it clicked. He took a step backward, away from his mother. Shit. If they didn't make their move now, Ash would lose his nerve.

"Let's jump." River started forward, into the fray, only to slam into a body that stepped directly in his path.

Cloud. The V-mark stood out against his pale skin. Guardian uniform, polished daggers catching manabee lanternlight. The Order of the Well's insignia gleamed in full sight. Not even attempting to disguise himself.

"For *Crimson's* sake." River and Ash dragged Cloud into the shadows between the nearest stall and the forest. "What are you doing here dressed like that?"

"Why not?" Cloud's voice was as flat as his gaze.

A sharp caw pierced the night. Then another. The warning multiplied, rippling outward from sentinel to sentinel. River risked a glance around the edge of their stall and glimpsed the Collector's gaze snapping skyward, searching.

He ducked back and summoned mana to create a silencing shield around them. "How did you sneak past the sentinels?"

"Doesn't matter," Ash said. "If you're here to fuck up our mission—"

"She doesn't have it here," Cloud said. "The cryptex."

Unease prickled River's skin. "And?"

"And I know where it is," he replied, eyes skating away. "I'm headed there later." He hesitated, fingers twitching at his sides. "But the tribunal…"

"Aren't you supposed to be there now?" Ash folded his arms.

Cloud took a step back and ran his gaze over Ash as if seeing him for the first time. His brows raised higher with each increment covered. "Why the fuck are you in Cardona ceremonials?"

"Fuck you, too." Ash scowled.

Cloud sent River a look that said, *What's up with him?*

He replied by flicking his gaze toward the Collector's last known location, hinting at the obvious reason. The silent communication settled something between them. Cloud's shoulders relaxed. Contentment curled around River's heart. Whatever rift had appeared would soon close. He knew it. It gave him hope. They would find time to talk properly later tonight.

"So why aren't you at the tribunal?" he repeated.

A hearing was notoriously closed to the public, except for individuals from the associated kettle. River and Ash had not been approached to offer defense, but that wasn't unusual. No one outside the Order gave a shit about a Guardian's opinion.

"I've said what I needed to say." Fingers tapped on leather-clad thighs. "But if you two go … it might help if you…"

"Speak on your behalf?" Ash raised his brow.

A curt nod. "Especially you, River."

"Why me?"

"You're the murder's golden boy, aren't you?" Bitterness laced his words. "You and your mate with her Well blessing."

Piercing blue eyes hardened on River, pushing unsaid accusations into his heart like daggers. Although no threat had been made, his body reacted as if it had. Mana surged to the surface of his skin, lifting every tiny hair on his arms. Perhaps thinking about reconciliation was premature.

Something felt off. First, Cloud turned up in his uniform, uncaring that it would ruin the Order mission he obviously knew about. Now he was asking for help? Since when did Cloud ask for help?

"Are you asking?" River ground out. "Or claiming the debt I owe you?"

"Forget it." Cloud tried to shoulder past, but Ash and River closed ranks to stop him.

The three of them stared at each other for a long moment, distrust lingering in the air. But if this was an olive branch, then they had to take it. Small steps forward were better than none.

"We'll go," River said. "Of course, we'll speak on your behalf."

"Wait here," Ash added, darting an almost relieved glance around the stall, tracking his mother's progress as she moved on from the trader. "When we return, you can take us to where the cryptex is."

Cloud's exhale was so small, it almost went unnoticed. "I'll wait here."

"We'll be back soon," River replied.

"Don't let her see you." Ash stepped backward, eager wings already flaring. "And don't let her leave."

"Oh, I won't." A wicked glint entered Cloud's eyes as he moved to a spot behind the next tented stall, which had a better view of the market. He leaned against a nearby tree trunk and folded his arms, staring into the distance.

Ash stalked off in the direction they'd arrived, but River hesitated. It wasn't as though he expected a spoken word of gratitude, but a hand sign might have been nice. Anger tried to force its way back into his heart, but he shoved it down.

"I know it's not the time," River said. "But I'm still willing to listen. Maybe we can talk on the way to the cryptex."

No answer. He sighed and snapped out his wings, ready to fly the moment he located an exit point through the canopy. The ruffling and rustling of feathers drew Cloud's attention.

"Your mate," he said, eyes taking in River's new primaries, "must be powerful to restore wings that couldn't be healed."

"Sparkles is." A pause. "But she doesn't think so."

Their eyes met. "I thought her name was Blake."

"I call her that because—" River gestured to his hair, warmth flushing his cheeks. Every crow saw different UV patterns. Why the fuck was he bashful over this? Maybe because he'd never felt this way about a female. Like she was his destiny and his doom all in one. Maybe because he still felt guilty. Sorry.

"Don't take all night." Cloud rotated on the trunk, facing the market.

Dismissed.

It was on the tip of River's tongue to say more about Blake, to tell Cloud that he'd get along with her if he gave her a chance. It only took a week of being in her presence, and vengeance had melted away. All he wanted now was for his triad to be back together. But he held back, even though it killed him.

"Cloud," he said, "we'll also speak on your behalf at the Order. Just so you know." He paused, waiting for acknowledgement. The only sign Cloud heard was a slight tensing of his jaw. Nevertheless, River plowed on. "When you're ready to face the consequences of your betrayal, we'll be there." He scrubbed his face. This was coming out wrong. "I mean, when you're ready to tell us how we can help, we'll do it."

Cloud's knuckles popped as he clenched his fist, still staring into the distance.

River sighed. At least he'd tried.

"Okay." He stepped back. "I'll … just head off."

Then he jogged in the direction Ash had gone. When he popped through the mana-enforced sound barrier cloaking the Shadow Market, he found a gap in the branches and launched into the air.

RIVER WASN'T FAR BEHIND ASH AS THEY FLEW OVER THE GREAT Murder. The storm clouds had receded, and a glimpse of moonlight illuminated UV trails left on the ground. The tiny glittering, intersecting lines were tracks left by rodents, other animals, and people. The more false light produced by campfires and manabee lanterns, the harder it was to see the tracks. The crow half of River wanted to chase down the freshest, brightest tracks to see what he could catch.

But the more human part only cared about one path—the one his matebond created, tugging his heart toward the Umbria roost. It took every ounce of control he possessed to resist going to Blake. The kernel of guilt he felt at leaving her so unsettled was blooming into something hard and frightening, something that confused his primal instincts. Something was wrong with her. He knew it in his soul. But a quick check with his senses revealed she was asleep. She

560

would want him to do everything he could to repair his broken triad.

Unsettled. Still.

Fuck it.

He had to see her. Just a little fly by past the nesting van. Ash won't even know. Two seconds later, he swooped and landed in the muddy field where they'd played Blake's game. Cold air bit his cheeks and nose, but it made him feel alive. Or maybe that was what being near his mate did. Without pausing to wave at his father chatting with Salvatore on the deck of their van, he jogged to the nesting van and frowned at the still-open door. Two steps and he was inside, breathing a sigh of relief.

There she was, head down on the table, cheeks flushed. Face smooshed on crinkled papers. Lightly snoring. Fast asleep.

Thank fuck.

He considered moving her to the bed, but that might wake her. He settled for closing the door. To ease his heart further, he checked that the proximity stones were still active around the roost.

No change was good, he supposed.

At least she was resting.

A tingling on his forearm announced an incoming triad message. Ash's scrawl appeared:

I'm waiting outside the pavilion. Where are you?

Oops.

ON MY WAY.

With a renewed sense of purpose, River launched back into the sky, picked up speed, and aimed for the tribunal pavilion at the center of the settlement. Colored flags and emblems of different family crests adorned the fabric segments, making it easily identifiable. As he descended, he almost clashed with another crow taking flight.

"Watch it!" River barked, but the floater didn't even look back, let alone hand-sign an apology.

Must have had an unfavorable tribunal outcome.

Ash stood outside the pavilion, arms folded, glaring at River's approach. The tent's entrance flap opened, and Carlotta and Ravi rushed out, almost bowling into Ash.

"Ma." River grabbed her shoulder, tugging her out of the way.

"What are you doing here?" Her eyes widened at him, then at Ash.

"We're here to put in a good word for the Cardonas at the hearing." River glanced at Carlotta. "And Cloud."

"You were?"

"Don't look so shocked." His smile dropped immediately when he realized her pale face had nothing to do with not expecting his aid. Ice trailed fingers down his spine. "What's wrong?"

"The tribunal hearing has been postponed," she replied. "It was supposed to begin over a turn ago, but Cloud never turned up."

SIXTY-ONE

Cloud remained beneath a dripping bough, surrounded by the scent of wet pine and decaying leaf litter. He silently tracked the bird-faced bitch, watching her intimidate vendors, cheat, and demand.

He watched, but his mind kept drifting to the things River had said.

When you're ready to face the consequences of your betrayal…

I would have followed you anywhere…

Pushed you into love, pushed you high, then watched you fall…

I'm sorry…

It was easy to apologize with new wings and a new mate by his side. Everything felt possible in those early years. River thought losing his feathers broke him. He didn't know the meaning of broken.

They thought Cloud *wanted* to become this?

He didn't plan the war.

He didn't wake up one day and think, *You know what*

would be fun? Treason. Mass murder. A bloody V painted on my fucking face.

He just wanted answers. To look in Rory's eyes as he squeezed the life out of her, to hear her deathbed confession.

Instead she—

A fierce ache gripped his throat, his lungs. He closed his eyes to ward off the memory, but the tree dripping nearby catapulted him further into his past.

Drip, drip, pip.

He saw Rory's cloudy, bloodshot eyes as he held her by the throat. Remembered how disturbing the color had been, how they'd once been like warm honey. They'd once shimmered with a whirl of colors so unique, so unheard of, that they hadn't been named.

They said a person's entire life flashed before their eyes just before their death. That's what Cloud had counted on when he dangled her over the airship's edge. No truer words had ever been spoken than a deathbed confession. They were supposed to have given him peace.

Closure.

Yet he still *felt* Rory's pulse throbbing against his fingers. He still heard his thundering wingbeat fight against gravity, still saw her hair blow from the convergence of clashing air, from his wings, from the airship, from the lake below. He still saw those eyes silently beg for him to let her go, to end her suffering.

Still heard her childhood, angelic voice in his memory, singing about flying away…

Pip, pip, pip.

P*IP, PIP, PIP.*

The curious rhythmic beat blended with the sound of singing.

Wind buffeted Cielo's body as he crawled up the glass-domed roof. He was up so high. The surface was slippery. This sky tower was trouble. He felt it in his bones. He'd only meant to map out the room below, but that voice … ferns and plants hid its owner.

Curious.

Maybe if he dropped through the open segment, just enough to see who was singing, he could retreat to safety quickly. The gap was wide enough to fit his wings—barely.

Pip, pip, pip.

That voice—that haunting, pretty song. She used the beat of the pipping steam in time with her lyrics, like drums.

Clever.

Cielo strained his senses, and when he was sure no other voice could be heard, he poked his head through the gap for a better look.

And gasped.

Not just plants inside, but treasure. Everywhere. A desk strewn with maps, baubles, strange human gadgets, and machines. The pip-pip came from a copper kettle chugging steam. He had no idea what the other machines did, but recognized forbidden substances—metal and plastic, enough to earn a Guardian's wrath if caught.

Well-dammit.

Half those items were useless to him. Worth nothing if he couldn't take them back to Elphyne and brag about the score. But maybe he could take them back. He'd crossed the wasteland after all.

"How'd you get up there!"

Cielo slipped.

He caught himself, went to dart back outside into the sky, but the sight of a human girl froze him in place. Warm skin, big eyes, and a dress miles too big. Her hair captivated him the most. Longish strands stuck out at all angles. Some seemed straight, some seemed crimped, defying the laws of nature. And the colors. The shine. Like the Northern Lights in winter.

He wondered how different she'd look in the full light of day.

He wondered if she was too big to fit in his satchel.

She pouted and pointed at him. "You should come down; otherwise, you might fall and hurt yourself."

"I ... um..."

If he went down, she'd know he was fae. But leaving now meant going home empty-handed. No fucking way.

The human girl was small. Weak. If Manfri were here, they'd each take her down with their eyes closed.

But Cielo couldn't move.

Those colors in her hair arrested every cell in his body long enough for fear to trickle in. What if she screamed, alerting guards? He'd heard stories of humans using weapons with flying bullets that moved too fast to dodge. Hadn't timed the guard's shifts. Hadn't expected this girl to be in here. He hadn't mapped out the room yet.

Maybe he should just cut his losses now, return to Elphyne, and teach Manfri how to cross the wasteland with him. He'd know how to deal with unexpected things like this. Cielo stretched his wings, ready to fly home. His feathers caught the icy wind and ruffled. The girl's gaze darted behind him, and she gasped.

"You're ... wow."

Wow?

Cielo blinked. He expected her to scream, to call the guards, but ... wow?

"I'm fae," he confirmed.

Her eyes narrowed. "Are you here to steal me away?"

He scoffed. "Why would I do that?"

"My dad says that's what fae do. But my moms say..." Her gaze turned distant. She shrugged. Frowned. *"I forget. What are you doing here anyway?"*

"Hunting treasure to rub in my dad's face." He glowered. *"And my brother's."*

"Oh." She went quiet. *"We don't have much treasure in here."*

"Everything is a treasure!"

"Like what?"

"Like that thing in your hand."

"This?" She held up a shiny, rectangular brick. *"It's a music player. From the olden days."* A sigh. *"I'm not supposed to play with it because it might break."*

"Music player. Was that where the song came from?"

"That was me." Pink bloomed across her cheeks.

"Oh." He paused. *"You have a nice voice."*

She went all floppy and looked at her feet. Her hair tried to hide her smile, but he'd seen it.

"What about that?" He pointed to the pip-pip machine.

"That's for the plants. Makes the air wet."

Dumb.

"And that?" He pointed to the desk.

She leaned closer, whispering loudly, *"Oh no. We don't go over there. That's my dad's stuff."* Her voice dropped lower. *"I'm not even supposed to play in here, so please don't tell anyone."*

"Why are you in here then?"

A spark of defiance lit up her eyes, making his stomach feel weird like he'd jumped off a cliff with no wings.

"Because he told me not to," she declared.

For some reason, that made Cielo laugh so hard that he nearly slipped again through the open glass segment.

"Please come down," she said, *"so I don't hurt my neck looking up at you."*

He surveyed the forest inside the room. "No one else is here?"

"All the grown-ups are in meetings. I won't hurt you. I promise."

Funny that she thought she could hurt him. He was the one with a dagger.

Unable to shift his wings away without access to the Well, he tucked them tight and slid head first through the gap between the glass segments. As gravity took hold, he somersaulted and landed on his feet—wings splaying for balance like an acrobat. He straightened, pleased with himself. That almost looked intentional.

The girl bounced on her feet and clapped hard, unruly hair bobbing.

"Your wings are so pretty," she gushed.

"Pretty is for girls," he growled, puffing out his chest. "I'm not a girl."

"I know that, silly. You're a boy."

He cleared his throat. "I'm a crow."

"A crow boy." She grinned. "Wow. My first crow boy friend."

He didn't want to break it to her, but they wouldn't be friends. He was here to steal from her.

Hand on **Murder's** *hilt, Cielo's gaze swept the room. Now that he was down here, a sense of urgency thumped through his veins. There were things on the walls he didn't notice before—things pinned to boards that looked disturbingly familiar and grotesque. "I should go..."*

"First, let me help you." She pointed to various objects, a devious glint in her eye. "What sort of treasure will make your father and brother eat their words?"

She had a funny way of talking.

"I don't know." He grinned. "There's so much."

"Hmm." She tapped her chin. "It has to be something my dad won't know is missing. Otherwise, I'll get in trouble."

"Anything old worldy."

She nodded and darted off.

Perfect. The human was doing his job for him.

While she searched, Cielo wandered the green-smelling room. When he passed the desk, his primaries clipped a brass cylinder, nudging it into a hairbrush. It ricocheted and rolled loudly toward the desk's edge. Gasping, he rushed to catch it before it fell. He braced for impact, for the pain of being disconnected from the Well as the forbidden substance connected with his skin. But as his fingers closed around the brass, nothing happened.

He'd forgotten he was already in pain. So much that he was numb.

But oh, what a prize. Multiple moving discs on the cylinder had letters inscribed on them. The craftsmanship was astounding. His father and Carmine would surely—how did the human say it? —eat their words.

"You shouldn't touch that," she said, frowning as she returned with a book.

"What is it?" he asked, turning the cylinder over.

"A cryptex." She gently pried it from his fingers. She was so close that her hair tickled his nose as she rotated the letter discs. "You have to spell the right word, or—" She deftly clicked the ends, opened them, then closed them immediately. "See?"

"Give me a turn." He snatched it faster than a hurricane.

"No!" She covered his hand, eyes widening. "One wrong move and it's ruined forever."

Cielo looked down at where she touched him.

He'd spent weeks conditioning himself to the pain of disconnecting from the Well. Weeks of repeatedly attempting to cross the wasteland. He'd almost given up. The task had seemed impossible. Every step away from the Well turned an ache into suffering. Suffering grew into agony. To torment. But his stubborn pride refused to let him give up, and his inability to think fast like Manfri left him with decision paralysis. But then something odd happened. Just as the pain was at its worst, it stayed at its worst.

Disconnection from the Well hurt, but he wasn't dead.

Once he'd made the realization, the pain became bearable. It took over all other sensations until he became numb to it all.

Until now.

"Trust me," she whispered. "He'll know this is gone. The prize isn't worth the pain."

"But … what if it is?"

She stared at him, long and hard. He stared back, refusing to cower, refusing to tremble for a small human girl. But when she tugged the cryptex from his fingers, he let her. And when she returned it to the drawer, he said nothing. He was too busy staring at his hand, frowning at the lingering tingle in his palm.

"What about this?" She held up her brush. Waggled her book.

"We have those in Elphyne." He shrugged.

"Ooh. I have a better idea." She skipped away. "I know what he'll never miss."

Cielo tried not to stare at the desk. He really did.

But a secret from the human leader would be the biggest treasure of all. Cielo was sure even the Guardians would forgive him if he brought that back.

And she'd left the drawer open.

"The cryptex is not for sale."

The voice snapped Cloud out of the past. His gaze narrowed on the source of his problems. The vendor had been forgotten, and the Collector now spoke with someone else. His Guardian senses picked up a wrongness in the stranger from where he stood, twenty feet away. She didn't belong in this world—a human or … something else.

"So you admit to having it," the woman said, triumph flaring in her eyes.

The Collector leaned toward the female and hissed, "Unless my son returns to his rightful place, it remains with me."

Cloud had once returned to this very market and begged the Collector to return the cryptex. Offered everything he had, and she replied with those exact words.

Still so fucking stubborn.

Still so fucking greedy.

"I promised you'd never be alone," River had said earlier. *"I failed you."*

His confession confirmed what Cloud had suspected all these years—River had been jealous.

He should be furious. Bitter. Seething. He should turn the lightning in his veins toward River again. For real this time. But instead of vengeance, of rage, he saw broken wings restored to wholeness, to glory, to flight.

Through Blake.

Through a Well-blessed mate.

Cloud used to hate his decision paralysis, but now he saw it for what it was—the blessing of time.

He strolled forward with deliberate casualness, each step measured and intentional. Lightning sparking beneath his skin, waiting to be unleashed, waiting for the Collector to notice.

Still, she haggled over her precious treasure.

"I'll bring him to you," the almost-human promised. "Tell me your son's name."

If Cloud were a better Guardian, he'd stop and figure out what this stranger was, why she was here. Maybe he would even use her to get to Nero and kill him, just as he'd done with all the other spies trying to slip into Elphyne.

But he was so close to gaining what he came for.

He kept walking. The market parted before him, vendors and customers alike pressing back against their stalls. Their eyes widened at his Guardian uniform, at the metal weapons openly displayed across his body. Fear rippled through the crowd.

Fear of him.

For what blazed in his eyes.

The Collector sensed his approach. Powerful beings always sensed the arrival of another. Her feathered head jerked up, beady eyes widening as he stopped before her and grinned. The last time they met, he was weak. Powerless. Just another crow bartering for scraps.

Lightning exploded from his fingertips, a force of nature he couldn't deny any longer. The blast caught the Collector directly in the chest. Her feathered form jerked as electricity coursed through her, wafting the stench of burned flesh and feathers.

Screams erupted. Music to his ears. Perfect chaos.

Cloud waited for the Collector to contact her son, to lay the bait. He waited for that infamous greed to reveal itself. Then he emptied his inner well.

CLOUD'S PATH TO THE UMBRIA ROOST STRETCHED BEFORE HIM, emptied from the chaos he'd created. Everyone had rushed toward the commotion, toward the Shadow Market to offer aid.

Just as he'd hoped.

No one noticed him descending on dark wings and landing on the muddy field where everything had changed. No one saw him approach the nesting caravan. No one saw his steps slow as he caught sight of River's mate through the stained glass window.

Hunched over drawings, brow furrowed as she slept. Her skin glistened with sweat despite the cool evening air. The fever was advancing faster than he'd anticipated. When a human burned like that, time was running short.

Cloud glanced around, searching for his triad in the darkness, waiting for them to rush to the rescue, to reveal what they'd always known.

It was never Cloud who'd been the hero. Never him the Well chose to keep its precious magic safe.

There was still time to walk away. To let nature take its course. To accept that some things couldn't be fixed. Some people shouldn't be saved. If only he'd learned that lesson himself, he wouldn't be in this mess alone.

The problem was that her voice still rang in his ear.

Not the angelic one singing, not the one screaming his name in pleasure, not the one taunting him as she plucked his feathers free, not even the one begging for her suffering to end.

If you hate me, then kill me!

Cloud flinched, turning his face as if slapped. But the memory was there, burning with brutal clarity. He closed his eyes and was back in his nightmare, reliving it as though it were yesterday. The airship, two lives slipping in his grip, wings beating furiously, deep blue water below. Rory gripping his forearms, using his own strength against him as she pulled herself up, tilting the world on its axis.

He knew what she was doing, knew *exactly* what truth she'd confess. The same words were pinned to his trove wall. The same words she'd repeated over and over in that Crystal City cell, making sure he'd never forget how little he meant to her. Making sure he could recall them as if written by his own hand.

If I can't…

She climbed higher, her fierce bloodshot eyes never leaving his.

If I forget…

Her lips moved toward his ear. He braced for her inevitable words.

Then let me go…

"Don't let me go," she'd whispered, and then plunged her dagger into his hand around her throat.

But it wasn't that pain reflexively opening his fingers. It was the pain in his chest, from the numb traitor he'd thought was dead. Her truest words exposed his greatest lie.

Every night, he replayed that moment. Every night, he watched her plunge, watched her watching him. Every night, those impossible words rang in his ears.

Don't let me go.

Don't let me go.

Now he finally knew why.

He forced his eyes open and then picked the lock on the caravan door. He stepped inside. Stopped. The feverish human slumped over papers—sketches of secrets stolen from his trove. Treasure maps. Anatomy diagrams. Blast radii. Lyrics to a song he'd never hear again. Letters she had no business reading, let alone copying. He traced fingers over paper, along words meant for his eyes only: *I'm learning to be better than him.*

He crumpled the paper in his fist.

A restoration gift was no coincidence. It was the Well's answer to an impossible prayer.

For five years, Cloud had been a villain. A traitor. A monster.

Tonight, he would become a savior.

SIXTY-TWO

"What do you mean, Cloud never turned up?" River asked Carlotta, then looked at his mother.

A flash of distant lightning revealed the whites of Ravi's eyes.

Wrong.

The single instinct of dread hit River before his mind caught up, screaming for him to pay attention. How could there be lightning without a storm, without thunder?

Activity around the tribunal tent increased. More people ran out from inside, heedless of those standing in the way. The mood quickly shifted from busy to one of panic. Like a shockwave, caws exploded from crow sentinels on the pavilion's rooftop, gaining in magnitude and scale as more throughout the Great Murder picked it up and repeated. Soon, the warning alarm of an attack echoed all around them, ringing in River's ears.

"Get back inside the tent," Ash ordered the females.

"Blake." River's wings snapped out, ready to fly to her. She'd been asleep. Vulnerable.

"Wait." Ash grabbed his arm, halting him.

The wind picked up, curling around their faces, ruffling their feathers. Ash's gaze grew distant, impossibly darker. The sense of mana swelled in the air, tingling on River's skin. A blue glimmer drew their gazes down to a rippling puddle—an incoming blood-borne communication.

Could be one of his siblings. Or Talo. River stepped closer, crouching to focus through the distorting water. He never expected the Collector's bloody face sharpening into focus.

"Always knew you were a coward," she warbled, eyes darting over River's shoulder. "Never thought you'd send another crow to do your dirty work—"

Blinding light arced through the puddle, forcing River and Ash to shield their eyes. When it was over, all that remained of the communication was a ribbon of blood diffusing into mud.

Another flash split the sky. No thunder. No sound. This time, there was no doubt where it came from. The wards keeping the market a secret had also been its downfall. A split second later, a golden orange glow backlit the trees.

The forest was on fire.

THE SCENT HIT RIVER BEFORE THE SCREAMS.

At first, it was the burnt ozone and scorched feathers, then came the tang of coppery blood. His wings faltered mid-beat as phantom pain splintered through his body, traveling to the tips of his wings—a*gonizing, nerve-frying pain.*

Cold dread coiled at the familiar and sickening.

"Fuck," he muttered, banking hard toward the Shadow Market's flaming entrance. He summoned mana and redirected every drop of water he sensed in the vicinity—from puddles, from the earth, from dewy drops on leaves—toward the fire. Steam hissed. Embers died. He tucked his wings and dropped through the smoking gap in the canopy, impact jarring his knees.

Vendors scattered like startled insects, faces frozen in horror. Stalls lay overturned. Charred fabric smoldered. A cage of contraband metal had melted into twisted, unrecognizable slag. Manabeeze popped from random corpses and floated, illuminating what hid in the shadows from flames and embers.

Not chaos. Carnage.

Lightning hadn't just struck. It had raged, jumped from stall to stall, body to body.

"Help!" Someone clutched River's sleeve. "Please!"

River shoved him aside, mind whirling and giddy from his instincts screaming at him. Not again. *Not again.* His gaze swept the devastation. Surely Cloud was attacked first. Someone must have provoked him.

He almost tripped over a female sprawled across broken wood, wings splayed at impossible angles, feathers smoking. Her eyes stared sightlessly toward the canopy. Another body curled beside an upended stall, chest rising and falling in shallow gasps.

Each victim carved fresh guilt into River's soul.

"What happened?" he growled, grabbing a nearby crow

shifter by the throat, lifting until his feet dangled and his wings drooped. "Who did this?"

The crow wheezed, eyes bulging. "Lightning ... so much lightning."

"I fucking *know* that." River's grip tightened. "Who?"

Don't let it be him. Don't let this be—

"Guardian." Fingernails scrabbled against River's wrist. "V ... bloody V."

River dropped him. Felt dizzy. Sick. The vendor crumpled, gasping.

No.

Not after their reconciliation.

Not after River's apology.

Not after Cloud had asked for help.

But the evidence lay scorched into flesh and fabric. Undeniable. Ringing in his ears multiplied. This wasn't a mistake. This was premeditated. It had to be. Cloud hadn't wiped the V from his face, hadn't turned up at the hearing, hadn't even claimed River's debt. No. That would be too easy. All this time, Cloud was still functioning with a single purpose—Vengeance.

"Please." A female voice croaked from beneath collapsed canvas. "My mate..."

Mate.

One word uttered from a distraught woman's lips was enough to put River's head back in the game. He forced himself forward. Each step felt like walking through quicksand. He crouched beside the wounded female and moved a column of splintered wood from crushing her chest. But the fool crawled back into the debris, clawing at wood and canvas and dirt, digging, crying for her mate.

River gently touched her on the shoulder and said, "I'll get him. Stand back. He'd want you to be safe."

Her bottom lip trembled. Tears spilled free over her soot-stained cheeks, but she nodded, shuffling backward. River used his gift to feel out the Well. He touched the earth, grounding himself, and sent his awareness through mana, into the destruction. An echoing ping of life was two yards away.

It took a hefty dose of muscle and mana to lift the entangled, collapsed framework from a mangled body. The male's breathing came wet and ragged. Blood and dirt matted his swollen face. Pupils contracted to pinpoint pain. His nails were torn, fingertips worn down to bloody stubs from trying to claw his way out—to reach his mate.

He tried to speak. Tried to go to her, but River pushed him down.

"Don't move," he said, and moved his hand to the male's grimy neck. He used his gift to sense the extent of injuries. No broken spine. "Some internal bleeding," he noted. "A good shift into your crow form will heal you better than I could. Well enough to fly out of the danger zone."

He glanced at the female and ushered her forward.

She ran over, sobbing as she collapsed on her mate. They gripped each other as if nothing else mattered. Not the pain the male surely felt with wounds like those. Not the sharp things she kneeled upon. There was only gratitude. Relief. Joy. Love.

Seeing it hurt River more than any wound, and he couldn't understand why, only that it made him ache to return to Blake, to be done with this job and its fucking miseries. To put this madness behind him.

"Go," he croaked, then cleared his throat. "Shift and return to the Great Murder. It's safer there. Be together."

The male quickly transformed into bird form, hopped, and cawed when the female hesitated.

"You're a Guardian." Recognition flickered in her eyes despite River's disguise. The mud must have come loose from his face. "But your friend … why?"

Her mate cawed again. She didn't wait for River's answer and shifted into her bird form. The two flew away, wings shadowing each other, whisking smoke with them into the canopy.

Boots thudded against packed earth behind River.

Ash surveyed the destruction, calculating. "How can we be sure it was him?"

River gestured irritably at the multitudes of blackened flesh, scorched wood—electricity's unmistakable signature. "Who else can fucking shoot lightning from their fingertips? I swear to the Well, I'll rip his throat out this time."

"But what if—"

"No." River shut that shit down. "I'd thought the same thing. Maybe he'd been attacked. Maybe he'd been provoked. Sooner or later, we need to face the truth."

Do we need to be worried? Jasper had asked him days ago.

Maybe, he'd replied. *But I can promise you this—no more innocents will lose their lives. If I find him, I'll stop him.*

SIXTY-THREE

Sentinels arrived and navigated the destruction, shoving past River and Ash with insults mumbled beneath their breath. Some fanned wings to clear the smoke. Others used precious mana to extinguish lingering fires and push off rogue manabeeze interfering with rescue efforts. But they were kittens amongst lions.

Ash flicked out his hand, and a gale blew forward, adding force to their efforts. River dug his fist into dirt and debris, connecting with the Well on a visceral level, ensuring no embers flared or fires sparked anew. The effort made him sweat and drained his inner reserves.

"Enough," he clipped. No one was dying. They'd survive the smoke.

Ash dropped his hand and stared bleakly ahead. Activity resumed, including more sounds behind them. They'd erected a makeshift triage at the market's entrance, and the injured lined up on palettes.

River jerked his chin toward the wounded. "Let's see if your ma survived."

Ash nodded, jaw tightening above the ceremonial feathered collar. The ridiculous mating outfit seemed obscene amid the carnage. But at least he'd rubbed the mud off his Guardian mark.

River pushed through the crowd, following burnt flesh and lightning's aftermath. Sentinels parted before them. Fear permeated the air with a sour stench. Getting in the way of Guardians now was suicide.

The groans of the wounded amplified beneath the triage tent. River caught sight of a feathered headdress first, once regal, now mostly gone, uneven clumps and burned skin laid bare. He wanted to feel triumphant. Satisfaction. Maybe relief at her injuries and hope that she'd fucking choke on them, but all he felt was a growing sense of confusion amongst his nausea.

If Cloud wanted her dead, she'd be dead.

The Collector was very much alive and on a palette, chest rising in shallow bursts. Beside her, another woman lay unconscious.

Ash stopped short and tucked his wings against his spine. His face hardened into a mask of indifference.

"My heir." The Collector's beak-like face turned toward Ash, dark eyes glittering despite her injuries. "Come … to witness … your handiwork?"

His fists clenched. "Not mine."

"You sent him." Blood-crusted feathers rustled as she attempted to sit, only to collapse with a pained gasp. "You sent the stormy one … because I refused him."

"I sent no one."

River's intuition prickled at the sense of wrongness nearby. Not from the Collector. His gaze drifted to the woman on the palette next door.

A single scorch mark across her left shoulder cauterized an open wound, giving the appearance of melted flesh. River's fingers drifted to his jaw line, where a spiderweb of thin scar tissue was all that remained of a similar injury.

He'd been so lucky to have access to a healer like Ada. He must have looked horrific when they'd brought him to her.

This woman's eyes remained closed, her breathing unnaturally measured. That wrongness amplified. There was still something off about her, other than the horrific melted flesh—something he couldn't place.

"She hasn't woken," a sentinel healer said, following River's gaze. "Took a direct hit, they say."

River frowned. Direct hits from Cloud's lightning usually meant death, not unconsciousness. It took a powerful fae like himself or the Collector to survive. He leaned closer, studying the wound through the torn fabric more closely. Something glinted beneath—something that wasn't flesh. And that sound. He canted his head. Was that ticking? Coming from her chest?

"How many dead?" Ash's strained voice turned River's head.

"Eight," another sentinel by the entrance replied. "Three vendors, four civilians, one sentinel ... who tried to intervene."

Innocents.

Ash's face paled. His gaze cut to River. "Why?"

"Because..." The Collector's talons flexed against the pallet, grating against wood. "He wanted ... what's mine. What he once ... traded away."

River tensed, suspicion rising as he faced Ash. "There's

something I haven't told you. About what Blake and I found in Cloud's trove."

"What?"

"Not just maps and blast calculations." Guilt squeezed River's throat. "Research notes, diagrams. Things suggesting the cryptex was the reason Rory was … punished. It's why Cloud went into Crystal City that day. He went in to rescue her."

Ash's jaw locked, vein pulsing at his temple. "So this is my fault."

"It's Nero's fault for being a sick bastard—"

"Nero…" The strange woman stirred, lips barely moving. "Needs…"

River's head snapped toward her, instincts flaring. "Who are you?"

Her dark eyes fluttered open, but stared at nothing. Her breathing remained steady despite her wounds, skin pale without pain's flushed heat, melted flesh a little too shiny for how River remembered his had been. The ticking intensified.

He reached for *Peacemaker* at his belt. "*What* are you?"

Before she answered, searing agony ripped through River's left arm, spreading to his heart. He doubled over, clutching at the blue mating marks spiraling beneath his sleeve.

"Blake," he gasped. That constant, comforting awareness of her sleeping presence had morphed into a sudden, visceral flash of shared terror, sharp enough to hurt him.

Then nothing.

No Blake.

An absolute, soul-crushing void.

"Fuck!" River stumbled against a pallet, knocking vials to the ground. "Fuck, fuck, FUCK!"

Ash caught his arm, steadying him. "What is it?"

"Blake." River tore at his collar, struggling for breath. The world narrowed to a single, horrifying point. "I can't feel her."

He shoved past startled sentinels, hurtled outside the triage area, and *ran*. He burst from the market's boundaries and launched into the night sky, wings beating hard, heedless of branches and twigs lashing his face. He sent mana through *Peacemaker* to blast anything in his way until he cleared the forest, and then his wings beat furiously, muscles burning as he raced toward their roost.

I need to finish these before I forget.

The words he'd never spoken clawed at his throat.

I love you.

The Umbria roost appeared beneath him, dark and quiet. He folded his wings and dropped hard enough to dent the soft earth.

Proximity stones were still dull and lifeless on the stakes. A flash of Talo sharing drinks with Salvatore on the van's deck hit him, adding to his dawning horror. It meant Talo had reconciled with the Cardonas enough to allow passage without triggering an alarm.

The nesting caravan door hung open, swinging in the night breeze.

"Blake?" River stumbled up the steps, heart hammering. "Sparkles?"

Silence.

Papers were scattered across the floor. The table where she'd fallen asleep was in disarray. Her ink pot had spilled, creating a black pool that soaked into half-finished sketches.

His boot crunched over something. A page. He bent to pick it up. Blake's neat handwriting labeled diagrams she'd copied from Cloud's trove. Not anatomy drawings. A map. A location.

There, in the corner, a circle around two points marked with an X. One labeled "Main Trove," the other, "Second location or fake?"

Blake's crumpled drawings lay everywhere, sheets spattered with ink as if someone had swiped them from the table in anger. But what froze his blood was the overturned eucalyptus. It had survived despite all odds. Blake's restorative magic had repaired it, just as she'd fixed his wings. Now it lay broken, soil scattered across the floorboards, pot cracked clean through, a familiar black, glossy feather amongst the debris.

"No." The denial tore from his lungs, hoarse and desperate.

Boots scuffed the caravan steps. Ash appeared in the doorway, fury finally showing itself on his face.

No words. No thoughts. River's body seized and went silent. Shock.

"No blood," Ash muttered. "She must be alive."

Alive.

"I can't feel her."

"She's probably disconnected from the Well."

Hope flared. Alive. Alive. *She's alive.* Must be. River's gaze darted about the room, desperate for answers, ending on what was in his clenched fist. The map. He thrust it forward, hand trembling. "Look."

Ash crossed the caravan in two strides and took the paper. His eyes narrowed as he scanned the marked locations. "This isn't..."

"He took her!" River slammed his fist into the wall, wood splintering. "That bastard took my mate."

"But why?" Ash's question cut through River's panic.

"Why the fuck does everyone take so long to point blame? Who gives a fuck why? No wait. I have a why for you." River grabbed Ash's feathered collar and shoved him against the kitchenette. "Why didn't your wind warn you about this?"

"It doesn't work that way."

"Why not?"

"Because it doesn't." Ash knocked River away. "I don't control it."

"Are you in on this?" he accused, eyes manic. "Was this why you two were so friendly during the game?"

"You're asking the wrong questions." Ash scrubbed his face. When his hand dropped, he leveled his stare on River. "Why would Cloud want to take Blake alive? At the market, what was the last thing he said to you after I left?"

River's mind whirled, traveling back.

"Fuck me." Bile rose up his throat. "I'm going to be sick."

He launched toward the kitchenette, braced himself, and breathed heavily as the truth settled.

"Cloud asked about her restoration power," he mumbled.

Sound of shuffling behind him. Ash picked up another of Blake's drawings—a detailed nuke component, but one part looked damaged, incomplete. "Maybe he thinks she can bring something back."

"What?"

Ash held up the schematic and said, "Don't you remember? Leaf's mate mentioned some kind of codes or a map inside the cryptex—Nero's backup plan. Wrong guesses opening the cryptex meant the ink inside ruined the contents."

River's gaze shifted to the broken eucalyptus vase. "You think he wants Blake to restore a war machine?"

"No. I don't think it's that." Ash's eye twitched. He searched the mess. "I don't think we were listening properly."

"What?"

"At the Shadow Market. Think about it. Think about the exact words he used. Cloud never said he was taking us to the cryptex. He said, 'She doesn't have it here—the cryptex. And I know where it is,' and we—"

"Made assumptions."

"Like we always do."

"I'm going there later," River murmured, repeating another part of Cloud's words. "That part was direct."

"Later could mean years. Decades."

River groaned. "This is impossible."

"You're just not thinking straight." Ash moved toward the door until a breeze brushed against him, ruffling his feathered collar. "I'm not hearing chatter. The wind might be fickle, but it's self-serving."

"The wind," River scoffed. "Just call it what it is—the Well."

"Whatever it is, I don't think this is Cloud wanting to burn the world down. Otherwise, I'd hear about it."

"You telling me you've known every time we've thought we were going to die, you knew we weren't?"

Ash frowned and looked away. "No."

"So you can't know for sure. All we're certain of is that he still wants that fucking cryptex. Right?" River spread the map against the table. "Your ma's second trove—where is it? Here?" He tapped at the location Blake had marked.

"I don't know."

"What do you mean you don't know? You lived with that psychopath for—"

"She never revealed it."

"But she never kept forbidden items at the place we found you, right?"

"I only know I saw her leave with a full satchel and arrive with it empty."

River traced a line across the map, finger following contours Blake had carefully reproduced. "Surely you know if this is a second trove, the one where forbidden items are kept?"

"You tell me."

"What's that supposed to mean?"

"Your bond. What direction did you sense her when it cut out?"

River swallowed hard. Sweat prickled his skin.

I should have said it. Should have told her every day since I saw her stabbing dick-face into a pulp.

"She's alive. Right?" The question came out broken.

"Focus." Ash pointed at the map, at the second location. "Did she write the word fake, or is that what you saw on the wall in Cloud's trove?"

"What difference does it make?"

"Unless she's psychic, Cloud is a meticulous planner. If he wrote the word fake, then it probably is."

"She's dead. What's the point?" The lines on the map blurred.

"Think." Ash flicked River's ear.

"Ow. Why did you do that?" He rubbed his boo-boo.

"Because you're giving up," Ash said, tone strained, eyes stark. "And if you give up, then what hope—"

His jaw clicked shut, and he looked away.

Well shit.

Ash was afraid, River realized. He'd never seen his adopted brother so openly vulnerable before. Not even just recently, at the Shadow Market, when he saw his mother, his abuser, for the first time in decades.

Dawn filtered through the stained glass window. Movement outside—his parents noticing the ruined nesting caravan's door, hugging tightly. Talo cupped Ravi's hair, whispering comfort into her ear. Probably something to help build courage and tell River about it. They didn't know he was inside.

Just like that couple at the Shadow Market, his parents seemed to find strength and solace in each other.

He looked around. Looked back outside.

This was it.

The mud. The mess.

And if River couldn't lead through it—he glanced at Ash, still scowling at the maps—what hope did any of them have?

River had a mate. He had an anchor.

Blake was alive. She had to be.

His resolve hardened. No more self-pity. No more feeling untethered. River's instincts were where he shone, where he flowed. His unhinged insanity could work to his advantage.

That's what makes you the best person for the job.

Blake's voice in his head spurred him on.

He closed his eyes, turned his focus toward that connection he'd once blocked. Was it truly gone or just muffled? He exhaled, followed the flow from his heart, down his arm. Thought about Blake. *I love you. I love you. I love you.*

A distant, muffled flicker answered like a voice underwater, too faint for words but unmistakably her. Alive.

He opened his eyes. "The second trove is fake." He pointed at the canyon. "She's there."

"The canyon." Ash's finger tapped the location, not far from the ruins where the kelpie had attacked the second time, from where Cloud's sanctuary lay hidden … from where the friendship of three foolish crow shifters had begun. "You sure?"

River stared at the map, pieces sliding into place. The old theme park ruins. The maintenance tunnels. Bioluminescent worms in abundance. Mana sometimes found ways to flow around the metal and plastic. It grew over it, reclaimed it. Even in desecrated places like Crystal City, mana flowed in spots that were fostered correctly. Ruins were the perfect hiding place for a forbidden trove. Metal in the surrounding environment would mask its treasures.

They'd seen it in action with Cloud's sanctuary, so why not for the Collector's hoard?

River grabbed his Guardian jacket and changed clothes. He strapped *Peacemaker* to his hip with steady fingers. No more trembling. No more hesitation.

"Wait." Ash still stared at the map, brows knitted. "After the battle with Maebh, the Order searched around here for years. Wouldn't they have found the hoard's location again?"

"Maybe she amplified the wards and we missed it."

"Wards won't hide metal from a Guardian."

"Then we confused it with the ruins."

Ash stilled. Stared vacantly.

"What?" River prompted.

"Clarke told me I'd find my destiny when I circle back home."

River shoved Ash's shoulder with a finger. "Your mother's trove isn't your fucking home."

"It's where my life began," Ash clarified, then glared at River's finger. "And if you shove me one more fucking time, I'm going to cut that digit off."

A grin split River's face. He clapped his brother on the shoulder, then grabbed him by the nape and shook. "I look forward to it."

"You're insane."

"You love it."

"River." A haunted look entered Ash's eyes. "There are places in my mother's hoard no one knows about. Tunnels beneath the spire, under the canyon. Cold spots. Bad places the wind refuses to go."

"Then that's where we go." River moved toward the door.

"We?"

River stopped, tensed.

Ash vowed never to return to the hoard. Even during their hunts over the years, he insisted that if they found it, he would call in the cavalry before entering.

River turned and met Ash's eyes with newfound authority. "You said it. Destiny awaits you or some shit. We do this together and we do this now."

Ash's unease flickered before resolve replaced it. He nodded once.

River stepped outside and launched skyward, wings catching the predawn air. Blake's fading presence guided him like a distant star, pulling him toward the canyon where everything had begun.

I'll find you, Sparkles, he vowed into the howling wind. *And this time, I'll say the words that matter.*

SIXTY-FOUR

A scream ripped its way up Blake's throat, but the wind snatched it away before she could make a sound.

Pain.

Sharp and absolute.

Like her soul was being ripped from her bones. *Too high.* They must be flying too high. The Well, her connection to it stretched thin. It felt like a raw, frayed wire about to snap. She instinctively reached for the comforting thrum of River's presence through their bond, but found only a terrifying, distant echo.

Black feathers—wrong, not River's, not blue—whipped her face, adding to the agony, hacking her consciousness into jagged pieces. Through the wind and the agony, she forced her eyes open.

Cloud.

Dark curls, wild in the wind. Jaw hard, set. The Guardian teardrop beneath his left eye looked dull. Oil-slick tattoos at his throat seemed to writhe in the gray, pre-dawn light. But the worst thing was the V-stain on his face, preserved to look fresh. That blood had once pulsed inside a person.

"It will pass," he said gruffly, eyes forward. "The pain."

Lies, she tried to say. Nothing came out.

He glanced down, only for a second before looking ahead again. She thought she noticed something flicker in his eyes then. Guilt? Or maybe just the reflection of her terror.

Then the pain, the speed, and the sheer wrongness of it all dragged her back under.

When she surfaced again, it wasn't to sharp, hot agony. This time it was different. A deep, rolling nausea. A bone-deep ache had settled in her joints, making every muscle scream. This was more than just a fever, or maybe the fever was just worsening.

Something cold with sharp edges bit into her back. She was staring at a blushing sky, lying on a mountain of junk. Piles and piles of it, resembling a dumpster after a flea market. She vaguely recognized some ancient objects, old-world glass Christmas baubles, broken ceramics, and decaying fabrics. Everything looked dull in the misty, grey light. Trinkets. Bits of treasure, maybe?

A rush of dopamine flooded her system, temporarily washing out the aches. She tried to reach for a smooth, glassy dome, but her limbs were so heavy. It felt like someone had replaced her bones with lead.

At least she felt connected to the Well again. It was a faint thrum in her veins, but not the vibrant, life-giving force she craved.

Then the smell hit her. Thick. Acrid. Cloying. A coppery tang underneath it all. She barely managed to roll onto her side before vomiting up bitter bile.

Shapes formed through her swimming vision. As she

blinked, they came into focus. Blobs of something dark were lying down. Little balls of light lazily drifted upward. Two hulking, black-furred … dogs? No, too big. Monstrous. Wounds oozed acidic blood from their mangled bodies and pooled in the cracks of junk. Sizzled. Oh god. Maybe the blood *made* the cracks.

Cloud methodically wiped dark stains from his daggers onto their hides, calm as anything. He didn't even look at Blake when he sheathed them. Each detached movement was a death knell to her hope. Nobody normal moved like that.

The fever that had been brewing all night, the one River had worried over, now raged in her body. Her borrowed shirt—River's shirt—clung to her clammy skin.

"Cloud…" she croaked, limbs trembling as she tried to sit.

"Quiet."

"Quiet?" She blinked.

"Did I stutter?" His words were flat, cold. "Shut up. I'm trying to listen."

He examined a ten-foot-high hill of treasure a few feet away, its pointed top half hidden in the mist. Cold wind gusted in, rattling trinkets. But all she could hear was Jeff's voice echoing in her head.

You just sound like an uneducated parrot…

Tears stung her eyes, and she shrank back into herself.

He's going to kill me. The thought landed with cold certainty. *I'm nothing to him.*

Blake's hand brushed against something cold and smooth. A big, dark gem, its surface polished like a mirror. It reflected a warped, hazy version of her face. Sweaty. Fever-bright. Puffy eyes. Hair a wild, tangled mess. *Not a beauty queen's daughter now, am I?*

Just a dumb bitch who couldn't stop herself from sketching out this man's private drawings. He must have found them, hated that she knew about his deepest secrets, and now he'd brought her here to dump her with the rest of the junk.

The Well-marks on her arm pulsed with a blue light that seemed too bright, too vibrant for this dim, miserable place, mocking her.

"You can't fix stupid." Her dad's voice was as clear in her mind now as it was in the Donna's hallucination. "But you weren't broke."

Scarface, her magpie, fell from the sky. She tried to reach for him, but then he soared away. His wings caught the sun. His warbling song faded the farther he flew.

"Two feet and a wingbeat, Bloss."

You're not meant to be here. The thought was a bitter certainty. *You're the one who's broken now.*

"He's going to kill me," she whispered to her reflection. "I'm … just a … a mistake."

Cloud finally looked at her then. For a second, just a heartbeat, she thought she saw confusion in his eyes. Hesitation.

Maybe he wasn't there either. Maybe she'd imagined everything—the world ending. This fantastical place.

Maybe her dad was sitting by the hospital bed, drinking bad coffee and watching the footy on the small TV above the bed. Maybe it wasn't her mother in the bed. Maybe it was Blake.

Cloud glanced down at his forearm and tugged his

sleeve up to reveal his triad tattoo. Something he read made his expression grow blank.

He moved then, all sharp action and cold purpose. Grabbed her arm, his grip like iron bands. He hauled her to her feet, but she stumbled.

"Sorry," she blurted, despite knowing she couldn't control her weak legs or feverish head. Every step dislodged another trinket or gem, yet Cloud wanted none of it. He shoved her towards a dark, gaping hole in the side of the mountain of treasure.

Just before they reached it, just before he thrust her into that suffocating blackness, he paused. Only for a second. His profile stood out against the deeper gloom of the passage, dawnlight tracing his unruly hair like a halo.

"This is why he's so afraid," she whispered, stupidly reaching for a lock of his hair blowing in the wind. "Why he's afraid to love me."

Grim, assessing eyes met hers, but he didn't pull away. It turned out, she couldn't raise her hand higher than her hip. "You don't have long," he noted.

"So just kill me now. Put me out of my misery."

"River has that effect on the ladies." A sharp laugh. A shake of the head. A deep, gathering sigh. "Remember when I said the pain would pass?"

Blake tensed. Held her breath.

"Yeah…" He stared into the gloomy doorway. "This is going to hurt again."

Before she could scream, before she could even draw a breath to protest, he shoved her forward.

Into the dark.

SIXTY-FIVE

CIRCA 200 YEARS AGO

anfri pushed through dense, thorny undergrowth. Branches whipped at his face, but he didn't slow. Cielo and Nikan were right behind him. Dirt and mulch stuck to their boots. The air was heavy with the scent of decay and a sickly-sweet smell that clung to the back of his throat.

Faster.

Had to be faster if they wanted to arrive before dawn, before they were caught and made to do this differently.

He glanced back.

Nikan was a hesitant silhouette, occasionally pausing as if listening to things Manfri couldn't—or wouldn't—hear. Cielo's outline was a tense shadow behind him.

"Any idea where you're actually leading us, Manfri?" Cielo hissed. "Or is this another one of your 'go with the flow' plans?"

"Worried you'll break a nail, pretty boy?" he didn't have time for doubts, not now.

He pointed at a faint, unnatural glow filtering through the trees ahead. There.

They continued onward until the sickly sweet smell intensified.

The oppressive predawn sounds of the forest gave way to a faint, almost inaudible hum, a thrumming sensation in the air as if the world held its breath. The glow ahead wasn't warm like a campfire in his home roost. It was a cold, pulsating bioluminescence. On the trees. In the underbrush. In the glimmering water beyond the forest's edge.

Behind, Manfri heard one set of footsteps halt. He turned and found Nikan stopped. His dark hair lifted slightly, stirred by an unfelt breeze. "The air here," he murmured, "it's ... listening."

"Everything in this damn forest is trying to kill us, Nik. Keep moving." Manfri pushed on, the glow drawing him. He wouldn't admit he felt the same unease they did. One sign of doubt and they'd all chicken out like a bunch of mouse-munchers.

Together, they burst from the treeline and onto the precipice of something vast and terrifyingly beautiful — the shore of the Ceremonial Lake.

"Fucking enormous," he whispered.

It had no right to exist here, no mountains feeding it, no sea nearby. But it was always plentiful.

The sheer power radiating from it felt tangible, like a living thing. This wasn't water, but a wound in the world, freely bleeding magic for its inhabitants.

The sacred, vibrant turquoise, blue, and purple water was impossibly vivid. It seemed to breathe. Steam coiled from its surface in ghostly tendrils and rose into a sky whorling with green, magenta, and indigo hues. Endless depths reflected the colorful sky. Or maybe it was the other way around. Hard to tell which came first.

"I thought we'd be too late to see it," Manfri murmured, nodding to the sky. During the equinox each year, the lights shone brightest. "The Donna says it's our ancestors protecting us."

"Ancient cultures believed it was a bridge to the afterlife," Nikan added.

"Protection," Manfri shot back, glaring. "It's protection."

Nikan's lips curved. "If you say so."

"Ugh." He rolled his eyes. "Always so pessimistic."

Cielo came to stand beside them, silent for once. He just stared.

Together, they watched the aurora's lights fade with the coming dawn. They might have stared, awestruck for half a turn of the hourglass. When the pretty lights started to fade from the sky, Manfri's gaze fixed on the long, dark jetty, a skeletal finger beckoning them into the endless abyss. There. That's where they'd do it.

He started toward the jetty without a word. His boots crunched softly through the sand until they hit the damp wood with a loud, jarring thud.

This was it. No turning back now.

He didn't look to see if they followed. They would.

As he continued along the jetty, he forced his eyes to focus ahead. He dared himself to chicken out. Water churned. Shadows slithered and coiled in the depths. The Inkeels, the Well Worms, or whatever their latest name was, waited for them. He tried not to think of the rumors of terror, whispers at storytellings of how they dragged Guardian tributes down, invaded them, and judged their souls.

As they reached the halfway point of the jetty, Nikan stumbled. Manfri's hand shot out, steadying him. A beat later, Cielo was on his alternate side, shoulder brushing his.

Nikan hissed, "The whispers … they're coming from the water. They know about the things we've done."

"Worried about your soul, princeling?" Manfri joked.

Nikan flinched but kept his expression hard. Their fear was a *mirror, and Manfri couldn't afford to look too closely. He kept walking. Walking. Until he stood at the jetty's end.*

The vast lake stretched before them. Tiny flares of luminescence bubbled and rippled on the surface, disturbed by what swam beneath. The air was colder here, the silence more profound, broken only by the faint laps of water against the pilings.

He knew each of them was thinking of what Nikan had just said ... wondering about the things they'd done, if any had made them unworthy of the blessing they each sought. Manfri thought of stolen kisses, bar fights, the reckless joy of breaking rules, and the shadows in his own heart. The guilt. The regret. The cowardice. He should have fought harder through the pain of crossing the wasteland to get to Crystal City. To rescue Cielo.

Will the Well see that?

"This is it," he mumbled, staring down at his boots. "Do we strip?"

Would the Well Worms care?

No one had an answer.

Eventually, Cielo said, "You're asking us to trust you with our lives."

Not an accusation, just a statement of fact. The weight of it settled on Manfri's shoulders.

Time. It was the greatest curse and blessing for the fae. So much space to drift, to be shaped by others, by circumstance, by regret. To feel powerless.

Nikan's whispering wind told him what to do, yet he seemed to do nothing. He was stagnant, or rather, happy to drift. Cielo spent so much time in his head that Manfri noticed he sometimes struggled to do a single thing, or struggled to enjoy a simple moment before it passed them by.

But Manfri—he knew time was long. It flowed like a river. It could sweep him along to surprising places he might end up loving, or places he might end up hating. Either way, it made him feel as though he had no choice in his life, no say in his final destination.

Time could get fucked.

The only way to control it was to become it.

Become the river.

"You're sure about this?" Nikan muttered.

So his wind wasn't giving him the answers. Manfri supposed that was a good sign. Another beat of silence passed, laden with unspoken fears and the vastness of their decision. If they failed to return, even if they did return, their families would be left behind. Only the three of them could fly this direction.

The lake seemed to hold its breath.

"No," Manfri answered. "But you fuck faces trust me."

Right? He glanced at them. Waited. Held his breath too.

"Ancestors save us, because I do." Cielo scrubbed his face, blinking widely. "I trust you fuck faces."

"Then we're really doing this, aren't we?" Nikan peered down into the depths.

"Yep." Manfri grinned, grabbing one of their hands in each of his. "We're fucking doing this."

Then they jumped, no wings.

SIXTY-SIX

River's frantic wing beats thundered as he climbed through the dawn sky. Each stroke drove him toward the canyon spires, a bruised and purple shadow against the horizon. No matter how hard he flew, the spires never seemed to get any closer. Blake's presence flickered through their bond like a voice calling from beneath ice. Barely there.

It didn't feel like a disconnection this time, but a sense of *her* fading.

His wings felt wrong. Too perfect. Too whole. They were nothing if they couldn't take him to where his mate was in time.

In time for what?

The dark, unknown answer propelled him onward.

"Faster," he snarled back at Ash, flying behind him.

Finally, they were there. River banked sharply upward, following the tallest spire's edge. Its circumference was as large as the Ring in Cornucopia, but narrowed the higher they flew. As the air thinned, a horrible thought occurred.

Mana flowed in natural, living substances. This rock technically fit the requirements, but would be riddled with unmined raw materials that could be turned into metal. Maybe even ancient ruins inside, just like Cloud's trove. The sense of being connected was less and often spotty, but still there. Air fae, avian shifters like him, would have no problem flying higher from the mana-abundant ground, so long as they remained close to the spire.

"He flew her this high." Panic tightened River's throat. "This must have been when—"

"She was cut from the Well," Ash confirmed.

Cut from magic as Rory had been. As Cloud, when he crossed the wasteland to rescue her, when she betrayed him, when none of his triad had his back.

River's jaw clenched as he spiraled higher, searching each craggy crevice in the clay and rocky surface just in case.

Their ascent took them through low-hanging clouds. Mana rippled across his skin like static electricity—the wards. He tensed, ready for pain or to suddenly find himself turned around and wondering where he was. But like the day they found Ash, he sailed right through.

The wards were definitely down.

He slowed his ascent, hovering upward until he cleared the mist.

The summit looked like a witch's hat. The pointed, rocky spire had shrunk to about thirty feet in diameter—large enough to contain tunnels and caverns. From memory, there was a doorway around the circumference that led inside. Treasure spilled from its side and settled on the surrounding platform. Gems, shinies, glass coins, painted porcelain goblets, mana-enforced weapons, and devices from every era were stacked in chaotic heaps.

The Collector's hoard.

River adjusted the angle of his aching wings and landed hastily on the slippery surface. His boots sent baubles scattering loudly. Lungs heaving, he squinted into the morning sun and scanned for threats. No one came running around the corner.

Ash landed beside him, far more deftly. Barely an item was knocked out of place, except for the feathers quivering on his ceremonial outfit. He could have delayed their departure from the Great Murder by stopping at his place to change into his Guardian uniform, but he didn't hesitate when River said it was time to go.

"It was here all along," Ash murmured as he crouched to pick up a gem and turned it in his fingers. "She must have changed the wards to block me."

"So why aren't they working now?"

Ash frowned as he stood and examined their environment. "Maybe when Cloud attacked her, the wards weakened too."

"Makes sense." River shook his head, annoyed he hadn't thought of that himself. Some wards could be tied off, left to run on their own almost indefinitely. But other wards, particularly those that included silent alarms written into the spell, must be tied to the caster's lifeforce.

The stench hit next—raw flesh and acidic blood.

River gestured toward the right and moved first, hand hovering on *Peacemaker*. They walked around the spire and discovered two dead Wellhounds, black fur matted with ichor. Stab wounds pierced their hides, ripped open their guts. No lightning scars, but Cloud's handiwork nonetheless. River had fought too many battles with him to mistake his favorite knife's shape, the entry angle of the wounds.

Their jaws still gaped in death, and their weeping acidic eyes stared blankly.

River crouched beside the nearest carcass and examined the killing strokes.

"Precise. Clean. Economical," he noted. Cloud had inflicted maximum damage with the least amount of stabs. He tested a clean part of the flank and found it still warm. His touch jostled a final manabee free from the body. River darted away, avoiding the hit. The mana could hold a vital memory, but the intoxicating effect wouldn't be worth the trouble. He needed his wits about him. Instinct was how River survived. He tensed, preparing for more. Nothing.

The beasts must have been killed only minutes ago, a quarter turn at most.

Considering the breadth of damage at the Shadow Market, Cloud's inner well must surely be close to depleted. Flying here wouldn't have allowed him to refill. Despite this, Cloud hadn't harvested the manabeeze. Ingesting them made one drunk, yes, but there were other ways to use the magic—powering a mana stone, for one.

"He's in a rush." River straightened. "But for what?"

Why kidnap Blake and bring her here?

Ash crouched to inspect a path of disturbed treasure showing where a body had been dragged. River didn't need to follow it to know where it led. Blake's presence, however faint, pulled in the same direction, toward a dark tunnel carved into the spire's central peak. The doorway inside. Every instinct of his screamed for him to rush forward, but he forced himself to scan first. To use his training.

Something dark stained trinkets near the doorway—fresh vomit.

River's blood ran cold. "Blake's still unwell."

Ash's head snapped up. He looked to where River gestured and failed to hide his concern. They both knew that a Well-blessed human shouldn't be sick, not like this. Before River could voice his fears, Ash strode toward the shadowed archway.

"This doorway leads down a spiraling staircase and splits into tunnels, leading far below the surface. Even into neighboring pinnacles."

"No shit?" River gaped, mind whirling. "It's like an ant farm in there?"

"That's one way of looking at it."

River entered after Ash and descended crude steps that appeared to be carved out by talons. Dark memories permeated the stale air. The space accommodated wings, barely.

River hesitated to shift his away. Being trapped here without escape, knowing Blake depended on him, made him cautious.

Their boots echoed. Feathers brushed the walls, dislodging dust. Each step drove them deeper. The temperature rose. The Well's presence thickened and pressed against River's skin like mud.

"Princeling," he murmured, gaze catching on skeletal remains embedded in a wall. "This place is fucked up."

A pause. "Yeah."

A few more steps ended in a landing, a fork in the path illuminated by blue glowworms crawling over the ceiling. Two circular passages vanished into darkness.

River strained his senses, checking for danger down each.

The right tunnel pulsed with twisted mana and smelled like a wet animal. A low growl echoed from its depths. Chains rattled. The left passage felt … cold. Dead. Deeper into the shadows, the lip of a massive rusted pipe protruded from the tunnel's wall. Like a storm drain.

Except, where the water near Cloud's trove had kept them sufficiently connected to the Well, here, it seemed like the pipe *was* the tunnel. The metal itself exuded the distinct sensation of wrongness. It felt empty, devoid of mana, yet smelled like ozone.

He had the sense that the shadows were hungry, waiting to siphon his mana and swallow it like breakfast.

"What is it?" he asked.

Ash paused. Fidgeted. "It's the bad place I told you about."

"Fucking fantastic."

"Which way?"

Cloud wouldn't have left a beast alive if he'd taken the right path, which meant he probably went left. River closed his eyes and reached through his mating bond. Nothing from the right passage, where magic seemed abundant, if not feral. On the left … she was there, faint like a dying ember.

He opened his eyes and scowled into the pipe. A few things didn't add up. "Your mother can survive being cut from the Well, right?"

"I don't know. Maybe."

"Cloud survived it."

"Cloud is…" Ash hesitated. "Different."

"Yeah. And he knows we're not." Bitter laughter escaped River's throat. "Of course, he'd choose somewhere he thinks we can't go."

Bastard.

"River—"

"Your ma is different, too," he said, cutting him off and pointing into the cold darkness. "My mate is that way."

Something like fear flickered in Ash's eyes. "You can't go in there."

"Watch me."

"You don't understand. It's not just metal. It's worse. Nothing lives there. Nothing grows. Even the wind stops at its edge."

"I'm still going."

"But—"

"Cloud crossed the wasteland for her." River's tone quietened. "He endured pain that would have killed most fae to rescue a woman who became his enemy."

"And maybe it drove him mad."

"I don't care. I'm going after my mate. You take the other passage if you want."

"She might not be alive—"

"Don't you fucking dare say that." River spun and seized Ash's throat. "Where is this coming from? This doubt? This fear? You were the one telling me to trust my bond."

Ash didn't fight the grip. "I'm just saying ... if she is alive—"

"Of course she's alive!"

"—prepare yourself for what state she'll be in. Prepare yourself for what he might be doing to her that requires a place beyond the Well's reach."

The notion hit River between his ribs. He released Ash and stepped back.

"I'm not leaving her." His jaw clenched. "Not like I left him."

"Like *we* left him," Ash corrected, expression unreadable. "Stop being a fuck face, taking all the guilt." Finally, emotion flickered in his eyes. "We *both* left him. The guilt is shared."

Ash was right. Just because he didn't reveal his emotions so plainly as River, didn't mean he felt them less. Usually, there was nothing River loved more than making his brother feel uncomfortable, but this time, it was his discomfort he couldn't stand.

He looked away and mumbled, "Whatever, princeling. Save your feelings for your journal."

"Fine." A soft laugh. "Take all the blame. But in case you're wrong, I'll check the other tunnel."

"Wait."

Ash turned back and met River's eyes.

"You're my brother," he said. "My home."

Ash's gaze flicked to the bad tunnel. "He is, too."

River stared at one of his longest friends. From the start, Ash had been a rock of fortitude for their triad, an ever-present company River and Cloud relied on for strength.

"We never deserved you," he blurted.

Ash stilled. "What?"

"I should have said this long ago." Now wasn't the time, but River was quickly learning that unspoken words were as powerful as silence. "Me and Cloud. We're fucked in the head. But you, your heart..."

A rueful, tragic yet knowing smile touched Ash's lips. "It wasn't my heart that saved us from floating."

"It wasn't mine."

They stared down the pipe. Into the darkness. Toward the one who'd refused to leave this Wellforsaken place without Ash on the day they'd first met. Toward the one who cried over being left behind as a fledgling. The one who *chose* to hurt himself rather than give up on Rory.

The one who kept the truth of his pain a secret, all these years, because he knew not even those closest to him would understand.

"If you find them first," Ash whispered. "Send me a message."

"You too."

CHAPTER
SIXTY-SEVEN

River ignited a ball of fire in his palm with mana. The moment he stepped into the tunnel's mouth, the sense of wrongness intensified. The expanse stretched ahead, rusty pipe walls catching light from his mana-fueled palm. A few more steps in, the light winked out.

He tried to summon mana again, but it sputtered and failed.

It shouldn't fail.

A Guardian can still be cut from the Well. Desecrated land is still desecrated.

River groaned at the memory. Scrubbed his face.

Fucking great.

One step.

Then another.

He forced himself forward until pain erupted, ripping through him like acid. He stumbled, catching himself against the corroded wall, and hissed when it burned. It shouldn't burn. He was a Guardian. He might feel the pain of disconnection in desecrated spaces, but not from contact with forbidden substances.

His wings spasmed, feathers shuddering. His stomach heaved, throat burning with bile.

He instinctively found *Peacemaker's* hilt.

The weapon responded in his palm.

Warm. Familiar. Present.

River gritted his teeth and forced another step. The pain doubled, then tripled. Wildfire consumed him from the inside. His wings thrashed, knocking loose rust scales that rained like blood flakes.

"You abandoned me," Cloud whispered from the darkness.

River's head snapped up, eyes narrowing.

Nothing. No movement. No further sound. He must be hearing things.

Another step. The floor sloped downward, descending deeper into the earth. His knees buckled, but he caught himself.

This time, the pain felt…

Off.

Too much of a burn.

"You weren't strong enough," the voice continued. *"Too afraid to suffer. Too afraid to save me."*

River pushed onward.

"Coward."

The rusted tunnel stretched endlessly, branching into smaller passages. Every inch was agony, every breath a struggle.

"You'll fail her, too."

The pain and emptiness morphed, turning thick and heavy like mud slowing his steps, dragging at his ankles, knees, and thighs. Soon, he was wading through it, sinking with each lurch.

"Blake," he pleaded.

The mud tried to engulf him, his identity, his power, his past. It all dissolved in the void—the hungry thing.

"You call yourself a Guardian," Cloud taunted from somewhere. *"You call yourself a protector of the weak, but when it mattered, when I needed you, you turned away. You watched me fall and had the nerve to tell me I wasn't alone."*

The tunnel walls rippled.

"But where were you?"

River saw himself standing on the airship's edge, watching a figure plummet overboard into darkness. Not Cloud. Not Rory.

Blake.

Her rainbow hair streamed upward as she fell, her hand outstretched. Through her billowing hair, he glimpsed glassy eyes and the terrifying truth. She felt betrayed, forgotten.

"No!" River lunged for the vision, but his fingers closed on empty air. Too late. Always too fucking late.

The hallucination shifted. The Ceremonial Lake materialized around him, vast and turquoise, steam coiling from its surface. Three crow shifters stood at the jetty's edge. Them, when they were younger. When they had other names.

"You're asking us to trust you with our lives," Cielo said.

"You're sure about this?" Nikan muttered.

"No," Manfri laughed.

"Of course you aren't."

River whirled around, searching for Cloud in the darkness. That sounded like he was here—an adult.

"Get over yourself."

Now it was Ash.

"Coward."

"Self-serving cunt."

The insults kept coming, peppering River like bullets until he collapsed onto his knees. He grabbed his ears to block the words, but they surrounded him. Whirled *through* him just like the Well Worms had, looking into his soul, judging, weighing, spitting out.

"Tell me how you really feel," Blake whispered.

The words he'd never said. The emotions he'd been too afraid to voice.

But now he was reminded of why he came here. He fought the oppressive weight and climbed to his feet.

"I love you," he choked out.

Pain.

Step.

Pain.

He staggered forward, deeper into the badness.

"Should have said it when you needed to hear it."

Step.

Step.

The hallucinations pressed closer, voices merging and growing vicious. *"We trusted you."*

"We followed you."

"We jumped."

"Now we're miserable."

"Now you're too late."

The attacks suddenly felt … performed. Crafted. Too specific to be mere pain-induced trauma.

A spell.

Which meant a caster.

Which meant mana.

Which meant—

River's hand closed around *Peacemaker's* hilt. The weapon sang in his grip, power flowing through the metal, an impossible and undeniable force.

I am the river.

His chakram cleared its clip in one fluid motion, splitting into twin crescents. Steel arced blue and sang with accumulated power, cutting not through rusted pipe but through illusion.

Dark magic.

He felt it disintegrate, and then he was slicing reality itself. The suffocating walls shimmered, revealing stone and earth beneath false metal. The dragging mud dissolved into mist. His mana flooded back, blazing through his veins. The pipe, the voices, the doubt. All gone.

Had never been there.

All that remained was an unassuming stone passage with ancient glyphs carved into its curved walls. Their ambient glow led toward a glimmer of sunlight at the end.

Real voices.

Blake.

River charged forward, reconnecting his blades, freeing one hand. He used a claw to carve a single word into the triad tattoo: *Here.*

The light brightened with every step. The voices grew louder, sharper.

"Try again," Cloud clipped.

"I can't." Blake's weak voice trembled. "It's never worked that way."

"But you restored his wings. He said it. He showed them."

"He *thinks* I did. But … I think … he self-manifested them."

"No. Try again."

Every muscle in River's body screamed in protest as he ran.

"Cloud … I saw everything on the wall," Blake continued. "Your glittery writing. Her letters. I'm so sor—"

"Shut up."

"This isn't going to work."

"Yes, it is."

"But—"

Cloud released a bellow of rage that echoed into the tunnel.

River's heart seized. He charged, erupting from the passage's mouth. Light blinded him. Unexpected pain and misery slammed into him, stealing his breath. Not his. Blake's.

His eyes adjusted, and the scene came together in an instant.

They were in a pit—the Collector's second, secret trove.

Light shards broke through thick roots and a metal grate above, blocking any hope of flight to the surface. Forbidden materials, but the land wasn't desecrated. Not yet. The air tasted of rust and a chemical odor. Blake sat hunched on a pile of old-world objects while Cloud stood over her. And between them, sticking out of the junk…

A brass cylinder. The cryptex.

River launched and swung, curved blade aiming for Cloud's throat.

SIXTY-EIGHT

River had dreamed of this moment for half a decade. He never imagined Blake's blood would be the price.

Peacemaker sang through the air, aiming for Cloud's throat, and then rainbow hair flashed, catching the light between them.

"Stop," she croaked, stumbling in the way of his blade.

River's fingers opened. Curved steel flew wide, clattering into shadows. He managed to avoid hitting her, but his momentum carried him forward. He crashed into his mate, pivoted with her in his arms, and used his body and wings to shield her from harm. They tumbled, falling onto rusted metal. He landed spine first, sharp edges biting through feathers and leather. Blake crumpled against his chest with a groan, her fever-bright skin burning through his clothes.

"Sparkles?"

"Hurts."

"Where?" He scrambled upright, cradling her. She

weighed nothing. Had she always been this thin? Her bones pressed against his palms. "Where does it hurt?"

She looked at him, *through* him, and then flopped. Her hair fell over her eyes, but when he lifted her chin, they were closed anyway.

"Blake, wake up." He gently patted her face.

"Fuck off, Dad," she groaned. "I fixed the bird feeder yesterday." She clawed clumsily at his chest, as if it were something else. "S'got glitter in the cracks. Check if you don't believe me."

"There's no one there, Blake." River's heart clenched.

The delirium was spreading. He pressed his palm to her forehead, summoned mana, and forced healing magic into her body. For a split second, she woke up, but then the power slid off like oil on water. Her eyes rolled back in her head. Lashes fluttered.

"Sparkles, stay with me."

But she started to convulse. It took all of River's willpower not to scream, to act like he had control of his wits. He held her through the fit and protected her from harm as she jerked with a strength he didn't think possible.

"Fuck, fuck, fuck." He'd never felt so helpless, so insignificant. "What do I do? What do I do?"

He glanced up, searching for help. Saw Cloud clutching the cryptex, his face pale beneath the blood-V, eyes never leaving River's mate. Reality crashed in.

He'd kidnapped Blake. This was his fault.

"I just need her," Cloud mumbled, "to restore what's inside. I just—"

"She's dying!" River bellowed, wings snapping wide.

The truth tore a feather loose. They watched it drift between them, black and blue against dancing dust motes.

Metal cracked as it warmed in the new sun. Time stretched as it fell, twirled, and finally landed between them.

Another convulsion wracked Blake's body. Her back arched. She clawed at her throat, at her lips. The sound she made wasn't human. A gurgling warble, as if she breathed underwater. River held her through it again, his own body shaking from the force.

When it passed, Blake groaned and mumbled about wanting to go home.

"It's okay, treasure. I've got you now. I'm taking you home."

His purpose clear, he gently rested her against the scraps and rushed to scoop up *Peacemaker*.

Now that he looked up with enough focus, he noticed more obstacles to freedom were in their way. Thick roots, vines, and foliage wove in and out of the pit's craggy walls. They choked the grate, hiding much of the blue. He'd thought from the way Blake's hair sparkled, that more sky was visible. But it was just her being her, caught in a shaft of sunlight.

He channeled his mana into it, feeling it drain from his inner well to virtual depletion. But escape demanded every drop. He blasted power at the grate overhead. Thanks to Trix's upgrade, it released precisely how and where he intended.

Metal screamed.

Debris rained down. Leaves. Sticks. More sunlight poured through the jagged hole. River sheltered Blake with his wings from falling wreckage. When it settled, he gathered her into his arms.

"No! Not until I open this." Cloud's eyes showed white. His fingers scrambled at the cryptex, rotating the keys. "It's not the codes, I promise. It's just her hair." A sharp laugh barked out. "From her fucking brush."

Holy Well.

Ash was right. Cloud had gone mad.

"Enough." River's wings mantled for balance as he stood with Blake in his arms. "Rory is dead, Cloud."

"I told you—"

"She's not coming back! Move on with your life."

Be happy.

"I can't!" Cloud's roar ripped from somewhere deep in his soul. Agony contorted his face. The cryptex trembled in his grip. "She begged me not to. The last thing she said—" He growled at himself. Clenched his jaw. Shook his head as if clearing his thoughts. "You don't know everything. You were too cowardly to ask, too cowardly to find me when it mattered."

"And lucky I was!" River adjusted Blake as she squirmed. "Otherwise, who would have cleaned up your piss and vomit while you refused to speak? While you screamed her name every fucking night, begging for her to stop hurting you?"

Cloud flinched.

"You think I wanted to become this?" He gestured with the cryptex at himself, at the preserved blood on his face. "You think I imagined this in my future?"

"I think you're so lost in your grief—"

"HATE!"

"—that you can't see what's right in front of you." River shook his head. "Regardless of how you feel, she's not coming back."

The cutting truth showed in the play of emotion on Cloud's face. In the way rage turned to despair, in how it switched to agony, how it faded to nothing. River stepped toward a large piece of debris, aiming to use it as a step up to a root.

But Cloud moved, blocking the way.

"We don't have time for this!" River glared at the cryptex. "My mate, my *alive* mate, needs help. She's in no condition to summon any kind of magic, believed or not."

"It's okay." Blake's weak voice muffled against River's chest. "The Well made a mistake. It's fixing it now."

"Don't say that." His voice broke when he lifted her chin and found tear tracks down her dusty cheeks. "You're delirious. You don't know what you're saying."

"I'm the crack, hun." A sad smile touched her lips. "The break that needed to happen. You can fill me with glitter now, make something beautiful." Her gaze defocused and drifted past him, toward the sunlight. She reached for it as if it were tangible. "See? The razz is here to take me away."

"No." River squeezed her. "You don't get to walk away!"

Cloud still blocked the passage. River saw it then, the same desperate terror reflected in his eyes. The two of them were the same, just at different points on the timeline of loss.

"If you want to stop me," he growled, "you'll have to claim the debt I owe you. You'll have to use my apology against me."

A tendon in Cloud's jaw worked. He seemed to consider the ultimatum, but River knew better. He wouldn't do it. For decades, *centuries*, he had every chance to claim Ash's debt from when they'd rescued him. But unless they'd kept it a secret, Cloud left it untouched.

Just as River had.

Cloud's chin dipped, but not in defeat. He gestured at the fake pipe tunnel and snarled low, "You'd cross the wasteland, face that pain for her. But not for me. Not to help me save my"—agony flashed on his face—"to save Rory."

"You never *asked*." River flared his eyes. "Sure, I might not have listened, but you never fucking asked anyway!"

"I shouldn't have to."

"You said it yourself." River shifted his mate's weight. More feathers scattered. "I wasn't ready for the mess."

"But now you are, because of her?"

"Because of *us*. All of us."

The words hung between them for a long moment. River honestly thought he'd have to carve his way out, but then Cloud's leather-clad shoulders sagged. His dark wings drooped, rustling as the primaries brushed the ground.

For a moment, River saw not the monster who'd rained lightning on innocents, who'd betrayed Elphyne, but the best friend who'd saved him from drowning.

Another blue-tipped feather spiraled to the junk-littered ground between them.

Pity filled Cloud's eyes as he tracked its descent.

"Go," he said, stepping aside.

River crouched, ready to launch, but then a shadow fell over them. Power. Thick, ancient, and twisted. It came in hot and harrowing, filling the pit and shattering the atmosphere like broken glass.

The Collector's squawk of rage reverberated against the walls. "Intruders!"

She fell through the hole he'd made. Arms splayed, fused to mighty wings so broad they spanned the entire width of the pit. Taloned hands at the wingtips gouged the rocky walls, slowing her descent. Her lightning-scorched feathers had regenerated with a speed that struck envy into River's heart.

She landed hard on a thick root jutting out from the wall. Clawed feet curved. Taloned toes gripped. Torn gown blowing. Her beak-like face contorted with rage as she took in the scene—her most precious treasure, the cryptex in Cloud's hand.

"You *dare* defile my sanctuary?"

She flapped in a tantrum. Just once. The action blew wind into the debris, kicking up sand and dust. In the cover, she hopped to a lower root, violence etched on her face. Another fast hop, and she was within range, swiping her razor-sharp winged hand.

River spun away, shielding Blake with his body. Talons raked air where his head had been. Cloud moved in perfect synchronization, his butterfly knife flashing in the sunlight as he drew her attention left.

Another shadow dropped from above.

Ash landed with a devastating, ground-trembling force between River and his mother. Junk went flying as air blasted outward. Even in that ridiculous outfit, even without being able to see his face, he looked like a vengeful god, straightening and mantling his wings to a span wider than his mother's.

Too big for the pit.

The display of power was impressive, but River caught the tremor in Ash's hands, the same tremor that had shaken him as a chained youth. His clothing was shredded. Blood seeped through the windway's pleats. Whatever feral beast he'd met in the other tunnel had not gone down easily.

"Still playing dress-up, little bird?" The Collector's tone oozed sarcasm. "Still pretending you're one of them?"

Cloud strolled between mother and son, within swiping

reach of talons. He gave her a pointed stare and then turned his back.

He said to Ash, "Took you long enough, fuck face."

"Missed me already?"

"Maybe."

A quick, tense pause made River suspect this wasn't rehearsed.

"Had to deal with one of her pets," Ash said, flicking dirt from his feathered shoulder.

To anyone else, the exchange seemed ill-advised, out of place—a fool's game in a hurricane. But River saw it for what it was. Enough time had passed since he'd contacted Ash that River knew the fae had avoided following him out of fear.

The Bad Place.

How many times had this mother used it as punishment against her child?

Cloud must have realized before River what Ash's delay meant. He offered his back to the enemy as another target, a distraction to buy time for Ash to gather his resolve. To remember he was a warrior, not a victim.

"One!" Her snorting laugh morphed into a screech. "Did you think I only had one pet? That I'd come alone after your little lightning display?"

Dark shapes poured through the opening, fangs gnashing. Wellhounds. Their eyes leaked luminous blue acid that dripped and sizzled on contact. One, two, three of them clawed down the hole, finding exposed roots instead of metal.

River summoned mana, but it sputtered like a dying flame. He'd used too much breaking through the illusion, blasting the grate, and attempting failed healings. Blake shivered in his arms, but it felt more like a convulsion running out of steam.

More feathers tore free.

"Get her out," Cloud clipped, moving to flank River on one side while Ash took the other.

Still brothers.

Still a triad.

Emotion clogged River's throat. His grip tightened on Blake. "I'm not leaving you crows alone."

"Yes, you are." Ash's wind slammed into an approaching hound, propelling it into the pit's wall. "We've got this."

Cloud's lightning crackled in his eyes, weaker than before but still deadly. "Go save your mate."

The Collector leaped. Three bodies moved as one—muscle memory from hundreds of battles. Cloud went low. Ash went high. River slung Blake over his left shoulder, unclipped *Peacemaker* with his free hand, and released a thin razor-sharp line of raw power that sliced a hound's tail clean off.

Empty.

Depleted.

"Now!" Ash bellowed.

He returned *Peacemaker* to his belt, slid Blake into his arms, and launched upward as his triad covered his escape. He bounced off exposed roots, his wings flapping to help him ascend. Wrong. They felt wrong. Should have propelled him higher.

No time to check.

Battle sounds echoed off cylindrical walls. Growls, acid dripping, hissing. Teeth gnashed for blue-tipped feathers when they flapped in range, and in this fucking pit, they were always in range. Somehow, he made it to the top.

Before he burst through the damaged grate, he looked down.

Cloud and Ash stood back-to-back, weapons drawn, united against the Collector's fury.

Up.

"River, wait!" Blake's panicked voice, suddenly clear. "The diagrams. Aeron."

"Later." He spread his wings wider. More feathers tore free. "Hold on."

Within moments, they were in icy morning air, flying hard. Blake's light weight felt like an anchor. His muscles screamed in protest.

Wrong.

"The caravan." Her words grew weaker, almost inaudible in the wind. "Diagrams. Aeron … needs them."

"You can redraw them." He banked hard, heading for Helianthus. For Ada. For hope.

"No." Her hands curled into claws against his chest. "There's no time."

"Exactly."

"Too late for me."

"It's never too late."

"Please." Trapped tears glistened in her rainbow-tipped lashes. "Let me do this one good thing…"

Her words trailed off. For a split second, he thought he had flown too far from the ground, cutting her off. But she wasn't in pain, not in that way. The agony came from her soul. It cut River to the core.

She still believed her ex's poison, still thought she wasn't enough. "Blake, I lo—"

Her head lolled. She went limp.

"BLAKE!"

Heart leaping into his throat, he flew harder. Why wasn't he moving faster? His wings protested. Black and blue feathers created a trail behind them. The moment he noticed, they lost altitude.

The ground, already closer than usual, slowly approached.

Falling.

Failing.

Scenarios and options hurtled through his mind. But he couldn't think of a way to save them.

Maybe Blake was right. He should have flown to the Great Murder. It was closer than Helianthus. The Donna might. But if she couldn't. Without a portal stone—

Why didn't River think of taking one before coming?

His right wing spasmed, tilting them to one side. He fought to correct, but more feathers stripped away, leaving patches of vulnerable skin exposed to cold air.

Then they were in free fall.

River's left wing, the only good wing left, beat frantically. It sent them spinning. Blake's hair whipped a rainbow across his face. Her fevered mumbling was lost in the roar of their descent. The ground rushed up, jagged rocks and death.

Blake's eyes fluttered open, focusing on something beyond him.

"Storm's coming," she whispered.

Impact never came.

Hands gripped beneath River's arms, jerking them back from the pull of gravity. Black wings above blocked out the sun. Cloud's shadowed face hovered over them, jaw set with determination.

"I've got you," he grunted, neck muscles straining as

molting feathers continued to fly into his face. "Tuck your wings!"

River pinned them to his back. Not enough mana to shift them away. Too terrified to borrow from Blake. But with them, they were too heavy. They dropped.

"You still have one good wing," Cloud shouted, and angled to River's right—the weak side. He deftly switched his grip, one now beneath River's armpit and the other beneath Blake's, sharing the weight of both.

A fleeting glance between them conveyed an unsaid promise, a vow. If it came to it, if River needed to let go so that his mate would live, then Cloud would carry her to safety.

Maybe he saw the defeat in River's face because he suddenly shouted, "Fly or die, fuck face!"

Fly or die.

Where was Ash?

And if you give up, then what hope—

The memory of his voice urged River to beat his good wing harder, to the point of pain. They almost fell, almost veered into a pinnacle that appeared from nowhere, but somehow, they found a rhythm. When he looked at Cloud, he was met with a carefully blank expression. Eyes straight ahead.

River wanted to speak—to thank him, to ask where Ash was, why Cloud's grip felt desperate rather than confident. But then he noticed Blake's rainbow hair had dulled.

In broad daylight.

SIXTY-NINE

Voices. Urgent. Familiar.

Blake struggled to focus. White ceiling. Moving fast.

"—get her to bay three—"

Did we make it? Did you get the diagrams? Her lips wouldn't work, and the thought dissolved when she landed on something soft.

Sand.

She was back on the sand. The mermaid lounged on her rock again, copper hair—no, she had blond hair.

Odd. Blake swore it was a different color.

This time, the mermaid waved.

"You came back," she said. "What happened to your clothes?"

My clothes?

Frowning, Blake glanced down and gasped. "Oh no, it's ruined."

Her sequins were tarnished and falling off. She'd spent so long sewing them on, giving it the razz. Now everyone could see the skeletal fabric had always been there, hiding beneath.

"Jeff's going to laugh at me," she groaned. "He told me this dress was cheap."

She plucked at the hem, pulling at the sequins. So many had lost their shine.

"—the anatomy diagram—" River's voice, desperate and distant.

Blake's head snapped up, searching. River?

He'd gone back for the diagrams. He believed in her.

"Blake," Ada's voice warbled from somewhere. "Some of these are smudged. I can't make out this section."

Relief curdled.

Of course, even her one good thing wasn't good enough.

Oh my God, babe. You're so clueless.

"Shh." The mermaid put a finger to her lips. "The tide's coming in."

Coolness touched Blake's forehead, then vanished.

"Something's wrong. The mana won't—" Ada's voice sharpened. "Find Clara ... *Go.*"

Blake shivered violently. The sand was so cold, colder than she'd ever felt on Perth beaches. But the sun still burned her skin, contradicting everything.

Someone screamed nearby—Trix.

She gets to stay, Blake thought distantly. *She gets to build something beautiful.*

The irony tasted bitter. Or maybe that was blood.

"You owe her!"

The shout was so loud.

"Dad?" she murmured, angry. "What are you doing here?"

"I can't find the workshop. Everything's underwater."

But it wasn't her father's hands holding hers. Through the blinding light, she tried to sit up. A gentle pressure pushed her back onto the cold sand. A shadow fell across her face. Black and white wings blocked out the burning sun moments before a bird landed beside her.

"Scarface? I thought you'd left me."

The magpie cocked his head, that damaged eye studying her. His feathers were ruffled, but she saw the fierce loyalty beneath his scars.

"You're not so scary," she whispered, reaching toward him. "It's okay. You should go and protect what matters."

She touched warm skin instead of feathers. The magpie's worried squawk sounded like her name.

Blake.

Blake.

Blake.

SEVENTY

River burst through the healing center doors with Blake limp in his arms. Bright white walls stretched before him. People were clustered at the far bay. Aeron, Jasper. Ada, kneeling. All were focused on a patient behind drawn curtains.

"Help!" he shouted.

They glanced over.

"River?" Ada's eyes widened. She glanced behind the curtain, then back at him.

A hand appeared on the fabric and dragged it back. Trix's surprised, mottled face emerged—dark curls to her sweaty skin.

River's stomach dropped. Her legs were bent, spread. She was about to give birth.

Shit. *Fuck.*

"Blake's dying." The confession scraped his throat raw. "I feel it through our bond. She's fading."

"Get her to bay three!" Ada pointed beside her, whispered something to her mate, then turned to Trix and continued talking.

It was all lost to the blood roaring in River's ears as he rushed Blake to the empty bay.

"Hear that, Blake?" His voice cracked despite every effort to steady it. "That's Ada. We're in Helianthus. You're going to be fine."

Jasper jogged over and cleared instruments from the bed, making room. River barely registered that the king was out of his fancy royal attire and in loose, training gear when he placed Blake down.

Her dull, dark hair fanned across a white pillow. No rainbow shine remained, not even with the afternoon sun filtering through a nearby window.

A feather drifted from his molting wing and landed on her chest. He flicked it away, but another followed. They were everywhere.

"What happened?" Jasper asked, voice gruff.

"She just started feeling sick." River rubbed his face. Tried to stop the emotion. "We thought it was the Donna's bat-shit paste, but…"

"Guano?" Ada arrived, wiping her hands on her apron.

"It's not supposed to be toxic," he replied.

"No. Not on Well-blessed humans." Ada's lips flattened. She placed her palm on Blake's forehead and closed her eyes to concentrate. Her frown deepened. "Tell me everything."

River paced alongside the bed, tugging at his hair, trying to piece it all into order. Still, all he ended up doing was spewing verbal diarrhea that made little sense. Ada and Jasper kept stopping him for explanations he couldn't provide.

"You're not making sense." Jasper's steady hand found River's shoulder, avoiding his wing. "You need to calm down. Sit."

"Don't tell me to calm down!" He shrugged off the king's touch. "She's my *mate!*"

"I know that," Jasper ground out, "but you're rambling and—"

"It's not the guano." A toneless voice drew every gaze to where Cloud stood in the shadowed doorway, shoulder propping it open, wings shifted away. His leather uniform was shredded in places from acid and talons, but his wounds had healed. Exhaustion was carved into every line of his bloody face. "She has a fever. The mortal kind."

"You came back," Ada said, blinking at Cloud. "What happened to your clothes?"

Violence rippled off her mate in waves. His upper lip peeled back, revealing elongated wolfish fangs. His guttural voice was too close to a beast's for comfort. "You have a lot of fucking nerve showing up here, crow."

Cloud merely crossed his arms and stared back, and repeated, "It's a fever."

"What?" Ada blurted. "But, that's not possible."

"Nova—" Trix's strained voice filtered from her bay.

"That was different," Cloud countered. "The taint."

He hadn't left River and Blake's side since saving them from falling. He'd even supported her continued, delirious pleas to collect the anatomy diagrams. When River protested about the risk, Cloud said, *If this is her final request, honor it.*

For once in his life, River listened.

But now this.

Now the light had faded from Blake's eyes and was barely there in her mating marks.

River scrubbed his face. Blinked. Stared at Cloud. At Jasper. At Aeron, who was angrily signing to his huffing and puffing mate. The two kings looked like they were about to throw down with Cloud. This could spiral. Fast.

"We don't have time for this shit!" he shouted, gesturing between them all. "Blake needs our help."

"I know that, River," Ada snapped, eyes flashing, her hand still on Blake's clammy forehead. "It's not like I'm knitting over here."

Blake tried to speak, but no words emerged, just breathy hissing. Her clawed fists tightened and raised, but then seized. Convulsed. Ada held Blake down. Each jerk vibrated the mattress.

When the convulsions subsided, Blake moaned and flopped. Her fisted hands spilling toward Ada.

"What's this?" She pried the crumpled paper from Blake's fingers.

"The anatomy diagrams." River pulled more folded pieces from his pockets and threw them at Ada. "Of the inner ear. You're fucking welcome. Here's everything she drew. Take it all. Just fix Blake. *Please.*"

I'm begging you.

I'll do anything.

River watched as Ada quickly gathered the papers. Her eyes raced over each diagram until she found one in particular. Her hands moved over the sketch. Hope flickered in her eyes, but then her shoulders sagged. "Blake, some of these are smudged. I can't make out this section of the inner ear."

"She did it?" Trix's elated screech transformed into a high-pitched scream of pain. "Oh—ow—oooh my *god* it's coming!"

River wanted to yell at them, to shake them. Blake was

more important than hearing, than a new baby, than the entire world. But he knew he was about to snap. If he did the wrong thing now, he'd surely make everything worse.

Aeron's hands flew in rapid signs at Ada. Then he grabbed Trix's hand and sat at her side, looking as lost as River felt. Trix's contraction ended, and she collapsed on her pillows, wincing and clutching her round belly.

"How's she looking, Erith?" Ada called out as she returned her palms to Blake's body, her brow creased in concentration.

River exhaled. Unclenched his fists. Ignored the bloody claw marks in his palms and watched Ada's face for any sign of good news.

A robed healer—mage by the blue mana-mark on her lower lip—bustled into the room from the bathrooms with a bowl of steaming water in her hands. She took one look at the chaos, and her entire demeanor changed. Her jaw hardened. Her nostrils flared. She put down the bowl, shoved Aeron aside, and bent to check between Trix's open legs. "She's crowning."

"Something's wrong," Ada mumbled. Her hand *glowed* against Blake's forehead, but then she jerked back. "The mana won't—" She whirled and shouted at the mage, "Find Clara. West Palace Wing. *Go.*" To River, she explained: "Clara's a fae healer. She's old. Has seen a lot. She might be able to help. Until she gets here, there's not much I can do."

The defeatist tone in her voice broke River's heart.

"Not much you can do?" He blinked. "Of course there is. You're the best."

Ada's rueful gaze dropped to River's molting wings. He tucked them behind him, out of sight, but velocity scattered more black and blue across the white tiles.

"I've never seen anything like this, River," Ada murmured. "She's not responding to mana. It's almost like she's"—her gaze dipped to the feathers on the floor—"rejecting it."

He stepped on them to seize Ada's wrist as she moved to leave.

"No!" His roar thundered off the walls. "Heal Blake *first*."

Jasper's warning snarl trembled the walls. Ada yanked her hand back, a fierce look on her face, and then stayed her mate with a raised palm.

"When Clara gets here, I might know more." Her expression softened upon meeting River's grief-stricken eyes. "I wish I knew more. I do."

She moved toward Trix. Turned her back.

"No!" River's second roar cracked something in his chest. "You don't walk away!"

He lunged after her—someone's grip caught him.

"River," Jasper's voice, calm now. But firm. That's what worried River most. "Ada has more than one patient."

Madness. This was madness.

"I don't give a fuck about anyone else." He punched the side table, scattering instruments and papers all over the place. "We *brought* you the diagrams. You *owe* her!"

Angst sliced into him from Blake, hot and sickly through their flickering bond.

"Dad?" she rasped. "What are you doing here?"

River shoved Jasper aside, rushing to his mate's bedside. "Sparkles, I'm here."

Her puffy eyes fluttered open and found his face. "Scarface? I thought you'd flown away."

The name hit him like a blade between the ribs. She

thought she was talking to her magpie—the one from her childhood. The damaged bird that protected what mattered. Three more feathers drifted to the floor.

"Never." He caught her reaching fingers. Gripped hard. "Where you go, I go, remember?"

You die, I die.

"You're not so scary," she whispered, hand falling limp. Her next words dissolved into incomprehensible murmurs.

"Blake, listen to me." His voice broke. "Blake. Blake? *Blake!*" He shook her awake. "You're not done yet. The diagram—Ada couldn't read it. She needs you to fix Aeron's ears. Stay with me."

His desperate words to grab her attention worked. Something shifted in her eyes. Focus flickered back, sharp and sudden.

"What?" she gasped, lucid. "I failed?"

"No. Just smudged."

Bolstered by her interest, River searched for the discarded papers. Some were missing from the floor. Where had Ada put the rest?

Cloud pushed off from the doorframe and pointed at a nearby table. At River's nod, he collected the sketches in two quick strides, placed them before Blake, and then retreated to his post.

"Okay, Sparkles." River cleared his throat, blinking rapidly to clear his vision. "We have your diagrams." He rifled through papers, all smudged. Well-damn him for letting her hold them on the journey, but it had seemed to calm her. He'd needed both hands to carry her through the portal from the Great Murder. "Which one?"

Blake's fight to focus was visible. Her muscles tensed, eyes strained. "Show me."

Hope exploded in his chest. She was rallying. Had to be.

He propped her up with pillows, then displayed each paper on her lap until she said to stop. She squinted, traced a wavering line with her finger. "That's the cochlea. The spiral should curve here, attach here…"

"Ada!" River called.

Trix's scream intensified. He glanced toward her bay. Only the top of Ada's blonde head was visible between spread thighs. Aeron paced, his usually neat braids were frayed. The shocked look on his face was worse than that of a rookie Guardian's after his first monster kill.

Jasper tried to calm him, but the Spring Court King glared at Cloud, signing aggressively and pointing. Jasper glared toward the door, a hard look in his eyes.

They were too busy worrying about Cloud to see the miracle Blake had offered them.

"Go show her," Blake insisted, breathless. "He needs to hear his baby."

River felt only peace through their bond, peace where panic should have reigned. She was better. Had to be. Maybe it was the paste after all. Maybe it just needed time to wear off.

"You sure?"

"I'm fine."

River pushed back his chair, stepped toward Ada, but then doubled back and kissed Blake. He murmured against her lips, "I love you."

"That's nice." He felt her lips stretch. She gave him a weak shove and said, "Go."

"Be right back." His heart somersaulted in his chest as he crossed to the next bay, shaking his head but grinning at Blake's answer. *That's nice?*

"Here." He handed the diagram to Ada. "Heal Aeron."

He explained the mistake as Trix released an ear-splitting scream. His eyes caught sight of something between her legs that made his mind stutter. Blood drained from his face. He quickly looked back at Ada.

"This is it," she gasped, reading the diagram. "Trix, I think she did it."

"I'll bloody well hold the baby in," Trix panted, clutching her belly. "Do it."

"You can't—"

"DO IT!" she bellowed.

Ada leaped up and placed her hands on Aeron's ears. Mana flowed. River sensed it in the air.

"Oh shit!" Trix's eyes widened. Clashed with River's. She made a constipated sound that turned into a squeal and ended with the rushed words, "I can't bloody well hold it!" She gasped. "The baby's coming!"

"River!" Ada barked, still working on Aeron. "I need your hands—"

He moved on instinct and caught the slippery form as it emerged from between Trix's legs. One blink, and it was in his arms. Eyes closed like a wrinkled, furless monkey. Face blue.

"It's..." His eyes widened. "Not breathing."

Behind him, another feather hit the floor.

The umbilical cord was wrapped around the baby's neck.

Silence.

Cut it.

River carefully cut the cord with a nearby scalpel and unwrapped it.

"Clean the airways," Ada clipped, concentration fracturing slightly on Aeron. "Hook your finger in its mouth."

River obeyed, but the baby remained quiet. Unmoving. A small, still weight in his palms.

"What's happening?" Trix cried.

"I'm almost done," Ada replied loudly. Sweat beaded on her upper lip. Aeron tried to look past her to see what was happening, but Ada blocked his view.

"Lift it upside down," she added quietly to River. "Smack its bottom."

A vague memory of his mother doing something similar guided him. He gripped tiny ankles in one fist, dangled the baby, head down. He smacked the bottom.

The baby's first, shrill cry pierced the air—strong, healthy, alive.

Aeron jerked his head toward the baby as River repositioned it and cradled it against his chest—tiny flailing fists aimed for his face. Aeron swiped Ada's hands from his ears and stumbled toward River ... toward his newborn as it wailed a second time. He blinked, tilted his head, and then his face crumpled with wonder.

"You heard that?" Trix burst into tears.

At first, Aeron hand-signed something, but then he froze mid-sign and slowly lowered his hands.

"Not like before," he answered, voice rusty from disuse and off-key. But he didn't care. He looked at the wriggling, fragile thing in River's arms, and his eyes glimmered. "It's muffled, distorted. Only in one ear, but..." He jiggled his finger in his ear. "But I hear *something*."

Joy flooded River's soul.

Blake had done it—stubborn, selfless mate. Even sick, almost dying, she'd given them this miracle. It wasn't perfect, but from the look on its parents' faces as River deposited the newborn into Aeron's arms, it was perfectly imperfect.

He spun toward his mate's bed, words tumbling. "Blake! Look what you—Aeron *heard*—it's a girl! You saved—"

Her chest wasn't moving.

Blake's eyes stared sightlessly at the ceiling, peaceful, empty, already gone.

SEVENTY-ONE

The incoming triad message whispered across Ash's forearm. He continued his descent into the dark tunnel beneath his mother's spire. Not the bad one, the other one. The one he'd made his friend. Manabee lanterns flickered along the walls. Their buzzing light cast dancing shadows that seemed to mock him.

Back again so soon, they taunted. *Hurrah.*

He stopped when the message started to itch, belligerent at being ignored. He yanked up the torn sleeve of his ceremonial garb. Letters had formed in the designated space:

WHY DO IT? WHY TRADE YOURSELF FOR THE CRYPTEX?

He stared at the words until his eyes burned. He traced his thumb across the fresh ink, as if he could somehow erase the question or the pain that prompted it.

Cloud.

The name settled on Ash's chest like a stone, growing

heavier with the memory of each choice that led him here. Back to these tunnels beneath the spire. Back to her domain, where ancient glyphs carved into rock watched his every movement with hollow, knowing eyes.

His clawed finger moved to trace a reply, hesitated, then began:

To save you.

He stopped. Deleted the words with another touch. The response tasted wrong down here, so he tried again:

Had no choice.

Worse. His hand trembled as he erased those words, too.

Sitting here in the belly of his mother's lair, those justifications became dirt in his mouth.

He slid his hand beneath the feathery ceremonial collar and checked that the thin lump remained beneath the lining.

Why do it? Why trade yourself for the cryptex?

His mother would accept nothing less. He was always destined to *be* the price. It was never a matter of if, only when.

Why?

Why now?

To save Cloud, Blake, and River's lives? Or because Ash had finally come to collect what had always been his? What he'd been waiting for his entire life.

His clawed finger hovered over the triad tattoo again. They deserved an answer, even if the truth would cut them. In the end, he couldn't do it. Not yet. But a cut had to be made, nonetheless. It just had to be clean, final, and with no room for guilt or rescue missions.

The triad might have a rocky relationship, but they were friends. Brothers. Family. More so than the female who inhabited these tunnels.

Frowning, he traced his answer, each letter deliberate:

Because this is my choice. Honor it.

He left it long enough to know it had been received, and then, before either could respond, he drew the feather quill from his collar. Ancient power thrummed against his fingers, waking at the touch of a descendant. He pressed the bony point to the triad tattoo and drove it beneath his skin.

Pain exploded up his arm as the sliver sliced through ink and flesh. The triad bond broke like a snapped string, leaving only silence in place of their presence. Blood welled around the quill, leaving a dark stain beneath Ash's skin, but the connection was gone.

Completely.

No more desperate reaches across the void.

No rescue.

He flexed his fingers. Ground his teeth. Swallowed.

Alright, fuck face, he imagined River saying. *You made your nest. Now go lie in it.*

He continued walking.

Air shifted, brushing against his face, carrying scents that brought him back to his past as if it were yesterday. The old bones of ancestors. Dust from artifacts that had crumbled to nothing in forgotten vaults. If he strained his hearing, he could almost hear the whispers threading through the darkness. *Blood calls. Home waits. Time to stop pretending.*

The corridor stretched ahead, leading deeper into the heart of his mother's life's work, leading toward the chamber where she waited, no longer performing weakness as she had at the Shadow Market.

Leading toward whatever reckoning had been building for hundreds of years.

Each step carried him farther away from the boy River and Cloud had rescued and closer to whatever he'd always been underneath the grateful mask.

Behind him, the manabee lanterns dimmed. The tunnel widened into a circular chamber carved from rock by claws —not his—along with patterns etched so deep that they seemed to suck in the fading light.

His steps slowed as ancient mana thickened the air. He waited for his eyes to adjust. Each breath tasted of copper and ozone. She emerged seconds later, as if woven from shadows, no longer the injured creature who'd writhed on a pallet at the market. Her dark eyes held no surprise, only satisfaction, as if she'd been counting down the moments until his arrival.

"There's my clever boy." She circled slowly, inspecting him.

Ash set his shoulders and straightened his spine, matching her posture. "Mother."

She trailed a talon along the carved wall. The scraping sound once grated against his nerves, but now it sparked something sharp and vigilant within him. His breathing adjusted without conscious thought, falling into rhythm with her movements—predator stalking predator.

"Two centuries of playing Guardian." Her voice carried amusement. "Such dedication to the performance. Did you think I couldn't feel you"—she paused, head tilting at that distinctive angle—"pulling strings across Elphyne like a spider in its web?"

Ash tracked her movements. "I don't know what you mean."

Her laugh echoed against the carved walls. "Oh, my darling heir. Still performing, even now."

"I'm not performing."

"Lies."

"Fae can't lie."

Another laugh, this one more like an incredulous cackle.

"You're so like your father." Her winged arm raised, hand reaching for his face. She traced her talon down his temple to his Guardian mark and smiled. "Wasn't it you, my heir, who taught me that the best lies are the ones you believe so deeply they become the truth?"

Her hand dropped, and she whirled with a dramatic flourish, a flurry of feathers and silk. She moved deeper into the shadowed chamber, toward something that made the mana pulse stronger.

With a heavy sigh, Ash followed until they met a skeleton embedded in the wall. Its ancient bones were black with age but somehow still vital, still radiating power in tangible waves. The same dark shade ran beneath Ash's skin, beneath the triad tattoo.

This was why it was never he who'd saved his triad from the Well Worms.

The Collector approached the remains like a lover, her palm settling against the skull with genuine tenderness. The gesture should have revolted him. Instead, his hand rose unconsciously, almost mirroring her touch. He jerked back, bile rising in his throat.

"Your father sends his regards." She stroked the bone

with the same affection Ravi showed Talo. "He's been so patient, waiting for you to stop pretending."

"I'm not—" The words died. Down here, wrapped in mana that sang the same song as his blood, the lie choked on his tongue.

"Not pretending?" Her fingers never stilled on the skull. "Blood calls to blood, doesn't it? And you've been calling for such a long time, haven't you, my love?"

The skeleton seemed to pulse in response. Power washed over Ash in waves. For a moment, just a moment, he felt complete. Understood. As though he were coming home after a lifetime of speaking a foreign tongue.

He stepped back, but the damage was done. The mana had recognized him.

And he'd recognized it in return.

Enough.

"Where?" His voice came out steady despite the tremor in his hands.

The Collector's smile could have cut glass. "Eager to collect your reward?"

He glared back until she gestured toward an archway hidden in the shadows. Despite knowing the way, Ash followed her through the opening into an antechamber, leaving behind the spiraling patterns of the main room.

Illumination came from the purple and midnight scales of a creature coiled on the floor before another door. Enforced ceramic chains thick as Ash's wrist circled the Shadowmaw's throat. More for appearance than purpose. Multiple rows of crystalline teeth caught the glow of its scales as it lifted its massive head. Dark eyes fixed on him.

No fear. No aggression.

Just the lazy contentment of a hound greeting its master.

Ash's steps slowed as he approached, something heavy settling in his stomach. The creature's deep rumble sounded like distant thunder and vibrated through the floor into Ash's bones.

He knelt, and it nuzzled his hand with serpentine grace. His fingers found the scar along its slippery flank automatically, tracing the precise line he'd carved there a mere hour ago. Again, more for appearance than purpose. Shallow enough to heal clean. Deep enough for the blood required to paint over his garb, fooling his brothers.

"Sorry about the scar, old friend."

The Shadowmaw huffed, a sound that might have been laughter in a creature capable of such things. Its hide was warm beneath Ash's palm, scales smooth as polished stone. He scratched behind the horned ridges of its skull. It pressed into the touch like a fee-lion seeking warmth.

Had to deal with one of her pets.

Ash's hand stilled. The Shadowmaw sensed his shift, nudging his shoulder with gentle concern. Real affection, even if their battle had been fake. Real trust, even though he'd used it to deceive the only family he'd ever known.

"What does that make us, Tenebris?" he whispered.

The creature only continued nuzzling Ash's hand, patient as stone.

He rose slowly, giving the beast one final pat. It settled back into its dark mana pool with liquid grace, content in its domain of shadows and ancient power.

The most honest relationship Ash had as a child was with a creature that helped him manufacture lies.

This was where his mother left him. Not a single word left her lips. No gloat. No snide remark. She had what she wanted, and now it was his turn.

He stepped over Tenebris and into another antechamber. This one, he'd carved out with his claws in his youth.

The space felt smaller than memory painted it. The single lantern of trapped manabeeze dangling over a closed and locked wooden door cast a twirling light. Each buzzing ball of energy struck its glass enclosure, eager to escape. Each soft *ting* created a rhythm, a melody he remembered well.

A mirror of polished obsidian dominated the opposite wall. Its black surface reflected nothing until he stepped into its range, and the blue glow of a Well-blessing revealed his face.

What a mess.

Ash smoothed his hair. Strands had fallen from the knot. He then adjusted his torn ceremonial garb, fingers moving with practiced precision. Each fold smoothed. Each crease aligned. Each feather was dusted. The actions felt natural, automatic—like breathing, blinking, or any other function his body performed without conscious thought.

He stilled and studied his hands. When had grooming become a ritual? When had preparation become an obsession?

Around the chamber, objects sat in perfect arrangement. Had his mother placed them there, or had he? The question lodged in his throat like a bone. He found himself adjusting a ceremonial dagger that didn't need adjusting, repositioning a bowl that was already centered.

His reflection caught his attention. Dark eyes glimmered in the black glass mirror. For a moment, the face looking back could have belonged to anyone.

Could have belonged to her.

His breathing stilled. The way he held his head, canted at that same predatory angle. He stepped closer to the mirror, studying the stranger wearing his face. Behind his reflection, the locked door stole his attention, reminding him of the day he'd carved those runes, not long before he'd met River and Cloud.

The first time he'd stood in this chamber was centuries ago, after carving out the space himself.

Nothing is truly yours unless you create it, she'd whispered into his ear as he marked his territory.

She'd spoken of rewards and patience and blood calling to blood. How easily he'd dismissed her then. How certain he'd been that rescue and captivity were opposites, not variations on the same theme.

Slowly, he walked to the door. His grip tightened on the handle until his knuckles blanched. Each breath came shorter than the last, his chest constricting like something vital was being slowly crushed.

I'm here to save—

The thought died unfinished. Even his mind rejected the lie now.

He straightened his ceremonial collar one final time, ready to meet his reward. Ready to discover which of them had been the prisoner all along. Distending claws from each of his fingers, he fit them to the hidden recess within the knob, then paused, remembering what happened when he'd opened this door only a few turns of the hourglass ago.

The scent had hit him first, like lightning. It made his soul sing and his bones ache with recognition. Then he'd noticed the knife aimed at his face with precision that spoke of training.

She'd struck, but he caught her wrist, stopping the point a whisper from his eye. Blue light exploded from the ground between them, magic older than his wrapping around their arms like chains.

Mine.

The thought had barely formed before her emotions flooded through the connection. Fear, rage, and determination burned bright as stars.

Mine.

This time, the thought grew teeth. Not protection. Not rescue. Possession.

He'd taken her weapon, stepped back, slammed the door, and locked it. He left his reward locked away while he processed destiny's gift.

What he'd always known would be his.

River would have torn down the walls. Cloud would have freed her immediately, consequences be damned. But Ash had kept her like his mother kept her treasures.

The wind whispered around him, messing the hair he'd just fixed.

Welcome home, little crow.

He turned the lock. *Click.* The door creaked open. Light spilled through the crack—not manabee glow but something steadier, brighter. Bluer.

Something blessed.

Beautiful.

He swung the door wider and stepped across the threshold, prepared to deflect another attack. Instead, he froze. He locked eyes with seething hatred five feet ahead, her pupils visible through a curtain of long, dark hair. A small smile tipped her lips. A sharpened bone fragment glinted in her hand.

But it wasn't her new weapon that stopped his breath. It was the spiral pattern carved into every surface of her cell.

The same pattern that decorated his mother's walls. The same pattern was tattooed beneath his clothes.

She'd been studying him through the bond. Learning from him. Preparing.

Impossible.

"Hello, mate," he said.

"Hello, monster," she replied. Her prison rags hung in deliberate tatters, revealing bare skin above her collarbone. "Let's test the strength of our bond, shall we?"

Then she pressed the bone to her throat.

SEVENTY-TWO

River's healing magic slid off Blake's skin. Again. He pressed harder against her throat, searching for a pulse that wasn't there. He poured mana into unresponsive flesh until his reserves screamed empty.

"Come on, Sparkles," he whispered. "Don't you fucking dare."

Birth fluids and sweat lingered beneath a sharp chemical scent. Behind open curtains, he glimpsed Trix cradling a tiny form while Aeron wept openly. The baby's wails cut through River's numbness. Ada smiled up at the new parents, instructing them on what to do next.

None of them had noticed that his mate lay still. Dull black hair against white sheets. Chest unmoving. Eyes vacant, fixed on nothing. Well-blessed bond a cold blue stain on her arm.

"Blake, wake up," he whispered again, too afraid to raise his voice. If he did, if everyone noticed, then it was real. "Blake, come on."

Footsteps. A compact, female wolf shifter shoved past

Jasper and Cloud's stunned faces in the doorway. Short, dark hair framed sharp eyes that cataloged the room in seconds. River's devastation. Blake's stillness. Ada across the room.

"What do you need?" the new female barked.

"Clara?" Ada's head whipped toward the newcomer. "I need you to—"

Her jaw clicked shut when she saw Blake.

"It's too late." River stumbled back from his mate's gray stillness.

A final feather fell from his wings. Raw pink skin gleamed where magnificent plumage once spread. He stood ankle-deep in his own molted shame, broken and pathetic.

Fire blazed across his forearm. He glanced down in time to see words forming on his skin, a reply to a message Cloud sent Ash earlier, one River hadn't noticed.

Why did you do it? Cloud had asked. *Why trade yourself for the cryptex?*

Ash replied, *Because this is my choice. Honor it.*

"What the fuck?" he gasped, gaze snapping to the bastard by the door. "Ash traded himself for your fucking cryptex?"

Guilty blue eyes met River's, no words needed. And then the final blow snapped across River's being—the triad tattoo went cold.

Dead.

Their link severed.

"Why is this happening to me?" The walls spun around him. The world tilted off its axis. He had to crouch and hold his head to stop himself from blacking out. *Why. Why. Why?* "Is it because we cheated to become Guardians?"

"You what?" Jasper growled from the doorway. He faced Cloud and pointed at the door. "Leave. Now."

But Cloud clenched his jaw and stood his ground. When Jasper raised a hand to force him out, Cloud dodged and ducked under his arm. He stumbled closer.

River's vision blurred red.

"You happy now?" His voice cracked. "We're all suffering the same as you! My mate's dead. Ash is gone. All because you're chasing ghosts!"

Cloud stilled. His gaze fixed on River's naked wings, the raw pink skin, the pile of scattered feathers. Something shifted in his expression—recognition. Understanding. Regret.

"I just wanted," he mumbled, "for her to do the same for me."

Ada looked up from checking Blake's pulse, a fire in her eyes. "His wings never grew back because she restored them. River did that himself. It was a mental block."

"What would you know!" he snarled. "You couldn't even heal her from a fever!"

Cloud's face crumpled. "So she can't bring back what's been lost?"

"She's fucking *dead!*" River grabbed Cloud by the collar and hauled him close. "She's gone! I said I love you, and she just—"

His words choked off. He couldn't finish.

Aeron approached, the baby swaddled in his arms. He looked at Blake, frowned, then faced Ada, his eyes widening.

"She had a fever?" he asked gruffly. Cleared his throat. "Did I hear that right?"

"Yeah." Ada pressed the heels of her palms into her eyes. "Manabeeze."

"What?" She lowered her hands.

"Where are her manabeeze?" Aeron gave a pointed look

around the empty air in the room. "If she died, she'd have—"

"She doesn't have manabeeze." River shoved off Cloud and braced Blake's bed. He bent his head low, studying the feathered floor, and sucked in a shuddering breath. "She's human."

"Jackson Crimson," Aeron said. "The journals. After the Fallout, the first humans who became fae had a fever first. They thought it was a plague. Crimson ... Leaf..." His eyes widened even further. "What if Blake isn't dying? What if she's changing into something new?"

"Is this true?" River's gaze snapped to Ada's.

A troubled look crossed her features. "That illness wiped out billions of people."

"Shit." River started pacing, kicking through his fallen feathers. "Shit. Shit."

"She is still connected to the Well, tethered to this world." Clara picked up Blake's marked hand. "The Spring Court King is right. It's not over until you see manabeeze."

"But I can't feel her..." River closed his eyes and hunted for their bond. Shook his head. His throat was too tight to speak.

She wasn't breathing. Her heart had stopped. Healing magic failed. It was only a matter of time before those traitorous balls of energy popped out of her corpse.

"She's not dying." Cloud pushed River aside. He *climbed* onto Blake's bed and straddled her. He flipped his knife and tore a line straight down her collar. Before he was done, he slid his free palm against her sternum—

River lunged forward. "Get off her, you sick fuck."

Death sang in his veins. Power flooded him from the Well's darkest depths, begging for release. River would take it all. He would plumb every drop from the world to save her.

"Trust me."

Two words sputtered River's rage. They shot him deep into the past.

Three crows. One lake.

"You're sure about this?" Ash muttered.

"No," River answered. "But you fuck faces trust me."

"Ancestors save us, because I do." Cloud scrubbed his face, blinking widely. "I trust you fuck faces."

All the pretense. All the betrayal. The bravado. The things left unsaid, the ego, the vengeance promised. It all stripped away with two words.

This right here proved it wasn't River who kept them from floating in the ceremonial lake. It wasn't Ash, either. It was the one who spoke the truth.

River stepped back, palms out in surrender. "What are you going to do?"

"Restart her heart," Cloud muttered, eyes closing as he repositioned his palms on Blake's body, somewhere by her ribs. "Think about it. She could see the UV writing in my trove."

Cloud … I saw everything on the wall.

Controlled lightning arced from his palms into Blake's chest. Her body jolted violently, spine bowing off the bed. Blue Well-blessed marks ignited with inner fire.

Your glittery writing. Her letters.

Blake fell against the bed, hair dull again. Light faded from their bond. River watched his mate. Willed her heart to start beating. Remembered Cloud was fucking right.

Details he'd missed. Not only did he overhear her tell Cloud she'd seen the glittery writing, but she'd drawn them out. In the trove, she commented on things written in UV ink. Fuck. Even earlier, in the nesting caravan, she noticed the painted UV marks on her skin.

That was days ago.

"She's not dying," he whispered, hope creeping in. "She's changing."

Another controlled bolt. She arched off the mattress. Collapsed.

"Come on," Cloud urged through gritted teeth. "Don't make a liar out of me, Blake."

His eyes filled with a blinding white light. Static skipped over his skin, illuminating the power-enhancing tattoos, lifting his dark curls as surely as if Ash's wind were here urging him on. He rubbed his palms and returned them to Blake's body. He held his breath. Hesitated.

"Do it," River said. "I trust you."

Power released. The scent of ozone sparked. Blue light and rainbow shards spliced through the room. Blake jolted, gasped … then fell and went still.

She stayed there, eyes closed. But her chest rose and fell in a shallow rhythm.

"Blake?" River ran to her side. "BLAKE!"

He shook her shoulders, but she remained unconscious. Cloud slipped from the bed, making way for the healers rushing in.

Ada checked Blake's pulse.

"She's alive." Her hand moved to Blake's forehead. "Still not responding to mana." To the smaller woman, she asked, "Do you have any insight?"

Clara's lips flattened. She stared at Blake for so long that River thought she was giving up. Then she ran her finger down the newly lit Well-blessed patterns on Blake's arm. She grabbed River's marked hand and pushed up his sleeve, baring as much as she could. Her eyes widened as she pulled his arm close to Blake's.

"Ada, come here." Clara waved her to the same side of the bed. "Bring Reed with you."

Jasper grumbled something about that not being his name anymore, but a stern look from Clara flattened his wolf shifter ears, and he pushed up his tunic sleeve to bare his marked arm. Ada did the same. Clara held them together and grunted with surprise.

"They're maps," she announced.

CHAPTER

SEVENTY-THREE

"Maps?" River stared hard at the Well-blessed marks. "I don't understand."

They just looked like glittering swirls.

"Oh my god." Ada's eyes widened. She flattened her palm against Jasper's and then aligned their arms. She rolled hers around his. Everywhere they touched, from her fingertips to her elbow, the blue lines met perfectly, as though they were two puzzle pieces fitting. "I always thought these looked like the contour lines of a map."

"Can you sense your mate, crow?" Clara brought River's hand to Blake's and laced their fingers together. "The Well has a hold on her. Use the map to find her, and then guide her home."

"How?" His throat closed. "I can't read that map. Can anyone?"

Blank faces.

Even Aeron shook his head.

"So then how?" he asked. "I already told her I loved her. And she said, 'That's nice.'" A manic, incredulous laugh burst out of him. *"That's nice.* Ha ha. What the fuck?" Then softer, more quietly. "Maybe she doesn't need me after all."

"Bullshit," Cloud growled. "Stop feeling sorry for yourself and sit the fuck down. Do the same thing you did for me when I needed it."

"What!" He was desperate now. "Do what?"

"Just be you."

"Right," River muttered. "Just be me. Easy. That's what I've been doing my whole life." He climbed over the pile of molted feathers and climbed onto the narrow bed beside Blake. "Yeah, sure. It's worked so far. It's worked great." He gathered her rapidly heating body against his. Her skin burned with fever again, but she was breathing. He laced his fingers through her hand again and kissed her knuckles.

Think.

Map.

Guide her home.

Okay.

He could do this.

He was born for this.

He was the river.

Right?

"I am the fucking river," he mumbled against her knuckles. "I am."

He was.

When chartered territory disappeared, he forged a new path. He jumped. No wings. *Fuck.*

Too many sets of eyes watched him. He needed a moment to think. To study the so-called map. That's what Cloud would do.

River lifted his outer wing over Blake like a canopy. Pink membranes filtered the harsh healing lights into a gentle amber, blending with the blue from their arms. He left the other wing hanging behind him, uncaring how pitiful they looked on the outside. All he cared about was right here, beneath them on the inside.

He buried his face into Blake's hair, kissed her neck, and then nuzzled toward her ear.

"I don't understand how to read this map," he whispered to her, "but I'll find a way. I promise."

She sighed.

Blake fucking breathed, and it was the most beautiful sound in the world. A sense of urgency filled him.

Read the map.

Read the fucking map.

Right.

I can do this.

But as River studied their marks beneath the shelter of his useless wings, all he could think of was that her skin had looked like this in Cloud's trove. Glowing. Smooth. Soft.

"You have a trove, too?" she'd asked him.

"Maybe."

"Will I get to see it?"

He should have shared more of himself when she'd asked, even the ugly parts he hated. He should have said yes. But he hadn't visited his trove for years. After he lost the ability to fly, the journey became a task. Besides, nothing had been worth collecting.

His trove was probably riddled with cobwebs, dust, and invasive sprites by now. There wasn't much for dust to settle on. Most of his treasures were the kind he'd painted on walls. Memories. Scenes. Faces. Places. Words.

It wasn't until he'd met Blake that he started collecting again. Even if his treasures were mostly cataloged in his mind, he'd hoped to paint them in his trove before she visited.

But again, time was not a friend. Contrary to his need to forge his own path through life, the inevitable conclusion remained the same. He could not control the journey. He could not bend fate to his will.

And he hated the feeling of being swept along. He hated the inevitable lonely end.

Where did that leave them?

Soft sounds of activity stirred outside his wing-cocoon. New parents murmured. Feet shuffled. A familiar rhythmic clink suggested that Cloud was nearby, flipping his butterfly knife.

It was his thinking habit—the flipping.

Painting was River's. He traced the pattern down Blake's arm, pretending his finger was a paintbrush. It was enough to keep his mind ticking over, thinking, too.

Cloud had betrayed them on the battlefield. He'd cost more innocent lives at the Shadow Market. Perhaps even more after the battle, if Jasper's soldiers were to be believed. And the rest? Frying River's wings? Kidnapping Blake? The cryptex?

The Six had woven the threads of fate long before Aleksandra and Maebh had. What was a little tug in Cloud's direction when the Six needed Rory to return Willow to Elphyne? What if the Six were the reason Cloud entered Crystal City in the first place? What if they're the reason Cloud fell in love with the enemy?

Was it fair to blame him when every mated male in this room would act the same if the woman they loved died? Even now, with Blake's life slipping away, River knew he would do anything—kill *anyone*—if it brought him a sliver closer to getting her back.

Cloud had loved Rory, and then she forgot him. She broke him. That messed him up.

As far as River was concerned, Cloud proved his heart by restarting Blake's.

There was hope.

"It's nice when you think about it." Blake's voice rose from a memory. River closed his eyes and sank into it, remembering how she'd touched items in Cloud's trove, treating the memories with respect. *"What I wouldn't give to revisit objects from me past—Mum's makeup brushes. Dad's hammer. I'd feel less alone."*

"Sparkles," River sighed. "I'm so ashamed I told you my trove was too personal to visit. After the … accident … nothing seemed worth keeping. I stopped visiting it myself. Stopped collecting. But I was wrong. Everything is worth keeping. And everything is worth sharing. Even the ugly bits, the painful bits. Even with your friends."

That's when the answer hit him. He knew how to guide Blake home.

He lowered his fleshy wing, and light flooded in.

Cloud still leaned against the doorway again, blocking the exit. Loose, black curls had fallen over his eyes as he flipped and toyed with his knife. *Clink. Clink.*

The curtain between Blake's bay and Trix's was not drawn as River expected. The new mother reclined on the bed, yawning, while Aeron paced beside her, gently rocking the baby in his arms.

Jasper sat beside Ada on a bench at the foot of the bay, leaning against the wall, staring at the ceiling. Ada's head rested on his shoulder. Her lashes kept drooping, but she flared them wide, trying to stay awake.

They should be resting, but they stayed.

For Blake.

For River.

"You should have a trove," he said to his mate, loud enough for everyone to hear. "I'll help you build one. Or you can share mine. I don't actually have many objects in mine, would you believe it?" He scoffed. "A crow without shinies? Anyway, I don't have physical mementos because I paint them. The early murals are fucking awful." He glided his hand across the air before Blake's sleeping face. "Imagine, if you will, a wall covered with crude drawings of thousands of cocks and balls. Impressive, I know. But in my defense, I was ten when I discovered the site."

Jasper gave a derisive snort. Ada smacked him on the chest.

"Ignore him, River," she mumbled, eyes drifting closed again. "Keep talking. She'll come home."

"Or fly away in horror," Jasper joked. A second swat forced a begrudging reaffirmation out of him. "She's right. Keep talking. You crows are like wolves—you need to know your pack is near."

"Pack is for pussies." River flipped up his middle finger at the king. "Murder is better."

A smile tugged at his lips when Jasper checked to see if his Ada watched, then mimed his hand talking and pulled a face at River.

"Don't keep us in suspense," Trix shouted.

"About what?" he teased.

"About what, he says." She rolled her eyes. "You know

bloody well what. Don't be a prick. Tell us what's in your trove."

"So impatient. But understandable." River nodded sagely. "Of *course* you're bursting with curiosity. A crow's sacred trove peels back layers of their soul, exposing every secret they've collected across centuries." Metal clinking stopped. "Treasures, memories, and dreams they only dare whisper to starlight, all gathered in one sacred space." Cloud's eyes narrowed, knuckles white around his knife. But River forged on. "Trespassing doesn't just break some unwritten rule. It slices open their heart and devours it raw."

"Oh no," Trix gasped, palms touching her rapidly reddening cheeks. "I didn't mean to pry. You don't have to tell us."

Nervous eyes darted around, checking reactions from the others—Jasper to Ada, Trix to Aeron, Cloud to everyone. Silence stretched. And just as the tension grew so thick they could choke, River's lips twitched in a half smile, and he shrugged.

"I suppose," he drawled, "if I can't expose myself around you lot, then who can I do it for?"

More than one of his friends groaned or rolled their eyes. Jasper might have palmed his face to hide an uttered threat. But Cloud, his shoulders loosened slightly.

He stepped aside and revealed people waiting outside the open door. Lark and Sera whispered to each other in the corridor, their expressions serious. A glimpse of the blue and black feathers revealed Ravi and Talo were there, but possibly talking to others.

Was that a flash of red hair?

Clarke peeked around the doorframe, saw River staring, and gave a hesitant wave. An enormous, masculine hand appeared above her head, dropped, and tugged her back out of view.

Two smaller red heads appeared lower.

"Fuck." Rush's grunt came seconds before the twins raced inside, squealing hurricanes.

"Uncle Wiver!"

Holly leaped onto Blake's bed with surprising nimbleness, considering one thumb was in her mouth. Hazel sniffed around the bed for a bit before climbing on.

Holly popped her thumb out of her mouth. "Mom said you're going to tell us stories."

"Are you?" Hazel demanded.

"Yeah," River said. "I am."

The girls hissed, "*Yes.*"

Emotion clogged his throat. Before he knew it, he was grinning, which was ridiculous considering the situation. But he wasn't alone.

Neither was Blake.

And that felt so fucking good.

He waved everyone in. "Find a seat, mouse-munchers. Storytime's about to begin."

Hushed questions multiplied as they filed into the room and crowded around the bed with worried looks. River made sure they left a spot for Cloud, even if he didn't take it. As his friends and family settled, he pulled out a folded note from his rear pocket.

His cheeks burned when he thought of reading it aloud, but if he lost courage now, then how would Blake know she had something to come back to? Something he'd been building from the moment he met her?

River laid his head beside his mate's on the pillow. The

folded note trembled in his grip as he held it where she would see it when she opened her eyes.

"Blake, I have a gift for you." He cleared his throat. "I'd originally planned to read this to you last night, even before I knew I could swoop you. I also had this whole rainbow thing planned. It involved some bioluminescent pigment and waterfall mist, but … yeah … I got a little distracted when you did that thing I love to my—"

"Pups in the room," someone barked.

"Right." River coughed. Oops. "Anyway, it's not perfect. But that's your thing, right? You make the imperfect perfect. I told you I love you, but I never explained how much or why. No wonder you were like, Oh, that's nice." He shook his head at his stupidity. "One day I want to paint the reasons in my trove—*our* trove. Not just for us to remember each other, but so that you'll always have a place to remember how much you were loved in your old life … and your new one. You know—" heat rushed to his cheeks "—I can't get the words out sometimes, so I wrote them down."

He cast a nervous glance around the room, but no one judged him. They listened patiently. Avidly. Rather, everyone did except for the twins. They plucked at the blanket with their claws and circled over Blake's lumpy legs to find a comfortable spot.

The moment they were done, he started reading.

SEVENTY-FOUR

Death tasted like champagne bubbles and salt water.

Swimming. She was always swimming.

Two feet and a heartbeat used to be enough, but Blake found neither in this freezing abyss. Her legs were numb. Her heart was silent. The ocean never ended.

Laughter.

Somewhere.

There.

A ray of sunlight broke through the clouds and landed on a boat, a yacht with the words "Boss Man" painted on the hull. Hope flared between her ribs. Jeff. He mustn't have seen her fall overboard.

"Oi!" she shouted, waving. "Hun, I'm over here."

She carved her arms through black water and swam to him. But lead weights had replaced her limbs. Her muscles screamed with each stroke. No matter how hard she tried, her legs remained numb, and the ocean remained an expanse of steel between her and the boat.

"Jeff!" Her voice broke as she floundered. "Don't leave me—"

The yacht's wake rolled over her head. Salt flooded her mouth, choking her.

Her husband's laughter drifted across the water. "You can't upcycle yourself, babe."

The prim and proper woman beside him cackled. Their champagne glasses clinked together.

"Look at her," the woman sneered. "She doesn't know when to give up."

"So clueless." Jeff clicked his tongue, judging Blake's struggle to stay afloat.

Something was wrong with this.

Hadn't she been here before?

Hadn't she chased after that boat until her legs went numb? But this time ... she was in the water. Last time, she was...

A shadow passed overhead. Then another.

Blake looked up, salt stinging her eyes. A familiar black and white bird circled tightly above. One eye peered down at her.

"Go away, Scarface," she mumbled. "Find something worth protecting."

Another bird arrived. Bigger. Blacker. It flew in a pattern that interlocked with the first. The larger bird cawed, desperate and demanding. Almost as if he had something to say to her. Like it was calling her name.

But that was nuts. Birds didn't talk.

Did they?

"*...from your old life...*"

Blake's head snapped up. That wasn't cawing. That was ... a man's voice. Warm. Inviting.

Much nicer than Jeff's.

"…and your new one."

Her legs tingled with the first hint of feeling. She twirled in the water, searching for the stranger, but only found more ocean. And now the yacht was getting away. She swam after it. One stroke. Two. Then stilled.

The circling crow's caws grew louder. Insistent. Calling her back. It changed into words again.

"Remember when we first met, and you said, 'Hell will freeze over before I take me clothes off for you.' Gentle reminder, Blake. You did take your clothes off for me. Often. Ergo … I'm painting a frozen hellish landscape in our trove. That way any time I want to look at your perfect ti—"

"For Crimson's sake." A deeper, gruff voice. *"Pups in the room!"*

Blake laughed. Water sprayed from her mouth. She wasn't sure why that was funny, but that voice. Not at the second, grumpy one. The first one. Every ounce of her being felt drawn to it. The warm timbre, the slight teasing note, the smile in it. The hint of male appreciation…

Heat flooded her body.

"Blake, every time you corrected 'me' to 'my' it was like you erased a part of yourself to please dickface."

Her hands fluttered, unsure which direction to swim.

"Hello?" she called. "Who are you?"

"I've been collecting each of your mys and burning them, keeping only the mes. I'm painting a whole wall of them in our trove next to my cock and balls wall. They'll be in a position of honor."

Another laugh burst out of Blake. What a weirdo. Who would want to collect her embarrassing words? To keep them?

"Her ex sounds like a right cunt, that one." A British woman's voice.

Yeah, Jeff *was* a cunt. And a dickface.

Blake was better than this. She stared after the yacht sailing away.

"Oi, Jeff!" she shouted, anger sizzling through her veins. "In case you missed it, you're a cunt! And I wouldn't get on your stupid boat if the world were ending."

She frowned. Kicked. Treaded water. Her legs weren't numb anymore.

"Oh yeah…" That sexy male voice deepened to a menacing purr. *"And your ex's boat? I'd paint it sinking. Over and over. In different ways."*

A loud crack thundered, startling Blake's heart. The circling birds released a cry of triumph as the yacht split in half, and water poured through the cracks. Beige suits soaked. The passengers cried out for help, calling her name.

But she didn't help.

"Screw those arseholes." She swam in the opposite direction, following the birds' flight path.

Pieces of debris floated past her, taking over with speed. Weird. Broken planks, a shattered mast, and fragments of cream-colored hull all drifted by. But instead of sinking, they bobbed on the surface like stepping stones.

She pulled herself onto the first piece of wood. It was solid. Real. Her bare feet found purchase, and she leaped to the next fragment, then the next. The birds spiraled upward, leading her higher.

"I'd paint your eucalyptus tree," the black bird said. *"Not the shitty one Trix gave you … the one from your old backyard."*

"Oi! She liked my tree!"

"Shush. I'm telling the story. She loves me more."

Blake smiled despite herself. The banter felt … nice. Familiar. Trix must be the British woman. Why did that name tug at something buried deep in Blake's chest?

Her feet found soft, springy grass. An assault of familiar scents hit her. Eucalyptus. Sawdust. Oil and cedar shavings. She closed her eyes and inhaled, long and deep. Her entire body sighed. *Home.*

When she opened her eyes, there it was: the eucalyptus tree from her childhood backyard, massive and gnarled, its silver-green leaves catching sunlight. She stepped off the grassy driftwood.

"I'd paint your porch and build actual steps you can sit on so that you can revisit any time you're feeling lonely."

The weathered porch materialized beneath the tree's shade, complete with proper steps instead of the broken concrete blocks she'd grown up with. She gasped at a sparkling light drawing her closer. Someone had glued glitter into the cracks, just like she used to.

"I'd paint your dad's workshop too."

Why did this stranger know her so well?

Blake climbed up the steps and found her dad's workshop, windows gleaming, door wide open. The smell of WD-40 was sharp in her nostrils. The radio crackled with golden oldies, a Frank Sinatra tune she remembered from Sunday mornings.

"Dad?" she called.

Her bare feet crossed the threshold. Tools lay arranged on the workbench in perfect rows. Things like chisels, sanders, and files. Things she'd been told not to touch. Her fingers hovered over her father's favorite hammer's worn handle, then jerked back. She glanced toward her old house, listening for his heavy footsteps. She didn't want to get in trouble.

Nothing.

She exhaled and turned back to the workbench. Half-finished projects waited on every surface: a jewelry box with its lid hanging crooked; a chair was missing its back slat; a miniature rocking horse had a splintered ear.

Blake traced the wood grain of the music box. The ceramic dancer was missing her skirt. She traced the broken wood and almost heard it whisper secrets. *Sand here. Glue there. New hinge.*

She knew exactly what it needed.

Her pulse quickened.

What if she fixed it? What if she saved it from the rubbish bin like all the other discarded things?

She turned the music box's winding key. A few broken notes tinkled out. The operatic tune made her chest ache with sudden, inexplicable loss and the memory of pancakes and maple syrup.

The birds landed on the windowsill outside. Their beaks tapped against the glass to be let in.

"You're not supposed to be here," she told them, and reached for the music box. She wanted to rewind it, to hear that tune.

It slipped from her hands.

The ceramic dancer's head snapped clean off, rolling across the workbench and onto the floor with a tiny clink.

"Oh no." Blake dropped to her knees and scrambled to collect the pieces. The dancer's painted face stared up at her, lifeless. "Shit, shit, shit. He'll be so cross at me."

Her father had carved the delicate wooden base by hand.

He'd sanded it smooth and started the restoration, but the box was half-finished. Deserted. Like he'd given up. Like he couldn't bear to touch something so precious when the person who loved it was gone. And now Blake had made it worse.

"Fuck'sake," she muttered, eyes stinging. "I can't do anything right."

Her hands shook as she tried to reattach the ceramic head to the tiny neck. Too small. The pieces wouldn't stay. She was making it worse, leaving fingerprints, getting it dirty.

He'll know.

Blake's gaze landed on her father's favorite hammer, the one she was never allowed to touch.

She grabbed it with trembling fingers, almost putting it immediately back down, but the weight settled into her palm like coming home. Perfect balance. The handle molded to fit her grip as if it had been waiting for her.

This—this felt right.

Not because it was forbidden, but because she was good at this. Because when she held tools, when she fixed things, she knew exactly what to do.

No one else's judgment mattered here.

The broken music box on the workbench looked different now. Less like a disaster. More like a possibility.

"Bloss?"

Blake whirled at her father's voice. He stood outside the workshop window, confused and frowning at her through the glass. "What are you doing here?"

The magpie and crow squawked outside, but she ignored them. Suddenly, she was seven years old again, tears burning her eyes. The hammer slipped from her fingers and clattered against the concrete.

"I'm so sorry," she cried. "I didn't mean to break it."

Her dad kneeled beside her on the floor, cradling the pieces. It was her mother's. She remembered now. Blake waited for his anger, but he sighed and tussled her hair.

"She'll be right, love."

"No, it won't." She shook her head. "It was Mum's, and I broke it."

He sighed. "It's my fault, Bloss. I was so worried I'd lose this part of your mum that I was too afraid to fix it."

"Now it's ruined," she wailed.

"The break will make it stronger, you'll see. Get me the special glue, would you?"

She scrambled to her feet and hunted through drawers and shelves. Everything felt slightly wrong. Tools were in the wrong places. Shadows fell at impossible angles. She found a small tube tucked behind paint brushes. Glitter glue.

"Mum would like it to sparkle," she whispered, then whirled back to her father with a grin. "We can make it pretty."

"Pretty won't make it strong, Bloss."

"Can't she be both? She's rough as guts now, Dad, but wait till you see what she looks like when we shine her up!"

Her father stared at her. "Is that what you want?"

Was that what she wanted?

"Show me how you work your magic." The familiar male voice, warm and encouraging. *"Talk to me like you would them."*

Blake's heart fluttered as a face came back to her, handsome and devilish. Blue-black hair. Smoldering eyes. Soft eyes. Eyes that looked at her as though she were his whole world.

Eyes that missed her. Needed her.

"There is no world without you, Sparkles."

An ache filled with longing bloomed in her chest.

"Yeah," she said. "That's what I want."

Blake stared at the glitter glue, then at the broken dancer. She squeezed silver and gold along every fracture, watching it catch the light.

BANG.

She startled.

BANG. BANG.

Her head snapped up. The birds were flying into the workshop window. Glass spider-webbed outward from an impact point, distorting her father's reflection into fragments. The cracks spread across the surface. Through them, she glimpsed black wings beating frantically against the glass.

BANG. BANG.

"Bloody nuisance!" Her father slammed his fist against the cracked window. "Mad as a cut snake, that one. Needs to be put down. Step aside, Bloss. Let me handle this."

"No." She stepped between her father and the broken glass, arms spread wide. "Stop."

"Blake, move. I need to protect you."

"I said, no." Her voice grew stronger. "I'm not a child anymore."

She reached for the window latch despite his protests. Outside, Scarface flinched but didn't flee.

"It's okay, little mate," she cooed. "Don't listen to him. You're not a nuisance."

Scarface landed on her outstretched finger, and the world exploded into color. Blake gasped as heat zipped up her arm. Every surface in the workshop shifted. Wood grain became rivers of gold. Dust motes transformed into diamonds. The air itself turned prismatic, fracturing light into impossible spectrums.

"Can't fix stupid." Her father's voice softened, and when she looked back, love filled his weathered features. Understanding. "Such a clever girl. I should have listened to you the first time."

Outside, the crow's cawing grew urgent. It wanted in, too. It swooped closer to the window, inside. Another crow arrived. Then another. Black feathers swirled through the open window, separating her from her father's fading image.

"Dad, what's happening?"

"Two feet and a wingbeat, Bloss?"

The birds circled faster, their cries layering into a symphony. Voices pierced through the whirling darkness, calling her name, but she was losing sight of her father.

"No! Don't go," she cried. "Don't leave me alone."

The male voice, desperate and raw. *"I saved this one for last. You said, 'I'm bloody well yours, arsehole. I'm not going anywhere.' Neither am I, Blake. I'm waiting right here until you wake up."*

"River?" She gasped as the name came to her.

She remembered. Remembered everything.

She shouldn't be here.

This wasn't real.

Blake was somewhere else. In a bed. Sick.

A baby's wail pierced the air, followed by a man's off-key, rusty voice singing a lullaby.

"Hear that?" River murmured near her ear. *"You made that happen."*

"River?" she called, tears in her eyes. "Where are you?"

He wasn't here. But she could feel him against her skin, holding her. He was everything right in the world, and he'd waited. He believed in her enough to trust her, trust that healing her sickness could wait because she wanted—*needed* — to prove something … that she mattered.

But she always had.

"You don't need to fill your cracks with something glittery, Blake," River said, a smile in his voice. *"You are the glitter. You are the shiny glue that makes broken things whole."*

Scarface pecked at her scalding hot skin, pulling away pieces that fell like ash. It didn't hurt. It helped. It relieved. It revealed something bright blue and sparkling in the cracks. Not flesh. Something beautiful.

"Fly home to me, Sparkles. For the love of the Well, fly home to me."

Other voices joined in, each telling her to listen to her mate, to come home. Aeron and Trix, Ravi and Talo, Sera and Lark, Jasper and Ada. All of them waiting. All of them wanting her back.

"…fly home to us…"

BLAKE'S CONSCIOUSNESS CLAWED ITS WAY BACK THROUGH layers of fire. Her skin burned. Every nerve ending screamed as awareness crashed over her like a tidal wave. Pain consumed her. Searing heat. Her bones were melting.

But River was there.

Wide blue eyes met hers the moment she stirred. His calloused fingers wrapped around her hand, anchoring her to reality in the white-walled healing center bay.

"Blake?" Tear tracks stained his stubbled cheeks. "You're awake? Everyone, she's awake!"

The rest of the room swam into focus. Trix sat on the neighboring bed, cradling a tiny bundle against her chest—the baby. Aeron was beside her, his face alight with wonder as he whispered to his child. Jasper and Ada sat close, her head on his shoulder, her eyes closed. Sera leaned against Lark, both watching Blake with barely contained relief. Talo and Ravi hovered near the foot of the bed.

Two strange, tiny redheads sat on Blake's legs, staring at her with big, puppy-dog eyes. Their mother—must be, her hair was just as red—called them over and smiled at Blake. One child went to her, the other to the tall, silver-haired man beside her. Blue teardrop beneath one eye. Another Guardian.

And there, behind everyone else, was Cloud. Relief flashed over his expression before he glanced away, scowling toward the door.

"I had the weirdest dream," Blake croaked, then coughed. Her throat felt wrong. Tight. Like something had shifted inside her vocal cords.

Jasper nudged Ada. She startled awake and immediately locked eyes with Blake. Two seconds later, she was at the bed reaching for Blake's forehead.

River's tears fell freely now. He wasn't even trying to hide them as he brought Blake's knuckles to his lips and pressed a desperate kiss there. "Oh yeah? What did you dream?"

"That I was home. In me dad's workshop. But you were there, too. As a crow." Blake frowned, her voice still not right. Each word felt strange in her mouth. "So was Scarface. And I think I exploded into glitter—*oh shit.*"

Her free hand flew to her lips.

"You gonna puke, Sparkles?" River gathered her hair. His

automatic care, even when she felt disgusting and sweaty and wrong inside, made her chest ache with love.

But it wasn't nausea that kept her hand over her mouth. It was something else. Something impossible. Her lips *moved* against her fingers. *Protruded.* Her jaw elongated with a sensation like warm clay being molded. Panic shot through her veins. Horror stole her voice. Was she still in the nightmare?

Wrong wrong wrong!

Her wide eyes found River's ocean blues and held.

Right right right.

He was her anchor. Her safety.

"It's okay," he murmured, never letting go of her gaze. "I'll be right here—"

Before he could finish, the transformation seized her completely.

"That's it, treasure. Let it happen. I've got you."

River's comforting words continued as bones shifted inside her body. They compressed with deep, wet, crackling sounds that made her want to scream despite feeling no pain. But River was there. He wasn't afraid—she sensed it through their bond. He was proud, excited even, as her flesh rippled and morphed, skin prickling from thousands of tiny points pressing from the inside out. Feathers. They grew beneath her skin, creating patterns of black and white and iridescent colors that glimmered like glitter.

It should have been agony.

Instead, it felt good. Like … becoming.

And then, as suddenly as it began, it stopped.

But everything was dark. Muted. She couldn't see past something heavy covering her body.

"Blake?"

River's voice came from outside the cover. Blake tunneled through the darkness, toward the light, and hopped out onto a giant bed. Wait. Everything was huge—the people, even the colors. They blazed with an intensity she'd never experienced, especially toward the window where sunlight streamed in, in places the warmth touched, in a sparkly way that called to her very soul.

"What the fuck kind of bird is that?" Jasper whispered.

"She's not a crow," Ada murmured, leaning closer with professional curiosity.

Blake turned her head toward them and discovered she could move it in ways that should have been impossible.

"The magpie collects..." River mumbled. "She's a magpie."

His deep voice sounded more like thunder. But nice thunder. Like the rolling promise of rain after a drought. His lips curved into the most beautiful grin Blake had ever seen. "Look at you," he gushed, so proud. "You're as big as a crow."

"I thought magpies were smaller," Ada mused.

"Not where Blake comes from." His eyes blazed with love and admiration. "Australian magpies are the most vicious, territorial, and fiercely protective creatures on earth. They'll defend what's theirs to the death." His teeth flashed in a grin. "And she's mine."

Blake opened her beak to tell him he was wrong—that they belonged to *each other*.

What emerged was pure music. The most beautiful song spilled from her throat. It was complex and melodic, like warbling wind chimes.

Everyone went silent, transfixed at the sound of notes that probably hadn't been heard for thousands of years, at the return of something lost.

CHAPTER
SEVENTY-FIVE

Blake watched the ceremonial lake swallow sunset the way the ocean had once swallowed her life—whole and without apology.

Six days had passed since her transformation into a magpie shifter. She still couldn't quite believe it, still caught herself holding her breath when UV light struck just right. Even now, a simple sunset became a light show. Colors she'd never known existed burst across her vision, flooding her bloodstream with liquid euphoria.

A crow cawed overhead, and Blake's lips curved instead of twisted. Funny how perspective changed everything. Back at that Perth jetty, when Jeff had abandoned her and sailed away, that harsh sound had felt like cosmic mockery, as if the universe itself was laughing at the girl who'd lost her husband, her iPhone, her whole world.

What a numpty she'd been.

Another crow joined the first, then another. Their wings cut sharp silhouettes against the dying light. These weren't harbingers mocking her misfortune. They were family calling their location to their murder, reminding themselves where they'd been, where they were going, and most importantly, who they were with.

They were the most loyal, protective, forgiving souls she'd ever met. They'd claimed her without question, made her understand that home wasn't a house with a workshop beside eucalyptus trees, or even this magical place.

Her windways whispered against her ankles as she moved closer to the water's edge, drawn by bioluminescence stirring beneath the surface like scattered stars waiting for darkness. A heavy weight tugged behind her. She glanced over her shoulder at the black and white feathers folded against her back.

Almost one of them, but not quite. Once she might have balked at the difference, but seeing it now filled her with fierce gratitude. Even though no other existed in this era, being an Australian magpie meant carrying home in her bones always. It meant she had a reason for feeling territorial and protective to the death. It meant she had purpose.

Losing everything when the world froze hadn't been the end.

Maybe it had been the beginning of possibilities she'd never been brave enough to imagine.

Everything here pulsed with life, with promise, with the kind of magic that made a woman believe anything was possible.

"She's got the razz, alright." Wonder threaded through her voice.

"Hey, flock-faces. Those aren't for yanking."

Blake's head whipped around to where River stood by the forest's edge, a few yards away, attempting a conversation with Rush about the evening's ceremony setup. Holly and Hazel were more interested in trying to steal River's newly generated, rather sparkly, blue-tipped primary feathers. They'd grown back fuller than ever within three days.

He'd been so proud.

Had attributed it to Blake's extra wing fondling every night since. Her wings ruffled, and she blushed at the memory. Tonight, there would be more of the same. She couldn't believe she got to spend the rest of her life with this hot, sexy, and loving crow shifter.

River had traded his Guardian leathers for simple dark trousers and a white linen shirt that clung to his torso in all the right places. Blake didn't blame the twins for their obsession with him. She was obsessed, too. He snapped his wings irritably, almost as if swatting flies. In reality, he was avoiding tiny grabby fingers.

Blake pressed her lips together to keep from laughing.

Farther down along the forest's edge, a platform rose under the hands of three shirtless, very buff Guardians. Some of the old-world, Well-blessed women Blake had recently met were gathered nearby to "supervise" their mates' building expertise. Laurel, the self-appointed supervising committee and liquid refreshments organizer, shouted over the rim of her cocktail glass for her mate to redo a particular low rigging. He'd not tightened it properly.

Thorne glared back, but scraped his hand through his ice-blond hair in a pose Blake had seen blokes at the gym use when they knew someone watched them. The other two Guardians, Leaf and Indigo, stopped rigging and added their glares to the mix.

Nova clapped her hands and ordered her mate back to work. Leaf doubled down on his glare, then paused to tie his long blond hair, flexing his biceps and grumbling something to Thorne. Indigo grinned at his mate, Violet, and tried to go to her. Leaf tugged him back by his leathery wings.

Blake had the urge to join them. These people had become her friends, welcoming her as easily as River's family. But first, she had something to do.

She refocused on the lake and fished a glass container from her windways pocket. The device felt warm in her palm—not really a device, but a thin, rectangular glass canister about the size of her old iPhone. Trix had outdone herself with this one. Even though they'd been using it to contact family for a few years, no one had named the invention.

So Blake called it a glasshole. River approved vehemently, and now the name had stuck.

She dipped the glasshole into the lake water and filled it to the rim. Bioluminescent flecks swirled through the liquid like tiny galaxies. Before she corked the gap, she held a finger before her face and concentrated. Mana rose from her inner well, swift and obedient, moving along her arm until it pushed out a claw from her fingertip. *Success.*

She let a few drops of blood fall into the water.

"Now for the finishing touch." Crystal beads were next. She watched them settle between the glass planes, corked it, then shook it to test the sparkle factor. Not enough razz. "Tomorrow I'm bedazzling you, okay?"

But first—she sent another sliver of power into the glasshole's water and asked it to reach out to any of her ancestors or family members that might be out there somewhere, frozen, just as she had been.

The water began to glow. She held her breath, too excited to hope.

No face appeared in the makeshift screen, just her

reflection staring back with eyes holding flecks of gold she'd not noticed before. Honestly, she didn't expect anyone to be on the other end, but had learned to hope for impossible things lately, which was why she continued talking.

"G'day, me little hidden gems." She drawled. "Did you miss me?"

Silence answered, of course.

"Right, well, I've got some bloody fantastic news." She tilted the screen toward her face, grinning. "Remember how the last time you saw me, I thought Jeff was about to propose again on that yacht? Well … that didn't happen." She frowned, realizing she didn't even want to talk about him, and waved her free hand dismissively. "Yeah, nah. I won't bore you with details about dickface. He's not worth it. But me new man is. Or should I say, me new crow boy? New fae? I dunno. Doesn't matter what you call him because check this stunner out."

She panned toward River and let out a soft "Awwww," then dropped the glasshole slightly as she became distracted by how cute her mate was being. The twins had upgraded from playful feather tugging to braiding his long primary feathers.

"Rush." River's voice held a warning tone. "Get them off."

Rush tilted his head and put his hand to his twitching fae ear. "What's that?" He spoke to no one. "You need my help to finish the setup." He showed his palms to River and made a disappointed face. "Gotta go. Duty calls."

"No one said anything!" River shouted, but Rush was already walking away.

Blake watched River stand there for a full minute before

he finally ground out, "Flock faces, those aren't for yanking."

Giggling.

"Fine," he sighed. "I give up. Go chase your daddy, and I'll tell you a story tonight."

The twins gasped and let go. Hazel bolted after her father, but Holly stumbled and scraped her knee on a jutting root. She looked up at River, tears welling in her eyes.

River shrugged. "You'll get over it."

But when she gave him those devastating puppy dog eyes, he made a constipated expression. Two seconds later, he checked to see if any of the male work crew watched.

"This should be good," Blake mumbled, raising her screen to capture the moment secretly. The blood connection was still in effect.

River crouched and pressed his palm to the little girl's scraped knee. Blue light flickered between his fingers. Then, with another quick glance around, he pulled a wrapped sweet from his pocket and pressed it into her palm. Whatever he said next was inaudible to Blake, but it put a mischievous and evil grin on Holly's face. Then she skipped off, too.

"I think me ovaries are combusting," Blake breathed as River watched the girls retreat, an unguarded smile touching his lips. She decided right then and there to make him paint this moment on her section of their trove wall when they visited later tonight.

"Hey, hun!" she shouted.

Her mate whipped around to face her, eyebrows raised, cheeks flushing pink.

"Wave for the camera and show the world how lucky I am."

He quickly flipped off both middle fingers but stretched those gorgeous lips into a fierce grin. It still didn't hide his embarrassment—she felt it through their bond.

Blake laughed, swinging the glasshole back to herself.

"Isn't he just the bee's knees? Acts all tattooed bad birdy and"—she dropped her voice to a growl—"*You die, I die,* macho man. But between you and me, he's a big softie. Thank fuck, too, because if he'd been proper obsessive, like he warned me some crows are, then after his best-mate Cloud restarted me heart a few days back, I might've woken up to some serious Romeo and Juliet bullshit. Who knows what River would have done if he truly believed I was dead."

The thought sent a shiver down her spine. Ada and Trix told Blake how River had almost lost it. But he didn't. And now they were here.

"Anyhoo, where was I? Oh yeah, funerals. The point is," she continued narrating, wedging her glasshole between her breasts and walking toward River, "about bringing back what's lost. I have sad news, for now—they told me I can't bring you back. Apparently, the only one who's done that besides the Well itself is Clarke and Rush's older daughter, Willow. But she's now off on an adventure with six hot blokes as her mates."

River's eyes sparked as she reached him. "Six mates, eh? Must be powerful magic she's got." His voice dropped to a wicked murmur. "Though I reckon it's not her mana keeping them all satisfied."

"Oh, stop!" Blake slapped a hand over her glasshole's speaker, blocking its nonexistent ears. "This is supposed to be a serious affair. Stop making me laugh."

"Never." His gaze lingered on her face with particular

intensity that made her stomach flip. When he reached out to tuck a strand of hair behind her ear, she went weak at the knees.

"The point is," she continued, taking River's offered hand and walking with him toward the gathering crowd, "whatever power Willow had to wake a civilization in another country was a freak of nature. It likely won't happen again. So, if me mates back home are somehow listening, I don't want them to get their hopes up. The Well has a plan, and—"

"Wants what it fucking wants," he finished.

The mood sobered as more people gathered quietly along the shore and the sun sank below the horizon. The playful atmosphere shifted, becoming something heavier, more reverent. Blake pulled her glasshole back out and spoke quietly into it as she captured the scene.

"We're here to hold a funeral, or rather, a memorial for every soul we've loved and lost, from the old world, and the new one." She tapped the glass with her newly bejeweled fingernails. "So yeah, I just wanted to show you all that you are missed. You may be hidden, but you're still gems. I love you all." Blake's throat clogged as she cut the blood connection and slipped the device into her pocket.

"You good?" River's eyes stayed fixed on her face. "We don't have to join them up front."

"Really?" She dashed away tears. "I'm just … a little emotional. I think I'd like to stand back a little. If that's okay."

"Whatever you want." He cupped her head and kissed the top. She sank into his side and slipped her hand around his waist.

Twilight had fallen. The ceremonial lake stretched beside

them like a mirror made of liquid starlight. Between them and the forest, fae from all around the Order of the Well campus had gathered—academics, Guardians, Mages, workers, and staff.

A hush fell over the crowd as members of the Cadre of Twelve and their families gathered in a loose semicircle near the wooden platform up front, their faces solemn beneath the new moon. Children pressed close to their parents. Mates held hands. Even the twins, Holly and Hazel, stood quietly beside Rush as Clarke stepped forward, onto the raised platform, and unfurled a scroll in her hands.

"Tonight," she announced, loud and clear, "we remember those who have returned to the Well. We honor their memory and carry their light forward."

The first name fell into the silence like a stone dropped into still water.

"Tinger."

"Oops, I'm on." River squeezed Blake's shoulder and jogged to meet Jasper a few yards along the shore. He raised his hands, the scent of ozone sparked in the air, and water erupted from the lake's surface like liquid fireworks. Bioluminescent particles swirled through the spray, creating dancing patterns of sparks of light before settling back into gentle ripples. But the most beautiful sight was when Jasper's magic joined in. He molded River's spraying water into shape. As they worked, Violet came to stand by their side. Then a miracle happened. Out of the lake, made simply from water, bioluminescence, and Violet's UV light particles, a glowing rabbit with wings and antlers formed. It bounded across the surface and somehow, even though the water returned to the lake, together, they made the illusion of

Tinger fly into the sky and explode into little stars— manabeeze—that joined the night sky.

A few sobs were heard around the group, and then more names followed, each one punctuated by the magical light show.

"Jackson Crimson."

"Aleksandra."

"Maebh."

"Dawn."

"Colt."

"Barrow."

Faces appeared, burst into stars, and then floated away. The list went on, encompassing all the fallen Order soldiers, the families the Well-blessed humans had left behind in the old world, the countless souls lost to war and time and heartbreak. Each name was a story cut short, a life that mattered, a person who deserved to be remembered. Some names without faces were listed on paper boats and set adrift on the lake. Blake wrote down each member of her family, her friends, and her followers. She even wrote 'Boss Man' on the side of one paper boat and watched it sail away.

Then Clarke's voice softened, carrying a particular weight.

"Aurora."

SEVENTY-SIX

Movement in the shadows beneath the trees caught Blake's attention. There, half-hidden in darkness, stood a familiar figure she didn't think was going to show.

Cloud's black locks curled at the edges, still damp from a recent shower or bath. He was clean and freshly shaven, but unlike the other Guardians, he still wore a uniform. The V marking bisected his face like a red scar. His eyes still held that same haunted emptiness she recalled from their last meeting. His frame returned to that unnatural stillness she'd come to associate with all the Guardians, particularly the most dangerous ones. Blake sensed tension radiating from him across the distance.

River was busy helping with the light show, but she wasn't sure she'd get another private moment with Cloud, so she slipped away from the gathering and dug into her pocket. She pulled out a folded piece of paper and smoothed the creases as she approached the tree line.

"Cloud."

He didn't startle, but his attention shifted to her. Up close, she could see the exhaustion carved into every line of his face, the way his power-enhancing tattoos seemed dulled without their usual greasy luminescence.

"I've been meaning to tell you something," Blake said softly, keeping her voice low so it wouldn't carry to the ceremony. "When I was in your trove, I noticed the lyrics you'd written on the walls. In UV ink."

"I know," he replied, flat gaze locked ahead.

"I'm not sure if you know, but they were incomplete," she continued. "It bugged me, so I wrote down the rest of the words, word for word." She held out the folded paper. "I asked Melody to sing it tonight. She'll start after the names are finished."

For a brief moment, Cloud's permanent scowl softened, revealing something raw and vulnerable beneath the blood-stained mask. It was the same face she glimpsed at the Collector's hoard.

His gaze flicked to her wings. His voice came out rough, barely above a whisper. "You really can't restore what's lost, can you?"

Blake's heart ached for him. "Not in the way you hope."

Cloud was quiet for a long moment, staring at the paper in her hands. Then he reached into his jacket and pulled out the cryptex, still sealed, still holding whatever secrets had driven him to such desperate lengths.

"Then here. Take it."

Before Blake could remind him that she couldn't touch metal, River appeared at her shoulder. Cloud's gaze shifted to him. Something unseen passed between the two males, yet it held the weight of years of friendship, of betrayal and pain that Blake would never fully understand.

"Fuck face," Cloud greeted.

"Fuck your own face," River returned, narrowing his eyes at the cryptex still hovering in the air. "You were supposed to return that days ago."

"Give it to Leaf and Nova." His eyes skated away, hand lowering with a shrug. "Or don't."

"Why don't you come with me?" River's hope threaded through their bond. "Don't you want to see what's in it?" He paused. "Without breaking the ink inside it?"

"I already know what's in it." Cloud's fingers moved over the cryptex's cylinders with practiced ease, clicking them into place. The device opened with a soft sound, revealing its contents.

Blake's breath caught. Inside, nestled against the crystal walls, lay a single strand of black hair. Just one.

Cloud tipped the cryptex, letting the strand fall into his palm. His fist closed around it, tattooed and scarred knuckles going white with the force of his grip. When he looked up, his smile was rueful, empty of anything resembling joy.

"It's useless to me now."

In the distance, a new voice began to rise over the water —rich and haunting, with the kind of power that made the air itself seem to vibrate. Blake turned to see Melody stepping forward, her platinum hair catching moonlight like spun silver, her curvy figure draped in flowing fabric.

The voice that emerged from her throat was nothing like the sultry, breathless tones Blake had remembered hearing on the radio. It sounded nothing like the original artist who sang it, either. Instead, it carried the deep, soulful resonance of heartbreak given form. It was raw and powerful and utterly transcendent.

The tune conjured memories of Blake sitting in front of the television as a child, eating pancakes, listening to her mum gush over how hot the musician was. But what struck Blake the most were the lyrics. The familiar words about wanting to fly away, to escape pain, and to find freedom took on a new meaning in this setting.

"That's it." Cloud's shocked murmur was barely audible over the song. His fingers traced the words he'd been trying so desperately to remember.

A lump formed in her throat as she turned away. She touched River's arm and gestured back toward the gathering. "We should give him space."

River's gaze lingered on his friend for a moment longer, then he nodded, allowing Blake to guide him away from the shadows and back toward the shoreline where the others had clustered.

They joined a small group that included Clarke and Rush. Aeron was holding baby Ivy while Trix stood beside him, head on his shoulder, eyes wistfully locked on Melody. The sight of the little family should have been heartwarming, but Blake found herself glancing back toward the tree line, that uncomfortable tightness in her chest refusing to ease.

"Will he be okay?" Blake asked quietly, keeping her voice low enough not to disturb the performance.

Her question had been for River, but Clarke answered.

"Not yet," she said, her gaze following Blake's to the treeline. The psychic's expression grew troubled.

"But he'd better be," Rush added quietly. "Because no one else can do what needs to be done to stop Nero."

"What does that mean?" River asked.

Aeron and Trix heard, both turning concerned eyes to Clarke.

"It means," she said, "that Cloud and Ash both need to sort their shit out soon." A glint of something flickered in her eyes, suggesting she was holding things back. "But now's not the time to push it. We have a little time before we need to worry."

When the song began to wind down, its final notes floating across the water, Cloud finally left the shadows and walked down to the lake's edge. A quick look around their group revealed no one else had noticed.

It seemed like another private moment, so Blake kept the knowledge to herself. Still, something kept tugging her gaze to the side, to where Cloud knelt at the water's edge, cupped water in his hands, and brought it to his face. Once, twice, three times. He washed away the V marking that had branded him for half a decade.

When he was finished, he remained kneeling for a long moment, staring out across the dark water. Then Blake saw his fist open over the lake.

The single black hair drifted down like a fallen star, disappearing beneath the bioluminescent surface without so much as a ripple. Cloud watched it sink, his shoulders rigid with the effort of letting go.

Blake felt tears prick her eyes. This was grief in its purest form, not the dramatic collapse she'd expected, but something quiet and devastating in its simplicity. She turned away. Hugged River's arm tighter.

As Melody's voice faded into silence and the gathered

crowd began to stir, Blake kept her gaze firmly fixed on the other mourners. Rush stepped forward, his jaw set with determination.

"I've had enough of waiting for Willow to get back to us," he announced to the gathered group. "We need answers."

"Rush," Clarke started. "I told you she'd contact us when she's ready."

"Don't care."

Blake pulled out her glasshole, offering it with a helpful smile. "You can use this if—"

"No," Clarke sighed, shaking her head. "I appreciate it, but I guess if he needs to do this, the lake will suffice." She glanced at River. "Stay with us? It might be handy having someone near who can transport matter through a blood connection."

"I've not tried it with blood other than my kin," River said. "But happy to give it a try if you need it."

River's hand found Blake's as they followed the others to the shore of the ceremonial lake. Residual magic from the memorial ceremony created patterns of light that—

Clarke stopped so abruptly that Blake nearly collided with her.

"What is it?" Aeron asked, shifting baby Ivy protectively to his shoulder.

Blake followed Clarke's gaze across the moonlit shore and felt her breath catch. Where Cloud had been kneeling moments before, a dark shape lay gathered on the sand.

Silently, they drew closer, as if sound would manifest the illusion of what they dared not name. The dark blobby shape resolved into something that made Blake's throat close completely.

"Cloud?" River's voice broke the silence.

No answer. Only the gentle lap of water against the shore and the distant calls of crows settling into their roosts.

There, on the sand, were piles of belongings. Leather. Black Guardian leather, carefully folded. Weapons arranged with military precision. A bandolier. Boots placed side by side as if their owner had simply stepped out of them and vanished into the night.

And there, placed with deliberate care atop the folded uniform—

His butterfly knife.

"I thought you were being dramatic," Blake whispered, tears blurring her vision as she looked at River. "When you said those things about crows being different. About them being obsessive to the point of—"

She couldn't finish. Couldn't voice what they all now understood.

"What?" Trix asked from behind them. "What do you mean?"

But Blake couldn't answer. Could only stare at the reason why River had been so afraid when they'd met.

River's hand closed over hers, his grip steady despite the storm of emotion raging through their bond. He was trying to comfort her, but Blake sensed the depth of his devastation. She squeezed back, letting him know without words that she wasn't going anywhere.

He knelt beside the pile, his hands hovering over the weapon as if afraid to touch it. Blake could see his shoulders trembling, could feel through their bond the way his heart was fracturing. First, Ash chose to remain with his mother. Now, Cloud had abandoned everything that once defined him.

River's fingers traced the knife's handle. Blue glyphs pulsed to life, revealing the weapon's name in a faint blue glow—a single word that seemed to mock everything Cloud had been, everything he'd chosen to leave behind.

Vengeance.

EPILOGUE

Nero stood in his tower's greenhouse, breathing rot and withering dreams. Decay crept across every surface. Plants that had once thrived now hung like corpses from their supports, their leaves brown and brittle. The stench of failure permeated the air, mingling with the sharp tang of chemicals and the persistent drip of something foul from the glass-domed ceiling above.

Yet amid the death, old-world technology hummed with stubborn life.

An ancient computer dominated the far wall. It was fortunate that he'd ordered the Tinker to revive it before she defected. Some parts were new, some were old, but somehow, it was functioning.

This. This right here was how he knew his plan was inevitable.

According to physics, this piece of equipment should be dead. But he'd cheated nature. He'd beat it. He'd replaced its rusted parts with new ones, and now the world's death rattle was prolonged.

Steam hissed from pressure valves. Gears clicked in measured rhythm. The old box screen flickered with static, casting shifting shadows across his face.

Tick. Tick. Tick.

Pandora sat motionless in the chair he'd positioned before the terminal. Copper cables snaked from the back of her neck to the machine's neural interface. Her dark hair fell across her shoulders, a little melted but otherwise pristine despite everything she'd endured. More of the Tinker's work was visible beneath her torn clothing and pulsed with soft blue light.

Tick. Tick. Tick.

Her clockwork heart beat steadily, but something in the rhythm felt wrong. Off-kilter, like a gear with worn teeth.

Nero's fingers hovered over the activation switches. Five years of work to get her functional again. Five years of rationing Guardian mana and salvaging parts while his people starved in the city. All for this moment.

He could simply wake her. Ask for her report.

But paranoia crawled beneath his skin like insects. The Tinker had been thorough, brilliant, and utterly untrustworthy. The Tinker didn't know what she was working on at the time. She didn't know all those little projects he'd given her were ultimately for Pandora's resurrection from the basement.

Still, what if she'd left surprises in Pandora's programming? What if his queen's memories had been tampered with?

Better to see the truth through her eyes. Raw. Unfiltered.

Nero threw the final switch.

The screen erupted in brilliant light, then settled into

grainy focus. Through Pandora's visual sensors, he watched her mission unfold in real time.

The Great Murder heaved with life around her. Stolen plumage adorned her shoulders as she moved between market stalls, mimicking the peculiar gait of crow shifters. Her internal chronometer marked each second, each heartbeat, each breath that brought her closer to her objective.

The footage jumped, skipped frames. Nero cursed and slammed his fist against the monitor's side. Ancient circuits clashed with new in a protest that ended in sparks, but the image stabilized.

A crow female blocked Pandora's path, eyes narrowing with suspicion. "Your feathers. They're not yours."

Pandora struck without hesitation. Her fingertips split open, revealing razor-sharp metal claws. Blood welled around polished steel as the crow shifter's struggles ceased.

Efficient. Clean. Perfect.

Another flicker. Another hit on the box screen. Another skip in the footage.

The scene shifted. Still at the markets, but now Pandora was eavesdropping on male voices.

"The Collector is here. She'll be at the Shadow Market tonight. Midnight."

Nero leaned forward. The Collector was exactly who Pandora had been sent to find.

Tick-tick-tick-tick.

The rhythm quickened as the footage jumped ahead. Pandora stalked through shadows. Twisted stalls flashed through her view. He watched it all, losing patience until finally, she located a hideous bird woman and attempted a trade.

"The cryptex is not for sale," the Collector hissed at someone off-camera.

"So you admit to having it." Pandora's voice, triumph evident even through the mechanical speakers.

The Collector leaned forward, talons extended. "Unless my son returns to his rightful place, it remains with me."

Nero's knuckles whitened as he gripped the terminal's edge. Hideous, *greedy* beast.

The screen flickered, went dark for three agonizing seconds. Nero could have sworn he saw his daughter's face in the dark reflection and checked over his shoulder. Empty, withering greenhouse. No. Her ghost hadn't returned since she'd put him in check.

When he faced the screen again, the footage had returned with crystal clarity.

Cloud now stood twenty feet from the Collector, every line of his body radiating controlled violence. A dark stain was painted on his face in the shape of a V.

Even through Pandora's sensors, Nero felt the wrongness in the air, the electric potential that he'd once witnessed firsthand.

Tick. Tick. Tick.

Lightning erupted across the screen in blinding sheets. When it cleared, chaos reigned. Stalls were being overturned. Merchandise was thrown and scattered—glimpses of destruction and agonized screams.

The footage skipped again, stabilized. Now he saw the aftermath.

Bodies. Smoke. The Collector and Pandora were both lying together on the ground, the night on fire around them. One sizzled and screamed in agony, the other pretended to do the same.

"All of this for your enemy's brass puzzle tube?" The Collector's *voice was weak but mocking, and directed at someone approaching.*

Cloud stepped into view, blood streaking his face. His expression was cold, remote, and utterly without mercy.

"Not the cryptex," Pandora croaked, *"but what was inside it."*

Nero almost bellowed at her stupidity—giving away their secrets—but then Cloud's head whipped Pandora's way.

"What did you say?" His eyes narrowed. His hand moved toward the dagger at his hip.

"All this for the last warhead."

Cloud's hand fell away from his weapon. For a moment, he dropped his head, shoulders shaking.

Silent laughter? Nero leaned closer to the screen.

Cloud crouched down, bringing his face level with Pandora's—level with the camera. His smile was sharp as broken glass, painted with someone else's blood.

"If that's what you think is still in there, then I guess she got what she wanted." The sneering words hit Nero like physical blows. Cloud's gaze seemed to pierce through the screen, through time and distance, to stare into his soul. *"She learned to be better than you."*

His dagger appeared before Pandora's face, its edge catching the firelight of nearby destruction.

"I should end you right now. But there's no need." A pause. A breath. *"You killed the only person who ever knew where to find your secrets. Poetic, don't you think?"*

Bootsteps. The image tilted as Cloud walked away, leaving Pandora bleeding oil on the ground.

Nero sat back in his chair, mind reeling. The only person who knew was Rory. But Nero never killed her. Sure, he'd intended to. It was the crow that let her fall. And she didn't know, for if she did, then Nero would know. He'd taken every last drop of her mana, held every last memory she had inside her body. None of them gave him a clue as to where she might have put the map to the last warhead.

Tick … tick … tick…

But neither did her mana hold memories of her time with the crow. He'd always wondered about that. Wondered if she'd found a way to suppress them. Wondered if maybe…

Tick … tick … tick…

The footage continued.

Pandora was now in a triage unit beside the Collector. There were hushed conversations, bargains offered and refused.

"What I seek is useless to us now," Pandora said. "Why would I help you in return for it?"

"If you believe him."

"Fae can't lie."

"Ah, but we can stretch the truth." The Collector's eyes glittered despite her injuries. "Even if he's not lying, I have something that will help you find what you seek. I will give it to you if you help me."

"What could you possibly have that will help us find the secrets of a dead woman?"

"Another dead woman."

Nero straightened, suddenly alert.

What?

The Collector's voice dropped to a conspiratorial whisper. "She is from the old world. Has a unique gift—tracking lost things, particularly those of the dead. It's how I found her. Poor, lost soul is a Well-blessed human. My son's … offering. Help me return to my trove and I'll—"

The screen went dark.

Silence filled the greenhouse except for the persistent drip from above and the whisper of steam through ancient pipes.

Tick.

Tick.

Tick.

Nero's shoulders began to shake. A sound escaped him, low and barely human. It built slowly, gaining strength and pitch until laughter erupted and filled the rotting space.

"Oh, my dear." He wiped tears from his eyes. "You were more like me than you let on."

His own daughter, the child he'd raised to be the perfect weapon, had been running her own game all along. While he'd tortured her, drained her, and finally dismissed her as useless, she'd been protecting secrets he'd never even suspected she possessed.

She'd stolen her own mana, stolen her own precious memories before he could access them.

But she'd made one mistake.

She'd died.

Nero pushed away from the terminal and crossed the greenhouse to where the chessboard waited. Rory's queen still held him in check from their last conversation. Cautiously, glancing around the greenhouse first to see if her ghost lingered, almost daring her to show her face, he reached toward the game and lifted the ivory piece. He studied the delicate carving one final time.

Then he set it aside and moved his king.

Check broken.

Game resumed.

Tick.

Tick.

Tick.

THANK YOU FOR READING BLAKE AND RIVER'S STORY. I HOPE you enjoyed the time in Elphyne. If you enjoyed the story, please help others find the series and share your thoughts online in a review.

ACKNOWLEDGMENTS

This book was dedicated to my Patreon supporters, who stuck with me through thick and thin while I had one of the toughest years of my life. I normally could put out four books a year, but with the extra pressure at home, I managed only one. (He's a thick one, but still...)

Without the support of my angels on Patreon, I wouldn't have been able to continue to write. I wouldn't have been able to push through until I found my creativity again, until I "refilled my inner well."

Here are the names of a few who have graciously agreed to let me name them, but there are more. Please know that though your name is not here, you are not forgotten in my heart.

Thank you to all supporters, including:

"The Smutty Professor," Abby DeVries, Amanda O'Banaman, Amanda Sternart, Amber McBride, Amy Kelly, Amy Rizzo, Angela Fagg, Angelica Luevano, Ann Hosler, Ann Hosler, Arysta, Ashley Berlin, Ashley McCormick, Barbara Schoonover, Becca Filippini, Billie Jean Foster, Billie Jean Foster, Bri Ilhan, Brit Irvin, Brittany Stephens, Carolin Kelley, Casey Young, Cass O'Hara, Cassidy, Cassy, Charlotte Tassan, Christina Cupp, Christina L Gallegos, Christine Jackson, Christine Pacelli, Christine Pacelli, Colleen Farrall, Dani Smith, Danielle Seitz, Dearna Mulvaney, Diana Baldrey, Diana Baldrey, Diana M, Dianna "Favourite Sister" Pecherczyk, Dj, Dj Weller, Ebatgirl3, Emily Darlene, Erin Pickering, Glorianna Marsteller, Heather Knechtges, Hope Becker, Jacynta Clayton, Jen Cerekwicki, Jennifer B, Jennifer B, Jesica Hereford, JF4, Jisselle Anne Metzdorf, Joanne Paton, Joddi Anderson, Jodi, Joy B Gallup, Joy Gallup, Kaitlin Wren, Kaitlin Wren, Katie Carlsoan, Kayla Mae Reid Chisolm, Kellie Hornick, Kelsey Crnkovic, Kerry Kelso, Kira McLemore, Kirianna Bekker, Kris Kenney, Kristen Grimes Ott, Kym Matuszak, Lacey Snyder, Lanette Lord, Laura Smith, Laura Waldmann, Lauren Penner, Leah DW, Leslie D. Nash, Leticia Vella, Lexi Graham, Lidiya Azhotkina, Lindsay Angsten, Lisa Wilson-Pennington, Madison, Maggie Asklund, Marisa Frazier, Mary Jo Laupp, McKenzie H., Megan Marshell, Melissa M, Melissa Ruzik, Michelle Anne, Mickyla Hatch, Monica Popescu, Monica Popescu, Morgan Weingart, Narissa Gonsalves, Narissa Kye Gonsalves, Nathalie Ulvstig, Nessa Ostrowski, Nico, Niki James, Nikki L. Hafliger, Peggy Hellenthal, Rachael Walsh, Rachel Joi Maples, Raeanna Williams, rebecca zeoli, Red Frost, Renee Floyd, Risa Joy Cavett, Robbie Dianne Cheshire, Robin Beckham, Robin Urstadt, Robyn Kehoe, Sacha, Sara Abel, Sara Garrett, Sasha Viers, Sharon, Shawnee S., Shelley Kinney, Shenia L., Sherri Richardson, Shery Werbelo, Sonia Johnston, Steph Blaauw, Stephanie Blaauw, Stephanie E., SunshineCat, Tami Newbold-Flynn, Tammy McGuire, Tarae Magras, Teela Mayne, Tinybeets, Traci Burch, Tracy Almond.

I'd also like to thank my Arc Angels (some are listed above as well) who always put up with me in deadline mode, going through my typos and dealing with last-minute changes. Also, thank you to Erika Robles, who always lets me prattle on about random shit and is far too encouraging of all the shiny new story ideas.

Thank you to Kelly Messenger, who's weathered the storm this year and adjusted her sails and still has not run away from me. I value your support (edits and proofreading), but most of all, I value your friendship. You're the best.

Thank you to Ann Harth, my developmental editor, who's also had way more hot messes of late. Ann has been with me since the beginning and always shines her great insight on these characters. They're better with her.

Thank you to my sister Heidi, who's worked tirelessly behind the scenes of my business (and often front of scene). She keeps the world spinning when my head stops. Love you sis.

Speaking of sisters. Thank you also to Nat and Dianna. They, with Heidi, are my rocks. When life goes to hell in a handbasket, I know they're with me.

And finally, thank you to my two boys, Harrison and Charlie. While they're teens not quite into reading books, they've come along and supported me at events, they've helped out at home with the business, and they've accepted and encouraged mum's random job with pride and curious wonder.

I look forward to sharing many more stories with you all.

Lana

xx

ABOUT THE AUTHOR

OMG! How do you say my name?

Lana (straight forward enough - Lah-nah) **Pecherczyk** (this is where it gets tricky - Pe-her-chick).

I've been called Lana Price-Check, Lana Pera-Chickywack, Lana Pressed-Chicken, Lana Pech...*that girl!* You name it, they said it. So if it's so hard to spell, why on earth would I use this name instead of an easy pen name?

To put it simply, it belonged to my mother. And she was my dream champion.

For most of my life, I've been good at one thing – art. The world around me saw my work, and said I should do more of it, so I did.

But, when at the age of eight, I said I wanted to write stories, and even though we were poor, my mother came home with a blank notebook and a pencil saying I should follow my dreams, no matter where they take me for they will make me happy. I wasn't very good at it, but it didn't matter because I had her support and I liked it.

She died when I was thirteen, and left her four daughters orphaned. Suddenly, I had lost my dream champion, I was split from my youngest two sisters and had no one to talk to about the challenge of life.

So, I wrote in secret. I poured my heart out daily to a diary and sometimes imagined that she would listen. At the end of the day, even if she couldn't hear, writing kept that dream alive.

Eventually, after having my own children (two fire-crackers in the guise of little boys) and ignoring my inner voice for too long, I decided to lead by example. How could I teach my children to follow their dreams if I wasn't? I became my own dream champion and the rest is history, here I am.

When I'm not writing the next great action-packed romantic novel, or wrangling the rug rats, or rescuing GI Joe from the jaws of my Kelpie, I fight evil by moonlight, win love by daylight and never run from a real fight.

I live in Australia, but I'm up for a chat anytime online. Come and find me.

Subscribe & Follow

subscribe.lanapecherczyk.com
lp@lanapecherczyk.com

facebook.com/lanapecherczykauthor
instagram.com/lana_p_author
amazon.com/-/e/B00V2TP0HG
tiktok.com/@lanapauthor
goodreads.com/lana_p_author
patreon.com/lanacreates

ALSO BY LANA PECHERCZYK

THE FAE GUARDIANS WORLD

Fae Guardians - Elphyne

(Fantasy/Paranormal Romance)

Season of the Wolf Trilogy.

The Longing of Lone Wolves

The Solace of Sharp Claws

Of Kisses & Wishes Novella (free for subscribers)

The Dreams of Broken Kings

Season of the Vampire Trilogy.

The Secrets in Shadow and Blood

A Labyrinth of Fangs and Thorns

A Symphony of Savage Hearts

Season of the Elf Trilogy

A Song of Sky and Sacrifice

A Crown of Cruel Lies

A War of Ruin and Reckoning

Fae Devils

(Fae Guardians Sluagh Spin-off)

Castle of Nevers and Nightmares

Trials of Dusk and Dreams

THE DEADLYVERSE

The Sinner Sisterhood

(Demon-hunting Paranormal Romance)

The Sinner and the Scholar

The Sinner and the Gunslinger

The Deadly Seven

(Fated Mate Paranormal/Sci-Fi Romance)

The Deadly Seven Box Set Books 1-3

Sinner

Envy

Greed

Wrath

Sloth

Gluttony

Lust

Pride

Despair

CONTENT WARNING DETAILS

This book mentions suicide, and the allusion to it. No details of the actual event are described explicitly or viscerally.

This book also has a scene featuring a newborn baby in distress. There is a happy ending for everyone involved in the birth.

www.ingramcontent.com/pod-product-compliance
Lightning Source LLC
Chambersburg PA
CBHW050557170726
48283CB00001B/7